THE MAID AND THE ORCS

A MONSTER FANTASY ROMANCE

FINLEY FENN

ALSO BY FINLEY FENN

ORC SWORN

The Lady and the Orc

The Heiress and the Orc

The Librarian and the Orc

The Duchess and the Orc

The Midwife and the Orc

The Maid and the Orcs

Offered by the Orc (Bonus Story)

THE MAGES

The Mage's Maid

The Mage's Match

The Mage's Master

The Mage's Groom (Bonus Story)

Sign up at www.finleyfenn.com for free bonus stories and epilogues, delicious orc artwork, complete content tags and warnings, news about upcoming books, and more!

ABOUT THE MAID AND THE ORCS

She's fallen for an angel... but he's mated to a monster.

In a realm of orcs and powerful men, housemaid Alma Andersson is drowning—in grief, debt, and drudgery. And when her awful employer makes his darkest demand yet, she flees for the forest, and tumbles toward her doom...

Until she's snatched to safety by a **huge, vicious green beast.**

An *orc.*

He's utterly terrifying, with his towering bulk, sharp teeth, and deadly black claws—but his touch is gentle, and his eyes are kind. And his scent is a deep, decadent sweetness, sparking a furious flame between them...

But it's only more disaster, because **Alma's shy, soft-hearted rescuer is already mated... to another** *orc.* A tall, silent, snarling monster named Drafli, who loathes Alma on sight, and clearly longs for her death.

Yet Drafli will do anything for his sweet mate, even if it means tolerating a weak, worthless human. So he makes Alma a cold, calculated offer: **he'll share his mate with her... but only on his terms.**

He wants her silence.

Her surrender.

Her servitude.

And with Alma's fate firmly in Drafli's ruthless hands, how can she face her own dark desires—or all the secrets hidden behind Orc Mountain's walls? **Can a lost, lonely housemaid come between two orcs... without being crushed?**

To Goddess Ruby Dixon
With all my most worshipful gratitude

1

Alma Andersson was about to be fired.

"I tried, my lord," her hoarse voice croaked, as her shaky hands wiped at her filthy, soot-streaked apron. "I was in the cellar when the fire started, but I called for help the moment I heard, and—"

"And by then, the entire kitchen was *destroyed*!" Mr. Pembroke shouted across the desk, his rounded, reddened face apoplectic with rage. "And that low-life, good-for-nothing Cook had already run for the hills, with all my finest silver shoved under her skirts!"

Alma opened her mouth to reply, but then thought better of it, choking the words back into her ragged-feeling throat. There was surely no explanation that would placate Mr. Pembroke now—not even the indisputable fact that he'd horribly humiliated Cook in front of his entire household staff the day before, and that he was damned well lucky she hadn't decided to poison his breakfast instead.

"At least we—we caught the fire before it spread into the rest of the house," Alma made herself say, over the ever-rising ringing in her ears. "And it doesn't seem like there was any serious structural damage. And my staff are already hard at work cleaning up the mess, and tomorrow we'll—"

"Tomorrow you'll *what*?!" Mr. Pembroke hollered, his clenched fist thumping against the desk. "You'll reverse the damage? You'll magically produce the outrageous amounts of coin this will cost me? You'll prove to me you're even half the housekeeper your idle mother was?"

Alma flinched back in her chair, and felt her eyes reflexively narrowing toward Mr. Pembroke's furious face. "My mother was *ill*, Mr. Pembroke," she blurted out. "For many, *many* years. And even so, she worked from dawn until dusk, every single day, to serve you and your household as best as she possibly could!"

But oh gods, what was Alma saying, because the rage only flashed brighter in Mr. Pembroke's eyes. "And what about *you*!" he shouted back. "It's been one failure after another ever since. The fires are never properly lit. The laundry is always late. The meals are constantly mediocre. You can't even keep on a basic skeleton staff, let alone properly *supervise* them!"

The thunder flared louder in Alma's ears, the wetness prickling close and threatening behind her eyelids. "I've been trying, my lord," she managed. "I'm doing everything I can. There's just—"

She had to bite at her lip this time, shoving down all the wrong, wrong replies. *There's never enough money. You've run off multiple good servants this month alone. You expect perfection when we don't even have the resources for adequate. You're the worst magistrate Ashford has ever had, you don't deserve a single copper you own, and this entire town hates you.*

I hate you.

But. Alma had worked in Mr. Pembroke's grand manor house nearly all her twenty-three years. She'd grown up here, spending her whole childhood in the cramped servants' quarters, learning at her sweet, soft-spoken mother's side. And just like her mother, she'd worked as hard as she could, first as a scullery maid, then a housemaid, then a chambermaid. And finally, six months ago—after her mother's endless, agonizing death—Alma had been appointed as Mr. Pembroke's interim Head Housekeeper. A spectacular opportunity to manage one of the largest households in Sakkin Province, while finally earning enough income to address the overwhelming physicians' bills that had accompanied her mother's later years.

And someday, when Alma had saved enough coin, she would buy a little house of her own. She would keep it neat and tidy, and decorate it however she pleased. She would plant a garden, perhaps, and make a private little shrine to her mother, and finally find a home for the deeply distressing jar of white ashes currently tucked away under her bed.

But now it was over, over already, because Alma had never managed to get along with Mr. Pembroke the way her mother had. She'd never found a way to soften his volatile moods, or soothe his many furious outbursts. And now her one hope, her one golden opportunity, was slipping away before her blinking eyes, as Mr. Pembroke whipped his grey-streaked head back and forth, and jabbed a thick, accusing finger across the desk toward her.

"You are a *failure* of a housekeeper, Miss Andersson," he hissed. "I should never have offered the position to someone so young, or so unqualified, or so utterly *inept!*"

Alma's swimming gaze had dropped to the desk, and she made herself nod, swallowing over the ever-worsening pain in her throat. Waiting for the inevitable final judgement, the rapidly approaching death-knell, dropping straight toward her pale, exposed neck.

And gods, what was she going to do now. Without a reference from Mr. Pembroke, it would be nearly impossible to find similar service work anywhere in the province—and she had no other experience, no other place to live, and no savings to support a long and dangerous journey elsewhere. And even if she'd somehow had the time or energy these past years to meet a potential husband, surely no respectable man would marry a mousy, impoverished, washed-up housemaid, who had little wit or beauty, and no more belongings than the ashes under her bed, and the soot-streaked clothes on her back.

"I have never before employed such an incurably incompetent *ingrate*," Mr. Pembroke railed on, with gut-swarming relish. "At this point, girl, I'd be well justified in hauling you off to the south, and throwing you out for the *orcs*!"

For... the *orcs*?! Alma's molten, pleading eyes had darted back toward Mr. Pembroke's reddened face, while a sharp, unbidden shiver ripped up her already-trembling back. Surely he wouldn't truly punish her with the *orcs*? The massive, deadly, terrifying brutes, whose massive, equally terrifying mountain was indeed only a day's journey south of Ashford? He would allow the orcs to hurt her, and drink her blood, and fill her belly with their huge, violent sons?

But no. No. Surely even Mr. Pembroke wouldn't do such a horrifying thing. He loathed the orcs, and often spoke of how many his militia had killed over the years, and how the foul beasts should be disemboweled on sight, and their vile spawn drowned, or left out for the crows. And how they didn't deserve the women they *did* manage to steal away, and how the Riddell heiress on the edge of town had turned into an orc-crazed trollop, and—

And gods, Alma had to pull herself together, because Mr. Pembroke was watching her with visible expectation in his eyes, clearly awaiting some kind of response to his appalling threat. And somehow, she found a way to gulp down another painful breath, while frantically groping for something, anything, to say.

"B-but surely you don't want to give the orcs any kind of— of support, my lord," she finally stammered. "And perhaps leaving me at Orc Mountain wouldn't—wouldn't work anyway, because didn't the orcs sign some kind of—of peace-treaty with the realm's lords, a year or two ago? Swearing not to take unwilling women anymore?"

But of course, it was again the wrong answer, always the wrong answer, because Mr. Pembroke's eyes bulged with black fury, his fist again banging on the desk. "Oh, those foul orcs may have wrangled the realm's lords into believing their treaty rubbish," he shot back, "but anyone on the ground knows the real truth. Those hideous beasts are planning to infiltrate our towns, steal away our women, and destroy our entire *civilization* with their dark magic, and their vulgar, barbaric practices! And I guarantee you, hardworking town magistrates like me are next on their list!"

Alma's headache felt like it was splitting her skull, and she could only seem to gaze speechlessly across the desk toward Mr. Pembroke. And perhaps he'd realized he was losing the thread, because he sat up straighter, gripping both meaty hands to his side of the desk. "And I said, the orcs are what you *deserve*," he snarled at Alma. "If you don't shape up, and start impressing me at *once!*"

If she didn't shape up. As if—wait, *wait*—as if there was still a chance. Still some hope. And Alma felt the sudden, tenuous truth of that leaping in her belly, firing painful clarity through her muddled, exhausted brain. She had to try to salvage this. Had to swallow the dregs of her pride, her dignity, her bitter helpless rage.

This was her survival. Her life.

"I'm so very sorry I've been such a disappointment to you, my lord," she choked out, her mouth twisting on the words. "If you would truly be willing to offer me one more chance, I—I'll do whatever I can to make this up to you. I will give it my absolute best effort. You won't regret it. *Please.*"

And yes, of course, *this* was what Mr. Pembroke had wanted to hear, because his corpulent body had relaxed back slightly in his chair, and a tiny, almost imperceptible smirk was finally curling at his mouth. And as Alma sat there, trembling and disgraced, she desperately fought the awareness that not only had Mr. Pembroke been waiting for her to start pleading, but that he was already *enjoying* it. That he *enjoyed* having her begging and broken before him, while he lorded his cold, cruel power over her.

And in Alma's most secret, shameful moments, alone in her cramped bedroom in the pitch-blackness, she could admit that the idea of that—of pleasing a powerful, confident male, and gaining his favour and protection in return—wasn't exactly an unpleasant one. But in those dark dreams, it was never a petty, paranoid, volatile little man, old enough to be the father she'd never known. It was never a man who looked at her like this, as though she was a silly, worthless trifle, who he'd just as soon cast out with the slops.

But at least Mr. Pembroke *was* still looking at her, his head tilting, that smirk still curving his lips. As if Alma was truly on the verge of salvaging this, saving her career, her future, her *life*. And she felt her breaths panting, her heart galloping in her chest, as she leaned forward, and fixed her wide pleading eyes to his.

"Please, my lord," she gulped. "I'll do whatever I can. *Please*."

And yes, this was what he wanted, it *was*—and Alma could have wept at that unmistakable flare of approval in his eyes, at the way he settled further back in his chair. Even at how the smirk was pulling up into a smug, triumphant little smile, toying at his plump little mouth, as he—as he—

As he dropped his hands, and began unbuttoning his *trousers*.

The sight was just visible over the desk, his thick fingers pulling at the buttons, his hand shoving the front fall downwards, and revealing the shocking truth beneath it. All while his beady eyes just kept gazing at Alma over the desk, glinting with challenge, with satisfaction, with *pleasure*.

No. *No.* Mr. Pembroke couldn't want—that? From her? *Now?*

A loud, ringing noise had begun rushing through Alma's hammering skull, and she could only seem to stare, frozen mid-breath on her chair. No. No, gods no, it had to be a mistake, some dreadful misunderstanding—and she abruptly glanced down at her filthy, soot-streaked apron, her black-rimmed fingernails, her decidedly frumpy-looking body in its unflattering uniform. And she could feel her frizzy blonde hair sticking to her burning cheeks, could feel her flailing heart trying to escape out her choked throat.

No. This couldn't be happening. It *couldn't.*

"Well?" Mr. Pembroke asked, his voice crisp, and wait, now *his* eyes were travelling down Alma's body, too. His gaze blatantly settling on the swell of her breasts beneath the filthy apron, and... lingering. *Leering.* Suggesting that he wasn't only enjoying this now, but he was actually—aroused. *Excited.*

Alma's eyes had briefly, painfully closed against that thought, because gods, was it even so surprising? In the six months since she'd taken this job, how many times had she seen that look in his eyes? How many times had he brought her into this office, watching coolly across his desk as she'd squirmed uncomfortably in this very chair?

But perhaps she'd been too naive to admit it, too afraid. Her mother had always been unusually stern about intimate relations in the house, about avoiding risky situations, about ensuring one was never fully alone with—with—

"I—I can't," Alma gulped, her body still frozen in her chair, even as her hands skittered against her filthy skirts, and gods, what had her mother taught her to say? "I—it's that time. With my courses. You can't want—"

But Mr. Pembroke's harsh laugh cut through the air, scraping more blistering terror down Alma's trembling back. "Of course I don't want *that*, you fool girl," he snapped. "But surely there's nothing wrong with your mouth?"

Her *mouth*. Alma's shaking hand had actually jerked up to cover it, as brackish bile surged sudden and powerful in her aching throat. No. No. *No*.

"I can't," she gasped again, and suddenly she was shivering all over, her heartbeat ricocheting through her chest. "I—I've never done such a thing to a man before. I don't—I don't even know *how*."

It was pure, unwashed truth, bitter and humiliating and thoroughly pathetic—but Mr. Pembroke only kept smiling, and oh gods, his hand had actually begun *moving*, blatantly tugging at what he'd exposed beneath his trousers. Again as if he were *pleased* by Alma's confession. By her foolish, shameful innocence. By her *fear*.

"Well, how old are you now, girl, twenty?" he demanded, his eyes once again dropping to linger on her heaving chest. "Clearly, it's about time you learned."

He might as well have slapped her across the face, and Alma reeled backwards in her chair, and fought down the awful, overwhelming urge to weep. She needed this job. She'd worked so hard for this job. And with her mother gone, there was no one left she could tell about this, no one to defend her—and this utter swine absolutely knew it. And if she agreed, he would use her and denigrate her, and he would enjoy it. And then he would expect it from her again, and again, and again...

A dark, unspeakable suspicion was suddenly curdling through Alma's shuddering brain, stealing away the last of her breath. Because this entire little scene was clearly familiar to Mr. Pembroke, expected by him, *normal*. And it was almost as though he saw that realization creeping through her thoughts, as though he could pluck it out as it passed.

"You don't *really* think you're any better than your mother, girl?" he drawled at her. "You think *she* didn't know who paid her coin, and filled her belly?"

The bile dangerously churned in Alma's throat, the revulsion roaring through her screaming skull. And before she'd even followed it, she somehow leapt out of her chair, staggering backwards, wildly whipping her head back and forth. The swine. The *scum*.

"My mother was *sick*," she rasped at him. "She was *dying*. You had *no right* to touch her, or ask *anything* else of her, beyond what she already gave you!"

The words came out loud, furious, ringing through the room—and she could see Mr. Pembroke stiffening, the anger crackling back into his glittering eyes. "I had *every* right," he snarled at her. "And I'll have you know, foolish girl, that your mother soon learned to enjoy it. *Long* before you were even out of the nursery!"

Alma's vision was spinning, her throat clawing, her heart raging against her ribs with overpowering force. "You foul piece of stinking *offal*," she hissed. "How dare you. How *dare* you. And I'll have *you* know"—she hauled air into her aching lungs—"I will never touch you. Ever. I'd rather damn well *starve!*"

Mr. Pembroke twitched, his eyes gone strangely still—and then he rose up out of his chair, too. The movement slow and menacing, his trousers still hanging wide open, his face mottled with red rage.

"Is that so, girl?" he asked her, all cold, deadly malice. "Then you can go right ahead, and get the *hell* out of my house, and waste away on the *streets!*"

Alma's battering heartbeat briefly stuttered—was she truly choosing possible starvation, over a few moments on her knees?—but it was too late, too late, because her frantically trembling hands were yanking at her filthy apron, dragging it off, and hurling it straight onto Mr. Pembroke's horrible, hideous face.

"With pleasure," she growled, as Mr. Pembroke floundered backwards, his arms flailing at the apron now wrapped around his head. "And if your entire house burns down tomorrow, it won't be soon enough!"

With that, she spun away, and rushed for the door. Her feet badly staggering, her shaking hands fumbling for the latch—while behind her, she could hear Mr. Pembroke knocking over his chair, and making a sound much like a roar.

"How dare you assault and threaten me, girl!" he hollered, his voice rising with every word. "*Guards!* Footmen! Help! I've been attacked!"

What? Alma's thundering head whirled around, her eyes and mouth agape—and Mr. Pembroke was *smiling* again, cold and vicious and terrifying, as he deliberately buttoned up his trousers.

"You don't think those murderous orcs will want you, girl?" he hissed, grim, satisfied. "Let's find out after all, why don't we?"

The terror screamed through Alma's entire body, blaring white panic behind her eyes. No, no, no, this couldn't be happening, this couldn't be the way her life ended, she'd worked so hard, given so much, and—

And somehow, somehow, her juddering hands found the latch, and yanked the door open. And without another look back, she snatched up her filthy skirts, and ran for her life.

2
___

Alma ran with desperate, feverish hopelessness. Tearing through the manor's corridors, down into the narrower servants' passages, and then bursting out the side door. Racing past two wide-eyed scullery maids, a stable boy, and the head groom, none of whom made any attempt to stop her, thank all the gods above.

And as she pitched across the grounds, her hair streaming out behind her in the chilly air, there was only one frantic hope, flashing through her panicked thoughts. If she could run far enough, fast enough, perhaps the guards and footmen wouldn't push. Perhaps they'd let her go, or at least only make a halfhearted attempt. She'd always done her best to be a genial and generous colleague, and there was no love lost between Mr. Pembroke and any of his staff, and she just had to give them a good enough excuse, make good enough time...

So she made straight for the thickest part of the approaching forest, fighting to ignore the distinctive sounds of voices and commotion behind her. Instead focusing on keeping her feet steady, dragging back ever more painful gulps of air, as she plunged into a dense stand of alders and birches against the edge of the forest.

Their thin bare branches whipped and scraped against her face, catching on her filthy skirts, but Alma ripped the fabric free, covered her face with her hands, and kept staggering forward. The men were still behind her, she had to keep moving, make it difficult, hopefully prevent Mr. Pembroke from having them caned for their failure, or worse—

But her breaths were already screaming in her lungs, her legs badly teetering beneath her. Fighting that damned fire had already taken so much of her strength, and she whimpered at the barrage of forest and pain, at the feel of hot, sticky blood now trickling down her hands, her cheek. She had to keep going, she knew what Mr. Pembroke was capable of when he was enraged and humiliated, if it wasn't the orcs it would be even worse, oh gods...

One of her staggering feet sank into a foxhole, wrenching her hard and sideways, and she had to clutch at a tree trunk for balance, scraping her already-bloody hands against the rough bark. While behind her, the men's voices kept shouting, and she had to keep going, please gods please—

But the terrain was only growing steadily worse, rocks and brush and pools of cold water flooding her flimsy shoes. Her entire body shaking and reeling, her breaths feeling like hot ash scraping down her throat, her lungs wheezing for air that felt thinner with every passing step. And when her floundering foot tripped on a root, she blindly shot forward, landing painfully on her hands and knees in rocky muck, while her breaths burned into hoarse, panting sobs.

She had to keep going. Had to. And there was a rushing sound up ahead, a muddy slippery bank, and Alma wept as she crawled toward it, dragging her gasping body over the grassy edge, slipping toward the churning, white-topped water below—

When suddenly, there was someone else. Someone running through the trees toward her, leaping over rocks and roots with light, astonishing ease. And it wasn't a guard, it wasn't a foot-man, because it wasn't—human.

It was—an orc?!

But yes, oh destroy her now, it was an orc. A tall, vicious, green-skinned orc, with glittering, terrifying black eyes. And he was coming for her, just like Mr. Pembroke had wanted, he was going to grab her, touch her, *kill* her, his sharp black claws snapping out of his huge deadly hands as he took one final leap toward her—

And with the very last of her strength, Alma pushed. Pushed herself off the slippery bank, toward the seething water below, as the orc lunged, his eyes wide and... afraid?

"No!" he was shouting, his voice slicing between them, his hand swiping uselessly through the air. "*No*, woman!"

But it was too late, it was over now, it was done. And Alma might have even smiled up at the orc's thwarted, wide-eyed face as she dropped back through empty air, and crashed into the deep.

3

Drowning, it turned out, was a terrible way to die.

The slam of the river's ice-cold water on Alma's back had felt like it was flaying her alive, breaking white-hot pain across her entire mangled body. So shockingly brutal that it left no room to move, let alone breathe or try to swim, and a desperate gulp for air only found sharp frigid water, swarming with devastating agony into her already-screaming lungs. Suffocating her in liquid death, in helpless shrieking panic, but her belated kicking and flailing was too weak, too useless, too late.

It was over. Finished. She hadn't done enough, worked hard enough. She'd failed.

And as she sank deeper, there was at least one small comfort, against the pulsing wheeling agony. Perhaps she would see her mother again. And they would run to each other, cling to each other, and never let go. And they would never speak of Mr. Pembroke again, even as he loomed and leered over them. *You think she didn't know who paid her coin, and filled her belly...*

Alma's mouth was silently screaming, but her body had seemed to lose the last of its will to fight, dragging her ever deeper. While her vision blurred, sparked, faded into the darkness...

When suddenly, something—*grabbed* her. Circling hard and powerful around her shuddering chest, and grasping tight. And somehow shoving upwards, away from the darkness, from her doom.

And in a shattering rush, there was open air again. Air, and warmth, from the solid strength against her, kicking her straight toward the opposite side of the river. Toward where the bank was thick with tall brown grasses, and she felt herself being dragged out onto them, while something firm and forceful slapped against her back.

The pain roared and ricocheted in its wake, but Alma was suddenly, violently coughing, vomiting out streams of water and blood and black clumps of ash onto the earth below her. While the thing that had slapped her—a hand?—rubbed large circles at her sodden back, steady and warm and reassuring.

"Good, woman," a voice breathed, low and vaguely familiar. "Good. I know this is pain, but you must cough all this from your lungs and belly, ach?"

The voice sounded regretful, but also as though it bore an edge of anger, too. And why did it sound *familiar*, why was more terror firing up her shivering back... and when Alma's stinging, streaming eyes somehow blinked open, they found...

The *orc*. The same huge, hulking, green-skinned orc, now with water dripping down his scarred face, streaking from wet wisps of thick black hair. And rather than being a proper distance away, he was right *here*, an orc was touching her, he was going to—

"No!" Alma tried to yell, but it came out as a hoarse, grating cough, wracking through her chest, streaming more water from her blubbering mouth. Oh gods, this couldn't be happening, what had become of her, what was he going to do to her—

But the warm touch on her back had swiftly, abruptly vanished, and when her blinking eyes found the orc again, he

was several arms-lengths away from her, kneeling on his
haunches in the tall grass, his eyes wide and intent on hers.

"Ach, I shall not harm you," he said, his mouth grimacing,
revealing a row of vicious, sharp white teeth. "Only need you to
be safe."

Safe. Alma's disbelief flashed with dizzying force, but she
was already coughing again, choking out more foul water onto
the ground beneath her. And when she tried to shove herself
up onto her shaking arms, she discovered that she didn't even
have the strength to do so—and she gasped with agony as her
shuddering shoulder slammed back to the earth.

"Ach, woman," came the orc's voice again, far too close, and
when Alma blinked up, he was here again. Hovering huge and
restless over her, his dark, long-lashed eyes frantically
searching her face. "You must not move. Only lie still, and seek
to breathe. *Please.*"

His concern seemed strangely, inexplicably genuine, and
even as Alma cringed back from him, she felt herself nodding,
and fighting to draw in one breath, another. The air felt like it
was made of knives, flaying her lungs alive with every inhale,
but the convulsive shudders had faded slightly, giving way to an
incessant, scraping ache.

"Ach, thus," the orc said, his voice fervent and approving,
his eyes flaring with visible relief. "Good woman. Brave
woman."

Another inexplicable shudder wrenched up Alma's throbbing back, but she was still taking breaths, holding the orc's
gaze. And he was nodding down toward her, again and again,
that approval and relief still shimmering in his blinking black
eyes.

So Alma kept breathing, kept looking, kept... living. And
the orc kept looking back, his breaths rising and falling with
hers, while his hanging black hair slowly dripped water onto
her heaving chest.

The forest had otherwise gone silent around them, but for

the rush of the nearby river. Suggesting, perhaps, that at least the men chasing Alma had abandoned the attempt, and she felt herself sag deeper into the earth beneath her, felt her own relief flaring through her aching body.

She was alive. She was breathing. This orc had—rescued her. Saved her.

And surely, if he'd meant to harm her, or take advantage of her, he could have easily done so by now. He was massive, and clearly very strong, he had those claws and teeth, and she was far, far too weak to fend him off. Gods, if he'd wanted to, he could have already yanked up her tattered skirts, and sired a son upon her...

But he was still just looking at her, breathing with her, his eyes so painfully intent on hers. And blinking back up toward him, it distantly, foolishly occurred to Alma that he had remarkably beautiful eyes. And that despite the stark lines of his face—and the various scars marring it—he wasn't nearly as hideous as she'd expected an orc should be, either. His green skin was smooth and even, his black brows thick and expressive, his nose straight, his mouth full and supple.

And that mouth was giving her a faint, twitching smile, making something stutter erratically in her heaving chest. "Good woman," he said again, soft. "This pleases me."

Oh. Alma's chest kicked again, but she somehow—impossibly—felt her own mouth twitching up, too. "Th-thank you," she croaked, her voice raspy and thin. "I am—I am indebted to you."

The truth of that seemed to fire another shudder up her spine, and she felt her breath catch, her eyes locked to his. She was indebted to an orc, she surely owed him her very *life*, and surely now he would call her on that debt. He would want to take her, use her, spawn his son upon her...

But above her, his eyes had sharply narrowed, his head whipping back and forth, hard enough to spatter water drops against her cheeks. "There is no debt," he said firmly. "Only—"

He broke off there, and huffed something that might have been a laugh. "I was once saved from a river also," he said, his voice now tinged with wry warmth. "I now only return this gift, ach?"

The sudden, incongruous vision of this huge, capable orc floundering helplessly in a river flashed across Alma's thoughts, and she felt herself wince, her eyes searching his face. "Were you—were you all right?" her hoarse voice asked. "You must have been—"

Gods, she couldn't even seem to finish it, to speak aloud what horrors must have befallen this powerful orc to make him suffer such a fate. And her thoughts had instantly jarred back to Mr. Pembroke, to the glee in his voice as he'd spoken of dying orcs, of the cruelties his men had eagerly committed against them.

Alma had found it distasteful then, but now it felt truly horrifying, the fear and the injustice of it clogging her aching throat. And above her, the orc was rapidly blinking, his mouth wincing too, his breath exhaling in a shaky, unsettled sigh.

"Ach, I am well now, thanks to the kindness of my brothers," he said, quiet. "And you ought not to be thinking of me, woman. Most of all when *you* are now the one suffering thus."

His clawed hand had given an unsteady-looking wave down at Alma's body, and she reflexively followed its path downwards—only to discover, oh gods, that her dress had been nearly destroyed. And while its remaining sodden, blood-streaked tatters still covered her waist and her groin, her full breasts were both fully exposed, their pink tips blatantly jutting up, almost as if inviting the orc to look his fill.

And then he—he *did* look. The glance brief and furtive, but most certainly intentional. And she could even see his throat swallowing, could see the flush staining his cheeks as he slowly, deeply inhaled—but then he shook his head, hard, and glanced back toward her face. His mouth betraying a tight, bitter wince, his eyes dark with unmistakable guilt.

Alma's shaky hand had only just now decided to obey, sliding awkwardly up to cover herself—and yes, surely that was relief, flaring through the orc's expressive eyes. As if he truly hadn't wanted to look at her, let alone take advantage. And amidst the mingled humiliation and exhaustion, Alma couldn't deny her own lurching relief, settling ever heavier within her aching chest.

"M-my apologies," she stammered at him, even hoarser than before. "I—I didn't realize I was so indecent."

The orc's blinking eyes had sharpened into something much like incredulity, and he jerked another shake of his head. "No, woman," he replied, his voice oddly strained. "It is I who ought to apologize. You are weak, and injured, and—"

He stopped and grimaced, his pained gaze briefly dropping back to Alma's arm clutched over her chest—and in an abrupt flurry of movement, he was yanking at his own sodden tunic, and dragging it off over his head. And after giving it a quick, forceful shake off to the side, he carefully draped it over Alma's front, like a large, wet, orc-scented blanket.

But once again, it was kind. So, *so* kind. And Alma could only seem to blink at his watching face, drinking up the faint flush still staining his cheeks, the way his pointed fang was biting at his full lip. The way his hand—now somehow with its claws drawn in—had awkwardly slipped up to rub against his bare, dripping-wet shoulder.

And curse her, *condemn* her, because now Alma was the one looking. Her tired, traitorous eyes dropping to the powerful bulk of that smooth green shoulder, the ease of its shifting muscle. And further down, the smattering of dark hair across his chest, the deep green of his pebbled nipples, the ripples of his slim waist, the line of black hair on his lower belly, trailing down toward his trousers...

Her swallow was surely audible, echoing shamefully in the sudden silence, and she felt her own cheeks flushing, her eyes belatedly squeezing shut. Gods, she had to be losing her *mind*, it had to be the exhaustion, the shock of it all, something...

The sound of the orc clearing his throat snapped her eyes wide again, and now he was giving her another little smile, wry, almost regretful. "Now I am the indecent one, ach?" he said, in a tone he surely meant to be light. "Forgive me?"

Something wildly swerved in Alma's belly, and she felt herself choke a laugh, or perhaps a sob. "Good gods, kind sir, you saved my *life*," she gulped, shaking her head. "At this point, I'll do absolutely anything you ask."

But wait, what in all the gods' holy names had she just *said*—had she learned *nothing* from Mr. Pembroke today?!— and suddenly the orc looked just as stunned as she felt, his half-bared body seized to stillness, his eyes frozen on her face. And now she could hear his swallow, could see his nostrils flaring, his chest filling with his slow, purposeful inhale. As that clawed hand surreptitiously slipped downwards, adjusting something at the front of his trousers...

And he saw her looking, he did, his hand spasming against his groin. Clutching against something long and shockingly thick, something that was visibly... swelling. And rather than being properly alarmed, or afraid, like she'd been back in Mr. Pembroke's office, Alma actually, *impossibly*, felt her tongue brushing against her lips, her breath scraping harsh and hungry from her throat.

A low, rumbling sound escaped the orc's mouth—a groan?—and in another flash of movement, he'd leapt away and up to his feet, his back turned toward her. His broad shoulders rising and falling, the ridged muscle shifting with every breath, and there was the strangest urge to reach for him, to beg him to come back, to begin weeping at his feet. Because wait, what if he already regretted his kindness, what if he realized how perverse and useless she was, what if he *left*...

"If you truly mean this offer, woman," his voice said, sounding far stiffer than before, "then you shall accept only—*only*—my help. You shall come to my mountain, and my brothers shall tend to you there, until you are well again. Until you"—his shoulders rose, fell—"you are able to return to your home again."

Oh. Alma kept blinking at the orc's rigid back, at his obvious discomfort, the unhappiness that felt almost strong enough to taste. And her own chagrined regret was rising nearly as sharp as her fear—did this lovely orc mean he felt obliged to take her to *Orc Mountain*, against his own wishes?—and she felt her head frantically shaking, her trembling hand clutching at his wet tunic, still clinging to her gasping chest.

"Th-there's no need for that, sir," she choked at his back. "You've already done more than enough, and I'm sure you wish to be—on your way again. I'll just rest here for a spell, and return to my—my home—when I'm able. Again, I am so very, very thankful to you, and hope the gods bless you for your great kindness."

Her breaths were panting by the end, hard enough that she had to lie fully back on the grass again, her swimming eyes blinking at the grey sky above her. But yes, this was the way forward, it had to be. She'd survived, this orc had saved her, and she couldn't bear for him to come to regret it, or feel obligated, or whatever else was bringing him such misery.

But suddenly he was here again, his face juddering back into place over hers, both his hands flat to the ground on either side of her head. "No, woman," he hissed down at her, his lips curled back, showing her all those vicious white teeth. "No. I shall not leave here without you. You are weakened, and ill, and mayhap yet at risk of death. You shall not seek to send me away, or *thank* me!"

Oh. Well. And blinking up at his harsh, angry face, Alma felt herself sagging harder into the earth, swallowing over the stabbing pain in her throat. "But you—you're sure," she croaked. "I would never wish to—to encroach, or interfere."

The orc barked a strange, shrill laugh, his head twitching

sideways. "You will not," he said, with an odd catch in his voice. "Now will you come with me?"

Would she come with him. To Orc Mountain. To the very place where Mr. Pembroke had threatened to abandon her, to leave her for dead...

But this orc had saved her. He'd been so impossibly kind to her. And against all reason, Alma somehow—somehow—trusted him. He wouldn't hurt her. He wouldn't.

"I will keep you safe," the orc breathed, as if she'd spoken that thought aloud. "I swear this to you, Bright-Heart. So you will come. Ach?"

Bright-Heart. She would come. She would come?

"Very well, sir," she whispered, to his beautiful, bottomless eyes. "Yes. I will."

4

Several moments later, Alma found herself curled up in an orc's warm arms, and being carried off toward Orc Mountain.

It was utterly, impossibly surreal, and as she felt the orc's smooth, powerful strides beneath her, it almost felt as though the world had cracked into jagged, irrevocable shards, never to be pieced together again. She'd been chased out of Mr. Pembroke's house. She'd lost her job, and nearly her life. And now she was willingly—willingly!—being taken off to Orc Mountain, by a lovely, bizarrely benevolent orc, who had so far defied every single preconception she'd ever held about his kind.

"Thank you again, sir," she said, muffled, into his smooth, sweet-smelling bare chest. "You are far too generous."

There was an instant's silence from the orc above her, a barely perceptible snap of tension through his solid striding warmth. "Ach, mayhap," he said, again with an obvious attempt at lightness. "This is what my mate always says, also."

His... *mate*?! As in... his *wife*? Alma had jerked to sudden, horrified stillness in his arms, her head twisting up toward his face. His grim, set face, already so inexplicably familiar, so easy to read. And indeed, he was telling her, shouting at her, that yes, he already had a mate. And that explained so damned much, of course it did, and it also meant that she'd been frightfully inappropriate back there beside the river, and oh gods, what must he think of her now?

And even worse, by telling her like this, he'd clearly meant to establish a boundary. To make it very clear to Alma, again, that this was only about his kindness, and nothing more. He was helping her until she was well, maybe as repayment for whoever had similarly rescued him, and then he would expect her to be on her way again. Out of his life. Back to her... *home*.

He was glancing uneasily down toward her now, perhaps following all her frantic, shameful thoughts—which had no doubt, once again, been entirely inappropriate. And Alma desperately fought to ignore the horrible churning in her belly, the shuddering humiliation, the twisting, dragging guilt. He had a mate. And she needed to respect that. She *had* to.

So she pasted on a smile, and surreptitiously drew back her hand, which had—somehow—been resting flat against his bare chest. "I—I'm so sorry, I didn't realize," she told him, her voice painfully thin. "If your mate is as lovely as you are, I very much look forward to meeting her. Before I return to my, er, home."

The orc's downward glance was accompanied by a wince this time, and she could see his throat bobbing, his chest hollowing against her. "Ach, my mate is not a woman," he replied, very smooth. "And he is not exactly *lovely*, I will confess. Rather the opposite."

A whisper of warmth had crept into the orc's voice as he'd spoken, softening his eyes and mouth—but Alma felt struck to stillness again, her gaze frozen on his face. Her rescuer's mate was a *man*? Or rather—surely—another *orc*?!

His glance down toward her was mulish now, his jaw set and grim. As if he was anticipating her response, and fully expected it to be shocked, or jeering, or horrified. Because surely, he had to know that such relations—while assuredly frequent among humans as well—were strictly forbidden by all the realm's laws, and therefore subject to any number of cruel, horrible punishments.

But Alma was already feeling inexplicably affronted on the orc's behalf, and she once again fought through her beleaguered, exhausted thoughts, and tried for another smile up at his set face. "So what is your mate's name?" her hoarse voice asked. "And I hope he's kind to *you*, at least?"

She could feel the orc's relief, settling heavy upon him, escaping in a husky laugh from his mouth. "His name is Drafli, of Clan Skai," he replied. "And ach, he is oft kind to me. Though he does not like to admit this, and thus"—his lips twitched a little higher, his cheeks unmistakably reddening—"he oft likes to make me beg for his favour also, ach?"

Wait. Alma's brain was wheeling, *again*, because was the orc saying—surely he was saying—that this was about his... *intimacy* with his mate? That this Drafli orc would command him? Make him *beg*?

But the orc's face was flushing even redder, the colour even reaching the tips of his ears, and he'd shifted her slightly in his arms, sheepishly rubbing a hand against his neck. Against where—Alma blinked to look closer—there appeared to be fresh *wounds* in his neck. And beneath them, many similar-shaped scars, all looking much like... *teeth-marks*?

A sharp, reflexive gasp had torn from Alma's throat, while her appalling thoughts now reeled relentlessly toward her own deepest, darkest dreams, back in her bed at Mr. Pembroke's. Serving a powerful male, pleasing him beyond all his expectations, and in return, he would...

She loudly coughed, shoving that vision forcefully away, and mentally flailed about for some kind of appropriate answer. "Er, I'm sure your Drafli cares for you very much," she said faintly. "Have you two been, er, *mated*, for quite some time?"

She couldn't quite meet the orc's eyes now, but she could feel the silent exhale from his chest. "Drafli and I have long been... close," he said slowly, as though he was choosing the words carefully. "But we spoke the vows of matehood mayhap half a year past. And thus, I should now never seek comfort or pleasure with any other but him, for these vows bear great weight to our kind, and to me. Ach?"

He was again making his position with her very, very clear, and Alma rapidly, earnestly nodded. "Yes, that makes perfect sense," she croaked, and suddenly she seemed far too aware of her staggering exhaustion, of the still-present ache in her pounding skull. "You two must be so happy to have each other to love like that. And thank you so much for telling me, before I—"

Before I made a complete fool of myself, she'd been about to say—but gods, surely she'd already done so, and she squeezed her eyes shut, swallowed over the fire in her throat. Waiting for the orc's judgement, perhaps, or his mockery, his contempt—

But there was only the steady roll of his steps beneath her, the slow rise and fall of his chest. The sound, perhaps, of his own throat swallowing, then letting out a heavy sigh. "Do you have someone, thus?" he asked, even more carefully than before. "Someone... to love? At your home?"

Alma's laugh scraped out on its own, bitter and broken, and far too late she choked it into a cough. "N-not yet," she made herself say. "But I'm sure I will, once I go back. Soon."

If she'd hoped that would soften the odd tension in the orc's body against her, she was mistaken—but she finally felt too tired, too worn and raw, to follow it further. He'd chosen to save her, he'd been kind enough to overlook her foolishness, he'd made his intentions toward her very clear. And suddenly there was only gratefulness left, pouring all through Alma's aching body, sagging her heavier against him. She was so, so lucky to have met him. So lucky he was still here.

"Thank you again, good sir," she mumbled, fervent. "Will—will you tell me your name, so I might better remember you?"

There was more inexplicable stiffness in his body, another slow sigh through his chest. "Baldr," he said, very quiet. "Of Clan Grisk."

Baldr, of Clan Grisk. An odd name, to be sure, but already Alma was brushing that thought away, and reorienting herself around it. Baldr, of Clan Grisk, who after her mother was quite possibly the kindest person she had ever met. Baldr.

"I shall never forget you, Baldr of Clan Grisk," she whispered. "Or your great generosity toward me."

He didn't immediately answer, his steps so steady, so careful. Lulling Alma ever deeper into the gratefulness, into this warm, rich-scented safety. Into the pain finally slipping away a little, twining into the dark...

"I shall not forget you either, Bright-Heart," said his voice, so distant now, shimmering through the air around them. "Now rest for me, ach?"

Rest for him. And yes, yes, Alma would do that, would do anything he ever asked—so she curled closer into his safety, and finally, gratefully, slept.

5

_____

When Alma next awoke, it was to the discovery that she was in... a bed. A very soft, very cozy bed, with something heavy draped over her, and a light, cheerful crackling sound tickling at her ears.

She twitched and blinked her eyes open, finding a mass of smooth grey stone above her—a ceiling? And wait, the room's walls were just the same, and there were no windows to be seen, which surely meant—wait—

She was in *Orc Mountain*.

The memories of Mr. Pembroke, the river, the orc—*Baldr*—were suddenly charging through her skull, and as she frantically blinked around her, the rest of the world slowly settled into sense again. Yes, Baldr had promised to bring her to his mountain—to his brothers—so that she could heal. And the room he'd brought her to was large and open, with a small fire burning at one end, and multiple metal-framed beds scattered throughout. As if this were indeed an actual *sickroom*. In *Orc Mountain*.

Alma dragged in a long, fortifying breath, willing her heartbeat to slow, and then she slowly, carefully shoved herself up a little in the bed. Noticing, distantly, how her body didn't seem to hurt nearly as much as it had before, and her headache had thankfully seemed to cease entirely. While her throat, on the other hand, still felt raw and inflamed, and every breath seemed to flare jagged pain ever deeper into her lungs.

"Oh good, you're awake," said a deep, unfamiliar voice, and when Alma snapped to look, she found herself faced with the sight of a huge, grey-skinned orc. He was bare-chested, with a long black braid hanging over his shoulder, and his harsh face bore multiple vicious-looking scars, giving him the precise look of the terrifying orcs from all the old tales.

But the orc was waiting a respectful distance away, and was giving her a careful, if alarming smile, and then—Alma blinked—even a curt little bow. "I'm Efterar, our mountain's Chief Healer," he said, in perfect common-tongue. "I've been caring for you since your arrival yesterday, together with our Ka-esh medics Salvi and Eben."

He nodded toward the other side of the room, to where— good gods—yet two more unfamiliar orcs seemed to be working over a large, stone-hewn workbench. Both of them were now looking toward Alma too, one of them with a rather stunned look in his dark eyes, the other with a wave and an easy smile.

Oh. Alma tentatively waved back, an action that caused the weight covering her to slip downward—and she grasped it just in time, because wait, she was *undressed* under this thing. This fur, apparently, and a surreptitious glance down at her bare body beneath it showed a variety of fading bruises, but no other obvious signs of injury. And she even somehow looked clean again, the caked-on soot and dirt seemingly vanished from her skin and her hands.

"You suffered multiple bruises and lacerations, but we've been able to heal the worst of them," the Efterar orc continued, his voice matter-of-fact. "I hope you'll forgive us for washing you as well. However"—his eyes narrowed toward Alma's chest through the fur—"your throat and lungs are another matter entirely. You were exposed to a fire, I presume? For quite some time?"

Alma grimaced, but nodded, swallowing against the sharpness indeed still scraping her throat. "Yes, in my employer's kitchen," she replied, her voice sounding astonishingly raspy and frail. "We fought it all afternoon."

The Efterar orc loudly harrumphed, his disapproval deepening the harsh lines of his face. "And then you fell in a river," he said crisply, "and fully flooded your already-damaged lungs with water. You've given us quite a job, woman. It's a miracle you're even still *alive*."

Alma couldn't stop her flinch, or the sudden, sickening plunge in her belly. "I—I'm truly sorry to have inconvenienced you, sir," her faint voice whispered. "If you'd be so kind as to draw up the bill, I will—"

But she broke off there, her eyes blinking hard, because good gods, what would she do? However would she find a way to pay him, with no job, and no reference? Not to mention the crushing weight of the physicians' bills she still already owed back in Ashford?

"Oh, don't be daft," Efterar replied, though his voice had slightly softened. "We don't expect payment here. And we're certainly not about to let you leave yet, not with your lungs in this state."

This revelation did nothing to soothe Alma's churning unease, and she glanced doubtfully around the room. There was no one else here, beyond this Efterar and the other two orcs. No humans, and no comforting familiar faces. No... Baldr.

But surely it was sheer foolishness to hope that Baldr might have stayed, or stopped by to visit. He'd made himself so very clear when he'd brought her here, and her behaviour around him had been unspeakably rude. Of course he wouldn't return. Gods, he'd all but said farewell, hadn't he?

"And beyond your lungs," Efterar continued, his voice still softer now, "extended smoke inhalation can often affect your mental state as well. If you haven't already, you might experience confusion, emotional changes, delirium, or worse. So I'd like to keep an eye on you for at least another week or two."

Alma couldn't seem to stop blinking at him—another *week* or two?—when suddenly, someone new burst into the room. Someone who seemed visibly agitated, and who was nearly sprinting across the floor, racing straight toward her.

Alma cringed back in her bed, clutching her fur up to her neck—but wait. Wait. It was... *Baldr*?

Her relief seemed to pour out like a flood, because yes, yes, thank all the gods, it was Baldr. Only looking rather different than before, what with the dry, looser-fitting tunic and trousers, and the way his long hair was now pulled back into a neat braid. And the look in his black eyes was almost panicked, somehow, his gaze raking frantically over Alma's face—and she felt her entire body relaxing under the strength of his obvious concern, her mouth curving into a true, genuine smile.

"Oh, it's *so* good to see you again, Baldr," her hoarse voice blurted out, before she could stop it. "But is something wrong? Are you all right?"

The panic seemed to drain at once from Baldr's face, leaving his green skin looking oddly pale. "Ach, I am well," he said, as his clawed hand came up to rub against his mouth. "But your scent—I tasted your—your *fear*. Your *anguish*."

He'd shot a sharp, accusing look over his shoulder toward Efterar, who abruptly raised both his hands, palms out. "I was only informing her about her condition, Grisk," he said, his voice curt. "But I do apologize"—his eyes flicked toward Alma—"if I alarmed you, woman."

Oh. It felt so easy to smile at Efterar, suddenly, and to attempt a dismissive wave of her shaky hand from behind the fur. "I only—I've just been a little overwhelmed, I think," she managed, glancing back toward Baldr again. "Mr. Efterar was very kindly telling me how all the smoke might have affected my—my mental state. So I suppose I'm bound to be rather unbalanced. Nothing for you to worry about, I'm sure."

She tried to smile again, but Baldr was still looking unnervingly pale, his hand twitching against his mouth. And then he took a large, purposeful step away from her, his shoulders squaring, as his uneasy eyes glanced deliberately toward the door.

And wait. That was because—there was yet *another* new orc, stalking tall and silent into the room. This one was lean and bare-chested, his grey skin latticed with visible scars, his claws curving like talons from his long, deadly-looking fingers. At his side hung a gleaming sword, belted to his low-slung trousers, and those were surely more blade-hilts, tucked into his soft black boots. And—Alma's gaze darted up again—his black hair was tightly pulled back from his face, accenting the sharp lines of his high cheekbones, his jaw, his hard, grim mouth.

But most compelling of all were the orc's eyes. Deep, glinting, long-lashed black eyes, which had already flicked to Alma's, and narrowed with dark, vicious danger.

"*Drafli*," Baldr said, his voice somewhere between strain and relief, and he strode straight toward the new orc, slipping his arm around his bare waist with smooth, familiar ease. And in return, the Drafli orc—yes, of course, Baldr's mate—slid his clawed hand into Baldr's hair, drawing his bowed head close into his shoulder.

The movement was firm, possessive, unflinchingly intimate—and Alma stared for a beat too long, her heart erratically skittering, her throat painfully swallowing. Until she realized, with a jolt of horrifying chagrin, that this Drafli was still glowering at her over the top of Baldr's head, with murderous rage flashing in his dark eyes.

Good gods, what was she *doing*, and Alma instantly dropped her gaze, and yanked her fur up closer to her chin. She most assuredly had no desire to make an enemy of Baldr's mate—quite the opposite—and truly, it was a wonder that Baldr had returned to see her at all. She needed to treat his boundaries with utmost respect, and make sure she offered the same to his mate as well.

So she waited, eyes downcast, until she was finally aware of movement, coming closer toward her. And when she risked a glance back up, and indeed found both Baldr and Drafli standing beside her bed, she took a breath, fixed her eyes to Drafli's angry face, and made her best attempt at a smile.

"You must be Baldr's mate," she said, as brightly as she could. "I'm Alma. Alma Andersson. It's so lovely to meet you."

She waited for his response, keeping the smile plastered to her mouth—but Drafli didn't move, or reply, or make any acknowledgement whatsoever that she'd spoken. Only kept glaring down toward her, dark and contemptuous, as though she were some silly, worthless little chit, who'd somehow stumbled her foolish way into his furious, disapproving presence.

"Drafli... does not oft speak aloud, the way we do," cut in Baldr's strained voice, and when Alma's startled eyes glanced toward him, he was looking even paler than before, his jaw taut. "But he watches, and listens, and sees much that others do not."

Oh. Baldr's mate truly didn't *speak*? By choice, or by necessity? And if he didn't speak, how in the gods' names did they communicate? How did he make Baldr... *beg*... for his favour?

Alma's eyes had reflexively darted down to Baldr's neck—to where there was a distinct set of fresh red teeth-marks, oh *hell*. And her traitorous brain was suddenly, wildly trampling with the vision of this lean, terrifying Drafli shoving Baldr against the wall, firmly pushing his head aside, sinking his sharp teeth deep into that smooth green skin...

Something had dangerously plunged in Alma's belly, and she couldn't seem to choke back the harsh, betraying little gasp from her throat. While before her, Baldr visibly winced, and Drafli's lips had curled into a vicious, silent snarl.

Curse her, what was Alma *thinking*—what had they even been talking about?—and she desperately groped for focus, words, *something*. "Er, I've often heard that people who are infirmed can develop other skills, to compensate for their weaknesses," she said thickly. "I'm sure you are very gifted in other ways, Drafli, and—"

And no, no, no, that was wrong, wrong, *wrong*, because Baldr's wince was more like a flinch this time, his clawed hand clutching to Drafli's arm—because otherwise, Drafli might have *lunged* at her. His teeth fully bared, his tall body taut and coiled, his eyes gone almost feral with black, vicious contempt.

Alma was suddenly shivering under the fur, her hand clamping over her mouth, while the implications of what she'd just said swarmed fully over her. *Infirmed. Weaknesses. Very gifted.* Gods, as if this powerful, deadly-looking orc was a wounded, precocious little pet, defined only by his inability to speak.

"And people like me," she belatedly managed, with a brief, mortified glance at Drafli's enraged face, "should learn to keep our foolish mouths shut, because that was very rude. Inexcusably so. I'm sorry."

Beside Drafli, Baldr's stiff shoulders had slightly sagged, and that was surely relief, flaring across his eyes—but Drafli's furious expression hadn't changed. And as Alma waited, still shivering under her fur, Drafli's hands snapped up, and made a series of swift, purposeful motions toward Baldr.

Baldr's wary eyes had followed them, his own hands making a slower, reluctant-looking gesture in return—to which Drafli's hands seemed to move even more forcefully, one sharp talon jabbing toward Alma, the other toward Baldr.

Alma watched in uncertain, awed fascination—was *this* how they communicated?—and yes, surely it was, because Baldr was now turning back toward her, his shoulders squared, his mouth tight and forbidding.

"Drafli and I serve our mountain's captain, Grimarr, as his

Right and Left Hands," he said, his voice formal. "In human terms, we are his chief lieutenants, mayhap. And thus, we have some questions for you."

A dark little shiver wrenched up Alma's spine, and she found her eyes darting uneasily between Baldr and Drafli. They were Orc Mountain's *chief lieutenants*? That sounded important, crucially so, and why hadn't Baldr mentioned that before? Unless—unless he'd had some reason to mistrust her? To *doubt* her?

"Of—of course," she stammered, her voice thin. "I—I'm happy to tell you whatever you like."

But again, this was perhaps the wrong answer, because Drafli's glower seemed to flare even sharper, and Baldr's clawed hand briefly rubbed at his eyes. "We need to know," he said, the words stilted, "why you were being pursued, in the direction of our mountain. And why the men chasing you were employed by Ashford's town magistrate, who has made no secret of his hatred for orcs, or his blatant disregard for our peace-treaty."

Alma blinked up at Baldr's stiff face, and then back to the still-enraged Drafli beside him—and then realized, in another rush of mortification, that not only did they mistrust her, but perhaps they suspected she was part of some kind of... plot? That perhaps she was a spy, or she'd been intended to draw out the orcs? Or—or worse, that she'd fully intended to be "rescued", so that the men could then turn around and accuse the orcs of abducting her?

"It wasn't a plan," she replied, in a rush. "It wasn't. I swear to you. Mr. Pembroke is my employer, and we had a—a disagreement, and I ran away. I will admit, I wasn't thinking very clearly at the time, and the men—"

Her voice broke off there, her eyes wide and appalled on Baldr's pained-looking face, because wait, whatever had happened with Mr. Pembroke's guards and footmen? They'd been close behind her, hadn't they? Had they seen Baldr rescue her from the river? Had they *followed*?!

"They—they didn't *see* you, did they?" she croaked at Baldr. "Or try to follow you, or attack you, or accuse you of abducting me? Oh gods, I ought to go back, before—"

Her voice had been rising, shriller and thinner, until it abruptly broke into a convulsive, wracking series of coughs. To which someone—Efterar—thrust a waterskin into her trembling hands, and she desperately fought to gulp the cool liquid down her spasming throat. She had to go back. She couldn't give Mr. Pembroke any reason to accuse Baldr of wrongdoing, after he'd been so impossibly kind to her. She *couldn't*.

"You aren't going anywhere, woman," interrupted Efterar's flat voice, as his warm hand reached out to briefly settle against Alma's gulping throat, his touch firm and businesslike before dropping again. "And look, do we really need to launch into an interrogation right now? You two *do* realize that she's still badly injured, and that losing her voice permanently is still a very real possibility?"

Alma blinked blearily up toward Efterar, who was now standing next to Baldr, and frowning down toward her. While beside him, Baldr was suddenly frowning too, his gaze fixed with hard, inexplicable intensity to Alma's neck—to where, oddly enough, Efterar had just touched her. And on Baldr's other side, Drafli just kept glaring, now looking as though he thoroughly despised all three of them, and would rather be anywhere else but here.

And suddenly, Alma only felt terribly exposed, and guilty, and exhausted. She'd disrupted all these orcs' lives, she'd unthinkingly put them at risk, and she'd grievously insulted Baldr's mate, after Baldr had been so good to her. She desperately needed to get out of their lives, and out of this mountain, as quickly as she possibly could.

"Look, I'm sure I will heal very soon," she choked out, into the silence around them. "And I fully intend to be on my way as soon as possible, back to my home. But if there is *anything* I can do, in the meantime, to prevent my employer from retaliating against Baldr in any way—"

Her voice had frayed into something unrecognizable by the end, and she had to stop there, struggling to pull in breaths. And though Efterar's hand had lifted toward her again, he'd suddenly seemed to think better of it, giving a long, unreadable look at where Baldr was now rubbing his nose, his eyes squeezed shut.

"We will—speak to our captain, of this," Baldr finally said, his voice still strained. "And then we will send you word, woman. Ach?"

Send her word. Meaning, surely, that again, this was good-bye. That this visit had been a one-time opportunity, or perhaps even a test—one that Alma had horribly, abjectly failed. But there was nothing for it now, nothing but to attempt another smile, and blink back the shameful wetness trying to escape down her cheeks.

"That's very thoughtful of you, thank you," she replied, her voice a brittle rasp. "And thank you for taking the time to visit. It was very good to meet you, Drafli."

And after one last, apologetic look toward Drafli's furious eyes, she slid back down under her fur, and made herself turn away, toward the stone wall beside her bed. And she waited, and waited, and waited, until she could feel Baldr and Drafli moving again, leaving her again, likely never to return...

The tears were finally streaking down her cheeks, dripping onto the bed beneath her, and behind her there was the heavy, distinct sound of a sigh. "You shouldn't pay any attention to Drafli, woman," said Efterar's low voice. "His clan—the Skai—aren't friendly to outsiders at the best of times, all right?"

But Alma was very near to full-on sobbing, now, and wiped an angry, shaky hand to her wet cheek. "But I insulted him, and now he *hates* me," she gulped. "And now I've pushed both him and Baldr away *forever*."

There was the sharp sound of a snort behind her, curt and

amused. "I don't think they'll be staying away long," Efterar said dryly. "And come to think of it, Drafli hated Baldr at first, too."

He had? Alma twisted around under her fur to look at Efterar—but he was already walking away, toward where the other two orcs were still working. "You worry about resting, woman," he said over his shoulder. "And healing. That's *all*."

And it was kind, it was so generous, and it should have helped. It should have. But it only felt like there was a growing, yawning ache in Alma's chest, dragging all hope into its depths. She'd lost her job. She'd lost her home, her future, even her mother's precious ashes. And now she'd probably lost Baldr, too, and it didn't make sense that it hurt so much, that she could still almost taste his unease, his misery, his pain. His pain that she'd caused, somehow, without at all meaning to, or even knowing why.

And before the despair could betray her to the room, Alma yanked up her fur over her head, buried her face in her hands, and silently, bitterly wept.

6

When Alma's awareness next returned, it came with the sound of voices. Or rather, one new voice, expressive and distinctly male, sounding audibly agitated as it seemed to flit back and forth across the room.

"And then, Roland just up and *left!*" it said, with feeling. "He said he'd done it long enough, and he was going to go put his feet up, and let his new *woman* take care of him!"

There was the sound of a familiar snort—surely Efterar—and then a wry laugh. "You can't really blame him, I suppose," Efterar's voice replied. "Old Roland's put in his time, hasn't he?"

"No, he has *not*," snapped back the first voice, "because he didn't even *try* to train anyone to do the job after him. No one knows how to manage this Keeping rubbish. He said maybe the Ka-esh would deal with it! As if he's never *met* a Ka-esh before!"

Alma's bleary eyes had finally blinked open, and found that the new voice was indeed coming from another new orc. One who was slim and bare-chested, his loose, long black hair whirling over his shoulder as he waved dramatically toward one of Efterar's medics, who was still working at his bench. The one named Salvi, Alma's foggy brain supplied, who was currently watching the speaking orc with his brows raised, his arms crossed over his chest.

"Is that supposed to be an insult, Kesst?" Salvi snapped back. "Because we *could* deal with Roland's job. If we wanted to."

"And that's exactly the problem," the Kesst orc retorted, with another vivid flourish of his hand. "If you *wanted* to. But we all know that you Ka-esh would spend *one day* washing clothes in that scullery, and then wander off to work some sums, or mix some potions together!"

The Salvi orc's eyes briefly dropped, to where there indeed seemed to be two potion-filled vials on the workbench before him—and his mouth twitched, even as he gave a dismissive shrug of his shoulder. "And why shouldn't we?" he countered. "We Ka-esh do *more* than our fair share of work around here as it is, without adding in laundry and floor-scrubbing and gods know what else. And"—his head tilted, his brows furrowing—"I thought the Keeping was supposed to be a Grisk job, anyway?"

"Yes, as did I," replied the Kesst orc, with an exasperated sigh. "But Roland said it was an unfair burden to just dump on the Grisk. And when I went and raised it to Grim just now, the big lout went and *agreed!* And then suggested"—he drew in a shuddering breath—"that maybe *I* could handle it!"

His voice had risen to a wail, his hands flinging up into the air—and across the room, Efterar barked a laugh, and then strode over toward him. "You know he was just baiting you, Kesst," he said lightly, sliding his arm around Kesst's shoulders, and drawing him close. "We all know you'd be the worst Keeper this mountain has ever had."

To Alma's vague surprise, Kesst didn't seem insulted by this, but actually looked rather mollified, his shoulders sagging, his body leaning into Efterar's. "I would be *dreadful*," he said, muffled, into Efterar's chest. "We would be rolling in filth. *Rolling!*"

Efterar gave a low, affectionate laugh, rubbing his big hand against Kesst's glossy hair. "So settle down, all right?" he said, his voice soft. "This isn't something you need to worry about. The captain will sort it out. He always does."

Kesst grimaced into Efterar's chest, his head twitching back and forth. "But how long is that going to take?" he asked plaintively. "And who's going to manage the laundry until then?"

Efterar blinked down toward Kesst, once—and then he threw back his head and laughed, the sound genuine and surprisingly contagious. "Oh, so *that's* why you're so worked up over this," he replied. "Let me guess, you're out of clean trousers?"

He'd clearly hit upon the truth of it, because Kesst loudly sniffed, narrowing his eyes up at Efterar's face. "Roland was already *weeks* behind," he said. "And I refuse to step *foot* in that filthy scullery. I'd rather walk around *naked*."

Efterar laughed again, palming his hand at Kesst's arse through his trousers, and in return Kesst sighed, even as he gave a small smile into Efterar's chest. "Yes, you'd like that, wouldn't you," he mumbled. "Typical."

Efterar's hand had spread a little wider, yanking Kesst closer—but then Alma saw him hesitate, his eyes flicking toward her side of the room. Toward—her?

She shrank back in her bed, pulling up her fur—but it was already too late, because this Kesst had turned to look too, his face brightening. "Oooh, our new arrival is finally awake!" he said, with a cheerful smile. "Yes, I suppose we don't want to alarm her into oblivion. *Yet*."

He accompanied this unnerving pronouncement with an exaggerated wink, and then untangled himself from Efterar, and strode over toward her. "Welcome to our mountain, sweetheart," he said, giving a fluid little bow. "I'm Kesst, of Clan Ash-Kai. Efterar's mate, and his favourite pain in the arse."

He'd smirked over his shoulder as he'd spoken, to where Efterar was rolling his eyes, even as a faint flush crept up his scarred cheeks. And despite the heat now flooding her own cheeks, Alma felt herself smiling back toward Kesst, and slightly relaxing under her fur.

"Th-thank you," she replied, her voice still rasping unnaturally in her ears. "It's so nice to meet you. I'm Alma."

Kesst's answering grin down toward her was approving, and unmistakably mischievous, too. "So tell me, Alma," he said lightly, "how have you been settling in so far? Have you met any of our orcs yet? If you're feeling up to it, maybe one of them could give you a tour? How about you, Eben?"

Across the room, Eben—who had been at the workbench with Salvi—abruptly fumbled with the jar of liquid he'd been holding, sloshing it all over the workbench. While beside him, Salvi cursed as he snatched up the open book that had also been sitting on the workbench, and then grabbed for a nearby rag, and tossed it into Eben's reddened face.

"She's still *recovering*, Kesst," cut in Efterar's flat voice. "And I don't think it's a wise idea for another orc to take her anywhere, until—"

He broke off there, his mouth grimacing, as if he hadn't wanted to speak further—but Kesst's brows had shot up, surprise flashing across his eyes. And then, as Alma uneasily watched, he stepped closer to her bed, leaned down, and *smelled* her.

It was unquestionably odd, and odder still was the way Kesst's eyes widened, his body jerking to stillness—and then he reared back up, and *laughed*. The sound warm and merry, his dark eyes dancing with amusement, his grin flashing toward Efterar behind him.

"Baldr?!" he demanded at Efterar, his voice sounding both disbelieving and delighted. "Oh gods, what I would have *given* to see Drafli's face. That smug Skai deserves to have his world shattered a little, don't you think?"

Efterar's mouth twitched, but that was surely a look of warning in his eyes, too—because wait, now all four orcs were suddenly looking at Alma again. At where she was sitting frozen under her fur, her heart painfully pounding, while something cold and uneasy snaked up her back. Kesst could *smell* Baldr on her? And that had somehow shattered Drafli's *world*?!

"I—I didn't mean to do anything," she rasped, her voice wavering. "I—I only fell into a river, and Baldr very kindly rescued me. I certainly wouldn't wish to obligate him in any way, or upset his mate, and I still mean to return home at once—"

But her rising voice had broken into coughs again, and Efterar shot Kesst a reproachful look as he grabbed for a water-skin, and strode over toward her.

"You aren't guilty of anything, woman," Efterar said, his voice clipped, his hand thrusting out the waterskin. "Scents are very strong for orcs, and mean more to some of us than others. But even for those of us who care about such things, there is *no* obligation—and no compulsion—in a scent-bond. *None.*"

A *scent-bond*? Alma's eyes were darting back and forth between Efterar and Kesst, catching on the grim certainty in Efterar's eyes, the sudden, inexplicable darkness in Kesst's. Did Efterar mean—he couldn't mean she was somehow *scent-bonded* to Baldr? And did he mean he and Kesst were scent-bonded, too? Or—or, judging by that look in Kesst's eyes—perhaps not?

And gods, could Alma *be* any more disruptive to these unexpectedly lovely orcs' lives, and she belatedly took a long, gulping drink from the waterskin. If she was truly going to be stuck here for a week, she ought to help. Ought to make some use of herself, and find some way—any way—to get out of these orcs' hair, and repay their astonishing kindness toward her.

So when she'd finished drinking, she squared her shoulders, and turned back toward where Kesst was still looking distinctly subdued, his gaze on the floor. "Did I hear correctly, earlier," she began, and then coughed again, cleared her throat. "That you're looking for someone to manage your house-keeping?"

Kesst blinked, and darted an uncertain glance at Efterar, whose frown was already deepening. "Yes," Kesst replied slowly. "But I assure you, sweetheart, that's nothing *you* need to worry about, all right? I was just flailing about and making a fuss. And annoying Eft with my drama."

He shot another brief, apologetic look toward Efterar, whose heavy brows had furrowed—and in a quick, purposeful step, Efterar slung his arm around Kesst's waist, pulling him close again. "Not annoying," he murmured, his voice light. "I want to hear your fussing, even if it's over laundry. But"—his eyes flicked back toward Alma—"we need to let the recovering human rest. Right?"

But Alma was sitting up straighter in her bed, drawing her fur up to cover her bare shoulders. "I'm actually feeling quite well, thank you," she replied, as firmly as she could. "And I also happen to have very extensive housekeeping experience. I would be more than happy to pitch in around here, even for a little while. Even just—just to earn my room and board, until you'll clear me to leave?"

Her voice had slightly faded as she'd spoken, wavering under the unmistakable, ever-increasing disapproval in Efter-ar's glare. "Or," she added helplessly, "maybe I could even just take a look around, and see what needs being done, so I could offer some guidance to Roland's replacement? Perhaps I could go on the—the tour Kesst suggested?"

She shot a pleading look toward Kesst, and thankfully his eyes had warmed again, his body leaning gratefully into Efter-ar's. "I could take her around, Eft," he said, glancing up at Efterar's still-narrow eyes. "Just for a bit. I'll bring her back as soon as I smell a whiff of tiredness on her, all right?"

Efterar's face had slightly softened, his head bending to nip at Kesst's pointed ear. "But she's to do *no laundry*," he said flatly. "Not even your favourite trousers. Swear it, Kesst."

"I swear, you overbearing tyrant," Kesst murmured back, but he was fully smiling now, his lashes lowered. "Though you'll come to regret it, once I'm flaunting your goods all over the mountain."

Efterar's low, disapproving growl seemed to light up Kesst's eyes, and he flashed a surprisingly dazzling smile toward Efterar's face, before briefly nuzzling into his neck. And when he glanced back at Alma, his eyes were warm and bright again, his mouth quirked back into a wry, mischievous grin.

"Well, I've sprung you, sweetheart," he said cheerfully. "Are you ready for Orc Mountain?"

A sharp, peculiar little chill raced up Alma's spine, but she lifted her chin, and swallowed hard. She'd already mucked up too much of this—most of all with Baldr—but surely, at least she could work. She could learn. She could find a way to at least partially repay these orcs, and then she would leave them forever, and find a new home, and never see them—or Baldr and Drafli—again.

She had to.

"Yes, of course," she said, her voice steadier than it had been yet. "I'm ready."

A lma was not ready for Orc Mountain.

First of all, the only mildly appropriate clothing the orcs had seemed to have on hand was a flimsy, floaty robe, which—while not quite indecent—certainly showed more of Alma's shape than she was accustomed to, curving brazenly over her ample hips, and the swell of her breasts. Not only that, but her shoes had apparently been lost, and despite Kesst's assurances that many orcs went barefoot in the mountain, it felt strangely precarious to be padding around without shoes, the stone floor feeling rough and cool under her feet.

But far more discomfiting than her ensemble was the mountain itself. Alma had already felt a distinct sense of size and weight and *life* about it, almost as if it had once been some ancient stone giant, now hunkered down to sleep—but as Kesst led her through the twisting, stone-hewn corridors, pointing out various features of interest along the way, Alma's bare feet stepped ever slower, her voice locked in her throat, her eyes gaping at the sheer unreality around her.

Because not only was Orc Mountain massive, but it was... *magnificent*. The corridors were wide and clear, their stone carved straight and smooth, and helpfully illuminated by a series of iron-wrought, wall-mounted lamps. And between the lamps, cut into the walls, were multiple large, square openings. Some were more corridors, Kesst explained as they passed, but most were rooms. Rooms all made of the same grey stone, with the same smooth floors and walls and ceilings—but all serving an astonishing array of different needs and purposes.

"This is the Grisk common-room," Kesst told her, waving casually toward a large, cheerful, firelit room, comfortably furnished with tables, benches, and furs. "And these"—Kesst waved at a row of close-set doors with no light beyond—"are Grisk bedrooms, and their latrine, and their main sparring-room. And over here is the Grisk forge."

He'd halted outside a warm, brightly lit room, in which several huge, bare-chested orcs were indeed smithing around a blasting furnace. The nearest orc was tall and broad, his muscular arm pounding out what appeared to be a shovel, glowing orange beneath his striking hammer—and as Alma stared, the orc's eyes flicked up, and met hers. And then he *winked* at her, his mouth quirking into a sly, sharp-toothed smile.

Alma twitched backwards into the corridor, her face heating, and beside her Kesst rolled his eyes, and waved her further down the corridor. "Grisk," he said, sounding half-exasperated, half-amused. "You bring *one* unmated woman through their wing, and suddenly it's like they're all in heat."

Alma's face burned even hotter, because so far, the various new orcs they'd met in the corridor had indeed been exceedingly friendly. Flashing her smiles that had ranged from shy to downright predatory, and many of them had even stopped to introduce themselves, giving her an assortment of odd-sounding names that had already begun to blur together in her stuttering brain. Eyarl. Tregmar. Valter. And now, this new one was Thrain? Or perhaps Thrawn?

"Thrain," repeated the tall, spiky-haired, kilt-clad orc, as he flashed Alma a warm grin, and rustled his hand against the braid of the shorter, broader orc beside him. "If you think that's odd, woman, how about Varinn here? I mean, what kind of name is *that*?"

The shorter Varinn orc rolled his eyes and ducked away from Thrain, smoothing out his mussed-up braid with a big hand. "I am named after an ancient Grisk battle-hero," he informed Alma, with a quirking smile. "Whilst Thrain, in our tongue, means 'stubborn oaf'. Or mayhap"—he raised his thick black brows toward Thrain—"a better translation should be, 'greatest pest amongst all his longsuffering Grisk kin.'"

Alma couldn't help a laugh—especially at Thrain's mock-horrified expression—and felt herself give a little curtsey toward them both. "It's lovely to meet you, Varinn," she said. "And you also, Stubborn Oaf, sir."

A bright, approving guffaw cracked from Thrain's grinning mouth, and without warning he lunged sideways toward Varinn, who just barely leapt out of the way. And then Varinn was calling a farewell as he pitched off down the corridor, with Thrain chasing close at his heels.

Alma chuckled as she watched them go, and belatedly drew her attention back to Kesst again. "So the orcs in this area are all Grisk?" she asked him. "And Grisk is one of your clans, right? Baldr's clan?"

The mirth in her voice had slightly faded at her mention of Baldr's name, and Kesst shot her a swift, sidelong look as he waved her down the corridor again. "Yes, there are five orc clans, and Grisk is the largest," he replied. "And as you've seen, usually the friendliest. These two things aren't unrelated, you can imagine."

His voice was amused, but Alma's thoughts had again seemed to darken, twining toward Baldr and his impossible kindness. "And how about the other clans?" she made herself ask, rubbing at her hot face. "You said yours was Ash-Kai, right? And Eben and Salvi are Ka-esh?"

Kesst's glance toward her was slightly surprised this time, but approving, too. "Yes, I'm Ash-Kai," he said. "Eft too. I like to think we're a decent bunch, but"—he gave an overly casual shrug—"we can also be selfish scheming bastards, so best not to take it too far. And the Ka-esh are our mountain's scholars— terribly handsome and clever, and excellent at keeping the place standing over our heads—but also completely useless when it comes to important matters like getting your trousers cleaned."

Alma couldn't help a reluctant smile at him, and in return he grinned back, waving her toward another adjoining corridor. "And then there's the Bautul clan—usually big and belligerent, but very useful in any battle, too, and good with hunting and gardens. And then"—his smile faded—"the last clan is the Skai."

The Skai. Kesst's voice had flattened as he'd said it, his eyes now looking straight ahead, his hands curled into fists at his sides. And Alma felt her head tilting as she studied him, her thoughts flitting back to that moment after Drafli had left the sickroom. To what Efterar had said.

"Efterar told me the Skai weren't... friendly," she said, her gaze dropping to the smooth stone floor beneath her feet. "I met Drafli yesterday, and..."

She thankfully bit the rest of it back just in time—gods, she surely didn't need to add gossiping about Baldr's mate to her ongoing list of blunders—but Kesst's answering snort seemed to suggest that he understood precisely her meaning. "Drafli was kind to you, I presume?" he asked, clipped. "Really welcoming? Understanding of the fact that you'd almost just *died*?!"

Alma winced, and kept her eyes fixed to the floor. "I was actually—quite rude to him," she said, her voice faint. "I—I commented unkindly on his—his inability to speak."

But Kesst only snorted again, and waved Alma around yet another corner. "Well, if it hadn't been that, I guarantee it would have been something else," he replied flatly. "You looked at him wrong, maybe. You wore your hair the wrong way. You didn't bow and simper at an arrogant Skai's *feet*, the way they all think you should!"

Kesst's voice had wrenched sharper as he'd spoken, suggesting that perhaps this went well beyond Drafli—and he paused mid-step, dragging a hand through his hair. "Sorry," he said, his voice gone carefully light again. "Too much history, you know. Do you want to see the kitchen, and the scullery?"

Alma belatedly nodded, and followed Kesst toward yet another door in the wall. This one opened up into a high, warm, cavernous room, with a blazing fire crackling in a large fireplace, and multiple shelves and barrels lining the walls. And working together at a long counter were two more new orcs, both of whom glanced up toward her. One of them with careful wariness in his eyes, and the other with abrupt, almost palpable hostility.

It was a disconcerting change from the other orcs—the *Grisk* orcs, Alma reminded herself—but Kesst didn't seem alarmed. "Alma, this is Gegnir, our mountain's Head Cook," he said, waving toward the wary-eyed orc, who seemed to be the older of the two, his grey-streaked hair pulled back into a tight bun. "He's Ash-Kai, too. And this is Gegnir's assistant Narfi. Of Clan Skai."

Again, Kesst's voice had definitely grown colder as he'd spoken, enough that this Narfi—a relatively smaller orc, with close-cropped hair—shot him a look of obvious animosity. "What do you wish for now, Kesst?" he asked flatly. "I told you, we shall *not* wash your clothes."

Kesst's lip curled, and he strode away from Gegnir and Narfi, toward the back of the kitchen. "I'm just showing Alma around," he said coolly. "She has actual housekeeping experience, you see, and therefore knows how to use a scullery, unlike *some* people."

Narfi made a noise rather like an affronted squeak, while

beside him, Gegnir gave a low, grunting chortle. "Do not launder Kesst's clothes, woman," he called after them. "It is a pit of doom you shall never escape."

A bubble of amusement escaped Alma's mouth before she could stop it, and she even flashed a reflexive grin over her shoulder toward Gegnir's face—but then her laugh broke in her throat, because Kesst had waved her into another room, tucked away behind a closed wooden door at the back of the kitchen. The... scullery.

Alma froze in horror, staring blankly at the newest sight confronting her blinking eyes. It was indeed a proper scullery, long and narrow, with a stone floor, worktables along both sides, and even what looked like a large stone sink. There were also several big wooden tubs for laundering, some rickety-looking racks on the walls, and an obviously human-made wringer for drying out clothes.

But Alma could barely even see it all, because the rest of the room was—a mess. A *disaster*. An utter affront to every sensibility she possessed, and she felt her hand clapping up to cover her mouth as she took in the damage. There was standing black water on the floor—gods knew how long it had been there, breeding filth and disease—and a huge pile of grey ash had seemed to grow against one wall, nearly reaching the height of the countertops. Several worktables were overflowing with a veritable mountain of dirty laundry—Alma could make out large bloodstains on multiple items—and another counter was dotted with vermin droppings. And, the entire room reeked, as though the drain had been clogged long ago, and the scullery left to rot in its wake.

"This," Alma said, her voice muffled from her hand still over her mouth, "is *foul*, Kesst. Quite possibly the most revolting thing I have ever seen in my *life*."

Kesst grimaced, frowning around at the room with equal-seeming distaste. "Yes, quite," he said, his voice thin. "But everyone else seems perfectly content to lock it up and pretend someone else is dealing with it, don't they?"

Alma shot a sidelong look toward Kesst, and it abruptly occurred to her that perhaps this had been about more than just his laundry. Because if she lived in this astonishing mountain—which had, until now, appeared acceptably clean throughout—and also knew that *this* was secretly rotting away behind the kitchen, she'd be upset about it too, wouldn't she?

"It's a *hazard*, Kesst," she said, through her hand. "Especially next to the kitchen like this. It could make you all sick! What in the gods' names was your Roland *thinking*?!"

Kesst jerked a shrug, frowning at the pile of ashes growing out of the wall. "It was never this bad before," he said. "Orcs care a lot about cleanliness, and most of us won't tolerate this kind of mess. But clearly at some point Roland just stopped caring, and didn't bother telling anyone. Let alone making sure it was dealt with after he was gone."

Alma's revolted gaze kept darting between Kesst and the teetering mountain of laundry, while her brain frantically grasped for purchase. "So did Roland work alone, then?" she asked. "Surely he must have had some kind of help? A few employees? *Something*?"

"If he did, I wouldn't know about it," Kesst replied, clipped. "And I don't know who else would, either. But at this rate, it's clearly only a matter of time before the rest of our mountain looks like this. And *smells* like this, too."

Good gods. Alma stared at Kesst, and the hideous room, and the open, comparatively pristine kitchen behind them. This was utterly unacceptable. These orcs needed help. And she could help. She could work to repay their kindness, by sorting out their filthy scullery.

"First, the ashes need to go," she said decisively, her hands now on her hips. "There must be some kind of chute around here, I presume? The room also desperately needs to air out—what do you do for ventilation in here? And then the drain needs to be fixed at once, before it poisons someone. Who do I talk to about that? The Ka-esh?"

Kesst's sidelong glance toward her was surprised, though there might have been a twinge of appreciation in it, too. "Yes, I suppose you could," he said thoughtfully, his eyes giving a slow, telltale flick up and down Alma's inappropriately clad form. "If you're sure you feel up to it, that is?"

But housekeeping was Alma's profession, her one and only area of expertise, and suddenly she felt more awake—and more enthusiastic—than she had since before she'd left Mr. Pembroke's. There was a job that needed doing, and she was going to do it.

"Oh, I'm certainly up to it," she said firmly, as she ducked back out the doorway into the kitchen again, and gratefully breathed in its relatively clean-smelling air. "I know house-keeping and cleaning—and food collection and preparation, too—isn't the most glamorous work, but my mother always said that it's important work, too. Honourable work, worthy of far more respect than it receives. It's what keeps us all going, don't you think? I mean, how quickly does everything devolve into chaos, when no one has any clean trousers? Or worse, any supper?"

Her impassioned voice had grown scratchy and high-pitched as she spoke, and she belatedly winced, because surely Kesst didn't care about her housekeeping philosophies, did he? But when she shot a chagrined look toward him, he was flashing her another grin over his shoulder, and his dark eyes had glanced, with unmistakable meaning, toward where Gegnir was standing stock-still behind his workbench, and watching. *Listening.*

"Keep that up, woman," Kesst said approvingly, once they were out in the corridor again, "and you'll have far more than the Grisk mooning about after you. When we go see the Ka-esh, perhaps you can tell them how much you appreciate their tunnel-digging? Or their potion-mixing, perhaps?"

He was tapping his claw to his chin, his brow furrowing, as though this were a legitimate strategy—and blinking at him, Alma couldn't help an astonished laugh, a sharp shake of her head. "I wasn't saying it just to be kind," she said. "I truly mean it, Kesst, cooks and cleaners and gardeners honestly run the *world*, and no one even notices, and—"

And there, in that instant, everything stopped. Alma's steps, her breath, her heart. Because tearing through her thoughts, her very being, ripping her in two, was—*Baldr*?

But yes, yes, it was Baldr. Baldr's voice, his harsh agonized groans, scraping with devastating power through the corridor around them. And Baldr was here, he was nearby, in trouble, in *danger*—

There was no thinking, no possible hesitation. Only sheer terror, kicking and screaming through Alma's frozen, distraught brain. Baldr needed help. Needed her. *Now*.

And with one last wide, horrified glance at Kesst, she whirled around, and ran.

8

Alma pitched down the corridor with staggering, frantic steps. Her hands in front of her face, her ears straining, her breaths dragging painfully into her gasping, heaving lungs.

Not here. Not there. Around this corner, yes, up here. Through here, that door, yes—

She only distantly noticed Kesst chasing after her, or his exasperated shout—because yes, finally, Baldr was here. In this large, unfamiliar, lamplit room, hot and muggy and heavily scented with sulphur, because there were huge steaming *baths*, cut into the room's stone floor. But Alma barely saw them, barely even noticed, because all that mattered was Baldr, there—

There. Baldr was *there*, leaning over what looked like a large square rock—a seat of some sort?—with both hands spread flat against it, his dark head bowed low. His long black hair hanging wet around his face, jerking sharply with his forceful, rhythmic movements, because wait, he—he was—

Unclothed. And standing tall and vicious behind him was—was—*Drafli*?

And yes, oh gods oh *disaster*, it was *Drafli*. His trousers dropped low on his lean hips, both his clawed hands clutched tight to Baldr's bared, convulsing waist. And Drafli's fluid grey body was snapping forward, again and again, powerful, menacing, merciless. *Against* Baldr. *Into* Baldr. While Baldr gasped, growled, groaned, and—took it. *Wanted* it.

And Alma truly couldn't move. Couldn't move her eyes, her feet, her wildly thundering heart. She was trapped, trapped and staring and silently screaming, and in that horrible, thrilling, deadly instant, Baldr—looked up. Found her. *Saw* her.

And gods, he was *stunning*. His hair long and loose and dripping around his face, his full lips parted with his moans, his lashes heavy and blinking. His dark eyes dazed with hunger and pleasure as they held her, knew her, *pierced* her—

Alma's gasp choked from her throat, juddering into the thick turgid air—and oh, gods curse her, now Drafli's head had snapped up, and he was looking at her, too. His glittering black eyes flashing with rage and contempt, his hips plunging forward even faster, his hand snapping for—for Baldr's *neck*. And as Alma gasped again, her entire body trembling, Drafli's hand curved possessively around Baldr's throat, gripping with palpable force—and then he yanked backwards, hard.

"No!" Alma gulped, unthinking—but wait, wait, it only meant that he'd pulled Baldr up, and now Baldr was... *standing*. No longer leaning over the rock like he had been, hiding his bared body in shadow—but now held straight and tall before his mate, and exposing everything for Alma's struck, staring eyes. And Baldr was still looking back at her, holding her gaze for one more brief, shuddering instant, before tilting his head back toward Drafli's shoulder, his lashes fluttering closed.

It meant Alma could look, he *wanted* her to look, to *know*— and gods above, she was looking, learning, drinking up the impossible, beautiful sight of him. His bare shoulders brawny and broad, his rippled abdomen flexing to meet every movement of Drafli behind him, his green nipples taut, his chest dusted with that smattering of dark hair. And rather than disappearing beneath his trousers, like it had back in the forest, Alma could now see the hair spreading, thickening, as it swarmed down to cover his bared groin.

And there—deep in the midst of it—was—*that*. A sight Alma had briefly glimpsed on several men before, including the horrid Mr. Pembroke—but this, a distant part of her was shouting, *this* was surely what it was meant to look like. Jutting out straight and shameless from that nest of dark hair, its thick length plump and smooth, and shaded a warm, rich green that grew steadily pinker as it tapered to its glossy, elegant tip. And from that tip's deep slit, there dangled a thick string of white, swinging brazenly back and forth with every slam of Drafli's still-driving hips.

And surely, *surely*, Alma should have been shocked. Appalled. Not only was she properly seeing a male for the first time, but he was also being coldly, brutally taken by another male, and he clearly, desperately wanted it. *Craved* it. The truth of it shouting with every clench of his torso, every flutter of his lashes, every harsh, guttural groan from his throat. Even with the way his muscular arm had reached up and back, finding Drafli's dark head behind him—and then dragging that head down, toward his own arched, exposed neck.

Drafli obliged without an instant's hesitation, his white fangs hungrily scraping against that already-scarred skin—and then his jaw snapped shut, firing even more frenzied intensity into Baldr's moans. His entire body spasming as Drafli's strong arm clapped tight and possessive around his waist, holding him in place as he drove against him, drank him, made that thick green length shudder and dance, dripping more of its viscous white toward the floor...

And then—Alma's breath stopped—Baldr again blinked his long lashes open, and *looked* at her. His eyes so hazy, so heavy, as if he were drowning in bright whirling ecstasy, in pure pummelling *life*. And in that instant, there was nothing Alma wanted more than to take the last few steps toward him, and perhaps touch a hand to his glistening, sweat-drenched chest, or his parted, gasping mouth. To feel this life, his freedom, his raw shameless abandon, if only for a moment...

And Baldr knew, he *knew*, with the way his eyes shifted, shuttered, broke. And maybe even Drafli knew too, his black gaze darting back to Alma's, and stabbing her straight through with his cold, vicious hatred. Saying, without words, *He's mine, always mine, he knows it, you know it, and I can prove it*—

And as Drafli looked at her, *mocked* her, he dropped one hand around to Baldr's front, finding that plump, bobbing green length with effortless ease, and gripping it in his long, sharp-clawed fingers. And with one single, smooth yank up, Baldr's voice rose to a shout, his entire body thrust to stillness, every muscle clenched and gleaming—

And then he... *erupted*. That glossy pink head spraying out long, powerful spurts of thick white, surging over the rock before them, flaring across the room. And even—Alma twitched, shuddered all over—catching on her bare *feet*, streaking straight across them with a slick-feeling string of warmth.

Behind Baldr, Drafli had stilled too, his lean body rigid and flexing, his head tilted back, his eyes squeezed shut—but when those eyes flicked open again, they were fixed to Alma. Or rather, to her... her *feet*.

And as Alma stared back, utterly transfixed, she found Baldr blinking at her too, his lips still parted, his eyes still hooded and dazed, and also held to her feet. And again, there was the strangest, most overwhelming urge to step closer, perhaps to loosen her robe, to see what else he might do with that beautiful mouth...

"Oh, *hell*," groaned a voice beside Alma, very far away. "Come *on*, woman. I do not want to even risk touching you right now, but I swear to the gods, I *will*. *This instant*."

Alma startled and blinked—had the voice been talking

before, too?—and found herself looking at Kesst, whose face was equal parts disgruntled and relieved. "Oh, *that's* what brings you back?" he asked, his voice clearly exasperated. "*Touch* threats. You're such a gods-damned Grisk already, woman, come *on.*"

Alma blinked again—wait, had Kesst seen all that, too?—and belatedly realized he was trying to make her *leave.* He wanted her to go away, away from Baldr and Drafli, after she'd just seen *that*—and what the hell did he mean by *touch threats,* and why couldn't she pull herself together—

But no, no, it was already too late, because Drafli had wrenched away from Baldr, and was stalking over toward them, yanking up his trousers. And his narrow black eyes were flashing with rage and contempt, his lips pulled back to show all his sharp white teeth. And one clawed hand was jabbing dangerously toward Alma's chest, while the other was gesturing with vehement meaning toward Baldr behind him.

How dare you, he might as well have shouted at her. *How dare you. He's mine. Mine. Get out.*

Alma shrank backwards toward the door, her heart plummeting, her head fervently shaking back and forth. "Oh gods, I'm so sorry," she gulped, squeezing her eyes shut. "I truly—I didn't realize—I thought Baldr was in trouble—I should have—should have left, I—"

Her wavering voice seemed to trip over itself, because gods, why hadn't she left? Why hadn't she taken one look, realized what they'd truly been doing, and then turned around and fled? Whatever could have possessed her to think that she had any right to invade upon someone else's—*intimacies,* most of all when she already knew how Baldr felt about this? When he'd already—*repeatedly*—made his intentions so blatantly clear to her?

"I'm so, so sorry," she said again, and she made her eyes open, made them find Drafli's furious face, still far too close. "It was completely inappropriate of me. Inexcusable. Again. I—"

But Drafli's hands were moving again, fast and forceful, surely still the equivalent of silently shouting at her. Telling her, perhaps, how shameful she was, how silly and undesirable and worthless—and she felt her mortification swarming her burning cheeks, prickling at her fluttering, trembling hands.

"I'm so, so sorry," she pleaded at him. "I was wrong. I swear I won't disrespect you again. I *swear* to you."

But it wasn't working, it wasn't, and Drafli actually spat on the floor this time, clearly even more enraged than before. And he was so close, and so *tall*, and what if he attacked her, what if he—

"Baldr!" snapped a loud voice beside her—Kesst's voice. "Get the hell over here, and call this prick off! Now!"

Alma's terrified gaze darted toward Baldr, who was still standing naked behind the rock, and staring toward them. His face gone distinctly harsh and haggard, in total contrast to his blissful expression from a moment before—and he truly looked as aghast as Alma felt, blinking between her and Drafli with wide, horrified eyes.

But then he jerked all over, almost as if jolting awake again—and he nearly tripped as he stumbled over toward them, the sight between his legs now dangling soft and slack toward the floor.

"Draf!" he barked. "Leave it! She didn't know!"

He'd clutched his clawed hand powerfully at Drafli's rigid forearm, enough to yank him a step backward, away from Alma's face. But Drafli's furious eyes didn't once leave hers, his mouth still silently snarling at her, and Baldr's brief, wounded glance toward her was almost worse, shouting of his helplessness, his misery. Of the sheer, broken *betrayal* in what she'd just done.

"I'm so sorry," Alma gulped at them, blinking hard. "I—I'll leave now. Back to my—my home. I'll go, and you'll never need to see me again. I *promise*."

She was backing toward the door, frantically waving her

hands—but she somehow, foolishly, bumped into Kesst. Kesst, who was standing there with his arms crossed, his eyes on Drafli, his own mouth pulled back into a snarl.

"You're not going anywhere, woman, until Eft approves it," he snapped, without looking at her. "He has *not* spent three full days saving your life for you to toss it away over this raging Skai prick. And if these two have a problem with that, they can damn well take it up with Efterar themselves!"

But if this was supposed to help, it most certainly didn't, because both Baldr and Drafli seemed to round on Kesst at once, and even Baldr's eyes were flaring with a sudden, surprising anger. "You take care what you call my mate, Kesst," he hissed. "And *you*, of all orcs, ought to have known better than to bring her here!"

Kesst visibly bristled, but when he spoke, his voice was very cool, very even. "Why should I, of all orcs, know better?" he asked. "Is that a reference to the rubbish *my* mate had to deal with, before Grim took over? No thanks to certain Skai bastards like *him*?"

Kesst had jerked his head toward Drafli, who was still snarling at him—but beside Drafli, Baldr was nearly snarling, too. "Ach, and the Ash-Kai were blameless in such things?" he demanded at Kesst. "It was your own clan who made you into their—"

He broke off there, grimacing, and Kesst gave a cold, chilly laugh. "My clan made me into what?" he said. "Their resident slag? Their *woman*?!"

There was an instant's ringing silence, in which Baldr—and Drafli too—looked at Kesst, not moving. And then Kesst laughed again, even colder than before, his eyes glinting on Baldr's. "And you think the Grisk were any better?" he demanded. "Oh wait, you weren't here to notice, because you were too busy hiding away with *your* woman, like a typical Grisk *coward*!"

Baldr reeled back like he'd been struck, and Drafli actually lunged at Kesst, who leapt backwards just in time. "That woman was my *mother*," Baldr growled at Kesst, from where he was once again holding Drafli back. "And I am not a Grisk coward, I almost *died* fighting to save her, and"—he dragged in breath, his eyes flashing—"these days I am barely even a Grisk at all!"

But Kesst's laugh was vicious this time, his lip curling. "We don't get to decide these things," he hissed back. "You're a Grisk, not a Skai. I'm a used-up Ash-Kai slag, not a lovely, scent-bound hearth-mate. And *this* lovely woman is scent-bound to *you*, and it's your own damned fault, whether you like it or not!"

And oh gods, now all three furious, enraged orcs were looking at *Alma*. And throughout all this, she had somehow felt wrenched bodily from her feet, and hurled headlong into the midst of these horrible truths, these horrible words being thrown about so carelessly. Kesst's clan had... *used* him? Baldr had almost *died* for his mother? And Baldr barely belonged to his own clan—his friendly, kind clan, who'd already been so welcoming toward her? And worst of all, she was still *scent-bound* to Baldr, and it was his fault?!

"Please, stop," she gulped at them, blinking desperately at their harsh, angry faces. "Please, don't say such cruel things to each other. I'm so sorry I began any of this, I'm so sorry to have ruined everything. And Kesst, could you please"—she fixed her molten eyes to his face—"*please*, take me back to the sickroom now, so I can speak with Efterar, and arrange my journey back home at once?"

There was another moment's fraught, dangling silence, and Alma cringed back a little more, because surely she'd said or done the wrong thing, again—and indeed, Baldr jerked a shake of his head, his hand rubbing at his eyes.

"You—ought to stay, woman," he said, his voice rough. "Kesst is right. You must heal. I—I shall speak with the captain, and seek to take some leave myself. Go back east for a spell, mayhap. Ach?"

He said this with a pleading glance toward Drafli, whose lean body had gone suddenly, strangely still. His eyes staring at Baldr, into Baldr, and Baldr winced, his hand twitching into a series of shaky, tired-looking motions. To which Drafli snapped something back, much sharper-looking, and Baldr winced again, and dropped his eyes.

"I must—go," Baldr continued, wooden, without looking up. "I am sorry we frightened you so, woman. And Kesst, I did not mean to wound you, and I thank you for your kindness to my—"

To his—what? To *her*? And Baldr had winced again, shaking his head as though it hurt—and without another word, he strode past Alma and Kesst, and out the door. And after one last seething, baleful look between Alma and Kesst, Drafli stalked after him, bumping Kesst hard with his shoulder on the way past.

Kesst glared after him, a surprisingly harsh growl burning from his throat—but then he abruptly seemed to wilt against the doorway, his shoulders sagging, his hand rubbing at his mouth.

"So, *that* went well," he said, with an attempted smile at Alma's face. "About as terribly as one could have possibly imagined, don't you think?"

Alma still couldn't seem to move, let alone speak, and Kesst's smile twisted into a tight, bitter little grimace. "Look, I'll apologize to Baldr," he said thinly. "I know I was out of line. That Skai, he just—"

And suddenly there was another horrible thought, shouting over the mess still swarming Alma's brain. "Drafli didn't—*hurt* you, Kesst?" she gulped at him, her voice hoarse. "Back then? With—with the others?"

The curt shake of Kesst's head was sheer sweeping relief,

spearing through Alma's chest—surely Baldr wouldn't swear vows to someone who'd done such things?—but there was still an odd darkness in Kesst's eyes, shifting in their depths. "*Drafli* didn't," he said, as he turned away from her, toward the corridor. "But he was still there, getting off with any Skai who would get on his knees. They were his clan. His *friends*. He still even *smells* like them."

Alma swallowed hard and followed Kesst into the corridor, her steps unsteady, her thoughts still swirling. Silently pointing out that he'd just said, moments ago, that one couldn't change one's clan, or one's past—but perhaps that was part of it, too, the wishing that one *could*. And now she was thinking of her own mother, and those awful secret choices her mother had made with Mr. Pembroke, and the misery churned even harder, sick and cold in her belly.

"Look, none of that was your fault, all right?" Kesst said into the silence, with a sigh. "The bond can affect people in unpredictable ways. And probably Grisk more than most."

The bond again. Alma wiped at her wet eyes, her hand jittery on her face. "I don't even understand," she whispered, "what a bond *is*. Or how it even could have *happened*, between us."

Kesst sighed again, led her around another corner. "Baldr touched you, when he pulled you out of that river, and brought you here," he said wearily. "Obviously at length, and on your bare skin. It means he smells like you, and you smell like him, and that's not something that will ever go away. Not for orcs."

What? It would never go away, *ever*? That was impossible, surely? But when Alma glanced back at Kesst, his face looked worn, strained. "And it's even stronger," he continued, with another heavy sigh, "when a person bears no other scents of mating. It's not just a bond—we call it *scent-bound*. It's so rare, and some orcs—especially the Grisk, but plenty of others too—have a real thing for it. Smelling only you when you touch someone. Knowing, with every breath, that you're the only one they've ever given themselves to."

Alma's wet eyes blinked at Kesst's drawn face, while yet more mortification, more humiliation, flooded through her thoughts. "So you *all* know I'm a—I'm *inexperienced*, just by smelling me?" she choked out. "And look, I didn't—*give* myself to Baldr like that. I only touched him, and surely I've touched a dozen other people similarly throughout my life?!"

But Kesst abruptly laughed, the sound cold and bitter. "Look, the bond doesn't just randomly *happen*, sweetheart," he said flatly. "For it to stick, there needs to be desire behind it. You wanted Baldr, he wanted you, he touched you naked for a few hours, so here we are. And him getting his scent on you like that"—his hand gave a dismissive wave toward Alma's feet—"is not going to help matters. At all."

The sudden slashing horror seemed to strike Alma to still-ness, her feet skittering to a halt, her eyes gaping downwards. Baldr had... gotten his scent on her? He'd truly built an irrevocable bond with her? He'd *wanted* her?

But yes, yes, her miserable thoughts were now caught on that moment on the riverbank, with how he'd touched that swollen heft in his trousers. With the way he'd looked at her, with that mingled guilt and pain and longing, not unlike how he'd looked at her just moments ago...

And Drafli would have... *known* all that. Good gods, Drafli *knew*, and no wonder he hated her so much, she would hate her too. And what the hell was she supposed to do now, Baldr couldn't leave his own home because of her, he couldn't leave his own *mate*?!

"I need to leave," she gulped at the floor, digging her palms painfully into her prickling eyes. "I need to go home. Today. My throat is already feeling much better, I'm sure it will be *fine*."

But Kesst's laugh sounded almost resigned this time, his sigh huffing out slow. "Nice try, sweetheart," he said. "But it seems likely to me that you don't even *have* a home right now. Do you?"

Oh. Oh. Another cold shudder ripped up Alma's back, her

shoulders bowing, her hands digging harder into her eyes. And she should have fought it, should have put up some kind of coherent protest, but if she tried to speak she was sure to start weeping, right here in the corridor.

"Come on, then," Kesst's voice said, softer now. "You need to rest. All right?"

And again, Alma should have spoken, should have found words to argue, or at least thank him for his kindness. But there was no way past the lurking sobs in her throat, the all-consuming knot in her belly—so instead she followed him in silence, her head bowed, until he led her back into the sick-room again.

And if Efterar had questions or censure for her, thankfully he didn't voice them, and only took one look, and waved her toward her bed. And Alma gratefully stumbled toward it, yanked the fur over her head, and finally sobbed into the darkness.

9

——————

Alma's sleep came in fitful bits and starts, swimming in and out of dreams. Glimpses of running helpless through the trees, sinking into the water, agony screaming in her lungs, Mr. Pembroke's face leering across the desk.

You don't think those murderous orcs will want you, girl? Let's find out after all, why don't we?

And mashed up into that, against that, there was Baldr's drawn face, his hand over his eyes, his bitter misery strong enough to taste. And beside him, Drafli's blazing fury, his mocking contempt, the ecstasy shattered into guilt and rage.

How dare you. He's mine. Get out.

And now, on top of all the rest, were more voices. Close, hazily familiar, curdling into Alma's ringing brain with more harsh judgement, more flat, impatient contempt.

"She's so sweet, it actually hurts my *teeth*," one of them was saying. "You should have heard her apologizing to those pricks. As if they didn't know *exactly* what the hell they were doing."

There was the sound of a heavy sigh, and then something that sounded oddly like a mewl. "Really?" said another voice, a woman's voice. "I can't see Baldr intentionally doing something like that to an *enemy*, let alone someone he likes. At *all*."

The first voice—Kesst's voice?—harrumphed, sharp and disapproving. "Yes, well, maybe *Baldr* wouldn't," it replied, "but that Skai bastard absolutely would, and *did*. He was making a damned point, is what it was. And it's not her fault it came back to smack him in the face. He had *no right* to fly into her like that."

There was another sigh, another odd little mewl. "Well, whatever the motive, Baldr was *not* happy about it," the woman's voice said. "He came to Grimarr this morning, and asked for a leave of absence. For a few *weeks*, he said. And as much as Grimarr would hate losing Baldr for all that time, you know he'd usually try to make it work, but"—she sighed again—"it's just the worst possible timing, now with Pembroke fired up like this. Just when we think we've got all those fool lords dealt with, *that* scum needs to stick his nose in?!"

Alma's heartbeat was abruptly pummelling against her ribs—they were talking about *Mr. Pembroke*?!—and she felt herself jerk upright in her bed, her scratchy eyes blinking wildly toward the voices. Toward Kesst, who was sitting sprawled on the bed across from hers, while beside him— Alma squinted—there was a tall, dark-haired, dark-eyed woman, who was holding something small, and green, and... *squirming*?

Both Kesst and the woman had snapped to look back toward Alma, both with surprise in their eyes—but then the woman's face softened into a broad, genuine-looking grin.

"You're awake!" she said warmly. "It's so lovely to finally meet you, Alma. I'm Jule, of Clan Ash-Kai, and I'm mated to our mountain's captain, Grimarr. And this"—she turned around the squirmy bundle in her arms—"is our son. Tengil."

Her *son*. Alma's shock was screeching through her skull again, because this woman's son was—an *orc*. A small, snub-nosed orc, with smooth greenish skin, tiny clawed hands, and delicate pointed ears. And his bright black eyes were looking back toward her with a surprisingly studious watchfulness, as if he weren't at all sure what to make of her, either.

"Or, as I prefer to call him," Kesst said lightly, as he reached over, and bodily snatched the little orc from the woman's arms, "Bitty-Grim. A weeny, grumpy version of his big, grumpy father. Right, little brother?"

The look on the serious little orc's face might have been almost disapproving this time, and Alma couldn't help a strange, stifled choke of laughter, even as her heart kept banging in her chest. This woman—Jule—had truly birthed an *orc baby*?! And now she was sitting here perfectly healthy and content and alive, as if this were a perfectly natural outcome of such a shocking development?!

But yes, clearly, this was entirely normal to them, and Alma fought back her bewildered astonishment, the urge to ask a dozen questions at once. "He's a beautiful baby," she belatedly told Jule, and she was distantly surprised to find that she meant it. "And it's lovely to meet you, too. But"—she glanced uneasily between Jule and Kesst, her heartbeat rising again—"did you just say that—that Mr. Pembroke has gotten involved? With—with *you*?"

Jule and Kesst exchanged a meaningful look, and Jule's mouth had visibly tightened, the warmth fading from her eyes. "Yes, horrid little worm that he is," she said flatly. "He's claiming that we forcibly kidnapped his head housekeeper—you, of course—and that we're refusing to give you back."

What?! Alma's shock was screaming yet again, her mouth fallen open, her heart plunging in her belly. Mr. Pembroke was truly claiming that the orcs had *kidnapped* her? That *Baldr* had kidnapped her, by saving her life?!

"And along with that," Jule continued, clipped, "Pembroke is also claiming that some irreplaceable valuables were stolen at the same time. Suggesting, oh so conveniently, that we're guilty of raiding *and* kidnapping. Both obviously in blatant violation of our treaty, and therefore clear grounds for retaliation."

Alma's heartbeat had seemed to ricochet into her skull, and she gaped between Jule and Kesst, twitching at the grimness in their eyes. "What the hell?!" she croaked. "Mr. Pembroke *fired* me. And then chased me, and then threatened to—to *compromise* me. And *Cook* stole his silver, and then set his kitchen on fire while I was in the cellar, and it had nothing to do with me, *nothing!*"

Her voice sounded frantic, incoherent, very far away, and Kesst and Jule exchanged another brief, meaningful look. "We never did think it had anything to do with you, sweetheart," Kesst finally said. "We've had enough dealings with these men to know what they're about. And when it comes to putting the hideous, depraved orcs back in their place"—he gave a not-quite-dismissive shrug—"any excuse will do."

Alma's heart was still flailing in her chest, and she swallowed over the painful knot in her throat. "But do you mean Mr. Pembroke is trying to *attack* you?" she whispered. "Because of Baldr's *kindness* to me?"

There was an instant's dangling emptiness, finally broken by Bitty-Grim—Tengil—whining as he reached back for his mother. "Pembroke isn't attacking, yet," Jule said, as she settled Tengil back onto her lap. "He's given us a fortnight to return you, along with compensation for his stolen valuables."

Oh, gods. Alma's heart kicked again, swarming her with more bitter dread, more trembling sinking terror. "Right," she said woodenly. "Well, I've been meaning to head back anyway, and I'm feeling much better, so I can certainly leave at once. Though"—she felt her clammy hands clutching at the fur—"I have no idea where Cook went, but maybe if we could find her, we—"

But she was interrupted by a loud, disbelieving snort, and

Kesst leaned forward on his bed, jabbing a claw toward her. "I keep telling you, you aren't going *anywhere*, sweetheart," he snapped. "Not until you're well again, and especially not back to that scum, who's likely to take out all his thwarted pettiness on you. It is *not* safe for you there. Eft, please come tell her she can't leave?!"

He'd shot an exasperated look over his shoulder, to where Efterar had just walked into the room—and though Efterar's brows went up, he indeed came over, and fixed Alma with a ghastly frown. "You'll stay until you're fully healed, woman," he said firmly. "Unless"—his dark eyes seemed to sharpen on hers—"you truly *want* to leave?"

Alma stared helplessly between the three of them, and desperately fought to dredge up a truthful answer. Yes, she wanted to leave, she needed to leave, but they'd been so lovely to her, she wanted to help them, but that *look* in Baldr's eyes, the pure rage in Drafli's...

I'll go, and you'll never need to see me again, she'd told them. *I promise.*

"I—I really do need to go," she said finally, her voice wavering. "But if you don't want me going back to Mr. Pembroke's, perhaps I could go elsewhere, then? Hide, until all this has blown over?"

But now it was Jule shaking her head, giving Alma a grim, regretful look. "I'm sorry, Alma, but I don't think that's wise," she said. "If we hide you away somewhere else, Pembroke's still going to keep claiming that we have you, or maybe even that we killed you. Kesst is right—you're a convenient excuse for that bastard, and he's going to milk it for all it's worth."

Oh. Alma felt her shoulders sagging, her eyes again blinking between Jule and the two orcs, her misery rising with every dragging breath. She was *trapped* here now? And not only was she breaking her word to Baldr and Drafli, but she was giving Pembroke a blatant excuse to attack? To possibly start another *war*?

"Look, the situation certainly isn't hopeless," Jule said brac-ingly, her eyes far too aware on Alma's face. "We've dealt with the likes of Pembroke before, multiple times—this kind of thing has been incessant, ever since we signed that treaty. But, attacking our mountain isn't easy or cheap, and we have a few friends in powerful places who might be able to help sway things, too."

Her calm confidence felt almost palpable, but Alma's unease was still jangling, and she couldn't help a swift, pleading look toward Kesst. "But—I still need to go," her voice said, before she could stop it. "I told Baldr and Drafli I would leave, at once. It would be—best, for everyone, if I go. I *promised* them, and Drafli said—"

She broke off there, because yes, she could still almost feel the strength of Drafli's furious command, the harsh intent in his glinting eyes, as if he'd silently shouted in her face.

How dare you. He's mine. Get out.

Kesst and Jule had exchanged another meaningful glance, and Jule's mouth tightened, a look much like impatience flashing through her eyes. "Drafli doesn't get to decide these things," she said flatly. "He won't go against Grimarr's orders on this. And he will *not* threaten you like that again, either."

Again, Jule's steely certainty should have been reassuring—especially along with Kesst's quick, teasing smile. "And besides," Kesst added, giving Jule another meaningful look, "Alma's promised to help sort out the mess Roland left behind, especially in the scullery. Have you seen that hole, Jules? It is vile. *Vile!*"

Jule wrinkled her nose, but her head had also tilted, her eyes on Kesst gone narrow and suspicious. "*Kesst*," she said, with tangible exasperation. "Is this about your laundry again?"

Kesst huffed and looked away, and behind him Efterar laughed, and stroked a big hand against his hair. "Foiled again, Kesst," he said affectionately. "And I keep telling you, she isn't supposed to be working. She's supposed to be *healing*. Especially after that stunt of hers yesterday, *running*. You *do* realize your lung capacity is still greatly reduced, right, woman? And that any over-exertion might send you right back to where you started?"

Now all three of them were looking at Alma again, Efterar with clear disapproval, Kesst and Jule with decisive expectation in their eyes. And Alma swallowed hard as she glanced between them, her thoughts still twisting, while more misery clenched in her stomach. She couldn't truly stay, not now, as much as some shameful, selfish part of her might want to. She *couldn't*.

"I truly appreciate your generosity," she said, hoarse. "And I truly do want to keep my word to you, and stay until I've healed, and help with the housekeeping. But you must see, I made a promise. And I can't bear for you all to suffer because of my foolishness, and Baldr's kindness. *Please*."

There was a moment's jangling silence, in which Kesst and Jule exchanged yet another look, and Kesst ran an impatient hand through his hair. "Grisk," he muttered, under his breath. "Unbelievable."

Alma wasn't following, and she drew in an unsteady breath, and glanced helplessly toward Jule. "There must be something," she said. "*Please*."

Jule sighed, and absently stroked a hand against Bitty-Grim's greenish back. "Well," she began slowly, "as loath as I am to suggest this—would you accept a compromise? Could you at least give us a few more days here? And perhaps you can stay here in the sickroom, well out of the way, so that there are no more unpleasant surprises? Baldr's already promised to keep his distance from you going forward, no matter what he smells. So it shouldn't be any trouble for you all to avoid each other, while we focus on Pembroke."

Alma's stomach had plummeted at that—Baldr had promised to stay away from her, no matter what?—but beside Jule, Kesst's eyes had lit up, his mouth quirking. "Ah, that's an idea," he said cheerfully. "And maybe we can bring over some orcs to keep you entertained, and you can see if any of *them* tickle your fancy?"

That thought only seemed to plunge Alma's misery deeper, even as Jule huffed a laugh, and rolled her eyes. "*Kesst*," she said irritably. "Alma's not here to pick out an orc, like a new *pet*."

"Are you sure?" Kesst asked, casting an impish glance over his shoulder. "I don't think Eben would mind being your new pet, right, Eben? *Especially* if there was a collar and lead involved?"

Eben, who had been intently mixing something together at the worktable, abruptly dropped his flask onto the table with a loud thunk, his face flushing bright pink. To which Jule elbowed Kesst sharply in the side, and fixed her attention back on Alma, her gaze watchful and intent.

"So you'll stay, then?" she asked. "If it helps, I'll tell Baldr and Drafli that this was my strong recommendation, and if they have concerns, or feel that this isn't in keeping with what you've promised them, I'll be sure to let you know."

Well. Alma swallowed through the ache in her throat, and searched Jule's flinty eyes. She wanted to help these orcs. She wanted to respect Efterar's expertise. She wanted to further explore this marvellous mountain, to fix that filthy scullery, to spend more time with all these lovely people. She wanted... she wanted...

She scrubbed hard at her face, and drew in a hitching, dragging breath. She couldn't have what she wanted. She knew that, she'd always known that. And she'd already made far too many mistakes here, and broken too many promises, and she had to try to salvage this. She had to.

"It'll be fine," Jule was saying now, her voice firm. "Baldr and Drafli will understand. So can you give it just a few more days?"

And blinking at the urgency—and perhaps even the

danger—snapping in Jule's eyes, Alma felt her shoulders sagging, her breath exhaling hard. She would find another way. She would.

"Very well," she said, a bitter, blatant lie in her throat. "I'll stay."

10

For the rest of the day, Alma stayed curled up in her bed. Drifting in and out of sleep, keeping herself quiet and unobtrusive, doing as she was told. Eating a bit of food, visiting the clever little latrine off the adjoining back room, washing her hands and face. Lying still as Efterar repeatedly stood above her, hovering his hand over her throat and chest.

And even as she felt something prickling deep inside her—almost as if Efterar was *knitting her back together*—she kept holding herself still and quiet. She'd already had some odd suspicions about Efterar—he hadn't yet used any medicines on her, or done any bloodletting, or any of the other things physicians usually did—and between that, and this, and all Mr. Pembroke's railing about dark orc magic, her suspicions had somehow settled into a strange, stilted certainty. But rather than feeling properly shaken, or afraid, her bizarrely blunted brain could still only seem to focus on listening. Waiting. Planning.

She had to find a way to leave, and fix all this. She'd *promised*.

Her opportunity finally came, many hours later, long after

Eben and Salvi had said goodnight. Leaving Alma alone in the sickroom with Kesst and Efterar, who had both gone suspiciously silent—at least, until Alma heard a muffled gasp from across the room. And then a shift of fabric, or perhaps furs, as one of the room's beds loudly creaked, and Kesst gave a low, husky moan.

"Fuck, Eft," his voice gasped, so hushed that Alma scarcely heard it. "Like being—split—in *two*. Every—damn—*time*."

Alma's body had snapped to attention, her gaze reflexively peeking out over her fur—but no, wait, Kesst wasn't hurt. He was—he was straddling Efterar's sprawled form on the bed, his head thrown back, his lean bared body gleaming in the dim firelight. And beneath him, Alma could see something shockingly long and slim, jutting up from Efterar's groin, and sinking bit by bit into—oh.

"Fuck," Kesst gasped again, as the hardness jutting out from his own groin abruptly bobbed and danced. "You—devious—*ack!*"

Alma couldn't see what Efterar had done, but she could still see Kesst writhing in response to it, his hair flying back behind him. While beneath him, Efterar grunted his satisfaction, his hips thrusting up a little harder. Sinking himself up slow but certain, Kesst's entire body shuddering as he took more and more of that impossible length inside, as—

"Efterar!" cut in an urgent, hollering voice. "Need you in the Bautul arena, *now*. Skai and Bautul got into it, and now Silfast's almost chopped Killik's *hand* off!"

Efterar's answering curse sounded surprisingly vicious, and Kesst gave a keening, high-pitched groan as he carefully began raising himself up again. "Damn those fool bastards," he finally said, breathless, once Efterar's shocking length had slipped fully free of him. "Again. They've been getting worse lately, right? Why the hell can't they ever take a damned day off?"

Efterar's cursing had darkened into what sounded like an ongoing stream of growling, to which Kesst made a soothing,

shushing noise, dropping his hand to stroke against the abandoned length against Efterar's belly. "There, there, Eft," he
murmured. "I'll come along, and finish you off while you work.
Who gives a damn if it slows you down. All right?"

Efterar's growls briefly stuttered, and Alma belatedly
yanked her fur back over her face, just in time—and soon there
were the distinctive sounds of footsteps, fading away down the
corridor. And when Alma finally peeked out from under her
fur again, she discovered that she was indeed all alone, the
room gone eerily empty in the light of the guttering fire.

Finally. This was her chance.

She silently slipped out of bed, tightly tied the sash of her
robe, and made her way to Salvi and Eben's worktable. Where
she pulled over a loose sheet of paper, and wrote out a quick
note with a piece of charcoal. Extending her deepest gratitude
to Kesst and Efterar and Jule for their kindness, and her heartfelt apologies for leaving them so suddenly.

After that came the most tenuous part of her plan, and
Alma felt her heartbeat rising in her chest as she made her way
to the sickroom's door, and carefully looked beyond. The
corridor seemed empty too, the light from its orange lamps
flickering steadily against the stone walls, and she took a deep,
bracing breath as she slipped out the door, and turned left.

It meant she was moving into the Grisk wing—or so she
thought, based on her foggy memories from Kesst's tour—but
unlike during the tour, the corridor also seemed to be entirely
empty. Only door after darkened door, lamp after lamp, and
Alma's heart thundered louder, her hands clutching tighter
against her robe. She had to make this work. She'd promised...

When up ahead, someone stepped out from one of the
doors, and looked at her. It was an orc, big and broad and bare-
chested, wearing only a kilt—but thank the gods, he looked
vaguely familiar, too. And after a moment's mental grasping,
Alma realized it was Varinn, the genial orc she'd met the day

before in the corridor. The one who'd teased his friend Thrain about his name. Varinn, a Grisk.

"Alma?" Varinn was carefully asking, his dark head tilting. "Is there aught that you need?"

Alma's relief kept clashing up against her surging unease, and she somehow gulped down another breath, and stepped closer toward him. "Y-yes, in fact," she replied, hoarse. "I have a—a proposal for you, Varinn."

Varinn's black brows were rising, his head cocking even more to the side, but he gave a wary nod, and waited. And Alma gulped back more courage, more breath, she had to try, she had to...

"It turns out that I need to return to Ashford, quite urgently," she managed. "Could I prevail upon you to escort me there, please? Tonight?"

Varinn blinked, and his uneasy eyes flicked down toward Alma's flimsy robe, and then her bare feet. "I should wish to help you, woman," he said, "but you ken—"

"Yes, I realize this is quite irregular," Alma interrupted, too loudly, before she lost the nerve. "But it's very urgent, and very important to me. And if it helps, I—I'm willing to make it worth your while, as well."

Varinn's brows had drawn together as he'd studied her, but at that, they shot back up again—and Alma plunged onward, without breath this time, her voice already wavering. "I—I have no funds, and I realize this puts me at quite a disadvantage. So I am willing to offer you"—she gulped down more air—"my—my affections. I have never been—intimate—with anyone before, and I've recently learned that this is—appealing, to some orcs. And most of all to the Grisk, so—"

Her voice was now shaking too much for her to continue, and she wiped her trembling hands on her robe, and attempted something that she hoped resembled a smile. While before her, Varinn's mouth had actually fallen open, and he abruptly looked away, dragging his clawed hand against his tightly bound black braid.

"You wish to *mate* with me?" he said, incredulous, as an unmistakable tinge of red crept up his greenish neck. "As *payment*, should I take you to *Ashford*?"

There was something Alma couldn't quite read in his voice, and she felt her stomach painfully plummeting, her thoughts helplessly swarming with sudden, incongruent visions of... Baldr. Of Baldr's warmth, his kindness, his bizarrely powerful beauty as Drafli had driven into him, his hungry, hazy eyes flashing on hers—

But no. *No.* That was over now. She'd promised. She'd *promised*.

"Er, yes," Alma belatedly replied, jerking a forceful nod, her eyes darting uneasily around the still-empty corridor. "Yes, exactly, thank you. Could we please leave at once?"

Varinn was staring at her again, his broad body unmoving, his hands now in tight fists at his sides. "You ken, woman," he said, very deliberate now, "that if you mate with me, this would very likely fill you with my *son*?"

Alma audibly gulped, but made herself keep nodding, even as she tightly crossed her arms over her chest. "Er, yes," she said again, over the ever-curdling fear. "And I realize that could create—complications, in Ashford. But I would hope—perhaps—if you were happy with me, you might send for me afterwards, or make some arrangement, or—"

Gods, she couldn't even bear to think of it, and she whipped her head back and forth, and forced herself to continue. "But if you aren't interested, of course I—I understand. And in which case, I would hope you could bring me to another orc—perhaps another Grisk—who might be willing. Or if not, I will keep searching, until—"

Varinn was now looking truly aghast, his wide eyes once again flicking up and down Alma's trembling body, and she fought the sudden, inexplicable urge to start weeping, or to throw herself at his feet.

"Please," she said to him, blinking hard, holding his eyes. "I—I'm desperate, and I have nothing else to offer. I realize I may not be what you want, but I am a quick learner, and a hard worker. I would do all that I can to please you, and make you happy with me."

And it was that, oddly enough, that brought a strange, inscrutable flash to Varinn's eyes, a new tightness to his jaw. And finally, finally, he jerked a curt, purposeful little nod, his hands flexing unnervingly at his sides.

"Ach, then, woman," he said. "We shall go."

11

A short time later, Alma found herself tightly wrapped in warm furs, and walking through a dark, dripping tunnel, with Varinn by her side.

He'd been surprisingly taciturn as he'd made their preparations, asking her to wait behind a long counter as he'd pulled out various items from what had seemed to be an astonishingly large stockroom. He'd found her warm wool socks, a pair of boots that somehow actually fit her, and a huge, hooded fur cape. He'd even somehow put together a pack full of dried fruit and meat, and had slung it over his shoulder, before grasping for the lamp he'd lit, and silently waving Alma back out into the corridor.

After that had been a twisty, confusing journey through a variety of smaller, unlit tunnels and rooms, until they'd reached this particular passageway, which had felt markedly different than the rest. It was long and straight, with rough-cut walls, and there was water regularly seeping from the earthen ceiling, and pooling beneath Alma's booted feet.

"Thank you for doing this, Varinn," she finally said, the first words she'd seemed able to speak since they'd left the stockroom. "I am truly indebted to you."

Varinn shrugged his bare shoulder and tilted his head back, almost as if welcoming the water dripping liberally onto his face. "There is no debt," he said, the words a sudden, unnerving echo of what Baldr had told her, the day he'd rescued her from the river. "Only brotherhood."

Alma shot him an uncertain, furtive look, and he must have somehow caught it, even as he kept his gaze on the ceiling. "You are Grisk," he said, quiet. "You bear my brother Baldr's strong scent, and his seed. Thus, I am bound to help you, as—I hope—Baldr would help me."

He—he hoped? That sounded... odd, and Alma angled another uneasy glance toward where Varinn was still walking steadily, still without even looking where he was going.

"Er, are you and Baldr close, then?" she asked, her voice scraping unpleasantly against her throat. "If you're friends, would that—it wouldn't affect this, would it? Our—agreement?"

Varinn grimaced, his gaze still firmly on the ceiling, but he didn't immediately reply. And Alma's heart was suddenly hammering again, her feet tripping to a halt on the wet earth, her eyes frantically searching his hard, unreadable profile, the unmistakable grinding in his jaw.

"Varinn," she choked out. "You—you *will* still do this. Won't you? Please?"

He'd stopped walking too, and his sigh was laboured and heavy, his eyes still not meeting hers. "I yet mean to help you, for as long as you wish," he said. "But I—"

His voice broke there, his breath inhaling sharp—and then his eyes darted back behind them, down into the yawning black corridor. "Ach," he said, in a tone that sounded almost... relieved? "Baldr has scented you, and is on his way. He shall be here soon."

Wait, what? Baldr had scented her? And was on his way here? *Now*?

"What?" Alma croaked, gaping at Varinn with rapidly rising

horror. "Did you—you didn't *tell* him about this somehow, did you?!"

Varinn blinked back toward her, his brows furrowing. "Ach, no," he said. "But this is *Baldr*. You surely knew he would scent you, ach?"

Alma stared blankly at him, at the confusion slowly creeping into his dark eyes. "*Baldr*," Varinn said again, slower this time. "Son of Barden, and Left Hand to the Captain of Five Clans. The best nose in all of Orc Mountain, and mayhap all the realm. You bear *his own* scent. Fresh. He could easily follow you across the *realm*, woman."

Alma's horror had abruptly begun flashing behind her eyes, and she had to clutch at the slippery wall for balance, gulping painfully for breath. "You *knew* Baldr would follow us, when you agreed to this?" she demanded at him. "Why didn't you *tell* me?!"

Varinn's eyes were looking rather hunted now, his brows still furrowed deep. "Ach, I thought you knew," he said. "But Baldr was off in the Skai arena, amidst that mess between the Skai and Bautul. So this was mayhap the best time you should find to do this, if you had some quarrel, and wished to make some play against him, or mayhap turn him closer toward you—"

He jerked a helpless shrug, waving vaguely back toward the mountain, while Alma gripped tighter against the wall, and fought to follow that through. Varinn thought she'd done this as some kind of—of game? Or some kind of ploy, to draw Baldr toward her? To draw him away from—from *Drafli*?!

"Oh, no, no, noooo," she moaned, wildly shaking her head, squeezing her eyes shut. "Oh gods, Varinn, I would *never*, I only needed to get back to Ashford, and they wouldn't let me leave! And Baldr didn't tell me anything about the—the *smelling*, or really even his job, we've only ever spoken a few times, and Drafli already hates me, and I—"

And she could... *hear* something, from behind them. Voices, and dull repeated thuds, as though someone was... running. Through the corridor. Toward them.

Alma shot Varinn a frantic, panicked look—and then shoved off the wall, and started running, too. Pelting off up the corridor, away from the voices, perhaps they were still a good distance away, she had to try, she had to...

The rock and earth was slippery and uneven under her racing feet, the light swiftly fading—but suddenly here was Varinn, loping beside her, holding up the lamp. And he *still* wasn't looking where he was going, and instead he was staring at her, the unease and confusion still palpable in his wide blinking eyes.

"You need not run thus, woman," he said, not even slightly short of breath. "This path is rough and damp, and not easy for human feet. Baldr should never harm you, ach?"

Alma fought back the rising urge to scream, and focused on pushing faster, dragging air into her throbbing lungs. "It's not about him," she gulped at Varinn, between painful breaths. "I need to go back. I need to see my employer. Don't you see, otherwise I'm going to start a *war*!"

Varinn visibly startled, even as he still kept pace beside her, still holding out the lamp. "Then we ought to stop, and speak of this," he said firmly. "You truly ought not to run thus, woman, for you shall never outrun Baldr, and this is not *safe*."

But Alma wouldn't stop, couldn't stop, not with the terror and misery and exhaustion now streaming into her lungs, into her sliding, pounding feet. Into the sound of voices coming closer, that voice, so familiar and yet so horribly, vividly painful—

"Alma!" he called, *Baldr* called, the word plummeting hard in her chest. "Stop!"

And suddenly, somehow, it was like that one word—that command, hurled out like a spear—had caught and hooked deep inside her, punching the last of the breath from her lungs. Powerful enough that there was nothing there, nothing left, not even beneath her feet, her entire body the entire world keeling sharp and sideways—

"No!" shouted the voice, but once again it was too late, because Alma was falling, sinking, breaking, and—

And stopping. Stopping, because familiar strong arms had somehow clutched against her, drawing her close. Into warm, rich heat, into solid safety, into quite possibly the most delectable scent Alma had smelled in her life...

"You are safe," Baldr's voice gasped, hot and close in her ear. "I am here."

12

Baldr was here.

And for a single, stunning instant, it was like everything else had blinked away. Like Alma was floating, where she'd once been falling, and breathing, where the air had once been barren. Like all the world had snapped into pure, perfect rightness again.

And blinking up at Baldr's blazing eyes, his flushed face, his parted lips, there was suddenly only craving, burning deep and brutal in Alma's belly. Yes, he needed to keep holding her like this. Yes, he needed to spread those strong fingers wider against her, let her feel the bite of those claws. And yes, he needed to bend down, to let her taste that mouth, to drink him until she burst—

But then—a sound. Nearby. Because someone was here, and where even was she, what was even *happening*—

Alma yelped and shoved at Baldr's warmth, his scent, his hands, scrabbling away, away—and by the time her tingling feet found earth again, the comprehension was already striking, setting her staggering. She was supposed to be running. Keeping her promise. Going back to Mr. Pembroke. Stopping the *war*.

"Gods damn it," she gasped, digging her palms painfully into her eyes. "How did you—"

But then, somehow, she was looking at Baldr again, and he was looking at her. And his face and his clothes were streaked with red—with blood?—his chest heaving, his hair messy and loose, his eyes dark and arrested in the lamplight, and slowly glancing toward something behind her.

And behind her—Alma nearly tripped again as she spun around to look—there was Drafli. Yes, gods strike her where she stood, there was Drafli, his hand clutched to the sword-hilt at his belt, his eyes glittering on hers with vicious, menacing rage. Because surely, *surely*, he too thought this was some kind of ploy. Some stupid plot, to draw Baldr after her. To steal him away.

And wait, perhaps even Baldr thought that too, because he was already advancing toward Varinn, his jaw set, his claws snapped sharp and deadly from his hands.

"What," he growled, "was this, Varinn. Why did you seek to run with her. You are supposed to be my brother!"

Varinn didn't move, but he didn't speak, either—and his eyes had angled, brief but telling, toward Alma. As if he wasn't about to tell Baldr anything, without her leave. And there was a sudden rush of deep, teetering gratefulness, even as Alma belatedly lurched forward, thrusting herself between them.

"Varinn didn't do anything," she gulped at Baldr. "I pushed him into this. I cornered him in the corridor. And I told him I would offer my—my *affections*—to any orc who would take me to Ashford."

But if she'd thought that would help, it accomplished the complete opposite, because Baldr's eyes flashed with fury, and he made to lunge around her toward Varinn again. "And you *agreed*, Varinn?!" he shouted at him. "Did you truly think you could take her far enough away that I would not *smell* it?!"

Varinn grimaced, but he still hadn't otherwise moved, or replied. He was still helping her, Alma realized, still showing her astonishing kindness—and without thinking, she clutched at Baldr's taut, blood-streaked wrist, digging her fingers into his skin.

"Varinn was only looking out for me," she gasped, glancing again at his eyes, suddenly seeing all this for the lowering, painful truth it had been. "I said, I told him I would offer a son to *any* orc. Anyone who would take me. And Varinn said"—her voice broke into a brief, rasping cough—"he said that by taking me, he was helping. Being a good brother. A good Grisk."

Beneath her touch on his arm, Baldr's body had gone very still—and when she blinked back toward him, the anger had seemed to drain away from his eyes. And in its place, there was something almost... shocked. Wounded.

"But why would you offer such a prize, woman?" he asked her, his voice strangely small. "And to—to someone *else*?"

Alma swallowed against her raw throat, and glanced reflexively up the corridor. "Because I need to get to Ashford," she croaked. "And I don't have anything else of value to offer. And I met an orc baby today, and he wasn't nearly as alarming as I'd first supposed, so—"

She could feel Baldr staring at her, could still feel that shock—that hurt—in his eyes. And then his hand abruptly came to his nose, rubbing hard against it, and his eyes were blinking over Alma's shoulder, still wide and wounded, as if they were speaking. Pleading.

And wait, wait, surely he'd been looking at *Drafli*—because suddenly Drafli was here, his clawed hand gripping at Baldr's arm, and tugging him out of Alma's grip. And then shoving Baldr bodily behind him, so that now Drafli himself could loom tall and terrifying over her, his eyes flashing, his lip curling with sharp contempt.

Why, he mouthed at her, the single word very clear, as his hand made a swift, purposeful gesture, and then repeated it. *Why you run.*

Oh. And yes, surely he thought Alma had been trying to

lure Baldr away from him, surely—and she squared her shoulders, and fought to drag up truth. "I swore to you I would go," she choked out. "Both of you. And I learned today that my employer is using my absence, and Baldr's kindness, as an excuse to launch more aggression against you. And the best way to stop him"—she painfully swallowed, but kept her eyes on his—"is obviously for me to make a public return to Ashford at once, and clearly proclaim your innocence."

Her voice had faded to a hoarse whisper by the end, her lungs dragging for air, and she braced herself for Drafli's certain retaliation, perhaps more anger or accusations—but to her vague surprise, there was something new shifting in his eyes. Something that looked more like... comprehension. Understanding.

"But it was clear that Jule and Kesst and Efterar wouldn't allow me to leave," Alma continued, even quieter now. "So I waited until they were called away, and then found Varinn. I realize it wasn't the best-laid plan, but I know my employer, and I know what he's capable of, and"—she painfully swallowed again, dropping her gaze to the floor—"he already destroyed my mother, and I couldn't bear for him to destroy you, too. Especially after you've all been so kind to me."

She reflexively sniffed, wiping a shaky hand at her wet cheek, and risked another glance up at Drafli's eyes. His glinting, unblinking eyes, which no longer looked understanding at all, but... speculative. Suspicious.

Then I take you, he mouthed at her, accompanying the words with more clear, purposeful gestures from his hands. *Now*.

Oh, thank all the gods above, and Alma's relief felt like a dizzying force, her body jerking a reflexive, reeling step toward Drafli's unmoving form before her. "Yes, please," she gasped, clasping for his hand with both of hers. "Oh, thank you so much. I would be so, *so* grateful to you."

But wait, had she done the wrong thing *again*, because

Drafli was suddenly sneering down at her, and yanking his hand away like he'd been stung. Even blatantly wringing it out, with pure contemptuous loathing in his eyes, as though Alma had somehow horribly tainted him with that single, stupid touch.

"Oh gods, I'm sorry," she groaned at him, pressing her shaking palms back to her eyes. "I'm so sorry, I just need to leave, and get out of your lives forever, and *will* you still take me? Please?"

But once she'd dropped her hands again, and found Drafli's glittering, furious eyes, here was yet more comprehension, plunging into her belly. Perhaps he'd never meant to take her, perhaps that had been some sort of—of *test*. And of course he wouldn't want to help her, not after she'd so repeatedly offended him, and she felt herself gulp a sob as she whirled around toward Varinn. Her last hope. She'd come so far, she had to try, please...

"Then will you still take me, Varinn?" she croaked at him. "Please. I'm begging you. You said you would help."

But oh gods, now even Varinn was looking angry, too. His hand dragging against his hair, his eyes gone grim and narrow on hers—and then flicking beyond her, toward Baldr and Drafli.

"Och, Baldr," he snapped, with surprising heat in his voice. "I ken we are brothers, but if you are too great a fool to speak your own truth to your own woman, then I shall do this. Ach?"

Alma blinked toward Baldr, who was in turn blinking blankly toward Varinn—who then spun back toward her again, his arms crossing over his broad chest. "Woman, you cannot go back to Ashford," he snapped. "I now see why you sought this, and thought it should help us. But it is not only for your own safety that you must stay. It is for *his*, and thus, for *all* of us."

His hard eyes had again flicked to Baldr, who still stood silent and unmoving behind Drafli, his eyes now unreadable on Varinn's face. And Alma wasn't at all following, and Varinn huffed a heavy sigh, and turned back toward her. "Baldr has built a mating-bond with you, and you are now scent-bound to him," he said firmly. "This is hard to break, for any orc. But for a Grisk, and most of all for *him*"—he jerked his head toward Baldr—"this bears more power than almost aught else. Should you go back to Ashford, and should this cruel man harm you, or force you to his bed, Baldr shall taste this with every breath, ach?"

He—he would? Alma shot another chagrined glance toward Baldr, who still wasn't moving, wasn't arguing this—and Varinn sighed again. "Few orcs can bear this," he continued, clipped. "And if Baldr should break under this, and follow you there, then Drafli shall follow *him*. And then the Skai, and the captain, and then all the Ash-Kai. And then we shall *surely* have a broken treaty, and more war. Ach?"

Oh. Alma felt pinned to the earth, suddenly, the understanding careening through her thoughts. They truly had been trying to prevent more war, by keeping her at the mountain. They'd been trying to protect Baldr. And even not letting her run and hide somewhere else—perhaps even that had been about Baldr, too.

"I ken the Ash-Kai can oft be overbearing schemers," Varinn said, with another sigh. "But they were not wrong in this. Any woman *he* built a bond with should soon become a risk to us all. It is far wiser to keep you close, and safe."

Oh, gods. Alma's trembling hands had fluttered to her thundering heart, and she felt her feet slightly tripping, her eyes snapped back to Baldr's stunned-looking face.

"But I—I don't want this bond," she croaked. "And Baldr doesn't want it, either. He already has a mate. They've sworn *vows* to one another."

She shot another pleading glance at Varinn, who was rubbing his head again, his shoulders sagging. "Ach, mayhap," he said slowly. "But then, mayhap you speak together of this. You mayhap find another way to break this. You do *not*"—his eyes flashed on Baldr's—"build a bond with a sweet, loyal woman, and next hand her off to the Ash-Kai, and scarce deign to *speak* to her! Mayhap this is what a Skai would do, but you are yet a Grisk, whether you like to admit this, or no!"

The anger was palpable in his voice, gone deep and forceful in the too-close tunnel, and now his eyes snapped even narrower, and flicked to Drafli's. "And why does this *Skai* deserve such fealty from you, brother," he hissed, "when he took *years* to grant you this in return? When I can still scent every Skai he took, whenever he was bored with you? Whilst *you* kept yourself true to only *him*?!"

Drafli's eyes were flashing dangerously on Varinn's, but Baldr was looking very pale, his face haggard, his mouth tight. "Drafli and I had an—agreement," he replied thinly. "He was keeping the Skai ways."

Varinn's laugh was hard and brittle, and he lurched a sudden, purposeful step closer to Baldr and Drafli. "Ach, then, so why can *you* not keep the Grisk ways?" he demanded. "Grisk care for our women, and honour them. And when a woman shows herself a Grisk, and makes a vow to us, we take this for the truth it is. *Your* woman"—he waved toward Alma—"vowed to you she would go away, and thus she did all within her strength to gain this, and you are a *fool* if you did not foresee it! What if she had found Ulfarr, instead of me? Or another Skai like Balgarr, or Skaap?!"

Varinn was truly shouting now, his voice echoing down the corridor, his eyes glowering between Baldr and Drafli. And Drafli was bobbing on his feet, his hands clenched to fists, looking as though he might lunge at Varinn at any moment—but Baldr's hand was gripping Drafli's arm, even as his head gave a hard shake, his mouth twisting, as if he were in pain.

And blinking back and forth between them, suddenly Alma only felt pain, too. Drafli had betrayed Baldr, for *years*? She'd been in true danger from the Skai, by leaving the way she had? And worst of all, not only had she and Baldr somehow built this ridiculous bond, but it was powerful enough that she was now a risk to his entire *mountain*?! And what was she supposed to do now, how were they supposed to deal with Pembroke, how had she once again bungled everything...

But she couldn't seem to find a way to speak beyond the mess, and no one else spoke, either, the silence gone dark and oppressive—when suddenly, out of nowhere, something shouted. *Someone* shouted, another deep carrying orc-voice from down the corridor, and Alma flinched backwards, her eyes frantically searching the darkness.

And yes, yes, it was yet another orc. A tall, vaguely familiar one, also wearing a kilt—and Alma realized it was Varinn's friend Thrain. And he'd clearly been running through the corridor toward them, but now his steps slowed to a saunter as he approached, his eyes sweeping back and forth between them.

"Och, there you are, brother," he said, clapping his big hand to Varinn's shoulder. "Smelled you raging all the way up in the Grisk wing, and I ken half the mountain's heard, too. Did someone die?"

Varinn twitched, but his shoulders seemed to sag under Thrain's hand, his eyes fluttering closed. "Not yet," he said, though his voice had dropped, too. "I am just down here raving at mayhap our kindest clan brother, for seeking to keep his vows to his mate. I ken I have frightened our new sister in this, also."

Thrain's eyes flicked knowingly toward Alma, and he drummed his claws against Varinn's shoulder. "Ach, this is the true fun we all seek," he said lightly. "But if you're finished, mayhap you can come spar for a spell? Nattfarr has just defeated Dammarr again, and thus he's due a good thrashing, I ken."

Varinn's shoulders sagged even more, and he gave a curt nod. To which Thrain bodily steered him around, and began marching him back up the corridor. And while Varinn seemed to go willingly enough, he cast a brief, regretful glance toward Alma over his shoulder.

"You three too," Thrain called back, with conspicuous casualness. "Else it shall soon be more than only me coming down here after you, ach?"

There was a sound much like a growl from Baldr behind her, but no one seemed to speak, or move. And finally Alma nodded toward the floor, and then followed after Varinn and Thrain, her head down, her arms crossed tight over her chest.

She'd failed. She'd tried so hard, and once again, she'd failed. And what was she supposed to do next? How would she ever find a way to leave now?

She couldn't help another reflexive sniff, and again wiped at her wet eyes. She would need to think of something. Find another way to keep her word, to get out of this mountain, forever.

"I am sorry, woman," came Baldr's low voice from behind her, close enough that she flinched, and darted a look over her shoulder. To where he was indeed following her, striding in step with Drafli, their fingers laced tightly together. "I ought to have spoken of this to you."

Alma shrugged and kept walking, her eyes back on the uneven earth beneath her feet. Because even if she said anything, it was sure to be the wrong thing, again. It was sure to lead to more mistakes, more anger, more misery.

"I had thought," continued Baldr's uneven voice, "that mayhap if I fought to ignore this, it should weaken. I thought this should help. I did not see that it should push you away to someone like Varinn, or make you seek to run."

Alma painfully swallowed, and briefly squeezed her wet eyes shut. "But I promised you I would leave," she managed. "You knew. I thought that was what you wanted."

Baldr made an odd noise behind her, almost like a growl. "No, I told you to stay," he replied sharply. "How could you possibly think that meant you should leave? Let alone wandering around the mountain *alone*, and offering another orc a *son*?!"

The harshness in his voice was surely genuine, dropping like a stone into Alma's belly, firing curdling ice up her back. And suddenly there was no resolve left, no other way through, and the wracking sobs were shuddering through her chest, escaping out her sore, gasping throat.

"I didn't only p-promise *you*," she gulped. "I have n-no desire to come between you two. I h-hate that I've hurt you, and p-put you at risk. I d-don't know why you didn't just l-leave me in the river, I—I would be with m-my mother now, and—"

And now she was weeping too much to speak, her shoulders convulsing, her wet face buried in her hands. And she could feel their eyes, the weight of their judgement, she'd been so foolish, so weak, worthless...

When suddenly, he was here. Baldr was here, his warm rich scent flooding her breaths, his arms circled close and powerful around her back. One set of claws digging into her waist through her cloak, the other clutching unevenly at her hair, tucking her head against his chest.

"Ach, ach, Bright-Heart," he choked. "Ach, do not weep. I am sorry. I never wished to bring you pain. I have been thoughtless, and cowardly, and afraid. I ought never"—he let out a heavy, shuddering breath—"unleash my weakness upon you, ach? Most of all when you have only sought to help me. *Honour* me."

His voice was fervent, his hand stroking her hair again and again, his chest heaving against her. As if perhaps he was weeping, too. And Alma should have pushed him away, should have thought of Drafli, standing there watching, his mate, his *mate*—

But instead she only clutched at Baldr's strong body, her lungs dragging in his scent with deep, gasping gulps. As if she was drowning again, and he was the only way out, the only hope left...

"Then what do we do?" she whispered, pleaded, into his chest. "How do we break it? Fix it?"

But Baldr's breaths only rose and fell, the sounds cracked and thin, his hands twitching against her. As if maybe he were drowning, too, with no hope of ever finding air again.

"I wish I knew, Bright-Heart," he whispered. "I wish I knew."

13

They returned to the sickroom in raw, ringing silence. With Baldr now walking at Alma's side, though he didn't touch her again, didn't speak.

And while Alma couldn't hear Drafli walking behind them, she could feel the strength of his eyes, the weight of his bare, bitter hatred. He would never forgive her for this. Ever.

Thankfully the corridors back toward the sickroom were mostly empty, with few passing orcs to witness Alma's wet, leaking eyes. And when they finally stepped back into the familiar sickroom, and came face to face with a frowning, tired-looking Kesst, Baldr forestalled any commentary with a surprisingly deep growl, a curt raising of his clawed hand.

"We shall not further speak of this tonight," he said flatly. "Alma must rest. And I must—*speak* with Varinn."

Kesst's eyes had gone rather speculative on Baldr's, but he twitched a dismissive shrug, and stalked over toward where Efterar appeared to be sleeping in one of the beds, his blood-streaked arm thrown over his eyes.

Alma went to her own bed without further prompting, pulling off her cloak and boots, and slipping beneath the fur. And then curling up and closing her eyes, perhaps waiting for

Baldr and Drafli to leave, waiting for that telltale angry prickle to finally fade from her skin...

But it only seemed to sharpen, somehow, scraping harder and colder, and that was surely the touch of Baldr's hand against her hair, fingers spreading wide. "We shall find a way, Bright-Heart," he whispered. "Now sleep, ach?"

Alma twitched a nod, and in return that hand patted her hair, and then lifted away. And finally, finally, there was only the exhaustion, swirling even stronger than the feel of Drafli's disapproval, and she gratefully sank into it, followed it into the darkness...

But when her awareness slowly flickered back to life, what felt like a long time later, the disapproval was... still there. Still *here*, so close Alma could taste it, deep and bitter in her breath.

Her arm reflexively snapped out sideways toward it, as if to reassure herself it wasn't real, it was some foolish construction of her too-tired brain—when she *touched* it. Warm, and smooth, and *alive*.

She lurched upwards in the bed, and just as quickly the warmth yanked away, recoiling from her touch. And blinking frantically toward it, Alma found... Drafli?

Yes, gods curse her, it was Drafli. Sitting stiffly on the bed across from her, his arms folded tightly over his bare chest, his eyes on hers still crackling with deadly rage. And there was no sign of Baldr anywhere, and no Kesst or Efterar either, and Alma cringed back in the bed, yanking her fur up to her chin.

"Oh gods," she gulped, and she was actually trembling under the fur, her teeth chattering. "I'm so sorry. For last night, and for—everything. I never meant—"

But Drafli's clawed hand had snapped sideways in midair, making a sharp, furious gesture that surely meant, *Stop*. And Alma's voice instantly broke, her eyes gone even wider, her body shuddering more powerfully than before. Had he come to threaten her, to punish her, to...

But then, without warning, he thrust something toward her.

A small square of folded paper, with a neat line of black lettering written across it. And after blinking uncertainly between Drafli and the paper, Alma turned it around, and read it.

We make new agreement, the script read, in careful, clear common-tongue. *You and me.*

Alma stared down at the paper for a long, twitching moment, and then blinked back up at Drafli's watching eyes. At their glinting, blatant anger, as he waved his hand toward the paper again. Meaning, clearly, *Keep going.*

So Alma unfolded the paper, and indeed found another line of neat black letters. And as her eyes read them, she felt her body stiffening in her bed, her heart thundering in her chest.

"What?" she croaked at Drafli, at those glittering, furious eyes. "Did you—*you* didn't write this?! Did you?"

But now there was contempt, flashing across his face, curling his lip. Surely saying, without speaking a word, that yes, he had written it, and why else would he be sitting here, wanting her to read it?

So Alma swallowed hard, dropped her eyes, and read it again. Fighting to follow the words, the impossible, unthinkable meaning behind them.

I give you my mate, it said, *if you give him a son.*

Alma blinked at those words again, feeling her heartbeat thunder even harder, her thoughts jolting and reeling through her skull. Drafli would give her *Baldr*, if she gave Baldr a *son*. One of those little green baby orcs, with sharp teeth and pointed ears, perhaps with Baldr's beautiful eyes...

And even as the longing seemed to shudder deep into Alma's belly—she surely didn't *want* that?—there was also disbelief, and maybe even anger, clawing at her choked throat. How dare he. How *dare* he.

"You would *leave* Baldr," she hissed at Drafli, "out of some misguided belief that he wants me more than he wants you? He would be *devastated*. He clearly *adores* you, even though the gods only know why!"

The certainty rang through her voice with alarming clarity, and she again winced backwards in her bed, her eyes wide on Drafli's face. Expecting his retaliation, surely—but instead, for the briefest of instants, there was something that might have almost been a grimace. While his eyes purposefully flicked away from her, his hand waving at the paper again, even more forceful than before.

So Alma unfolded it, her heart still thudding erratically, her eyes racing over the new lines of script. *I no leave him for you*, it read. *He would no bear this. He stays my mate, and you will honour this.*

Oh. So Drafli was suggesting—he was suggesting that Baldr would keep her on the side, as some kind of... *mistress*? As a *kept woman* of some sort, good only for sharing Baldr's bed, and giving him a *son*?

But then Alma's shaking fingers opened the last fold in the paper. And as her wide eyes rapidly scanned down the multiple rows of text filling the page, the humiliating certainty of it seemed to strike hot, then cold, then hot again.

It was a list of terms, broken out with clear, devastating callousness. She would swear to stay at Orc Mountain for one full year, at minimum. She would stay in a designated, defensible room, and sleep alone. She would submit to the best possible medical care, and do her best to birth a healthy, hale son. She would honour the orcs' beliefs and practices. She would never taint Baldr's scent with another's. She would never seek to run away again, or take Baldr's son away from him, no matter the circumstances.

And at the bottom, with a thick line scored beneath it, was one last demand, perhaps the most appalling of them all.

You will honour and obey me, in all things.

She would honour and obey him. She would obey... *Drafli*?!

Alma's incredulous eyes had snapped back up to his,

searching them with desperate disbelief—but yes, yes, surely he meant that. He meant all of this. He wanted to turn her into his mate's servant. His... *harlot.*

The vivid vision of Mr. Pembroke was suddenly swarming Alma's thoughts with horrifying, sickening strength—and twisted with it, tangling with it, was the vision of her mother. Her sweet, lovely mother, so unflinchingly kind and generous, *You don't think she knew who filled her belly?*

Alma's hand had somehow clapped over her mouth, and she fought to focus her swarming gaze on Drafli again, on the cold, distant hardness in his watching eyes. "Why," she whispered, "would I *ever* agree to this?"

Drafli's eyes didn't change, but his hand abruptly reached toward her, his long fingers flipping open to show her something in his palm. Something small, and bright, and glittering.

Alma's throat audibly choked, her eyes gone wide, because those—those were *jewels.* A necklace, and earrings. And while Alma had cleaned Mr. Pembroke's jewels on multiple occasions, she'd never before seen any so stunning as these. They were made of intricately twisted gold, and they each boasted a large, perfectly cut, gleaming blue stone, surrounded by smaller stones of bright sparkling green. Sapphires, surely, with emeralds, and together they flashed almost like water, glittering beneath a sunny sky.

They were quite possibly the most beautifully crafted things Alma had seen in her entire life, and she felt herself swallow as she stared at them, her breath caught in her throat. Drafli was offering her these? In exchange for becoming Baldr's... *kept woman*?

"These are... yours?" she somehow asked, glancing toward Drafli's forbidding eyes—and he jerked a nod, hard and grim.

Yours, he mouthed at her, slowly, jabbing a clawed finger toward her. *If you agree. One year.*

Good gods. Alma swallowed again, her eyes fixed back on the jewels, while something clutched painfully in her belly.

She'd known how much coin Mr. Pembroke had gained from selling far less spectacular jewels than these, and these would surely be worth far more. Enough for her to live on for multiple years. Enough to buy a little house of her own, with a little garden, a little place for her mother's ashes, if she could ever find a way to retrieve them again...

But it was wrong. So wrong, to even consider such a thing. Those terms had said Alma couldn't take the child away with her—so Drafli meant he would trade her these jewels, for her *child*. She would sell him not only her body, but her *son*.

"But what if," Alma rasped, and why was she asking this, even *considering* this, "what if I don't *want* to leave my son, after?"

Drafli's mouth betrayed another unmistakable grimace, even as his shoulder gave a deceptively fluid shrug. *Then you no leave*, he mouthed at her. *You choose.*

Oh. He meant—he meant Alma could stay, if she wanted. He meant he would pay her, either way, for her year, for her son. He was handing her... a future. A house. A way to pay off her mother's debts. A way to be *free*.

Alma squeezed her eyes shut, and whipped her head back and forth. Because gods, that was even assuming she survived it. A pregnancy was no small commitment on its own, but to willingly become pregnant with an orc's son? And even if Jule had apparently somehow survived such a birth, that truly didn't mean anything, did it?

"But giving birth is dangerous," she managed, plaintive. "Even with human children. You—you're asking me to risk my *life* for this."

Drafli's eyes had narrowed menacingly on hers, his lip curling with clear, disapproving contempt. *You offered this to Varinn*, he mouthed at her. *Varinn. For no jewels, and no vows. I give you good terms, and good care. I keep you safe. I keep my word.*

And blinking at Drafli's snapping eyes, his angry mouth, it distantly occurred to Alma that she—believed him. Gods, in the midst of whatever bizarre absurdity this was, she believed him. But it didn't make sense, Drafli couldn't truly be offering to care for her like that, to share his *mate* with her, indefinitely. He *hated* her, he'd hated her from the very first moment they'd met...

And Alma was clinging to that, suddenly, with all her strength, and she pulled up straighter in her bed. "You can't truly want this," she countered, and that had to be true, it *had* to be. "You would never choose for me to interfere with your life like this. With your own *mate*."

But Drafli gave another fluid shrug, his eyes again flicking to something beyond her. *He longs for you*, he mouthed, accentuating the words with more pointed jabs of his claws. *He longs for a son. Thus, I grant you to him. I give him this. Not you.*

More comprehension was flashing through Alma's thoughts, stark and brutal. So by doing this, Drafli would still be upholding his superior place as Baldr's mate. He would be the one giving Baldr these gifts, and thereby taking the credit for Alma's body, and her sacrifices. For her *son*.

But it still didn't make sense, it didn't, and Alma desperately grasped for more comprehension, more truth. "But Baldr's your *mate*," she gulped. "How could you bear for him to—to be intimate—with someone else?"

Drafli grimaced again, even as he gave another one of those casual, too-dismissive shrugs. *He has oft borne this from me*, he mouthed at her, again clarifying the words with sharp movements of his hands. *Thus, I shall bear this for him.*

Varinn's accusation from down in that corridor had been swirling through Alma's brain—*I can still scent every Skai he took, whenever he was bored with you*—but even if this was about somehow making things fair between Drafli and Baldr, it still didn't make sense, did it? She'd seen how Drafli looked at her, she'd felt his hatred, his contempt. And gods, she could even still feel it in this very moment, still pinned like this under his scornful, disapproving gaze. Still as though she were some foolish, worthless trifle, who'd stumbled her way into his cold, superior presence.

"But you hate me," she said, or perhaps pleaded. "You *hate* me, Drafli."

His body's sudden spasm at her use of his name felt almost visceral, and his lip had snapped up again, baring all his sharp white teeth. Very clearly proving her exact point, and she could see the recognition of that flaring across his eyes, and then vanishing again. Leaving behind something that looked almost—worn. Tired.

I hate all women, he finally mouthed, and she saw his throat convulse, quick and furtive. *All humans. But*—he frowned down at the jewels still glittering in his hand—*if naught else, I know you will keep your word to me.*

She would keep her word. Because of the night before, Alma realized, blinking at his bowed black head. She'd promised Baldr and Drafli that she would leave—and even when Baldr had absolved her of that promise, she'd still kept her word to Drafli. Even when it had put her at risk, and put his entire mountain at risk, and...

"Wait," she croaked at him. "Is this—is this just about finding a way to keep me here, after last night? Is this just a way of keeping your mountain safe? Keeping *Baldr* safe?! From Mr. Pembroke?!"

And yes, oh gods, yes, surely it was, and that—that explained *everything*. And Alma abruptly thrust her fur back, and leapt up to her feet. Just needing to move, to do something, to shout at him, to escape...

But before she'd even seen him move, Drafli was on his feet, too. And gods, this close he was so tall, looming well over a full head above her, the tension crackling through his too-near, too-large body.

"No," something hissed, hoarse and vicious. "You sit. You *listen*."

Alma froze in place, her eyes seized to Drafli's face—

because yes, somehow, that had been him. He'd spoken. He could *speak*?

But yes, clearly, he could—even though his clawed hand was now rubbing hard at his throat, his face contorting with brief but visible pain. And between the shock, and something that felt dangerously like sympathy, Alma twitched a shaky nod, and sat.

But Drafli didn't sit this time. Just kept standing there, glaring down toward her, his arms crossing tightly over his bare chest. "I tell you," he continued, in that harsh, rasping voice, barely more than a whisper. "He is *mine*. I swore vows to him, I give all for him. This is *my* right. *Mine*."

Alma's hands were gripping together, her mouth perhaps opening to speak—but he silenced her with the already-familiar sideways slice of his fingers. "I will no see my mate further suffer for any of this," he hissed, "and most of all for a fool woman such as you, who no even *sees* the debt she owes him. But for him, you should now be a corpse floating down the river, and I should be *glad* of this!"

The pure venom in those words seemed to strike Alma straight across the face, and she couldn't hide her flinch, the fearful clutch of her hands to her chest. But Drafli wasn't done, he was stepping even closer, his legs very nearly touching her knees, his clawed fists deadly weapons before her eyes.

"I shall fix this," he whispered, his strained voice almost inaudible. "I shall see my mate happy and safe again. If you no agree to this with me, then I shall find another woman to cover your scent upon him. Mayhap one who sees him for the prize he is!"

What? The sheer unfairness of that snapped Alma's head back, her anger lurching in her chest, churning against a sudden, blazing jealousy. "I *know* what a prize Baldr is," she growled. "But I have been trying to do *everything* in my power to ignore that. Because I know he's committed to *you*, you arrogant prick, and I want to respect his wishes! And"—she clutched her shaking hands tighter together—"if Baldr truly wants this so much, then why isn't he here with you? Why isn't *he* the one making me this offer?"

Drafli kept sneering back down at her, and his lean body before her seemed to coil with his rising rage, his cold contempt. "You ken you know my mate's wishes better than I?" he breathed. "You ken he should *ever* ask this of you, even if this is what he most longs for? You know *naught* of this, or of him. And I ken I am just as great a fool as you are, if I thought you might see the honour in what I offer you!"

His voice had fully faded by the end, sputtering into silence—and though he twisted away, his long black braid whirling behind him, his hand clapping over his mouth. And Alma could see his shoulders wrenching, the muscles clamping tight and rhythmic in his bare back, as a strange, scraping noise rasped into the silence. He was—*coughing*.

And despite everything he'd just said, and the misery still curdling in Alma's belly, she couldn't suppress the sudden, overwhelming surge of knowing. Of *understanding*. And she fumbled around for the waterskin—yes, there, just beside her pillow—and thrust it out toward his back. Realizing, too late, that surely he wouldn't take it, surely this was just more foolishness on her part, and—

And then he snatched the waterskin away, without even slightly turning, or looking at her. And with a swift bite of his teeth, he'd pulled out the stopper, spat it away, and poured the water down his spasming throat.

Alma watched in silence, not missing the winces of pain in his profile as he swallowed, or the sheen of sweat that had broken across his cheek. And again, the sympathy kept rearing up, scraping against her ribs, feeling brittle enough to break—

But then Drafli lowered the waterskin, dragging a shaky-looking hand against his braid before tossing the empty waterskin down toward Alma's feet. And as her eyes followed it, his hand reached down, and snapped the paper from her fingers.

Crumpling it in his fist as he spun on his heel and strode for the door, without a single look back.

He was—*leaving*. He was taking away his offer. He was going to find another woman for Baldr, he would cover Alma's scent forever. Only one year, what Baldr most longed for, keeping him safe, repaying the debt she owed...

Suddenly it was like Alma's misery cracked, splintering her apart, tearing her open from the inside out. She was a fool. She'd failed again and again. She'd put Baldr in danger, and possibly ruined his life—and Baldr's mate was giving her a way out. A way to salvage this. To... *stay*.

"Wait," she croaked at Drafli's back, the word a bare, broken plea. "Wait. Please."

And when Drafli turned around, the movement slow, measured, she could almost taste the hostility in his eyes. The sheer, sweeping loathing, nearly strong enough to make her retch.

"If I did it," she gulped at him, "would you treat our son with kindness? Would you care for him? Or would you treat him like—like—"

She waved frantically at herself, at the clear object of Drafli's hatred. A hatred that could surely, so easily, extend to her son, and grant him an entire lifetime of certain misery, caught in the cruel, callous contempt of his own father's bonded mate.

But to Alma's vague surprise, Drafli's shoulders dropped, his eyes briefly closing, as if he were in pain. And one hand, oddly, had come up to rub again at his throat, while the other came to a fist over his heart.

"I shall treat your son as my own," he whispered, barely audible to Alma's ears. "I shall care for him, and give all for him, and guard him with my life. This I swear to you, and to my father Skai-kesh."

His fist had thumped gently against his chest as he spoke, his head bowing low. As if this were some kind of vow, both to

Alma, and to his god. *I shall treat him as my own. Guard him with my life.*

And again, may the gods curse her, Alma believed him. She believed him, and she was shivering beneath the strength of it, her own hand somehow come to rest against her furiously beating heart.

"Then I agree," she whispered, into the stuttering deep. "I'll do it."

14

For the next quarter-hour, Alma and Drafli avoided one another's eyes, and worked through the details of their new plan with stiff, mutual bitterness.

It ought to have felt like negotiations, like an actual agreement—but so far, it had been Drafli telling Alma how it would be, while she'd capitulated to every one of his terms. She would share Baldr's bed on the schedule that Drafli set, and otherwise would avoid distracting him, or seeking him out. She would bear Baldr his son, under the medical supervision that Drafli demanded. She would sleep in the Grisk wing, in the room of Drafli's choosing. She would say a prayer each morning to Drafli's god, Skai-kesh. She would leave Mr. Pembroke to the orcs to sort out, and stop worrying about his demands, or his deadlines.

And finally, perhaps most unsettling of all, she would obey Drafli's orders, without question or hesitation. Even if the orders appeared to contradict the rest of their contract.

"What—what kinds of orders might those be?" Alma tentatively asked at that, searching Drafli's forbidding eyes—and he glanced away with unsettling intent, even as he gave one of those fluid, dismissive shrugs.

Whatever he wishes, he mouthed at her, *I will give*.

Drafli accompanied the "he" with a graceful gesture over his heart, one Alma had seen him use multiple times now—and she carefully repeated it, raising her eyebrows toward him. Earning a ghastly scowl in return, but then another one of those shrugs, sharper this time.

My mate, he mouthed at her, as a very faint flush crept up his neck. *Pure-Heart*.

Oh. He called Baldr *Pure-Heart*. And it again seemed to crack something in Alma's chest, something that wanted to laugh, or perhaps weep. But thankfully she somehow managed to keep her expression neutral, and nodded as she repeated the gesture over her heart.

"Pure-Heart," she echoed, quiet. "It suits him."

Drafli jerked yet another sharp shrug, but at least he didn't argue. And somehow it seemed to give Alma the courage to finally ask for one request of her own, her eyes dropping to her hands, still clutched together on her lap.

"Could I at least," she ventured, "still spend some time with Kesst, and help out with the housekeeping, like I promised I would? That scullery truly is a travesty, and he and Efterar have been so lovely to me."

She fully expected Drafli to mount some kind of argument—to perhaps demand that she wait alone and ignored in her room until he called for her—but after another moment's frowning at her, he again shrugged, cool and uncaring.

Only if you no touch them, he mouthed at her, as he again reached over, and plucked his list of terms out of her fingers. *You only touch Pure-Heart. Or mayhap me*.

With that highly unnerving statement curdling between them, he strode toward the fire, still flickering low on the opposite side of the room—and then he tossed the paper down into its crackling orange flames.

Alma yelped, and belatedly leapt out of bed after him—he was burning their *contract*?!—but she was far too late. The

paper already flaring up with a single bright flame, its thin
edges licking away into ash.

"What the hell," Alma gulped, but Drafli entirely ignored
her, and spun toward the door. As if he were just going to *leave*,
after that?! And when she reflexively snatched for his arm, he
yanked away from her with palpable disgust, shaking out his
hand as he stalked out into the corridor.

Alma stood there staring after him for a hanging moment,
caught in mingled frustration and humiliation—but then
Drafli sharply waved toward her, the command all too clear in
his glinting eyes.

Come, it said. *Obey me.*

Oh. It obviously meant that their contract was still fully in
force after all, even if he'd gone and *burned* it. And as Alma
grudgingly followed him down the corridor, turning into
another passageway she hadn't yet seen, it occurred to her that
by burning his list of terms, Drafli had been hiding the
evidence. Keeping it secret. From... Baldr?

"Does Baldr know *anything* about this contract of yours?"
she tentatively asked, toward Drafli's suddenly stiff shoulders.
"Are you sure he'll agree to it?"

Without warning, Drafli whirled back around toward her,
his eyes sweeping uneasily over the empty corridor—and then
he gestured toward a nearby door in the wall. Clearly ordering
her to go in, and Alma stared at him for an instant, gritting her
teeth and silently cursing her foolishness, before turning and
walking inside. Finding herself in an entirely empty room,
which suddenly felt very small, thanks to Drafli's tall body
towering far too close to hers, and backing her into the nearest
wall.

You never again speak of contract, he mouthed at her, his
words barely visible in the corridor's distant lamplight. *Most of
all to Pure-Heart. This was* vow. *To me.*

Alma eyed Drafli with increasing uncertainty, searching the

grim lines of his harsh, frowning face. "You mean," she whispered, "you want me to *lie* to Baldr about this?"

Drafli's mouth instantly contorted into a terrifying scowl, his hand again making the sideways gesture that meant, *Stop. No.*

You no lie, he said, as his hand kept sharply signing. *You speak only of vow, when you ask him for this.*

When she asked him for this. *She.* And once again Alma was gaping up at Drafli's infuriating face, at the already-familiar stubborn glint in his eyes. "You expect *me* to ask Baldr for this?" she squeaked at him. "You want *me* to suggest that I share his bed, and give him a *son*? For *pay*?!"

Drafli's soundless but very real snarl sent a vicious chill up Alma's back, and his hand again snapped that disapproving sideways gesture. *You never speak of pay, or jewels,* he silently hissed at her. *You say I swear to help you, after. This is all.*

Alma's discomfort was rapidly rising, creeping in cold shivers under her skin, but Drafli only leaned closer, his breath hot and strangely sweet on her face. *You will ask Pure-Heart for this,* he continued, jabbing his clawed finger toward her chest. *He will no accept this from me.*

Wait. *Wait.* So not only did Drafli expect Alma to conceal critical aspects of this from Baldr—but he wasn't even sure if Baldr would *accept* it? If Baldr even wanted it? Wanted *her*?

And despite the tall, muscled, deadly orc trapping her against the wall, his claw still aimed menacingly toward her heart, Alma's defiance was rapidly rising, the clarity juddering through her thoughts. This had already been a terrible plan. The worst plan. And now Drafli wanted to make her a liar, as well as a harlot? Toward Baldr, who'd saved her *life*?! Good gods, what had she been *thinking*?!

"Look, I—" she began, as she rubbed painfully at her hot cheeks. "I'm sorry, but I actually—I don't think I should do this, after all. I don't want to lie to Baldr. He doesn't deserve that from me, the rest of it is already bad enough, and—"

She rubbed harder at her face, and had to drop her gaze from Drafli's dangerously glinting eyes. "You said you could find another woman for him," she whispered, toward the smooth, scarred skin of his too-close chest. "So you should do that, I think. I'm sorry."

With that, she ducked away from him toward the corridor, keeping her eyes on the floor. She would go back to the sick-room, she would ask to meet with Jule, to come up with some other solution, she had to—

When suddenly, something *grabbed* her. Two strong, powerful hands, gripping at Alma's shoulders, whirling her around, and shoving her roughly back against the wall. And she was already shivering, her heartbeat galloping in her chest, as Drafli once again loomed close over her—and then snapped up his hand, and circled it around her *neck*.

Alma instantly froze, her eyes wide and panicked on Drafli's harsh, horrifying face. On all those sharp white teeth, bared toward her in a true, terrifying threat. Silently shouting the sudden, sheer precariousness of this moment, of what she'd been trying to do. She'd broken her word to an orc who already hated her, and they were alone, he was a Skai, he was going to punish her, or worse—

But as Alma cringed against the wall, bracing herself for his certain retaliation, something abruptly shifted in his eyes, in his tall body against her. His shoulders sagging, his throat convulsing, his mouth twisting into a furtive, unmistakable grimace as his eyes squeezed shut. As his head twitched back and forth, like he was trying to shake something out of it.

And when his eyes flicked open again, holding bright and glittering on Alma's, it was almost as though she could see through them, into them, down into the dark, broken desperation tainting his soul. The determination. The... *fear*?

You will speak what I tell you, he silently hissed at her. *If you fail in this, I shall make you suffer, and I shall be glad of this.*

He would make her suffer. It was a threat, it was, and Alma

should have surely still been terrified, and fighting to escape for her life—but she couldn't stop noticing, strange and distant, how that look in Drafli's eyes didn't at all match his words. And even his fingers' sudden, menacing flex against her neck didn't flash more fear up her spine, or more churning in her belly. Because she was still looking at him, into him, seeing...

So you will tell Pure-Heart I made this threat, Drafli continued, slow. *If ever he claims you have spoken false to him.*

And yes, surely, there was the truth of it, flickering deep in his eyes. This threat—this orc's hand circling Alma's neck like this, pinning her to this wall—this was an... *escape.* A way for her to tell Baldr, truthfully, that Drafli had pressured her into this. That he'd threatened her. Promised to make her suffer. To perhaps even *kill* her.

But Alma still couldn't seem to stop searching Drafli's eyes, fighting to follow this, to understand—and she could almost feel his surging unease, his defensiveness. He didn't want her to know it was a false threat, a way out. He wanted her to be able to say this to Baldr, with all truth behind it.

I only lied to you, because Drafli threatened my life.

"Ach?" Drafli rasped at her, out loud, his voice so low, so pained. And then he abruptly leaned in closer, almost near enough to touch. His breath hot against her ear, his tall body so rigid and stiff and cold. But also, that distant traitorous part of Alma pointed out, so strong, so sure. So warm...

"Ach?" he demanded again, close in Alma's ear this time, as his long fingers again flexed against her neck, all deadly ominous intent. "You shall obey me in this, fool woman, or you shall weep and plead at my *feet.*"

And gods curse her, but Alma—*gasped.* The sound far too ragged and raw between them, not hinting even slightly at fear—but instead at something else entirely. Something horribly and devastatingly shameful, that had somehow begun pooling hard and hot in her groin, flushing bright and betraying on her cheeks. Drawing up furious visions of her darkest, deepest dreams, of a powerful commanding lord, bending her to his will...

And against her, Drafli's tall, menacing body shot to sudden, curious stillness. His fingers gone taut and unmoving on her neck, his breath utterly vanished from her skin. While the traitorous heat just kept pooling harder in Alma's belly, in her slow, shuddering exhale against his bare chest. Which had somehow seemed to ease even closer, the smooth, scarred skin almost near enough to touch her lips. And suddenly she could even smell him, rich and musky and surprisingly sweet...

And when his firm grip on her throat slowly tilted her head sideways, away from his too-close mouth, she didn't even try to resist. Only felt her eyes fluttering, her breaths still shuddering, as his other hand snapped up, brisk and businesslike, to brush the loose hair off her neck with a single flick of his sharp claw. And as his head bent closer, Alma almost seemed to arch into it. Almost... *welcoming* it.

The first light, searching scrape of Drafli's teeth against her bared throat felt like a thunder-clap, like a blistering flash of heat exploding in her groin. Driving a hoarse, helpless groan from her mouth, a convulsive, thrilling shudder up the entire length of her body. While those teeth dragged again, sharper this time, as if seeking the best place to strike, to sink deep. And, perhaps, as if revelling in her reflexive shivers, her harsh gulping breaths, her *fear*...

And when Alma moaned again, the sound low and almost pleading this time, there was something else, brushing against her belly. Something long and hard and powerful, spasming as it filled, as it strove and swelled against her. Something Alma had never before felt from a male, and oh this was unthinkable, he hated her, he was *threatening* her, and...

And her trembling, shivering fingers were *reaching* for him. For *that*. Needing to feel it, to know it was real, to drink up the truth of it. Touching her. Wanting her?

Her fingers' brush against it was brief, skittering, uncertain—but more than enough to prove its existence. Its long, hard, pulsating strength, bobbing out into her, against her, almost like a weapon. Like something he would revel in wielding against her, just like his teeth dragging ever harder against her neck, and what if he yanked open her robe, if he...

Alma's other hand had somehow reached for him too, fluttering against his bare chest—and in that instant, Drafli froze. The stillness in his lean body feeling far different than before, the claws on her neck suddenly prodding with true danger, his low growl grating into her ear—

And then he was gone. His entire body recoiling out and away, reeling multiple steps backwards, his head shaking. His hand frantically wiping at his mouth, and then he actually spat onto the floor, his face contorted with bitter, vicious disgust. With... hatred.

Alma couldn't seem to move from the wall, her body shivering with genuine fear this time, her belly plunging as she watched Drafli spit onto the floor again, and then again. As if he truly couldn't bear even the taste of her.

When he finally looked back at her again, his loathing was almost visceral, almost sickening. And Alma's trembling was only making it worse, and why was she doing this, why had she done that, why could she never do anything right...

You will ask Pure-Heart for this, Drafli finally mouthed at her, his eyes still flashing with fury. *Now.*

And why wasn't Alma fighting him. Why wasn't she disagreeing, rushing for the door, leaving this patently foolish plan forever behind her. Why wasn't she taking this orc's hatred for the threat it clearly was, the very real risk it was. Why was she thinking instead of his teeth, of how they'd felt, scraping against her skin...

And why was she nodding. Nodding, agreeing, saying yes, she would. Even as her trembling hands clutched at her robe—at where it had somehow fallen slightly open—and yanked it closed again. As if trying to hide herself from Drafli, protect

herself, and she could see how it only flared more scorn
through his eyes, more contempt. As if he would never truly
want her, no matter what that had just been.

Now, he repeated, as he smoothly stalked for the door
again, jabbing his claw toward her. *Obey me.*

And again, Alma didn't fight him, didn't try to escape. Just
nodded, ducked her head, and went.

15

———

Without once again looking at her, Drafli led Alma ever deeper into Orc Mountain. Through an incomprehensible array of twisting, darkening corridors, until the blackness was so complete that Alma had to stop walking, her eyes squinting uselessly into the emptiness.

She could feel Drafli's disapproval, his contemptuous exasperation—and then a light, quick movement in front of her. And then, abruptly, something was pulling her by the waist, tugging her down the corridor again.

Alma briefly stumbled, her hands groping the empty air before her, and thereby discovering that the sash tying her robe was pulled straight out before her. Meaning that *Drafli* had to be holding the other end of it, and using it to drag her through the corridor. Because clearly he couldn't bring himself to touch her again, let alone do something helpful, or kind.

But again, Alma somehow couldn't find the urge to protest, or argue. Just kept her head down, her feet moving, even as her face burned with humiliation, with defeat. She had to ask Baldr for this. And gods, what would she say? How was she supposed to explain this—whatever the hell this even was?

But already it was too late, because Drafli had jerked her

sideways, and the air suddenly felt different, smelled different, than before. And when light once again flashed before Alma's eyes—it was from a candle, flaring up beneath Drafli's clawed fingers—she found herself in yet another stark, stone room.

This one was slightly bigger than some of the others she'd seen so far, and it had a few simple furnishings—a chest, a shelf, a rack of shining weapons, a fur rug, and a large fur-covered bed. And lying sprawled on the bed—now sitting up, and rubbing at his eyes—was Baldr.

He was bare-chested and barefooted, wearing only a low-slung pair of trousers, his long braid untied and loosening at the end. And his bleary-looking eyes were blinking blankly, uncomprehendingly, toward Alma, as though he didn't quite believe she was real.

"Bright-Heart?" he asked, hoarse, almost wondering. "Why do you smell like—"

His voice broke off there, his eyes visibly sharpening, narrowing as they flicked over toward Drafli. Who was still standing beside the shelf, and lighting another candle with what looked like excessive casualness.

"Draf?" Baldr's voice said, with far more of an edge than before. "What is this?"

There was visible suspicion in Baldr's eyes now, and he was glancing repeatedly between Drafli and Alma, his eyes lingering with almost palpable awareness on Alma's neck, where Drafli's teeth had scraped her. And then dropping to her belly, where—Alma felt her face flushing—that other part of Drafli had nudged at her. And then, oh gods, even to her hand, where she'd so briefly touched him, felt him flex and fill under her fingers...

Baldr's gaze snapped back up to her face, and surely that was shock—and perhaps something almost like hurt—flaring in his eyes. As if he'd somehow just followed all that, as if he'd realized that Alma had just been blatantly groping his own damned mate down the corridor.

Alma could feel Drafli's eyes on her now too, boring into her with unflinching disapproval—and a swift glance toward him only confirmed it, his silent command almost painfully clear, ringing with urgency and contempt.

You will ask Pure-Heart for this. Now.

Alma gulped for air, and felt her clammy hands clutching at her robe, pulling it tighter around her. "Um," she croaked, fixing her blinking eyes to Baldr's again. "Drafli and I have been—talking. And we have a—a proposal. For you."

Baldr was staring blankly back toward her, the hurt now glimmering with confusion in his eyes, and Alma drew in more air. "I—like you, Baldr," she managed. "A lot. You're so kind, and very handsome, too. And we've somehow made this—this bond, between us, and I now understand that this is very difficult to break. And that it's quite dangerous for me to leave, because of the effect it might—inadvertently—have on you. So as a solution, Drafli and I thought—"

Her breath had seemed to run out, her face burning hot and painful—but the deepening confusion in Baldr's eyes somehow hurt even more, so she dragged in another breath, and ploughed onward. "We thought, perhaps," her chagrined voice whispered, "that I could spend some time with you. In bed. With Drafli's permission. And as part of that, perhaps I would even—bear you a son. If—if you were interested."

Her voice had gone very small by the end, her eyes blinking uncertainly at Baldr's face—because rather than looking pleased, he was suddenly looking... angry. His eyes rapidly narrowing, darkening, and in an abrupt, fluid movement he leapt off the bed, and stalked across the room toward her. Or rather—oh. Toward *Drafli*.

"What in the gods' names is this, Draf," Baldr hissed, his voice surprisingly dangerous, his claw forcefully jabbing into Drafli's bare chest. "We have *spoken* about this. At length!"

But Drafli's too-casual stance didn't change, even as he slowly turned to fully face Baldr, his eyes gone guarded and watchful. And his hands carefully raised up, and snapped out a smooth, swift series of movements, far too fast for Alma to even try to follow.

"That changes *nothing!*" Baldr exploded back at him. "This is *not* your choice to make. I swore those vows to you, and I mean to keep them!"

Drafli's eyes were still careful—too careful—and he snapped out another intricate series of gestures. One of them, this time, clearly directed toward *Alma.*

Alma's eyes were frozen on the two of them, watching as Baldr barked a bitter laugh, and gestured something back. His hands also pointing toward Alma, his movements rushed and angry, his fingers visibly trembling with rage.

And as Alma stood there staring at them, it occurred to her, with gut-twisting ferocity, that Baldr didn't actually want her. That Drafli had been wrong—horribly and brutally wrong—about this. And gods, why hadn't she even considered that possibility? How brazenly presumptuous had it been for her to assume that of course Baldr would want her, because he was an *orc*? As if she was some kind of prize, with her truly laughable lack of wealth or wit or beauty? With her destroyed career as a housemaid?

Alma was slowly backing away from them, blinking hard, and even worse when Baldr laughed again, whipping his head back and forth. "She could *smell worse*?" he demanded at Drafli. "You think that will sway me? I *know* how you feel about women, her most of all—and there is *nothing* you can do to fool me otherwise!"

There was another sharp, sickening plunge in Alma's belly, and she backed away further, groping for the doorframe— when abruptly, both Baldr and Drafli snapped to look at her. Drafli with unmistakable wariness, verging on disapproval— and Baldr with clear, blazing fury, plummeting even more misery deep into her gut.

"P-please, don't," she said, breathless, toward Baldr's eyes. "I didn't—I didn't realize. I would never have asked if I didn't think you might be—interested. I see now that I was deeply mistaken, and I will gladly rescind my offer, and leave you."

She helplessly waved toward the door, and made to move toward it—when in a breath, Baldr lurched across the room, bobbing with visible agitation before her.

"Please, wait," he said, his voice rough, his face grimacing. "I am not angry with *you*, ach? And it is not as though I hold no"—his grimace deepened—"*interest*, or that I am not grateful to you for offering. I only know Drafli far better than you do, ach?"

Oh. Alma stood immobile, her eyes darting toward Drafli, who looked almost as uncertain, as unsettled, as she felt. And as he briefly met her gaze, she could again almost feel that same inexplicable desperation. The *fear*.

This was still important to him. Crucially important. And even if he hadn't truly explained why, he'd perhaps admitted some of it, hadn't he? *I will no see my mate suffer*, he'd told her, with such hard, purposeful urgency. *I shall see my mate happy and safe again...*

Alma dragged her gaze back to Baldr, who was still studying her, again with far too much awareness in his eyes. "What did Drafli tell you?" he asked, and he suddenly just sounded weary. "Did he threaten you? Offer you some kind of payment? Coin? Jewels?"

Alma didn't dare look at Drafli now, but she could again feel the strength of his tension, his watching waiting eyes. She'd promised. She'd meant it. But...

"Drafli suggested we could try it for a year," she said, slow and careful. "And we agreed—I agreed—that if I decided to leave after a year, he would offer me financial support. But if I stay here, as long as I stay here, he will provide for me, and care for me."

It wasn't quite what Drafli had said, not in the least—but suddenly Alma was firmly, thoroughly committed to it. If she ended up deciding to stay here, after a year—if she truly found happiness here—she would not take Drafli's payment. She would *not*.

"Drafli promised to protect me, and my son," she continued, faster now. "And to give me a secure room of my own, and food and clothing, and good medical care. And"—she felt her face heating, but she made herself say it anyway—"and pleasure. With you."

Baldr's eyes on hers were genuinely astonished, and he shot a swift, accusing glance toward Drafli. And though Drafli's expression had gone suspiciously blank again, he gave a slow, careless-looking shrug. As if to say, *Yes, I did, and so?*

Baldr stared at Drafli for a long, thudding instant—and then frowned back toward Alma again. "And you *wished* for that," he said, the disbelief still far too close in his voice. "You agreed to that. Even knowing"—his gaze briefly dropped to her waist—"what could come of that."

Alma swallowed, but felt herself nodding, jerky and quick. "Yes," her quiet voice replied. "I mean, Drafli made the fair point that I offered the same thing to Varinn, for far less in return. And obviously"—she felt her already-hot face flushing even hotter—"I would far rather you. No offense to Varinn, of course, but—"

She swallowed again, her eyes perhaps almost pleading on Baldr's—but he was still staring back at her with marked disbelief, his hand rubbing at his mouth. So Alma took another breath, kept going, digging herself deeper.

"And I know I told you I had a home," she whispered, "but I don't really, not anymore. Other than my mother's ashes, there is only debt and misery for me there. And it is quite lovely here, far more than I would have expected. And I even met an orc child, and he wasn't at all what I expected, either. And I'm sure your son would be even sweeter, so—"

She couldn't seem to find words beyond that, beyond perhaps shameful begging—and before her, the disbelief in

Baldr's eyes had shifted. Twisting into something like pain, or regret.

"Ach," he said, his hand again rubbing at his mouth. "I am—honoured, woman, that you should say you wish for this. But I have a mate, ach? I have vowed to stay only true to him, until my breath fails me. And I will *not* forsake him to share your bed, even if"—his eyes flashed back toward Drafli—"he *claims* he wishes for this."

Oh. Of course. And Alma had already begun to nod, angling again toward the door—when her eyes, again, caught on Drafli's. On that fear, shimmering sharp enough to taste, bitter and strange on Alma's tongue.

Drafli still wanted her to keep talking. To keep fighting for this. But gods, what else could she say, she'd surely made every possible argument—

But then Drafli's eyes dropped, brief but purposeful, to her neck. To where he'd almost—almost—bitten her. Before snarling at her, and spitting away the taste of her. And Alma closed her eyes, drew in another breath. She surely wouldn't go there. She wouldn't...

"What if you didn't... need to forsake Drafli," she croaked. "What if he was... part of it. With us."

And yes, that had done it, because now they were both staring at her, Baldr with more disbelief in his eyes, Drafli with a grim, bitter resignation. Blatant enough that when Baldr whipped around toward him again, he surely saw it—and then barked a brittle, high-pitched laugh.

"Ach, so *that* is why you put your scent on her," he hissed at Drafli. "Let me guess, this comes with more pay for her, after a year? Or mayhap more threats? And what, you shall lie there and watch, with your prick always soft, whilst the taste of your rage and revulsion chokes my throat?!"

Baldr was truly angry again, Alma realized, and Drafli actually took a very slight step backwards, even as his hands gave another swift flurry of motion. Including several pointed gestures toward Alma, and Baldr laughed again as he spun back toward her, even sharper than before.

"He says you have *tested* this," Baldr spat, his voice low, unusually hard. "So you could be sure, before you came to propose this to me. And he says that you were more than willing, and so was *he*."

Baldr was looking for confirmation, Alma realized, for her agreement to this claim—and searching his glittering eyes, it occurred to her that this wasn't only anger, but also hurt, and betrayal. He truly thought that Drafli was lying, trying to deceive him, to gain some kind of upper hand. That perhaps Drafli had some other plan, some secret he wasn't telling. Perhaps, even, that Drafli wanted to break those vows they'd made.

And gods, how had Alma ever thought it would be a good idea to tangle herself up with this, in the midst of whatever this was? But she was, and maybe it was already too late, maybe Drafli had already just destroyed whatever little trust Baldr clearly still held for him. And suddenly Alma couldn't bear to see Baldr suffer under that, she couldn't, she *couldn't*.

"Drafli—was willing, I think," she gulped. "And I—I was. I mean, I know nothing of these things, but"—she squeezed her eyes shut, made herself keep talking—"but he is very tall, and powerful, and he smells very good. And though he's perhaps not handsome, not the way you are, he's still quite striking, don't you think?"

There was a ringing, dangling silence, and when Alma peeked an eye open, both Baldr and Drafli were staring at her again, and she could see Baldr's throat convulsing, his clawed hands flexing at his sides. "And he did not offer you more coin for this," he said, voice still hard. "Or threaten you. Or frighten you."

A hot, thoroughly ill-advised shiver rippled up Alma's back, and surely Baldr saw it, his eyes narrowing, his body whirling toward Drafli again—but before he could speak, Alma choked a cough, and lurched closer, raising her hands.

"A little," she blurted out, "but I—I liked it. I wanted it, I *did*. I *do*."

And now they were both gaping at her again, both with sheer, stunned astonishment. Even Drafli, but he recovered quickly this time, and when Baldr spun to look at him, he'd schooled his face to blankness again, and gave another careless, dismissive shrug.

Baldr looked at him for a long, unblinking moment, and then slowly turned to Alma again. And now his eyes were oddly blank too, holding on her with chilly, unnerving emptiness.

"If this is truth," he said, slow, "then you both will prove this to me. *Now*."

16

They would prove this to Baldr. Now.

Now?!

Alma couldn't help a wide-eyed, terrified look at Drafli, who was again looking just as stunned as she felt—but again, it smoothed away just as quickly, and he gave another fluid, offhanded shrug. And then, with a careless flick of his fingers, he waved Alma toward the *bed*.

Alma couldn't move, couldn't stop staring at Drafli—wait, he truly didn't mean to do this, while Baldr watched?!—but yes, yes, he did, his hand giving another purposeful wave, sharper this time. And his eyes on hers were just as sharp, saying, very clearly, *Obey me.*

And gods curse the slimy bastard, because surely—surely—Drafli had known it would come to this. He was the one who knew Baldr best, he must have understood how Baldr truly felt, how he would react. And even if Drafli had perhaps given Alma that tiny bit of warning—*or mayhap me*, he'd said—he most certainly hadn't suggested it would lead to anything like *this*?!

"Ach, and already she *reeks* of fear," Baldr's voice snapped, dragging Alma's gaze back to his face, already drawn tight and angry again. "Can we now leave this farce? Please?"

Drafli's eyes were glittering dangerously on Alma's, boring into her, all but shouting his silent command. And without at all meaning to, Alma felt herself groping reflexively for Baldr, clutching for the warm strength of his hand, and dragging in long, steadying breaths.

"Look, I—I want to," she gulped, and she was distantly surprised by how much she meant it. "I do. I'm just—a little nervous, you see, because I—I've never done anything like this before, not really. Ridiculous, I know, and quite embarrassing, I'm twenty-three years old, and I've never even—"

And gods, she sounded utterly pathetic, and she belatedly clamped her mouth shut with a snap. Though her face just kept heating, her hand still shamefully clutching at Baldr's—and as he blinked down toward her, his fingers very slowly curling around hers, she could almost see his eyes softening, flaring with something much like... understanding.

"Ach, there is nothing to be ashamed of," he said, quiet. "We were all once thus, ach? And I know Drafli"—his eyes flicked up, hardened—"would be gentle with you. *If* you truly still wanted this."

Alma risked a glance at Drafli, whose eyes had gone fully unreadable again—but his hands were moving, far slower than before, accentuating the silent words from his mouth.

I only touch you, he said. *Only so Pure-Heart can see.*

Oh. He would only touch her. Alma felt her shoulders sagging with genuine relief, her hand briefly squeezing tighter on Baldr's still-present, still-warm fingers. And when Drafli jerked his head toward the bed, she somehow found the where-withal to nod, and even walked toward it with slow, careful steps.

Baldr had followed behind her, with no apparent resistance, his hand still clasped in hers. And when Alma tentatively sat down on the soft, fur-covered bed, he even sat beside her, his body close and deeply reassuring. His eyes angling up toward Drafli, who had stalked to the bed's other side, and signed another curt, silent order toward Alma with his clawed fingers.

Lie down, it clearly meant. *On your back.*

Alma fought the disbelief lurching in her throat—she couldn't be doing this, was she truly doing this?—and made herself slide sideways, and then sink back onto the fur. Her hand still thankfully clasped in Baldr's, and he was still sitting close on the bed beside her, his eyes now flicking between her and Drafli with unreadable intensity.

Drafli was looking back at Baldr, one eyebrow raised, and he slowly put his trousered knee to the bed, and gracefully sank down on Alma's other side. And then, with a smooth flick of his hand, he'd reached down for the sash tying her robe, and pulled out the knot.

It hadn't actually exposed anything—the robe was still lying closed, still thoroughly covering her—but Alma felt herself freeze on the bed, all the same. And she could feel both Baldr and Drafli freezing as well, Baldr's eyes instantly gone narrow and suspicious again, Drafli's flaring with brief, unmistakable disapproval.

"What is it?" Baldr said to her, clipped, his eyes searching hers. "You wish him to stop?"

Alma shook her head, but she couldn't seem to stop glancing between them, either. Feeling the lingering unease between them, the weight of everything that hadn't been said, everything they were about to change...

"I just—I truly don't want to come between you two," she whispered. "And you won't be—angry, if Drafli touches me? Or jealous? I mean, I certainly would be if I were you, I wouldn't be able to bear him touching anyone else at *all.*"

But to her vague astonishment, Baldr gave a twitchy shrug, and a low, hoarse laugh. "I have watched him do far worse, many times," he replied. "Having him touch my"—he halted, made a face—"such a sweet, lovely woman, who is scent-bound to me, and now mayhap also to him, this shall—"

He broke off there, his throat convulsing, his eyes glancing warily over at Drafli's equally guarded face. "This shall not," he continued, quieter, "be a hardship, ach?"

Oh. Alma's relief seemed to be echoed in the slight settle of Drafli's shoulders, the softening of the tightness around his mouth. His gaze on Baldr looking almost—warm, suddenly, or perhaps even wicked. And when his lips twitched up, showing just a hint of sharp fang, Alma actually felt her breath catch, the heat pooling hard in her groin.

Because in that instant, Drafli truly looked like a *devil*. Like a devious, bright-eyed fiend from the old tales, come to steal away her innocence, and hand it over to his favourite watching worshipper...

But just as quickly, it was gone. His expression abruptly flattening, hardening, as his eyes dropped to her again. As he glanced dispassionately up and down the length of her, almost like he was deciding which part of her would repulse him the least.

Alma swallowed, a movement that snapped Drafli's gaze up to her throat—and perhaps that had decided it, somehow. Because as she stared up at him, her breath locked in her lungs, Drafli dropped his hand, and gently, deliberately, traced his claw across the front of her neck.

It felt like a threat—perhaps it was a threat—but it still seemed to spark something hot and powerful beneath it. Something that dragged a shaky, desperate groan from Alma's mouth, and fired a fierce, rippling shiver all the way down her form.

It could have been construed as fear, surely, surely—but when Alma's eyes darted back toward Baldr, that surely wasn't concern on his face. No, he was looking—shocked. His mouth fallen slightly open, his own eyes snapping almost accusingly to Drafli's face.

And suddenly Drafli looked fiendish again, and surely smug, too. His eyes glinting, holding to Baldr's, as he again traced his claw back across Alma's neck, this time without even looking at her.

But her answering shiver was still the same, and even worse when those claws made a little brushing motion against her skin. As if drumming against her, taunting her with their sharp, deadly threat.

Alma's throat once again swallowed, audibly convulsing beneath his touch. And Drafli's mouth twitched up even higher, his eyes still on Baldr's shocked face, as his other hand came up, and very gently traced its claws along the still-clothed line of her shoulder.

It was such a ridiculous thing, such an unimportant place—but another furious shiver still raced out from around it, as more heat pooled to Alma's belly, her cheeks. As her entire body almost seemed to lean into it, arching toward it, craving more...

And oh, hell, Drafli was giving more. That claw tracing back up her shoulder, back toward his other hand still stroking against her neck—and then slipping lower. Straight down from her collarbone, toward where she was thankfully still hidden by her robe...

But a brief, chagrined glance downwards showed that her nipple was brazenly, blatantly visible, jutting up beneath the robe's thin fabric—and that Drafli's claw was going straight there. Gently scoring up the swell of her breast, and then dragging, lingering, as it scraped over that too-sensitive peak.

"Oh," Alma gasped, straining all over, the heat surging and flaring—and Drafli's mouth was fully smirking now, his gaze still fixed to Baldr as he scraped that claw back up. Doing it again, the utter bastard, and Alma's tingling body gave the exact same response, her hand now clamping tight against the strength around it.

And wait, that was Baldr—Baldr was still holding her hand,

thank the gods—and he almost looked as flushed as she felt, his eyes dropping toward hers with a knowing, twinkling warmth. His hand even giving hers a reassuring squeeze back, as if to say, *Yes, Bright-Heart, I know. I understand...*

So Alma clung to that, to him, as Drafli's sharp claws kept toying with her. Flicking over that nipple again and again, until it felt almost unbearable—and then he slid the claw over to the other side, and repeated it all again. While his other hand kept smoothly, casually stroking and scraping at her neck, dragging out more gasps and shivers and swallows, the heat pooling ever harder, the sparks flashing and fluttering beneath her skin.

And when that claw finally drew the top part of her robe aside, baring Alma's flushed, damnably peaked breasts to the air, she almost—almost—didn't care. Especially with Baldr's hand again squeezing hers like that, his eyes hazy, half-lidded on the sight. On his mate's claws still casually stroking and plucking at her bared, swollen nipples, as if showing them off for Baldr's hungry eyes. As if they were his to use, to exploit, to share.

Drafli's words from what felt like an age ago were suddenly echoing through Alma's thoughts—*I grant you to him, I give him this, not you*—and rather than feeling offended, in this moment, she almost felt—honoured. *Prized.* As if Drafli had personally selected her, chosen her, for his mate. And as if he were now flaunting her attributes, playing her like an expensive instrument, showing off this rare new gift...

And when Alma shot another furtive, heated glance up at Drafli's face, this time he was looking back at her. As though he'd somehow followed her thoughts, and his glittering, narrowing eyes were confirming them, speaking them aloud.

I give him this, they seemed to say. *Show him. Obey me.*

And his eyes stayed on hers now, glinting with that silent command, as his hand slowly, carefully slid lower. Scraping along bare skin this time, lower and lower, parting her half-open robe as he went.

Alma's shivers had hardened into full-on shudders, her muscles tautening as those claws scraped slow but inexorable over her navel, her lower belly—and then sideways, toward her hip. Scattering gooseflesh in their wake as they traced down the front of her thigh, flicked the robe aside...

Oh. He'd been *undressing* her. And already he'd done the same to the other side, pooling the robe off onto the bed, so that Alma's entire lower half was also bared to the room, to their eyes. To *Baldr's* eyes.

And oh, Baldr was looking. His hooded gaze sweeping up and down Alma's naked body with blatant, shameless fascination, while Drafli once again watched him, with just as much intensity. His claws almost following along with Baldr's eyes, brushing over her breasts, her torso, now even with distant, casual purpose over the dark hair at her groin...

Look what I've brought for you, his gleaming eyes almost seemed to say to Baldr. *You like?*

Baldr had actually let out a low, husky groan, his eyes back on Drafli's face. And even as his hand again squeezed Alma's, his other hand eased up, and made a fluid series of motions toward Drafli. Speaking, with words that Alma couldn't follow.

But Drafli surely did follow, and again that astonishing warmth seemed to flash across his eyes, the wickedness curling at his lip. And then he raised his own hands from Alma, and signed back a reply, the movements somehow both languid and predatory all at once.

Baldr's cheeks visibly flushed, his head ducking—but Drafli made the motion again, more imperious this time. And Baldr groaned again, his throat bobbing, as his half-lidded eyes dropped back to Alma's face.

"Drafli wants me to," he began, and then swallowed again, gave his head a wry little shake. "He wants me to—grant myself relief. While he grants this to you."

Oh. And he couldn't mean, surely—or wait, perhaps he did. Because Drafli's eyes were looking with cool, peremptory purpose toward Baldr's groin. To where Alma could see a very thick, very visible bulge, jutting sideways beneath his very tight-looking trousers.

"Should this—alarm you?" Baldr asked her, as his big hand went—perhaps self-consciously—to adjust that bulge through the fabric. "Or upset you?"

But Alma's eyes were very firmly fixed to his hand, still hovering awkwardly around his swollen groin. And the shivering sparking craving had somehow wrenched even stronger than before, thundering in her chest, deep in her belly...

"I would—like to see that," she heard her voice say, liquid and low. "Very much."

There wasn't even room to be ashamed, not even when she furtively glanced back at Drafli's face—because yes, yes, that was surely approval, flaring oh so brief through his eyes on hers. And then, once again, that watchful, almost predatory hunger, as his eyes slid back to Baldr, his fingers making another fluid, commanding gesture.

You heard her, it perhaps meant. *Show her.*

Baldr's face flushed even redder, but he jerked a curt, shaky nod. And even as his left hand seemed to grip Alma's tighter, his other hand fumbled for his trousers, loosening them with unsteady fingers...

And then he shoved them downwards. And the bulge behind them suddenly sprang to life, bobbing out thick and straight and impossibly close. While a musky, heated scent swarmed the air, fluttering Alma's eyes, flooding her breath...

Gods, it was... *big*. And so strangely compelling, so close like this, dipping and flexing under the light touch of his clawless fingers. Its base hidden and dark green beneath his thick coarse hair, its length jutting out smooth and plump, and growing lighter as it went. Until the tip of it, just peeking out from beneath the skin, was all that plush rosy pink, not unlike the pink staining Alma's own flushed, still-peaked nipples.

Alma truly could not look away, could not risk missing a

single instant of this—and when Baldr's skittering, careful fingers lightly slid up its length, she couldn't help a choked, broken moan, echoing far too loudly in the silence. To which Baldr twitched her a shy, self-conscious smile, his cheeks and ears now a bright red, before his eyes once again darted toward Drafli's. Almost as if asking for permission, or even forgiveness.

But Drafli's eyes on him were sheer, burning appreciation, his hand giving a wave that surely meant, *Continue*. And his brief glance down at Alma was again smug, or perhaps even triumphant. As if to say, perhaps, *Look how beautiful my mate is. Now you shall thank me for this, ach?*

And Alma would, she *was*, and she fervently nodded toward Drafli, her eyes wide, her breath shuddering ragged from her throat. Almost as if begging him for similar permission, for forgiveness, for...

For this. For his claws again tracing down her belly, with far more purpose this time. Not slowing as they carded through the coarse hair at her groin, as they slipped down to the join of her thighs. As their sharp tips abruptly pressed sideways on her left thigh, in a silent but very real order. *Open*.

And once again, Alma nodded, and... obeyed. Her thighs badly trembling as she slid them slightly apart, felt the cool air pooling between them. And then felt herself shiver all over as Drafli's claws nudged again, even harder, clearly saying, *More*.

Alma again obliged, her face flooding so hot it was painful—but this time, Drafli's claws just kept nudging, wanting more. Until Alma's thigh was splayed up and wide, blatantly exposing *everything* between her legs—and even worse when he did the same on the other side, his touch efficient and merciless. Leaving Alma shamefully bared and open, and there was the almost overwhelming urge to drop her hand, to hide her humiliation behind it—

"Are you well, Bright-Heart?" came Baldr's hoarse voice, snapping her eyes toward his face. Toward where he was watching her very closely in return, his mouth parted, his sharp tooth biting at his lower lip. "Wish him to stop?"

His own hand had stopped moving on his own thick, swollen arousal, which now had a shiny bead of white growing at that pink tip—and Alma dragged for breath, dragged her eyes back to his face. And then shook her head, hard and forceful, because she couldn't bear for this to stop, not now, please...

"If you change your mind upon this," Baldr murmured thickly, his eyes fervent, "you only say this, ach? Drafli shall stop, whenever you wish. *Always*."

And glancing again at Drafli, at his suddenly forbidding eyes, it occurred to Alma that perhaps he himself would never have granted her such a caveat, prior to this—but now that Baldr had said this, promised this, he would. *Whatever he wishes*, he'd told her, *I will give*.

And Drafli was indeed nodding, brief but certain, his eyes again angling to Baldr's face. To where Baldr gave him a quick, genuine smile, his eyes warming with tangible affection, while Drafli's mouth again twitched up, his eyes giving a devious, purposeful glance down at Baldr's bared, leaking heft.

Baldr huffed a shaky sigh, the wry smile still pulling at his mouth, as his hand curled tighter around his length, and slowly, smoothly slid up. While Drafli's clawed fingers once again carded into the coarse hair at Alma's groin, and slipped downward.

He was moving with far more speed and intent this time, perhaps as some kind of retaliation against that fail-safe Baldr had just given her—and Alma felt herself quiver and keen as he stroked down over the open, exposed curve of her. His fingers smoothly sliding against where it felt strangely wet and swollen, and where Alma had never, ever before been touched, by any hands other than her own.

And oh, it felt *impossible*. It felt like a million racing flashes of light, like something hot and raw and desperate had fluttered awake beneath her skin. Like Drafli's strong, capable fingers were all that mattered in all the world, like they were bringing her to life, after she'd so long been asleep...

And in this sudden, impossibly surreal moment, Alma didn't care if Drafli saw her weakness, her shame. If she blinked up at him with open, pleading longing in her eyes, with the craving far too close in her racing, pounding heart.

"Oh, my lord," she breathed at him, as her thighs somehow spread wider, as her body arched up beneath his fingers' caress. "Oh, please. *More.*"

And yes, yes, he was already doing it, those fingers delving deeper, stroking smooth and steady against her swollen, convulsing crease. Opening her up more with every breath, sliding easy and purposeful past the hot clutching core of her, *taunting* her—

And as Alma stared at him, gazed into his glittering eyes, she realized he *was* taunting her. He knew exactly what he was doing to her, what that teasing little dip of his fingers felt like. And he was *enjoying* it, he was *enjoying* her discomfort, her weakness, her shame...

A brief, horrid memory of Mr. Pembroke flashed across Alma's thoughts, cold and far too vivid, freezing her limbs in place—and wait, perhaps Drafli had somehow caught that, his head tilting, his eyes shifting on her face. And his fingers' touch had suddenly softened, stroking with far less command, less power, than before. His gaze searching her, seeking her, searing deep inside. As if he wanted to—to *know*.

And the awareness of that, the bizarrely potent conviction of that, seemed to thrust the awful vision of Mr. Pembroke away entirely. Because in this moment, Drafli *wasn't* like Mr. Pembroke, and Alma was utterly, inexplicably certain of it. He wasn't taking this from her. He was—*giving* it. *Sharing* it. She was—*safe.*

So Alma felt herself draw in breath, her chin lifting—and somehow, she stroked back at Drafli's touch. Her slick, wide-open wetness clutching at his gently delving fingers, gripping at them with greedy, lurid intent. Almost as if... kissing them. Wishing for more...

And the concern—the *concern*?—that had been darkening Drafli's eyes abruptly gave way to awareness, to a cool, dismissive quirk of his eyebrow. To his other hand making a graceful, circular gesture that surely meant something like, *Why did you stop begging me.*

And Alma somehow *smiled* at him, even as she gasped, and again shivered all over. "Please, don't stop," she breathed. "Please, my lord."

Drafli's eyes shifted again—did he *like* that?—and yes, yes, those stroking fingers were finally, properly lingering, seeking just where Alma most wanted them. Not feeling even slightly sharp now, just warm and clever and perhaps almost eager, nudging her open around them, oh, oh...

But Drafli was waiting, waiting again, raising an eyebrow at her this time, and Alma frantically nodded, opened herself wider. "Please, my lord," she gasped. "Please, grant me this. *Please.*"

And yes, that was what he wanted, that was surely triumph, flashing in his wicked eyes. As those warm fingers nudged just a little deeper, circling slightly, as if making sure of their place—and then they drove all the way inside, solid and shocking and deep.

Alma's entire body froze and flared, her eyes wide, a shrill shout tearing from her throat—but oh, oh, it was still there. *Drafli* was still there. He was *inside* her, oh gods, with two whole fingers, and it felt so strange and so full and so unreal, and oh, so gods-damned good...

"*Draf,*" came a distant, breathless voice, with something almost reproachful in it—and when Alma's wide eyes blinked toward it, it was Baldr. Baldr, whose too-bright eyes were looking down at where Drafli's hand—Drafli's *hand*—was wedged tight between Alma's legs, his two middle fingers entirely vanished, because they were *inside* her.

Baldr was chiding Drafli, Alma belatedly realized, for
perhaps not being gentle with her, not taking this slowly—but
Drafli's eyes were pure blazing power as his fingers began
sliding softly out of Alma again. And oh gods, he couldn't take
this away from her, he couldn't, and her cursed mouth was even
groaning at him, her eyes pleading at him...

But he wasn't looking at her, he was looking at Baldr, that
silent command again flaring between them—and once again,
Drafli drove his fingers deep. Dragging another loud, shameful
shout from Alma's throat, her body again coiling up around
him, writhing beneath the impossible feeling of it. At how
those fingers were curling a little inside her this time, stroking
her, wringing up something even hotter and higher, oh
please...

"Please, my lord," she gulped, but Drafli still wasn't even
looking at her. Even with his hand grinding against her like
this, impaling her upon it, he was still looking at Baldr,
commanding Baldr. Clearly saying something, something new,
something that was suddenly, crucially important.

She is mine, it meant. *I give her to you. I do whatever I wish
with her.*

Alma could see the understanding flaring across Baldr's
eyes—and with it, to her distant surprise, the relief. His head
briefly nodding, ducking low—but in his slack hand, that
swollen heft seemed to be bulging even fuller, visibly vibrating
against his fingers, shuddering out a splutter of white from its
rosy tip. Earning an approving nod from Drafli in return, his
hand again giving a commanding wave toward Baldr's groin.
Meaning, surely, *Keep going. Like I told you.*

Baldr's groan was guttural, deep, but he nodded too—and
obeyed. His hand smoothly stroking again, sliding up and
down with familiar, fluid ease, even as more thick white spluttered out of him, running sticky down his fingers.

And suddenly, between Alma's legs, Drafli was doing the
same. Sliding in and out with the exact same fluent rhythm,

keeping perfect time with Baldr's strokes. His fingers plunging into her again and again, claiming her, *owning* her. While Alma trembled and gasped, flailing up with his every thrust, her invaded heat clutching helplessly upon him, the sounds slick and shameful and obscene.

And Drafli just kept watching Baldr, matching Baldr, biting his own lip, his eyes fluttering. His other hand making a quick, meaningful gesture up and down Alma's convulsing naked form, to which Baldr moaned, desperately shook his head— but Drafli nodded, vicious and powerful and all-commanding, as Baldr's hand fisted up, one more time, his body jerking up onto his knees on the bed, nearly bending double over Alma, and—

And then, that dripping, flexing heft in his hand exploded. Spurting out rope after rope of hot, sticky white orc-seed, all over Alma's bared, shuddering body. Catching on her breasts, her belly, in her navel. Even on Drafli's hand against her, his palm now grinding in steady circles, his fingers deep inside, curling and stroking, ramping her higher, higher, tighter, closer, oh—

Her own release shot hard and white, blasting out with whirling, world-spinning ferocity. Clamping again and again around Drafli's firm invading fingers, the ecstasy flaring out in shock after shock, consuming her, convulsing her whole...

Baldr was still pumping himself, his spurting liquid now slowed to a drizzle, pooling on Alma's belly—while across from him, Drafli had risen to his knees, too. His free hand suddenly shoving down his own trousers, giving Alma a brief glimpse of thick, dark veined hardness—before his own hand gripped it, pumped up once, twice—

And now he was the one spraying out, all over Alma's trembling, already-sticky body. But he was aiming it, the bastard, his strings of darker white painting back and forth over Baldr's— and then even up toward her *face*, oh gods. And his other hand was here, on her bottom lip, his claw curtly yanking it downwards, so he could blatantly pump himself out all over her cheeks and chin, and deep into her waiting, open mouth.

His eyes looked almost terrifying as he did it, flashing with vicious satisfaction, with *victory*. As if he had truly conquered Alma in this, humiliated her beyond all fathoming, painted her in his cruelty, and his contempt.

And as if to accentuate his point, his claw shoved up under her chin, snapping her mouth closed again. And for the first time in the stunned stuttering silence, Alma could taste him in her mouth, warm and slick and surprisingly sweet.

"*Draf*," Baldr's voice said again, almost pained this time— and when Alma blinked her sticky-feeling eyes toward him, she found that he was leaning over her, his hand flat to the bed beside her head, his chest heaving with his breaths. But he was looking at Drafli, at where Drafli had suddenly gone very still, his eyes dark and unblinking on Alma's messy, dripping face.

And in an abrupt, astonishingly fast movement, Drafli was off the bed, and striding away. His hands yanking roughly at his trousers, and then snatching for where there was a pitcher of water on the shelf—and then he dumped it fully out over his head. Sending water splashing down over his hair, his bare shoulders, down onto the floor at his feet.

Alma just kept staring, blinking again and again, while her awareness seemed to slowly creep closer, colder. Drafli was... washing himself. Washing off the scent of her. And now even grasping for what looked like a rag from beside the water, and scrubbing off his hand. *That* hand.

Baldr was still watching too, his eyes gone dark and pained, his breath shuddering out in a slow, ragged sigh. And when Drafli tossed the rag over his shoulder toward them—without even looking—Baldr instantly caught it, his gaze finally dropping back to Alma's face.

He looked at her for a long, dangling moment, his expression somewhere between dazed and resigned. And when he leaned down and slowly inhaled, his nose nearly touching hers, she could feel the judder in his chest, the rumbling heat in his throat.

"Ach," he breathed, still dazed, or maybe almost reverent. "You smell so *good* thus, Bright-Heart."

Oh. Some of Alma's humiliation had seemed to ebb away, and she managed a twitch of a smile up toward him—which had the unintended effect of dripping more of Drafli's slick liquid into her mouth. And it was still impossibly sweet, unfairly so, and Alma somehow found her tongue brushing against it, almost as if seeking for more...

"He tastes so good, ach?" Baldr murmured, as his finger lightly nudged at her cheek, coating itself in the mess—and then slipped into her mouth. And gods curse her, but Alma was eagerly sucking his finger, swallowing more, distantly noting that somehow it tasted even better like this, with a twinge of salty richness, too. And oh hell, that would be because this was the hand Baldr had used on himself, and that was *his* taste, too...

And it occurred to Alma that if they kept doing this—if she hadn't somehow just ruined it all—that she might get to truly taste them both. To feel them both. To have more impossible moments like these, Baldr now gently slipping his finger out from her lips, coating it in more of his mate's fresh seed, feeding it back into her mouth...

But that all depended on Drafli, surely—and an uncertain, furtive glance showed him still standing with his back toward them, his hands gripping at the shelf, his head bowed, his shoulders visibly heaving. As if—as if he were trying not to be *sick*.

The sight of it seemed to drain away the last of Alma's whispering pleasure, leaving a cold, brittle emptiness in its wake. Drafli hadn't truly wanted to do that. He hadn't truly wanted *her*.

Baldr was looking at Drafli again too, his mouth tight, his other hand still clutching at the rag. And after another heavy, juddering sigh, he slipped his finger from Alma's mouth, and began carefully wiping at her face.

"You know this was not an—insult, ach?" he said to her, low, as he gently dabbed at her eyes, her cheeks. "I know it is mayhap—strange, to humans. But among orcs—and most of all among the Grisk—this is a sign of honour. Of favour. Any orc who now scents you, or sees you, shall know you are ours, ach?"

Ours. That single word sending a dazzling, wonderful shiver up Alma's spine—but then it ran cold again, as she once again glanced over to Drafli. Drafli, who still wasn't looking at them, who still almost reeked of anger and bitterness. Of regret.

Surely Baldr saw it too, and after another heavy sigh, he brought Alma's hand to the rag, clearly meaning for her to continue. And then he stood, yanking up his own trousers with shaky hands as he strode over toward Drafli, straight *into* Drafli, and circled his arms tightly around his stiff waist.

It was as though the touch had cut through a tautened string, sagging Drafli's tall body against Baldr's slightly shorter one, his arm curling around Baldr's shoulders with genuine-seeming relief. Pulling Baldr closer into his chest, and Baldr willingly went, his hands stroking firmly up and down Drafli's back, one even dropping to grip possessively against the hard curve of Drafli's arse.

It was a scene of undeniable intimacy, of almost visceral affection—and as Alma shakily wiped at the sticky, sopping-wet mess covering her front, she couldn't help but compare it to her own experience from only moments before. Which hadn't been about affection in the slightest, but about lust. About ownership. About Drafli setting the boundaries, the expectations, between his mate and his new gift. His servant. His... *harlot.*

And perhaps even this moment was part of that, and Alma wiped at herself faster, harder, until the rag was a sopping, dripping mess. And by the time Baldr and Drafli finally pulled apart, and turned to look at her, she was standing tall beside the bed, her robe wrapped around her still-sticky front, her arms folded tightly over it.

Baldr's head tilted as he looked at her, his brow furrowing with visible concern—but behind him, Drafli's chilly eyes met Alma's, and darted brief, but very clear, toward the door. While his hand made a quick, surreptitious gesture, in time with a silent order from his mouth.

Out, he said. *Now*.

And Alma had sworn to obey, she had—and somehow she swallowed, and clutched her robe closer. "Er, that was very— lovely, thank you," she said thickly. "But I'd probably best be going now. I'm quite tired, and I promised Efterar I would return soon for a checkup, so..."

Her voice awkwardly trailed off amidst its lies, her eyes darting helplessly between Baldr and Drafli. And while Baldr was still looking concerned—or disappointed?—Drafli's eyes remained narrow and disapproving, as though Alma still repulsed him, even in this.

"I do hope I'll see you again soon, though?" she made herself say, attempting a smile toward Baldr this time, and not missing how his eyes had already softened at the words. "And Drafli, would you mind walking me back to the sickroom? Please?"

Drafli's disapproval flared even sharper, but Alma stared straight back toward him, because surely he couldn't expect her to wander around in the pitch-darkness alone, until she stumbled across the sickroom again? And thankfully Baldr glanced questioningly up toward Drafli too, which seemed to immediately clear away the reluctance in Drafli's eyes. And after a purposeful gesture between Baldr and the bed—*Go back to sleep*, it surely meant—Drafli even inclined his head toward Alma, and gracefully waved her toward the door. As if to say, with all courtesy, *After you, then*.

Alma gave Baldr another quick, foolish-feeling little smile, and then ducked her head, and went. Fighting to ignore her awareness of Drafli's tall, silent body behind her—and then the sudden, alarming feel of his claws, poking hard into her back, steering her down the corridor.

At least he was deigning to touch her this time—perhaps that was some kind of improvement?—but as Alma walked, slightly twitching under the steady press of those claws, it occurred to her that beyond the crucial part, it had only ever been his claws touching her back in his bed, too. As if, perhaps, he truly couldn't bear to touch her. As if she truly had repulsed him, no matter how he'd pretended otherwise.

"So was that what you—what you expected from me?" she heard herself ask, tentative, into the stilted darkness. "Was there anything I could have—improved?"

There was only silence behind her, of course, and Alma sighed, and blinked toward where she could finally see distant light again, from further up the corridor. "Or do you even—still want to keep doing it?" she continued, even quieter, as her heartbeat suddenly seemed to pick up speed. "Perhaps now that you've, er, seen more of me, you've—changed your mind?"

And gods, as bizarre as it was, that was surely fear, flooding fierce and unnerving into her belly. What if Drafli called it all off? What if she'd truly been too repulsive or too foolish for him to bear? What if she never got to feel such things again, to taste such things again, to know the glory of such rampaging pleasure destroying all else in its wake?

From behind her, there might have been a sigh, huffing warm against her hair—and when Drafli's claws shoved her sideways, she went. Finding herself in yet another empty room, this one featuring several unused-looking bunks. And instead of crowding her against the wall, like he had last time, Drafli hovered a good distance away from her, his body once again stiff and taut, his hands already gesturing sharply before him.

You no understand, he mouthed at her. *I never change mind. We make vow. We are now bound to this.*

Oh. Alma couldn't deny the surge of relief, exhaling from her mouth, even as she kept searching Drafli's hard eyes. "But you didn't—like it," she said, chagrined. "Me, I mean."

Surely, that had once again been the wrong thing to say, because Drafli's lip curled, his eyes narrowing with that familiar disapproval. *No*, he silently snarled back. *I already tell you, I no like you. I hate you.*

Alma flinched backwards, her stomach plummeting, the hurt flooding up with astonishing, unnerving strength. "Even after—after something like that?" she whispered, and oh gods, here was the horribly unhelpful vision of his hand, grinding hard and purposeful against her, his fingers buried deep inside. "We can't even find a way to be—friends? Find some kind of—understanding, together?"

Drafli's sneer of cold, impatient contempt felt almost like a slap, cruel and vicious across her face. *We have vow*, he mouthed back at her. *You obey me. Honour me. Seek to please my mate. This is all.*

Alma's hurt seemed to be twining even deeper, her hands trembling against her robe. "But it doesn't seem right," she said, her voice almost pleading. "B—Pure-Heart—obviously wants this to be—equal, between us. And it's also clear that he's already been hurt by you, and he doesn't trust you, so why—"

But before she could finish, Drafli actually *lunged* at her. His hand wildly making that *stop* gesture, his eyes blazing with disbelief and rage and sheer, burning hatred—and if he hadn't reeled back, just in time, he might well have sliced Alma straight across the neck.

She belatedly flinched and stumbled away, her eyes shot wide and horrified. That was the same hand, the same one, oh gods, oh gods, and would he truly have used it to—

She'd clutched her own hand to her neck, foolishly, as if to somehow protect it—and now Drafli was rubbing his face, hard, whipping his head back and forth. Perhaps as if he regretted that, as if he hadn't meant to hurt her—but when his eyes snapped back to hers again, there was still nothing but hatred in them, and purest, deepest loathing.

You never again speak this, he mouthed at her. *To me, or Pure-Heart. You honour me to him. You obey. This is all.*

And without waiting for an answer, he spun on his heel toward the door, and sharply waved her after him. And when she didn't move—couldn't move—he whirled around again, his eyes reddened, almost frenzied with rage.

Come, he silently hissed at her. *Obey me!*

And with a lurching stagger, a gulping choke in her throat, Alma finally nodded, and obeyed.

lma awoke the next morning feeling tired, achy, and miserable. Her eyes swollen and scratchy, her front covered with a sticky-feeling film, her groin feeling decidedly flushed and tender where Drafli had touched her. *Taken* her.

Even now, the memory of it was far, far too powerful, too painful, and she dug her palms into her eyes as she fought to shove it away. She'd already spent far too much time last night weeping over that prick, curled up alone and empty in her bed, until her eyes had felt empty, too.

And by the end of it, she'd felt even more helpless, more resigned, than before. She still had no funds, no resources, nowhere else to go. She'd made that fool promise to Drafli, and then she'd gone and convinced Baldr of it, too.

And perhaps most horrible of all, Baldr clearly *had* been convinced, in the end. He'd clearly wanted it, and welcomed it. And how would he feel, how hurt would he be, if Alma were to turn around and walk away now? After all the kindness he'd shown her?

She groaned aloud and rubbed again at her eyes—and then heard a wry, familiar laugh, from close beside her bed. And when she twitched up to look, there was Kesst, placing a bulging waterskin next to her pillow, and eyeing her with tangible amusement.

"Rough night?" he said, with a wink. "It certainly smells like it was quite a time."

Alma blinked blearily at him, and fumbled to uncork the waterskin. "Um," she said. "It does?"

"Indeed," Kesst cheerfully replied. "I'm sorry to tell you this, sweetheart, but you positively *reek*."

Alma flinched, and reflexively bent her head to sniff at her shoulder. Which perhaps smelled slightly sweeter than it usually did, but it wasn't a *reek*, was it?

Kesst chuckled again, and shook his head as he sank down onto the bed opposite, his elbows on his knees. "Not like that," he said. "Like *them*. Like Baldr and Drafli. Like they each took a few good long turns with you."

He accompanied this shocking statement with another knowing, approving wink, and Alma felt her face furiously flushing as she took a long, long drink from the waterskin. Yes, Baldr *had* mentioned about her smelling like them now, but this—this—

"So how were they?" Kesst continued, clearly undaunted. "Let me guess, Baldr shy and worshipful, that Skai prick ordering you around like he owns you, and neither of them having the sweetest clue what the hell they were doing?"

Alma's face surely could not feel any hotter, and she had to choke down the rest of the water, fighting to find some kind of answer. "Um, it didn't go—quite that far," she finally managed, with a furtive glance at Kesst's curious eyes. "And Drafli *definitely* knew what he was doing."

Her voice had gone rather bitter at that, because surely it would all be far easier to mentally deal with, if Drafli's *attentions* had been fumbling or unpleasant or genuinely painful—and across from her, Kesst blinked, his brow furrowing.

"Really?" he asked. "That Skai doesn't smell like any women, at *all*. And believe me, these things *linger*."

Kesst grimaced as he spoke, and Alma's flailing brain abruptly flicked back to his bitter words from several days before. About how his own clan had taken advantage of him, and left their scent upon him. Of how he would have liked, perhaps, to be scent-bound. Like—like she was.

"So you're staying here for a while after all, then, I take it?" Kesst continued, with a rather forced-sounding cheerfulness. "How do you feel about that laundry, then?"

From across the room, there was a loud, exasperated groan, and when Alma glanced over, it was Efterar, standing up from where he'd been bent over a bed. A bed which—Alma tilted her head, frowning—seemed to be occupied by a vaguely familiar-looking orc.

"Don't you start, Eft," Kesst said, his voice both teasing and offended. "I am *one day away* from smelling just as strong as *she* does. No thanks to *you*, I might add."

Efterar rolled his eyes, but that was surely a flush creeping up his neck as he turned back to the orc in the bed. "I think you're fine to go, Grisk," he said. "Only take it easy for a few days, all right? I've kept your actual seed cut off for now, but your loads should still smell and taste about the same. Come back once you can't feel any pain, and I'll fix the rest of it then."

Alma blinked—surely she hadn't heard all that properly? But wait, the orc in the bed *was* familiar, it was *Varinn*—and he was sitting up on the bed, and giving Efterar a rueful, grateful smile. "Thank you, brother," he said. "I am much indebted to you."

Efterar waved it away, and strode off to wash his hands in the nearby basin. While Varinn stood up and stretched, rubbing a tentative-looking hand over his groin—and then caught Alma staring at him, and dropped his hand, and gave a sheepish-looking wave as he came over toward her.

"Ach, it is good to see you again, sister," he said. "I hope you are well again?"

"Yes, thank you, Varinn," Alma said, with a careful but sincere smile. "I truly appreciated all your help the other night. But"—she glanced up and down his bulky form, which seemed entirely uninjured—"how did *you* end up in here, too? Are *you* all right?"

Varinn's face visibly reddened, but he shrugged, and gingerly sat down on the bed beside Kesst. "Ach, much better now, thanks to Efterar," he said. "Only went a little too far with the sparring, ach?"

Kesst loudly snorted beside him, and shot Alma an amused, conspiratorial look. "What the poor fellow means is," he said, under his breath, "that he was very nearly *castrated*. By someone who smells a lot like *you*, sweetheart."

Wait. Alma twitched an uncertain frown at Kesst, and then back to Varinn. "Truly, Varinn?" she demanded. "*Drafli* did that to you?"

Varinn winced, but didn't actually reply, and again it was Kesst who spoke. "Not the Skai, believe it or not. No, this was an unprecedented level of Grisk-on-Grisk violence, am I right, Varinn?"

Alma's mouth dropped open—*Baldr* had done that to Varinn? To his friend? "But—but *why*?" she demanded. "Baldr doesn't usually do such things—does he?"

Her eyes were darting uncertainly between Kesst and Varinn, and again Varinn winced, while Kesst gave her a wry, teasing smile. "Not usually," he said. "But you can't think of any reasons why Baldr might have lost his mind on *him*?"

Alma's hand clapped over her mouth, her eyes again gaping at Varinn's face. "Because of *me*?" she squeaked at him. "But— me running away was all *my* fault, Varinn. Not yours! And Baldr *knew* that!"

Varinn winced yet again, and gave a twitchy shake of his head. "There is no *fault*," he said. "My brother was under duress, after all this, and only needed some release. I was happy to offer him this."

But Kesst huffed a laugh, and arched an incredulous eyebrow. "Oh, don't be such a Grisk, Varinn," he said. "Baldr fights like a Skai, *not* a Grisk, and he had no business taking his rubbish out on you. He nearly rendered you incapable of fathering orclings forever. Do you know what a job Eft's had sorting you out?"

Varinn shot a regretful look toward Efterar across the room, even as his bottom lip jutted out, his eyes narrowing back toward Kesst's face. "My brother was not... himself," he said stubbornly. "It was not good for an orc like him to be scent-bound, and then kept apart from his woman thus, while she yet stayed near. This will fray at his mind, ach? I am glad"—his gaze flicked toward Alma—"that he saw sense, sister, and came to terms with you upon this."

What? Alma was staring again, and suddenly she could hear her heartbeat, echoing too loudly in her ears. Baldr's mind had begun to... *fray*? Enough that he had nearly castrated Varinn? Because of *her*?

"Baldr didn't come to terms with me," she heard herself say, her voice hollow. "It was—Drafli. All Drafli."

The understanding flared across Varinn's eyes, and he gave her a quick, knowing smile. "Then I am glad Drafli was wise enough to see this," he said firmly. "And their scent blends well upon you, ach? This is always a good sign. I ken they shall keep you fat and content, and full of good seed. And mayhap soon, a hearty, hale son."

He smiled again, and then carefully stood up, and walked with a rather bow-legged gait toward the door. Leaving Alma staring after him, appalled, while memories of Drafli's urgency—his *fear*—swarmed across her thoughts.

Was *that* why Drafli had pushed so hard for this? Why he'd been so determined with it, so ruthless, even when he'd so obviously loathed it? Loathed *her*?

A new, grudging commiseration toward Drafli was clanging unsteadily through Alma's chest, and she rubbed at her face, and tried to steady her breath. So did this mean—she *had* to stay? Had to keep making this work? Not only because of her debt to Baldr, and the vow, and Mr. Pembroke... but so Baldr's mind wouldn't fray? And possibly... *snap*?

"And how are you, Grisk?" broke in a voice—Efterar's voice—and when Alma glanced up, he'd come back over, and seemed to be talking to her. "Are you feeling any pain in your throat or lungs today?"

It took Alma a moment to follow that, and she belatedly swallowed, touching a careful hand to her throat. "A little," she replied. "But it is still feeling progressively better, thank you. I do apologize for running like I did, and possibly affecting your hard work."

Efterar thankfully waved it away, and moved his hand to hover over her neck. "These orcs give me far more work than you do," he said. "But still, you need to be careful with it, all right, Grisk? No more running, no yelling, try not to speak if you feel pain. Maybe have your Skai teach you his way of speaking with his hands."

Alma's brain still seemed to be scattering in a dozen directions at once—*her* Skai? And surely Drafli would *not* welcome teaching her his language? But Efterar was still looking expectantly toward her, and she felt herself grimace, even as she attempted a nod.

"I can try, I suppose, thank you," she replied uneasily. "And, er, is there a reason you keep calling me *Grisk*?"

Efterar gave a distracted half-smile, his hand now hovering over her neck. "Old habit," he said. "Easier than remembering names when you're tired and trying to focus. The scents are so much clearer, especially on humans."

Alma was feeling even more befuddled than before, and she shot an uncertain glance toward Kesst. "But didn't you say I smelled"—she could feel her face heating—"like *both* Baldr and Drafli now? Not just Baldr?"

Kesst shrugged, and briefly met Efterar's eyes before looking away again. "Baldr touched you first, and made that first scent-bond," he said dismissively, "so his scent blends the deepest, right, Eft?"

Efterar absently nodded, his eyes still focused on Alma's neck. "Doesn't mean the Skai isn't there, though," he said. "And by putting his scent in your mouth and womb before Baldr's, he's given it a nice, smooth, sensual balance. It's good work. Thoughtful, too, for a scent-sensitive mate like Baldr."

Wait. Efterar could *smell* that Drafli had done such things? And it was *good work*? *Thoughtful*? As if, once again, Drafli's actions had been pure, purposeful calculation, as opposed to any kind of actual emotion toward Alma? Let alone desire?

"But believe me, sweetheart, being claimed as a proper Grisk mate is your best option, in this particular scenario," Kesst's voice said, with a rather false-sounding cheerfulness. "You'll want to avoid actually ever becoming a Skai's mate, by all possible means. Their 'ways' of claiming their mates are generally *ghastly*."

They were? Alma felt her head tilting, her eyes darting between Kesst and Efterar—and above her Efterar audibly sighed, and shot Kesst a pointed look.

"Look, that's not always the case, Kesst, and you know it," Efterar said. "Many Skai—*including* Drafli—have been working lately to change the old Skai traditions. To do better by their mates."

"Yes, *goody*," Kesst replied, his voice surprisingly sharp. "They got rid of *one* ritual from the dark ages. So instead of being *hunted*, Alma, or passed around to Drafli's friends while you scream, you can now look forward to"—he counted on his fingers as he spoke—"oh wait, *still* being hunted, or, even better, shown off to Drafli's friends while you scream. *Such* improvement."

Alma surely wasn't following, her throat spasming, her hands clutching together in her lap. "Hunted?" she repeated, high-pitched. "*Shown off?*"

Kesst's mouth pursed into a not-so-nice smile, his shoulder shrugging. "Hunting, stalking, same thing," he said flatly. "Essentially, your Skai picks you out like a choice bit of meat, and then secretly creeps about after you until he finds a way to get up your skirts. And being shown off in a Skai rut"—his smile curled even colder—"is just what it sounds like. Naked, on your knees, while your Skai flaunts your various offerings, to anyone who cares to watch."

What? Drafli's clan truly did such things? *Drafli* did such things? *Supported* such things? But yes, the glittering look in Kesst's eyes suggested that perhaps he did, even as Efterar gave another heavy sigh, and dropped his hand from Alma's neck.

"Look, Kesst, you're making it sound far worse than it usually is," he said. "And the rest of us haven't always done better. Maybe the Ash-Kai most of all."

Alma's whirling thoughts had flashed back to that point about Kesst's own clan—the Ash-Kai—being the ones who'd hurt him. And clearly Kesst was thinking of it too, because he loudly laughed, the sound ringing far too harsh through the room.

"Yes, perfectly understandable for you to think so, Eft," he said coolly, "because we all know it's mostly the stink of old Ash-Kai you notice when you take me. But those Skai bastards can be even worse, and Alma deserves to know what her new, oh-so-*thoughtful* Skai bedmate is likely to do to her, over in the Skai common-room!"

A hard chill wrenched up Alma's spine, her heart thundering in her chest, and above her Efterar actually hissed a low growl, his eyes narrowing on Kesst's reddening face. "You're scaring her, Kesst," he said. "Drafli is *not* likely to do anything she doesn't want, especially not with Baldr as his mate. And I smell *you* when I take you. *You.*"

Kesst's answering laugh was chilly and bitter, and still far too shrill. "Yes, and you also just said that the first scent always goes deepest! And that Alma smells nice and smooth and *sensual*, and when have you ever said something like that about *me*?!"

Efterar stared at Kesst for an instant too long, his mouth tightening—and at that very moment, there was a commotion at the door. With multiple orcs staggering into the room, some of them arguing, some of them bleeding, and two of them carrying a massive, shouting orc with a horribly unnatural bend in his leg.

"Efterar!" called one of the orcs. "Silfast went and broke Grum's leg! In three places!"

Efterar was looking distinctly aggrieved, his eyes briefly closing, even as he jerked a nod, and turned to leave—but then he whirled back again, as if thinking better of it, and squeezed his big hand to Kesst's shoulder, giving it a firm little shake.

"Later, all right?" he said roughly—and then he did turn and stride off, his hands clenched to sharp-tipped fists at his sides.

Kesst watched as Efterar walked away, his own hands gripped tight on his knees. And when he eventually glanced back at Alma, it was with eyes that were rapidly blinking, and unmistakably bright over his flushed-red cheeks.

Alma's own unease had given way to a jolting, plunging sympathy, and she searched Kesst's face, the misery in his eyes. The way he intentionally looked away, his face flushing even redder, his hand rubbing at his mouth.

"Um, so I was wondering," Alma blurted out, "if you might take me back to the scullery? I would *love* to take another look at the laundry. Maybe find your favourite trousers, and see if they can be salvaged?"

Kesst's brows shot up, his wet eyes glancing back toward her—and that was surely a reluctant smile, pulling at his mouth. "Nice try, sweetheart," he said, a little hoarse. "No one *wants* to go see that disaster. But I will take you, if you actually want to get out of here."

"Yes, please," Alma said firmly, and thankfully Kesst stood, and strode for the door. And after making sure her robe was tightly tied around her waist, Alma followed him toward it, not missing how Efterar had looked up from his work to watch them, his eyes still dark, his mouth pressed tight.

"Sorry about that," Kesst said to her, clipped, once they were halfway down the corridor. "I am clearly on a frightful spiral lately. It's bad enough that Eft has to deal with it, I certainly don't need to involve you, too."

Alma shrugged, but found herself carefully glancing toward him, taking in the hard set of his jaw, the way it was visibly grinding in his cheek. "Well, I do appreciate you looking out for me," she said quietly. "And I'm so sorry that you've had to deal with so much. And that you're constantly reminded of it, just because of how you *smell*. It seems so horribly unfair. So *cruel*."

Kesst shrugged too, and gave another one of those hard, brittle laughs. "Well, that's life as an orc for you," he said. "Your mother dies young, giving birth to yet another son she didn't want. Your father's always off at war—not to mention addled from all the death and trauma—and your obnoxious blood-brother's vanished too, gone off to gods know where. *And*, your horrid captain decides you make for excellent entertainment, and thus shares you with his Hands—including the foulest Skai alive—until their scent will never, *ever* fade from you, long after they've all gone and rotted into dust. You know"—he gave Alma a wan smile—"the usual."

Alma's steps had stumbled to a halt on the stone floor, her eyes gaping at Kesst's drawn face. "That is *horrifying*, Kesst," she said, her voice cracking. "I'm so, *so* sorry. How *awful* for you."

Kesst twitched another jerky shrug, his eyes now fixed on the corridor up ahead. "It was years ago," he said, "and I should probably be over it. I should at least *not* be giving Eft hell over it. Not after everything he's done for me. Not after he *saved* me."

Kesst's voice had gone hard and fervent, his arms crossing over his chest, his shoulders hunched. And looking at him, Alma felt herself sinking into the same pose, her heart clanging miserably against her ribs. "I'm sure Efterar understands," she said. "He obviously loves you dearly, Kesst. He would never hold something like that against you."

But that was another jerky shrug from Kesst's shoulder, a bitter laugh from his mouth. "Eft would never admit it," he said flatly. "He would *never* say it. But they were absolute pricks to him too, especially about me, because they *knew* how he felt about me. And Eft is a saint, Alma, a gods-damned *saint*, and he deserves so much better than smelling those swine on me every time he touches me. He deserves a devoted, scent-bound hearth-mate. A *real* one."

A *hearth-mate*. Alma vaguely recalled Kesst using that phrase before, and she glanced again at his hunched shoulders, the tightness in his jaw. "A hearth-mate?" she repeated, quiet. "Is that the same as being scent-bound?"

Kesst barked another laugh, and kicked at the floor with his foot. "No," he said. "It's a stupid old orc thing. A sweet, loyal, beautiful woman, who tends your hearth, and makes it your home, and eases your pain, while also shamelessly blowing your mind in bed, and all that rubbish. I could tell you twenty-odd ancient tales waxing poetic about them, complete with all their nauseating pet names and useful skills and bedroom tricks and heart-stopping beauty. While Eft would be listening with *stars* in his damned eyes."

Oh. It took too much effort for Alma to find words, to speak over the constriction in her throat. "But Efterar said he cares for *you*, Kesst," she said helplessly. "And that's so obvious to me, even though I've really only just met you. He clearly *adores* you."

Kesst shrugged again, but didn't reply, so Alma kept going,

her voice slightly faltering. "I can't—I can't even imagine what that must be *like*, Kesst. To know that the person you care for chose *you*, wanted *you*. Rather than just being caught in some random physical compulsion, and possibly being driven *mad* by something he can't even *control*!"

Kesst's eyes had angled toward her, his head tilting, and suddenly it felt like all the chaos—all the unease—of the past few days was choking up, spilling out of Alma's mouth. "Especially when he's made it quite clear," she continued, "that he doesn't even really want *you*, and he'd far rather have the mate he actually *chose*, who in turn would have been *more* than happy if you'd just gone off and *drowned*! And no wonder, because your very *existence* is now a hazard to his lovely original partner, and he's now obligated to welcome you into their *bed*. When in truth he secretly *hates* you, and would far rather throw you away to his horrible clan, so they can do to me what they did to *you*!"

Her voice had grown louder with every word, until it was somehow shouting, carrying through the corridor, ringing of regret and anger and bitterness. Astonishing even herself with its strength, and she felt her steps falter, her hands scrubbing at her face.

Gods, what had she gotten herself into. What had she been thinking. How would she ever find a way through this...

And it was then, without warning, that someone stepped out of the nearest door. Someone so beautifully, painfully familiar, who was meeting Alma's eyes with a cold, flinty glare.

It was Baldr. And he'd heard *everything*.

lma flared to utter stillness in the corridor, her eyes seized on Baldr's stiff, angry face.

Gods, what had she just said. *Some random physical compulsion. He doesn't even really want you. More than happy if you'd gone off and drowned.*

And worst of all, *He's now obligated to welcome you into their bed, when he secretly hates you, and would far rather throw you away to his horrible clan.*

Alma's hands belatedly clapped over her mouth, because oh gods, why had she just said all that. She'd sworn to honour that contract, to honour Drafli, most of all toward Baldr. And she'd surely just broken the contract, she'd betrayed her promise, she'd probably just destroyed everything?!

"Where the hell did you even *come* from?" Kesst's blank voice was asking, with an obvious edge of irritation. "There was *no* scent of you around here. *None.*"

But Baldr didn't even look at Kesst, and instead kept his glittering eyes on Alma. And for an instant, she was forcibly, viscerally reminded of Drafli, with his command, his censure, his *hatred.*

"Could we talk for a moment, Alma?" Baldr's voice asked, cold and flat. "Now, please?"

Alma swallowed, but reflexively nodded, even as she shot Kesst an apologetic, sidelong look. Which he returned with an equally apologetic grimace, and a twitch of his head up the corridor. "I'll wait for you around the kitchen," he said coolly. "Bring her there when you're finished, Baldr, will you? And if she's more upset than she is now"—he gave a chilly, rather unpleasant smile—"I'll happily tell a *very* good story to your boss."

With that, he spun and strode off, leaving Alma alone with a clearly furious Baldr, while she miserably wrung her hands together. "I—I'm so sorry," she breathed. "I shouldn't have said all that, I don't know what I was thinking—"

Baldr cut her off with a sharp wave of his hand—Drafli's motion, *stop*—and Alma choked the words back, and nodded, bowed her head. Waiting, surely, for him to say it was over, that she'd insulted him beyond repair, and betrayed the mate he truly loved, and ruined *everything*...

"Will you come in here, please?" Baldr's voice finally said, very controlled and careful, and when Alma glanced up, he was waving toward a nearby room, one with a rough-hewn wooden door. "So we can speak in private?"

Alma again nodded, and went for the room, her head still bowed. And it was only once she heard the door shut that she looked up again, and found Baldr setting down a flickering lamp onto a nearby shelf, and then turning back around to frown at her.

"You told me yesterday that you *wanted* this, with us," Baldr said, his voice still unnaturally steady. "With *both* of us. You were very, very clear about that, and worked *very* hard to sway me to this. Now tell me, Alma, was any of this actually *truth*?"

Alma's stomach plunged, and she felt herself frantically nodding. "Yes," she gulped, "it was. I meant it, I *did*."

Baldr didn't look even slightly convinced, his arms folding

tight over his tunic, and Alma desperately searched his forbidding eyes, while her thoughts twisted and wailed. She'd sworn that vow to Drafli, she'd promised to stay, she had to try, why was this such a mess—

And as Baldr's eyes kept darkening on hers, obviously reading into her hesitation, Alma suddenly couldn't bear to lie to him any further, to make this any worse. She had to try for honesty. She had to.

"I did want it, yesterday," she began again. "Very much. And what we did together, it was"—she dragged in a breath—"it was *everything*, Baldr. It was like nothing I have ever felt before. Both of you. But then, after—"

Baldr's eyes had shifted—listening, he was listening—and Alma heaved another breath. "But after," she whispered, "it felt more as though perhaps I was—intruding on you, after all. And that perhaps Drafli—regretted it, and dislikes me more than he wants to show. And then I heard how you *attacked* Varinn, because of how all this was affecting you. And *then*, how Drafli might want to—to share me, or humiliate me, in front of his whole clan, and—"

Her voice broke there, a shiver rippling hard up her back, and she made herself keep going, getting it out. "And then Kesst was upset about something," she said, "and I was just trying to comfort him, and I—well, I clearly got carried away with it all, and said some things I shouldn't have. *Especially* in a public place like that. I'm so sorry, Baldr."

It came out sounding genuine—it *was* genuine—and after an instant's too-stiff silence, she could see Baldr's shoulders sagging, his breath shuddering out in a slow sigh.

"Ach, you are not fully at fault for this," he said heavily. "I ought to have spoken to you of all this. I was on my way to do this, once I had tasted you were awake, but—"

He bit his lip, shaking his head, and his eyes seemed to harden on Alma again, his big body pulling up taller. "But before we go any further with this," he said, "I need you to understand—truly understand—where I stand with Drafli. Ach?"

Alma managed a nod, jerky and quick, and Baldr ran a hand roughly through his hair, and gave another heavy exhale. "I know Drafli is not—easy, or even oft kind," he said. "He can be stubborn, and rude, and angry, and cold. I know how he tasted after this yesterday, how this must have felt to you. I *know*. But—"

His eyes had fixed back to Alma's, glittering narrow and hard. "Drafli shall always be my mate," he said. "I will never choose you over him. I *cannot*. And this is not"—he again pulled a hand through his hair—"only about my vows, or about his rule over me, ach? To me, Drafli is pleasure, and safety, and joy. He cares for me. He is part of me. He is *home*."

Oh. Alma's stomach had plummeted further, and she felt herself blinking hard, and attempting a nod—but again, Baldr's hand gave Drafli's sharp sideways motion. *Stop*.

"And thus, if you truly still wish to do this with us," he continued, "I cannot hear you freely speaking ill of my mate thus. Or claiming that he hates you, or wishes to harm you, or means to run a Skai rut upon you."

Alma's throat convulsed, because Drafli *did* hate her, he'd told her so multiple times himself—and surely Kesst hadn't been lying about that *rut*, had he? Even Efterar hadn't said it wasn't true, even as he'd tried to defend it, right?

But perhaps Baldr had followed that, exhaling another slow sigh. "I understand your fear of this," he said. "The old Skai ways of claiming their mates were indeed oft harsh and cruel. But Drafli would never, *ever* run a Skai rut upon you thus, or share you with his clan. He did not bear these ruts amongst his kin, long before they were stopped, and he would *never* bear this with a woman who carries his scent, or mine. He would gladly *die* first. Ach?"

Oh. Alma swallowed again, the feeling almost painful this time, and she shouldn't ask, she shouldn't—but the words were already here, curse her, tumbling out her mouth. "So Drafli *didn't* do such things with you?" her voice croaked, her eyes searching Baldr's. "He didn't properly claim you as his mate, before his clan, like Kesst said they do?"

And that, surely, was a wince, twisting at Baldr's mouth. "Drafli would not share me," he replied slowly, "but he did show me, and claim me. The Skai have... changed this rut, you see, and now the one being claimed makes the choice of who partakes. Thus, it is now most often only the one Skai who performs the rut, while his clan bears witness. And after this, the vows are spoken, and the mating-bond is complete."

The vision of all that—of Drafli showing Baldr off, claiming him, while all his clan watched—was pulling at something raw and shameful in Alma's belly, and she squeezed her eyes shut, whipping her head back and forth. "So how can you know for certain," she whispered, "that Drafli wouldn't do such a thing to me? How do you know for certain that he can be trusted, especially after—"

After he betrayed you with other orcs for years, she'd been about to say, *and when he's still lying to you*—and gods, what the hell was she doing, she was not supposed to be digging herself deeper, or hurting Baldr even more. But curse her, he was already wincing again, and it looked truly pained this time, his eyes shifting heavy and dark.

"Drafli has kept his vow to me, and stayed faithful to me, in the moons since we did this," he said woodenly. "And he would *never* take you as a true mate himself, so you have nothing to fear upon this."

Oh. And perhaps Baldr hadn't meant to speak with such callousness, but it still dragged more heaviness in Alma's belly, more bitterness in her churning thoughts. And for an instant, there was the absurd impulse to laugh, to say, perhaps, *Oh, Drafli was faithful and honest to you for a few months before he started lying to you again, what an accomplishment, what a gods-damned prick.*

But thankfully Alma had choked the words back, even as new ones poured from her mouth. "But that's—that's part of it too," she gulped. "Drafli—regretted it, yesterday. Touching me. Like I—repulsed him. And if he doesn't actually *like* women, if he isn't even *attracted* to me, and would never *consider* taking a woman as his mate, it surely isn't right for him to—to—"

She couldn't seem to finish, flapping her hands down at her robe instead. And she could feel her face burning again, her own thoughts belatedly flailing back to how she and Drafli had worked together—*conspired* together—to convince Baldr that Drafli had truly wanted her. And now here she was, once again ruining everything?!

Baldr's sigh was slow and resigned, his hand again dragging at his hair. And though his eyes were still dark, still tired, they at least didn't seem *more* angry, did they?

"It is not that Drafli is not—*attracted* to women," he said finally, his voice stiff. "It is only that he—"

Alma waited, watching, unmoving—and Baldr abruptly bit his lip, and glanced away. "It is not my tale to tell," he said, quiet. "But Drafli has suffered much, at the hands of a woman he cared for. And this has brought him deep distrust of you. *Fear* of you. Ach?"

What? Incredulity was jolting through Alma's stilted thoughts, and she felt her brow furrowing, her head shaking. *Drafli* had been harmed by a woman? *That* Drafli? Enough that he feared them? Feared *her*?

"But—" Alma began, and then bit it back, shook her head again. "But he still didn't—seem attracted to me, yesterday. Did he?"

Baldr's shoulder shrugged, and his mouth made a sound that might have been a laugh. "Mayhap not after," he replied. "But you did not smell him, when we were in the midst of this. Had it not been for the strength of how he tasted, I would never have—"

He grimaced and looked away again, but surely he'd meant

that he wouldn't have finished the way he had, spraying out his scent upon her. Feeding her his mate's seed. *You smell so good thus, Bright-Heart.*

"But as good as this was," Baldr continued, his shoulders squaring, his voice hardening, "I yet cannot risk Drafli in this. I cannot see him hurt further. I cannot *bear* this."

That last bit was near to a growl, Baldr's hands clenching at his sides, his eyes now fixed on something beyond her. "So if you truly yet wish to do this with us," he said, "these are my terms. You will honour Drafli. You will honour what he is to me. You will seek to trust him, and earn his trust in return."

Alma swallowed, her mouth opening to speak—but Baldr again made that *stop* motion, his gaze still not meeting hers. "Not only this," he continued flatly, "but you will welcome his touch, and accept what he offers you with willing eagerness. You will obey him, and appreciate him, and *worship* him with me. You will make every effort upon this. *Every effort.*"

Alma's heart dropped—he truly didn't think she'd been giving her best effort?—and her body shot to chagrined still-ness, her breaths far too loud in the silence. And when Baldr's glinting eyes flicked back to hers, brows raised, Alma was again suddenly, bizarrely reminded of Drafli. Of his expression, his determination, even his words.

We have vow. You obey me. Honour me. Seek to please my mate. He has borne much. I give all for him.

And it was so absurd, and confusing, that Baldr should be here, speaking alone to her, making almost the exact same demands that Drafli had made. And if they both felt this way, why weren't they just speaking to each other, why hadn't they made these damned proposals to her together, side by side, like the mates they were? The *real* mates they were, because clearly Alma had no hope of ever becoming that, for either of them?

"Now that we are clear upon this," Baldr continued, his voice wooden again, "do you yet wish to continue this, with us? If you do not"—something moved in his eyes—"I will not hold this against you. We will find another way forward, and part as friends. Ach?"

As friends. And blinking at Baldr's drawn face, his tired eyes, it occurred to Alma that they were barely even friends. Gods, they still barely even *knew* each other. Even though he'd saved her life, he'd covered her with his tunic, chased after her into that tunnel, sprayed his pleasure upon her, fed her his mate's seed...

And suddenly there was just longing, deep and instinctive, crushing Alma beneath its weight. She wanted him so much. She wanted to get to know him better, to truly become the friends they ought to be. She wanted to find a way to make this work, a way out of this mess, with him. As friends, as bedmates, even as co-worshippers of the cold, cruel, untrustworthy mate he seemed to love so much.

She wanted it all, she craved it all, so much it ached. Pleasure, and safety, and joy. A family. *Home.*

"I understand, Baldr," she whispered, holding his eyes. "And as long as you're sure *you* still want this, I truly would still like to stay. To try to make this work, between us."

She could see Baldr's eyes slightly fluttering, his throat bobbing. "And you will agree to my terms," he said, his voice almost tentative now. "You will honour Drafli, and seek to gain his trust, and make a true friend of him."

Alma twitched at the thought of making friends with Drafli—*friends*, with *Drafli*—but she nodded, kept holding Baldr's gaze. "I understand," she said again. "I'll try."

She couldn't quite read his eyes, the way they were searching her, as if seeking some kind of crack, some weakness, some falsehood. But then he gave another careful nod, another hard swallow in his throat.

"Then we will try," he said, his voice very even. "Mayhap for one month, before any lasting choices are made."

For *one month*. Wait. As if Baldr was proposing a—a trial. A challenge. A test of Alma's ability to honour Drafli, and make friends of him, and gain his *trust*. In one *month*?!

Alma's throat had spasmed, her eyes gone wide on Baldr's face—he truly didn't trust her, he was testing her, one *month*— and she again felt her stomach plummeting, her gaze dropping, her clammy hands twisting together. One month, to make friends of Drafli, when he'd told her again and again that he hated her. That there was no way they would ever, ever be friends.

It was impossible. Impossible.

"I am sorry, Bright-Heart," came Baldr's low voice. "But these are my terms. You can yet say no, with no consequence."

But his voice had very slightly wavered at the end, and when Alma glanced back up, it was to the sight of him biting his lip, his eyes blinking toward her. As if he truly were sorry. As if he truly did care. As if the way he'd fed her his mate's seed, with such approving, affectionate tenderness, was still true, somewhere below all this tangled, twisted muddle of a mess.

And Alma had already come this far, already dug herself this deep, made all these foolish promises. And it wasn't like she had any better options, did she? Did she?

No. She had to try. She had to.

"I understand," she whispered again, to the floor at her feet. "One month. I'll try."

19

B aldr led Alma back to the kitchen in a stilted, awkward silence, neither of them quite meeting the other's eyes.

It was as though his ultimatum—his deadline—had irrevocably changed whatever warmth had existed between them, and turned it into something hostile, something heavy and cold. And as much as Alma wanted to find something to say to him, every possible thought brought up only more potential risk, more potential pitfalls. Drafli. Varinn. Mr. Pembroke. One month. And then what?

"Here you are," Baldr said, with genuine-sounding relief, as he waved her into the kitchen. "I can smell Kesst near the back."

Alma thanked him, with equally genuine relief, and stepped past him into the kitchen's familiar, reassuring warmth. "Morning, Gegnir," she said, with a cautious wave toward where he was chopping parsnips at the counter. "And Narfi. How are you two today?"

Narfi returned this with a suspicious, narrow-eyed glower, his nose abruptly sniffing the air—while beside him, Gegnir actually smiled at her, and jerked his grey head toward the scullery. "Kesst is over there," he said. "Despairing over the laundry again, no doubt."

At that, Alma reluctantly smiled back, and went for the half-open scullery door—and only then did she realize that Baldr was still here. Still following her, his lamp still in hand, his eyes meeting her surprised glance with a look that was rather—mulish. Or perhaps even... guilty.

"I just wish to make sure you are safe," he said, as his gaze purposefully shifted away from hers, and frowned toward the scullery. "Also, why are you going in *here*?"

Alma attempted a shrug, and a wan smile toward him. "I promised to help sort out the scullery," she said. "It's, well— you'll see."

She was already opening the door, confronting her and Baldr at once with the sight and stench of the still-vile scullery. If it was possible, the pile of laundry on the counter had seemed to grow even higher, and the giant mound of ash had seemed to expand, too. And in the midst of it all stood Kesst, staring at the mountain of laundry with abject hopelessness all over his face.

"I can't even *smell* my trousers in this," he said mournfully to Alma—and then his eyes flicked behind her, slightly stilling as they caught on Baldr in the doorway. And when Alma glanced back too, Baldr was standing there gaping wide-eyed at the room, his hand clapped over his nose.

"You are not *staying* in here?" he demanded toward Alma, with surprising vehemence. "*Helping* in here, you said?!"

Alma blinked at him, and then back at Kesst, and the scullery. "Er, yes, if that's all right?" she said uncertainly. "And wait"—her eyes were searching the dirty but dry floor, and then Kesst's face—"what happened to the water, Kesst? Did the drain get fixed somehow?"

A brief flare of smugness crossed Kesst's mournful eyes, and he strode over to kick at a now-visible metal grate in the floor. "Looks that way," he said. "I *may* have mentioned it to your most devoted Ka-esh admirer, and let him know you would be *eternally* grateful to have it dealt with. He must have sent someone up."

Alma couldn't help a delighted grin toward him, even as there was the odd, unnerving sound of a growl behind her. "Who?" demanded Baldr's voice, and when Alma twisted back toward him, he was glowering at Kesst with surprising anger. "*What* Ka-esh?!"

"Eben, of course," Kesst replied, coolly raising his arched brows toward Baldr. "He's spent the past week pining over Alma in the sickroom, which you would know, if you ever came to visit. Lovely fellow, though, isn't he Alma? So handsome, too. Maybe"—he glanced purposefully back to Alma again—"maybe we can ask him to come join us, and find the chute for the ashes, and whatever the ventilation is supposed to be in here?"

Alma had begun to nod back—that *would* be a significant help—but behind her Baldr had growled again, set down his lamp, and stalked across the room with astonishing speed. And after kicking at the pile of ashes against the wall—and whirling up a thick cloud of dust in the process—he yanked out a steel shovel from deep within the ashes, heaved away several large shovelfuls of ash, and then repeatedly banged the shovel against the floor. And suddenly, there was indeed a visible, stone-lined ash chute cut into the lower wall and floor, and extending down into blackness.

"How did you know any of that was there?" Kesst asked suspiciously, as Baldr kept shovelling ash down into the chute. "Did you work with Roland on the Keeping somehow? A Grisk thing, maybe?"

"No," Baldr replied, without looking back toward them. "I barely knew Roland. I only remembered how the room smelled before."

Oh. That seemed very impressive, to Alma's mind, and her

eyes seemed trapped on the sight of Baldr's quick, efficient shovelling, his broad back shifting with each movement. "Also," Baldr continued, even more clipped than before, "it is obvious that it would be here, in this wall behind the oven. The oven's ash chute connects to it also, ach?"

It was a fair point, and likely one Alma should have thought of herself, and she attempted a smile at Baldr's back. "This is so helpful, Baldr, thank you," she said. "I don't suppose you might have any idea how the room ended up like this? Surely Roland wouldn't have *wanted* to work in this kind of state?"

Baldr shrugged, and kept shovelling. "I can scarce even smell Roland in here," he said. "His scent is strongest out there, around his desk."

He'd jerked his head back toward the kitchen, and Alma met Kesst's equally confused eyes before glancing to Baldr again. "Roland had a *desk*?" she echoed. "Might you be willing to show us? If you have another moment to spare?"

Baldr shrugged again, but then propped the shovel against the nearest wall, grasped the lamp, and strode back out into the kitchen. Going toward the very back of the room, which clearly extended further than it appeared at first glance, into an area that obviously served as the kitchen's pantry. It was tightly packed with a random-seeming mess of casks and crates and barrels, but Baldr easily wove his way through them, following what seemed to be a barely discernible path. And when he finally halted, it was indeed before a small, tucked-away wooden desk, surrounded by tall stacks of barrels and hanging, fragrant herbs.

It was a surprisingly cozy-looking place, almost a little barrel-walled room of its own, entirely hidden from the larger kitchen behind them. And upon the desk, there were even several large, roughly bound books, and a variety of writing implements.

"Oh, these must be Roland's ledgers!" Alma said eagerly, as she moved around the desk, and carefully opened the uppermost book. It was indeed a housekeeping ledger, with long columns of text and associated numbers. And though Alma couldn't even slightly read the messy scrawl—let alone the language it was written in—it was suddenly so ordinary, so blessedly familiar, that she almost felt faint.

"Can you read these?" she demanded excitedly at Kesst, who was still blinking bemusedly around the tiny room. "Do they list purchases or services? Or names, perhaps?"

Kesst obligingly elbowed past Baldr, and came over to frown down at the book. "Gods above, Roland's penmanship is a *travesty*," he said, running his black claw down the page. "These are trading-credits, I think?"

"Trading-credits?" Alma asked, glancing toward Kesst again—but before Kesst could reply, Baldr cleared his throat, and lurched over to stand stiffly on Alma's other side.

"Trading-credits serve as our mountain's currency," he explained. "An orc offers a good or service—hunting, mayhap, or gathering food or firewood or furs—and in return, he earns trading-credits to spend on other goods or services. The captain has worked with the Ka-esh to make these sums standard, and fair to all orcs."

Alma shot Baldr a quick, grateful smile, but still found him not quite looking at her, his eyes intently dropping to the open ledger. "The credits are now managed by each clan, most oft through the porters of the trading-rooms," he continued. "Roland must have been granted some by the Grisk porter to use toward the Keeping."

"That does make sense," Alma said thoughtfully, with another furtive smile that Baldr didn't seem to see. "This is such a large mountain—probably bigger than any estate in the realm—and I had been wondering how on earth Roland had been managing it all. A property this size really needs an entire team, and the housekeeper should be focused on that—hiring and directing staff, managing maintenance and repairs, planning and budgeting and prioritizing. Making sure the property stays viable, and keeps its inhabitants *safe*."

Her voice had risen as she'd spoken, surely betraying far too much enthusiasm on this—and beside her, Baldr's brows had furrowed together, his gaze darting between Alma and the ledger. "Wait," he said slowly. "You surely are not implying that *you* mean to take over the Keeping? As well as cleaning that filthy scullery?"

Alma blinked uncertainly toward him, and then glanced at Kesst, who was suddenly eyeing Baldr with palpable distaste. "Yes, Alma was implying exactly that," he said coolly. "As again, you would know, if you ever bothered to visit, or properly speak to her!"

Baldr grimaced, but his eyes on Alma's were flinty, his jaw taut in his cheek. "You are not here to clean our mountain for us, Alma," he said, voice flat. "You are *not* our scullery maid, or our *servant*."

It shouldn't have mattered—Alma should not have cared—but she still felt herself blanch, her hands clutching reflexively at her robe. Not only at Baldr calling her a *scullery maid*—a job she'd done when she was twelve—but at how she'd just told him what a real housekeeper did, what she'd been doing for years. And worst of all, between the various demands and ultimatums Baldr and Drafli had made—*honour me, obey me, these are my terms, you will make every effort*—was Alma not rather like a servant, after all? To *them*?

"*We* aren't treating her like a servant," Kesst's cold voice broke in, with particular emphasis on the *we*. "Was it Grim who told you that Keeping doesn't matter, and is on a level with servitude? Or was that your Skai? It certainly doesn't sound like something a Grisk would say."

And now it was Baldr blanching, and giving Alma a chagrined, shamefaced grimace. "It just—this was not part of our agreement," he said, under his breath. "There is no need whatsoever for you to—to work here, Alma, or to earn your keep."

Alma tried for a smile, but couldn't seem to make it work. "I—I *like* working," she said wretchedly. "I would far rather be busy, than waiting around for"—*for you*, she'd been about to say, but she caught it just in time—"for something to do. And Drafli said he didn't mind, so I didn't think you would either, so please—"

She didn't know how to finish, suddenly—*please don't take this away too*, she might well have said, *please don't demand even more of me*—and somehow found that she was very near to weeping. It had already been such a distressing and disorienting day, in an increasingly long line of them, and she'd thought Baldr was an ally, a friend, someone who understood. But here he was making demands of her too, putting her on trial, one measly month, and then—

"Come on, Alma," Kesst cut in, as he sharply slammed the ledger shut. "Let's go find Eben, and see if he can shed some light on this credits situation. If not, he can surely help us with the scullery's ventilation and water pump, at least."

With that, Kesst stalked back around the desk, toward the kitchen. But when Alma made to follow, her head bowed, she suddenly found that she'd been blocked in, by—Baldr. His big body twitchy, tense, far too close.

"I am sorry, Bright-Heart," he said, his low voice hurried and hoarse. "I did not mean to—insult you, or thrust more demands upon you. I only"—he dragged his hand against his hair, his throat audibly convulsing—"did not mean for you to feel you *must* do this. As some kind of—payment, or *penance*, for us."

Oh. Alma blinked up at him, at where he was blinking back down at her, his eyes just as bright as hers felt—and it occurred to her that this was *guilt*, glimmering in his eyes, contorting his mouth. And it looked wrong, so wrong, upon his lovely face, and she attempted her best smile, and perhaps almost succeeded this time.

"There's no need to apologize, Baldr," she told him, and she meant it, her hand briefly coming up to squeeze against his arm. "I understand. And I truly do appreciate your thoughtfulness."

She gave him another watery smile, and then made to step around him. Toward where Kesst was waiting with obvious impatience, giving an exaggerated roll of his eyes—when Baldr abruptly blocked Alma again, his big hands gripping at her shoulders this time.

"I could—help you," he said, in a rush. "Should you wish. This scullery vent shall not be hard to find, and the water pump ought to be easy as well. I could also clean out this ash for you, as you ought not to work in a room full of this, given your wounded throat. I shall also ask the captain about some trading-credits for you. Ach?"

That was almost panic in his eyes now, frantically searching hers, and Alma felt her tension pooling away, her shoulders sagging under his touch. It was the first time he'd touched her since his bedroom, since he'd so sweetly fed her Drafli's seed, and she could almost feel his awareness of it too, the shift in his watching, waiting eyes.

"Oh, it's so lovely of you to offer," she told him, and her smile felt fully genuine this time, slow and warm on her mouth. "I would be so happy to have your help. Especially when you already seem to know so much of these things."

Her relief seemed to be reflecting in Baldr's eyes, curving up his mouth, too—at least, until Kesst loudly snorted behind them, and jerked his head toward the kitchen. "I think Eft needs me," he said, with deliberate blandness. "I'll leave you two Grisk to... whatever the hell this is. Baldr, bring her back to the sickroom when you're done, will you?"

He didn't wait for a reply, and instead spun and strode off, leaving Alma and Baldr alone. And Baldr surely looked even more relieved than before, giving Alma a swift, sheepish smile, his hands gently squeezing her shoulders.

"Finally," he said, under his breath—and then he bit his lip and shook his head, smiling even more wryly than before. "Now. Will you teach me how to housekeep, Bright-Heart?"

And suddenly Alma was smiling back, so broadly it felt like it was cracking her face. "Of course," she said. "I'd love to."

20

For the rest of the afternoon, Alma worked with Baldr in the scullery, talking and laughing until her throat ached.

It should have been tedious, tiring work—in truth, it probably still was—but Baldr's cheerful, reassuring presence made it all so much easier, and so much more interesting, too. He indeed found the scullery's vent—it had been tucked under one of the workbenches—and then showed her how to turn on the water, as well. It actually ran straight into the large stone sink from the wall above it, and it was controlled via a thick brass plate in the adjacent wall. And, it turned out, there was also apparently an ingenious steel storage basin in the wall above the kitchen's fire, so the water would be heated, as well.

"Our Ka-esh engineers are careful to work with the streams and passages that were already here," Baldr explained to her, as he slid the plate open and closed, while the steaming hot water poured into the sink and then—after a moment's delay—stopped again. "Thus, their workings may not always be obvious, but they wear better this way, ach?"

Alma nodded at him, legitimately impressed, as she knelt to look at the vent again. "And are the vents all throughout your mountain as well?" she asked. "Or just in certain areas, like this?"

"No, all through," Baldr said, as he again picked up the shovel, and began heaving more ash down into the chute. "Again, they are not always obvious, but we cannot risk poisoning ourselves with stale air, ach?"

It was utterly brilliant, and Alma fervently told him so, as she once again reached for the broom, and began sweeping up the area he'd cleared. They'd been dealing with the ashes in shifts, clearing out what they could until the air became too dusty to breathe, and then going back out into the kitchen until it settled again. Baldr had also insisted that Alma cover her nose and mouth with a rag he'd given her, and it did help, even though she cringed at the thought of adding it to the teetering mountain of laundry.

"How do you know so much about these things?" she tentatively asked, as she swept her pile of ash toward him, and he obligingly shovelled it into the chute. "You said you didn't know Roland, right? Or anything about the house-keeping?"

Baldr shrugged, the back of his tunic now soaked with sweat, and streaked with smudges of grey ash. "I am the captain's Left Hand," he said. "And thus, as part of this, I serve as his nose. I seek to know all who enter this mountain, and where they are, and what they do, within it. Thus, I know most of our mountain's secrets, and its air and its streams"—his head jerked toward the wall—"are always speaking their truth to me, ach?"

Oh. A curious little chill had quivered up Alma's back, and she stopped her sweeping, so that she might better stare at his muscled, sweaty, unbelievably impressive form. "That's incredi-ble, Baldr," she said. "Varinn told me that you could also follow—well. You're like a—a *god*."

Baldr barked a laugh and shook his head, even as a faint flush crept up his greenish neck. "Ach, just an orc," he said dismissively. "Grisk oft have good noses. Varinn could find any scent through all the mountain also."

Alma's head tilted, considering all that, her sweeping still forgotten. *These days, I am barely a Grisk at all,* Baldr had told Kesst that day, while today Varinn had stubbornly defended Baldr, and made excuses for him. *My brother only needed some release. I was happy to offer him this...*

"So is that why Varinn found me in the corridor, the other night?" Alma asked carefully. "And not... someone else?"

Baldr curtly nodded, though he didn't meet her eyes as he kept shovelling. "Ach," he said, with a wince. "Had I been thinking clearly, I should have understood this kindness, and left him be. I was a *beast*, toward him."

There was hard, genuine bitterness in his voice and his form, and perhaps despair, too. And gods, why was Alma dragging up these unpleasant things, when they'd finally been getting on so well, and finding a way to make things easy again between them?

"Well, at least you only suffered your lapse of judgement with Varinn, who seems to have already fully forgiven you," she said, as lightly as she could. "Whereas I"—she gave a mock bow, complete with a silly little flourish of her broom—"upon meeting the mate of the lovely person who saved my *life*, told him that he was *infirmed*. I don't think I shall *ever* live that down, Baldr. "

Baldr huffed a short chuckle, and wryly shook his head. "It was not the best beginning, I ken," he said, as he shovelled another pile of ash down the chute. "But Drafli has heard far worse. From those far closer to him."

That wasn't actually comforting—and also, how lowering was it to realize that Alma wasn't actually *close* to Drafli, despite having gotten a faceful of his seed—and she grimaced as she searched for anything else, please gods, to say.

"So Efterar thinks," she began, "that it would be good for me to try to learn your sign language. That it might help with my throat. And I was thinking"—she grimaced again, made herself keep going—"that maybe it would help with Drafli, too? In gaining his trust, I mean? Or do you think he might find that frustrating, or annoying? Or presumptuous?"

Baldr had given her an unreadable look over his shoulder, and Alma braced herself for his certain refusal, or maybe even his censure—but then he spun around to fully face her. "You would truly try?" he asked, his voice and eyes unmistakably suspicious. "You would not give up, after you had learned a few basic signs?"

Alma blinked, and felt herself shrink a little inward, her eyes searching his face. "Er, I hope not?" she said uncertainly. "I mean, I've learned a few already, things like *stop*, and *keep going*, and *honour you*, and *come with me*, and *I understand*, and *vow*"— she made what she hoped were the correct signs with her shaky hands as she spoke—"and—and *you*."

She made the *Pure-Heart* sign, carefully moving her fingers over her heart the way Drafli always did, and for an odd, hanging instant Baldr didn't move, and just stared at her, at where her hand was still hovering over her breast. So she made the motion again, slower this time, while Baldr kept watching, his sharp tooth now biting at his lip.

"Er, and I was wondering," she ventured, "if you might show me your sign for Drafli's name, so I could at least follow that, too?"

Baldr seemed to twitch all over, as if jerking awake—and then he nodded, and gave a quick, fluid flick of his fingers, very near his mouth. And then again, slower this time, as if he truly meant for Alma to see, to follow. To learn.

So Alma copied the motion, moving her fingers in the way he had—and then watching intently as he did it again. With his thumb actually touching his lips, she realized, so she pulled down her makeshift mask and repeated it again, and this time Baldr twitched a nod, his tooth again visible and sharp against his lip.

"What does it mean?" she asked, as she again made the motion, and earned another twitchy nod in return. "Is it just his name?"

Baldr's face was slowly turning scarlet, and he shook his head. "It means—Golden-Tongue," he said his voice low. "It is what I call him, like this."

Oh. *Golden-Tongue*, for an orc who struggled to speak—and suddenly Alma felt her own face flushing, too, while a distant part of her marvelled at the warmth in that name, the inherent intimacy of it. The suggestion of other uses of Drafli's tongue, surely—but also, perhaps, the respect it implied, as well. That Drafli's words were still sweet, still golden, still bearing true value, even when they weren't being spoken aloud.

"It's a lovely name," Alma said, quiet, and she repeated the motion again, this time seeking to catch more of the fluency, the sensuality, of Baldr's version. "And you truly don't think he would mind if I used it for him, too?"

Baldr gave a shaky-looking shrug, his eyes still fixed on her hand at her mouth. "We can try," he said, and as he spoke, his hands moved along with his voice—clearly showing her the words, helping her learn. "He will tell us, if he does not wish for it. And I would never"—he half-smiled, the flush still darkening his cheeks—"*never* speak it aloud to him, ach?"

Right. So it was only used like this, a secret name only between them—and now Baldr had shared it with her. And Alma felt her own face heating too, her mouth curving into a shy, grateful smile, as she made the sign for *I understand*.

Baldr's eyes had darted to her hand, and then up to her eyes. And she could see his throat bobbing as he eased closer, his lips parting, his breath filling his chest...

But then he twitched, and abruptly plucked the broom out of Alma's slack hands. And as she stood there, her face still unaccountably hot, he swiftly swept the last of the ash down into the chute, leaving the floor still streaked and dirty, but entirely, blessedly clear.

"There," he said, without quite meeting Alma's eyes. "Tomorrow I shall find you a cover for the chute, so you shall not risk breathing any more ash, ach? I shall also find you those trading-credits, so you can seek the help you need. Mayhap I can send you some fresh ledgers and inks, as well."

Wait, he could really do all that? Alma couldn't help a delighted smile toward him, and an enthusiastic nod. "Yes, please," she said, with feeling. "Thank you so much. For that, and for this today, too. It would have taken me *days*, without your help."

She waved at the much-improved scullery, which, while still unpleasant, wasn't nearly as revolting as it had been—but in return, Baldr only shrugged, and glanced uncomfortably away. Looking almost guilty, suddenly, and Alma followed that all too easily, back to his demands. His deadline. One month, to make friends of Drafli, to gain his trust, or...

Alma's own smile had abruptly faded, her eyes dropping to the floor, and before her Baldr cleared his throat, and leaned the broom against the wall. "Ach, I ken we now *reek* of this room," he said, with an obvious attempt at lightness. "I am coated in ash, also. Shall you mayhap come, and bathe with me?"

A bath suddenly did sound like a wonderful idea, and Alma willingly followed Baldr back out into the kitchen. Saying a quick farewell to Gegnir and Narfi on the way past, which—oddly enough—seemed to result in Baldr huffing out a low growl, and then slipping his hand around her waist, and drawing her closer against him.

"Drafli *did* speak to you," he began, a little stilted, once they were out in the corridor, "about scents, ach? About you—only touching us, and none else?"

Us. Alma swallowed, but nodded, and fought to ignore the delicious nearness of his warm, shifting body, his arm close and safe against her, his rich scent filling her breath. "Yes, it was part of the—of our discussion," she said, silently cursing her near-lapse. "And I can assure you, Baldr, I have no other interests on that front whatsoever. *None.* Only you."

Her face was heating again, her eyes on the floor, but she could feel Baldr's relief beside her, his hand briefly tightening against her waist. "I—thank you," he said stiffly. "This is a true kindness, toward me."

Alma waved it away, earning another squeeze of his hand against her, perhaps even an inhale of his nose against her hair—but then he was guiding her into another room. Into the lamplit room scented of sulphur, with the huge steaming baths carved into the floor. The room where Alma had found him and Drafli together that day, Baldr spraying his pleasure across the room, Drafli snarling with rage, *Get out*—

Alma's steps briefly faltered, her eyes caught on the rock where they'd been, and she could feel Baldr hesitate too, the stiffness returning to his body against her. "Drafli and I oft come here together," he said, his voice gone flat and defensive. "It is—calming, for me."

Oh. Wait. He thought Alma was—upset by that, perhaps, or jealous. And gods, she couldn't bear to bungle this up even more, and she took a deep breath of the strong-smelling air, and attempted a jaunty smile toward him. "Even with this smell?" she asked. "I hate to tell you, Baldr, but it's nearly as bad as the scullery."

And thankfully, Baldr's smile back toward her was surely relieved, and perhaps teasing, too. "This is not even *close* to that rancid rathole," he informed her. "And here, there is water to block the scent, ach?"

And with that, he abruptly shucked his tunic and trousers, giving Alma a brief view of his muscled back and bare arse as he turned, and dove headfirst into the pool. Making impact with barely a ripple, and then vanishing fully beneath. And when Alma lurched closer to look, she could only see the room's dim lamplight, reflecting on the surface of the steaming water—so she waited and waited, her heartbeat erratically

pulsing, until Baldr's head finally reappeared, at the opposite
end of the pool.

He didn't speak, his eyes closed, his head tilted back, while
water streamed down his face—until he dove in again. But this
time, he stayed near to the surface of the water, his powerful
arms slicing again and again as he swam with astonishing efficiency to the pool's opposite side. And then, with a fluid-
looking flip of his big body, he kicked off the wall, and did it all
again.

Alma had never seen anyone swim so beautifully in her life,
and she crouched down to watch more closely, as a hard lump
seemed to grow in her throat. As her thoughts kept lurching
toward a river, those strong arms around her waist in the darkness, dragging her to safety...

When Baldr finally resurfaced again, nearer than she
expected this time, she felt herself caught on the sight of him,
her eyes sweeping over his face, his long-lashed eyes, his
streaming wet hair, his broad shoulders. Gods, he was stunning, and she swallowed hard, and cleared her throat.

"I think perhaps you *are* a god, Baldr," she said, hoarse.
"That was *spectacular*."

Baldr's wet shoulder twitched a shrug, but he did indeed
look more relaxed than before, his eyes warmer and easier on
her face. "It is only swimming," he said lightly. "Do you not do
this also?"

Alma shook her head, giving an uncertain glance at the
large, steaming pools. "I never learned," she said. "My mother
so rarely had time off when I was a child. And once I began
working in earnest, I never had the time, either."

Baldr's eyes flared with unmistakable sympathy, and he
gave her a quick, understanding smile. "Then you shall learn
now," he said firmly. "Unless"—his head tilted—"you do not
wish to, after all this with the river?"

After she'd nearly drowned, he meant—but suddenly there
was only the overwhelming urge to please him, to see that

smile lighting up his face again. "I—I'm happy to try," she replied. "Though I'll warn you now, I'm likely to be horrendous at it."

But yes, that was another smile, even warmer on his mouth. "We shall take our time," he said. "Now undress, and come in?"

He'd held out a hand toward her, his brows raised—but suddenly Alma was frozen in place, her hand clutched at her now-grimy robe, her eyes angling toward the opening into the corridor. Where anyone could walk by, or walk in, or...

"There is no shame in this here, Bright-Heart," came Baldr's low voice. "None shall condemn you, or mock you. And I swear that none but me shall touch you. Ach?"

None but him. *Bright-Heart*. Those words resonating almost painfully in Alma's thundering chest, her eyes caught on his. On his kindness, his reassurance, his safety.

So she gave a heavy, shaky exhale, nodding, as her hands fumbled for the sash of her robe. As she awkwardly yanked it off, her body still crouching, her knees now pulled up tight against her chest, hiding herself away.

But Baldr had leaned up out of the pool, his fingers closing around hers, drawing her toward him—so Alma nodded again, and scooted closer, and closer. Until Baldr's big hands finally reached up, grasped her by the waist, and slid her into the water against him.

And—oh. Oh. He was so close, so alive, and the feel of his smooth bare skin, all against hers, was truly, bizarrely breathtaking. Gods, it felt good—it felt *glorious*—and for a frozen, dazzling instant, all Alma could do was stand there and feel it, revel in it, drag in deep, gasping breaths.

Baldr wasn't moving either, his own eyes gone rather glazed, his hands still clamped at her waist—until Alma felt something, something new, nudging close and powerful against her belly. Something that seemed to swell larger with every breath, flexing and filling, flaring wild streams of heat all through her groin—

But then, without warning, it was gone. Gone, because Baldr had wrenched himself away from her, leaving her fully untouched in the water. And suddenly Alma felt cold all over, despite her belated awareness that the water was very hot, and dampness was already dripping down the back of her neck.

"Ach," Baldr said, with a rueful half-smile, half-grimace toward her. "I swore to Drafli that I would never touch you thus, without him."

Right. Of course Drafli would demand something like that, and Alma swallowed down her own grimace, and again made the sign for *I understand*. And then stood there, not meeting Baldr's eyes, and instead glancing uneasily around at the pool, at the too-close water that nearly covered her shoulders.

"Er, so," she said, as steadily as she could, "what does one *do* to learn to swim, exactly?"

Baldr gave an odd little cough, but then began to explain that learning to swim really began with being comfortable in the water, and trusting one's body within it. "So I would not worry too much about learning, yet," he said. "Mayhap we only play, for now?"

His voice was hopeful, his eyes still a little regretful on hers, and Alma tried for a nod, and a smile. And when Baldr suggested that perhaps she could try to catch him, she agreed with a rather forced-feeling eagerness, and then staggered her way toward him.

He made it easy for her, at least, allowing her to block him into a corner—where he rewarded her with a wry, approving grin, before raising his hands, and waggling his claws at her. Clearly turning the tables, and Alma yelped as she flailed backwards, and rushed for the opposite corner. And though Baldr almost instantly caught her, his hands slightly lingered at her bare waist, the hopeful smile still pulling at his mouth.

"Good, Bright-Heart," he murmured. "Again?"

It felt even easier to oblige this time, and Alma's laugh when she caught him felt far more genuine—especially when he again bared his claws at her, complete with a mock growl this time. And soon they really were just playing, teasing and laughing and dunking each other, and splashing around the pool. And though Alma fought very hard to respect Drafli's no-touching rule, it seemed increasingly difficult to stop her hands from lingering on Baldr's strong arms and shoulders, or to keep herself from leaning into where his own hands seemed to keep catching on her waist, that too-obvious hardness at his groin still nudging against her belly.

"Ach, Bright-Heart," Baldr finally said, as he once again wrenched himself away from her, dragging both hands through his wet hair. "Drafli is coming. Thank the *gods*."

Alma blinked uncertainly toward him, the smile on her face fading—had he not enjoyed this time with her, after all?—and Baldr winced as he stepped closer again, his hand cupping against her full breast beneath the water.

"I only mean," he murmured, as his thumb stroked at her peaked nipple, firing shards of heat in its wake, "that mayhap he shall grant us some relief, ach?"

Oh. Alma felt her breath shuddering, her body shamelessly leaning into his touch—and he grimaced again as he dropped his hand, and jerked his head toward the pool's edge. "Drafli is not likely to swim now," he said, as he gracefully heaved himself out of the pool, and then knelt to pull Alma out after him. "So let us be ready for him, ach?"

Alma gave a shaky nod, even as her eyes seemed suddenly fixed to the sight of Baldr's tall, broad, fully bared body, standing so close and shameless and dripping wet. With that smooth, plump heft at his groin jutting out straight toward her, and—Alma's breath caught—already pooling white at the tip.

Alma bit her lip, her eyes guiltily darting up to his flushed face—but oh, his smile was so warm, so sheepish, so *hungry*. His own eyes briefly dropping down Alma's equally bared front, as his hand eased down to circle around his dripping heft, and slowly squeezed up. Milking out more of that thick white, and oh, he wanted her to look, he wanted to—

"Ach, Bright-Heart," he murmured, as he abruptly dropped his hand, and reached behind him for a large cloth—a towel—and tossed it toward her. "You are far too beautiful, you ken."

Alma choked a strange-sounding laugh—no one had ever called her beautiful before, *ever*—and began wiping herself dry with clumsy-feeling hands. "You're the beautiful one, Baldr," she said thickly. "And far too kind, as well."

Baldr had snatched for a second towel, riffling it through his wet hair, his face gone even redder than before. And though he swiped for his trousers, clutching them in his fingers, he didn't actually make any move to dress, his eyes now searching toward the corridor.

And that—Alma yanked her own towel close—was because Drafli was here. Stalking tall and bare-chested through the door, and then pausing, his mouth pursed, as his glinting eyes swept over the room. Over his mate, standing there fully bared, with that heft now visibly bobbing at his groin—and beside him, a slightly quivering Alma, clutching her towel against the proof of her shame. Her *guilt*.

Drafli's lip slightly curled as he looked at her, the contempt flashing through his eyes—and beside Alma, Baldr cleared his throat, and strode straight toward him. Not stopping until he'd tucked himself close against Drafli's stiff form, his arms circling around his waist, his face ducking into his neck.

"*Finally*, Draf," Baldr said, his voice barely audible. "Did not expect you to take so long, ach?"

And once again, Alma could almost feel Drafli's tension pooling away, his shoulders sagging. One of his clawed hands sinking into Baldr's wet hair, the other sliding around to grip with proprietary ease against his firm bare arse. And when he bent his head back toward Baldr's, Alma realized Drafli was actually speaking to him, though she couldn't hear even a whisper.

But Baldr had given a reflexive shudder against Drafli, a low, heated growl hissing from his throat—to which Drafli looked grimly pleased, his hand tightening on Baldr's arse. Until his eyes abruptly lifted, finding Alma's—and the pure, glittering hatred in them felt almost alive, like something that desperately longed to devour her. To *destroy* her.

And far too late, Baldr's demand—his ultimatum— swarmed to the front of Alma's thoughts. *You will honour Drafli. Seek to make a friend of him. One month.*

So Alma desperately attempted a smile toward Drafli, and even a stupid little wave—which only had the effect of flaring even more contempt across his furious eyes. *Foolish woman*, they seemed to say. *Silly. Worthless. I hate you.*

Alma's gaze belatedly dropped, while damnable wetness pooled behind her eyes, and she was vaguely aware of Baldr pulling away from Drafli to look at her. And when she gave another chagrined glance up, that was surely concern on Baldr's face, while Drafli betrayed an unmistakable grimace.

"Are you all right, Bright-Heart?" Baldr asked, while behind him, Drafli gave a small but purposeful twitch of his head, his eyes on Alma's now hard and urgent with meaning. Saying, surely, *You're fine*, and also, *Come here, now.*

"I'm fine," Alma managed, and she stumbled over toward them, as though being pulled by a string. "I'm just—I realized that I'm still—undressed. In public."

And while still foolish, surely that had been the right thing to say, because Baldr's concern had softened into understanding, while Drafli's urgency now looked more like grudging relief.

"Ach, we know comfort with this shall take time," Baldr replied. "Do you wish to again dress, until we reach our room?"

Their room. A sudden shiver of fear—or perhaps anticipation—wrenched up Alma's back, as Baldr gave her another too-understanding smile. "But as I told you, there is no shame in any of this," he said. "Ach, Draf?"

Drafli's expression had again shifted, his eyes on Baldr gone half-lidded and surprisingly light, his mouth quirking at the corner. And then, as Alma blinked, he reached down to grasp that still-jutting hardness at Baldr's groin—and then, keeping his hand gripped tight, he turned, and walked toward the door.

It meant that he was pulling Baldr—by *that*—out into the public corridor. Like *that*. And Baldr wasn't even pretending to argue, and instead shot Alma a rueful glance over his shoulder as Drafli drew his fully bared body out the door.

"You come too, ach?" he called, and Alma belatedly hurried to grasp her robe, wrapping it tightly around herself as she rushed to catch up. Though it did seem rather ridiculous to be worrying about her own propriety, when the orc beside her was being led down the corridor by his—well.

But Baldr certainly didn't seem to mind, his face gone even more flushed than before, his eyes lingering with visible hunger on Drafli's straight back, on the strangely compelling casualness in Drafli's easy, silent gait. In the way he coolly nodded at a random passing orc, who stared openly toward Alma, but didn't even seem to notice the shocking sight beside her.

But Alma couldn't seem to stop noticing. How Baldr's big, brawny body seemed even more coiled and muscular than before, despite being so clearly overpowered. How his breaths were coming even heavier, his glances between Drafli and Alma dark and hungry, his rich scent seeming to twine through the air around him. And wait, he was even leaking white liquid into Drafli's hand, which Drafli was occasionally using to slide up his plump length, the movements careless but intentional, as if slicking him with his own seed...

And then it occurred to Alma, sudden and hot, that this was exactly the same way Drafli had led her to their room the day before. Except that it had been the sash of her robe, rather than... *that*. And as the corridor deepened into full darkness—

closer, closer—there was the odd, wondering question of whether Drafli had... liked that? *Wanted* that?

But then they were already turning, Drafli leading Baldr sideways, while Alma silently followed. Into that same room, *their* room. This time already illuminated with several tall candles, casting a flickering orange glow over the stone walls, and the huge, fur-covered bed.

Drafli's strides hadn't faltered, pulling Baldr straight toward that bed—and then glancing, narrow and purposeful, toward Alma. While jerking his head toward the bed, making his meaning very, very clear.

Go on, it meant. *On the bed.*

And though Alma took a tentative step closer, her heart was suddenly roaring in her chest, her eyes wide and unblinking on Drafli's stern, commanding face. While the memories from the day before seemed to crash over her all at once, hard enough to make her sway on her feet.

The way he'd touched her. The way he'd taunted her. The blazing hunger, the power, in his eyes. *Look what I've brought for you. Show her. Oh, my lord. Oh, please. More.*

You did not smell him, Baldr had said, *when we were in the midst of this. Had it not been for the strength of how he tasted...*

And was it there again in Drafli's glimmering eyes, perhaps, perhaps it... *was*. Perhaps there was still hope. One month, to gain Drafli's trust. To obey. To *honour*.

So Alma gathered her courage, and silently nodded. And then she dropped her robe, raised her head, and walked toward the bed.

She could feel their eyes on her, prickling over her bare breasts, her hips, her arse—and her heart seemed to thunder even louder as she carefully sat on the bed, and looked back toward them. Toward where Baldr suddenly looked just as nervous as she felt, his tooth biting his lip, his eyes angling toward Drafli—while Drafli looked even more dangerous, more determined, than before. His glinting gaze still fixed on Alma, his jaw tight, his hands betraying perhaps the faintest tremble as they snapped out something—surely an order—in the air between them.

It was too swift for Alma to follow, her eyes again darting toward Baldr—and she could feel his swallow, could almost taste his hunger, unspooling sharp but uncertain beneath her swarmed-hot skin.

"Drafli wishes you to lie back, Bright-Heart," Baldr whispered, "so he can grant your maidenhead to me."

21

Lie back, so he can grant your maidenhead to me.

Alma didn't know how long she stared at Baldr, while he stared back toward her. While the nervousness, the uncertainty, the fear, seemed to swell higher, shouting with every hammer-strike of her desperate heart. They were going to do that? Here? Now?

And gods curse her, but *how*? Alma had truly never witnessed such things in her life, it had all been furtive whispers, laced with lewdness and mockery. And that—that *thing* of Baldr's, still lying thick and swollen in Drafli's familiar fingers, was so intimidating, and so damned massive, so how—*how*—

When between them, Drafli rolled his eyes, gave an exasperated-sounding sigh, and took a sudden, swift step toward Alma on the bed. His clawed hand snapping out, snatching for her *neck*—and then slightly *pressing*. Guiding her upper body down and back, toward the furs beneath her.

But despite its abruptness, the movement was thankfully gentle, even reassuring. And as Alma sagged back against the bed, with Drafli's warm strong hand still circled firm around her throat, she almost—as bizarre as it was—felt herself relaxing. Her eyes softening on Drafli's hard face, her mouth twitching into something that might have been a *smile*.

And in return, as Drafli blinked down toward her, surely, that was... comprehension. Recognition. An instant's unmistakable acknowledgement that he saw. He *understood*.

But then his gaze swept intently away, to Baldr. And when he waved Baldr toward the foot of the bed, the movement curt and commanding, Baldr instantly obliged, awkwardly kneeling his big body on the furs, very near to Alma's feet. But he didn't otherwise move, or make to touch her—and once again, Alma could almost taste his trepidation, his fear, ringing far too close to her own.

But she had Drafli's touch, while Baldr didn't, and there was an odd, tenuous safety in that—and Alma found herself swallowing, the movement convulsing against Drafli's hand.

"Are you—still sure you wish to, Baldr?" she heard herself blurt out, hoarse. "I mean—I certainly wouldn't blame you if you'd changed your mind, or—or you'd rather wait, or go about it differently—"

Baldr blinked down at her, once, and then his gaze flicked, brief but meaningful, to Drafli. "Ach, I wish to," he replied, just as hoarse. "I only—I also have never before—done this, thus. *Taking*."

His face had flushed even redder, his eyes on Drafli gone almost guilty this time—but Drafli's face remained cool, implacable, as his hand slipped away from Alma's neck, and reached over to brush against Baldr's mouth. Earning a harsh, heated gasp from Baldr, his lashes wildly fluttering—and then a low, guttural groan as Drafli leaned in, and... *kissed* him.

It was slow, soft, surprisingly sweet—but Alma could see their kiss deepening, hardening, as Drafli's hand slid into Baldr's hair, drawing him closer. His tongue clearly slipping into Baldr's mouth, his sharp teeth scraping against Baldr's lips, while Baldr moaned and clutched at him, his claws digging into Drafli's bare shoulder, the still-swollen sight at his groin visibly bobbing with hunger.

When Drafli finally pulled away, there was a trickle of red running down Baldr's chin, and his previously fearful eyes had gone heavy and glittering. Looking at Drafli with a hard, worshipful longing that felt almost painful, plummeting something deep in Alma's belly.

"Will you grant her a kiss thus, also, Draf?" Baldr murmured, his voice husky and melodious, as his eyes glanced toward—toward *Alma*. "Please?"

And suddenly the hazy hunger swarming the room had cleared away, leaving even more uneasy fear in its wake. While Drafli's body beside Alma had gone very, very still, every muscle locked and clenched, as though he might bolt for the door at any moment—

"Please?" Baldr said again, as something shifted in his watching eyes—something that perhaps hinted at *suspicion*. And surely Drafli saw it too, because he was already inclining his head toward Baldr, his hand making a motion that perhaps meant, *Very well*—and then he turned, slow and controlled, to face Alma.

And Alma could see, while Baldr now surely couldn't, how the tolerant warmth had entirely vanished from Drafli's eyes, leaving only a cold, dangerous fury behind. Very clearly telling her, *I will do this, but only for him. Not you.*

And gods, Alma might have even nodded, her head bobbing against the fur still behind it, her heart again galloping in her chest. She could manage kissing Drafli, surely. And should she sit up again, should she meet him, what the hell was she supposed to *do*—

When suddenly, Drafli was here. Bent down over her, so close. His long fingers cradling her jaw, tilting her head up—

And that, oh gods, was his *mouth*. His warm, supple, succulent mouth, brushing gently against hers, tasting of iron and sweetness...

Alma reflexively gasped, parting her lips further—and oh gods, oh hell, that was Drafli's *tongue*. Feeling impossibly long and slick and powerful, curling like that *into her mouth*. And her gasp this time might have been a groan, escaping dark and betraying from her throat.

That was surely a silent scoff, or even a laugh, from Drafli's mouth against hers—but he still didn't pull away. His lips and tongue now moving together, exploring her, caressing her, willing her to open more for his taking. And it was like Alma was falling apart beneath it, like the rest of the world had shattered away, and she just needed more, more, *more*—

But then it was—gone. *Drafli* was gone, pulling just slightly up and away from her, his long braid tickling at her cheek, his eyes still cold and mocking on hers. As if to say, *Fool woman, so spineless, so weak, to give so much for a kiss*—

And without thinking, without at all realizing what she'd done, Alma lurched up, and found his mouth again. Meeting those warm, clever lips once more, tasting their impossible sweetness on hers. And for the briefest of instants, that was surely his tongue again, sliding out to brush against hers, almost as if he wanted to taste her again, too—

But then there was something sharp, nipping hard and painful at her lip, and strong fingers, clamping again at her neck, shoving her away. And when Alma's blinking eyes focused again, Drafli was sitting up, scowling back down toward her, with yet more rage in his eyes, and fresh *blood* smeared against his lips.

"*Draf*," croaked a voice—Baldr's voice—and both Alma and Drafli snapped to look at once. To where Baldr's eyes seemed to be shifting between rapt and reproachful, flicking from Drafli's mouth, to Alma's, and back again. "Be gentle with her, ach? Did he hurt you, Bright-Heart?"

Alma belatedly brushed her tongue against her lip—good gods, he really had *bitten* her—but Drafli's eyes on her were hard and mulish, his jaw set. And it didn't really hurt—really only a sting, and it was already rapidly fading—and Alma shook her head, and tried for a smile toward Baldr's worried face.

Baldr smiled too, his relief almost palpable, his own bitten lip still steadily dripping red down his chin. "Drafli does not always bear sudden movements well, ach?" he said to her, soft. "You ought to ask first, until he grants you leave otherwise. And we cannot take his kisses from him thus, for these are gifts, ach? Rewards, for when we please him."

We. It should have been absurd—that *was* absurd, they had rules for kissing, that Alma was now expected to follow?—but her mouth still felt strangely tingly and swollen, and Baldr's eyes on hers were quietly serious. While Drafli still looked angry... but behind that, perhaps almost wary, too. He *feared* women, Baldr had said.

"R-right," Alma stammered, to Drafli's eyes, her voice not quite her own. "For-forgive me, I—I didn't realize. That was just—very lovely, and I didn't—I didn't expect—"

Gods, what was she even *saying*, and she was thoroughly unsurprised to see yet more contempt, flaring through Drafli's frowning eyes. But down by her feet, Baldr gave a choked little laugh, his hand brushing gently against her bare ankle.

"This was your first kiss, ach, Bright-Heart?" he murmured. "Draf is good at this, is he not?"

Alma gratefully nodded toward Baldr, and yes, surely that was understanding, wry and rueful in his eyes. "So you shall seek to please him," he continued, "so he shall kiss you again, ach?"

Oh. Yes. Yes, Alma would, surely, and she felt herself nodding again, her eyes darting to Drafli's this time. To where he didn't look quite so contemptuous as before, but perhaps more commanding, as he coolly dropped his hand to her bare thigh, and smoothly pulled it to the side.

Alma's body was suddenly shivering—they were doing this, already?—but yes, clearly, they were, because Drafli's hand had swept to her other thigh, and spread it wide, too. Opening up everything in between, showing it brazen and obscene for Baldr's blinking, watching eyes—and Alma could see Baldr's throat bobbing, his gaze suddenly fixed, frozen, on the sight.

And for a fraught, horrible instant, Alma could again almost taste Baldr's unease, his rapidly rising panic. His body gone rigid, his clawed hand rubbing at his mouth, his wide eyes flicking a look toward Drafli that felt almost pleading.

Drafli surely saw it, huffing out a heavy, impatient-sounding sigh—and then he smoothly slid his hand down between Alma's spread thighs. The movement easy and capable, finding her slick, exposed heat with familiar, proprietary ease.

There was no teasing this time, no warning. Only those warm, deft fingers settling against the place they wanted, deep within Alma's parted crease—and then driving up inside. Filling her with sudden, shocking tightness, dragging a help-less cry from her mouth—but if Drafli noticed, he didn't acknowledge it. And instead began slipping those fingers in and out of her, efficient and purposeful, and now even spreading even wider, pressing her apart.

Baldr was blatantly looking again, his eyes hooded and hungry, his tooth biting at his still-dripping lip. Watching Drafli's fingers as they plunged into her, played with her, made wet, obscene sounds with her. And then, as Baldr stared, Alma could feel yet another finger, brushing alongside the first two—and then that sank inside, too, while she arched and cried out, far too loud and shameful, with three whole orc-fingers buried deep between her legs.

And curse him, but this time Drafli held them there, watching her writhe and gasp upon him, while certain amuse-ment flashed in his eyes—and then, oh gods, he did it all again. Dipping and swirling those three fingers against her, inside her, stretching her open around them. Truly making a wet, blub-bering spectacle of her, her entire body flailing and clamping and leaking upon him, lost to his callous humiliation, his amusement, his contempt.

And when she felt his fourth finger brushing up against her, so much, so menacing, Alma bore down hard, and some-how—somehow—pushed him away, out of her altogether. But her triumph was short-lived, because Drafli coolly raised his brows at her, and only began teasing her open again, impaling her easily now on his three fingers, while her clenching, mind-less heat clutched at him, milked at him, drowning.

"He seeks to open you for me, Bright-Heart," Baldr breathed, his voice hitching, his hand skating against his own swollen, dripping hardness, still jutting out from his groin. "If you wish for this, you shall welcome him, ach? Drink him deep inside you? For me?"

Damn him, but it was the right—*wrong*—thing to say, because it fired another furious, glorious thrill up Alma's back, and sent a hard rush of blood toward her still-impaled heat. Enough that she felt herself jerking a shaky, furtive nod toward Drafli's cold eyes, telling him, perhaps, *Very well*—and then even making the sign, with her jittery, tingling hand. *I understand.*

Something shifted in Drafli's eyes, his fourth finger again settling close and menacing against her—but this time, like Baldr had wanted, Alma sought to welcome him. To drink him. To feel herself being filled with orc, taught to accommodate him, to please him. To hold her gaze to his eyes, to show him her trust, her obedience, as he slowly sank those four long, powerful orc fingers inside her.

"Good woman," she heard Baldr breathe, as Drafli held his fingers there, her body stretched and pinioned and frantically clamping upon them. "Good. You are so pretty, opened so wide thus upon him."

Alma gasped a desperate moan, but she couldn't seem to look away from Drafli's cold, commanding eyes. Saying, surely, *Yes, I am opening you as I please, and yes, you will welcome it for me. Yes, you will shout for me, you will long for me, you will be mine*—

Alma was nodding back, again making the sign for *I understand*, her eyes reverently blinking toward Drafli's face, the pleasure rising, rocking, roiling. And if he would hold it there, hold her there, keep her like this, warm and stretched and safe upon him, for only one more moment—

But then, no, *no*, he was gone. Pulled out. Away. Leaving her swollen, quivering body entirely empty and untouched. While Drafli coolly leaned toward Baldr, brought up his hand, and slipped a wet, glistening, pink-streaked finger deep between Baldr's parted, gasping lips.

Baldr sucked it off without hesitation, his lashes fluttering, his eyes blazing on Drafli's—and then again, as Drafli fed him the next one, and again. Until Baldr had licked all Drafli's fingers clean, and had even ducked his head to lap at Drafli's palm, as though drinking up every last drop.

Alma's heartbeat was lurching again, her thwarted craving still juddering and jolting through her still-sprawled body, escaping in a guttural moan—and after another instant, both orcs looked back toward her at once. Drafli's eyes wholly unreadable, Baldr's with a burning, barrelling hunger.

And when Drafli's hands dropped to Alma's trembling thighs, spreading them wider, she didn't resist—even when it showed Baldr more of her shame, now stretched and slick and slavering for him. And when Drafli reached for Baldr, and nudged him over to kneel between Alma's splayed thighs, Baldr didn't resist that either, his eyes still fixed and fluttering on what Drafli had opened for him.

Drafli was waving him forward—*Do it*, he meant, *take what I am giving you*—but Baldr had once again stilled, his eyes catching on Alma's flushed, hot face. And again, flaring to life between them, was the uncertainty. The fear. Perhaps even... the *guilt*?

Until beside them, Drafli once again huffed a harsh, exasperated sigh—and then he reached one hand down for Baldr's thick, bobbing, leaking heft, and the other for Alma's clenching, empty heat. And as Alma and Baldr both stared, frozen and gasping, Drafli's deft fingers spread Alma even wider, and then drew Baldr forward, and settled his slick, sputtering pink tip against her.

Alma's moan sounded more like a shout, scraping high over Baldr's low, rasping growl—but oh, they were still touching, he was still there, still jutted up warm and alive against her. And it felt so different than Drafli's fingers had, so much smoother and sweeter, and she could actually *feel* him pulsing against her, spluttering that thick liquid straight into her grasping, greedy caress.

"Oh gods," Alma gulped, as another desperate, wracking shudder shook her all over, coiling in the clutch of her body against Baldr's, in the responding sustained vibration of that slick head against her. "Oh please. *Please.*"

And she wasn't looking at Baldr now, but back at *Drafli*. Drafli, who was somehow—impossibly—looking cool and unaffected, as he arched a brow toward her. And then he calmly drew his hand away from her, and made a familiar, circular motion, all distant, composed command.

Keep going, it surely said. *Beg me to give him to you.*

Again, Alma was nodding—and even signing, *I understand*—as she gulped for air, for words. "Please, my lord," she managed. "Please, give him to me."

Between her legs, Baldr had given another low, throaty groan, that slick head again vibrating hard against her—but somehow she knew he wouldn't defy Drafli on this, either. He would wait, he would obey, as long as it took...

"Please," Alma gasped again, her blinking eyes held to Drafli's, to that smug, dismissive smirk on his mouth. "He feels so good. So—so—"

There weren't even words, suddenly, only chaos, only Baldr's shuddering heft against her, the sputtering liquid now slipping thick down her open crease—but Drafli again made that *keep going* sign. Even as Alma felt—saw—his other hand stroking up and down the rest of Baldr's pulsing length against her, as if to comfort him, to claim him.

He's still mine, it meant, *even if he's almost inside you.*

"I know he's yours," Alma breathed, begged, her eyes now pinned to the breathtaking sight. "I know. I can only have what you give me. But you can give me to him too, my lord, can't you? You can"—she dragged for more air—"you can give him my maidenhead, please, because it's *yours.*"

And oh, yes, yes, that was what Drafli wanted, and that was satisfaction—*approval*—flaring across his glittering eyes. And when those eyes next slid toward Baldr, brows still raised, he didn't even need to ask—because Baldr was already clearing his throat, and fervently nodding.

"Please, Draf," he croaked. "Please, grant me this. You know it is still you. Always you. Ach?"

Oh. And even as the truth of those words scraped somewhere deep in Alma's brain, far closer was Drafli's slow nod, the triumph curling at his mouth. The glance toward her that surely said, *Think upon that, fool woman, while I break your maidenhead upon him.*

But Alma didn't care right now, she couldn't—because Drafli's hands had moved again, one settling on Baldr's arse, one stroking against where Baldr's spluttering head was still nudged up against her shuddering, waiting heat. And then, keeping his eyes steady on Baldr's, Drafli slowly, smoothly, drew him forward toward her.

It meant he was pushing Baldr against her, *inside her*, that slick, rounded head sinking its way deeper, breath by breath. And it felt utterly unreal, it felt impossible, like a whirling towering invasion, like being seized, split apart. Like being impaled on something huge and foreign and strange, something hot and hard and alive, and Alma was fighting it, craving it, clutching it, milking it...

And oh, oh, Baldr's *face*. His glimmering eyes, his sharp tooth again biting at his already-marred lip. His big body finally leaning forward over her, his hands skittering against the furs beside her shoulders, his huge, throbbing heft now half-buried between her legs.

"Ach, Bright-Heart," he breathed, his gleaming chest heaving, every muscle taut and ridged in the candlelight. "Ach. You feel so good. So sweet. So *alive*, upon me."

Alma had to gulp for more air, desperately nodding beneath him, as her hand fluttered up to brush against his face—and then froze in midair, just in time, her eyes darting toward Drafli beside them. Asking his permission to touch his mate, because surely that still mattered, even now.

To her surprise, Drafli gave her a curt, jerky nod, his gaze flicking purposefully away, even as she felt his hand spasming down between them—and Alma was taking it, oh she was taking it, her fingers finally, finally stroking Baldr's beautiful face, feeling the smoothness of his skin, the hard lines beneath. And then sliding against his scarred neck, his broad shoulders, the strength of his upper arms as he held himself above her.

"You feel so good too," she whispered, arching and gasping as Drafli's hand between them kept guiding him deeper, deeper, *oh*. "Both of you. You—you feel like... life. Like *home*."

Perhaps that was the wrong thing to say, spasming like that across Baldr's mouth—but when Alma's hands fluttered back up to stroke against his face, he bent into her touch, his eyes squeezing shut, his exhale shuddering from his lips.

His hardness halfway inside her was still shuddering too, vibrating powerfully from base to tip, and Alma could almost feel the liquid wringing out, soaking her, easing his way. Drawing him forward, fuller and tighter and deeper, until she was shouting again, her stretched, invaded body flailing and convulsing upon him, surely pushed to its limit—

And yes, Baldr had stopped again, his tooth again biting his lip, his body wedged so tight within hers. But still not all the way, because surely it was too much, surely she couldn't possibly take any more—so why was she looking at Drafli like this, pleading at his oddly distant eyes, at where they were staring off at something beyond them.

"Please, my lord," she whispered, snapping his gaze back toward her. "N-need you. *Please.*"

And what was she saying, and why was she relaxing at that shift in his eyes, that contemptuous little curl on his mouth. At the feel of his hand again spasming between them, guiding Alma even wider apart, pushing Baldr deeper...

There was a dense, dull ache now, whispering deep within, but somehow Alma was welcoming it, pressing into it, into them. Into Drafli's clever touch, into Baldr's brutal invasion, opening herself up, deeper and deeper, *theirs*...

And with one last, heavy push, Baldr sank fully inside her. His warm groin, those full bollocks, lodged tight against her, against Drafli's hand still caught between them. Jamming Alma impossibly full, her writhing body stuffed to bursting, her maidenhead irrevocably pierced, forever changed, in this screaming, impossible moment.

And surely there was no moving beyond this, no way for Baldr to risk drawing out again, without blood or pain—and even a small, tentative circle of his groin against hers swirled up more of that ache, scrabbling against the burning, beautiful pleasure.

Beside them, Drafli's hand had moved in a shaky-looking gesture toward Baldr—*stay*, it surely meant—while his other hand, the one still wedged between them, began to circle, slow but steady, against Alma. Just above where Baldr was stuffing her full, that deft warm palm circling again and again, pooling up yet more juddering swarms of heat beneath it. Wringing up something even higher and hotter, closer and brighter, and Alma was babbling again, begging him, writhing against his touch his mate his control, the silent, snapped-out motion of his other hand, surely an order, one Alma couldn't at all understand.

"He commands you to reach your peak for him," Baldr's voice gasped at her, between frayed-sounding breaths. "To milk the seed from me. Now."

Oh. Oh. And those words, that command, the flash in Drafli's eyes, one last, powerful circle of his palm—and Alma was screaming, and breaking apart. Her body writhing up, clamping again and again against the shuddering heat invading it, each convulsive beat a rush of trammelling ecstasy—and oh, gods above, suddenly Baldr was breaking, too. That rammed-tight heft flailing and jerking inside her, pumping out his molten liquid deep within, while his head arched back, his eyes shut tight, his teeth bared with his hoarse, guttural howl.

It went on for far longer than Alma would have thought, his pulses inside her coming slower and slower—until finally, they subsided. And Alma could feel him softening, the pressure steadily lessening—but in its place, there was a slick, sticky wetness, already seeping out between them, pooling onto the furs below.

Alma's breaths were badly heaving, her eyes blinking hard at Baldr's taut body still over her, at his flushed cheeks, his closed eyes, the sweat glistening on his face and his chest. At his tooth once again biting his lip, his head twitching back and forth, his shoulders erratically convulsing with his breaths.

Alma's uncertain glance at Drafli found him studying Baldr too, his brow furrowed—and he swiftly leaned up, and then guided Baldr back, away. Drawing him out of Alma's still-quivering heat, the movement slow and gentle and still oddly painful, emptying her breath by breath—and with a humiliating squelching sound, Baldr finally slipped out entirely, while a furious rush of hot, sticky liquid bubbled out in his wake.

Alma couldn't seem to move, her body sprawled and stunned as it kept spurting out what he'd left inside her. And there was the jolting, distant realization that Drafli's hand was still there, still curved against her, feeling his mate's seed streaming through his fingers. Almost as though he—liked it, there. Wanted it there.

But Baldr still hadn't opened his eyes, his head still jerking back and forth—and Alma could feel Drafli's fingers briefly clenching against her as he leaned forward, his other hand tilting up Baldr's chin toward him. And then Drafli once again kissed him, the touch of his lips almost achingly soft and sweet, surely speaking of his approval. Of his reward.

You pleased me, it surely meant. *I love you, Pure-Heart.*

And suddenly Baldr seemed to flare to life again, his hard groan growling between them, his lips meeting Drafli's with almost panicked desperation. His clawed hands scraping against Drafli's chest, clinging to him as he drank his mouth—and then one hand fumbled down inside Drafli's trousers, dragging him out.

Alma only caught a glimpse of dark, scarred skin before Baldr's trembling hand closed around it, yanking up hard once, again—and oh, Drafli was already spraying out, spurting ropes of thick, sticky seed all over Baldr's bare chest and belly. While their mouths kept crushing together, Drafli's other hand still clamped close between Alma's legs.

And then, perhaps, it was over. With Drafli abruptly drawing away from both Baldr and Alma, yanking up his trousers, tying them with visibly shaky hands. While all the fervour in Baldr's body seemed to dissipate at once, his eyes again squeezing shut—and without warning, he collapsed down onto the bed beside Alma, rolling onto his back as he heaved for breath, his arm flung over his eyes.

Alma still felt strangely slow, stunned, as though the world had suddenly turned to water—and she couldn't seem to look away from Baldr, now lying so close beside her. At how his mouth was twisting, perhaps even trembling, as those hard, strange breaths kept shuddering through his bare chest.

He was—*weeping?*

But yes, yes, those were surely sobs, ripping from his mouth, even as he clearly tried to choke them away, to hide. And Alma's own misery was suddenly swarming with astonishing force, because did this mean he hadn't liked it, perhaps he'd been disappointed with it, with *her*?

Alma's panicked eyes were abruptly searching for Drafli—Drafli, who was now standing close beside the bed, and blinking down at Baldr. And for an instant, he looked nearly as panicked as Alma felt, his gaze sweeping wildly up and down Baldr's shuddering form—and then he actually flinched all over at the sound of a harsh, ragged sob, escaping from Baldr's mouth.

Alma had to do something, *something*, oh gods—and she grimaced as she tentatively touched a hand to Baldr's sticky, heaving chest, bracing for Drafli's response, his certain disapproval. But Drafli still wasn't even moving—he looked almost helpless—so Alma let her fingers spread wider, felt the strength of Baldr's thundering heart beneath.

"Baldr," she whispered, wavering. "Did I—did we—do anything wrong? Did we offend you? Hurt you?"

Another glance up at Drafli showed him still staring at Baldr, his eyes still so dark and wide, as if waiting, too, for this answer—and finally, thank the gods, Baldr shook his head behind his arm. "Nothing—wrong," he croaked, between breaths, his voice hitching. "Just too—too—"

He didn't finish, his mouth again contorting, his chest shuddering under Alma's hand, and she abruptly felt herself nodding, her own bottom lip trembling. "Too much?" she whispered, and Baldr's sharp, shaky nod was sheer, shining relief, flashing up her spine. And another glance at Drafli showed him looking unmistakably relieved, too, his shoulders dropping, his lashes fluttering heavy against his cheek.

"I fully agree," Alma heard herself say, her voice still quavering. "I have never—*ever*—felt anything like that in my *life*. It was so good, wasn't it? So *good*."

Baldr's chest heaved again, and he jerked a hard nod, under his arm—and when Alma shot another look at Drafli, this time he met her eyes, and signed an order at her. *Don't stop*, it meant. *Keep going.*

So Alma gulped down the still-present lump in her throat, spread her fingers wider against Baldr's sticky chest. "You were perfect," she whispered. "You were so, *so* beautiful. And now I'm completely convinced that I was right, and you truly are a *god*, Baldr."

She tried to make her voice light at the end, and yes, that might have been a bitter little twitch, at the corner of Baldr's mouth—and Alma didn't even need to look up to see Drafli's repeated order, out the corner of her eye. *Keep going.*

"And your mate," she breathed, with a furtive glance up toward his face, "is clearly a *devil*. Goading us like that. *Tormenting* us. Bringing us both firmly to heel, and laughing all the while."

And yes, surely that was another twitch on Baldr's mouth, higher this time—so Alma drew in more air, kept going, not quite daring to look at Drafli's face, now. "And you were right," she whispered, "because his kiss was *glorious*, and now I feel unfairly compelled to please him, so that I might earn another one. Or maybe"—she did meet Drafli's watching eyes this time—"I could earn another kiss for *you*, because seeing you two like that, it—"

She couldn't quite finish, her eyes now caught on Drafli—because while his expression wasn't quite approving, it surely wasn't *disapproving*, either. And there was perhaps even a hint of that familiar command again, as he casually waved his hand at Baldr's sticky, messy chest... and then jabbed his claw toward Alma's *mouth*.

"And *now*," Alma heard herself say, her mouth twitching too, her eyes still on Drafli's, "your devil is ordering me to *clean* you, Baldr. To lick off the mess he made of you, if I want to earn you another kiss."

Baldr spasmed beneath her, his arm very briefly lifting up, showing her narrow, reddened eyes, a sudden thinness on his lips—but before he could speak his certain protest, Drafli dropped a casual hand to clamp tightly over his mouth. And Alma's glance up toward Drafli was almost grateful this time, and she actually heard herself laugh, husky and low.

"No need to defend me," she murmured. "I'm happy to oblige him. I'd do far, *far* more than that, to please you."

But surely that was speaking too far, risking too much. And before she could foolishly betray anything else, she ducked her head to Baldr's sticky, still-heaving chest, and gave it a careful little lick.

And oh, Drafli's seed tasted just as good as she remembered—even better, maybe, mixed with the salt and musk of Baldr's silken skin. And Alma let out a slow, shaky sigh as she licked him again, broader, harder. Feeling gooseflesh rising beneath her tongue, Baldr's breath exhaling in a rush, and she chuckled another little laugh as she licked him again, again, again.

And thank the gods, she could feel Baldr relaxing as she did it, too. His breaths gradually steadying, his clawed hand even slipping into her hair. And surely, this was one of the most unreal moments of Alma's life, comforting her new lover by cleaning his mate's glorious-tasting sweetness off his chest, while said mate stood there, and dispassionately watched.

When she'd finally finished, leaving Baldr's chest sticky but clear, her jaw and tongue were aching, and her belly felt uncomfortably full—but Baldr's breaths were deep and slow again, his lips slightly parted. And Alma's glance toward Drafli was met with a short, almost imperceptible nod, as he bent down, and pressed a soft, gentle kiss to Baldr's mouth.

Baldr groaned, low and husky, arching up into it—and Drafli seemed to meet him with equal willingness, his hand spreading against Baldr's cheek, his tongue slipping deep. Giving as much as Baldr wanted, tasting, lingering, until the softened, glistening heft at Baldr's groin had swollen to full hardness again, dripping yet more wetness onto his still-sticky abdomen.

But just before Drafli pulled away, his gaze once again flicked toward Alma—and then, hard and meaningful, toward the door.

Get out, it surely meant. *Now. We're done.*

Oh. Alma's chest seemed to clamp against her ribs, her eyes fixed blankly to Drafli's face—he truly wanted her to *leave*, after all that?—but yes, yes, that was absolutely what he meant. His gaze purposefully holding on hers before dropping back to Baldr, his hand caressing Baldr's cheek as he gently drew away, pausing to brush a light kiss to the tip of Baldr's nose.

And it was that tiny, affectionate movement that finally made Alma swallow, and slide herself toward the edge of the bed. They were mated, they loved each other, and of course Drafli would want to keep comforting his mate without her interference. And when Baldr abruptly moved his arm from his face, blinking dazedly toward her with puffy, bloodshot eyes, Alma's smile toward him felt almost painfully genuine, wavering on her mouth.

"I think I ought to leave you two alone for a while," she said thickly. "Your mate will take good care of you, I'm sure. Perhaps I'll see you again tomorrow?"

Baldr's eyes still looked dazed, and perhaps a little disappointed, too—and Alma blinked back her own disappointment, and gave him another trembly smile. "This was so— lovely," she said, and though that was absolutely the wrong word, she couldn't seem to find anything else. "Thank you so much. Both of you."

With that, she spun, and frantically fled for the door—only to find that it had suddenly been blocked by Drafli. Drafli, feeling far too tall and intimidating, frowning down toward her, and clutching her forgotten robe in his claws.

Oh. Right. She hadn't even thought to dress—foolish,

foolish—and she gave him a wincing little grimace as she took the robe, and wrapped it around herself. And then made to step out around him, her head ducked low—but again, somehow Drafli was already there, blocking her path. And he wasn't even looking at her, but he was looking at Baldr, and signing something with his hands. Something thoroughly unexpected, that perhaps meant, *I shall take her back, you wait here.*

Baldr's response was languid enough that Alma could even follow it—*I understand, Golden-Tongue*, it meant—and then he cleared his throat, and again met Alma's eyes. "I thank you, for all these unthinkable gifts tonight," he rasped, his voice thick. "Sleep well, sweet Bright-Heart."

Alma attempted a smile back, but already Drafli was moving again, nudging her toward the door. So after one last, furtive little wave toward Baldr, she went, stepping out into the dark corridor, with Drafli close behind her.

But now it was over, really over, and as Alma walked, she again felt her head bowing, her thoughts fighting to ignore the feel of Baldr's hot slickness streaming down her thighs. He'd made love to her—*they'd* made love to her, they'd taken her *maidenhead*—and in the midst of it all, she'd thought that surely it was about more than just the contracts, the ultimatums, the bond, the son. That on that bed, in too many of those brutal, beautiful moments, they'd... seen each other. They'd... understood.

But that certainty was already wavering, faltering, draining away. Leaving only the cool, uncaring efficiency in Drafli's steps, the almost imperceptible press of his claws against her back, as he guided her down one corridor, and then into another. And now into an unfamiliar one, tilting downwards—and Alma blinked over her shoulder in the steadily increasing lamplight, searching Drafli's unreadable eyes.

"Where are you taking me?" she asked thickly. "This isn't the way back to the sickroom, is it?"

Surprise flared in Drafli's eyes, but it flattened just as quickly, his head giving a quick little shake. *No*, he mouthed at her, curt, his hand making a sign similar to *stop*. *I take you here.*

Here, it turned out, was a small, low passageway, leading into utter darkness—but then there was a candle-flame, flaring to life beneath Drafli's claws. And in the flickering light, Alma could see a small, unfamiliar, stone-walled room, furnished with a surprising assortment of wooden, human-made furniture—a bed, a shelf, a chair, a trunk. There were no other visible belongings, beyond a wash-basin, a chamber-pot, and the candle Drafli was setting on the shelf—but the bed was generously covered with soft-looking furs, and even a familiar-looking pillow. And wait, was that the pillow Alma had had in the sickroom? And beside it, her waterskin?

Alma shot Drafli a confused, questioning look, which he blatantly ignored—and instead, he reached over and plucked away her robe, and tossed it aside. Not sparing a single cursory look at her bared, dripping body as he waved her toward the bed, the command sharp and imperious.

Get in, fool woman, he might as well have said. *If you cannot follow this, there is no hope for you.*

Right. He had promised to give her a room in the Grisk wing, hadn't he? So no more sickroom, then, no more comforting awareness of Kesst and Efterar while she slept. And Alma felt herself give a weary little nod, her hand signing *I understand*, as she went for the bed, and slipped her sore body beneath the furs.

And gods, she *was* sore, especially down there, and exhausted, and suddenly, horribly miserable. She'd given Baldr and Drafli her maidenhead, she'd kept to both their terms, she'd done everything she possibly could to please them—or so she'd thought. But now, blinking up at the unfamiliar stone ceiling with watery eyes, there was the sinking, bitter realization that perhaps this was how it would be. She would keep trying, keep working, keep fighting to please them—and it would never be enough. She would always be foolish and worthless, she would only earn dismissal and disdain, she would be their *servant*—

When above her, something moved. *Drafli* moved. His tall, silent body standing close over her, his eyes shifting, distant, entirely unreadable—

And then he bent down, and *kissed* her. His mouth so soft, so gentle, so sweet, his tongue brushing against hers, his long fingers skating against her cheek. Just the same way he'd kissed Baldr, oh gods—and just like Baldr, Alma felt herself arching up to meet it, her tense body unspooling beneath it, her moan gasping hoarse and desperate into his mouth.

He drew back far too soon, and though his mouth released hers with astonishing gentleness, Alma was sure he would mock her again, meet her with coldness and contempt. *Fool woman, to give so much for a kiss*—

But then he—didn't. He only stood there for another long moment, his breath exhaling in a slow sigh—and then he signed something toward her. Something new, something that had the flat of his hand pressing against his heart, and then tightening into a fist, as he silently mouthed the words, so she could understand.

Thank you, he said. *This honoured me.*

And with that, he spun around, snuffed out the candle, and stalked out of the room. Leaving Alma stunned and silent and blinking in the darkness, her lips still tingling, still whispering their memory of his kiss.

22

Despite Alma's exhaustion, it took far too long for sleep to come that night.

She couldn't seem to stop dwelling, lingering over Drafli and Baldr's words, their touches, the way they'd felt. The way they'd opened her, filled her, poured this truth inside her. Like a gift. An offering.

And here in the safety of the darkness, Alma's trembling fingers were even slipping down to the mess still between her legs, feeling the raw, undeniable truth of it. How it felt so tender, stretched open, her maidenhead forever gone—and in its place, this. An orc's seed. And perhaps, an orc's *son*.

And though none of them had again mentioned the son, the weight of him had surely still hung there, hovering so heady and powerful above them. This was their bargain. Their contract. And that was all.

But as Alma's fingers slid a little deeper into her clenching heat, feeling yet more thick liquid pooling out onto them, the certainty of that was wavering again. The way Baldr had looked at her. The way he'd touched her. And most of all, the way Drafli had kissed her. *Thank you. This honoured me.*

Maybe—maybe there was still hope. Maybe she could still do this. One month.

So Alma clung to that, cleaved to that, as her slick hand skated back up her front, and found her mouth. As a rich, musky new flavour—*Baldr's* flavour—flashed across her tongue, dragging a hoarse, hungry moan from her throat.

It led to her blatantly seeking her own pleasure, shuddering beneath the furs, her dripping-wet fingers slipping again and again into her mouth. And when relief finally came, with it came enough sagging exhaustion that Alma finally, finally closed her eyes, and slipped into sleep.

She had no idea how long she slept, or when she woke again—but when her eyes blinked open, it was to the realization that two people were striding into the room. One of them was carrying a lamp—it was Drafli again, Alma realized, bare-chested as usual, with his gleaming sword strapped to his hip—and the person behind him was... Efterar?

"Morning, woman," Efterar said to her, giving a curt nod, and a brief, approving glance around at the room. "Nice new little place you've got here. Your Skai wanted me to come see you, though I can't see why you couldn't—"

He broke off there, his nose wrinkling, his eyes flicking down toward Alma's body beneath her fur. "Ah," he amended. "Right. Do you mind if I take a look at you, then? Settle any pain or swelling?"

Alma was still blinking between them, caught on that odd mention of *Your Skai*, on the way Drafli's cold eyes were very intently not meeting hers. On how his hands had thrust down the lamp onto the shelf, and were now giving a sharp, imperious motion toward her fur.

Off with it, he meant. *Now.*

Alma's face flushed hot—Drafli wanted it off, in front of Efterar?—but yes, that was most certainly what he meant, and he'd even made the motion again, more impatient this time. So

Alma gingerly slid down the fur, exposing her still-bare, slightly trembling body to the room.

But as Efterar came a step closer, his eyes narrowing on her groin only showed a detached, assessing watchfulness. "Looks like they were careful with you, at least," he said, "but that should still be healed. Mind if I touch you, Grisk?"

Grisk again. Alma's face was still burning, her eyes darting an uncertain glance toward Drafli. Who didn't, in fact, seem to be arguing this Grisk point, but was instead signing something else toward Efterar. Something that perhaps meant, *No. You don't touch her. Never.*

"What?" Efterar replied, frowning at Drafli with obvious confusion. "I thought you *wanted* me to heal her?"

Anger snapped across Drafli's eyes, and he made the signs again—but Efterar only looked more confused, and this time glanced uncertainly toward Alma. And after belatedly clearing her throat, she attempted what she hoped was a conciliatory smile.

"Er, I think Drafli means he would rather you didn't touch," she said carefully. "If possible. Please."

Drafli didn't even acknowledge that Alma had spoken, and kept his narrow eyes steady on Efterar. But Efterar was thankfully nodding, and now jerking a wave toward Drafli. "Didn't think you Skai cared about that," he said, with a shrug. "Over your hand, then?"

Alma wasn't following, now, but Drafli made a face, and then stepped closer, beside the bed. And then, to her complete astonishment, he nudged her thighs apart, and dropped his hand deep between them. Curving flat over her. *Covering* her.

It was a deeply humiliating position, especially with Efterar still standing right there, and with Alma's still-wet, still-swollen body suddenly clenching and spasming against Drafli's touch. Almost as if greeting him, or *wanting* him there, oh gods—and his brief, chilly glance toward her eyes said that he absolutely knew it, and couldn't care less.

Alma's face surely could not go even hotter, but it somehow did anyway, especially when Efterar's big hand dropped down to cover Drafli's, his eyes intent on whatever he saw behind their fingers. While also surely seeing how Alma's humiliating heat was still gripping and clutching at Drafli, blatantly begging him, craving him.

Her thoughts had somehow streaked back to the night before, to the gentleness of Drafli's kiss, the truth of his approval. And how now this—this dismissive detachment, written all over his body and eyes—should likely have been insulting, or upsetting, but instead felt like something else entirely.

"That should do it, then," Efterar finally said, as he drew his hand away. "Do you feel any pain, Grisk? In or out?"

He and Drafli were both looking at Alma now, Drafli with a rather mocking arch to his brows—and before she could reply, Drafli smoothly slid a finger *inside* her. Moving it around, up and down and sideways, as if testing this, the utter bastard— and Alma barely choked back her moan, and somehow twitched a shaky nod.

"Er, all good, thank you," she croaked toward Efterar. "Very grateful to you. Again."

Efterar gave a dismissive wave, his eyes now flicking to Alma's neck. "Just keep taking care of your throat," he said. "Keep it up with that sign language, so you can give your voice a break. And I'd still like you to come by the sickroom regularly, so I can look you over."

Alma nodded and thanked him again, and Efterar made to leave—but then Drafli's other hand snapped out something else. Another question for Efterar, clearly, and one that involved pointing at Alma's belly, and—oh.

Efterar's confusion was again all too apparent, his eyes frowning toward Alma's face—so she swallowed, and again made herself speak. "I think Drafli wants to know," she began, "if I'm—pregnant."

Efterar's expression instantly cleared, and he shook his head. "No, not currently, I'm afraid," he replied. "You'll need to release your own seed first, and based on the current state of your cycle, that likely won't be for a week or so yet. Orc-seed can sometimes help things along, but there's no guarantee."

Oh. And wait, was that *relief* in Drafli's eyes—did he not *want* Alma to be pregnant?—and he even nodded toward Efterar, and made that same sign he'd made toward Alma the night before, his hand flattening against his heart. *Thank you.*

Efterar seemed to follow that one, because he nodded, and then strode out again. Leaving Alma alone with Drafli, who— she choked a gasp—was still cupping his hand over her, still with his finger *inside* her. And his eyes were back on her face again, as his other hand snapped up, and tugged at her bottom lip. Pulling her mouth open, and then leaning down and inhaling, almost as if... smelling her?

Disapproval suddenly flared across his eyes, quick and dangerous, even as his finger twitched inside her. *No,* he signed at her with his other hand, matching the word with his mouth. *You no taste Pure-Heart, unless I tell you.*

Wait. He meant—did Drafli mean he could *smell* Baldr on her mouth? He could smell what she'd done alone in the dark last night, her shameful secret weakness, oh gods—

"I—I'm so sorry," Alma gulped at him, her face now painfully hot, her body trembling beneath him. "I—I know I shouldn't have. I know it's profane, and *wrong*, and a woman should *never*—"

But Drafli's hand had again made that sideways motion—*stop*—and before Alma could quite follow it, he'd grasped for her own hand, and brought it down to... *there.* To brush close against his, to where his finger was still inside her.

Alma stared at him, her eyes wide, her fingers shaky, uncertain—and Drafli signed another order, cool and distant. *Keep going,* it surely meant. *Do it.*

She shuddered all over—was he testing her, punishing

her?—but he kept watching, waiting, commanding. And when she finally slid a tentative finger downwards, brushing carefully against her slick openness, that was surely the faintest twitch of approval in his eyes, in the slight circle of his own finger inside her.

And gods, now that she was touching there, she could *feel* Drafli's hand moving against her, could feel his warm strength opening her, jutting into her, like he owned her. And like he truly wanted her to do this, to touch herself like this, to feel his authority, his *permission*...

And it felt so good, his strong hand with hers like this, his so coolly invading, hers stroking and seeking, Rubbing hard against where it felt best, at the top of her crease, while Drafli dispassionately watched, and then—she gasped—he began sliding his fingers in and out, moving in perfect time with hers.

Alma's moan was hoarse, unfettered, and for an instant that might have been amusement in Drafli's eyes—but then it was back to chilly, distant challenge, as he deliberately nudged a second finger against her. And Alma slid her own hand down to feel it, to feel him gently easing against her clutching wetness, opening her further—and then sinking slow and powerful inside.

"Oh," Alma gulped, as she felt his knuckles settle close against her, his fingers buried within. "Oh, my lord. *Gods*."

His mouth slightly quirked, his other hand making that commanding, circular *keep going* motion. And Alma was desperately nodding, slipping down her other hand to join the first, one still grinding, the other just blatantly feeling him touching her, filling her. Him *approving* of her, wanting this from her—and when her own finger perhaps nudged too close, he somehow caught it between his, and then drew it inside. *Together*.

Alma's moan was more like a shout this time, and Drafli's mouth was definitely smirking now as he pumped her finger in and out alongside his. Making her do this to herself, wanting to see her do this, so shameless and brazen and obscene. Her thighs spread wide, her lord's long clever fingers plunging up between with her own, making her use herself, debase herself, for his command, his *entertainment*. Moving faster and faster, the heat wrenching whiter and wilder, she was going to bend she was going to break—

She pitched over the edge with a shrill, broken shriek, with Drafli's fingers gouging deep inside her, holding, holding. Feeling her clamp and clutch against him, as if she was seeking to milk more pleasure out from him, and suddenly there was the sharp, surging craving to feel his own groin pressed there instead, to feel that part of him buried inside, to drain out all of that hot sweet seed, to make him *hers*—

But then it was shifting, slipping away, sinking into the rapidly returning reality. Alma was bared and sprawled on a bed, and Drafli's hand was very swiftly yanking away from her. And he'd leapt to his feet—when had he moved to sit beside her?—and he was snatching for what looked like a rag from her shelf, and purposefully wiping off his fingers, one by one.

Oh. Alma watched it with blank, frozen uncertainty, her heart thudding louder and louder in her ears. Had he been mocking her, after all? Punishing her? Shoving her face in her shame, and making it clear that was where she belonged?

The certainty seemed to grow as she watched Drafli's stiff shoulders, his still-scrubbing hand. And here, flooding her, were his own words, and Baldr's, all mixed up and mashed together.

You will honour him. Make a friend of him. Obey me. I hate all humans. One year. One month.

"I'm sorry if I offended you, my lord," Alma choked, to Drafli's back. "I didn't mean to shame you, or myself. I—I'll try to do better. Whatever you wish."

Drafli's shoulders visibly sagged, and she could see his head tilting back, his eyes closed, almost as if begging his god to grant him patience. And then he abruptly strode back toward her, and thrust his rag into her hand.

There is no shame in pleasure, he mouthed at her, matching his words with signs—the last one a deeply distracting, fluid grip at his own visibly bulging groin. *But Pure-Heart's seed is mine alone to give. You will honour this. Honour me.*

Alma's relief felt like a tangible force, like a rush of warmth washing her into her bed. "Oh," she replied, as her mouth curved into a genuine smile, her shaky hand making the sign for *I understand*. "Yes, of course. I should have realized. Thank you, my lord."

Drafli's expression had gone entirely unreadable, his eyes fixed on her face for an instant too long—and then he signed something else, a question. *You pray to Skai-kesh today? Tell him your fear, your longing, and your thanks?*

Right. That had been part of their initial contract—their vow—and until this moment, Alma had entirely forgotten it. She'd never been much for gods or prayers, but the stubborn glint in Drafli's eyes suggested that clearly, he was—so she promptly ducked her head, and said a silent prayer. Telling this unknown Skai-kesh god of her strongest fear—Mr. Pembroke, always—and then her longing, and her blessing. Baldr, of course, for both.

When she looked up again, Drafli was giving a jerky nod, and then he spun and strode away, toward the door. Briefly pausing beside that large wooden chest, flipping the heavy top up with an easy flick of his hand—and after one more purposeful glance over his shoulder toward Alma, he stalked out, leaving the chest open and waiting behind him.

It was surely another order, and after a moment's careful wiping with the rag he'd given her—it did feel far less tender down there, thankfully—Alma pulled on her grimy-feeling robe, and ventured toward the chest. Discovering, to her surprise, that it was filled nearly to the top, with a remarkable variety of items—some looking familiar, and some entirely foreign.

She blinked down at them for an instant, and then glanced uncertainly toward the door, where Drafli had disappeared. Had he truly meant these things for her use? Or perhaps— perhaps even as her *possessions*?

Alma belatedly shook her head—he was planning to pay her with those priceless jewels, so surely these were only loans—and gingerly began sifting through the chest's neatly stacked contents. On one side, there was a variety of rags, a wool blanket, and multiple large, soft, clean-smelling furs. While on the other side, there was another full waterskin, a stoppered glass bottle of what looked like oil, a gigantic packet of dried fruit and meat, and even several intriguing-looking pamphlets, with vivid illustrations of orcs on their pages.

And at the very bottom of the chest, tucked into a cloth bag, were two odd, polished stone objects. One was long and rounded at both ends, looking rather like a pestle, while the other seemed to be a curved sculpture of some sort, with a flared base on one end, narrowing to a smoothly rounded tip on the other.

Alma was still frowning down at these—had Drafli meant her to display them, perhaps?—when she heard a purposeful tapping at the door. And once she'd glanced up to look, she found herself staring at... women?!

But yes, there were three unfamiliar women, standing clustered together in her doorway. They were all around Alma's age, or perhaps a little older—and they were all dressed in highly unusual clothing. Two of them were sporting what looked like oversized men's tunics, both pulled taut over their visibly pregnant bellies, while the third—a buxom, very pretty woman with wild, reddish-blonde hair—wasn't wearing proper clothes at *all*. Instead, there was a little fur cape tied around her shoulders, and a very short kilt slung low on her hips—and glinting all over her, where clothes should have otherwise been, were instead flashes of *gold*. Gold dangling from her ears, her neck, her wrists and ankles, even her blatantly bared *navel*.

"It's Alma, right?" the woman was saying, fixing her with a warm, stunning smile. "Welcome to our mountain. I'm Ella, and this is Rosa, and Maria. We've all been *dying* to meet you."

"Yes, for *days!*" interjected the shortest of the women— Rosa, who had blonde hair and sparkling blue eyes—as she swept into the room, her hand outstretched toward Alma. "But Efterar is *such* an old grump, and kept railing on about how you needed rest. Which I'm sure you did, and we hope you've fully recovered now, but *still*. And ooooh"—Rosa paused her enthusiastic shaking of Alma's hand to glance down toward the open chest beside them—"you have some of my introductory pamphlets! How *wonderful!* Did Baldr bring you these?!"

Alma was still distractedly shaking Rosa's hand, and felt herself giving a bemused but sincere smile. "Er, I actually think Drafli left them," she replied. "I haven't had a chance to read them yet, but I certainly will. Did you write them?"

If possible, Rosa's beaming face seemed to brighten even more, and she eagerly nodded. "Yes, indeed," she said. "It's one of my life's goals to correct the realm's *many* preposterous preconceptions about orcs. Although"—her blonde head tilted—"it was truly Drafli who left you those? As in, *angry* Drafli? The one who can barely stand to be in the same room with a woman? He's giving you *informative literature*?!"

Rosa's obvious astonishment at this felt oddly reassuring, and Alma barked a hoarse laugh, her head nodding. "Er, maybe? And also"—she glanced back down at the stone sculptures still in her other hand—"these? Whatever they are?"

All three women glanced down at once, their eyes widening on the sight. And then Ella abruptly grinned, Rosa gave a delighted-sounding squeak, and the third woman—Maria, tall and handsome and dark-haired—looked legitimately shocked, one hand come to her heart, the other to her pregnant belly.

"Oh, Drafli's given you *tools!*" Rosa said blithely, still

smiling warmly up at Alma's face. "For your personal pleasure, of course—you can see how each one would best fit each anatomical place? They'll also help prepare you for various orc-related activities, because"—she actually *winked* at Alma—"their own anatomy can be quite intimidating at first, haven't you found?"

Oh. Well. Alma's rattling, thoroughly confounded brain was darting back to Drafli—*there is no shame in pleasure*, he'd told her—and now he'd gone and reinforced that by giving her... these? Gifts? For... each *anatomical place*?

And yes, gods curse her, Alma could see how that might be the case. The cylindrical, pestle-like one for where Baldr had taken her, and then the flared-out one... well. And in Alma's thoughts, where there should have been shock, or revulsion, there was only a strange, stilted warmth. Drafli had given her *gifts*. For her *pleasure*.

She'd been blinking down toward them, a foolish little smile pulling at her mouth—and when she belatedly glanced up again, both Rosa and Ella were still smiling too, as though fully following her thoughts. While Maria was still looking genuinely stunned, her awestruck brown eyes darting between the tools, and Alma's face.

"*Drafli* gave you these," she said to Alma, her low voice thick with disbelief. "*Drafli*. Who's mated to *Baldr*. Who's been... *scent-bonded* to you."

Right. Alma couldn't hide her wince—so these women knew about that, then—but she made herself nod uncertainly between them. "Er, yes, I think so? We've, er, come to an agreement, between us. The three of us."

All three women were looking astonished again, Maria most of all. "And you've... *seen* Baldr and Drafli together, right?" Maria said, her voice suddenly careful. "With the... fighting. The begging. The *blood*."

Something flared low in Alma's belly, and she felt herself swallow, her face once again swarming with scarlet heat. "Er, a little," she replied uncertainly. "They're really quite compelling together, don't you think?"

For an instant, no one spoke—Maria's mouth had actually fallen open—and then Rosa smiled again, her eyes warm and appreciative. "They are, most assuredly," she said firmly. "Many people from my clan—the Ka-esh—also take great joy from more, ah, *intense* pleasures. I swear, Drafli could have been a Ka-esh in another life, I could certainly see him giving Baldr a *kraga*, couldn't you?"

As she'd spoken, she'd touched reverently at her own neck, which was encircled with a slim, close-fitting gold ring. And Alma somehow seemed caught on the sight of it, and then on the memory of those blue-and-green jewels, glittering in Drafli's outstretched hand. And then on the realization that she'd never seen Baldr wear any gold or jewels at all. Had she?

"So are jewels a Ka-esh custom, then?" Alma asked, before she'd quite realized it, as her eyes slid back toward Ella, with her remarkably gilded attire. "Are you from the Ka-esh clan, as well?"

Ella laughed aloud, and shook her head. "No, thank the gods, I'm not *nearly* clever enough," she said, with a teasing glance toward Rosa. "I'm Grisk, like Baldr, and my mate Natt serves as the clan's Speaker. I think you've met some of his guard, Thrain, and Varinn? And Grisk orcs love jewels, and piercings, too—it's traditional to give them to your mate, as a show of your affection."

She'd given a rather self-deprecating wave down at her own jewel-bedecked ensemble, and Alma again felt oddly caught on it, her head tilting. Thinking, with a strange pang in her chest, of how Baldr had said that day, *I am barely Grisk at all.*

"It's a lovely tradition," Alma said, and she meant it. "Your mate must care for you very much."

A pretty flush stained Ella's cheeks, though she waved it away with a dismissive, glittering hand. While beside them, Rosa, who had begun sifting through the pamphlets in Alma's chest, gave another squeak of excitement, waving a sheet of paper in midair.

"Ooooh, look!" she exclaimed. "Did you see this, Alma?"

This? Alma hadn't in fact seen it—she must have missed it among the pamphlets—and she stepped a little closer, and peered uncertainly down toward it. It had some familiar-looking writing on it—Drafli's writing?—along with a few lines of text, a number, and what might have been a signature.

"It's an authorization for trading-credits," Rosa explained, her finger enthusiastically tapping at the number. "The orc equivalent of coin, you know. So you can go buy things!"

Buy things?! Alma blinked bemusedly at the paper, and then back at Rosa's beaming, expectant face. "But there must be some mistake," she said. "Drafli already left me"—she flailed at the chest—"all of this."

Ella and Maria had both leaned over to look at the paper, Ella's brows rising, Maria's mouth again falling open. "Unbelievable," Maria muttered. "It says Alma's to use it for *clothes*. And that you're to dress to please *Baldr*?!"

What? Alma frowned down at the paper again, but yes, impossibly, that did seem to be what was written there. And yes, her makeshift robe was surely due for a wash by now—and even as she grimaced at the thought, something new and unfamiliar was leaping in her chest. Drafli had truly given her such a gift? Truly?

"But how does one even *do* such a thing?" Alma asked, with a tentative glance between her new friends. "Find new clothes, in Orc Mountain?"

But Ella's grin was immediate, and perhaps rather wolfish, too. "You're talking to the right people," she said firmly, as she linked her arm with Alma's. "Come on. Let's take you shopping."

23

S hopping in Orc Mountain, it turned out, was *marvellous*. Together with Maria and Rosa, Ella had escorted Alma a short distance down the corridor, into a room that she vaguely recognized. It was in fact the same stockroom Varinn had taken her to the other night, before her ill-fated escape—but now that she was in a far fresher frame of mind, she found herself staring around at the room with sheer, staggering wonder.

It was rather like one of Ashford's most well-stocked shops, with its multiple rows of shelves, fronted by a long counter. But the orc now standing behind the counter—a harsh-faced, older-looking fellow named Ymir—didn't ask Alma to wait while he went and fetched items, like Varinn had done. Instead, he'd peered darkly at the paper Ella handed over, and then waved them all behind the counter with a sharp flourish of his talon-like hand.

"We welcome you to our clan, woman," he said to Alma, his voice gravelly. "I hope you shall dress yourself as best befits a Grisk."

He did? But yes, he'd given a grudgingly approving glance toward Ella's ensemble as he'd spoken, and Ella had warmly thanked him, and eagerly hauled Alma around behind the counter, with Rosa and Maria following behind. Into a truly dazzling mass of shelves, all bursting with an astonishing array of goods.

There were bags of flour and oats, baskets of dried meat and fruit, barrels of pork and ale. And cooking pots and pans, and weapons and tools and lamps and tarps and supplies. And then boots and shoes, and—Ella pulled Alma to a halt—rows and rows of fabric. Of *clothes*.

They were all neatly arranged, with some folded and stacked on shelves, and some pressed and hanging, not unlike in Mr. Pembroke's extravagant wardrobe back in Ashford. And beyond that wardrobe, Alma had truly never seen so many clothes in one place in her life, and she stared at it with wide eyes, her mouth fallen open.

"So the Grisk are absolutely the squirrels of Orc Mountain," Ella said cheerfully, as she began rummaging through piles. "They love clothes and goods, and they *never* throw anything away. Because of the scents, you see—they'll linger on textiles for *years*—so to Grisk, your possessions are almost an extension of your family, and your home. But anything that's here is free for all to use, not even just Grisk, so you needn't worry about wearing someone else's heirlooms! Do you see anything you like?"

Alma was still feeling thoroughly stunned, blinking at the astounding array of clothing and furs around her. "Er, I'm not sure," she said, as her thoughts darted back to those instructions Drafli had written. "If I'm to dress to *please Baldr*, what kinds of clothing would he like? I mean, we've certainly never discussed such things, so how—"

She waved helplessly at the surrounding bounty, and belatedly noticed that all three women were exchanging meaningful glances. "Well," Ella said bracingly, "I suppose Baldr *is* Grisk, right? And traditional Grisk clothing is, well, *this*."

Her hand had given an all-encompassing flutter down

toward her own ensemble, with its skimpy cape and too-short skirt. And looking at it again, at the striking, carefree shame-lessness of it, there was something almost like longing, or perhaps even envy, clutching in Alma's belly.

"But—Baldr himself doesn't dress like that," Alma said uncertainly. "Does he? He dresses like—like a human. Does *he* ever come shopping here?"

The three women exchanged glances again, though this time they looked more uncertain, as if they'd never before considered that point. "You know, I'm not sure," Ella said slowly. "Baldr doesn't spend much time here in the Grisk wing, or seem to pay much attention to Grisk traditions. But"—she'd grimaced, shaking her head, as if she regretted saying that—"I do know he didn't grow up here at the mountain, either. So perhaps he's just more accustomed to human clothes."

Alma's uncertainty was only increasing, her eyes now glancing between Rosa and Maria, both with their oversized, far more modest tunics. "So perhaps he would prefer human clothes, then? Or"—she felt her face slightly flushing—"maybe he would like traditional *Skai* clothes? Whatever those are?"

Ella and Rosa both glanced expectantly at Maria, who was giving Alma a wry smile. "We can certainly help you dress like a Skai woman, if you like," she said, in her low, warm voice. "But be forewarned, you'll be walking around like *this*."

With that, she promptly reached for the hem of her baggy tunic, and lifted it to her waist. Showing her ample thighs and rounded belly, and... the small piece of leather fabric hanging over her groin, barely covering the crucial parts.

It was... a *loincloth*. With a *dagger* tucked into the side of it?!

"I'll often just wear this in the Skai wing," Maria was saying, as she dropped her tunic again. "But I still find it's a bit much to wear through the rest of the mountain. Though Simon—my Skai mate—would very much like it if I would."

Beside Maria, Rosa gave a knowing laugh, and a roll of her blue eyes. "Of *course* he would," she said dryly. "No offense,

Maria, but if I were Alma, I would be choosing the Grisk path here. No question."

Maria didn't seem offended, giving a low chuckle too, but her eyes had narrowed on Alma, her dark head tilting. "But perhaps Alma would prefer to wear human clothes, too," she said. "You shouldn't feel that you need to oblige Drafli in this. Or anything else, for that matter. He can be..."

She didn't finish, frowning and glancing away, and Alma felt her stomach flipping, her heartbeat rising. She *had* to oblige Drafli. Honour him. Obey him. *There is no shame.* One month.

"No, I want to," she said, too quickly, darting her eyes back to Ella again. "To try the Grisk clothes, I mean, if you might be willing to help me find something appropriate? Though I'm sure I'll never look as lovely as you do in them, Ella."

Ella snorted, even as she flashed Alma a dazzling grin. "Rubbish," she said. "You'll look marvellous. And I'm sure we'll find *just* the thing."

Alma didn't voice her misgivings, but instead gave a grateful smile back. And soon she was caught up in a delightful whirl of flaring fabrics and furs, in a breathtaking variety of colours and lengths and styles. All of them unquestionably revealing—not to mention the process of changing between them—but the other women didn't seem to even notice. Instead, they enthusiastically compared colours against Alma's skin and hair, interrogated her on whether she was itchy or cold or uncomfortable, and tested whether she could move around properly. Soon Maria had even taken Alma's hair out of its old messy braid, and begun brushing it out with oil, and even carefully slicing at it with her *dagger*. While Rosa had somehow, somewhere, scrounged up a book with old Grisk illustrations, and was excitedly brandishing it before Ella and Alma's eyes.

"So *useful* to shelve a book on Grisk dress with the Grisk clothes!" she exclaimed, as she began carefully flipping through pages. "Oooh, this looks so similar to what you're doing now, Ella! Have you studied this book, perchance?"

Ella laughed and shook her head, but she was looking at the book with interest, glancing back and forth between the page and Alma's current ensemble. "Oh, it *is* close, isn't it?" she said. "And perhaps if we add a leather belt here..."

This led to more enthusiastic rummaging through the piles, and soon a similar-looking belt was found, as well as a long leather strip that was wrapped around Alma's forearm multiple times. "This is in case you need to bind something, or hang something, or put your hair up," Rosa supplied, still reading from the book. "And you can see how the belt has these loops as well, in case you want to carry tools, or weapons. So clever, you Grisk!"

It *was* clever, and it occurred to Alma that such things would probably come in handy with her housekeeping efforts, too. And once she'd voiced that thought aloud, the women all eagerly agreed, and soon launched into an intensive conversation about the housekeeping, and how they too had begun to notice Roland's absence.

"The floors in the Skai wing are a *disaster*," Maria confided, with a grimace. "I mean, it's our own fault, I'm well aware, but I didn't realize that Roland somehow had huge parts of the mountain *flooded* one night each moon, did you?"

The other women shook their heads—and this was certainly news to Alma—and Ella was grimacing, too. "And he switched out all the fur rugs and bedding regularly, too," she said. "Believe me, you can tell."

"Yes, and the *fires!*" Rosa added, wrinkling her nose. "The Ka-esh don't use them that often, but the other day John—he's my mate, Alma, and he's *frightfully* busy—he got called to three separate fireplaces because they wouldn't light! Which was because no one had bothered taking out the ashes! John was in a *ghastly* mood after that, I can tell you."

Alma was rapidly taking mental notes, and asked for as

many details as she could, which the women readily supplied. However, it turned out that none of them had actually been involved in the housekeeping, or spent any time with Roland themselves.

"I honestly took it for granted," Rosa said, making a face, "which is a *grievous* oversight on my part, because I know how much work these things are. If we can help you at all, Alma, please, let us know."

The other two echoed this, and Alma thanked them, and promised to keep them informed. And at that point, Maria had seemed to finish whatever she was doing with Alma's hair, and Ella had collected a variety of similar items—changes of clothes for multiple days, she explained—before stepping back, and giving a critical, assessing glance up and down Alma's form.

"I think this works," she said. "Come on, let's take a look."

With that, she pulled Alma toward the rear of the room, to where there turned out to be a large looking-glass, propped against the back wall. And in the glass' reflection, surrounded by three lovely women, there stood a complete *stranger*.

Alma gasped, putting her hands to her bare torso—and the stranger in the glass did the same, because it was... her. Oh gods, it was *her*, and she was indeed dressed much like Ella was. Like a... a *Grisk*. With a short, silvery fur cape tied around her shoulders, and clasped together with a black leather tie in front. Her thick, low-slung belt was black leather too, generously studded with leather loops and silver metal rivets. And hanging below the belt was a short, flared black kilt, scarcely reaching to her mid-thigh.

It was indeed shockingly revealing, showing off alarming views of her bare arms and legs, and the entirety of her torso. And—Alma stilled as her gaze lifted to her face in the glass— her eyes were shining, her cheeks flushed a becoming shade of pink, and her pale, frizzy hair had somehow been tamed into a mass of shining waves, curling over her shoulders, looking almost white against the rich grey fur.

"So what do you think?" Ella asked, grinning with satisfaction at Alma's reflection in the glass. "It suits you, doesn't it?"

And blinking at herself like this—*herself*, like this, bared and brazen and shameless—there was suddenly a tight, twisting longing, deep in Alma's belly. This couldn't be her. It couldn't. The person in the mirror was brave, bold, perhaps even beguiling, with her lovely flowing hair, her capable hips and shoulders, the weight of her full breasts just peeking out from below her cape. With the definition in her arms and legs and abdomen, borne of many hours' hard work, contrasted with that pleasing flush in her cheeks, the surprisingly dark lashes held low over her eyes.

"But surely I couldn't go in public like this, or—or do *housekeeping* like this," protested the woman in the glass, glancing uncertainly toward the similarly dressed, reddish-haired beauty beside her. "And surely—surely Drafli and Baldr wouldn't—*approve* of this?"

But Ella just laughed, the mirth lighting up her eyes in the glass. "Nonsense," she said firmly. "These clothes will allow you to freely do any activity you wish. And I suspect that this was *exactly* what Drafli had in mind for you."

Alma couldn't stop staring, as a bright, shivery chill seemed to dance up her spine. *Exactly what Drafli had in mind.* It didn't seem possible, it seemed utterly unfathomable—but he *had* clearly ordered Alma to do this. Or something like it. Hadn't he?

"I can't imagine that Drafli would have given it that much thought," she heard her faint voice say. "I mean, he doesn't even—"

Like me, she'd been about to say, like the perennial fool she was—but thank the gods she bit it back, just in time. Or perhaps it hadn't been in time at all, because Ella and Rosa had exchanged uncertain glances, and Maria was looking suddenly, decidedly grim.

"Then there's only one way to know for certain," Maria said flatly. "Let's go find Drafli now, and see what he has to say for himself."

24

A few short moments later, Alma was being marched through the corridors by a grim, glinting-eyed Maria. Rosa and Ella had clearly intended to tag along as well, but upon leaving the storage-room, they'd been confronted by a big, bare-chested, rueful-looking orc, who was holding a tiny, frantically squalling orcling in his powerful arms. The orcling turned out to be Ella's son—his name was Rakfi, Ella supplied, while the orc was Nattfarr, her Grisk mate. And, Alma couldn't help noticing, just like Ella, this Nattfarr was wearing a similar short kilt, and also seemed to be festooned with jewelry, including a thick gold ring through his greenish *nipple*.

"We have heard much of you, woman," Nattfarr had said, inclining his head toward Alma as he'd tucked Ella close beneath his big arm, while Rakfi had eagerly latched to Ella's breast below her cape, nursing with all apparent glee. "We hope you are happy to be here, amongst our Grisk kin?"

There'd been something unnervingly compelling about Nattfarr's eyes as he'd spoken, and Alma had felt herself fervently nodding, without at all intending to. "Yes, you Grisk have all been *so* kind," she'd replied. "Thank you so much for welcoming me here."

Nattfarr and Ella had both looked genuinely pleased by this, while beside Alma, Maria's eyes had seemed to go even darker than before. And after a quick farewell to Ella and Natt-farr—and to Rosa, as well, who'd begun to look a bit peaked—Maria had steered Alma down the corridor, in the direction of the Skai wing.

"Look, I—I'm actually not sure this is a good idea," Alma said, glancing uneasily around the corridor. "I don't think Drafli—"

She abruptly shut her mouth, wincing, but Maria's too-aware eyes suggested she'd fully followed anyway. "If Drafli doesn't like it, he can go chew on a sharpened blade," she said coolly. "He does *not* control this mountain, as much as he likes to think he does. I presume he hasn't sworn a vow to you, either? Or allowed Baldr to? Or even given you a written agree-ment of some sort?"

Alma fought back her wince, and uselessly searched for some kind of appropriate answer—when thank the gods, Varinn and Thrain strode out of a door in front of them. And though both orcs were blatantly blinking at Alma's new ensem-ble, her relief at the interruption felt palpable, and she waved warmly toward them.

"Very nice, woman," Thrain said back, waggling his black eyebrows toward her. "I really, *really* hope you're off to see Baldr. Can we come, mayhap? I have a feeling this could be entertaining."

Alma's face heated, her eyes dropping, and beside her Maria loudly harrumphed. "No, you can't," she said flatly. "Though I don't suppose either of you might know where Drafli is?"

Alma's tentative glance upwards found Varinn inhaling deep, even as his eyes stayed unnaturally fixed on Alma's outfit.

"In the Ash-Kai meeting-room," he said. "With Baldr, and the captain, as well."

He still hadn't looked away, and Alma found herself flushing again, and fighting the urge to cover herself. While beside Varinn, Thrain elbowed him hard in the side, his eyes darkening with something that might have been... envy?

"Thank you," Maria said brusquely, herding Alma back to a walk again. Even as Alma shot a regretful look over her shoulder toward Thrain, who gave an unmistakable wince back—and then a shrug, and a halfhearted little smile.

Oh. Alma found herself frowning as they walked, considering that, and beside her Maria audibly sighed. "Would you rather stay here in the Grisk wing with them?" she asked. "I'm sorry to be carting you off like this. I just—Drafli has some nerve, you know? He has *no right* to be throwing vague orders at you like that, when he clearly hasn't even given you some kind of surety about all this. Like you're his *servant*."

Alma again had to search for an answer, swallowing down her grimace. *Honour him. Obey him.* One month.

"Er, I really don't mind," she made herself say, through her too-tight throat. "Drafli's actually been quite—quite good to me, considering."

But there was no mirth in Maria's laugh beside her, and she steered Alma around another corner, the floor now tilting steadily upward. "And did he tell you to say that, too?" she asked, clipped. "Or threaten to harm you if you refused?"

Good gods, this woman was unnervingly astute, and suddenly highly intimidating, as well. And Alma truly couldn't find words to speak—couldn't even look at her—as Maria ushered her toward the door of a large, unfamiliar room. It had a fire crackling in the opposite wall—which was also banked heavily with ash, Alma's distracted brain noted—and in its middle was a large, low square table. And sitting on the floor around the table were three orcs, two of them indeed Baldr and

Drafli, while yet another familiar orc paced back and forth before them. It was—Kesst?

"He's barely slept in a *week*," Kesst was snapping, his arm wildly waving, his eyes glaring down toward the table. "I'm doing what I can, and gods know I've tried to give those brawling pillocks the benefit of the doubt. But they need to lay off for *one damned day*, and let Eft *rest*, or at least get a load off without being interrupted once in a while! And if it means you need to shut down the arenas, Grim, you *should*!"

Alma and Maria had stilled in the doorway—Alma was already fervently wishing herself elsewhere—but both Baldr and Drafli's eyes had snapped over toward them. Toward *her*. Drafli's gaze cold and assessing, flicking dispassionately up and down her brazenly clad form, while Baldr—Alma's cheeks flushed again—Baldr looked like he'd been struck straight across the face, his mouth fallen open, his cheeks flooding with red.

But the third orc at the table—a huge, hulking orc, who clearly had to be Jule's mate, the orcs' captain—only spared them a brief, curious glance before returning his gaze to Kesst before them. "I wish I could call for this, brother," he said, his voice measured and deep, "but you ken I have no power upon this. The clans train as they do to defend us all, most of all against the new threats of men. If I seek to stop this, you ken they shall claim this is a grievous Ash-Kai overstep, and do this all the more."

Kesst gave a surprisingly menacing growl, his hands clutched to fists at his sides. "And will it be an Ash-Kai overstep if they end up *dying* for their stupidity, too?" he demanded. "What if Eft just cracks one of these days, and fucks off for good, just like Roland did? What then? We're just happy to live in a disgusting *dump*, while our brothers bleed to death in the corridors?!"

Alma's heart was suddenly pounding, her eyes frozen on Kesst's stiff back, and she barely heard the captain orc sigh.

"The Ka-esh are some help, are they not?" he asked. "Are not Salvi and Eben in the sickroom each day?"

"Yes," Kesst replied thinly, "but their work supplements Eft's, and expands it. They are *not* a replacement for him. No other orc *alive* can replace him, and you damn well know it!"

The captain sighed again, slow. "I shall spend more time in thought upon this, brother," he said. "I thank you, for raising this."

It was clearly a dismissal, and Kesst stiffly turned, and stepped toward the door—and then hesitated as he caught sight of Alma. His eyes flicking up and down, almost as dispassionately as Drafli's had—and then meeting hers with an odd, glinting bitterness.

"Lovely," he said thinly. "As if you really *needed* to be any sweeter."

And with that confusing statement ringing through the air, Kesst elbowed past Alma and Maria, and strode out the door. Leaving Alma feeling even more uncertain and exposed than before, especially when the captain orc stood and came over to loom above her, too.

"This is your new woman, ach, brothers?" he said, flashing a toothy grin over his shoulder toward Baldr and Drafli. "Welcome to our mountain, woman. I am Grimarr, Captain of Five Clans. I am glad my faithful Hands have found you, and I hope you are well pleased with them. They are a great gift to me, and I am sure they shall be to you, also."

With that, this Grimarr gave Alma a rather terrifying wink, and then walked out, too. Leaving just Baldr and Drafli at the table, and Alma and Maria by the door.

And while Alma's brain was now frantically whirling in a dozen directions at once—poor Efterar, and poor *Kesst*, and what had Grimarr meant about the new threats of men, and why was Baldr still *looking* at her like that—Maria didn't seem the slightest bit discomposed. And instead, she'd stalked further into the room, and was now glowering down toward Drafli's seated form, her hands on her hips.

"I've just had the pleasure of meeting Alma this morning," she said to him, without preamble. "And in this short time, not only did you subject her to a random, poorly explained order, but it became very clear that she felt very, *very* compelled to follow it, to your satisfaction. And that you *expected* that from her. Or else. With *nothing* in return."

Alma badly blanched behind Maria—gods, had she truly betrayed that much?—and she didn't miss the sudden flash of displeasure in Drafli's eyes, narrowing over Maria's shoulder toward her. While beside him, Baldr—who had still been looking at Alma with flushed cheeks and half-lidded eyes— had slightly paled, his gaze suddenly darting between Alma and Drafli. Looking almost... *guilty*.

"Do I need to bring Simon in on this?" Maria was demanding at Drafli, her hand slipping to clutch to her hip—to her *dagger*, good gods. "I know he's willing to overlook a hell of a lot when it comes to you, and only the gods know why—but I think he needs to take a *serious* look at the precedent you're establishing here, don't you? Suggesting that Skai can just go off and make women their *servants*, rather than their *mates*?"

Drafli's eyes gazing back up at Maria had gone deceptively steady, but Alma could almost taste his malice in the air, sharp and furious. But instead of snapping back at Maria, as Alma was almost certain he wanted to do, he unfolded his lean body from the floor, and gracefully rose to his feet. And then, without the slightest change in his expression, he strode straight past Maria, toward—toward Alma. And before she could blink, or take a breath, Drafli bent down, and *kissed* her.

Alma choked and shuddered all over, freezing against him—but at the insistent brush of his tongue against her lips, she melted into it, into him. Moaning aloud as she met his clever, glorious warmth, even as his teeth gave a painful, surreptitious bite at her tongue. *Obey me*, it meant. *Honour me*.

It meant this was still the lie, still the game, but when Drafli gently drew away, and coolly patted Alma's cheek with his hand, her heart was still thundering, her eyes still wide and suddenly starving on his distant, dispassionate face.

You understand, he signed at her, without moving his lips this time. *Why this.*

This was a wave at her clothes, and then a very brief angle of his eyes toward Baldr behind him. Baldr, who was still staring toward Alma with unblinking eyes, his expression still straddling something between obvious guilt, and bare, blatant *longing*.

And Drafli was clearly making a point with this—*honour me*—so Alma fixed her eyes back to his, and even attempted a smile. *Yes, I understand*, she signed back at him, her hands slightly trembling. *For Pure-Heart. Thank you, Golden-Tongue.*

There was a very faint shift in Drafli's eyes, there and gone again, as he gave a short, almost unnoticeable nod. *This honoured me*, he signed. *Now, speak this, to Pure-Heart.*

Oh. It was surely more of the game, and Baldr had surely followed that part at least, his head tilting—but then he glanced, very briefly, toward Maria. Who, Alma belatedly realized, was watching her and Drafli with her mouth hanging open, while genuine disbelief flared across her eyes.

Alma had to bite at her lip, not at all missing the flash of cold satisfaction in Drafli's gaze, and then nodded, and again signed, *I understand*. And then she stepped away from him, around both him and Maria, and toward Baldr. Who slowly stood up as she approached, his movements far jerkier than Drafli's had been.

"So Drafli asked me to dress in something that I thought would please you," Alma said, a little shyly. "I wasn't sure what that meant, but Ella and Rosa and Maria very generously helped me"—she shot a sheepish-feeling smile over her shoulder toward Maria—"and we came up with this."

She gave a reflexive curtsey toward him, briefly dropping

her eyes, and then meeting his again. "Do you like it?" she made herself continue. "It's traditional Grisk dress, apparently, but we thought perhaps we'd best come and ask before going much further with it, in case it wasn't to your liking."

And before her, Baldr... shuddered. His entire body almost rippling with the strength of it, his sharp tooth biting at his lip, his eyes fluttering. And his hand abruptly dropped to his groin, squeezing with painful-looking pressure against—oh. His swollen, visibly bobbing heft, which was currently streaking a dark patch of wetness against the front of his trousers.

"Ach, I like this," he whispered, with another hard, shuddering exhale. "You are *stunning*, Bright-Heart. You steal away all my breath, ach?"

Oh. Well. Alma couldn't help her shaky, relieved grin, or the way her own body seemed to shiver all over at the words. "Oh, I'm *so* glad," she whispered back. "Do you think, then, that I might be able to convince your too-clever devil to grant me another reward?"

She couldn't help a quick, teasing glance over her shoulder toward Drafli, whose eyes had instantly shuttered, hiding away whatever had been glinting there. And his gaze now slid blandly, purposefully toward Maria, who—Alma grimaced—had still been standing there watching all this, still with utter disbelief in her dark eyes.

Drafli gave a curt flick of his long fingers toward her—*Now run along*, it surely meant—and Alma again had to bite her lip as Maria actually snarled back at him, her hand again clutched at her dagger-hilt. "I'll leave it this time, you smug prick," she hissed at him. "But rest assured, Simon is still going to hear about this. And even if he's not watching you, *I will be*."

With that, she spun on her heel, and stalked for the door— and then briefly hesitated, and glanced back again. "And you watch yourself too, Alma, all right?" she said, her voice dropped to softness again. "And let me know if this devious bastard does *anything* you don't like."

With that, she tossed her hair over her shoulder, and flounced out. Leaving an instant's uncomfortable silence behind her, ringing through the room—at least, until Drafli turned back toward Alma and Baldr, and gave an elaborate roll of his eyes.

Finally, he mouthed, matching it with a sign Alma hadn't seen before. *Thank Skai-kesh.*

Alma gave a choked, reluctant laugh, while Baldr did the same beside her—though his eyes were rather pained, too. "Drafli and Maria have long been at odds, ach?" he told Alma. "You cannot trust a word one says upon the other. And this is a shame, for Maria"—Baldr's now-reproachful eyes angled back at Drafli—"is a very lovely and kind woman, Draf."

Drafli didn't even pretend to hear this, and instead strode over toward them, his eyes oddly glinting as he studied Alma again, flicking up and down. And when he signed something— at Baldr this time—Baldr's face again flushed red, his eyes fixed back to Alma, too.

"Ach, she does look like a true Grisk," he said quietly. "And that—it pleases you too, Draf, I ken?"

Baldr's eyes were suddenly, intently searching Drafli's face—and wait, was that jealousy, or perhaps even *hurt*, glimmering in Baldr's eyes?!—and Alma didn't miss the very faint twitch of tension through Drafli's form, in his gaze darting to Baldr, in his slightly tightening mouth. In the almost, *almost* convincing casualness of his shrug.

Wished her to please you, *Pure-Heart*, he signed, the movements almost too quick for Alma to follow—and then she did lose the thread, his hands flashing into incomprehensibility. But whatever it was, it seemed to reassure Baldr, his expression slowly clearing, and then shifting back into... hunger. Into *craving*.

"Draf tells me you have been tasting me without his permission, Bright-Heart," he murmured at her. "Is this truth?"

Alma's body instantly seized to stillness, her eyes darting

guiltily between Baldr and Drafli—and Baldr huffed a low, approving laugh, while Drafli dispassionately brought his claw to her lower lip, and tugged it open. While his other hand signed something else toward Baldr, something that had him blushing even redder, and licking at his lips with a long sweep of his hungry black tongue.

"And now he says," Baldr whispered, "that you will spend the rest of the afternoon choking on orc-prick, until you learn."

lma's moan was hoarse, involuntary, impossible to hide. Betraying her with such sudden, vicious ferocity that she clamped her hand to her mouth, her eyes snapping wide and horrified between Baldr and Drafli's watching faces.

But to her distant, bizarre gratefulness, neither of them laughed, not even Drafli. Instead, he arched a cool eyebrow toward her, and nudged her back toward the low table close behind her. Until it hit the back of her knees, and she felt herself stumble a little, sagging down until she was sitting on it.

But yes, that was surely what Drafli had wanted, based on that faint flare in his eyes—while beside him, Baldr groaned under his breath, his hand again skittering against his still-tented groin, as his eyes darted toward the... the door. Open. Behind them.

But before Alma could turn to look—before the whispering shame could swarm into a flood—Drafli's strong hand grasped her chin, and tilted it up. Making her look at him, and suddenly, vividly, calling to mind that very morning. Gods, had it been just that morning, when he'd blatantly filled her with these very fingers, and said, *There is no shame. Honour me.*

Alma swallowed and nodded, taking a deep breath—and then, for a reason she couldn't at all follow or identify, she felt her tongue slipping out, and flicking at where his palm was brushing against her mouth. As if to say, *Yes. I know. I remember.*

Drafli jerked a nod, and dropped her chin—and then his hand snapped down, and with an unexpected, purposeful tug, Alma's silver fur was sliding off her shoulders. Baring her even more to the room, to Baldr, to whoever might happen to walk by, or walk in.

She had to fight the urge to cover herself, to hide her exposed, shamefully peaked breasts away. Because the cool command in Drafli's eyes was still there, still far too clear, flashing even harder as he reached for Baldr, and drew him close. His hand now purposefully palming at Baldr's swollen groin, surely about to take him out, to teach her, oh please…

But then Baldr fumbled against Drafli's touch, pushing him away. And Alma saw her own confusion reflected in Drafli's eyes, though he very quickly covered it again, his head tilting as he studied Baldr, his mouth pursed.

"You made it all about me yesterday, Draf," Baldr said, low. "Today, I want it to be about *you*."

Drafli's hands hanging before Alma's eyes had abruptly clenched, his claws digging into his palms—but his expression had remained impressively bland, even as he slightly shifted on his feet, as if itching to move away from the grave danger Alma presented. And when his hands snapped up to sign at Baldr, his claws had pulled in again, the movements fluid and convincingly careless.

I wish her to please you, Pure-Heart, it clearly said. *Not me. You.*

But Baldr's bottom lip was jutting out, his arms folding over his tunic, his head shaking. "It will be you, or nothing, Draf," he said flatly. "You said this would be both of us. You *promised*."

He wasn't wrong, Alma's stilted thoughts pointed out, but she still found herself bracing against Drafli's certain refusal, his retaliation. He clearly didn't want to touch her again, not in the slightest, and it belatedly occurred to Alma that she'd almost been... forgetting that. That to Drafli, she was still repulsive. Still just a means to an end.

I hate you. You obey me. Seek to please my mate. This is all.

But Drafli was still looking at Baldr, his jaw set very tight— and to Alma's utter astonishment, he finally shrugged, sharp and dismissive. To which Baldr's mouth curved into a slow, relieved smile, his hand slipping close around Drafli's waist, his head bending low into his shoulder.

It was once again a moment of almost achingly powerful intimacy, enough that Alma had to drop her eyes—but then, suddenly, there was the feel of weight, of warmth, settling close. *Baldr's* weight, now seated on the table beside her, his powerful thigh brushing hers through his trousers.

"Now, Bright-Heart," he said firmly, glancing toward her with surprising slyness, "I shall teach you how to suck our devil. Properly."

His teasing gaze had flicked back up to Drafli, who had been watching with chilly eyes—but then he exhaled, slow. And that was surely fondness, or even indulgence, stealing across his face, as his hand slid up, and rustled against Baldr's hair.

Baldr leaned into Drafli's touch, his lashes fluttering, his mouth still curving. "Drafli is a very exacting mate, in this," he murmured, his gaze shifting back to Alma's. "But if I can learn, so can you, ach?"

Alma swallowed and nodded, and in return Baldr shot her a swift, approving smile. "First," he said, "you must ask him. Always."

Alma swallowed again, watching—and not quite breathing—as Baldr leaned closer toward Drafli's groin before him. Toward where there was now a long, visible ridge in Drafli's trousers.

"May I suck you, Draf? Please?" Baldr murmured, as he

made the matching signs with his hands. *Suck*, an obscene-looking nudge of his own finger into his mouth, while *Draf* was replaced with that now-familiar *Golden-Tongue* motion. And *please* was said with Baldr's hand on his chest, slightly higher than for *thank you.*

Drafli's breath had exhaled again, his hand still stroking at Baldr's hair, but he briefly, curtly nodded. And now Baldr was looking expectantly at Alma, and she fought through her sudden flailing heartbeat as she raised her eyes to Drafli's cold, dispassionate face.

"May I suck you, my lord?" she whispered, as she repeated Baldr's signs with her trembling hands. "Please?"

Drafli's eyes had remained very still, almost blank, almost as though he hadn't seen her, or heard her, and Alma's heart seemed to judder faster, audible in her ears. What if she'd asked it wrong, what if Drafli couldn't stomach it after all, even for Baldr. What if he flat-out refused...

But then he exhaled again, hard enough to flutter Alma's hair, and gave a shuddery shrug of his shoulder. Releasing Alma's own choked-off exhale, too, and she couldn't help a warm, grateful grin up toward him, a touch of her hand to— she twitched—her bare breast. To say, *thank you.*

Drafli's blank eyes didn't change, but Alma could see his nostrils flaring, his throat bobbing. While beside Alma, Baldr gave her a companionable little nudge with his shoulder, and lifted his hands to untie Drafli's trousers.

"You must undress him with care," Baldr murmured toward her, as he slowly pulled at the strings, keeping his eyes on Drafli's face. "Again, best not to make sudden movements, ach?"

Alma nodded, her own eyes intently fixed to the sight. To Baldr's deft hands drawing those trousers downwards, moving with a gentle, steady reverence. Revealing Drafli's taut navel, the hard ridges of his lower abdomen, the thickening line of coarse dark hair, and then... *that*. Bobbing out swollen and shameless above Drafli's heavy bollocks, and jutting straight toward Baldr's face.

And it was—different, than Baldr. Surprisingly different. Even longer, perhaps, but slimmer, too, with more visible veins, and tapering to nearly a point at the head. And it was a much deeper shade of grey, and the hint of its tip beneath the outer skin was darker still.

But most surprising of all—Alma shot Baldr an uncertain look—were the scars. Laddered all up that veined grey shaft, and looking almost—almost like *teeth-marks*.

But Baldr didn't seem even slightly disconcerted, and his fingers slid up the full length of it with slow, easy eagerness. Pulling the hood back, and fully revealing a smooth, glossy grey head, split by a deep cleft, with just a glimpse of white hidden within it.

But even this part of Drafli was scarred, too, and Baldr seemed to catch Alma's uncertain look this time. "I ken he looks different than I do," he murmured. "But he shall feel just as good within you. And taste even better, ach?"

Oh, hell. Alma's craving seemed to surge with irrational force, but she bit her lip, and angled an uncertain glance up at Drafli's face. "And it doesn't hurt him?" she asked, almost a whisper. "With all the—scars?"

Drafli's eyes—which had been watching them with surprising intensity—purposefully angled away at that, and beside Alma Baldr betrayed an unmistakable wince. "No," he replied, far flatter than before. "These are all old marks. Many orcs like to bite, for pleasure."

That shouldn't have been surprising, perhaps, but Alma still couldn't hide her shocked gasp, her eyes again searching the mess of scars on Drafli's skin. As if he'd liked it, too. Many, *many* times.

"And is that something he... still likes?" she asked uncertainly. "Or expects?"

Because perhaps Baldr had done some of that, perhaps it

was part of their pleasure together? But beside her, Baldr had gone noticeably stiff, his eyes distant and shuttered.

"No," he replied, clipped. "He does not allow me to bite him. I ken he would not allow you to, either."

Oh. Alma's glance up at Drafli seemed to confirm this, his eyes briefly narrowing on hers, and slipping away again. But there was still something in that, in the tightness of his mouth, the bitter glint of his eyes.

"Because you're special to him, right?" Alma heard herself ask Baldr, without at all meaning to. "Because you're his sworn mate, so you're different than anyone else. He wants your kisses, perhaps, rather than your teeth."

Baldr had turned to look at her, his head tilting—and then he was glancing back up at Drafli, something Alma couldn't read passing between them. And Drafli's hand—which had still been in Baldr's hair—slipped down Baldr's cheek, his jaw, until his clawed thumb was brushing gently against Baldr's mouth.

Alma could feel Baldr's body slightly relaxing against her, his breath exhaling. And perhaps Drafli even looked more relaxed too, his eyes now half-lidded on Baldr's, his thumb slipping into Baldr's mouth.

Baldr sucked on it without hesitation, his gaze still locked to Drafli's—and not blinking, not faltering, as Drafli tugged his thumb away, and smoothly replaced it with the tip of his scarred, glossy cock.

Baldr moaned aloud, his mouth already tasting and kissing, soft and hungry and familiar. His black tongue visibly swirling at Drafli's scarred head, seeking, caressing, without even the slightest hesitation. As if this were the most divine thing he'd ever tasted, as if he would do anything to worship at his mate's altar...

Drafli clearly liked it too, his eyes still hooded and glinting, his scarred length visibly shuddering against Baldr's kissing mouth. His hand in Baldr's hair slipping around to the back of his head, as if bracing him—and then Drafli slowly, steadily eased forward. Sliding himself deeper and deeper and deeper, until—*impossible*—he'd fully vanished inside Baldr's mouth, his length clearly jutted all the way into Baldr's visibly convulsing throat.

But Baldr was moaning again, the sound low and garbled, and Drafli was caressing his hair, his face, even as he kept himself pressed there, plunged all the way inside. Clearly revelling in this, in his beloved mate so eagerly swallowing him into his very throat, and Alma had surely stopped moving, stopped breathing, her eyes seized on the sheer, stilted unreality of it.

Drafli finally eased backwards again, sliding himself out smooth and effortless, his scarred length now slicked and glossy all over. While Baldr kept sucking, kept kissing, and when Drafli pulled himself fully free of Baldr's mouth, his hand still firm on Baldr's head, Baldr then licked at what Drafli allowed him to reach, his tongue just brushing against that slick cleft, against where it was now pulsing a steady stream of white.

And again, Drafli was clearly enjoying this, his scarred heft bobbing and nudging against Baldr's tongue, almost as if it was another tongue, licking and kissing back. And then slipping back into power, into casual command, as it again slid deep into Baldr's mouth. But faster this time, harder, burying itself with sharp, deadly ease into Baldr's forcefully convulsing throat. While Baldr breathed hard through his nose, his chest heaving, his lashes fluttering.

Alma had somehow forgotten to breathe, her eyes again darting up to Drafli's face—and finding, to her distant surprise, that he'd glanced toward her, too. And his eyes weren't speaking of mockery or contempt, not quite—but instead, perhaps, of possession. Of pride.

Look at my beautiful, sweet mate, they seemed to say. *He shall never do this for any other. He is mine.*

Alma could easily follow that, could even appreciate it—

and her traitorous hands had somehow signed back an answer, quick and furtive. *Yes. I understand. Pure-Heart is beautiful.*

Drafli's gaze shifted, angling back to Baldr again, to his heft still buried in Baldr's spasming throat—but wait, that was a nod. A *nod*, surely saying, *yes*. Approving.

And the approval only deepened as Drafli slid backwards again, easing out of Baldr's mouth, his watching eyes gone perhaps warmer than Alma could ever remember seeing them. As if this moment, with him so utterly in control of his pliant, worshipful mate, had dropped away all his chilly distance, leaving only that glinting-eyed devil behind.

Baldr seemed to know it too, his mouth still softly kissing at Drafli's tip, even as his sparkling eyes finally glanced back toward Alma. "Now you try?" he murmured, between kisses. "You can see how it pleases him, ach? Calms him?"

Alma's heart had skipped a beat, but she felt herself nodding, her breath shuddering out slow. And Drafli had even leaned a little toward her, oh gods, making this easier for her— and she flashed him a sheepish little smile, and leaned closer. Toward that scarred dripping power, its sweet scent suddenly flooding her breath...

The first brush of her mouth was tentative, careful, barely a touch—but oh, the *taste* of him, sparking sweet and glorious across her tongue. And against her, Drafli had shuddered hard against her lips, and that—that was because he'd sputtered out another delectable surge of white, sudden and strong enough that it dribbled down her chin.

There was an instant's jangling stillness, Alma's wide eyes darting up to meet his—and then he yanked away, his head snapping sideways. While Alma's face instantly flooded with heat, because clearly she'd done it wrong, and already failed, oh gods—

But suddenly there was something warm—Baldr's hand— gripping gentle around her wrist. Pulling it away from where she'd been about to wipe off her chin, to perhaps attempt to cover her shame.

"This was good," Baldr murmured at her, and when she glanced toward him, his eyes were warm, earnest. "You keep this slow and sweet, ach? If he wishes you to stop, he shall tell you. And you *never* wipe away his seed without his leave, ach?"

Baldr's eyes had dropped to her chin as he spoke, holding there with meaningful intensity, and Alma felt herself slightly relaxing, and nodding, and furtively glancing back toward Drafli. Who had indeed eased a little closer again, that dripping heft only a breath away from her mouth—so she again leaned forward, and pressed another soft, tentative kiss to its dripping-white tip.

It shuddered again, pulsing out even more rich sweetness, but Alma was prepared this time, and perhaps even craving it, as she carefully sucked it inside. As Baldr gave an approving grunt beside her, his hand now rubbing at her back.

"Ach, this is it," he said softly. "He tastes so good, ach? Keep kissing him, and he shall grant you more."

Oh, *hell.* Alma's moan was far too loud, thoroughly shameful, but Drafli's heft only pulsed harder against her kissing mouth, and Baldr huffed a low, indulgent laugh. "Ach, thus," he breathed. "You look so pretty, Bright-Heart, with my mate's prick kissing your sweet little lips."

Alma moaned again, even louder than before, and Baldr laughed again, hot and husky, his hand still stroking at her back. "You shall taste so good after this, too," he purred. "If you can gain a full load of his seed thus, his sweet scent shall then *always* linger upon your mouth, ach?"

Gods, that should *not* have felt as appealing as it did, and Alma felt herself kissing harder, taking Drafli a little deeper. Earning another approving laugh from Baldr beside her, now close enough that she could feel his warm breath against her ear.

"And I shall tell you a secret," he whispered. "It shall help, I ken, if you use your tongue deeper. If you seek *inside* him, for his seed."

A distant part of Alma was suddenly quaking—Drafli could surely not want her *seeking his seed*—but somehow, somehow, she was already obeying. Her tongue stroking closer against that slick, oozing cleft, tentative at first, but then a little deeper. Feeling how it almost seemed to convulse around her, kissing back against her, granting her even more impossible heady sweetness...

"Ach, thus," Baldr was saying now, his hand still stroking at her back, his breath so close, as Alma kept tasting, licking, seeking. "Our orc-tongues are too large for this, but your little human ones are perfect, ach? If you keep seeking, mayhap he will open even more for you?"

Another hard, shameful moan escaped from Alma's mouth, but again she instantly obeyed, nudging her tongue even deeper against that slick, pulsing slit. Feeling how it did seem to soften at her touch, even slightly opening for her, so she might taste further inside. To where it felt tight, hot, silky-smooth, pulsing against her, *around* her, with every splutter of hot sweetness. As if she truly were seeking it from him, coaxing it out stronger and faster, drinking him from the inside out...

"Ach, thus," Baldr repeated, sounding rather ragged this time. "This is called a true orc's kiss. And should you fondle him here"—he brought Alma's tingly fingers up to Drafli's swollen bollocks, almost too large to fit in her hand—"this shall bring out even more."

Oh, gods, he was right, and these almost seemed to pulse beneath Alma's fingers, too. Surprisingly soft and heavy, covered over with thick dark hair, and Alma could almost feel the seed juddering up, pumping up the full length of him, out into her kissing mouth...

"Good woman," Baldr breathed beside her. "Now, if we pump his shaft as well, he will surely grant us all we wish. Just like a sweet milch cow, ach?"

He'd cast a sly, taunting look up toward Drafli as he spoke—and when Alma glanced up too, Drafli's gaze was glinting dangerously on Baldr's, clearly caught somewhere between incredulity and amusement. His brows sharply rising as he tugged himself away from her with a little pop—he'd been *on* her *tongue*, oh gods—and leaned back toward Baldr again.

And as Alma stared, awestruck, Drafli casually took himself in hand, his capable fingers circling close around his base—and then he swung himself sideways, and slapped his scarred heft straight across Baldr's *face*.

It must have stung—Baldr's head had snapped sideways at the impact, a low groan easing from his throat—but his eyes on Drafli's remained bright, taunting, hungry. Waiting, wanting this, as Drafli blatantly slapped him back across the other side, hard enough to again whip Baldr's head sideways, another growl burning from his mouth.

But that was still only pure, potent craving in Baldr's eyes, blinking with heated reverence on Drafli's imperious face. And when Drafli again thrust himself between Baldr's lips, far harder this time, Baldr's moan was deep and perhaps even grateful as he eagerly sucked Drafli down his throat.

Drafli stayed there even longer this time, pressing Baldr's flushed, gasping face tight against his groin, clearly as retaliation for his sheer audacity. Or, perhaps, for his betrayal, in teaching Alma to do such secret things. And she felt herself shuddering all over as Drafli's eyes flicked toward hers, dark and crackling, even as he kept grinding himself deep into his mate's throat.

But then, without warning, he'd yanked out of Baldr's mouth with an obscene squelching noise, his brows raising toward Alma. And oh hell, she was already obeying, lunging forward to kiss at him again, at where he'd just been buried down Baldr's throat. Her tongue again seeking that sweet bounty, slipping and slurping inside, feeling him pulse and dribble against her...

And then he was gone again, leaving Alma flushed and thwarted and gasping—but oh, that was because he was once again finding Baldr's parted lips, and plunging deep. While Baldr moaned and gasped as he sucked, his hands clutching hard at Drafli's thighs, his eyes worshipful on Drafli's face.

When Drafli yanked out again, with another obscene-sounding pop, Alma knew it was coming—and somehow that ramped the hunger even harder when he swung himself back toward her. That pulsing, sputtering heft again finding her mouth, kissing so filthy and lurid upon her hungry seeking tongue. While Baldr's hands kept rubbing up and down Drafli's thighs, and Alma's hands somehow found those heavy hanging bollocks again, eagerly caressing them with her fingers.

And when Drafli yanked away again, plunging back into Baldr's mouth, Alma kept both hands there, fervently stroking him, watching with wild, careening craving as he so deftly plundered his mate's throat. Making Baldr groan and drag for air, before again yanking out—now dripping a long string of Baldr's saliva, as well as his own thick white—and finding Alma's mouth, clutching and kissing at her tongue.

He still hadn't used her throat yet, not like he had with Baldr—and it meant there was still so much of him to touch, to learn. And somehow Alma had tugged Baldr closer, too, and oh, now he was licking Drafli *with* her, moaning as he slipped his long tongue almost fully around that scarred, veined, shuddering shaft, while she sought to lick inside it.

It meant their hungry mouths were brushing, their hands and fingers sliding together as they stroked and caressed at Drafli's thighs and bollocks, learning him together, worshipping him. And Alma's fervid, desperate glance upwards found Drafli watching them with almost feral intensity, his teeth bared, his lean body taut and ridged all over, his mouth contorting as his pulsing slit against Alma's tongue almost seemed to open wider, welcoming her inside—

And then, without warning, he *sprayed* her. That dark, secret channel suddenly spurting out a hot stream of sweet molten heat, so powerfully that it shot Alma's tongue away, and then flooded into her empty, unsuspecting mouth. And even as she fought to follow, to swallow, there was surely far too much, spilling out between her lips, spitting back onto him, and dribbling hot and sticky down her chin.

Drafli's eyes glittered even harder, as if rapt, or almost triumphant, on the sight—and he abruptly yanked his still-spewing heft away from her, and thrust it between Baldr's waiting lips instead. And Baldr frantically, eagerly swallowed, sucking him to the base, guzzling down the rest of his mate's sweet spurting seed, as his own eyes rolled back, his body arched and juddering all over...

And oh, that was because he was spraying out too, the wet liquid staining the front of his trousers in an ever-widening pool. And Drafli *liked* that, he'd wanted that, and his commanding, glittering eyes flicked back to Alma, as if to say, *Look at my mate, look how he pleases me, what about you—*

And it was shameful, abominable, but Alma's hungry, shaking hand had dropped to her own aching groin over her short skirt, rubbing hard once, twice. And then her own relief was shouting, spiralling, escaping coarse and desperate from her throat, and thoroughly, brutally betraying her.

But again, that was surely another twinge of unmistakable triumph in Drafli's watching eyes, or perhaps even... *approval*. And Alma felt herself shuddering beneath the strength of that, lost in the lingering tremors of pleasure, of *peace*.

Thank you, Golden-Tongue, she signed at him, without at all meaning to, and again, that had to be more approval in those eyes. Reluctant, perhaps, or grudging—but surely still there. And when his eyes flicked back to Baldr—who had been intently watching all this, still with Drafli's clearly softened length in his mouth—Drafli slightly jerked his head toward Alma, and briefly touched his thumb to his own lips.

It was some kind of sign, perhaps an order—and Baldr exhaled hard as he nodded and slowly drew away from Drafli, that slack, scarred, glistening heft slipping from his mouth with shameless ease. And then Baldr leaned forward, his sticky hand slipping around to the nape of Alma's neck, as he drew her close, and *kissed* her.

It was so soft, so tentative, so sweet—but it still felt like a frantic grappling explosion, rushing from the press of Baldr's lips, to every tingling nerve beneath Alma's skin. Because oh, he hadn't once yet kissed her, *ever*, and this careful, searching gentleness was at utter, staggering odds with Drafli's smooth, bone-melting certainty. But just as glorious, just as dizzying— and perhaps most of all in the way they both tasted of Drafli, the way his fresh seed still painted both their mouths with rich, decadent sweetness.

Baldr's eyes were dazed and heavy-lidded as he drew back, his gaze intent on Alma's swollen-feeling mouth, his tongue brushing against his own swollen lips. And when he glanced back up at Drafli, it was with palpable gratefulness in his eyes, or perhaps even adoration.

Thank you, Golden-Tongue, he signed, just the same way Alma had. And then, something new, something that had his wrists crossing against his own chest, his fists clenched tight. And then both hands lifted up, pressing the same sign in the same place against Drafli's chest, too.

I love you, it surely meant—and perhaps even more when Drafli's hand gripped Baldr's crossed wrists, and held them there. Making the words ring and resonate between them, hanging and flickering in the silence.

Alma's eyes seemed fixed on it, drinking it up just the way they were. And in this quiet, shimmering instant, she was distantly surprised to find that the swarm of emotion churning in her chest wasn't envy, or jealousy, like she might have thought. No, it was almost like... gratitude. Relief. Happiness.

Because surely, she hadn't yet come between them, in the way she'd feared. She hadn't stolen Baldr away, or turned him against his mate. He and Drafli still loved one another, so powerfully she could taste it—and she could almost see, perhaps, how she could fit into that, or even complement that, without at all taking it away from them.

And when Drafli finally dropped Baldr's hands from his chest, and briefly met her eyes, she wondered, for a breath, if perhaps he'd been thinking that, too. And while she braced for him to frown, or turn away, he just... didn't. Just exhaled, long and heavy, his chest slowly hollowing.

"You are a quick learner, Bright-Heart," Baldr murmured beside her, one of his hands still caressing Drafli's thigh, the other gripping gently at her knee. "Mayhap next time, once you have his leave, you shall seek to touch him even more? Only, no further back than here"—he gave Drafli a quick little smile as he again cupped at his still-bared bollocks, now looking shockingly large behind his softened heft—"and never to his neck, ach?"

Oh. And wait, that was new, surely—and as Alma glanced back and forth between them, she found Drafli suddenly frowning again, down toward where Baldr's eyes had gone a little stubborn, or maybe even defiant. As if this was something Baldr had wanted to tell her. Something she ought to know.

And now Alma's eyes were searching, finding Drafli's neck. Studying where his throat was visibly bobbing within it...

And wait. There—where she hadn't noticed before—was a very thin, very faint scar, drawn straight across the front half of Drafli's neck. As if it had been sliced, or sawed into, by a long, sharpened blade.

Comprehension swarmed Alma's thoughts, flooding in a sudden, sickening rush. So *this* was why Drafli struggled to speak aloud. Why he coughed as he had. Why he spoke with his hands. And whatever Alma had distantly attributed it to—some kind of unfortunate birth defect, perhaps—abruptly felt almost painfully laughable. Drafli had surely almost *died*, and it had taken his voice, and perhaps—perhaps his ease, as well. And perhaps this was why he was so twitchy, why Baldr always insisted on asking him, *he does not bear sudden movements, he has suffered much...*

Alma belatedly realized that they were both still looking at her, Baldr clearly tentative, Drafli with rapidly narrowing eyes. As if testing her, or fully expecting her to once again bungle this, one month to gain his trust...

"I understand," she said quietly, signing as she spoke, and feeling her mouth give a rueful little twist. "Just like a sweet milch cow, right?"

Beside her, Baldr huffed a choked, astonished laugh, but Alma was still watching Drafli. Drafli, whose eyes had briefly betrayed disbelief, or perhaps even—amusement? And before she'd quite followed it, he'd smoothly clutched at his softened heft, and swatted it straight across her *mouth*.

It didn't actually hurt—it had really felt more like a nudge—but Alma still gasped aloud, her body gone stiff, her eyes frozen on Drafli's face. On where he was coolly signing something down toward her, the movements far too fluid for her to follow.

"He says that if you ever *dare* to call him a cow again," Baldr murmured, his voice still edged with mirth, "he shall forego all the kindness he showed you today, and use your throat until *you* cannot speak, either."

Oh. Drafli had shown her *kindness* in this today? And even more importantly, was—was he now *teasing* her about it? Making a *joke*?

And blinking up at his carefully dispassionate face—yes, yes, surely he was—Alma felt herself bark a hoarse laugh, her smile bright and genuine and perhaps even grateful on his.

"Just like the degenerate devil he is," she murmured, and

gods, did she sound *eager*? "Though"—she cast a shy glance at Baldr—"*your* throat still seems to be in good working order, despite his use? Perhaps you could teach me a few tricks, just in case?"

And oh, Baldr's answering grin felt like light, like a shuddering, stunning flame in Alma's chest. "Ach, should you wish," he murmured. "Though this is much hard work and practice, and much gagging upon his prick, you ken?"

Alma's gaze had angled back to Drafli—Drafli, who was still standing here, watching, listening, for her answer—and she felt something like longing, or perhaps even craving, twisting low in her belly. "I wouldn't mind," she murmured, and though it was shameful, she couldn't seem to look away. "I truly want to learn to please you, my lord."

Drafli's mouth pursed, his eyes purposefully angling beyond her—but Baldr's hand was flexing at her knee, surely speaking of his silent approval. "Then we shall practice," he said. "And Drafli told me he left you some tools today also, ach? These should help, if you truly wish. For opening not only your throat for his taking, but also your other holes, as well."

He said this with firm, matter-of-fact ease, as if Alma opening her—*holes*—for his mate's taking was an ordinary, unremarkable request. And despite her frantically flaming cheeks, there was the inexplicable need to meet it with the same ease, or even eagerness.

"I understand," she said, signing as she spoke, glancing between them. "I'll do my best."

And yes, yes, that was grudging approval in Drafli's eyes, and most certainly in Baldr's dazzling, indulgent grin. "This pleases me, Bright-Heart," he murmured. "And we have some time left before we need to go out, ach, Draf? What do you say to one more round? Teach her how to take you a little deeper?"

And before Alma's face, Drafli's previously soft length... leapt. Twitching and shuddering, swelling and hardening, as though it couldn't think of anything more it wanted, than to plunge itself back into Alma's mouth.

And Alma's mouth had gone bone-dry, her eyes locked to the thoroughly thrilling sight. Drafli wanted her. He *wanted* her.

Her smile up at his face felt truly grateful, bare, shining from her eyes. And she kept her gaze on his as she leaned forward, inhaling, craving, longing. *May I suck you, my lord?* she asked, with only her hands this time. *Please?*

And Drafli's nod felt like a thunder-bolt, like the sun streaming on a bright summer morning. *Ach,* he signed back. *Kiss me.*

26

W hen Drafli finally walked Alma back out into the corridor again, she couldn't seem to stop smiling, despite the soreness in her lips, and the throbbing ache in her jaw.

They'd indeed done it all over again, much like the first time—but this time, Drafli had borne down far deeper into her mouth, stretching her around the full width of his shaft, gently nudging that shuddering slit into her throat. Coolly watching as she'd desperately sucked him, while Baldr had alternately murmured instructions and praises, and rubbed her back, and reminded her to breathe.

In the end, Drafli had finished the same way he had the first time—with Alma kissing at his head, her tongue sunk deep into his slit, while Baldr licked and lavished the rest of him. But this time, Alma had managed to swallow much more of Drafli's hot surging sweetness before he'd pulled out, and poured the rest into Baldr's mouth instead.

Along the way, Baldr had somehow again spilled into his trousers, without once being touched—and after Drafli had finished emptying into his throat, he'd demanded that Baldr hand the trousers over. And as Alma's reward—her *reward*, good gods—Drafli had allowed her to taste the seed on Baldr's trousers, while Baldr had sat there and watched, his eyes glittering with thwarted hunger, his now-bared heft swollen to full hardness again.

And Drafli clearly *was* the devil incarnate, because he'd only smirked at Baldr—and swiftly signed at him to stay—as he'd roughly tugged Alma's silvery fur cape back on, and guided her back out of the room. Leaving Baldr to laughingly huff behind them, and then loudly clear his throat.

"See you tonight, Bright-Heart?" he called after her. "After supper, mayhap?"

Alma eagerly nodded, flashing him a delighted smile over her shoulder, and then hurried to catch up with Drafli. And as he silently walked her down the corridor, Alma's grin truly felt like it was splitting her face, her eyes stealing regular glances up toward Drafli's surprisingly appealing profile. They'd had fun together. She'd pleased them. She'd see them again tonight. This was still doable. One month.

But Drafli hadn't once looked back down toward her, or acknowledged her searching glances. And the further they walked, the more Alma could feel him stiffening, his shoulders squaring. His previously easy strides becoming tight and controlled, his claw-pricks becoming ever more pronounced against her back. Until his hand dropped altogether, his body easing away from her as they walked, putting a small but palpable distance between them.

Alma couldn't seem to hide her wistful sigh, or her reproachful, lingering grimace toward him—to which Drafli instantly glared back, his hand making that so-familiar slicing gesture. *No. Stop.*

Right then. Alma swallowed, fighting to ignore the hard drop in her belly, the clench of her fingers against Baldr's trousers. Wait, she still had Baldr's *trousers*, and she suddenly felt her face burning at the memory, and then at her belated understanding of Drafli's implication in giving them to her.

Because surely, he'd done it so Alma could *wash* them. He'd been—*mocking* her. Reminding her of her place. As their *servant*.

And Alma would not give this prick the satisfaction of knowing he'd hurt her again—she would *not*—and she gritted her teeth, and stared at the corridor up ahead, while the mingled misery and frustration pulsed deeper. She was supposed to be honouring him, gaining his trust... but obviously this was how he wanted it to be, right? And gods, why keep pretending otherwise, why keep handing her heart to him, when he clearly couldn't care less?

"So Pure-Heart didn't know you were going to send me off shopping like that today, did he?" she heard herself mutter at him, under her breath. "I don't suppose you've ever thought to do the same for *him*?"

It was a question that had been scraping at the back of her mind, ever since she'd seen that twinge of jealousy—or perhaps even hurt—in Baldr's eyes. *She does look like a true Grisk*, he'd told Drafli. *And that pleases you too, I ken?*

Drafli certainly hadn't missed the accusation in Alma's voice, and he was already easing a little further away from her, angling her a look of deep dislike. *I have offered*, he mouthed back at her, matching it with sharp movements of his hands. *But Pure-Heart refused this, and I no wished to push him.*

Oh. The truth of that answer—laced, surely, with defensiveness—caught Alma up short, her eyes again searching Drafli's harsh profile. "Then why do you think he refused?" she asked, still with an edge on her voice. "Because he didn't want to take your coin? Or he didn't like the idea of you dressing him? Or"—her voice dropped lower—"*he* didn't want to feel obliged to dress like a Grisk, too?"

Drafli didn't look at her this time, but his mouth had visibly spasmed at the last bit. Suggesting, surely, that it was indeed the Grisk point that had been the issue, because of course

Baldr would otherwise welcome such attentions from the mate he loved so much, wouldn't he?

"And he couldn't dress more like... a Skai, then?" Alma asked, frowning at Drafli's perennially bare chest, at the low-slung trousers that always seemed to show off far more than Baldr's did. "Maria showed me how Skai orcs like their mates to dress, so...?"

Drafli's glance toward her was pure withering derision now, his lip curling. *Ach, no,* he mouthed and signed at her, the movements forceful. *Pure-Heart is my mate, but he is yet Grisk, not Skai. He shall never be Skai, and I am glad of this.*

Despite her still-present irritation, Alma carefully watched the movements of Drafli's hands, especially on the clan names—*Grisk* a fluttering little wave over his heart, *Skai* a quick movement that surely echoed a blade-strike. And she found herself thinking, distantly, about what Kesst had said to Baldr, days before. *You're a Grisk, not a Skai. I'm a used-up Ash-Kai slag, not a lovely, scent-bound hearth-mate.*

"Then do you know why Pure-Heart feels as he does about his clan?" Alma asked, surely pushing it now, but suddenly this seemed crucially important. "Why he apparently avoids everything to do with them? Is it related to what Kesst said, about"— she didn't say it aloud, but made the *Grisk* sign instead—"being cowards?"

Drafli made a face, and gave a jerky shrug of his shoulder. *Mayhap,* he mouthed, with a corresponding, wishy-washy sign. *But Pure-Heart no like to speak of this. And*—his eyes narrowed dangerously toward her—*you shall never again call Grisk cowards. Grisk are oft sweet and faithful, but this no mean weak. Pure-Heart is no weak.*

Oh. Alma grimaced and nodded, though she couldn't seem to stop searching Drafli's face. Realizing, with more blunted surprise, that he clearly cared about this, and perhaps this had been bothering him, too. And perhaps—Alma's eyes darted down toward her own ensemble—had this perhaps even been part of it?

"So did you *mean* for me to go off and dress up like a Grisk today?" she asked him, her voice rising. "As some kind of—of statement to him? Or a *test*?"

Drafli's frown etched even deeper, and something flexed in his jaw. *I no tell you to dress thus*, he signed back. *You do this.*

Right. But searching his hard profile again, Alma couldn't quite shake the feeling that he'd still perhaps wanted it. *Dress to please my mate*, he'd written. And *had* it all been play-acting, back in that meeting-room, when Drafli had come over and kissed her, *rewarded* her, said she looked like a true Grisk...

"Well," Alma continued, before she lost the nerve, "if you haven't already, then I think you should try giving him some jewels. Ella said it was traditional to give jewels and piercings to your Grisk mate, as a sign of your affection, but"—she hauled in another breath, speaking faster now—"Pure-Heart doesn't wear any, does he? And I mean, maybe he wouldn't want those either, maybe he really *doesn't* care about Grisk traditions at all, and of course that's fine. But—if he sees you give those ones you had to *me*, and you've never offered any to *him*, well—"

She belatedly snapped her babbling mouth shut, because surely she wasn't foolish enough to accuse Drafli of failing his own mate in this, or failing to see the potential pitfalls in such a plan? But beyond another dark frown toward her, Drafli didn't actually retaliate, and instead nudged her around a corner, back toward the Grisk wing.

"Er, actually," Alma cut in, her voice flattening as she glanced down at the trousers still in her hand, "didn't you mean to take me to the scullery?"

Drafli shot her yet another dismissive frown, and kept walking. *Why*, he signed at her, *would I wish this.*

"Um, because of these?" Alma said, waving Baldr's sodden trousers at him. "Because you wanted me to wash them, right?"

Drafli gave her an impressively bland look—good gods,

now he was going to pretend like didn't even know what she was talking about?—and Alma felt her feet skittering to a halt, her hands clenching to fists. While all the combined emotion and confusion of this utterly unreal day bubbled and churned, jostling for escape out her still-sore throat.

"You gave me your mate's dirty clothes," she hissed at him, "to remind me of my place. Remember? To make it extra clear, in case I wasn't already well aware, that I'm here to be your *servant!* Just like Maria said!"

Drafli's steps had abruptly stilled, too, his dark eyes narrowing toward her—and without warning, he yanked her sideways, into another empty, abandoned-looking room. This one featuring a few low tables and stone stools, as though it might have once been a dining room.

Why you think this, he signed sharply at her, as he loomed before her in the faint lamplight, his shoulders hunched. *You are no servant. I swear* vow *to you. You say I no keep my word?*

Alma blinked down at Baldr's wet trousers, and back up at Drafli's face—but before she could speak, Drafli's hand snapped sideways. *No. Stop.*

I only give you these to tease Pure-Heart, he silently mouthed and signed at her, the movements pointed, but slow enough for her to follow. *Because now he think of you smelling these. You tasting these, and thinking of him. This is all.*

Oh. Wait. Drafli meant—he hadn't meant Alma to do the laundry? He had meant—

I no seek to make you servant, foolish woman, Drafli continued, silent and furious, his hands now wide and wheeling. *I seek to make you his hearth-mate!*

Wait. He was—Drafli was trying to make Alma into Baldr's *hearth-mate*? And a hearth-mate was—*a sweet, loyal, beautiful woman*, Kesst had said, *who tends your hearth, and eases your pain, while also shamelessly blowing your mind in bed...*

And wait. Even this morning, with Drafli so blatantly using

his fingers on her, *there is no shame, dress to please my mate, I want her to please you...*

And as horribly lowering as that awareness suddenly was—Drafli had still been doing all that for *Baldr*, and not for himself in the least—far more powerful was the truth of Drafli stepping closer, his hand reaching out, and gripping Alma's chin with surprising strength. Tilting it up toward him, making her meet his glinting, bitter eyes. And, perhaps, making himself look at her, too, as though he loathed the very sight of her.

"You ought to *thank* me, foolish woman," he rasped at her, out loud this time, his mouth contorting. "I shall make you all Pure-Heart deserves. You shall be one he can trust. One who shall please him without shame. One who shall *never* betray him, or bring him pain!"

And at that last word, Drafli's voice broke, his head snapping sideways, as a series of ugly, grating coughs barked from his throat. While Alma had seized to stillness before him, feeling his fingers convulse on her chin with every wracking cough, her own thoughts gone stilted and strange.

Because Drafli was comparing her to... *himself*. Wasn't he? He himself had failed Baldr, betrayed Baldr, so now Alma was some kind of... of apology? Compensation? And perhaps even a punishment to himself, something he would be forced to endure for the rest of his *life*?

And staring at Drafli like this, at his other hand now clasping against his own neck—his horrible, devastating scar—it occurred to Alma that he'd been betrayed, too. *By a woman he cared for*, Baldr had said. And then Drafli had turned around and betrayed Baldr, for *years*, and now this. All these lies, that vow, those rules he'd given her... to keep his mate safe. To protect Baldr from what Drafli himself had suffered. From *him*.

"So you... you didn't drag me into all this just to give Baldr a son, then?" Alma heard herself say, her voice very thin. "Or to deal with the bond? I'm also"—she felt herself swallow—"your chance to do it all over again? Your penance? Your—your *absolution*?!"

Drafli's hand had dropped from his neck, his head twitching as he glared back at her. "I already tell you, I give all for him," he hissed, now barely audible. "I give him son. I give him *peace*. And, ach, it is too late for me, so I give him *you*!"

As he spoke, his eyes raked up and down Alma's body, lingering not only on the beautiful new clothes he'd given her, but on the swell of her breasts, and her bared waist. His eyes again glittering with bitterness, with loathing, with... *envy*.

And wait, now his hand had dropped to follow his eyes, skating just as coldly down her front. Pausing to jiggle at her heavy breast, and then to pinch at her peaked nipple, before slipping further downwards. Flipping up her skirt like he owned it, like he owned her—and oh, hell, touching her like he owned her, too. His cool fingers efficiently skating over her swollen, slick-feeling crease, while she gasped and shuddered against them. *Wanted* them.

His cruel mouth had curved into a mockery of a smile, even as one of those delving fingers split from the rest, and slid up inside her. Dragging another hoarse, hungry moan from Alma's throat, and in response Drafli's mouth twisted higher, that bitter envy glinting harder in his eyes.

"See?" he whispered at her, his finger plunging deeper, while she helplessly twisted and writhed against him. "I make you into Pure-Heart's dream. Into all he has ever *wished* for!"

Alma couldn't stop shuddering, staring, while the comprehension kept blooming through her thoughts. *Pure-Heart's dream. His hearth-mate. One he can trust. All he has ever wished for. It is too late for me.*

And perhaps it was the sheer audacity of this, of the blatant, casual ownership in how Drafli was touching her. Or perhaps it was the truth of him indeed touching her like this, *again*, almost as if he *wanted* to be there, despite all his mockery, all his anger...

But whatever it was, as Alma stared up at this deadly, duplicitous orc—whose finger was still toying *inside* her—she suddenly felt almost breathless with clarity... and with a rapidly rising, dizzying rage. This bastard. This complete and callous *bastard*.

"You lying, self-absorbed *prick*," she hissed at him, her voice cracking, her body clamping hard against him. "It is not too late for you. It is *not*. Pure-Heart wants you. He *loves* you. And he has clearly chosen to forgive you for your awful past actions, even if you don't deserve it! So why the hell can't you take that for the incredible gift it is, and try to make *yourself* worthy of him, rather than dumping all your rubbish on *me!*"

Something flared in Drafli's eyes, and his hand abruptly yanked back from her, stealing his strength away—but Alma was in this now, the words spilling from her mouth. "You could stop lying to him, to start," she hissed. "You could stop making all these vows and threats and schemes behind his back. You can treat him with the respect and the honesty and the *love* he damn well deserves!"

Drafli's eyes flashed again, his hand now snapping sideways, saying, *Stop*—but Alma's rage just seemed to kick higher, clamping at her chest. "And if you're still so hell-bent on making me part of this, then maybe you could stop lying and pretending with me, too! We both know you don't exactly *mind* touching me, and lording your power over me, and teaching me how to please you! And, you *wanted* me to dress up like a Grisk today, whether you admit it or not! So why the hell can't we just be honest with each other, and make the best of it?! For Pure-Heart's sake, if nothing else!"

There was a brief, stilted silence, another menacing judder of Drafli's hand in midair. And suddenly Alma's thoughts had leapt back to that morning, to Drafli asking Efterar if she was pregnant. To that look in his eyes when Efterar had said no. That *relief*.

"And," she continued, her voice hardening, "for our future

son's sake, as well. Because if you think your son will be well-served by one of his own *fathers* being a total scheming bastard, and lying up and down to his other two parents to assuage his own ridiculous guilt complex, then you've lost your damned *mind*!"

Drafli's eyes were looking truly murderous now, his mouth curling with certain, vicious bitterness. *Your son*, he signed at her, and oh, *son* was like he was rocking a little baby, protecting it in his arms, *will no be mine. He will be Grisk. From Pure-Heart, and you.*

Alma was again struck momentarily speechless—wait, her son would be Grisk, Baldr's son would be Grisk, of course, of *course*—but then she found her hand signing back at Drafli, sharp and furious. *Stop. Stop.*

"Oh give it up, you prick," she snarled at him, and suddenly she was somehow even angrier than before. "How *dare* you say our son won't be yours. It's only thanks to you that he'll even exist! And I've sworn to hand him off into your custody *forever*, and you've sworn to protect him with your *life*. You promised!"

And even Drafli couldn't argue that, his eyes gone unnervingly still on hers, with something dangerous lurking beneath—but Alma was not done, not even close. "So of course you will be our son's father," she hissed, "and you had damned well better start accepting it. Or else"—she dragged in another breath—"I will call this entire deal *off*, Drafli! I will run off back to Ashford, and leave you to wallow here in your guilt and your lies, *forever*!"

Her words seemed to ring painfully through the air, pinging back and forth between them. And for a stilted, hanging moment, Drafli just... looked at her. Looked at her, as though he'd never quite seen her before.

Until without warning, his hand snapped out, straight toward her neck. Circling around it with taut, barely restrained strength, his long fingers flexing, his claws prodding into her skin. Clearly making a statement, reasserting his authority, reminding Alma of her place. *You swore a vow. Honour me. Obey me.*

But even as that familiar hot shudder rippled up Alma's back, her heartbeat skipping in her chest, she felt herself raising her chin, holding his eyes, perhaps even pressing her neck tighter into his touch. "I *am* honouring you," she said, her throat moving close against his warm, flexing fingers. "I'm keeping my vow to you, in every way I can, and you know it. Now you need to keep yours, and get over your own rubbish, and be the mate you swore to be. The *parent* you swore to be. For Pure-Heart, and your *son!*"

Drafli had moved closer toward her, his lips pulling back into another silent snarl, a threat—but the dregs of Alma's rage were still lingering, just enough to raise her chin even higher. "And unless you want me to go tell Pure-Heart all of this," she breathed at him, "you *will* go back to him, now. You'll tell him that you've been thinking about your son being Grisk, and how because of that, you've been wanting to learn more about Grisk culture together with him. And if Pure-Heart is willing, you *will* go get him something gold and shiny. And then you will tell him how much you love and appreciate him, and pound him into your bed until he *screams* your name!"

And again, for another long, tangled instant, Drafli just stared at her. But this time, somehow, Alma could almost read the emotions, passing one by one across his too-bright eyes. Rage. Disbelief. Frustration. Regret. Recognition. Longing.

Longing.

"Please," Alma heard her voice say, far quieter than before. "For them. My lord."

And finally, Drafli grimaced, and snatched for Baldr's trousers, yanking them out of Alma's slack hands. Leaving her untouched, unanswered, as he spun on his heel and stalked out, without looking back.

27

A lma felt cold and shaky all over as she staggered out into the corridor again, rubbing her hand at her hot, prickling face.

She had one measly month to make friends of Drafli. To gain his trust. And it had all been going so *well*, and then she'd gone and shouted at him like that? Made demands of him? Threatened to tell Baldr everything, or call the entire plan off? To break her own vow? To *leave*?! To run back to Ashford?

And now here was the spectre of Mr. Pembroke, looming up far too strong in her thoughts. And with it, the realization that she hadn't heard anything about him these past few days. Had she? And yes, she'd sworn to Drafli that she would stop worrying about him... but *had* Mr. Pembroke ever stopped looking for her? Or stopped accusing the orcs of kidnapping her? And if she asked Baldr or Drafli about it, would that make Drafli even angrier? Even more displeased with her than he already was?

It was all so unsettling, and so confusing, and Alma somehow made her shaky way into the kitchen, and into the filthy scullery. Where she promptly dove into her lengthy mental list of long-overdue tasks with desperate abandon, fighting to forget the words she'd shouted at Drafli, the fury in his crackling eyes.

She'd ruined everything. He would never forgive her. *Ever*.

"Gods above, sweetheart," cut in a blank, familiar voice behind her, some time later. "What the *hell* are you doing?"

Alma guiltily whirled around, her hands wet and reddened with lye—and found Kesst standing in the doorway, eyeing the scullery with awed, blinking astonishment. His gaze lingering first on the four huge tubs full of steaming water and soaking laundry, and then on the soap Alma was currently mixing together, thanks to the buckets of lye and lard she'd found beneath the counter. And then Kesst's disbelieving eyes glanced to the spotless counters, and the equally spotless floor, and the large assortment of wet, wrung-out clothing now hanging on the rickety racks she'd pulled out from the wall. And then up to the mountain of laundry, which, while still enormous, now looked slightly less malevolent than before.

"The laundry, of course," Alma replied, with a halfhearted attempt at a smile, and a bracing breath. "And I've discovered, Kesst, that unlike with human—er—*spend*, orc-seed seems to be entirely water-soluble, and dissolves away with almost no effort whatsoever! I cannot tell you how deeply relieved I am. That is an *unimaginable* gift from the gods to your kind, you must know."

Kesst kept blinking bemusedly toward her, and Alma lurched for the sink again, and rinsed off her reddened hands in the basin. "But the blood is still just as stubborn as ever," she continued, "and I've no idea where to air out the furs. And I realized that I also have no conception of whose laundry is whose, or which wing to send it back to. I presume Roland must have sorted it all by scent?"

Kesst was still gaping around at the room, and then down at Alma's reddened hands. "Yes, no doubt," he said. "And honestly, there's no point in taking bloodstains out from most of these, because those constantly brawling pillocks will just put them back again. And look"—he wrinkled his nose, now eyeing the certain mess of Alma's frizzy-feeling hair—"weren't you supposed to be getting some help for all this anyway? Wasn't your fellow sickly-sweet Grisk supposed to be sorting that out for you?"

Gods, Alma had very nearly forgotten about that, amidst the rest of the miserable mess swarming her thoughts. And the surprise of it almost drowned out the sudden twinge of hurt at Kesst's words—*sickly-sweet*, he'd called her—until she caught the look in his eyes as they flicked dispassionately up and down her still scantily-clad body. As if he was... *judging* her.

And yes, good gods, Alma had almost completely forgotten about her new clothes, too—they really had turned out to be quite comfortable—and for the first time since that morning, she felt the inexplicable urge to cover herself, to hide away her shame.

There is no shame, Drafli's distant voice hissed—but Drafli surely hated her now, and Alma's eyes had already dropped, her wet hands rubbing against her skirt. "Um," she said, "right. I should have checked with Baldr on that. It's just been really busy, and..."

"But not too busy to go off dressing up like every Grisk's wet dream, right?" Kesst's cool voice interjected. "And then to suck some Skai cock, too? I *dearly* hope Drafli didn't bruise your already-wounded throat, at least, because more pointless work is *just* what Eft needs right now, you know."

Oh. There was a sudden hot prickling behind Alma's lowered eyes, and while there was a ridiculous urge to insist that she *liked* her new clothes—and Drafli *had* actually been gentle, at least in that—she couldn't seem to speak over the lump in her throat. And before she could fully betray her weakness, she spun back around to the mountain of laundry, and frantically began sorting, even faster than before.

"Shit," came Kesst's low voice behind her, and then a heavy

sigh. "Shit, sweetheart, I'm sorry. I really am. I'm just being a petty jealous prick, all right?"

Alma swallowed hard, but couldn't seem to turn around, and Kesst gave another heavy sigh. "Just—seeing you in this getup, volunteering to do all this heavy labour, being your impossibly sweet scent-bound self"—his voice cracked—"gods, you're so perfect that even a *Skai* apparently dotes on you! Is it true that he gave you *four hundred* trading-credits so you could deck yourself out to please him? I mean, what the *fuck*, sweetheart. I can't even afford a clean pair of *trousers*."

Alma's hands had frozen on the laundry—had anyone ever explained how much of Drafli's gift she'd spent, or how much she had left over?—and she bit her lip, her heart beating erratically in her chest. "Believe me, Drafli does *not* think I'm perfect," she said, her voice wavering. "And truly, Kesst, if I have any credits left, I'd be more than happy to share them with you. There were so many clothes in that storage-room, I've never seen anything like it in my life. And Ella said anyone was welcome to shop there, and—"

But Kesst was loudly groaning behind her, the sound deep with exasperation. "No, sweetheart," he snapped. "No. Stop it right there. I will *not* take your credits. *Ever*. For fuck's sakes."

Right. Alma couldn't seem to find an answer for that, and Kesst groaned again. "And you look marvellous like this," he said thinly, "and Eft was right, because your scent is beautifully balanced, too. And as loath as I am to admit it, that Skai bastard clearly knows what he's about—and I clearly don't. So ignore my rubbish, *please*."

Alma's breath was coming a little slower, and she attempted a smile that Kesst couldn't see. "It's all right, Kesst," she said, and she meant it, though her voice still wavered. "I know you've been dealing with a lot lately. And"—her thoughts flicked back to that meeting-room earlier, to what Kesst had been telling the captain—"it really does seem like Efterar has been working way too much, hasn't he? That must be so difficult and exhausting. For both of you."

Kesst barked a hoarse laugh behind her, and that might have been the sound of him kicking one of her overloaded wash-basins. "For *him*, you mean," he said. "Whereas I—you can ask Grim, because I quote—am quite possibly the most useless orc in this mountain."

What? Alma whirled around to frown at Kesst, her own hurt entirely forgotten beneath her rising indignation—and he frantically waved it away, in a motion that was rather similar to Drafli's *stop* sign. "Just—forget it," he said thickly. "And look, how much longer do you think the rest of this will take? I've been wanting to bring in the sickroom bedding, it's such a vile infection hazard at this point, but—"

He bit his lip there, blinking his too-bright eyes up at the mountain of laundry, and Alma felt her indignation jolting even higher, and with it a tight, gut-swarming sympathy. "I'll ask about getting more help," she said firmly. "And you're absolutely right, the sickroom bedding should be a major priority, and I can't believe I didn't even think of it. Is there anything else over there that ought to be dealt with?"

Kesst looked like he was about to speak, but then clamped his mouth shut, and shook his head. "Just—stop, sweetheart," he said, choked. "Gods. It's *fine*. I just—"

He gave another frantic wave of his hand, and then whirled around, and rushed out. Leaving Alma staring at the empty doorway after him, her thoughts again churning up with miserable helplessness, a hard lump forming in her throat.

Gods, could she not do anything right? First Pembroke, and then Baldr and Drafli, and now Kesst, and even the damned laundry, too?

Foolish woman. Sickly-sweet. Shameful. A servant.

And suddenly Alma's shoulders were shuddering, her hands over her face, her head whipping back and forth. She couldn't do this. She was ruining this. One month...

"Hey, Alma," interrupted a vaguely familiar voice. "Is everything all right?"

Alma's head snapped up, her heart thundering—but no, it was only Ella, leaning against the scullery door, her head tilted. "Varinn mentioned—well. Is there anything I can help you with? Maybe I could send for Maria again?"

Ella's eyes twinkled at that last bit, as if she knew exactly what chaos might next ensue—and Alma couldn't help a choked laugh, even as she winced, and shook her head. Gods, she could not risk angering Drafli even further, what if he never forgave her for this, one month...

"No, I'm fine," she replied, though the words were brittle, a lie. "I just..."

And gods, she couldn't even finish, her eyes helplessly searching Ella's—and Ella's shoulders slightly sagged, her mouth twitching into not quite a smile. "You know, I missed my prayers this morning," she said, "so I was just on my way to the Grisk shrine. Perhaps you'd like to come along?"

Alma couldn't seem to find a reason to refuse, and soon she was numbly following Ella down the corridor, and into a new set of rooms she hadn't yet encountered. They apparently belonged to Ella's mate Nattfarr, due to his role as the Grisk Speaker—but, Ella explained, they were open to anyone who wished to visit, the shrine most of all.

Alma had listlessly nodded at all this, though she felt her attention slightly sparking as Ella led her into the cozy, sweet-scented shrine. It was lined with soft furs and colourful wall hangings, and along one side there was a long table with a row of carved figures, each more fantastical than the last. And Ella had gone to stand before perhaps the most astonishing figure of them all—a beautiful human woman, with disproportionately large breasts, and a blatantly bared, swollen belly.

"This is our goddess Akva, the mother of all five clans," Ella said, as she sank to the fur-covered floor before the goddess, her hand over her heart. "She sees us as her daughters, and welcomes us, just as we are, without shame."

Without shame. Those words pulling painfully in Alma's chest, and she found herself carefully studying the carving, taking in the strange, surprising freeness of it. In the fact that it was just sitting here, out in the open like this, not only for the Grisk to see, but to *worship.* A human, and a goddess. *There is no shame...*

"She's lovely," Alma said, though she couldn't help an uncertain glance toward where Ella was still kneeling, her head lowered. "But—Drafli asked me to honour *his* god in my prayers. Skai-kesh."

She winced as she spoke, fully anticipating more censure, more questioning of Drafli's surely questionable motives in such a command. But Ella's glance upwards was surprised, and perhaps also... pleased?

"Oh, that's very thoughtful of him," she said, to Alma's vague astonishment. "Of course he would want to teach you about his clan, and their god—Skai-kesh is very important to the Skai. But if you like, you're welcome to honour both, because Akva is Skai-kesh's mother, you see. And Skai-kesh often stays close to her, protecting her."

With that, she'd waved up at the figure after Akva in the row—the taller, leaner orc, who had gleaming, black-painted eyes. Eyes that almost seemed to look into Alma, through Alma, down into the chaos and confusion, and the cold, curdling misery crowding at her heart. As if he... saw her.

Alma felt herself swallow, her eyes glancing down at her still-surprising ensemble—and then she furtively nodded, and knelt beside Ella on the furs. And when Ella closed her eyes, her hand still over her heart—*thank you*, it was saying—Alma did the same, breathing in deep.

And to her distant surprise, it helped. The quiet, the steady breaths, the easy companionship of Ella beside her. The comfort in even the idea of this Akva, a brazen, sensual, much-loved human mother, who saw her daughters without judge-ment or shame—and close beside her, a fierce, all-seeing Skai, defending her, keeping her safe.

And for the first time in perhaps days, Alma even allowed her thoughts to circle toward her own mother, and that urn of ashes, still hidden under her bed back at Mr. Pembroke's. Toward how her mother had also loved her, seen her, accepted her—but then, how she'd still stayed at Mr. Pembroke's. How she'd stayed in a situation that had surely hurt her, and would surely someday hurt her daughter, as well.

And gods, Alma missed her mother, and loved her, and somehow still wanted to shout at her, to rage at her, just the way she'd shouted at Drafli. *You could stop lying. You need to step the hell up, and be the parent you swore to be...*

The strength of that conviction felt almost alarming, suddenly—but also, perhaps almost reassuring, too. If nothing else, Alma had defended her son today, even if he didn't exist yet. She'd sought to protect him, to keep him safe. To honour him, as best she could.

There is no shame.

And when there was a loud squalling at the door—Ella's little orcling Rakfi again, trying to escape from the arms of a rueful-looking Varinn this time—Alma found herself smiling, and wiping at her eyes. And then agreeing, with genuine will-ingness, to Ella's cheerful offer of a late lunch, and perhaps some entertainment, too.

The entertainment turned out to be a good-natured wrestling-match in an adjacent sparring-room, pitting Varinn and Thrain against two genial Grisk orcs Alma hadn't yet met—Thrak, Thrain's blood-brother, and his heavily pierced, sharp-eyed mate Dammarr—while Nattfarr officiated. And by the end of it, Alma was laughing so hard her stomach hurt, and she'd somehow even made a friend of Rakfi, who'd happily squirmed between her and Ella while they'd watched.

And once they'd finished, Alma still felt easier—lighter,

somehow—as she made her way back to the kitchen again.
Saying a brief hello to Gegnir and Narfi, who were both now
cleaning up after the main meal of the day, and then settling
herself to work in the scullery again, diving back into her list of
projects with single-minded purpose.

And this helped, too. Just working, moving, doing, until
there was only one task after another. So simple and straight-
forward, so surprisingly comforting—and in its steady accomplishment, there was somehow a steady rising certainty, too.

She would keep honouring Drafli, and seeking to gain his
trust, as she'd promised—one month—but she would not
repeat her mother's mistakes, either. She would *not* stop
demanding Drafli do better, both for Baldr, and their son. She
would try to do better. She *would*.

"Still at it, sweetheart?" broke in a quiet, tentative voice at
the door, and when Alma looked up from her washtub, it was
Kesst again. His face looking markedly subdued as his hand
thrust out a chipped cup full of beautiful pink flowers.

"Here," he said. "Camellias, from the garden. To brighten
up your lovely scullery."

He'd cast a grimacing glance behind her, surely betraying
his true thoughts on said scullery, but Alma was already
standing and wiping her hands, and gratefully taking the cup
of flowers. "They're so pretty," she told him, with a smile.
"Thank you."

Kesst grimaced and shook his head, his eyes flitting up to
the mountain of laundry. "I just—wanted to apologize," he
said. "Again. You're lovely, and I'm a crusty bitter arsehole."

But Alma waved it away, and set her flowers on the counter.
"It's forgotten," she said. "You're lovely too, Kesst. And look"—
she couldn't help a pointed glance toward him—"you really
ought to bring the sickroom bedding by, sooner rather than
later. If you don't mind."

Kesst loudly snorted, shaking his head, though his eyes
were again looking oddly bright. "And you desperately need to

be stopped, sweetheart," he said, choked. "Before all our teeth rot out of our heads. Gods. The bedding's *fine*."

But it clearly wasn't, and *he* clearly wasn't, and Alma eyed him for another long, hanging instant before loudly clearing her throat. "Well then," she said, "it's been a while since I've last eaten, how about you? Do you think Gegnir and Narfi would mind if we cooked something, as long as we stay out of their way?"

Kesst blinked at her, but then slowly shook his head. "No, I cook at odd hours all the time," he replied, his voice still hoarse. "What were you thinking?"

It was the first hint of cautious optimism Alma had caught from him in this whole miserable day so far, and she attempted another smile, a jaunty tilt of her chin. "Well, why don't we go see what's there?" she said. "And you can tell me what your favourite human meal is?"

That was definitely interest in Kesst's eyes this time, even though he clearly tried to hide it—and his brief tour through the kitchen, showing Alma where various stores were kept, was genuinely helpful. After a while Gegnir even began tagging along, darkly pointing out that Roland had previously managed all the kitchen's inventory and food-delivery credits, and that while he'd tried to take it over in Roland's absence, he scarce knew what was where, or whether he'd paid out the proper amounts for it.

"I'd honestly be happy to help with that while I'm here, Gegnir," Alma told him, as she and Kesst peered into crates and baskets and barrels. "It's the kind of work I always did back in Ashford. To start, though, I'd need a list of items and amounts, if that might be something you can pull together for me?"

Gegnir readily grunted his agreement, and then heaved out a large barrel of salted pork, and then an overflowing basket of fresh berries. And upon seeing Kesst's eyes light up at the sight, Alma announced that she was in the mood for some pork pie and berry cobbler, if anyone else would like some?

It turned out that Gegnir was quite eager for a meal too—Alma well knew how wearying it could be for cooks to be always making their own meals—though Narfi, who had been furtively lurking about, loudly sniffed, wrinkling his nose at her. "I should not eat *anything* a human makes," he declared, to the room at large. "Her foul reek shall taint it all."

Alma felt herself blanch, but thankfully Kesst had whirled around toward Narfi, baring his surprisingly sharp-looking teeth. "Oh, shut it, you slimy little toad," he snapped. "The only thing Alma reeks of right now is Skai, and you damn well know it. You only *wish* you smelled like her."

Narfi scoffed a laugh, and curled his lip back at Kesst. "Ach, I yet bear far more of our Right Hand's sweet scent than *she* does," he hissed, jerking his head toward Alma. "There is *naught* of him on her womb, ach? And, for one who *dares* to besmirch Skai scent thus"—he took a menacing step toward Kesst—"you still carry so much of this, that I oft ken the great Ofnir yet walks among us!"

There was an instant's ringing stillness, in which Alma felt her own indignation rising—wait, did Narfi mean he'd taken *pleasure* with Drafli?!—while beside her, Kesst had gone markedly pale, his claws digging into the wooden counter. And though his mouth slowly opened, nothing seemed to come out, and Alma was deeply relieved when Gegnir barked something at Narfi in the orcs' language, and sent him scurrying out the door.

"Pay him no heed, either of you," Gegnir grunted, with a dark look toward where Narfi had gone. "I smell naught that he spoke of, and he likely only seeks to rile you. Now, woman, here is the flour and lard. What more do you need?"

Alma gratefully returned her attention to the task at hand, again sinking into the familiar, comforting rhythm of work, of doing, of creating something real and useful. This pork pie had been one of her mother's favourite recipes, and she even found herself humming a little tune as she worked, and chatting easily with Gegnir beside her. Asking him for more details about how the kitchen and supply stores usually ran, and what else he could recall that Roland had previously done.

But Kesst remained unusually subdued throughout, despite Alma and Gegnir's attempts to involve him in the conversation. And he only seemed to revive himself when Alma had finally finished packing a fragrant, steaming basket of food, and then thrust it into his slack hands.

"For you, and Efterar," she said firmly. "And there's a little empty dining room just down the corridor, and I *insist* that you two go eat it there, *alone*. And ignore any and all demands for Efterar's attention until you're done. Or else."

Kesst was blinking blankly down at the basket—Alma had stuffed it with several pork pies, and the cobbler, and some biscuits she'd thrown together with the leftover flour and lard. "Um, sweetheart," he said, his voice choked, "this is—"

"Your supper," she repeated. "And gods only know when you and Efterar have last eaten a proper meal, and that would make anyone tetchy, all right? Now go. And remember, *no working*. For either of you."

Kesst was still giving Alma a bemused, blinking look, but after she shooed him toward the door—and then threatened to go for her broom—he finally turned and went. Leaving Alma alone with Gegnir, who was giving a low chuckle beside her.

"I commend you, woman," he said, as he sliced out a piece of steaming pie with his claw, and took a gigantic, rather terrifying bite. "That boy needs strong handling thus. Seems you are learning well from your Skai, ach?"

Alma had been giving a flushed-feeling smile, but felt it swiftly fading at that mention of *your Skai*. Drafli. She'd been desperately trying to avoid thinking about him while she'd worked—about that look in his eyes, about how he'd walked away—but now, it seemed as though he was swarming all her thoughts, flooding her with fury and contempt.

Foolish woman, he'd said. *Obey me*.

But Alma still wanted to do better. She needed to do better. And as part of that—yes—she still wanted to try to keep her word to Drafli, too. To try to honour him. One month.

"I was thinking, Gegnir," she said, tentative, her eyes fixed blankly on her pies, "of sending some of this over to Baldr and Drafli's room. Though I'm not sure they'll be there? Or whether they've already eaten, or if they'd, er, even want something like this?"

"Ach, they shall surely welcome this, no matter what they have yet eaten," Gegnir replied, his eyes twinkling as he bit into yet another gigantic piece of pie. "And if they are not there, they shall soon come at the scent alone. Not even the cruelest orc in this mountain would turn away a sweet hearth-mate like you, bearing such riches."

The hearth-mate again. But that only seemed to twist harder at Alma's uncertainty, dragging up all those memories of all Drafli's horrible intentions, his horrible words. *I make you into his hearth-mate. One he can trust. His dream. All he has ever wished for. It is too late for me.*

And gods, surely this was the worst idea, but suddenly Alma was just doing it, as rapidly as she could. Grasping for another basket, packing up her food, carefully layering it inside. And then saying a quick, heartfelt thank-you to Gegnir before turning and stalking out into the corridor.

She'd thankfully begun to acquire a passable mental map of the mountain—or at least, of the areas she'd encountered so far—but with every breath, every step further into the murky darkness, her heart seemed to pound louder in her chest, her hands gone cold and clammy on her basket.

What was she thinking. What if Drafli raged at her for coming to them, and then turned down her peace offering, and sent her away. What if she'd already ruined this beyond repair, and destroyed everything between them. She'd promised him she would honour Baldr, she'd promised Baldr she would try, one month—

She'd almost made up her mind to turn around again, to rush back to the safety of the kitchen—when out of nowhere, one of the corridor's shadows *moved*. Swirling out of the darkness before her, looming tall and deadly in her path.

And even as Alma yelped and scrambled backwards, she could taste him in the air, could feel him in her bones...

It was Drafli. And surely, he was furious.

lma stood in the corridor with her knees buckling, her heartbeat ricocheting in her chest. Drafli was here.

And clearly, he'd come to meet her... or intercept her. And his eyes were glittering, surely with unbridled rage, and surely now he would send her away, tell her that yes, indeed, she'd ruined everything, and now it was over forever, and...

"I only—wanted to bring you some supper," she managed, as her shaky hands thrust out the basket toward him. "Just as a—well. You certainly don't need to eat it if you don't want to, or if you've already eaten, but I just thought—I hoped—maybe—"

And gods, her voice was wavering so badly she could barely form the words, and the basket in her hands was trembling, too. And suddenly she could feel her eyes prickling, her tooth biting hard at her lip, driving back the shameful urge to beg his forgiveness, to apologize. No. She hadn't been wrong. She hadn't...

When to her astonishment, Drafli swept the basket out of her hands, grasped her arm, and steered her down the corridor. Not back toward the kitchen, but toward—their room?

"Um," Alma protested, glancing uncertainly toward his hard profile, that distinct frown of his brows. "Are you sure— you don't want—"

But it was too late, because Drafli was already ushering her into their familiar, lamplit room. Into where Baldr was leaping up to his feet, a bright grin breaking across his face—while hanging up on the wall behind him, Alma couldn't help noticing, were his trousers from earlier that day. Looking distinctly wet, and... clean?

"Bright-Heart!" Baldr exclaimed, his voice warm. "I hoped you were coming to see us. And ach, Draf, what has she brought?!"

He lurched over to take the basket from Drafli, his chest filling with his breath, his grin still broad and contagious on Alma's. And then he went to sit on the thick fur rug beside the bed, waving both Alma and Drafli down after him.

To Alma's continued astonishment, Drafli actually nodded as he obliged, his tall body leaning back against the bed, his long legs sprawling out on either side of Baldr. To which Baldr nudged Drafli's ankle a little wider, and gestured for Alma to sit on the fur beside him.

Alma shot a fearful look toward Drafli, but he hadn't even seemed to notice—so she gingerly obeyed, settling herself close beside Baldr, between Drafli's actual bare *feet*. A position that suddenly seemed oddly, unnervingly intimate, and she ducked her head as she quickly began unpacking her basket, while the succulent smell of fresh pastry and tender pork unfurled through the room.

"Ach, you... *made* all this, Bright-Heart?" Baldr asked faintly, once she'd thrust a pie toward him. "And you are giving it—to *us*?"

"Yes, of course," Alma replied, her voice still a little shaky, as she carefully handed a pie toward Drafli, who seemed to accept it willingly enough. "I was in the mood to cook something, and Gegnir and Kesst very kindly showed me around the kitchen. Hopefully you like pies? And cobbler?"

She darted another uncertain glance at Drafli, who was now studying his pie with intent, unreadable eyes—and beside her Baldr chuckled, and nudged at Drafli's foot with his knee. "Ach, human food is always a rare treat," he said. "Even Draf should never refuse such a gift, ach?"

He was giving Drafli a teasing, toothy smile, to which Drafli rolled his eyes—but then, indeed, he'd somehow produced a gleaming knife from his belt, and was swiftly cutting out a small, steaming piece of pie.

Baldr kept watching with visible amusement as Drafli ate, chewing for what seemed a rather long time before slowly swallowing. His face slightly grimacing as he did so, and for an instant, Alma felt a swarming, irrational fear that he would spit it out, tell her that it was awful, that she'd still ruined everything—

But wait, Drafli had flipped his knife in his long fingers, and was already slicing another piece, even larger than before. And this time as he ate, his eyes fluttered with something that looked much like... pleasure?

"Eating is oft painful for him, ach?" murmured Baldr's voice beside her, his eyes still warm on Drafli's face. "But cooked food—and thus human food—is much easier. It was very kind of you to bring this."

Predictably, Drafli had paused his chewing to glower at Baldr, clearly displeased by him again sharing such secret revelations—and though Alma instantly froze, her thoughts again screeching with panic, Baldr's look back toward Drafli was surprisingly flinty, his hand giving Drafli's ankle a brief, meaningful little shake.

And again, Drafli... didn't argue. Only looked at Baldr, with slowly softening resignation in his eyes. And Alma's scattering thoughts were suddenly flashing back to earlier today, back to before that horrible fight, to when Drafli had been so unexpectedly patient. Indulgent. *Kind*...

"Well," Alma heard her shaky voice reply, without at all meaning to. "He fed me quite a lot earlier today, didn't he? And he was very generous about it, too. So it seemed only fair to return the favour."

She even managed a tentative smile at Drafli as she spoke, a hope, an *offering*—and in return, Drafli coolly raised his eyebrows at her, his eyes dangerously glinting. And then, as he took another sharp bite of her pie, he reached for his trousers, untying them with an easy flick of his claw, and...

And. There he was, so bizarrely familiar now, and yet so shocking, jutting out long and scarred from his trousers with bare, blatant shamelessness. And as he took another large bite of Alma's pie, he jerked his head downwards, his meaning far too clear, without him even signing a word.

Suck it, it meant. *Now.*

"*Draf*," Baldr breathed, surely a protest—but Drafli didn't even look at him, his eyes fixed steady and commanding to Alma's. Still silently ordering her to do this, while he and Baldr sat here and watched, and casually ate the food she'd brought them.

And surely, Alma's distant brain protested, it was some kind of statement. A punishment, perhaps, for how she'd shouted at him, and made all those demands and accusations. It was Drafli firmly putting her in her place, once again.

Or... or was it? Because he wasn't demanding apologies, was he? And had he truly shown her any cruelty yet tonight, or anger, or genuine retaliation? And perhaps she was imagining it, but that brief, glinting look in his eyes almost looked like... acknowledgement. Recognition. *There is no shame*...

And somehow, Alma felt herself nodding—nodding!—as she awkwardly shifted herself closer, bending low between his sprawled knees, inhaling that already-sweet, so-close scent.

And then careful, so careful, brushing her lips against that smooth, scarred tip.

It leapt against her mouth, its sweetness sputtering between her parted lips, and oh, it tasted good, it felt good. Even if it was still some kind of statement, it was still Drafli acknowledging her, giving her this, it *was*—and she suddenly, eagerly delved her tongue a little deeper. Feeling him again clasp and clutch around her, spurting yet more hot rich sweetness against her tongue.

Gods, it tasted even better, the more he gave her—but a tentative glance up at Drafli's face showed him not even looking at her. Instead, he was carving yet another bite of her pie with his knife, and snapping into it with his sharp white teeth. And his briefly fluttering eyelids were surely from the taste of Alma's pie, the bastard, and not from her actually sucking him off while he ate.

"You remember how to do this for him, ach, Bright-Heart?" came Baldr's voice, slightly garbled, because wait, now *he* was eating, too. "How to use your hands, and seek for his seed? Mayhap take him a little deeper, also?"

Alma's low moan escaped on its own, and somehow she was already obliging, obeying. Shifting her hands up to stroke at Drafli's shaft and bollocks, bearing down a little deeper upon him, while behind her Baldr made a noise that might have been approval. "Ach, this is good," he said, again clearly around another bite. "Good for you too, ach, Draf?"

Alma could somewhat see Drafli signing something back, and then cutting yet another bite of pie, while Baldr gave a half-laugh, half-groan. "I meant her mouth," he protested, "not her cooking."

But Drafli only smirked at Baldr, reaching over to swipe something from the basket—a biscuit—and then biting off half of it with a single snap of his teeth. Chewing and swallowing with all apparent nonchalance, while Alma kept desperately stroking him, and sucking him, and seeking inside him with her tongue.

And surely, she should have felt denigrated, humiliated, ashamed. She'd bitterly fought with this infuriating bastard, she'd finally found the strength to call him out on his rubbish, and now he was retaliating with this? By making her drown in her inferiority, her shame?

But... there was no shame. He'd said that, a true Grisk goddess had echoed that, it had to be true. And as more hot sweetness spluttered out onto Alma's tongue, it occurred to her that no, this almost felt like... like indulgence, like decadence. She'd argued with her lord, made uncomfortable demands of him—and instead of punishing her as a result, or refusing her, he was willingly accepting her gifts, and enjoying her mouth. He was lying back and luxuriating in her, he was revelling in her efforts, in her worship...

And that meant, perhaps, that he wouldn't give her his release, not yet, no matter how desperately she sucked and stroked, no matter how deeply she dared to delve inside. No, he was going to relax and eat her food, and use her mouth, and now—Alma betrayed another low, helpless moan—he was going to sign smoothly at his mate, and have a casual conversation while he did so.

"No, no pain still," Baldr replied back, to whatever Drafli had asked. "Still feels very... strange, though, ach? Very... strong."

Drafli's smirk had curled higher, his brows actually waggling at Baldr as he tossed the rest of his biscuit in his mouth, and swallowed it in a single satisfied gulp. And Alma's angling eyes had narrowed on his smug face, searching how he was finally, finally glancing down toward her, even as he coolly signed something else toward Baldr. Something that surely included her.

"Ach, Bright-Heart," came Baldr's voice behind her. "Whilst we were out today, Drafli gave me a... a gift."

A *gift*. Alma's mouth had hesitated on Drafli's heft, her eyes again darting up toward him—and that little flicking gesture surely meant, *Yes, I will allow you to stop and sit up, to listen to my mate.*

So Alma slowly, carefully drew away from him—giving him one final, furtive little lick as she did so—and then pushed herself up to sitting, now close between Drafli's sprawled thighs. While before her, Baldr had paused his eating, his face gone a deep shade of red, his eyes darting between Drafli and Alma.

"Drafli gave me a... ring," Baldr continued, his voice lower, huskier. "Of gold. One that he has had, he said, for some time. And he even had this engraved, with his vow toward me."

Truly? Alma's glance between Baldr and Drafli was first astonished, and then delighted—Drafli had actually *listened* to her on this, and gone and given Baldr jewelry?!—but when her eyes dropped down to search Baldr's hands, they found... nothing. Nothing?

"Not there," Baldr added, with a choked little laugh, as those hands slipped downward, toward... his *trousers*. "Here."

And as Alma stared, her eyes gone wide, Baldr slowly reached inside his trousers, and drew himself out, too. Showing that plump, swollen heft, long and thick, with its glossy pink head... but embedded in that pink head was something new. Something thick and gold, glinting bright in the lamplight.

It was... a ring. Curving out from deep inside Baldr's slit, and then plunging back down into the skin of him on top. It was... in him. *Inside* him. *There.*

"Draf told me he granted you a gift today, with these Grisk clothes," Baldr breathed. "So he wished to give me a Grisk gift, too."

Alma's sore jaw had dropped open, her eyes frantically darting between the ring and Baldr's face—and Baldr was still smiling, wry and rueful, as his hand slipped down, and gently rubbed against it. Against where it went *into* him.

"Doesn't it... hurt?" Alma's thin voice asked, far too high-pitched, as she shot an accusing glance toward Drafli. But Drafli was still purposefully watching Baldr, his eyes intent on where Baldr's face had gone even redder than before, his hand again reflexively stroking against the gold jutting *into* him.

"No, not now," Baldr replied, hoarse and low. "Orcs heal far faster than humans, and Efterar addressed it once we returned, also. Though"—his voice dropped even lower—"I ken it shall yet take some getting used to, ach?"

Across from him, Drafli was actually smirking again, and making a sign above his own still-bared, still-swollen heft. Something that looked rather like an explosion, his long fingers flaring out, straight toward Alma's face.

"Ach, thus," Baldr said, his eyes again gone rueful, flicking between Alma and Drafli. "I shall mayhap never be able to spray straight again, ach? And never again without thinking of you, Draf. Even if it is not seed I am trying to spill."

Oh. Oh, gods. And the thought of that—the sheer *power* in that—seemed to steal away the last of Alma's breath, catching her here frozen between Drafli's thighs. She'd demanded that Drafli give Baldr a gift—something gold and shiny—so he'd gone and done *this*. A thick gold ring, embedded deep in Baldr's actual *prick*, that would remind him of Drafli every single time he—well.

And perhaps even more crucial, every time Baldr took Alma from this point onward, it would be there, between them. Silently shouting Drafli's name, his strength, his superiority. His *ownership*.

And again, it should have been shocking. Humiliating. Another punishment, perhaps, another immutable, implacable reminder of Alma's place. This was surely Drafli staking his claim, and again leaning back, and revelling in it.

But something was thundering in Alma's chest, fierce and volatile, and she felt her shaky finger reaching out, almost as if to touch it—but then stopping, just in time, as she darted a searching look back toward Drafli. "May I," she whispered, "my lord?"

That might have been surprise, flaring across Drafli's watching eyes—but then he jerked a shrug, cool and dismissive, and that surely meant *yes*. And yes, oh gods, Alma could touch it, bless him, *bless* him.

"Thank you," she whispered, as she watched her tentative fingers reach toward Baldr again—until they just brushed against that smooth shining gold, embedded inside his very *skin*. And in return, that swollen heft leapt, almost as if she'd touched *him*, rather than the gold within him.

But Drafli had only given permission for this, so Alma very carefully kept her fingers only on the gold, stroking up and down. Just seeing the edge of the engraving inside it, the words written in curling, unfamiliar script. And seeing how Baldr twitched and flared at her touch, his breath sharply catching, a low growl now hissing from his throat.

"What does it say?" she whispered. "The engraving, I mean?"

Even that made Baldr twitch up, the gold pressing hard against her finger. "It says," he breathed, "*I see you, my sworn mate. I pledge you my troth, and my favour, and my fealty.*"

Oh. His *fealty*. And wait, if Drafli had truly had this ring for some time, it meant he'd been planning for this, he'd been wanting to give it to Baldr, and he hadn't. Until now. Until... her?!

"You like it?" Alma asked Baldr, still strange and breathless, and she felt him again twitching up at her words. "Having your mate's gold within you? His vow?"

"Ach," Baldr said back, his voice ragged. "So much. I never thought I should wish for aught like this, but—"

He didn't finish, but it didn't matter, because Alma so vividly understood, so perfectly she almost felt faint. "But it's so beautiful," she murmured. "And so thoughtful, too. Your mate always with you, *inside* you, reminding you of his love for you, and his vows toward you. Even when he himself isn't there to do so."

Baldr silently nodded, his eyes holding brief but fervent to Alma's, while appreciation—*affection*—flashed so fiercely within them. And then flicking up toward Drafli, holding on Drafli, and wait, that was actually a *tear*, streaking swift down Baldr's greenish cheek.

"I have never had such a generous gift, from anyone, in all my life," he whispered. "Thank you, Draf."

And when Alma glanced up toward Drafli too, that was surely something unguarded, something genuine, in his glittering eyes. Something that made his throat swallow hard, as he brought both his arms up, and crossed them over his chest.

I love you, it meant, so strong Alma could taste it. *I love you, Pure-Heart.*

And in this unreal, thoroughly unthinkable moment, Alma was... smiling. Smiling between them, bright and delighted, while something seemed to spasm deep in her belly. Drafli had listened to her, he'd given Baldr such a lovely Grisk gift, and Baldr had welcomed it. And she'd made them supper, and they'd liked that too—indeed, Drafli was *still eating*—and surely, nothing could be better than this, *nothing*.

At least, until Drafli's eyes flicked downwards, finding her, seeing her. Seeing how she was still here, still sitting close between his sprawled legs, eagerly awaiting his command. And his hand had reached for her chin, again catching it in those long fingers, casually tilting it up for his eyes.

And Alma met him without reluctance, without shame. She'd asked him to do this, to be a better mate, and he'd... he'd actually *listened*. And surely this was still tenuous, still treacherous—but she'd meant it, she would keep her vow to him, as long as he kept his. And Drafli knew it, he meant it too, he *did*.

And Drafli's fingers flexing on her chin might have been familiar, or perhaps even approving, as he coolly raised his other hand, and signed something toward Baldr behind him.

Something Alma couldn't follow, but Baldr surely did, what with the low gasp behind her, the gentle brush of a new, tentative hand to her thigh.

"Drafli says we please him, Bright-Heart," Baldr breathed. "And as our reward, I shall now share his gift with you, and teach you to welcome it inside you."

lma's moan felt more like a cry, scraping hungry and desperate from her throat. Oh, gods, they were going to do it again? Baldr was going to put that *inside* her?

Beneath Baldr's tunic, his own chest was shuddering a hard exhale, his tooth biting his lip. His eyes gone heavy-lidded as they slid back toward Drafli, who was signing again, his hands fluid and swift.

"Draf says," Baldr began, breathless, "that he wishes *us* to begin this, this time. To show him what we have learned."

He what? Alma darted an uncertain look toward Drafli—surely they couldn't do such things *without* him?—but his gaze back at her was utter distant blandness. One of his hands coolly reaching for another biscuit, while the other one made a few sharp, very clear gestures.

I am waiting, he surely meant. *Lie down, and spread your legs for him.*

Oh. Oh, hell. The heat seemed to flood to Alma's groin in a rush, her face burning. And when she didn't move—perhaps couldn't find a way to move—Drafli's hand shot out, and grabbed a fistful of her *hair*. And then drew it downward, not hard enough to be painful, but enough that Alma instantly, shakily complied. Sliding down to lie on her back between his legs, her own legs spread, her head now resting on—on Drafli's *thigh*.

But Drafli didn't seem to notice, or care, and was already signing at Baldr again. And Baldr was nodding, his face also flushing red, as he pulled off his tunic, and then shoved off his trousers, too. Leaving him kneeling and fully bared between Alma's legs, his broad shoulders heaving with his breaths.

And *gods*, he was gorgeous. His greenish body hard and rippled and gleaming in the lamplight, the swollen heft at his groin looking even more compelling, more stunning, than before. Jutting out so smooth and plump from his dark hair, shuddering with every breath, its glossy pink head now crowned with that bright, glinting gold. Gold that was already—Alma gasped aloud—dripping a string of thick white, dangling down toward the fur.

Damn. Alma's shaky fingers had spasmed against her own thigh, perhaps seeking toward it—and now Baldr's gaze was on her hand, and then on the skirt still covering her groin. While above her, Alma could just make out Drafli's signed order at Baldr, while his other hand reached for yet another biscuit. *Keep going*, it meant.

Baldr's head ducked low, his pointed ears gone bright red, and his hands dropped to Alma's belt. Unfastening it with careful movements, before pulling both it and the skirt aside— and then his hands skittered upwards, and did the same with her cape.

It meant she was suddenly, utterly exposed, lying helpless on her back between Drafli's sprawled legs. Her bare breasts shuddering, their nipples hungry and peaked, while the heat between her parted legs was already convulsing, as if begging for Baldr's attentions, his touch. And indeed, oh gods, he was looking, his eyes heavy and hooded, his tooth biting at his lip.

But he wasn't moving, not even his breaths now, and his eyes had flicked, brief and perhaps almost beseeching, up to

Drafli. To where Drafli had pulled over Alma's pan of berry cobbler—which had gone untouched, so far—and was now eyeing it with unmistakable skepticism, flicking at the crumbly crust with the tip of his knife.

"*Draf,*" Baldr's voice breathed, somewhere between laughing and pleading—while in return, Drafli only made his *keep going* motion with one hand, while the other deftly sliced out a bit of cobbler, and brought the knife to his mouth. Sliding the sharp blade with alarming deftness against his own tongue, his eyes slightly fluttering as he swallowed.

Gods, he was such a devious bastard—clearly saying, challenging, that they were currently less interesting to him than her *food*—and gods, Alma should not have been shivering like this, her hands reflexively clenching against her thighs. So near to her swollen heat, wide open and waiting, pleading to be touched. *Show him what we have learned...*

And before she could think better of it—*there is no shame*—her trembling hand slid over, and did it. Brushing softly against her slick, parted crease, slipping up and down. Feeling the astonishing wetness there, how she was wildly clenching, against even her own touch...

Baldr had twitched and gasped aloud, his eyes now fixed to the sight, and Alma dragged in a bracing breath as she delved her fingers a little deeper. There was no shame, there wasn't—and Drafli surely wanted her to do this, he'd taught her to do this. They had to show him what they'd learned, to entice him, to please him...

And yes, yes, her glance up at Drafli above her found him meeting her eyes with brief, grudging approval, as he again bit off more cobbler from his glittering knife. And Alma held his gaze this time, drinking him up, as she slowly slid down her other hand to join the first. Touching herself, showing herself, and now even slipping another finger inside. Readying herself for Baldr, opening herself wide for him, just as Drafli had shown them.

The sounds were already thick and obscene, the wetness dripping, and she dropped her pleading eyes back to Baldr's face as she finally slipped her slick fingers out again. And then used them to spread herself even wider, parting her folds for him, waiting.

And yes, oh gods, yes, Baldr was finally leaning forward, closer, closer. His gold-tipped head bobbing and dripping as it aimed toward her, as if seeking her all on its own—and then settling, oh so gently, against Alma's parted, open heat.

Alma's moan rose in time with his, because oh, it felt good. The brush of hard, unyielding gold such a strange, compelling contrast to the rest of his smooth warmth, nudging so slick and alive against her. Already spluttering out its thick liquid into her, and oh Alma could already feel how it was different, with the ring. How the seed was pulsing wider and messier, how more of it was already streaking down her crease.

"Oh," she gasped, as Baldr gently eased closer, prodding it just slightly deeper. His eyes blinking and intent on the sight, perhaps on the way Alma's opened heat was clutching and milking at him, perhaps kissing at his mate's gold, drinking it inside her, just as he'd commanded...

Another glance up at Drafli—who was still eating, damn him—showed him watching now, too. Watching how Baldr was slowly, slowly pressing a little closer, a little deeper. Sinking inside Alma, opening her around him, breath by breath. His shoulders shuddering, his tooth again biting hard at his lip, his body leaning closer over her. Enough that his hand clutched at Drafli's shin for balance, his eyes darting up toward his watching face.

Drafli was looking back, his eyes glinting on Baldr's with bright, fiendish intent. And with a cool flick of his hand, his sharp knife was once again dripping with steaming berry cobbler—but this time, the knife was hovering before Baldr's mouth. Surely a command, *come, eat it*—but when Baldr leaned a little forward, Drafli swiftly drew it further back, his lips curving up into a sly smirk.

He meant he wanted Baldr to follow it, oh hell, like a pet with a treat—and Baldr was, he did, his lashes fluttering, his body easing ever more forward. And sinking ever deeper inside Alma's frantically clutching heat, slowly filling her, splitting her open upon him. Sliding far easier than before, smooth and slick and succulent, until—Alma cried out, and shuddered all over—he was fully seated inside her, his swollen bollocks pressed hard below, his mate's gold surely kissing at her womb.

Baldr was groaning too, that swollen heat inside her flexing and squeezing out its bounty, so powerful, so *alive*. But his eyes were still on Drafli's, his face now so near to Drafli's, both his hands clutched to Drafli's legs, holding his upper body high over Alma's. And as she watched, trembling and gasping, Drafli lowered his knife to Baldr's lips, and fed the rich, juicy cobbler into his mouth.

Baldr's moan of pleasure was fierce and guttural, his long tongue licking with frantic eagerness at the sharpened steel, his heft between Alma's legs swelling and juddering even harder than before. His hips grinding himself a little deeper, and Alma's shrill cry tore from her mouth, her own hips reflexively arching up to meet his.

Fuck, that was good, and surely Baldr thought so too, his gaze fluttering on Drafli's, the groan burning from his throat. And Alma could see Drafli's satisfied smirk quirking higher as he fed Baldr more, from his fingers this time, the juices streaking dark and messy down Baldr's chin.

And gods, this should have again felt thoroughly degrading, humiliating, *shameful*—Drafli was blatantly encouraging Baldr to ignore her, to focus on the pleasure he was offering instead, the pleasure she'd *made* for them. But gods, the sight of it, the feel of it, the craving clawing and raging, there was no shame, and she needed, she needed...

"Feed him your seed," she whispered, pleaded, into the suddenly choked silence. "Please, my lord."

And oh gods, oh hell, what was she even *saying*—and both Baldr and Drafli instantly stilled, both staring down toward her. Baldr's hazy eyes flashing with even more hunger than before, while Drafli's brows slowly rose on his forehead, his berry-stained fingers making a clear sign toward her. *Say that again.*

"Feed him your seed, my lord," she whispered at him, small, ashamed—but there was no shame, and surely that was more approval, or even amusement, in Drafli's surprisingly indulgent eyes. Still glinting on hers, surely wanting more, so Alma gulped back the mortification, fought for air, for words.

"Please, my lord," she whispered. "I would—I would like to see that again. Very much."

Her opened, impaled body had clenched hard around Baldr as she'd spoken, making him hiss through his teeth. And his gaze still fixed on hers was pure, craving reverence, so deep it took her breath away. She was doing this to him. They were doing this to him, and...

And above her, Drafli was shrugging, *agreeing*, oh gods above. And his lean form was shifting, his legs slipping out from under Alma's head, from beneath Baldr's hands. Slowly rising to his knees, just behind Alma's head on the fur, as his long fingers shoved his trousers downwards. Fully releasing that scarred, sweet-scented grey length, jutting straight out from the dark hair at his groin, just above her watching eyes...

And as Alma kept staring, heaving for breath, Drafli coolly grasped one hand to Baldr's head, the other to his own thick base. And then he drew Baldr forward, and slowly but surely fed him the full length of his pulsing, gleaming prick. Sinking deeper and deeper, until it was fully buried in his mate's gagging, convulsing throat.

Damn. Alma had never imagined such an impossible sight in her life—and surely never from such an impossible angle, hovering directly above her eyes. Giving her a shocking, utterly obscene view as Drafli slowly drew himself all the way out again, his length now slick with Baldr's saliva, a long string of white dangling down toward her face.

And surely Drafli couldn't begrudge her tasting it, surely—because he was watching, again almost amused, as Alma licked for it with her tongue, and moaned at its faint but still-rich sweetness. But then it was gone, vanished, because Drafli was again bearing down into Baldr's throat, while Baldr's thick strength still buried inside her shuddered and vibrated. Pushing forward even harder than before, his hips canting against hers—wait, because Drafli was still moving Baldr's mouth back and forth upon his length, easing him into a slow, agonizing rhythm.

And Alma was meeting it, caught in it, lost in it. In the impossible, surreal sensation of Baldr plunging so deep and heavy within her, pierced with Drafli's gold, while Drafli kept plunging so deep within him. The three of them smoothly rocking together, following Drafli's lead with surprising ease, with Baldr and Alma's gasps and moans rising together, fraying together. While snatches of liquid pleasure kept dripping from Baldr's swollen lips, pooling down onto Alma's face and mouth, teasing at her eagerly seeking tongue...

And Drafli liked it too, Alma's distantly screeching brain noted. His sharp cheeks very faintly flushed, his head tilted back, his intently watching eyes hooded to narrow slits. As his hips rolled forward even faster, sinking deeper into Baldr's moaning throat, driving Baldr harder inside Alma. Doing it again and again and again, making Baldr use her like this, take her like this, and oh gods Drafli was signing at her, something blatantly filthy that her shouting brain vaguely recognized...

Milk him dry. Now.

And fuck, fuck, how was Alma arching up like this, screaming like this for her beautiful generous lord, while her split-open heat frantically, furiously obeyed. Convulsing against Baldr's still-driving power with shrieking, surging desperation, while Baldr's motions against her staggered to sharp, sudden stillness. His big body arching up over her, his blocked throat audibly choking on Drafli's invasion, as his own heft inside her sprayed out its release in wild, chaotic streams of heat.

And now it was Drafli's turn, both his hands gripped tight to Baldr's head as his lean body drove forward once, twice more—and yes, yes, Alma could see his scarred length visibly pulsing now, streaming out into Baldr's mouth. But not feeding it all the way down his throat, not like the other times, because this way some of it spilled out between Baldr's lips, splattering down onto Alma's flushed, watching face.

And it was a gift, oh gods, Drafli was *giving* her this, and Alma eagerly sucked and licked for it, even as the dregs of her own ecstasy kept rippling and roaring wide. And wait, Drafli had even pulled away from Baldr, hovering himself over Alma's parted lips, so that the last of his bounty, now bubbling out in a long thick string, could pool down into her waiting, open mouth.

The pleasure swerved and stuttered as Alma licked up every drop, took all he would possibly give her, while Drafli signed something at Baldr—and then the euphoria smashed into utter, screaming insensibility as Baldr slowly bent his head down, and *kissed* her. His mouth still full of Drafli's seed this time, and oh hell they were still giving it to her, still rewarding her. Baldr's mouth purposefully soft and open on hers, letting her drink from him, taste him, feeding her just as generously as Drafli had fed him...

Alma's conscious thoughts had somehow seemed to flutter away, all awareness of time or reality whirled elsewhere, lost. Leaving only this, the steady sweet feeding of her beautiful lover's mouth, sharing his beautiful mate's succulent fresh seed. Speaking so deep of their approval, their affection, their safety, her *home*...

But then, no, no, Baldr's mouth gently pulled away. Leaving her unfilled, unkissed, alone. And Alma felt herself whimpering aloud, her shaky hands suddenly clutching helplessly back toward him, toward Drafli above her. No, they couldn't leave her like this, *no*—

But then, oh thank the gods, there was the feel of a warm arm, settling heavy across her waist—and even stronger, another capable, long-fingered hand, sliding close against her straining neck. Holding her with firm, steady certainty, claws gently pricking against delicate skin.

And it made no sense, a distant voice shouted, that was *Drafli's* hand, he might still be angry with her, he could strangle her, she should be terrified—but the relief was crashing into Alma like a physical force, sagging her against the fur. They were here. Safe.

"Ach, Bright-Heart, we are here," came Baldr's low voice, as if speaking her thoughts aloud. "Mayhap only rest here for a spell, and breathe for us, ach?"

Breathe for them. Alma instantly fought to obey, dragging in hoarse, gulping breaths, and thankfully Drafli's hand on her neck stayed firm and still, while Baldr's stroked up and down her bare flank, smooth and reassuring.

"Mayhap you should have had more to eat," Baldr said, husky. "It was very selfish of us, to eat all that you so kindly brought thus."

Another convulsive quiver quaked up Alma's already-trembling back, and she felt her head frantically shaking, back and forth. No, Baldr couldn't possibly think it was selfish, he was so lovely, he'd felt so *good*, he ought to know the truth, it was for, for...

"B-brought it for you," she gulped. "Wanted to m-make up with—with Drafli. Make—*peace* again."

Wait. Her distant, stilted thoughts were suddenly shouting somewhere, screeching dark, dire, desperate warnings. But she couldn't seem to follow why, to pull them together—

Until Drafli's hand on her neck abruptly snatched away. While Baldr's hand stilled its stroking, its previously relaxed weight gone tight and tense.

"Make up with Drafli," Baldr's voice repeated, slowly, far flatter than before. "And make peace. Why would you need to do this?"

Something sharp and dangerous sliced through the haze clouding Alma's thoughts, and her eyes snapped open. Finding the room, still here in the too-bright candlelight—and Baldr, still here too, though his hand was slowly drawing away from her. And on her other side, Drafli was sitting up, his trousers again fastened tightly around his hips, his eyes gone cold and forbidding on hers.

Oh, gods, why couldn't Alma *think*, and now Baldr was leaning closer over her, his jaw set, his eyes flicking with purposeful intent between her and Drafli. And though Drafli gave a dismissive shrug—*I no ken what she speaks of*, it meant—Baldr's gaze dropped back to Alma's, shimmering with certain, rising *suspicion*.

"What do you need to make up to Drafli, Alma," he said, low, but suddenly, devastatingly compelling. "You have done all you can to please us—to please *him*—today. And these past days also. You have honoured us in this. Have you not?"

And wait, wait, Baldr was—was he *smelling* her? Inhaling like this, so slow and deep above her, while that suspicion kept hardening in his eyes. As if he could taste Alma's fear, or even her lies...

And oh gods, did Baldr think she was hiding Drafli's lies from him? That she was covering for Drafli, and supporting his ongoing deceptions and betrayals? Or—or even worse, did Baldr think she was breaking her own promises toward *him*?

You will honour Drafli. One month. I understand. I'll try.

"Tell me the truth, Alma," Baldr said, the words a heavy, terrifying thud against her heart. "*Now*."

30

Tell Baldr the truth. *Now.*

And staring up at his waiting, dangerous eyes, there was only more fear, ricocheting against Alma's ribs. Baldr thought she was lying to him. He thought she was deceiving him. And what would he do if she told him everything, would he send her away, back to Mr. Pembroke's, forever?

But wait, surely Alma could say, *It's Drafli's fault. We fought over all his lies today, he's made a secret vow to me, he's only doing this with me for you...*

But then she made the fatal mistake of looking at Drafli. At the glinting, shifting intensity in his eyes upon hers... and just for an instant, the vivid, unnerving glimpse of fear.

Don't, those eyes seemed to say. *You promised. Please.*

And Alma *had* promised, and suddenly she couldn't bear the thought of what would come next, if Baldr knew the whole truth about that secret vow. If it ended up breaking Baldr and Drafli apart, if it meant Baldr would lose the mate who brought him such pleasure, such peace. And it had all been going so well, Alma couldn't ruin this for them, she couldn't bear to never see either of them again, she *couldn't...*

"I only meant," she somehow gulped, her voice cracking, "that I wanted to make up with Drafli—because of *humans*. Because of women."

It didn't make sense, surely, and Baldr's brows had pulled together, clearly not following—so Alma fought for more air. For truth. Other truth.

"Because Drafli's been hurt by—by women," she choked. "Betrayed, you said, by women like me. So I want him to—to have better. To know we're not all like that. To know he can—trust me."

And it wasn't a lie, not quite, not at all. And perhaps it had been enough, or close enough, because that cold suspicion was surely fading from Baldr's eyes, and in its place was a visible, palpable relief. But still with a tinge of darkness, a brief glance toward Drafli that Alma suddenly couldn't at all read.

"I am glad you wish to honour Drafli thus, Bright-Heart," Baldr said, his voice quiet, his eyes shifting on hers. "And you know this honours me, also. But you are not at fault for the deeds of other women. Ach?"

Alma's throat convulsed, and she searched for a reply—but Baldr's gaze had flicked back to Drafli, his shoulders squaring. "And most of all," Baldr continued, "you do *not* need to make amends for the choices of Drafli's mate. Ach?"

Of Drafli's... mate. Wait. His *mate*?

And no, Baldr surely couldn't mean that, surely—but he was still looking at Drafli, his gaze unflinching. And now he was even pushing himself up to seated, perhaps so he might better meet Drafli's eyes.

"*She* was the one who chose to betray Drafli, and their unborn son," Baldr continued, even quieter. "This wrong was hers, and hers *alone*."

Wait. Wait. The last of Alma's haziness had abruptly wrenched away, her eyes snapping wide and shocked to Drafli. To where he had suddenly gone markedly pale, his eyes flashing, his hand stuttering sideways with none of his characteristic gracefulness.

No. Stop.

But Baldr slowly shook his head, his jaw set, his eyes flinty on Drafli's pale face. "She might as well know, Draf," he said, still so quiet. "She will hear it sooner or later, ach? But this is *not* her sin to pay for. And it is not yours, either."

Alma's heart was horribly hitching in her chest, her eyes still frozen on Drafli's ashen face, her thoughts now tumbling back to their earlier fight. To all that talk of penance, of payment, of absolution...

"But what," Alma's voice croaked, without her even realizing it, "did Drafli's mate *do*?"

Baldr didn't immediately reply, his jaw still hard and square, waiting. And Drafli now wasn't looking at either of them, his gaze fixed on the wall beyond. But wait, that might—*might*—have been a shrug, shivering from his bare shoulder.

"His mate... sold him," said Baldr's voice, finally, heavy and low. "To the militia of the town nearest their home. Almost half a year after they had spoken vows. And"—Alma could hear him swallow—"you can guess what some men would do, with a live unarmed orc, in the midst of a brutal war against our kind?"

Alma's body jerked up to sitting too, her hands clapping over her mouth, the shock and the revulsion surging up in her suddenly spasming throat. No. No. Drafli—*this* Drafli—had had a mate, a woman he'd sworn *vows* to, a woman he'd wanted to have a *family* with—

And his mate had sold him. *Sold* him. To men who had clearly taken his voice, and his ease... and surely much else, besides.

I hate all women, Drafli had told her, with that darkness in his eyes. *All humans.*

And once again, Alma's thoughts were churning with

visions of Mr. Pembroke. Of his careless, casual brutality toward orcs, of the glee in which he'd spoken of such atrocities. As if the orcs weren't real. Weren't real people, with real homes and families, who had already borne so much suffering.

"That is—*heinous*," Alma gasped toward Drafli's stiff, distant-eyed form, still seated here on the rug beside them, and yet gone perhaps a hundred leagues away. "That is *horrific*. How did you—how did you escape? And what happened to your son? To *her*?"

Drafli didn't move, didn't even glance toward her, and Baldr sighed again. "He escaped because he is *him*," he said, with a skittering wave at Drafli's lean body. "And his mate, she—she sought to have their son... *removed*, and succeeded in this—but then she died of infection, soon after."

Good gods. Alma again had to choke back the bile in her throat, her hands still fluttering against her mouth. "But— why?" she croaked at him, at them. "Why would she ever go and *sell* you?"

And wait, here were the visions, sudden and almost dizzying, of all Drafli's growls, Drafli's threats, Drafli's rage. *Drafli is not easy*, even Baldr had told her. *He can be stubborn, and rude, and angry, and cold...*

But Baldr had seemed to follow those thoughts, his head giving a meaningful little shake. "I could yet smell his mate's strong scent upon him, when first I came here," he said. "And there was no lasting fear or misery in this. She freely longed for Drafli, and for the care and pleasure he gave her. We ken"— Baldr's voice flattened—"it was mostly the coin that swayed her, in the end."

The coin. And suddenly Alma truly felt like she would be sick, right here on their fur, and she again clapped her hands to her mouth, just in time. The coin. And what had Drafli offered her, for his payment, for his penance? Even today, for her clothes? *It is too late for me, in this. So I give him you.*

Drafli had... *paid* her, because *that* was what he believed would last. What would matter most. What would keep her loyalty to his beloved mate.

There was suddenly no way for Alma to speak, her head whipping back and forth, her thoughts whirling and wailing in her skull. Gods, how had she ever become part of this, how had she ever thought it would be a good idea to take Drafli's payment, to sell her loyalty, to be his penance, to *lie*?

And the only possible refuge in the deluge was here beside her, it was Baldr, so steadfast, so loyal, so kind. "But you," she gulped at him, please, *please*. "You've been so good to him since then. Haven't you? You've helped him. Given him comfort. Earned his trust. He swore *vows* to you. Even after all that."

And this seemed so desperately important, suddenly, Alma needed this to be true, to hear it said aloud—but Baldr's eyes angling toward Drafli were oddly bright, his lips pressing together in something that could have been a smile, but surely, surely wasn't.

"I have sought to help," he replied, hoarse, with an attempt at a shrug. "To be a true partner and friend. To be worthy of Drafli's trust, and his loyalty."

But... in the face of all that, Baldr still hadn't been enough. Not for years, he'd said, because Drafli had betrayed him again and again, perhaps even with orcs like Narfi. *I can still scent every Skai he took,* Varinn had said, *whenever he was bored with you. Whilst you kept yourself true to only him...*

And surely that had been why Baldr had demanded Alma's truth, just now. He'd questioned her because he still didn't trust Drafli. And Drafli had surely seen that, and known it. He'd been *afraid* of it.

And Drafli still hadn't moved. Still hadn't even looked at them, or acknowledged anything they'd said. And Alma might have almost thought he hadn't heard, but for—she felt herself blanch—the way his clawed hands were digging into his knees. The way there were spots of... *blood*, pooling beneath those flexed claws, and spreading into his trousers.

And suddenly there was the urge, almost dizzying in its strength, to touch him. To shout at him. To throw her arms around him, and bury her head in his stiff shoulder, and shake him, and make him do something, *say* something. To make him explain, to make sense of this mess, to at least see him again say, *I love you, Pure-Heart, I love you.*

But he didn't, and she couldn't, and there was just this hanging, horrible silence—and now the faint, bitter taint of blood, curdling in the air. And in the helplessness, Alma clutched for Baldr's slack hand, and clasped it in both of hers, squeezing as tight as she possibly could.

"And you *have* helped," she told Baldr, her voice thick and vehement. "You *have*. Do you know what Drafli said to me, when we first discussed our proposal to you? He told me he would do anything for you. That he would never, ever leave you, or break his vow to you. That you would be his mate, always. That you are a *prize*."

Baldr's hand spasmed in hers, his eyes darting uncertainly toward Drafli's distant face—and beyond a swallow in his throat, Drafli still didn't look, didn't move. But Alma was in this now, still needing this, still grasping almost painfully at Baldr's hand.

"And even today," she gulped, "Drafli told me he wants you to have everything you deserve. That he wants to keep you happy, and *safe*. And that"—was she going to say this, she was—"that he wants to be the very best mate he can be for you, and for your son. So that you can be the best possible fathers to your son together. And you will be. I *know* you will be."

And gods, why was she saying these things, and why did they feel so powerful, so true. Why were her fingers almost numb as they gripped Baldr's hand, so tightly it was trembling against her.

"You two have found *peace* in each other," she insisted at him, pleaded at him. "You love each other, and you bring each other such joy. And your son will adore you, both of you, and you'll be such a happy family together. I know it. I *know*."

But instead of Baldr relaxing, or agreeing, or perhaps even smiling, he somehow looked even paler, and more haggard, than before. And Drafli had finally, *finally* glanced at him, and Alma couldn't even begin to read that look in his eyes, or the way his claws were flexing against his still-bleeding knees.

And perhaps—perhaps they just needed to make this up together. To sort this out alone, without Alma bumbling in between them. So she abruptly, belatedly stood, swiping for her clothes, fighting to ignore the mess now streaming down her thighs. The proof, perhaps, of that future, of that son...

"I think I'd best leave you two alone," she told them, her voice wavering. "But please, work through this, all right? Be here for each other. And just"—she hauled in another breath, she would say this—"just be *honest* with each other. Trust each other. Tell each other the truth. Everything. *Please.*"

And with that still quivering through the room, Alma clutched her clothes to her chest, and shot Baldr and Drafli one last silent, helpless plea. And then she whirled toward the door, and rushed away into the darkness.

Alma's sleep that night was scattered, broken by dark dreams, and bitter, blistering guilt. Why had any of them done this. Why had she agreed to this. *It is too late for me. She sold him. I have sought to help. I can still scent every Skai he took.*

Obey me. Honour me. One month.

And surely it was wrong, it was *depraved*, but Alma finally lurched out of bed, and went for the chest Drafli had given her. Finding those hard stone tools, hidden in that soft bag, and staggering back with them toward the bed. And then slicking them all over with Baldr's spent seed, and slowly, painfully impaling herself upon them in the darkness. Until she was writhing in dark, heated agony, lost in something that indeed felt almost like justice, like penance. Like absolution.

And once the release had torn through her wracking body, and she'd furtively washed the tools and hidden them away again, there was at least an odd, stilted clarity, whispering deep in her exhausted brain. She couldn't control Baldr and Drafli. She couldn't change their horrifying pasts, or their hidden motivations, or this convoluted mess they'd dragged her into.

But her thoughts had again flicked back to her own mother,

to the goddess Akva in the Grisk shrine. To how today, she herself had somehow found the courage to be honest with Drafli, to do better, and to demand that he do better, too... and how instead of truly retaliating, Drafli had actually seemed to *listen*. How he'd finally gone and given Baldr that beautiful ring, and brought him such joy.

And surely, Alma could keep seeking that honesty between them. She could stop lying, and covering for their lies. And most of all, she would *not* take any of their coin, at any point, for any reason. She would find a way to pay Drafli back the full cost of her lovely new clothes, and keep working to earn her own keep. Her *own* place.

And with that settled, Alma finally managed to sleep for what felt like a significantly long time. And when she awoke again, it was still with that same stolid determination. She would do better. She would.

So she first said her morning prayers—now both to Skaikesh and Akva—and then washed and dressed, and sat down to read one of the pamphlets Drafli had left her. It was an extensive account of the war between orcs and humans, but written from the orcs' perspective. And while Alma had never known much about the war—in truth, her world at Mr. Pembroke's had been very small—she found her horrified disbelief abruptly rising as she read, her hand covering her mouth. Her thoughts wrenching again toward Drafli, toward—

"Bright-Heart?" came a tentative voice from the door. "Is aught amiss?"

It was Baldr, wearing a dark tunic and trousers, with a long, gleaming scimitar hanging from his belt. And while Alma had seen Drafli with multiple weapons now, she hadn't before seen Baldr wear one, and she felt herself swallow, her thoughts again skittering toward this war. Toward how it had hurt Drafli. Toward...

"I was just—reading," she belatedly said, lurching to her feet. "About the war. It's all so horrible, isn't it?"

She tried for a smile at him, but certainly failed, and Baldr gave her a wan, too-knowing smile back. "I am sorry if I threw too much of this upon you, last eve," he said. "But I thought it was better if you heard it from us, ach?"

Alma fervently nodded, searching his tired-looking eyes. "I'm so glad you told me," she replied, low. "But I've been worrying about it, and about him, and *you*, and"—and she was going to be honest, she was—"and look, do you really still think it was a good idea, bringing me into all this? I must be dragging up so many awful memories for him, and I can't even *imagine* what he must have been feeling all this time, and—"

But Baldr's hand was slicing sideways—*stop*—though the movement was soft, his eyes again far too understanding on hers. "I feared this too, at the start," he said. "But he fought me again and again on this, and now"—he shrugged, and ruefully rubbed at his neck—"I ken mayhap this is his own push back against it all, ach? His own stubborn vengeance, against that woman's power over him."

Oh. And surely that wasn't why Drafli was doing this—he was doing it for Baldr, to protect him, to give him a son, to gain his absolution, *it is too late for me*—but before Alma could speak, to try to argue that, Baldr's hand again said, *stop*.

"You cannot smell him, when we are in this," he continued. "You cannot smell the strength of his hunger, or his relief. His... *victory*, mayhap, when you plead for him, and obey him. When you show yourself so kind, and eager, and sweet."

Alma should likely have been disconcerted by that—was it even worse, if Drafli was using her as some kind of vicarious vengeance against a dead woman's sins? But again, she was thinking of all he'd said the day before, of all that talk of penance. Of absolution. Of justice against himself... or maybe *for* himself, too.

"But last night," Alma began, uncertainly searching Baldr's eyes. "He was so... upset. And I certainly didn't help matters. At all."

Baldr barked a short laugh, his hand again rubbing awkwardly at his neck. "You did," he said firmly. "You did, Bright-Heart, with all that you said, with such sweet truth and kindness. And once you left, ach, we fought, but then—"

He pulled his hand away from his neck, and wait—Alma frowned, and stepped closer—he was still *bleeding*. Because those were deep, fresh teeth-marks, ravaging his throat. *Drafli's* teeth-marks. And Baldr... liked them there. He'd *wanted* them there.

"But then he took me so hard I can yet feel this," Baldr whispered, his eyes glittering now, his face flushing with pink. "And he near bit my new ring out of me—this, when he almost *never* uses his mouth thus. And when I unwittingly sprayed him in the face—after he commanded me against this—he swore that next he shall pierce my teats, and use these to truss me to the wall whilst he ploughs me, and I ken"—his voice dropped, heated and husky—"I ken he *meant* this, Bright-Heart. He means to grant me more gifts, to wear *inside* me."

It was almost as though Alma could see these thoroughly shocking scenes as he spoke, could feel their power flaring to life—and curse her, but that was a moan, escaping out her throat. "Truly?" she heard herself whisper, her hand fluttering almost reflexively toward Baldr's chest—and then away again, just in time. "Oh, I'm *so* glad, Baldr. That sounds so—*wonderful.*"

And surely, *wonderful* was completely the wrong word, but Baldr was already nodding, his eyes still shining with happiness. "And after this, he repeated all you said," he confided, even huskier. "Even though he scarce has signs for such things. He told me I was a true prize, and that he shall never, ever forsake me. And that even if I were not his heart, he should forever treasure me for my deep throat alone, and for my tight arse, and my sweet, fat, pretty Grisk prick. Which now, with his gift, shall always"—Baldr's head ducked—"*always* scent of *him.*"

Oh, hell. Another hoarse gasp had choked from Alma's throat, her breaths heaving far too fast, her hands coming to her burning cheeks. And Baldr was glancing up at her again, his eyes dark and heated beneath his long black lashes, and Alma actually had to take a quick, purposeful step away from him, her head shaking, her hands fluttering. *No touching, no touching, honour him...*

And wait, was she signing that with her *hands*, oh gods, she was, she *was*—but suddenly, somehow, Baldr was... *laughing*. His shoulders shaking, his eyes crinkling at the corners, his grin broad and approving. His gaze so warm, so indulgent, as he signed back at her. *I know. I understand.*

But within that had been a new sign, one Alma hadn't seen before—and clearly Baldr had noticed her attention to it, and he repeated the sign, slower this time. A little explosion of fingers, flaring out wide over his heart.

"It means, *Bright-Heart*," he said softly. "You. Draf and I decided it last night, after."

Alma blinked at it for a long instant, her head tilting, because it had almost—almost—been the same sign Drafli had used the night before, when he'd been teasing Baldr about the side effects of his new gift. About the mess, exploding from... well.

Alma had reflexively glanced downwards, and oh, Baldr had followed that, too. And yes, yes, that was the same damned sign, now exploding out from where he was tented, and very visibly *throbbing*, the hard line of his new ring very obvious through the too-tight fabric.

"Ach, it is the same," he murmured. "I spray for you, you ken? Because of him."

Oh. Oh, hell, oh sweet gods above. They'd named her together, with something that spoke of both of them. Something that also spoke of desire, and of affection, of *approval*. And the smarting heat in Alma's cheeks seemed to suddenly be spilling up, and escaping out her eyes, and she couldn't stop smiling at him, or sniffing, or rubbing at her burning cheeks. And Baldr was smiling too, blinking his own too-bright eyes, and suddenly Alma just wanted to rush at him, and squeeze him until she burst—

When at that moment, Drafli strode in. Tall and bare-chested and imperious, his narrow eyes instantly catching on Baldr, and then flicking dark and dangerous toward Alma.

What, he mouthed and signed, glaring thunderously between them, *is this?!*

Alma sniffled and smiled at him, wiping at her watery eyes, and she could see Baldr's hand skating over his eyes, too. "Ach, Draf," Baldr replied, his voice hitching. "I was telling Alma of the joy you gave me last eve. And I just showed her the name we chose for her."

He made the sign again, his fingers slightly trembling as he did so—and Drafli stared at him for a long, disbelieving moment. Looking not quite angry anymore, but rather almost bewildered—and then, perhaps even incredulous, as he whirled back toward Alma, and found her still standing there smiling, and wiping at her uselessly leaking eyes.

"It's the loveliest name," she told him, and she meant it. "I'm truly honoured. Thank you. Thank you both."

She signed the *thank you* as she spoke, bowing toward Drafli—and found, when she met his gaze again, that his incredulity had briefly stuttered, into something she couldn't at all read. But then it was gone again, just as quickly, and he gave an exaggerated, longsuffering roll of his eyes.

Foolish Bright-Heart, he signed at her, and oh hell now *he'd* said it, those long fingers flaring out over his own heart. And Alma had choked a reflexive gasp, staring at it, and in return Drafli actually smirked at her, before tilting his head, and signing something else. *You pray today, Bright-Heart? To Skai-kesh?*

Alma nodded, and felt her cheeks again heating, her eyes again caught on the sight of him saying her name, her *name*.

"And to Akva as well, if you don't mind," she said. "And I used your—your *tools*, my lord, in both places, as you wished. And read one of your pamphlets, too."

Drafli's eyes had briefly gone unreadable again, but then he inclined his head, almost as if he—he *approved*. And then, as if he couldn't bear to allow such a concession to stand, he abruptly spun back toward Baldr, yanked him bodily against his side, and signed something else at him, too fast for Alma to read.

"Ach, there is again much we must attend to today," Baldr replied, easing his arm around Drafli's lean waist, before glancing warmly toward Alma. "But Draf says that if you bring us some supper later, Bright-Heart, mayhap he shall again reward us."

Reward us. And wait, that meant Drafli had liked her cooking, he'd wanted more, he would *reward* them—and not only that, but he'd given her such a lovely name, he'd given Baldr such a lovely gift, and told Baldr all the things he ought to have been saying, all this time. He was being a better mate, they were making this work, and she was honouring them, learning to be honest with them, they were going to be a *family*—and suddenly Alma was smiling again, so wide it was hurting her face.

"Then I'll see you at supper, my lord," she said, with a curtsey, her hand over her heart. "I can't wait."

32

After such a splendid morning greeting from her orcs, Alma couldn't have possibly wanted for anything more—at least, until Baldr and Drafli had escorted her to the kitchen, and Baldr gave her another warm, sheepish smile.

"Oh, and I meant to tell you, Bright-Heart," he said. "I have finally gained you some trading-credits from the captain, and put the note upon your desk, along with some fresh ledgers and inks for you. If you would kindly use them to write up a Keeping budget for this week, as you spoke of, I shall take this tomorrow to the captain and the porters, and apply these credits as you wish. The captain said you are to work upon the Keeping as you see best, and hire whoever you wish to help you, also."

Alma's answering gasp of delight wasn't at all put-upon, and she profusely thanked Baldr for his help, and then wished both him and Drafli a most productive day. And then watched them walk away together, their steps perfectly aligned, while something knocked erratically against her chest. They'd given her a name. They were making this work. A *family*.

She found herself humming and smiling as she first threw

herself into another round of laundry, and then sat down at the desk—*her* desk, Baldr had called it—and reviewed the credits Baldr had left her. Comparing them against what she could make out of Roland's previous expenditures, and then breaking them into a preliminary budget, covering what had so far seemed to be the most urgent priorities. And then she went back to tackle more laundry, now folding and stacking the dry clothes into neat piles, while also darkly eyeing the fresh vermin droppings on her previously spotless scullery floor.

"Still here, sweetheart?" cut in a familiar voice—Kesst's voice—some time later. "All by your lonesome again, too?"

Alma had just finished yet another round of floor-scrubbing—and was indeed in the process of filling her four steaming tubs with yet more laundry—and she shot a quick smile over her shoulder. To where Kesst was frowning back toward her, and also lugging a large, heavy-looking bucket toward the ash chute.

"Er, yes, for now," Alma belatedly replied, watching as Kesst carefully dumped his bucket of ash down the chute. "But Baldr did arrange those credits for me, which should be a great help. And I've even decided on my first Keeping employee."

"Oh?" Kesst asked vaguely, as he snatched for the nearby shovel, and jabbed it down at the full-looking chute. "Let me guess, another peppy, impossibly sweet Grisk, with unfairly impressive cooking skills?"

"No, you ornery Ash-Kai," Alma shot back, half-laughing, even as she put her hands to her hips, and attempted a glare at him. "I'm hiring *you*."

Kesst froze, his shovel hovering in midair—and then he whirled around with impressive speed, giving her a surprisingly vicious glower. "Very funny," he said flatly. "Sorry, sweetheart, as much as I realize I owe you, I am *not* about to wade into your hell of stinking, seed-stained laundry. Ever. I'll happily *croak* first."

But Alma laughed again, and shook her head. "No laundry,

I swear," she replied. "I've decided to hire you as Orc Mountain's official Infirmarian."

Kesst's frown sharply deepened, his brows angling together. "As our *what*?"

"Our Infirmarian," Alma repeated, as she turned back to her tub, and kept dropping laundry in. "The manager of the infirmary. Or in your case, the sickroom."

"But—*Eft* manages the sickroom," Kesst said from behind her. "And Salvi and Eben."

"No, actually, they don't," Alma replied, as she reached for the soap, and dropped it in, too. "Efterar is your physician, and Eben and Salvi are his assistants. And *you*"—she turned back to Kesst—"are the manager."

Kesst began to protest again, but Alma's hand snapped sideways, saying, *stop*. "You *are*, Kesst," she insisted. "When I was ill, you regularly checked on me. You brought me food and water. You showed me the latrine, and got me up and moving around. You've been monitoring the sickroom's capacity, and Efterar's capacity, and advocating about it to your captain. You've also been keeping an eye on the laundry, and now here you are cleaning out the *fireplace*. You even told me yesterday that you often come here to cook at odd hours, and I *guarantee* that's not just for yourself, is it?"

Her voice had risen as she'd spoken, her hands back on her hips, and Kesst was blinking uncertainly at her, and then down toward the empty bucket at his feet. "Look, none of that is important," he replied, with a shrug. "I'm just trying to help Eft."

"Yes, because as you know, Efterar is irreplaceable, and apparently being *shamefully* taken for granted around here!" Alma countered. "And if good medical care is so important to your captain, and all your clans' ability to train as they do, then they ought to make an effort to better support it. And pretending that crucially important work does itself, for free, is blatant mismanagement, and I will *not* stand for it, Kesst!"

Kesst blinked at her for another long instant, his hands clenching on his shovel, while unmistakable suspicion crept across his eyes. "Wait," he said slowly. "This is all just some kind of sickeningly sweet scheme, isn't it? All my bellyaching has made your soft Grisk heart feel sorry for me, so now you've come up with some underhanded ploy to get me new *trousers*?"

He cast a dark look up at the still-looming mountain of laundry, and Alma heard herself make a sound much like a growl. "It's not a ploy," she said flatly. "It's proper housekeeping, Kesst. It's taking care of a house's most important needs first, and making sure its inhabitants stay safe! And if you want to talk about ploys, let's discuss the one where you made a big fuss over your trousers, because you were worried about the state of the sickroom's bedding, but didn't want to add to Efter-ar's stress! So"—she hauled in a breath, and pulled herself taller—"you *are* going to oblige me on this, because you are *crucial* to that sickroom's operations, and to your patients' health. And if *you* decide to run off like Roland did, we would be in a sorry state, with no one to replace you! So I will *not* hear another word about it! *None!*"

She nearly barked the last word, loud enough that Kesst startled, and almost dropped his shovel. "Good gods, sweetheart," he said, wiping nervously at his brow. "You have clearly been spending *far* too much time with that Skai."

Alma belatedly grimaced, and gave him a wincing, apologetic smile as she stepped forward, and took the shovel out of his slack hands. "Sorry," she said. "I just—I do feel quite strongly about this. So will you please just indulge me? Your first pay should be with the Ash-Kai porter tomorrow, and if you *are* still legitimately in need of trousers, there's no need to purchase new ones, because I'm sure I *will* get to yours soon."

Kesst groaned aloud, muttering under his breath about Grisk and his teeth, but then he finally threw up his hands, snatched up his now-empty bucket, and stalked out. And Alma was taking that as a victory, damn him, and she found herself smiling toward where he'd gone, and again humming a cheerful little tune as she set back to work.

Yet another welcome development came a short time later, with the sudden appearance of Varinn at the scullery door. He was flashing Alma an easy smile, and he had his bulky arm slung around the shoulders of a new orc. A *young* orc, Alma realized, with unmarked grey skin and long gangly limbs, who was eyeing her with a mixture of curiosity and trepidation.

"Good day, sister," said Varinn, inclining his head toward her. "I wish you to meet our little brother Timo. We heard that you might need some help with the Keeping, and thought mayhap Timo could be of use. Rather than"—he ruffled Timo's hair—"running about causing mayhem all day, ach?"

Timo cast Varinn a reproachful look, his face slightly reddening. And Alma felt herself smiling warmly toward him, and even giving him a quick little curtsey. "I'm honoured to meet you, Timo," she said. "And I would be even more honoured to have some help. Especially"—she glanced at her neat stacks of folded laundry—"with all these clean clothes, because I have no conception of who they belong to, or where they ought to go! Is that something you might be able to guide me in?"

Timo took a tentative step toward the laundry, and bent down to sniff the nearest stack. "Ach, woman, you have mixed them up quite badly," he said, with a shy glance toward her. "This is Skai—Killik's, I ken—and this is Ka-esh, Gary's. And this"—he yanked out a kilt from halfway down the pile—"is Thrain's! Ach, Varinn?"

He'd excitedly thrust the kilt into Varinn's hands, and Varinn raised it to his nose, and took a rather deep-looking inhale. "Ach, it is," he said to Timo, with an affectionate smile. "So mayhap you shall kindly help our sister sort these, and deliver them for her?"

Timo eagerly nodded, and Varinn took his leave, waving away Alma's heartfelt thank-you. And leaving Alma alone with

Timo, whose shyness quickly crumbled after a few curious questions, and who was soon regaling her with enthusiastic descriptions of his friends, and the new sparring-sword he'd gotten at Yule, and how he and his best brother Trygve had recently sneaked into the Skai arena.

"They didn't even smell that we were there," he gleefully informed her, "and we got to see Drafli fighting against three Skai at once! It would have been a *bloodbath*, had they been armed. Our Right Hand is *terrifying*, ach?"

Alma's interest had reflexively sparked, though she found herself wincing at the memories of all the bloody orcs in the sickroom. "Hopefully there were no lasting injuries, at least?" she asked. "I saw some of your Grisk brothers sparring yesterday, and that seemed quite safe?"

Timo loudly scoffed, and immediately launched into a detailed breakdown of the differences between the clans' fighting styles, followed by an exuberant recounting of the match he'd seen. Down to how Drafli had run one orc so ragged he couldn't breathe, and then had thrown him into a wall by his hair while he'd laughed. And despite the vivid brutality in this lurid tale, Alma felt herself smiling, and even telling Timo, with all honesty, that she'd wished she'd been there to see it.

"Ach, mayhap we can sneak you in with us, next time," said Timo, with another shy smile. "Of course you should wish to witness your mate's fierceness, ach?"

Her mate. Alma's face was suddenly flushing, her mouth opening to protest that, but Timo was already speaking again, his eyes thoughtful. "But we shall need to do very good sneaking, for no doubt Drafli will not wish to frighten you. He will wish to keep safe such a pretty, scent-bound mate."

Alma's cheeks had gone even hotter, and thankfully at that moment Gegnir poked his head into the scullery, and informed her that there were a few pantry deliveries, if she'd be willing to handle them. So after a quick farewell to Timo, who promised to deliver the clean laundry at speed, Alma found herself back out in the kitchen, and meeting with three new orc arrivals, by the names of Kalfr, Eyolf, and Iyolf. They were all apparently from Clan Bautul, and they were carrying several overflowing baskets of produce between them, as well as an alarmingly fresh-looking deer carcass.

"Thank you, woman," said Kalfr, with a careful smile, once Alma—under Gegnir's direction—had shown them where to leave their harvest, and had written up their corresponding credits in a separate kitchen ledger. "We look forward to working with you."

Alma returned this with a genuine smile of her own, and then turned her attention to several more orcs Gegnir was ushering over—and soon, she was fully caught in a bustling rhythm of productive activity. Alternating her pantry-stocking with more laundry, a few updates to her budget, some more small jobs for Timo, and even with helping Gegnir and Narfi pull together the orcs' supper.

It was helpful to see their usual process for preparing the meal, but it turned out that most of the food was indeed served raw. So while Gegnir and Narfi turned their attention to the ever-growing lineup of chattering orcs out the door, Alma threw together some custard tarts, fried up some fresh venison, and once again took a steaming basket over to Baldr and Drafli's room.

She found them again sitting on their fur together in the candlelight, swiftly signing back and forth to one another. And while Drafli's glance up toward her was carefully blank, Baldr instantly leapt to his feet, flashing her his broad, toothy smile. And then he tugged her into the room, and pulled her down to sit beside him between Drafli's sprawled feet.

"And let her eat this time, Draf," Baldr said, gripping his hand at Drafli's ankle, and giving it a cheerful little shake. "At least for now, ach?"

Drafli's slow, answering smirk sent a delicious thrill up

Alma's back, and so did the eagerness with which he pulled over her basket, and began unpacking it. Not even bothering to inspect her cooking this time before taking a massive bite of venison, the juice dribbling down his chin.

"Ach, that *is* good," Baldr said, once he'd bit off a piece, too. "You are too kind to us, Bright-Heart. Now tell us, how did you spend your day?"

Alma hesitated at that—surely they didn't actually care to hear about her housekeeping efforts?—but they were both watching her expectantly, even Drafli. So she obliged, speaking tentatively at first, but then more confidently. Telling them about her decision to hire Kesst, and how she'd taken over the pantry, and how there was still an irksome vermin situation, and how Varinn had brought Timo by to help her.

"It was so thoughtful of Varinn," she told them, between careful bites of venison. "He's just been *so* generous toward me. And Timo was such a help, and so sweet, too. And he obviously thinks very highly of you, my lord, and told me that you are quite possibly the fiercest orc in this mountain."

She accompanied this with a shy smile toward Drafli, who until now, had appeared to be listening with surprising magnanimity—but at that, his eyes had alarmingly narrowed, and he snapped a large chunk of venison between his teeth as he signed something at Baldr. Some kind of question, perhaps, about whether *he* had done that?

"No, I did not ask Varinn to bring her help," Baldr said, and his eyes had gone rather disapproving, too. "Mayhap he again meant to be... *kind*."

This was again said with disconcerting disapproval, and a dark glance back toward Drafli. And when Drafli sharply signed something else at Baldr—something that almost looked like, *Get on her, now*—Baldr instantly obeyed, and plucked the venison from between Alma's fingers, and popped it into his own mouth. And then he promptly grasped both her ankles with strong warm hands, and drew them wide apart.

"Oh," Alma gasped, blinking at him with mingled shock and eagerness as he shucked his own trousers, and eased his powerful, gleaming body between her legs. "Truly?"

Baldr returned this with an unexpectedly deep growl, his hands now pulling at her skirt with purposeful efficiency, baring her lower body for his eyes. While another hand—Drafli's hand—tugged off her cape, and dropped his hand to give her exposed, jutting nipple a curt little tweak.

Baldr gave another growl as he watched, his eyes hooded and intent, and oh, Drafli did it again. Tweaking a little harder this time, rolling that peak between his capable fingers—and even tugging it up a little, toward Baldr's eyes. As a command, perhaps, or an offering—and Baldr accordingly bent his head, and sucked it into his mouth.

Alma's moan was harsh and far too loud, because oh, *hell*, that felt good. So, so good, Baldr's hot mouth and tongue covering her, tasting her, while Drafli's capable hand gripped the soft flesh a little lower, guiding it deeper. As if he were *feeding* her to Baldr, easing ever more of her inside Baldr's eager mouth, while Baldr's groans vibrated deep into her very skin. And while something else—something with a hard tip of gold—prodded hungry and meaningful between her spread legs.

Alma's shaky hands were already dropping toward it—gods, she needed more, *more*—and she furtively found that hot, swollen head, and guided it to where she most wanted it. Darting an ashamed glance between Baldr and Drafli as she did so, but Baldr was busy sucking more of her into his mouth, while Drafli was giving a speculative glance toward her untouched other breast, and dropping his hand to give it an almost-painful pinch.

Alma's groan was even louder this time, her back arching, and oh, that meant Baldr's smooth, pulsing head was pushing even harder against her. And now slowly sinking its way inside, breath by dazzling breath—and when Alma squirmed down a little more, taking more, Drafli's answering pinch felt more like a caress. Like... approval.

And Alma basked in it, revelled and writhed in it, as Baldr's warm, vibrating power kept filling her, opening her around him. Sliding in even smoother and easier than before, as though he had been made to fill her, his gold meant to sink as deep as it could go, kissing dark and secret at her womb.

He finally had to release his mouth's hold on her breast, his upper body now held high over hers, but oh, Drafli was still stroking her other side, gently kneading her with those long, clever fingers. While his other hand had hooked on Baldr's bottom lip, drawing his gaze up—and then Drafli signed something at him. Something that looked thoroughly obscene, something like...

"Ach," Baldr croaked back, between heaving breaths, his lashes fluttering. "Ach, yes, Draf. *Please*."

But Drafli's brows were coolly rising on his forehead, his hand clearly saying, *Keep going*. And Baldr shuddered as he nodded, his hips canting a little harder into Alma's, his moan low and ragged alongside hers.

"Please, Draf," he whispered, blinking at Drafli's eyes. "Please, take me. Plough me. Make me feel you, inside me, with me inside her. *Please*."

And oh, were they truly going to *do* that, and Alma's already-writhing body was flailing up at the very thought, wringing itself even deeper onto Baldr's pulsing heft. Again making him pulse and throb inside her, while Drafli's cool, questioning eyes dropped to hers, waiting.

"Yes, please, my lord," she gasped up at him, without thought, without hesitation. "Please, give him this. You promised you would reward us, and you always keep your word, don't you? And I want to see you do it, want to be with you in it, because you're both so, so perfect. So gorgeous. *Please*."

And was that satisfaction in Drafli's eyes, oh, oh surely it was, as his fingers gave her nipple one last hard, merciless twist, and then a firm little pat. And then he smoothly rose to his feet, and strode over to stand behind Baldr, casually kicking Baldr's legs wider apart. And giving Alma a perfect, shocking view as his clawed hand reached inside his trousers, and drew out his own hard, scarred length. And then began brazenly pumping it up and down, stroking it with firm, deft fingers.

And wait, he was *milking* himself, he was bringing out that thick white sweetness, so he could catch it in his hand, and smear it all over. Slicking himself for this, for his mate, who was still bearing down deep inside Alma, and had now tipped his head back, closing his eyes, inhaling slow and reverent. Surely scenting his mate's arousal, his fresh seed, so close...

And when Drafli dropped to his knees behind Baldr, Alma could feel Baldr's answering full-body shudder, the swell of his strength inside her. And then again as Drafli pressed a strong hand to Baldr's bare back, pushing him further downwards, until he was hovering close over her, his breaths stuttering hot in her ear.

Alma's breaths were stuttering too, her gaze caught on where Drafli was still lingering between their legs, his eyes gone half-lidded as he surveyed the sight he'd exposed. Looking at her own wide-open thighs, perhaps, with Baldr buried all the way up inside her, his thick bollocks pressed hard against her crease. And, perhaps, at Baldr's own spread legs above her, at what was waiting deep between his muscled arse-cheeks. At how it was surely as eager and hungry as Alma felt.

And when Drafli leaned forward, clearly notching himself there, Alma could feel Baldr's answering heave above her, *inside* her. His breath hissing hard in her ear, his heft within her flaring and flexing, the rest of his warm body gone hard and clenched all over. Waiting, surely, bracing himself, as Drafli drew in a breath, and slowly pressed forward.

Fuck. Baldr and Alma both seemed to wrench up at once,

Baldr's voice crying out, while inside her, he seemed to bulge and surge and harden even more. Swelling fuller than he'd ever been yet, stretching her tight and thin around him, and she could feel the seed spasming out of him, wringing from base to tip. As if rather than Alma milking him, pulling it out from the front, Drafli was now driving it into her, pushing it out from behind. Almost as if he were making Baldr into an extension of himself, as if he were mounting him, charging him, using him as a weapon against her...

And when Drafli drove in the rest of the way, snapping himself deep inside, Alma was suddenly, desperately sure of it. Because already it was different, already Baldr was grinding and gouging against her in a way he never had before, his hips pushing fierce and demanding against hers. And when Drafli slowly drew back, his eyes now chilly and intent on Alma's face, Baldr drew back too, taking himself away from her, his breath rasping, his head thrown back, waiting...

Until Drafli plunged forward again, burying himself deep—and inside Alma, Baldr did the same, ramming himself firm and solid against her. While she shouted and arched up, clinging to his shifting shoulders with all her strength—but not strong enough to keep him from pulling away again, emptying her again, nearly all the way this time—

Drafli's next thrust forward shot stars behind her eyes, Baldr's growl rumbling deep into her chest, his heft again slammed to the hilt inside her shaky, writhing body. While Drafli just kept looking down toward her, holding her in his satisfaction, his triumph. *His own stubborn vengeance*, Baldr had said, *against that woman's power over him...*

And in this stilted, completely overwhelming moment, flush with chaos and sensation, suddenly Alma... welcomed it. Welcomed Drafli's vengeance, his rage, the way he was wielding his mate against her. The way he was sinking in again, again, even harder and harder, until he was pounding Baldr's massive, rock-hard cock into her in a raw, relentless rhythm. Silently shouting that this was still what he thought of women like her, what she'd earned from him, what she deserved.

She deserved to have Baldr's sweetness wielded against her. She deserved to shout and shudder beneath Drafli's agonizing onslaught. She deserved to be used, and railed, and broken open upon the mate he truly loved. And she would take it, she would pay it, she would hold his furious eyes and beg for more as her ecstasy grasped and shook, hurling up with whirling abandon against the weapon stabbed deep inside her, welcoming it, *cherishing* it...

Baldr's explosion inside her came without warning, hot and wild and roaring. Spurting out in burst after burst of slick molten seed, flooding her even fuller with him, while his eyes rolled back, and his roar echoed through the room. And behind him, Drafli's body had juddered to stillness too, his eyes squeezing shut—and then he pitched forward over Baldr's back, his hair fallen loose down over Baldr's shoulder, his face buried deep in Baldr's neck.

And then, suddenly, all was still, but for their breaths. Their deep, dragging breaths, seeming to rise and fall together, as one. All three of them held together, locked together, and somehow Alma's trembling hands had curled against both their dark heads. Drawing Baldr closer against her neck, and Drafli closer against Baldr's.

And no one argued, no one protested, or even spoke. Only kept breathing, in and out, in and out—until finally Drafli lifted his head, and looked at her.

And—oh. Oh. His sharp cheekbones were flushed with pink, his long black hair adding an astonishing, alluring softness to his harsh face. And his mouth, his hard mouth was stained and dripping with red, because he'd been—he'd been biting Baldr. *Drinking* him.

And that red was even dripping down onto Alma, pooling from both Drafli's mouth, and Baldr's shoulder. And she should have been repulsed, she should have balked and condemned this, whatever the hell this had been...

But most powerful of all, glittering here above her, was that look in Drafli's eyes. The regret. The... guilt. Almost as if he hadn't actually meant to use her like that. Hadn't meant to be so angry. To turn her into someone she wasn't, to make her pay for someone else's sins.

But suddenly, again, Alma didn't care. She didn't, and despite the intensity of this—and yes, the pain—she felt herself smiling up at him, careful but genuine, her hand spreading wider against the back of his head.

"So I brought dessert, too," she whispered at him. "Did you try it? I think you'll like it."

And that was... *relief*, surely, in Drafli's shifting eyes. Gratefulness. And maybe even a ghost of a rueful smile, passing brief and surprisingly stunning across his mouth before vanishing again.

No, he signed at her, his hand's movement easy and languid. *No yet.*

And before Alma could find a reply, he drew back from Baldr with a slick-sounding squelch. And then Alma could feel his strong fingers between her legs, circling around Baldr's softened base against her—and then popping him out, too. Releasing the flood of pent-up seed inside her, spurting it out in hot, sticky streams. Feeling even thicker and messier than usual, flowing all over her aching, gaped-open heat—and wait, that was surely because Baldr was dripping *Drafli's* seed, too. Pooling it from where he was perhaps stretched and gaping too, leaking liberally down onto Alma's thighs and belly. While Drafli knelt behind and watched, his eyes hooded and surely even approving on the sight.

When it felt like the worst of it had subsided, Drafli purposefully nudged Baldr away, off to the side. An order Baldr promptly obeyed, wincing as he settled beside Alma, his hazy eyes darkening with concern on her face. "Are you well, Bright-Heart?" he breathed. "Do you have any pain, from this?"

Alma did, a little—but her answer was abruptly whirled away, deep into the abyss. Because Drafli, who had still been kneeling between her legs, was ducking his dark head down, and—

He *licked* her. *Drafli* licked her, *there*.

Alma's yelp was sharp and frantic, her whole body seizing up in the impossible, unreal furor of it. Drafli was between her legs, his mouth was *between her legs*, his tongue had touched her, *there*—

And as Alma stared helplessly down toward him, shivering all over, he did it *again*. That long black tongue darting out—from *Drafli's mouth*—and tasting her. *There*.

Alma's cry again tore from her throat, ringing through the room, while Drafli just did it again, even harder this time. His tongue dragging smooth and deep into her leaking, tender crease, and flaring out fiery streams of raw, ruthless pleasure in its wake. While his glinting eyes held to hers, slipping back into cool mockery—and even moreso when he raised his hand, and signed something she couldn't follow.

"He says," murmured Baldr beside her, because oh, Baldr was still here, he'd propped himself on his elbow to watch this, his eyes just as dazed—and just as astonished—as Alma felt. "Draf says he is—having his *dessert*."

Fuck. Alma arched up again, her throat again crying out, while another spray of shuddering sparks seemed to soar from Drafli's sliding tongue. Lingering even longer and harder this time, before he briefly drew back, and blatantly licked at the slick wetness on his mouth. At the sure tinge of fresh new *pink* smeared against his cheek. From... her.

And oh, he was licking that, too, together with his mate's spent seed inside her. His *dessert*, he'd said. And why was Alma crying out again, why was she so arrested on the sight of it, the truth of it, oh he was going to do it again, the ache and the ecstasy flashing up like lightning, striking hot and blazing against her...

"Ach, you must breathe, Bright-Heart," whispered Baldr beside her, and her desperate glance toward him found him still looking dazed, but perhaps amused, too. "Lie back, and take joy in this great gift he grants you."

Oh. Alma fervently nodded, and fought to obey—at least, until that relentless, glorious tongue stroked again, even deeper this time. Driving a full-on shriek from Alma's mouth, to which Baldr gave a low, indulgent chuckle, a wry shake of his head.

"Breathe into this, Bright-Heart," he murmured. "If you relax and open more for him, he may drink from even deeper within you, ach?"

Oh hell, and Alma's nod felt like a hammer-thrust, her eyes squeezing shut, her legs instinctively snapping wider. While beside her, Baldr laughed again, his body shaking with mirth. "Not quite thus," he whispered. "Deep breath, Bright-Heart. With me. Ach?"

At that, he took a long, deliberate inhale, his warm chest filling against her, while her entire body kept shuddering at Drafli's continued onslaught between her legs. But she'd somehow managed to drag in air with him, earning a purr of approval beside her, while Drafli's tongue indeed seemed to swarm deeper and hungrier inside her.

"Good," Baldr murmured, as she trembled and arched, revelling in it, *destroyed* in it. "His tongue is just as sweet as his scent and his seed, ach? It is"—his voice hitched—"a rare gift, and his greatest reward, ach?"

This was said with a heated, meaningful glance toward Drafli, as though this were a truth they shared very intimately—and of course they did, because Baldr was the one who'd named Drafli *Golden-Tongue*, wasn't he? And Drafli surely was in full agreement with this, his eyes glinting as he kept licking ever deeper inside Alma. The tip of his thick, writhing tongue curling up just where it felt the fiercest, again and again, the maelstrom juddering up higher and higher, tighter and tighter—

It flashed to earth with a roar, with a booming clamour of pelting, mind-melting ecstasy. Wringing Alma out again and again and again, careening light behind her eyes, raw thundering heat ripping and tearing her apart. While that tongue just kept vibrating inside her, *laughing* at her, while she shattered into pieces upon him.

It left her feeling limp and trembly all over, thoroughly and utterly spent. And when Drafli finally, slowly drew away, his cheekbones still slightly flushed, his tongue blatantly licking at his lips, there was no other truth left, no other reality, beyond him...

But he wasn't even looking at her, wasn't even acknowledging what he'd done to her—but instead, he was looking at Baldr. And when he beckoned Baldr forward with an imperious flick of his finger, Baldr immediately obeyed, rising up to his knees—and then Drafli grasped the back of his neck, dragged him forward, and kissed him.

It was hard and forceful this time, and Alma could almost feel the plunge of Drafli's slick tongue, the bite of his sharp teeth. While Baldr moaned and clutched at him, his own tongue desperately licking and seeking back, even as a fresh streak of bright red ran down his chin.

It wasn't until Drafli finally drew away—licking up that streak of red as he went—that he finally looked back at Alma, his gaze sweeping up and down her limp, messy, thoroughly debauched body. And the pure, glittering triumph on his face was so vivid, so vicious, it stole away the last of her breath.

He's mine, it seemed to say. *Mine. And so are you. Look at you, so destroyed by my tongue.*

It was surely mockery, surely dripping with icy, arrogant contempt. And perhaps it was even a continuation of before, of how he'd surely meant to punish her, to put her in her place. To use Baldr against her.

But there was no against. Not anymore. He and Baldr loved each other, they needed each other, they were going to be a family. And Alma would be honest with them, she would be true, she would do better. *There is no shame.*

And she didn't care if it was obscene, if she spread her legs wider to show Drafli where he'd tasted her, where she was still dripping his mate's seed. Or if she stroked her full breast with one hand, displaying it for him, while the other hand spoke to his glinting, victorious eyes.

Thank you, she signed at him. *Thank you, Golden-Tongue. I am yours.*

And oh, his eyes. His eyes, blazing bright with triumph, with satisfaction, and with... *relief*. Relief, as his clawed hand moved, and signed something new. Something that set her heart fluttering, the warmth curling dark and deep and whole.

Yes, he said. *You are mine.*

33

You are mine.

Those impossible, unthinkable words kept whirling and ringing as Drafli finally rose to his feet again, and waved for Alma to follow. Surely about to take her back to her room for the night, as usual—at least, until he glanced coolly at Baldr, and beckoned for him to follow, too.

You are a mess, again, he signed at them. *Come with me, and bathe.*

Alma and Baldr exchanged delighted grins, and soon, all three of them were traipsing down to the baths together, Alma wearing only her skirt, and Baldr entirely unclothed. While Drafli—still in his trousers—strode tall and imperious before them, inclining his head toward the various orcs they passed, and thoroughly ignoring the two messy, happy, flush-faced Grisk trailing along behind him.

Once they were all in the pool together, Alma soon discovered that Drafli was almost as accomplished a swimmer as Baldr was, his lean bared body slicing through the water beside Baldr's with fluid, dazzling ease. And finally even Baldr stopped swimming to watch him, his eyes warm on Alma's, his hand furtively spreading against her bare waist beneath the water.

"You two are incredible," Alma told him, a little shyly. "How did you ever learn to swim like this?"

Baldr shrugged, his gaze flicking back to Drafli again. "My mother raised me alone, in a cave by the eastern sea," he said, "and there was oft nothing else to do there, ach? So I spent my days hunting, and tracking, and most of all swimming. And"—he grimaced—"waiting for my father to come."

Oh. Alma felt her head tilting, her thoughts catching and circling around that. Wait. Had Baldr ever mentioned his father before? His *Grisk* father?

"So you *did* know your father?" she asked, quieter now. "Did he come to see you often?"

Baldr grimaced again, his eyes still very intent on where Drafli was doing a beautiful little flip at the end of the pool. "Sometimes," he said vaguely, as something tightened in his jaw. "But my father was very busy serving his clan, and it was a long journey. How about your father, Bright-Heart? Did you oft spend time with him?"

Alma's eyes had flicked back to Drafli too, her head shaking. "No, he died before I was born," she replied. "But I was fortunate, because my mother was always very good to me. At least, until—"

She broke off there, wincing as Pembroke's horrible face loomed up in her thoughts, and she could feel Baldr's hand spreading wider against her, drawing her a little closer. "Ach," he said, quiet, with far too much understanding in his voice. "Mine, also. And ach"—he cleared his throat, his eyes still on Drafli—"look at Draf! You would never ken *he* had not learnt to swim as an orcling."

It was clearly an intentional change of subject, and Alma certainly wasn't arguing it, giving Baldr a wan, grateful smile. "He's brilliant," she said. "How did *he* learn to swim, then? Did you teach him?"

Baldr nodded, his eyes softening as he again watched Drafli flip over, and kick off the edge of the pool. "He only learnt it to humour me," he replied. "But now we come here near every day. He says it is only to keep up his strength, because it helps him in combat, but whenever I do not join him, he—"

This was broken by another gigantic splash, as Drafli suddenly resurfaced before them, bodily tackled Baldr, and dragged him below the water. And when they bobbed up again, Baldr was both gasping and laughing as Drafli spun him around, clasping Baldr's muscled back tight against his front. His hand blatantly seeking down between them, clearly again finding that secret place between Baldr's arse-cheeks, oh *hell.*

"He does—*this*," Baldr huffed at Alma, his eyes fluttering, his body scrabbling in the water—and then he flailed up as Drafli drove forward, slamming himself deep and powerful inside. "He—"

His voice again broke there, his dripping-wet face now flushed a deep pink, his eyes rolling back as Drafli eased into a swift, punishing rhythm. "He—*pounces* on me," Baldr continued, still with laughter in his hitching voice. "Says I need to stop smelling all the time. Stop *thinking* all the time. So—"

Behind him, Drafli's face had gained that distinctly devilish look, and he coolly eyed Alma as he gripped for the back of Baldr's neck. As he unceremoniously shoved Baldr's *head* under the water, while he kept driving away behind him.

And at this point, surely, Alma might very well have been shocked, or repulsed, or terrified. But she could only seem to keep watching, drinking up the sight, as Drafli's long, lithe, gleaming wet body kept thrusting into his mate, making him his.

Mine, his glinting eyes told her. *Mine.*

Something swelled in Alma's chest as she watched, something that might have been relief, or even gratefulness—and she somehow felt herself smiling at Drafli, slow and warm. *Yes*, she signed back. *Yours.*

That might have also been relief, flaring in Drafli's glittering eyes—and when he finally allowed a gulping, gasping Baldr to resurface again, Alma found herself moving closer, her hand reaching for Baldr's dripping-wet face. While her eyes glanced back at Drafli, asking his permission—and when he gave a noncommittal shrug, her other hand came forward too, tilting up Baldr's chin, making him look at her.

"It's so good of your mate, to care for you like this," she murmured at him, at his rapt, blinking eyes. "And you look so beautiful when he's taking you, too. When he's reminding you who *owns* you."

Baldr gasped, low and hoarse, his eyes fluttering harder as Drafli pounded deeper into him, as Alma's hands caressed his wet, gorgeous face. "So pretty," she whispered at him. "So *perfect*, with our lord so deep inside you."

Baldr's answer was a raw, broken moan this time, his body reflexively flailing up at every drive of Drafli's hips. And Alma was moaning too, still caressing him, adoring him, adoring *them*. "So pretty," she breathed. "With your tight arse. With your sweet, fat Grisk prick, with your mate's gold buried deep inside it. So now you'll spray for him, won't you? Show us how much you honour him?"

And oh, it was working, Baldr's head nodding, his eyes squeezing shut, his tooth biting his lip—and Alma could feel his body convulsively jerking as he emptied himself, spilling out into the water. While behind him, Drafli's eyes had rolled back too, his hand flexing on Baldr's neck—and he again thrust Baldr's face down under the water as he sprayed out his own relief inside him, his lean body bucking and gleaming in the lamplight.

Drafli held him there for a long, breathless instant, his eyes briefly blazing on Alma's—and then he drew Baldr up out of the water again, and pulled him close. And Alma could see how Baldr had gone just as limp and relaxed as she'd felt back in their bedroom, how his big body sagged into Drafli's with visible, visceral gratefulness.

And this time, Alma didn't wait for Drafli to ask her to leave. Instead, she managed to climb out of the pool herself, and then smiled warmly toward them as she wiped off with a nearby towel. "Thank you for this," she said. "Both of you. Enjoy the rest of your evening. And"—she fixed Drafli's unreadable eyes with a mock glare—"maybe go a little easier on him, your next round?"

But Drafli's eyes on hers had gone rather saucy, his claws visibly digging into Baldr's skin. *Pure-Heart loves it*, he signed back at her, with a certainty that should have felt arrogant, but didn't. *He loves me.*

If he'd again meant it to be a challenge, Alma certainly didn't care, and she couldn't help smiling at him again, and giving a fervent little nod. *Yes*, she replied. *He loves you.*

It felt a little odd, crossing her arms like that over her chest, and extending them toward Drafli. And perhaps he'd thought so too, his gaze instantly dropping, his hand caressing Baldr's wet head with studied casualness. So Alma quickly took her leave, her heart still unaccountably skipping as she crept through the corridor, back to her quiet, dark room.

But it felt so much easier to fall into bed this time, and to sink away into the lovely, floating safety of sleep. *He loves you.* A family.

Mine.

And when Alma blinked awake again, what felt like a long time later, she almost felt eager as she slipped out of bed, and washed and dressed. And then made thorough use of Drafli's tools, and read Drafli's pamphlets, before making her way into the Grisk shrine. Finding several Grisk already kneeling there—Varinn, Ella, and Nattfarr among them—and when Ella grinned up at Alma, and waved her over, she gratefully went to kneel beside them.

The prayers to Skai-kesh and Akva again seemed to clear

her thoughts, settling them quiet and calm. And she was once again humming a jaunty tune as she stepped back into the kitchen, and said a cheerful morning hello to Gegnir and Narfi.

"Morning, Keeper," Gegnir replied, while Narfi twitched and glowered beside him. "I put a few more delivery notes on your desk, ach? And here. Eat."

At that, he tossed a round red apple toward her, and Alma gratefully caught it, and then munched away as she set to work. First at her cozy little desk, logging the deliveries Gegnir had mentioned, and then in the scullery, putting in yet another load of laundry, and frowning at the new vermin droppings under her counters. But before she'd even reached for the shovel, there was a sudden commotion behind her, and three more orcs spilled into the room.

"Here, Boss?" one of them was demanding, his voice incredulous. "Doing *that* laundry? Can you not *smell* that shit?!"

The speaking orc was tall and lean, his long black hair tied up in a messy knot on his head—and wait, the orc he was talking to, the orc he'd called *Boss*, was *Drafli*. But before Alma could properly register that, the third orc—one with stooped shoulders and a shock of grey hair—had stepped closer toward her, looking her up and down with vague, cloudy eyes.

"Room has... human," he said unhappily, curling his lip, and thereby showing several missing teeth. "Human *attack*."

"Ach, Duff, she won't attack you," broke in the first orc— and now that Alma had had a moment to study him, she realized that despite his height—and many obvious scars—he was probably a little younger than she was, with sharp, boyish features. "Can't you smell Boss all over her? No way she'll risk attacking you, if she's in *his* bed every night."

This was said with a rather impish glance up toward Drafli, who didn't seem nearly as irked by all this as Alma might have supposed. Rather, his expression had remained perfectly bland, or perhaps even *tolerant*, as he signed something at this orc. Something that looked rather like, *Get on with it*, and the new orc heavily sighed, and purposefully shifted his gaze to Alma's.

"Hullo, woman," he said, in the bleak tones of one who'd been sentenced to a grim, horrible punishment. "Boss here says you need help with the laundry. And since I went and busted my knee in the arena last week"—he grimaced, and frowned darkly down toward his trouser leg—"here I am, at your service. Tryggr, by the way, of Clan Skai. And this here is Dufnall. He's gonna help, too."

He was? They were?! Alma's astonished eyes were flicking between Drafli, and this Tryggr, and now this Dufnall. Who certainly looked older than most orcs she'd seen in the mountain so far, his eyes pale and rheumy, his nose and ears very large, and sprouting many grey hairs. And his gaze on Alma had gone increasingly suspicious, his nose abruptly snuffling at the air.

"I no smell Skai scent on human," he said darkly. "Only smell Grisk. *Danger*."

"Grisk ain't dangerous, Duff," interjected the other orc— Tryggr—with a meaningful glance up at Drafli. "Not to us, anyway. And you remember your nose is a bit wrecked, ach? This human *definitely* reeks of Skai. Boss has been having some good fun with her."

He was flashing Drafli a sly, amused grin, which Drafli returned with a crisp sign that looked rather like a ribald *affirmation*. Making Tryggr bark a merry, contagious laugh, while beside them Dufnall sniffed, and rubbed ponderously at his nose.

"*Danger* human," Dufnall said woefully. "*Attack*, soon as back turns. Then we *die*, in filthy washtub."

Alma could feel Drafli's exasperated sigh as he snapped his long fingers in front of Dufnall's mournful face, and signed something else. Something that Alma didn't follow, but clearly Dufnall did, his mouth pursing, his cloudy eyes again flicking toward her.

"If you prove Skai loyalty," he said, glancing stubbornly back at Drafli, "*then* I help. *Only* then."

Drafli sighed again, heavy and clearly resigned—and then, to Alma's ongoing astonishment, he flicked those fingers toward her, and then the floor. Clearly telling her, *Get down, and suck me.*

Alma twitched and startled—Drafli wanted her to *what*?—and he repeated the command, even sharper than before, his eyes glinting with sudden, surprising menace.

Get down, he snapped. *Now.*

And oh gods, Tryggr and Dufnall were watching all this, Tryggr with bright curiosity, Dufnall with ever-deepening suspicion. And Drafli with that same chilly menace, as if he truly wanted Alma to do this, without Baldr here, with these two strange orcs watching. As if he wanted... her.

Mine, he'd said. *Mine.*

And somehow—*unthinkable*—Alma felt herself slowly nodding, holding Drafli's imperious eyes, as a quick, curious shudder raced up her spine. And she kept her gaze on his as she carefully knelt down on the hard floor before him, and then signed up at him, as Baldr had taught her. *May I suck you, Golden-Tongue? Please?*

There was a low, approving whistle from Tryggr beside them, but Alma kept her eyes on Drafli's, and waited. While her heart thudded louder and louder in her ears, her face flushing ever hotter, her tooth biting uncertainly at her lip.

But then, oh thank the gods, Drafli gave a minute nod, and smoothly reached down into his trousers. And Alma's blinking eyes barely saw that scarred, dripping, rock-hard heft before it was sliding between her parted lips, and bearing down toward her throat.

Alma heard herself moan, the sound thoroughly betraying, her face still painfully hot. But surely Drafli was giving her a chance with this, he was *acknowledging* her with this, and he'd given her breathtakingly glorious—and very comparable—

pleasures just last night, had he not? And gods, what had Baldr taught her, use both her hands, caress those heavy bollocks, seek her tongue within him, find that oozing sweetness at its source...

And yes, surely it was right, because Drafli's hardness was shuddering against her tongue, and spluttering out more rich sweetness into her mouth. While beside him, Alma heard Tryggr chuckling, the sound low and husky, surely even *approving*.

"Ach, Boss, you and your pretty Grisk pets," he said admiringly. "You do know how to train 'em, though, don't you? Look at her, Duff, kissing him with her sweet little tongue like that."

Alma's face was smarting with heat now—they were all watching her, *judging* her—but Drafli still clearly wanted this, and Drafli mattered most. Drafli whose eyes had shifted with something almost like satisfaction, while his hand coolly signed another order down toward her. *More*, it meant. *Keep going.*

Alma attempted a nod—as much as one could, with this much hard orc in one's mouth—and indeed fought to do more, to take more. To sink her tongue deeper into that dark clenching heat, to drink him from the inside out, while her hands stroked and fondled, pumping him, pleading him...

"They are even prettier with Skai in their mouths, ach?" Tryggr continued, his voice even huskier than before. "I ken she was a good choice, Boss. Don't s'pose you might be willing to share that little tongue of hers for a spell?"

There was an abrupt shift of Drafli's body above her—because wait, he'd punched Tryggr in the *arm*, and Tryggr was loudly yelping, and frantically rubbing at where Drafli had hit him. "Just joking!" he squeaked. "We all know you like 'em scent-bound to you. And by the smell of her, she likes it too, ach?"

Drafli's eyes, which had been crackling rather dangerously, had flicked down toward Alma again—and they seemed to shift as they watched her, perhaps even softening again. And his hand coolly signed something else toward Tryggr beside him, even as his heft bore down a little deeper onto Alma's tongue, sputtering out more hot, succulent sweetness against it.

"Ach, this is truth, Boss, I *could* get my own," Tryggr replied thoughtfully, and when Alma darted a furtive glance up toward him, he was again eyeing her, with far more shrewdness than before. "A sweet Grisk like one of yours would be quite nice. Or maybe a Ka-esh? I've seen a few *very* pretty ones down there, and lots of 'em like it rough, too."

In response to that, Drafli's hand had coolly reached up, and grasped for a handful of Alma's *hair*. Tilting her head back, just hard enough to tease at the edge of pain, while he pushed past her still-seeking tongue, and drove down deep and merciless into her throat.

Alma's moan was muffled, choked off around the shuddering heat filling her mouth, and above her Tryggr barked another amused laugh. "Now you're just showing off, Boss, really. And Duff's gotta be satisfied at this point, right, Duff? You don't really still think she's gonna drown you in a washtub?"

Dufnall muttered some kind of skeptical-sounding reply, to which Tryggr laughed again. "Ach, I'll drown you myself, if you keep that up. Now are you gonna feed her, or what, Boss? You really do like to make 'em work for you, don't you?"

But to Alma's amazement, Drafli was actually *smirking*, his hands pulling back a little harder on her hair, his eyes gleaming on her face. His hand again signing at her, and saying, *You like this, Bright-Heart. You want this.*

Oh, hell. And Alma was somehow dragging him even deeper, all but choking on his pulsing length as she frantically fought to nod. *Yes*, she signed back, her hand trembling in midair. *Yes. Please. More.*

And Drafli shrugged—*shrugged!*—as he thrust in deep once, twice, again. And suddenly Alma's mouth was swarming with surge after surge of hot, delectable sweetness, flooding her cheeks, pouring down her throat.

But this time, she managed to swallow it in gulp after gulp, dragging in deep breaths to help, like Baldr had shown her. Until Drafli had finally stopped oozing, and she was gently sucking at his softened heft, and holding his eyes. Seeing, for the briefest of instants, another flare of warmth, or even approval, as his cool hand gently patted her hot, sticky cheek.

Thank you, Golden-Tongue, she signed at him, as well as she could, with him still in her mouth—and that earned her one last little splurge of sweetness from his softened heft, another brief pat to her cheek. And then he was briskly popping himself out of her, tying up his trousers again, and signing something at Tryggr and Dufnall before spinning on his heel, and walking out.

Oh. It left Alma kneeling there shivery and red-faced, her tongue licking at her still-sticky lips, her own groin feeling rather swollen, and thoroughly thwarted. While both Dufnall and Tryggr eyed her, Dufnall now with a mulish-looking resignation, and Tryggr with palpable admiration.

"Um," Alma said thickly, as she staggered to her feet. "Thank you both so much for coming. Er, perhaps I'll start by showing you the usual process for the laundry, then?"

They agreed easily enough, even Dufnall, and soon the two orcs were hovering over the tubs together, working with surprising efficiency. And as Alma turned her attention to the latest round of clean, dry clothes, she couldn't help noticing how the two of them seemed to communicate in an odd, seemingly random blend of speaking and signing. Many of the signs ones that she now recognized, but mixed with many unfamiliar ones, too.

"Do *all* orcs speak your sign language?" she asked at a break in their conversation, before she could catch herself. "I thought it was... *Drafli's* language?"

"Ach, no," replied Tryggr, with a shrug, and a half-smile.

"Though Boss knows lots more than any of the rest of us, on account of his throat getting slashed, you know? But lots of Skai learn it—even just in bits and pieces—because it's damned useful when you're out there hunting or fighting, and trying to talk across distances while humans are trying to slaughter you. And that's also why"—he signed along as he spoke—"so much of it is one-handed, see?"

Alma had nodded along, wincing at that mention of murderous humans, but Tryggr didn't seem to notice, and was now nodding toward Dufnall. "'S good for orcs like you too, right Duff? Duff has good days and bad days, and sometimes the signs come easier than the words, don't they?"

Dufnall nodded too, and opened his mouth to reply—but then he abruptly began sniffing at the air, and signed toward both of them, saying, *Stop*. Leaving Alma and Tryggr glancing warily at each other, as Dufnall silently eased sideways—and with astonishing speed, he swiped his clawed hand beneath the counter, and brought it back holding a large, squirming black rat.

Alma stifled a yelp, her body lurching backwards, while beside her Tryggr crowed aloud. "Nice one, Duff!" he exclaimed, as Dufnall brought the rat to his mouth—and thankfully Alma squeezed her eyes shut, just in time, as she heard a decisive-sounding snap. "That's a big one. Must be a nest around here, ach? Oooh, he's juicy, too."

"I'll just—" Alma interjected, keeping her eyes closed, as she fumbled toward the door to the kitchen. "Leave you two for now. I hope you enjoy, Dufnall."

She could hear Tryggr hooting with laughter as she left, but not quite loudly enough to cover up the distinctive sound of Dufnall's continued crunching. And Alma gladly fled to her desk, where she was soon distracted by the return of Timo— who shyly offered to take around more clothes—and then by several more pantry deliveries. One of these was from Kalfr, the tall, charcoal-skinned Bautul orc Alma had met the day before, and after a few moments' pleasant conversation, he tentatively asked if she might like to see the Bautul garden, to gain a better sense of the food supplies?

Alma certainly wasn't about to refuse such an intriguing offer, and soon, after another short trek through the mountain, she found herself taking deep, cleansing breaths in a truly stunning, sunlit, walled-in garden. It was tucked up against the mountain's south side, ensuring plenty of light and warmth for its spectacular bounty of trees and plants.

It also turned out that there were two more new women in the garden, both of them having just returned with their orc mates from a trip to the south. One of the women, plump and heavily pregnant with doe-like eyes, was named Stella, while the other, tall and lean and dark-haired, introduced herself as Gwyn, the mountain's midwife. And once Alma had shyly given them her own background—briefly mentioning Baldr and Drafli—Gwyn's brows shot up, and she rushed off to collect her own mate, a tall, sly-eyed orc named Joarr.

"You say *Drafli*, witch?!" this Joarr demanded at Gwyn, his mouth quirking up as his eyes swiftly surveyed Alma—and then he broke into gales of bright, merry laughter, his hand clutching at his waist. "Ach, we welcome you, new woman, and wish you best luck. Now"—he grinned delightedly between Alma and Gwyn—"I ken I have pressing work in Skai wing, ach? You wish to help, brother?"

This was said with a gleeful smirk toward Kalfr, who was already nodding, and twitching an equally amused grin. To which Joarr hooked his arm around Kalfr's neck, dragging him back toward the mountain with impressive speed, while Gwyn laughed and rolled her eyes after them.

"Please, ignore him," she told Alma, with a knowing smile. "And pity Drafli, who's never going to hear the end of this. Now, come see the rest of our garden! And did you say you were taking over the mountain's *Keeping*?"

Alma had found herself smiling too, and soon they were all

cheerfully chattering together as Stella and Gwyn showed
Alma around the garden. Plying her with multiple fresh fruits
and berries as they went, and expressing their fervent appreciation for her efforts with the Keeping.

"I hate to bring this up, but you really ought to see the
Bautul fighting-pit," Stella said with a grimace, once they'd
wrapped up their lovely tour, and Alma had eaten so many
delicious snacks she'd begun to feel rather queasy. "I have no
idea how Roland cleaned it, but gods, it's a *travesty*."

This was not an exaggeration, Alma soon discovered, as
Stella and Gwyn happily offered to extend their tour, and soon
ushered her into what indeed seemed to be a flat, deep pit, at
the bottom of a huge, cavernous room. It was surrounded by
thick-cut angled stairs, surely meant for watching the goings-
on below—and while there was no fighting happening
currently, the floor beneath their feet was covered with a crusty,
blackish layer that was churning at Alma's already-unsteady
stomach.

"There are still grates in the floor here, somewhere," said
Gwyn, who had begun to look just as ill as Alma felt. "Somewhere. We hope."

Alma's hands had clutched over her nose, her head shaking
back and forth. "You really mean orcs are still fighting here?"
she demanded. "And that they're... getting wounds? In *this*?
And then dragging their filthy wounded selves up to *Efterar*?"

Gwyn and Stella exchanged a wincing look that surely
meant yes, they most certainly were. "If it helps," Gwyn said
hopefully, "I don't think the Skai arena is quite as bad? And the
main one probably isn't either?"

But Alma was staring at Gwyn with deep distaste, her
hands still held over her mouth. "You mean," she gulped,
"there are *others* like this, too?!"

But yes, to Alma's horror, there were indeed others. A main
arena, which was apparently shared by all the clans, was only
slightly less vile—and the Skai arena, surely the one Timo had

mentioned, thankfully turned out to be the least repulsive of the three. However, it was also truly massive, with multiple fighting areas, and therefore multiple varying degrees of foulness.

To make matters more difficult, the Skai arena was still very much in use, with many shouting, bleeding orcs viciously brawling all about. However, none of the orcs were Drafli or Baldr, and Alma wasn't sure whether to be disappointed or relieved by that as she studied the unfolding mayhem before them.

"Maria mentioned, the other day," she began, flinching as she watched one orc hurl another one onto his head, "that somehow Roland used to flood the mountain, once each moon. I'm assuming he must have cleaned these arenas, too? Surely more often than once a month, given their current state?"

Gwyn shot a questioning glance at Stella, who in turn was looking thoughtful, her large eyes distant. "I *do* remember Silfast—my mate—saying something about that," she said. "Perhaps we can go ask him?"

This led to a jaunt back through this side of the mountain, which Alma hadn't yet seen—and upon noticing her interest in the various rooms and passages they passed, Stella and Gwyn continued their expanded tour. Showing Alma the Bautul forge, the Bautul trading-room—far smaller than the Grisk one—and the firelit Bautul hearth, which also featured several massive, muscled orcs flagrantly taking their pleasure together.

But the sight was only making Alma think of Drafli—he'd done that earlier today, with *her*—and when Stella's huge, hairy, deadly-looking orc mate strode over, and blatantly groped Stella's plump body as he introduced himself, Alma scarcely even blinked. And after a shy smile and curtsey toward the orc—Silfast—Alma asked whether he might know anything about the floor-flooding, or how Roland managed it.

Silfast didn't know details, it turned out, but suggested that they ask Uglak, the Bautul trading-post porter. And a visit to

Uglak confirmed that indeed, he and Roland had been paying another orc—Gaukr—to help implement it throughout the Bautul wing. And that in fact, Gaukr had been managing the Bautul fires as well, but that he was at heart a lazy arse, who in the lack of ongoing direction had taken to lounging about in the arenas all day instead.

This led to another quest throughout the mountain, seeking out this Gaukr, who was nowhere to be found—and finally, upon encountering Varinn and Thrain in the Grisk wing, Alma enlisted their help, too. And Varinn's excellent nose indeed proved highly useful, and soon they found Gaukr snoozing in an empty bunk, and seeming entirely undaunted by the group of women and orcs standing over him, and demanding he tell them everything he knew.

"Ach, I helped with the flooding," he replied, yawning, and rubbing contentedly at his generous belly. "But I only did as Roland and the Ka-esh told me."

The Ka-esh?! Alma and Gwyn and Stella all stared at Gaukr, and then at each other—and then burst into helpless, astonished laughter. And soon they were traipsing down to the Ka-esh wing, now with Gaukr in tow, and seeking out Rosa. Who turned out to be highly affronted that her mate John hadn't once told her about the Ka-esh's involvement in such an intriguing project, and then flounced off to find him, with the rest of them trailing after her.

"And by the end of it," Alma told Baldr and Drafli that evening, as they once again shared a supper together, "we *finally* sorted out how Roland's floor-flooding had been done, and who had been involved in it. Twelve Ka-esh orcs, with support staff from each of the clans! And none of them had thought to pursue it without Roland's ordering them about! And since it hadn't been on John's list to manage, he hadn't realized it needed to be picked up. No wonder Kesst didn't think the Ka-esh could handle the Keeping, he said they've probably never even *seen* inside the arenas before!"

She'd surely been speaking with far too much enthusiasm, her voice breaking into occasional bubbles of laughter. But beside her, Baldr was grinning as he took another bite of the fresh bread she'd brought them, and even Drafli was looking reluctantly amused, a muscle twitching in his cheek.

"And then what, Bright-Heart?" Baldr asked her, nudging his knee against hers. "Did you set them all straight again?"

"Yes, I'm afraid so," Alma replied with a wince. "In truth, I think likely I came on rather too strong about it, because I told them all we would be shutting down the arenas in three days' time, and doing the floor-flooding, along with a thorough cleaning. Or else."

"Or else what?" Baldr prodded, his eyes dancing, and Alma winced again, and glanced guiltily toward Drafli. Whose brows were raised too, clearly waiting for her answer, even as he took another long drink from the tureen of hot soup she'd brought.

"Well," Alma said sheepishly, "I *might* have told them I would bring it to *you*, my lord. And that if your clan's crucially important arena was allowed to become any fouler, you would surely be very, *very* displeased. And you should have seen them jumping into action after that, it was like they were *possessed*!"

Beside her, Baldr howled a sudden guffaw, so hard he nearly spat out his mouthful of soup, and even Drafli's mouth had quirked up, giving her a glimpse of a sharp white fang. Firing a flare of hot, shuddery relief low into Alma's belly, and she smiled back at him, even warmer than before.

"Even Gaukr told me he would report for work tomorrow," she informed him, "and Eben, who I have never heard *speak* before, told me that you are the most fearsome orc he's ever seen in his life! Between them and Timo and Tryggr—who clearly worships the ground you walk on, my lord—I think we ought to start a society."

Drafli's eyes were still glittering on hers, and after another long drink of soup—draining the tureen—he beckoned her closer. And when Alma tentatively obeyed, shuffling up between his sprawled legs, he grasped for the long leather tie looped around her wrist—the one that was part of her traditional Grisk outfit, which had indeed come in handy for a variety of tasks—and after clutching her other wrist close, Drafli circled the leather tie around both her wrists, and pulled it tight.

It meant that Alma's wrists were *bound together* in front of her, oh gods—was Drafli punishing her, for using him as leverage in her housekeeping?—but his eyes were still glinting on hers, and he signed something new, something she hadn't seen before.

"He says," Baldr breathed behind her, "you are a presumptuous little human, Bright-Heart. And as redress, you will now present yourself for my ploughing. On your hands and knees, arse up."

A furious shudder licked up Alma's spine, shaking her all over—Drafli wanted *what*?—but yes, he was signing the order toward her again, slower this time. A single meaningful motion, ending with the direction he wanted her to... *present* in. Toward Baldr.

Alma's breath was heaving, her heart frantically thudding, but Drafli's purposeful tug on the cord—on her wrists—had her abruptly skittering forward between his thighs, catching herself on her bound hands. Her arse indeed up, facing toward Baldr behind her, and oh, she could feel him looking, her skin shivering hot beneath his gaze. And after another silent command from Drafli, that was Baldr's *hand*, sliding up under her skirt, rucking it up to her waist.

Alma shuddered again, blinking uncertainly up toward Drafli—but his eyes were sweeping dispassionately up and down her kneeling body, almost as if *judging* her. And when he signed another casual order toward Baldr, Alma could hear Baldr's breath catch, as both his warm hands again settled to her bare skin, his touch gentle but firm.

"Draf said, arse up, Bright-Heart," he murmured behind

her, as he pressed down on her lower back, making it arch. "And legs wide, also. When he orders you to do this, we ought to be able to see all of you, and be free to plough either hole, as we wish."

Oh, *fuck*. Alma's moan escaped on its own as she sought to assume the pose Drafli wanted. Widening her legs, tilting her arse up and out, exposing everything hidden between. While she desperately fought to ignore the feeling of cool air pooling against her splayed, already-pulsing heat, and the certain truth of Baldr's hungry, prickling gaze upon it.

"Like this, my lord?" she whispered, pleading up at Drafli's bland, assessing eyes—and the bastard only raised an eyebrow at her, and then yanked the leather in his grip further forward. Making Alma slip down to her elbows on the fur, leaving her arse jutted even higher in the air behind her.

"Fuck," she gulped, without meaning to, and in return Drafli smirked at her, and signed something at Baldr. Something that might have asked whether she was *ready* for him.

"Ach, I ken," Baldr breathed, his breath hitching. "She is wide open, and dripping wet. And her hungry womb seeks for aught to milk within it."

The words fired another flash of heat up Alma's shivering spine, and she could feel her blatantly exposed body clutching even harder, as if showing itself for Baldr's eyes. As if it did, indeed, want something to milk inside it, oh gods...

But before her, Drafli was looking thoroughly unimpressed again, and he casually signed something else at Baldr. Something with two long fingers extended, that looked like...

"Ach, I shall test her," Baldr replied, hoarse, and Alma choked a low gasp as she felt his warm, tentative fingers brushing against her, just *there*. So easily finding her slick, convulsing heat, and sliding slow and smooth up inside.

"Ach, Draf, she is good," he breathed, as those fingers slid in a little more, spreading a little wider. As if learning what this felt like, perhaps, because he'd never touched her like this before, had he? No, no, it had always been Drafli—and oh, Baldr felt so different, so *good*, his movements inside her slow, careful, reverent.

And the other one? Drafli signed now, his brows still raised, and Alma felt herself clutching against Baldr's fingers, as if seeking to keep them safely inside her. But no, they were already obeying, easing out of her, away. Leaving her wide open and empty as they slid deliberately upwards, further up her parted crease, to... *there.*

Alma yelped and froze all over—they really wanted this? But oh, hell, Baldr's blunt, slick fingertip was indeed circling there, nudging soft and gentle against her. As if seeking its way in, oh gods above, and it felt so strange, so foreign, so *dangerous.*

"Breathe, Bright-Heart," Baldr murmured, as that finger stroked and teased against her. "Think of opening up for me, ach?"

Alma trembled and gulped for air, dragging it down harsh and bracing, and Baldr's finger nudged a little deeper, his other hand caressing up her flank. "Ach, this is it," he purred. "A little more. Think of how good I shall feel inside you. How pleased our devil shall be, if you welcome this for him."

Their devil. Because yes, yes, Drafli did look much like a devil in this moment, his eyes gleaming, his hand still lightly gripping the leather binding Alma's wrists. And looking up at those eyes, at his sharp, beautiful, commanding face, Alma felt herself fervently nodding, and slightly relaxing, opening, against Baldr's touch.

And she kept looking at Drafli, holding the strength of his eyes, as Baldr's slick finger sank inside her. Feeling so wrong, so *right*, as it delved deeper and deeper, into where no other living being had ever gone. Filling her, impaling her—*keep going*, Drafli's hand was saying—until she could feel Baldr's hard knuckles brushing against her skin.

She was shivering again, scrabbling on the fur between them, but Drafli wasn't even looking at her now, and was again watching Baldr through hooded eyes. Signing something else, to which Baldr's finger twitched a little inside her, making her keen and arch up against him.

"Ach, she is good here too," he breathed. "So soft. So tight. She shall feel so sweet upon you, I ken, when you take her here."

When *Drafli* took her there. *When.* And oh, Alma could feel Drafli's hard exhale, rippling at her hair—and then he signed another command, one that made Baldr moan, raw and ragged. And then he was shifting behind her, his warmth settling closer, until—

That. That smooth, prodding, gold-tipped head, delving against her exposed, dripping, clutching heat, finding its place—and then slowly, smoothly pressing inside.

Alma's shout tore from her throat, because it felt truly shocking from behind like this, so different, so powerful. And driving that power stronger, deeper, was how Baldr's finger was still buried all the way inside her, while his thick, pulsing heft kept easing itself in below. Filling both places at once, oh gods, and Alma's shout again filled the room as he sank the rest of the way inside her.

And oh, she had never felt anything, *anything*, like this. The sensation sheer and screeching, her body clamping and seizing at all that solid strength opening it, using it. Her hands reflexively pulling against their bonds—against Drafli's bonds—but in response he only yanked the leather a little tighter, tugging her hands forward, arching her back up even more. While Baldr moaned and bucked even deeper inside her, his hips grinding against hers, his heft shuddering out base to tip.

Alma's shout was more of a scream this time, the pleasure blaring and barrelling—and when her desperate blinking eyes found Drafli's again, he was actually *smiling* at her. Smiling, dark and wicked and dangerous, as his other hand easily caught her chin, and tilted it up.

And wait, wait, he wasn't making her look at his eyes—he

364   FINLEY FENN

wanted her to look at *this*. At the bared, scarred, swollen length
of him, jutting out from his groin, and bobbing straight toward
her face. Her mouth.

"Oh," Alma somehow gulped, through the wheeling, flying
sensation. She was already being filled with orc, split open
upon Baldr in two places at once, and surely Drafli didn't think
she could possibly take any more—but his smile at her was so
fiendish, and perhaps even *fond*, as he tugged her bottom lip
down, and slowly fed his hard, pulsing heft between her parted
lips.

Fuck. Alma's shout was muffled this time, her eyes frantically fluttering, her body wracking against this shocking,
surreal onslaught. Baldr's massive thickness grinding hard
between her legs, his finger now twisting and curling inside
her, his other hand gripping tight at her shuddering arse-
cheek. While Drafli eased into a smooth, fluid rhythm on her
mouth, one hand still pulling the leather, the other again
caught in her hair, pulling her head back, making her meet his
glinting, approving eyes.

And as he kept using her throat, now moving in perfect
time with Baldr behind her, he moved a little closer, straddling
wide over her bound, outreached hands. And his other hand
had released the leather for an instant, before snapping down
to catch it behind his sprawled knees, pulling her even harder
apart as he made her look at him, made her writhe and flail
upon him, made her scream at her own undoing—

Her release hit like a blow, screeching and slamming in
strike after strike of hot, staggering pleasure. Her entire
impaled body writhing and flailing, furiously seizing against
the orcs inside it, so hard that she surely would have collapsed,
without their strength holding her up between them. But oh,
now Baldr was buckling too, pitching forward over her, his
jammed-deep heft shuddering as it sprayed out hot inside
her—and fuck, now it was Drafli, his strong hand gripping at
the back of her head as he poured himself deep into her throat.

Alma swallowed as much as she could, while her own body kept wringing out the dregs of her pleasure. But there was so much hot sweetness, far too much, and finally she felt it spilling out her mouth, in bizarre tandem with the feel of it spluttering out below, escaping around Baldr's slowly softening heft inside her.

And when the awareness slowly filtered back in again, it was to the realization that Drafli's hand had slipped around to her chin, tilting her face up. Surveying her with eyes she couldn't at all read, lingering on her burning cheeks, the certain mess of her hair, the hot slickness still dripping down onto the cool touch of his fingers…

And then he bent down, drew her up—and oh, oh, he *kissed* her. His mouth so deft and warm on hers, so gentle. Rewarding her—rewarding her!—because he'd liked it. He'd *approved*.

And even as he drew away, coolly patting her cheek and rising to his feet before her, the swirling, swimming conviction of that only seemed to deepen. And she was smiling at him, truly smiling, as he efficiently lifted her up onto her feet too, and then guided her unsteady body toward the door.

Alma managed a furtive little wave back toward Baldr—who was looking just as dazed as she felt—before realizing that her hands were still bound together, and she was still streaked and sticky with their mess. And that just like the night before, Drafli almost seemed to be enjoying this, prowling tall and silent beside her, his fingers gentle but firm against her back.

It meant that Alma once again got many long, lingering glances from the various orcs they passed in the corridor—some curious, some approving, some perhaps even envious. One of them was Gwyn's mate Joarr, delightedly waggling his brows between them, and another one was Narfi, glowering darkly as he scuttled past. And soon after that came Tryggr, striding beside a tall, unfamiliar orc, and giving Alma a conspiratorial wink before signing something at Drafli that looked a lot like, *Good work, Boss. Very pretty.*

And to Alma's rising astonishment, Drafli actually half-smiled as he signed something back, something familiar from earlier that day. *Get your own*, it meant.

And oh, it meant that Alma was *his*, that Drafli truly liked this, liked showing her off, and proving his ownership of her. His protection. And in truth, he *had* sworn that vow to her, hadn't he? He'd promised to care for her, and keep her safe. His.

And when Alma leaned herself a little closer into him, into that steady touch of his fingers against her back, he didn't resist this time. Didn't flinch away, or frown down toward her. Only kept walking with her, with the proof of his pleasure all over her.

They seemed to reach her room far, far too quickly—and as Drafli coolly nudged Alma inside, clearly intending to leave again, she found herself clearing her throat, and searching for his eyes.

"Th-thank you, my lord," she stammered up toward him. "For that, and for—for everything, today. For—listening to me. Bringing me help. And even"—she attempted a smile toward him—"allowing me to use you as a threat."

Drafli's eyes shifted, his shoulder rolling an indifferent shrug as he angled toward the door again—but suddenly Alma needed to keep talking, needed more, only for a moment—

"And Tryggr and Dufnall were so helpful," she told him, her voice cracking. "They did more laundry in one day than I've done so far *combined*. And Dufnall caught four more rats, and even said he was looking forward to coming back tomorrow, because they were so very fat and tasty."

She was still smiling at Drafli, her eyes oddly blinking, and almost—*foolish*—reached up to touch him. But she still wasn't supposed to touch him without asking, and thankfully her hands were still bound together anyway, so she dropped them again, and swallowed as she searched his unreadable eyes.

"I think it was the loveliest day I've spent," she whispered, "since my mother died. Thank you, my lord."

There was an instant's stillness from Drafli before her, another casual shrug from his shoulder. His eyes now dropped to her wrists, and she could see his throat convulsing as he reached and plucked at the leather cord, and pulled it off. Studying the red marks beneath for an instant, and then rubbing them with firm, purposeful fingers, watching with surprising attentiveness as they slowly began to fade again.

But then, to her bewilderment, he didn't give the leather back. Instead, he looped it around his own wrist, and slid it up onto his lean, muscled forearm. And Alma looked at that, and then up at him, as he intently avoided her eyes, and signed something toward her.

Enough, Bright-Heart, it said. *Go to bed.*

But it wasn't angry. It wasn't cold, or even dismissive. It was Drafli caring for her, speaking to her, with her leather on his arm. Hers.

I understand, she signed back, with another trembly little smile. *Good night, Golden-Tongue.*

And even as Drafli shrugged again, and walked away without another word, Alma couldn't seem to stop blinking, and smiling at where he'd gone.

34

If Alma expected her newfound happiness to be short-lived, she was very swiftly proven wrong.

She spent the next morning in the kitchen, alternating between her cozy desk and the scullery, and laughing at the ongoing antics of her new helpers. Timo had clearly found a new friend in Tryggr, and had begun drilling him with incessant questions about Skai fighting and weaponry, all of which Tryggr answered with good-natured ease, his arms buried to the elbows in soapy water. Dufnall also did his fair share of washing, though he was frequently distracted by his rat-hunting efforts, and he had begun to glower balefully at a large crack in the stone beneath the counter.

"Need small creature to sneak in, and chase rats out," Dufnall announced out of nowhere, halfway through the morning. "Need cat. Why you no have cat, human?"

This was said with a suspicious frown toward Alma, who half-smiled over at him from the fresh batch of soap she'd been making. "Er, because you don't have any cats here, do you? Maybe out in the stables? I did meet Ella's little dogs there yesterday."

The stables had been a new discovery the day before—

their quest for floor-cleaning assistance had truly taken them all over, and Ella's dogs had been utterly adorable—but Dufnall's frown only deepened. "No cat in stables," he corrected her. "Need cat *here*. Humans *always* have cat."

Alma couldn't help a pleading glance toward Tryggr, who was looking rather thoughtful, his soapy hand drumming at his chin. "You know, Duff, that's a fair point," he said slowly. "Seems to me like there's more than one rats'-nest in there, and at this rate, they're probably getting deep into the food stores, too. You know how to get us a cat, woman?"

Alma shook her head—she didn't, beyond perhaps returning to Ashford, and raiding Mr. Pembroke's stables. And even the thought of Mr. Pembroke was making something plummet hard in her belly, and Tryggr eyed her as he wiped his hands on a nearby rag.

"S'pose we can't very well expect her to pull out a cat from under her skirts, can we, Duff?" he said, with a quirk of a teasing grin. "C'mon, let's go ask Boss, he'll know how to sort it out."

But wait. Boss was *Drafli*, and Alma froze in place, her stomach flopping frantically in her gut. "We can't just go *ask Drafli*," she said, her voice sounding thin and scandalized. "Especially about a *cat*."

"Ach, sure we can," Tryggr replied, with clear surprise in his eyes. "Boss shall help with anything. Most of all if you're a clan brother, ach? Or"—he flashed Alma another cheeky grin—"working hard to honour him each day, as you are."

With that, Tryggr strode toward the door, blithely beckoning the rest of them after him. Both Timo and Dufnall instantly complied, apparently seeing no potential pitfalls in this ridiculous plan, while Alma belatedly trailed along behind them, her face already heating, her hands rubbing uncertainly at her skirt.

Because surely, even after the sheer, tilting wonder of the night before, Drafli's position toward her hadn't actually changed. Had it? He was still the one in charge, and she was expected to obey. And beyond their various arguments, Alma had scarcely even *spoken* to him outside the bedroom, let alone interrupting him in the middle of the day, right? About a *cat*?!

Her uncertainty on that front only worsened when they found Drafli in the Ash-Kai meeting-room, indeed in the midst of what was clearly an important meeting. There were multiple now-familiar faces present, including Nattfarr, Joarr, Silfast, John, and Jule, who smiled and waved toward the door from where she was pacing back and forth with a fussing Bitty-Grim. And once again, Baldr and Drafli were seated on either side of their massive captain, and Drafli was currently signing toward the captain's face with furious fluency, while Baldr's low voice swiftly interpreted aloud.

But Baldr's voice had slowly trailed off, and both he and Drafli were looking toward the door, Baldr's brow creasing with visible concern, while Drafli's eyes narrowed into dark, suspicious slits. And even as Alma felt herself shrinking further back into the corridor—gods, this had been the worst, *worst* idea—Tryggr casually leaned against the open doorway, and flashed the room's assembled occupants a careless, cheerful grin.

"Sorry to interrupt," he said lightly. "Skai business, you know."

As he'd spoken, he'd signed toward Drafli with something that hadn't at all matched the rest—*Come for a moment, Boss*—and in return, Drafli smoothly rose to his feet, and strode out to join them in the corridor. His eyes still narrow and angry as they flicked back and forth between the three orcs, and then toward Alma, who was currently slinking against the opposite wall, and grimacing guiltily toward him.

"So we need a cat, Boss," Tryggr was saying, seeming entirely undaunted by Drafli's murderous expression. "Vermin situation's out of control over in the scullery, and even Duff can't keep up with it. Not good to have the rat-scat stinking up the place when we're trying to work, let alone having the little buggers munching away at the kitchen stores, right? And you'll soon be growing your son in your woman, if you ain't already—and you're not gonna want her on her knees cleaning up vermin shit every day, are you?"

Alma had listened to this appalling monologue with ever-increasing alarm, her eyes snapped wide on Drafli's frowning face. And then on Drafli's hands, which were signing back at Tryggr with purposeful urgency, far too quickly for her to follow.

Alma fully expected Tryggr to shrink backwards in response, perhaps to finally apologize—but then, unbelievably, he grinned up at Drafli with smug, jaunty satisfaction. His hand signing back... *Thank you*?!

"Knew you'd agree, Boss," Tryggr said cheerfully. "Thanks. Now, you three need anything else, or are we good?"

This was said with a questioning look over at Dufnall and Timo and Alma, but Dufnall was gazing vaguely down the corridor, while Timo was blinking between Tryggr and Drafli with worshipful awe in his eyes. And Alma was still standing there frozen, digesting all this, as Drafli tilted his head, and beckoned her closer.

She might have cringed back even further, had she not caught sight of something familiar, wrapped around Drafli's bare forearm. That long, thin strip of leather, from the night before. *Her* leather. He was... still *wearing* it.

It was enough to send her stumbling over toward him, to where he firmly grasped her chin, tilting it up as he fixed her with his dark, disapproving glare. *You never touch rat dung*, he mouthed at her, accompanying the words with sharp signs from his other hand. *Or cat dung. You ask them for help.*

Them meant Tryggr and Dufnall, and Alma gulped down a swallow as she nodded—to which Drafli nodded back, spun on his heel, and stalked back into his meeting. Leaving Alma feeling oddly hot and shivery all over, while Tryggr smiled complacently toward her.

"See?" he told her, as they made their way back toward the kitchen. "Boss always helps. No point in mincing away from asking either, 'cause he'll only flay you worse once he finds out you've been keeping secrets from him. Now, I wonder what kind of cat he'll get us?"

Alma's thoughts were flailing far too much to answer that question, but thankfully both Timo and Dufnall chimed in with a variety of eager suggestions. And soon they were spilling back into the kitchen again, and Gegnir was calling out about a few more pantry deliveries, and Alma was caught up in another busy bustle of productive, entertaining activity.

"How are you holding up, Alma?" asked a familiar voice, perhaps halfway through the afternoon—and when Alma glanced up from her desk, there was Jule again, smiling down toward her, with Bitty-Grim squirming in her arms. "I hope we aren't working you to the bone with all this?"

Alma smiled back and shook her head as she stood, reaching over to tickle at Bitty-Grim's plump little belly. "I've honestly been having so much fun," she told Jule. "Though now that the laundry's being handled, and we have plans for the floors, I've been wondering what else has missed being done around here. I don't suppose you've seen anything?"

Jule had, of course, and soon she was taking Alma on a comprehensive, highly informative tour of the Ash-Kai wing, while Alma took notes in the ledger she'd thankfully brought. It turned out that since the Ash-Kai wing was the highest up in the mountain, it was also the coldest—and therefore had the foulest, most ash-filled fireplaces she'd seen yet.

"We should be able to get started on those tomorrow," Alma told Jule, as they walked back toward the kitchen again. "It would be good to have them dealt with, before—"

She stopped there, twitching at sight of the corridor up ahead—to where there seemed to be a small, furry mountain, growing in the middle of the floor. And as she and Jule approached, Kesst's tall form suddenly stalked out of the nearby sickroom door, and he unceremoniously dumped several more furs onto the pile.

"I am *not* touching these any more than I absolutely need to," he announced at Alma and Jule, tossing his hair over his shoulder as he stalked back into the room. "I *refuse* to smell any fouler than I already do, thank you very much."

Jule and Alma exchanged glances, and followed Kesst inside—where they found him scooping up yet more furs, and stomping back toward the corridor. While Efterar, who had been hovering his hand over the unfamiliar sleeping form of a big, bloody orc, looked both pained and amused as he watched Kesst stalk back over toward them.

"I have no idea what you've unleashed upon us with this, Grisk," he said to Alma, with a tired half-smile toward her. "But it does smell much better in here. Smells more like *you*, Kesst."

This was said with a careful glance toward Kesst, who was busy yanking furs from the nearest bed, and avoiding Efterar's eyes. "Love you, Eft, but you don't need to keep saying it," he said. "Now, sweetheart"—his eyes flicked toward Alma—"if you really are planning to wash all the floors, can you make sure you get in here, too?"

Alma agreed willingly enough, and after promising to send Tryggr for the furs, she headed back for the kitchen again. Where she now found Gaukr, the indolent Bautul orc from the day before, mulishly rubbing his belly and lounging against the counter, and informing Tryggr that he was actually too busy—and hungry—to help out with the Keeping after all.

"Bollocks, you lazy arse," Tryggr was snapping back, as he hurled an armful of clothes toward Gaukr. "How much of Roland's credits did you keep taking, while you lolled around here doing jack squat? So you're gonna grab a basin, and"—his eyes snapped toward the door—"oooh, Boss, you found one!"

Alma whirled around to look too, and yes, Drafli was

striding into the room—and dangling from his clawed hand, pinched by the scruff on its neck, was a squirming, squalling black *cat*.

"*Cat*," Dufnall said happily, as he lurched forward to collect the cat—and upon being released from Drafli's iron grip, the cat instantly raced up Dufnall's arm, clamped onto his grey head with all four paws, and began furiously hissing at Drafli. To which Drafli rolled his eyes, spun around, and strode back out the door again.

"Thanks, Boss!" Tryggr called after him, reaching up to stroke at the cat—and earning for his trouble another frantic hiss, and a swipe of a little black paw toward him. "Ooooh, she's a feisty one. What are you gonna name her, Duff?"

"Cat," said Dufnall happily, as he returned his attention to his washing, seemingly unperturbed by the cat still perched on his head. "*Cat*."

Tryggr's mouth was curving up, his eyes angling toward Alma's with impish amusement—at least, until he caught sight of Gaukr, who amidst the distraction had attempted to sidestep toward the door. "Like hell you're taking off now, Bautul," he snapped. "Now *get to work*."

To Alma's surprise, Gaukr actually obliged, and grudgingly began scrubbing clothes—at least, until the cat suddenly leapt off Dufnall's head, and scrambled away beneath the counter. Prompting Tryggr to start crowing aloud, calling out rat-hunting encouragement, while Dufnall dove under the counter to watch. And in the ongoing hubbub, Gaukr made another unsuccessful attempt to escape, but was soon thwarted by Tryggr, who had noticed just in time, and lunged over to block the door with a washtub.

"And by then," Alma shyly told Baldr and Drafli that evening, as they sat together eating the roasted quail she'd brought them, "Tryggr was in a *mood*—justifiably so, after all the work he's done—so he told Gaukr that if he was really that hungry and lazy, he might as well suck it up, and get on his knees for Dufnall while *he* worked! Which, then, Gaukr *did*! While Tryggr *watched*, and gave them *pointers*!"

Her face had surely gone scarlet as she'd spoken, the memories of that completely shocking incident flashing through her still-jolting thoughts. While beside her, Baldr was merrily chuckling as he chewed, and even Drafli was quirking a reluctant, twitching smile around his bite of quail.

"And then what, Bright-Heart?" Baldr asked, nudging her knee with his. "Was Dufnall pleased with this?"

"He was delighted!" Alma exclaimed, with a flushed, chagrined smile. "I could not have *conceived* that he could work so fast. And then your cat—which Duff has named *Cat*, by the way—brought him not one, but *two* fresh rats, so Dufnall started slipping foul little bits and pieces down to Gaukr for *him* to eat, too!"

Baldr was still chortling, his hand over his mouth, while Drafli signed at her, his mouth still quirking. *And what he say?* he asked, and it took Alma an instant to realize that *he* was *Tryggr*, a cheerful little whirl in front of his mouth. A perfect sign for Tryggr, truly, and Alma laughed and shook her head, her face again flushing hot.

"Tryggr told Gaukr he'd turned out to be a half-decent help after all," she replied, "and that he ought to come back again tomorrow! Which I do *not* think is ethical at *all*, and now I shall have to bar Timo from the scullery while he's there—but Dufnall looked so pathetically hopeful, that I *agreed*! So now Gaukr is apparently my employee too, but I have *no conception* of how to put him in my budget for your captain!"

At that, both Baldr and Drafli broke into genuine-looking laughter, grinning at one another. And Alma was strangely, suddenly caught on the sight of Drafli's shoulders shaking, the grin pulling up at his mouth, turning his face into something almost... handsome.

"And according to Tryggr," Alma continued, still smiling warmly at Drafli's face, "this is probably the best day Dufnall has had in *years*. And he even took Cat back off to his bedroom with him! It was"—she felt herself swallow, her eyes searching Drafli's—"very, *very* kind of you, my lord. Thank you."

Drafli's eyes angled away at that, his hand giving a dismissive wave—but Baldr chuckled aloud, and prodded Drafli with his elbow. "Tell us, Draf, how many Skai scouts did you set to work on that cat today?" he said lightly. "Four? Six??"

Drafli's eyes had dangerously narrowed on Baldr, even as his mouth kept quirking—and in a sudden, vicious flash of movement, he'd lunged at Baldr, and tackled him to the floor. And after a few moments' wrestling, Drafli had tied up Baldr's hands with the leather—*Alma's* leather, which had still been wrapped around his forearm—and gave Baldr the same silent order he'd given Alma the day before.

Present yourself, Pure-Heart, it meant. *To me.*

Baldr immediately complied, his breath heaving—and soon, they were lost in another heated, glorious tryst on the fur together. This time with Baldr kneeling between Alma and Drafli, his tongue frantically lapping between Alma's legs, while Drafli viciously drove into him from behind. Until Baldr was a shaking, gasping mess on the fur between them, his face reddened and slicked all over, his shuddering body coated with ropes of glossy, fragrant white.

Afterwards, Drafli threw Baldr onto his back, and ordered Alma to lick up the mess, even as he himself buried his face in Baldr's neck, flashing yet more pain and pleasure across Baldr's eyes. And once Baldr had swollen to full hardness again, Drafli even gave Alma leave to use her mouth on him, for the very first time—and oh, it was spectacular, Baldr twisting and writhing beneath every gentle stroke of her tongue, sputtering out hard and furious around that smooth, gleaming gold inside him.

Once Baldr had again finished—Alma had nearly swallowed all of his hot richness, but not quite—he seemed truly, utterly spent, his eyes blinking hazy and unseeing toward the ceiling, his muscled body sprawled and trembling and thoroughly debauched. And when Alma glanced up at Drafli, licking at her still-wet lips, she found him looking straight back at her, and licking his own reddened mouth, too. His eyes glinting with just as much satisfaction as she felt, his hand languidly signing between them.

This was good, it said. *Look at him. He is so pretty.*

Alma was looking, and nodding—gods, Baldr was quite possibly the most beautiful thing she'd ever seen in her life—and signing back. *So good*, she told Drafli, as she watched him slipping the leather off Baldr's hands, and wrapping it around his own forearm again. *He is so pretty. He loves it. He loves you.*

And this time, as she made that motion toward Drafli—*loves you*—she could see his throat bobbing, his tongue again brushing out against his reddened lips. And his hand had slid down to caress at Baldr's face, his mouth dropping a kiss to Baldr's forehead, before he smoothly rose to his feet, and beckoned Alma after him toward the door.

She willingly complied, and when she instinctively leaned into Drafli's touch as they walked together through the darkness, he didn't seem to mind, either. And back in Alma's room, he even tucked her into bed—and then bent down to press a gentle kiss to her forehead, too.

It was so easy to fall asleep, flush in the warmth of that kiss—and even easier to wake up the next morning, and do it all again. Settling into her already-familiar morning routine—tools, reading, prayers and good-natured banter in the shrine with Ella and the other Grisk, while cuddling a happily squirming Rakfi in her arms. And then back to the kitchen again, reconciling a few pantry deliveries, chatting companionably with Kalfr and Gwyn, catching up with Tryggr, Dufnall, and Cat—and then even with Gaukr, who indeed showed up for "work" again, much to Dufnall's delight.

Another welcome development came later that afternoon, with Baldr poking his head into Alma's office, and shyly asking if she might be able to spare some time for a swim. She eagerly agreed, of course, and soon she was splashing in the pool with Baldr and Drafli, and laughing as they once again frolicked and fought in the water.

It helped that she was becoming more comfortable in the water too, just like Baldr had promised, and she was both surprised and pleased when he and Drafli turned their attention toward teaching her a few specific points. How best to breathe in between strokes, how to tread water, how to sink underwater and rise again.

A little deeper, Drafli signed at her as he hovered before her under the water, his hair swirling around his head, his movements barely visible in the lamplight from above. *Ach. Thus.*

He proved to be a surprisingly patient teacher, and his praise—though sparing and succinct—somehow felt just as rewarding as Baldr's more effusive grins and caresses. Enough that Alma perhaps pushed herself a little further than was wise, and somehow ended up sucking down a full mouthful of water—a choking, horrifying feeling that instantly snapped her back to Pembroke, to the river, to the feeling of liquid death, strangling her from the inside out—

When she'd finally stopped coughing and shivering, she somehow found herself desperately clinging to Drafli, her fingernails digging into his solid back, her legs locked around his. "Sorry," she wheezed, before breaking into yet another round of painful coughing. "Sorry. Not supposed to—"

She winced down at where she was still clinging to him— blatantly breaking that rule about not touching without asking—and shakily attempted to extract herself. An effort that instantly failed, because Drafli had yanked her close again, his strong hand firmly caressing her back.

"No," he breathed, into her ear. "I no mind your touch. You no need to keep asking, but for fun."

Oh. She didn't need to keep asking... almost as if Drafli *wanted* her to touch him. And gods, Alma might have almost been weeping as she clung to him, the fear almost entirely forgotten in this beautiful, blazing new truth. She could touch him without asking. He didn't mind. She was his.

"I wish we could stay longer," Baldr regretfully told her, once they'd all climbed out and dressed again. "But we have yet more work to address with the captain today. We shall see you for supper tonight, though, ach?"

Alma eagerly agreed, and then willingly threw herself back into the rest of her afternoon's work, which turned out to be mostly consumed with her upcoming floor-flooding project. It was still on track for the following morning, and it had somehow grown into a massive undertaking, involving a good two dozen participants from across all five clans. And between them, Alma had assigned a variety of tasks—including clearing the drains, managing the waterworks, draining the baths, preparing cleaning equipment, and even warning the clans of the forthcoming deluge.

And while Alma continued to run into several complications throughout the afternoon—including with Stella's mate Silfast, who had taken severe umbrage at the prospect of the Bautul arena being closed for an entire day—it all somehow seemed to come together by evening, with plans for a bright and early start the next morning.

"I'm terrified that it's going to be such a mess," Alma confided to Baldr and Drafli over supper, as they rapidly consumed the admittedly delicious roasted duck she'd brought them. "I mean, I've done my share of housekeeping projects, but flooding an entire *mountain*? Gods above, what was I *thinking*?!"

Baldr returned this with a sympathetic grimace, and a reassuring pat to Alma's knee—while before them, Drafli's eyes had narrowed as he snapped off a large hunk of meat. *You no fear this*, he signed at her. *You are smart. You are strong. You learn fast, and work hard. You are good Keeper.*

Oh. Alma couldn't help a surprised, questioning smile

toward him—Drafli truly thought all that about her?—and in return, he gave a sharp, decisive nod. And then raised his brows at her, and coolly signed that if she was done eating, she might as well undress and touch herself, and thereby offer them some amusement while they finished.

Alma complied, shyly at first, because surely, it should have been humiliating, blatantly stroking and fondling herself like this—putting on an actual obscene *show*—while Baldr and Drafli just kept on enjoying their supper. But between their rapidly tenting trousers, and those telltale glints in their eyes, and all the combined things Drafli had told her today—*you are smart, you are strong, you no need to ask*—it soon felt almost... safe. Exciting. A challenge.

And even after Drafli had finally rewarded her—teaching her how to ride Baldr on top this time, while he himself stood over her, and made thorough use of her mouth—that same certainty seemed to keep lingering, settling quiet and deep. Drafli had *complimented* her. He had faith in her. She could do this.

Alma slept long and deep that night, and was awoken early the next morning by Varinn, who together with Thrain had volunteered to be one of her principal helpers. And who now ruefully informed her, with a regretful smile, that there were already a dozen orcs amassed in the kitchen, and waiting for her.

Alma quickly washed and dressed, while Varinn waited outside in the corridor—but once she'd stepped out to meet him, she was surprised to find herself once again confronted by Baldr and Drafli. Both of whom were hovering just outside her doorway, and who were also both glaring toward Varinn with tense, dangerous disapproval.

"We have come to wish you luck today, Bright-Heart," Baldr said, a little stiffly. "We would offer our help, you ken, had we not more urgent work today for the captain. And yet..."

His eyes had gone even narrower on Varinn, while Drafli

purposefully elbowed Baldr in the side, and then stalked over toward Alma. And before she'd quite realized what had happened, Drafli had backed her into the wall, shoved her to her knees on the floor, and yanked down his trousers. While Baldr, who had caught up with astonishing speed, was now leaning against the wall beside them, and dropping his hand to Alma's mouth.

"Open up, Bright-Heart," he ordered her, his voice surprisingly deep, his strong finger tugging down her bottom lip—and oh, that was so Drafli could lean forward, and sink his bared, swollen heft deep into her mouth. "Ach, thus. You suck your Skai, as you ought."

Alma moaned helplessly around Drafli's invading strength, which was indeed already gouging against her throat—and when she belatedly brought up her hands to stroke at him, caressing his heavy bollocks, he slid his own hand deep into her hair, and picked up speed. Blatantly using her, right there in the damned corridor, while Baldr purred approvingly beside them.

"So pretty, Bright-Heart," he crooned, as his hand wiped away some of the liquid pooling down her chin. "You keep sucking thus, and mayhap Draf shall grant you a sweet Skai breakfast, ach?"

Oh, hell. Alma moaned again, nodding as well as she could—when out the corner of her eye, she briefly caught sight of Varinn, who was still standing there, and looking rather stunned. And perhaps Drafli had seen it too, his rhythm briefly stuttering—and without warning, he loudly popped himself out, and held Alma's mouth open as he yanked Baldr closer. So that *Baldr* could sink inside instead, oh hell, his plump heft smoothly parting Alma's lips around him, his hard gold sinking into her throat.

"So pretty," he gasped again, as Drafli's hand in Alma's hair tilted her head upward, giving them a better look at her flushed, frantically sucking face. "So sweet, Bright-Heart. *Ach.*"

He was surely already close, his eyes fluttering, his head tilting back—when Drafli coolly reached down to grasp him, pulling him out again. So that *he* could slide in for another turn, oh hell, and Alma eagerly sucked and lavished him, sinking into the wonder of it, the unthinkable, impossible craving. Her orcs were blatantly using her, trading her back and forth between them, taking their pleasure with her. Where anyone, everyone, could see...

And when Drafli abruptly poured out, flooding her mouth with thick molten heat, Alma frantically, desperately swallowed—but before she'd even finished, here was Baldr again, pumping in with steady, powerful strokes. Until he too was spurting out into her mouth, the taste of his rich seed swarming with Drafli's still-present sweetness. And it was so good, so *so* good, that Alma's own release somehow sparked, and then pitched into swell after swell of shuddering, head-spinning ecstasy.

And oh, Baldr and Drafli had surely both seen it, glancing toward each other with smug, smirking satisfaction. And once Alma had finally finished swallowing everything in her mouth, Drafli calmly pulled her back up to her feet, gave her cheek a firm little pat, and wiped her face clean. And then flashed a rather vicious, terrifying smile as he spun her around, and thrust her back toward Varinn again.

"Good luck today, Bright-Heart," Baldr called behind her, and when Alma looked over her shoulder, he was sheepishly waving, while Drafli kept giving that dreadful smile beside him. "See you tonight for more, ach?"

Alma twitched a shy, furtive wave back, and then an apologetic, flushed-feeling wince toward Varinn—but thankfully, he didn't seem offended. In truth, he looked almost... wistful, somehow, his eyes angling toward hers, and away again.

"I am glad to see you so content here," he said, his voice a little hoarse. "Mayhap soon you shall choose to make a son after all, ach? This should bring you all much joy, I ken."

Alma blinked uncertainly toward Varinn, her face heating—because wait, was he commenting on the slowness of her forthcoming pregnancy? The... lack of it? And gods, that had nearly escaped Alma's mind in the midst of everything else, but surely it should be happening soon... shouldn't it? And yes, Efterar had mentioned it might take at least another week or so, but a week had surely passed by now, hadn't it? And while Drafli had still never taken her that way, Baldr had done so multiple times now. And yet...

"Forgive me," Varinn said quickly. "I ought not to pry—of course you may wish to keep this secret. Ach, here we are."

This was said with a relieved-looking gesture toward the kitchen, which—Alma blinked, while warmth flared in her belly—was indeed overflowing with helpers, several of them eagerly calling her name. And in the rising hubbub, she soon forgot Varinn's odd statements, and found herself completely engrossed in preparing for the busy day ahead. Dividing the orcs and women into teams, making sure everyone had tools and cleaning supplies, and then herding them into position, all over the mountain.

The flooding itself wasn't quite as shocking as Alma had expected—it was more of a steady stream of water, pouring cooperatively down a single route of corridors, and providing a highly convenient water source for scrubbing the adjoining rooms. Each clan's members had been ordered to clean their own personal spaces as needed, while Alma and her teams focused mostly on the mountain's shared rooms—the common-rooms, the trading-posts, the baths, the sickroom, and of course, the filthy arenas.

Thankfully, the orcs who would otherwise have been fighting in the arenas had been sent to help as well, scrubbing floors and sluicing water down the arenas' conveniently placed drains—and nearly all of Alma's new friends had joined in too. Many of them her fellow Grisk—including Ella, Nattfarr, Varinn, Thrain, Thrak, Dammarr, and Timo—but also Tryggr,

Dufnall, and Gaukr, and Gwyn, Stella, Rosa, and Maria. And together, they made slow but steady progress as they moved their way down the mountain, talking, laughing, and scrubbing, leaving the floors behind them damp but sparkling clean.

By the time the Ka-esh finally turned off the water that evening, it felt as though several full days had passed, and Alma was sweaty and shaky all over, and barely capable of standing upright on her feet. But they had done it—she'd done it!—and once she had finally set aside her mop, and thanked the last of her helpers, she felt almost giddy with sheer, staggering relief.

"We did it!" she told Baldr, smiling blearily but happily toward him, after he'd come to collect her from the Ka-esh wing. "Though wait, how late is it? Did I miss supper? And oh no, I didn't cook for Drafli!"

Baldr firmly shushed her, slipping his hand around her waist, and guiding her through the lovely clean corridor. "Do not fret over this, Bright-Heart," he said firmly. "You have already done more than enough for us today. Draf has gone and found supper for us, ach?"

That seemed absurd, surely—Drafli had made *her* supper?—but once Baldr had ushered her back to their room, it turned out that this was indeed the case. The food was nothing elaborate, but there was fresh fruit and slightly charred meat for Alma, and a hunk of raw red meat for Baldr and Drafli. And though Alma could see Drafli faintly wincing as he chewed, he didn't complain—and when he caught her watching him, his expression went very carefully neutral, even as she could see the hard shifts in his swallowing throat.

Once they'd all finished eating, Alma somehow ended up leaning back against Drafli, her tired head lolling into his strong shoulder. The room briefly flickering, fading away into darkness—until she was abruptly snatched up, and caught close against something solid and warm. Against—him.

And oh, was Drafli putting Alma in their bed, was he

allowing her to *stay*?—but no, no, he was signing one-handed toward Baldr, and striding for the door.

"I'm sorry, my lord," she mumbled, as he stalked down the corridor, with her curled close in his arms. "We didn't even—Pure-Heart—"

But she could feel Drafli shaking his head, his strong arms hoisting her a little closer. Carrying her, Drafli was truly *carrying* her, like she was *his*—so she let herself sink into it, into the truth of this moment. He might not yet want her to stay, but he was taking care of her, again. And he thought she was a good Keeper, he wanted her to touch him. His.

And when he tucked her into her bed again, this time he smoothed her hair back, his soft kiss gently brushing against her lips. "Sleep, Bright-Heart," he breathed, his voice a soft, broken croak. "We shall make you scream for us tomorrow, ach?"

Oh. *Oh.* And Alma was smiling wearily up at him, the relief so visceral she almost felt faint. "I can't wait," she whispered back. "And you'll still take good care of Pure-Heart tonight, won't you?"

That might have actually been a small, genuine smile in return, curling at Drafli's mouth. *I always do*, he signed at her. *He shall scream enough for both of you.*

Alma laughed—laughed!—as she gave him a shaky little wave goodbye. And as she swiftly sank into sleep, there was again only contentment, and satisfaction, and peace.

She was doing good work, and she was making this work between them. And most importantly, she would meet her one-month deadline with plenty of room to spare. She *would*.

35

If it was possible, Alma awoke the next morning feeling even happier than she had the day before. Eagerly resuming her already-familiar morning routine—tools, reading, prayers in the Grisk shrine—and then heading for her desk in the kitchen. Where she discovered, in a pleasant surprise, that Kesst was already there waiting for her, perched precariously on her desk with his arms crossed.

"You are a devious, dastardly genius, sweetheart," he snapped at her, before she'd even had a chance to sit down. "Thanks to you shutting down those arenas for your floor project yesterday, Eft slept for the entire day. The entire *day!* And then"—he jabbed an accusing finger toward her—"once he woke up, he went and kept *me* awake for half the night, the greedy bastard. Of course, after I'd spent the whole day worrying he was *dead!*"

This was said with an indignant snort and a toss of his head, but Alma didn't miss the faint flush staining his cheeks, too. "And I did not hear one complaint," he continued. "Not one, not even from that Bautul menace Silfast. Apparently, come to discover, the Keeper has always gotten final say on cleaning-related closures, and even the captain isn't supposed to argue with you! So"—Kesst's brows snapped higher on his forehead—"you're going to keep this up, right? Maybe you can close the arenas on a regular basis? Every week, ideally?"

Alma couldn't help a laugh, though she tilted her head, considering it. "Honestly, those arenas really *should* be cleaned every week," she said. "And if that would help you and Efterar, Kesst, you know I'm all for it. Of course."

Kesst slightly twitched on the desk, his throat bobbing— but then he nodded, quick and fervent. "Well, in return," he said firmly, "I'll keep trying to be the best damned Infirmarian who ever walked this realm, all right? Speaking of which, I really do need a regular laundry rotation. And some kind of meal fix as well—all these fools with broken jaws and teeth can't chew the food the kitchen's making them, and how are they supposed to heal, and get out of Eft's hair, if they can't eat?!"

It was a fair point, and one that had been nagging at Alma since she'd seen Drafli eating the night before, too. "It's a really good point, Kesst," she said. "There are others—women like me included—who can't eat raw food as well. I wonder..."

She was still tilting her head, tapping at the ledger with her charcoal, when Tryggr abruptly poked his head around from behind a barrel. "Sorry to interrupt," he said, "but just wanted to let you know Duff can't come today—just not feeling sound enough. Think he mighta pushed himself a bit too hard yesterday."

Alma winced, sitting up straighter in her chair—but Tryggr was already giving a dismissive wave, and leaning against the stack of barrels marking her door. "Ach, he was happy to do it," he said, "and he'll come round again in a day or two, he always does. I took him some food, and he told me we could borrow Cat—she's skulking round the scullery now—so maybe she'll catch a nice juicy rat for him, too. And I know Boss and Simon will check on him later today, they always do, so no need to fret, ach?"

He flashed Alma a reassuring grin as he spoke, while Kesst—who was still perched on the desk—gave him a cool, tight-lipped smile. "Oh, you *Skai*," he said. "Always so *attentive*, so *concerned*, when it's one of your own in trouble, aren't you?"

Tryggr didn't seem to notice the edge on Kesst's voice, and gave a dismissive shrug. "Ach, we try, I ken," he said. "We all have our troubles at some point or another, don't we? No good in leaving a brother behind over something foolish like *that*."

Kesst returned this with another smile, even more brittle than before. "Quite," he said coldly. "Now, if only you showed such magnanimity toward the rest of us, hmmm?"

At that, Tryggr's head cocked sideways, his brow creasing. "Ach," he said slowly, "we don't?"

"No, you don't," Kesst replied, this time with a barely perceptible hitch in his voice. "Especially when it's one of your own precious *Skai* who's at fault. And when it's somebody *else's* troubles they're causing. Somebody you don't need to *bother* caring about, because they're not one of *you*!!"

Kesst's voice had risen as he'd spoken, scraping through the too-small room—and in return, Tryggr blinked once, twice. And then, to Alma's vague surprise, he stepped closer toward Kesst, leaned forward, and... *smelled* him. His nose wrinkling as he inhaled, his mouth faintly grimacing.

"Ach, I see," he said to Kesst, quieter now. "That's Ofnir, ain't it?"

Kesst flinched away, while visible chagrin flashed across his eyes—but Tryggr's expression had gone uncharacteristically dark, his hand rubbing at his mouth. "Yeah, Ofnir was a right bastard, wasn't he?" he said. "Only met him a few times myself, but my Pa's told me tales. That scum never shoulda been allowed to run around as long as he did. Thank Skai-kesh"—he put his hand to his heart—"that Boss finally got to him. But you're right, it shoulda been sooner. We were all terrified of him too, I ken."

Tryggr gave a genuine-looking grimace as he spoke, his

hand even signing *sorry* over his heart. While Kesst again flinched on the desk, his brows furrowed hard together, his arms now tightly wrapped around his chest.

"Where are you getting this rubbish, Skai?" he said, his voice thready and high-pitched. "Your Boss—*Drafli*—did *not* get to Ofnir. He did *nothing*."

Tryggr blinked at Kesst again, and then gave a short little laugh. "Sure he did," he replied. "Ofnir's dead, ain't he?"

Kesst twitched again, his eyes squeezing shut, his head shaking back and forth. "Yes, Ofnir's dead, because he *drowned*," he retorted. "In a *hunting accident*."

But Tryggr laughed again, and shook his head, too. "And you believe that?" he asked, with wry astonishment in his voice. "Thought you were Ash-Kai, you're the most suspicious bastards of us all, aren't you?"

Kesst was staring at Tryggr now, unmoving, and Tryggr's smile was a little reluctant this time, maybe even sympathetic. "It was only a moon or two after Boss took up with his Grisk, remember?" he said. "And you've seen the two of 'em swimming, haven't you? Like fish, they are. And with everything being the mess it was at the time, water was the best way to get rid of Ofnir, 'cause it helps cover the scents, right? Add in Boss' Grisk, and all he can do with scents"—Tryggr gave a dismissive shrug "and ain't nobody could pin it on Boss. Let alone say he shouldn't become Right Hand after, either."

Alma was also gaping at Tryggr now, her heart skittering erratically in her chest. Wait. Was he really saying that Drafli had... *killed* this horrible Ofnir? And Baldr had... *helped* him?

But Alma's shocked look at Kesst found his throat convulsing, his mouth opening and closing. Not protesting this, as she'd surely expected, but instead... believing it? *Accepting* it?

"Why," Kesst said finally, his voice wavering, "did no one *tell* me?"

Tryggr gave another pained smile, his shoulder shrugging. "Probably thought you liked the old bastard," he replied.

"Handsome, powerful sort, wasn't he? And you Ash-Kai are real good at your play-acting, aren't you? Making out as though everything's fine, when it's really not. And never letting on when you need help, either."

There was an instant's stunned, dangling silence, Kesst's mouth half-open as he stared at Tryggr—but then a shrill, distant caterwauling tore through the air, from the direction of the scullery.

"Ooooh," Tryggr said brightly, his head snapping over his shoulder. "Cat musta got another one! I better go see."

With that, he sped off toward the scullery, leaving Kesst and Alma both sitting there in silence behind him. Kesst still staring blankly at where Tryggr had gone, while Alma's heart kept thumping uncertainly in her chest.

"You really think that's... true?" she whispered, into the silence, after another long, stilted moment. "That Baldr and Drafli *killed* that awful old orc?"

Kesst startled on the desk, almost as though he'd forgotten she was there, and roughly ran a hand through his hair. "You know what, yes, actually, I do," he said, hoarse. "I can't believe I didn't see it. I—I need to go see Eft."

With that, he lurched off the desk, and out the door. While Alma blinked uncertainly after him, and strange, scattered thoughts seemed to twitch through her skull. Of course she was happy, and so, so *relieved*, that Drafli had helped Kesst, even if that had meant *killing* someone... but then, the thought of that, the vision of it. Baldr and Drafli splashing and playing in the water, Drafli's mouth kissing hers with such sweetness, liquid flooding her lungs as she'd sunk into the deep...

It was some time before Alma seemed able to rouse herself enough to go back to the scullery. Where she found a trembly, flush-faced Eben, thrusting a fresh bucket of lye into Tryggr's hands, before scurrying past Alma out the door again. While Tryggr frowned after him, his eyes gone rather calculating—

but then blinking, refocusing, as he glanced back at Alma again.

"You all right, woman?" he asked, his head tilting. "Want me to send for Boss?"

Alma shook her head, and started pulling dry clothes from the racks. "I'm fine, thank you," she replied. "I think I'm just"— she took a breath—"Tryggr, do Baldr and Drafli... *often* kill people?"

She couldn't quite seem to look at him as she asked, and she could hear him huffing a sigh behind her. "Ach, I shoulda thought about that, before opening my big mouth," he said. "But you ken, I really don't think they do much of that now. Not anymore. Not with that peace-treaty being signed, and all."

But Alma's breath was still oddly hitching in her throat, her hands trembling on the laundry. Because Tryggr meant, surely, that Baldr and Drafli *had* killed people before. Right?

"And look, it's not like they'd run off doing it willy-nilly, you know?" Tryggr continued behind her. "They'd have a good reason, like being attacked, or like what they did with Ofnir. But they're still the captain's Left and Right Hands, which means they're still gonna get their own hands dirty sometimes, on his behalf. You know?"

But Alma... didn't know. Did she? And it was that awareness, more than anything else—more than the actual *killing*, good gods—that had her blinking uncertainly down at her laundry. Because while Baldr had often spoken in vague terms of their work—suggesting, surely, that it was both busy and important—he'd never shared specifics like this, had he? And why hadn't he—or Drafli—ever told Alma more about their day-to-day activities, or their lives outside the bedroom? Their *real* lives, *together*?

But the more Alma considered it, the more something seemed to plummet, tight and painful in her belly. Because beyond that conversation the other night about Drafli's mate, had they *ever* discussed such things with her? Did she really know *anything* about their families, their upbringings, their daily work for their captain? And gods, the few times she'd tried asking, Baldr had almost always dodged the questions, and had instead turned them back toward her, or toward their pleasure together. And then Drafli would take her away afterwards, and put her in her own bed, and...

"Look, I'm gonna go find Boss," said Tryggr firmly. "Seems to me like you two oughta have a talk. Ach?"

Alma should have protested—Drafli was *sure* to be displeased with that—but instead she felt herself shamefully nodding, and clutching reflexively at the counter. And there was the feel of Tryggr walking out—moving almost as quietly as Drafli did—and leaving her alone in the empty scullery.

She stared at the wall for far too long, almost as if she was *waiting*, good gods—but when Tryggr didn't immediately return, she belatedly forced herself to start working again. Folding clothes with fumbling, shaking hands, one piece after another, keep going, keep working. Drafli had to see that she was trying, he'd said she was still doing good work, she wasn't worthless, only their servant, she *wasn't*...

And when there was finally a sound at the door, Alma whirled around, her heart juddering in her chest—but it wasn't Drafli, or Tryggr, or even Gegnir. It was—Narfi?

Alma froze in place—why was Narfi here, surely he wouldn't offer to *help*—and when she attempted a smile toward him, he returned it with a chilly, dismissive frown, his eyes blatantly flicking up and down her form.

"You ken our Right Hand shall now rush to your side, whenever you call for him?" Narfi asked coldly. "You ken he shall be pleased to keep lowering himself thus, for a *human*?"

Alma swallowed, her eyes angling helplessly toward the door behind him—but it remained stubbornly empty, and Narfi snorted, or perhaps laughed. "Ach, Drafli is not coming," he said. "You ken I could not smell this, after how much of his seed I have known?"

Alma couldn't help a flinch—surely this was rubbish, surely Narfi was just trying to upset her again—but he was smiling now, thin and unpleasant. "Ach, I have tasted him many, *many* times," he continued, his voice a slow, taunting drawl. "Our Right Hand has mayhap the sweetest seed in all the mountain, you ken? It is a gift from the gods, and one he is meant to bestow freely upon all Skai who wish for this."

And clearly, that was something Narfi very much still wished for—and thank the gods, Alma's indignation was finally rising, drowning out the disbelief, the still-bubbling *hurt*. "Well, as I'm sure you're aware," she said, her voice only slightly wavering, "Drafli's *gifts* now belong only to Baldr. And Baldr is *very* particular about sharing."

But Narfi's answering laugh was snide and mocking, his head shaking. "Ach, that spineless Grisk knows well how to share," he said. "You ought to have seen him sulking and brooding about, whenever our Right Hand gave another Skai his due, and filled our throats with his good seed. The taste of his Grisk envy only made that sweet Skai seed all the sweeter, ach?"

Alma found herself frowning darkly at Narfi, and abruptly spun away from him, back toward her folding. "And then Drafli came to his senses, and swore *vows* to Baldr," she snapped. "*Forever*. So you've had your last taste of him, I'm afraid."

There was a low growl behind her, but Alma didn't turn around, and determinedly kept folding. "Ach, mayhap not," Narfi's cold voice said. "Drafli tempts the gods with this Grisk vow, you ken. When a Skai breaks our ways in secret, Skai-kesh shall hurl this into the light, and smite his son with all his strength."

Now Skai-kesh would do *what*?! Alma's hands twitched on her folding, her head jerking a quick shake. "That's absurd," she said sharply. "Why would Skai-kesh *ever* smite his own loyal son, for publicly making a vow to someone he loves, and then keeping it?!"

She could hear Narfi growling again, lower this time. "The Skai *share*," he hissed. "We have *never* sworn fidelity to other orcs. Drafli may have swayed some Skai to accept this on our behalf, but Skai-kesh yet sees this sin, and shall judge him. As he has before."

There was dark satisfaction in Narfi's voice, and Alma felt herself bristling, her shoulders gone tight and square. "Bollocks," she snapped, without turning around. "And utterly pathetic, honestly, if your jealousy of Baldr has warped into some kind of vile quest for divine punishment. You only *wish* Drafli cared for you, the way he cares for Baldr. You should *see* how much Baldr enjoys his—"

But the words suddenly died in her throat, because somehow Narfi was here, directly beside her, with his claws and teeth bared. And though he was far shorter than Drafli, he still loomed deadly and terrifying above her, his beady eyes crackling with rage.

"You foul little wench," he hissed. "No wonder our Right Hand only uses you for his pleasure, and refuses to truly take you as a mate, or grant you his son. Shame, for otherwise I should wait and *pray* for the day we run a Skai rut upon you, whilst you scream and weep and *plead* at our feet!"

Alma's horror surged and flailed, her feet staggering backwards—she'd heard those words before, had *Drafli* said them before?—but there was only the solid stone counter behind her, oh gods. And Narfi was stepping even closer, bending over her, near enough that she could smell his sickly-sweet breath. His lips curling up in a horrible mockery of a smile, showing her all his sharp teeth, and—

"Instead, mayhap, we shall sell you back to that man," he crooned, in a sing-song voice. "I hear he shall pay a pretty price to have his sweet little servant back. I wonder what he shall do with you, when he has you alone in his bed?"

Wait. Narfi was talking about—about *Mr. Pembroke*. And gods curse her, Alma had somehow shoved Mr. Pembroke's various demands from her mind almost entirely—like Drafli had *wanted* her to, her distant thoughts chanted—but wait, what had Jule last said? That Pembroke had demanded Alma be returned, yes, along with whatever valuables Pembroke had claimed she'd stolen. And wait, there had been a *deadline* on that, hadn't there? A fortnight, Jule had said, before Pembroke decided to attack?

And how many days had it been now? Seven? Ten? And had Alma ever heard any news on that? *Had* there been a bounty? Gods, had she even bothered *asking*?

And even worse... had Drafli and Baldr *known*? Had Drafli truly meant to keep this from her, along with everything else? Had he meant to keep her so ignorant, so foolish? Like a servant? A harlot? A *pet*?

It suddenly felt hard to breathe, Alma's throat gone tight and choked, and she clutched at the counter behind her, frantically shaking her head. "I'm not going back there, *ever*," she gritted out. "And Pembroke doesn't care about me. He would never pay real *coin* for me. I'm only an excuse for him. A means to an *end*."

Her voice was far too fervent, as though if speaking these things, wishing these things, would surely make them true. *Pembroke doesn't care. I'm only an excuse. Never going back...*

But suddenly she was coughing, her throat painfully spasming, for the first time in days—and Narfi's loud, grating laugh seemed to slice open her convulsing chest, spilling her fear dark and wide.

"Foolish human," he hissed. "You shall go back there, before the next moon. For there is a price upon you, and soon, *it shall be paid*."

oon, it shall be paid.

Alma's terror felt alive, like a cold creeping thing, crawling in her exposed belly. Paid. Back to Pembroke. *No.*

But Narfi was laughing at her, and stepping even closer, his breath nauseating on her face. "You like that, fool wench?" he purred. "You wish to see what this man—"

But his voice halted there, cracking into silence—and somehow, suddenly, he was gone. Gone, wrenched away from her, because of—Drafli?

And gods, yes, it was Drafli. Tall and silent and terrible, hurling Narfi bodily to the floor with fluid, shocking ease. And then—Alma flinched—Drafli kicked him in the side with a hard drive of his booted foot, while Narfi yelped and cowered, his arms thrown over his face.

Alma stared, aghast, her hands fluttering between her mouth and her eyes—and without warning Drafli was here again, looming before her, snatching her wrists, and holding them above her head. While his face leaned down close into her neck, and inhaled.

Alma couldn't even follow anymore, her entire form

trembling, her neck and shoulder twitching up toward Drafli's warmth. To where she could feel something soft and slick—his tongue—and the too-hot shudder of his slow, stuttering exhale.

"He no touch you?" Drafli's voice hissed, a harsh whisper in her ear, and Alma shivered again, and shook her head. And then perhaps wished that she hadn't, because Drafli had yanked back again, whirling entirely away from her, and once again kicked Narfi's still-cowering form with terrifying force.

Narfi was muttering some kind of apology, but Drafli didn't seem to be listening—instead, he was stepping toward the door of the scullery, and reaching out his hand. To where—Alma twitched, stared—Baldr was rushing in, his eyes wide and searching, sweeping between Alma and Drafli, and Narfi on the floor.

"Ach," Baldr said, squeezing his eyes shut, clutching tight at Drafli's outstretched hand—and then keeping it clasped in his as he strode toward Alma. "Are you well, Bright-Heart? What has happened? I could taste your fear like a—"

He grimaced, breaking off there, and though Alma attempted a smile toward him, she abjectly failed. "Narfi says that Skai-kesh will—*p-punish* Drafli," she gulped. "And that Pembroke's placed a b-bounty on me, and you're going to—to send me b-back."

The fear was again tainting her voice, choking at her throat—and suddenly Baldr was looking pained, and angry, and grim. His eyes glancing toward Drafli, who was sharply signing something toward him, to which Baldr swiftly signed back. And somehow, despite all the chaos screaming through her skull, Alma was almost painfully grateful for them, and their competent understanding of one another, their *safety*.

"Come, Bright-Heart," Baldr said firmly, gripping her hand, and guiding her toward the door. "We shall meet Drafli at the Skai shrine, ach?"

The Skai shrine? Alma blinked uncertainly toward Drafli over her shoulder—she hadn't seen a Skai shrine yet, had she?—but Drafli was slowly advancing on Narfi again, his body coiled and deadly, his claws jutting long and menacing from his fingertips.

The fear again surged in Alma's belly—Drafli was a killer, was Drafli going to *kill* him—and she could hear Baldr hiss under his breath as he drew her faster into the kitchen. Into where Gegnir was frowning at them, his head tilted, and Alma couldn't even muster a smile as Baldr dragged her past.

"Breathe, Bright-Heart," Baldr said, once he was guiding her up the corridor, his arm tight around her back. "You are not in danger, ach? We shall never send you back to that man. *Ever.*"

His voice was low and fervent, enough that Alma's swirling brain couldn't seem to argue it, not with his arm around her like this, not with that hard, furious set to his jaw. But. But...

"But is it really true, though?" she asked him, her voice almost inaudible. "That Mr. Pembroke still wants me back? That now he's promising *coin* for me?"

And beside her, Baldr... flinched. Flinched, as though she'd struck him, and his throat was visibly swallowing, his gaze angling toward her. "I thought," he said, "you knew this. The captain's mate spoke to you of this. And Drafli said—he said you agreed to forget this man, and leave him to us to address. Ach?"

And now Alma was the one flinching, because yes, she had agreed to that, hadn't she? And yes, Jule *had* talked to her about it, all those days ago—but she certainly hadn't mentioned the bounty, which seemed a highly crucial development. And surely Baldr and Drafli could have said something, *anything*, and Baldr knew it, he did, he *did*.

"I am—sorry, Bright-Heart," he said, his voice catching, his eyes now staring straight ahead. "I ought—I ought to have spoken to you more of this, ach? I only—I was selfish. *Greedy.* I did not wish to taint the—the short time you stay with us— the pure *joy* you grant us—with this. And after, you—you always leave us, and I ken this is not your doing, I *know*, but—"

His voice broke there, his eyes blinking hard, and still not looking at her. And Alma was blinking too, her mouth quivering, her arms circling tight against her chest. "You could have," she whispered, "come to see me. Spent more time together. Talked more. Gone swimming more, maybe. During the day. If you'd ever—wanted to."

But Baldr was wincing again, twitching his head back and forth. "You know I should wish for this," he said. "I have longed for this, with all my heart. But since this man began all this, many days past, near all our days have been spent—"

He again broke off mid-sentence, his mouth twisting—and here, like a slam to the gut, was the horrible, sickening realization that Baldr had been spending all his time dealing with... this. With Mr. Pembroke. With... *war*?!

"But what," Alma breathed, "what has Mr. Pembroke *done*?"

Baldr's shoulders jerked a shrug, a sigh heaving from his chest. "It is not," he said, "much altered, since your first days here. He demands your return, in five days—only now he has set a bounty upon you, for any man who should gain this. And he has sent bands of his men to camp around the mountain, knowing that we will not attack them, and risk breaking our treaty."

Oh. Oh, *gods*. And Alma's fear was swirling and spiralling again, screeching bitter through her gut, and beside her Baldr had actually clamped a hand to his mouth, his head frantically shaking. "Please, Bright-Heart," he gasped. "Please, do not fear this, do not taint your sweet scent thus, ach? This man shall not have you, he shall not harm you, you shall never see him *again*. We have faced this many times before, these men are all the same, and Drafli and I shall never allow this to touch you, *ever*. You are ours. *Ours*, Bright-Heart. We shall keep you safe. For *always*."

Theirs. For... always. *Safe*. And Alma wanted to cling to that, she needed it more than she'd ever needed anything in her life, but they'd been hiding this, they'd been lying to her, Drafli had even built her ignorance into his damned *vow*...

And speaking of Drafli, he was suddenly here again, striding tall and silent beside her, his eyes also fixed straight ahead. But he was signing, his still-clawed fingers moving so rapidly Alma could only catch pieces of his words.

"Draf says," Baldr supplied on her other side, quiet, "that Pembroke is scum. He is not worth your fear, or your time, or even your *thought*. And instead of this man, Draf wished you to think"—Baldr's voice hitched—"of me. Of us. Of your new life here. Your new work. Your new *home*."

Oh. But surely this was more of Drafli's lies, more of his play-acting, performed for Baldr's benefit alone—he'd built this into their *vow*—but Drafli's eyes had cut sharply toward her, searching her with narrow, glinting intensity.

This is truth, he signed at her, slower now, as Baldr nudged her into an unfamiliar, sweet-scented room. *I wished you to forget that man. He hurt you. He made you afraid. He near killed you.*

Alma's throat convulsed, her mouth grimacing, and she held his hard, glittering eyes. "But you still," she gulped, "should have told me about all this. I had the right to know. To decide what I wanted to know."

She braced herself as she spoke, waiting for Drafli's retaliation, for yet more of his lies—but then, unexpectedly, he winced. Shook his head. And then glanced, brief but far too telling, toward Baldr beside her.

Ach, he signed back. *This is truth, and*—

His signs again skittered into illegibility, and when Alma looked toward Baldr, he nodded, cleared his throat. "Drafli says, this is truth, and he asks your forgiveness. He is not— good, at thinking of these things, or speaking of them, amidst his need to see us happy, and safe."

Oh. And suddenly here was the memory of Drafli hissing at

her, saying those same words, back when he'd first made Alma that offer. *I shall see my mate happy and safe again.*

"But he says," Baldr added, his voice lower, "that he is trying to learn. That he wishes to be a better mate, and a worthy father to our son."

And surely Drafli was lying now, surely, he had to be—so why was he glancing sideways, his hand come to his heart, his head giving a little bow, as though...

And wait. This room—this had to be the Skai shrine. And blinking around at it, Alma discovered that it was carved in a circle, with multiple doors in the rounded wall, and several large, fur-covered benches spread about. All facing toward the room's very middle, toward where there stood a cluster of carved stone figures—but unlike in the Grisk shrine, these ones were life-sized, all taller than Alma. And none of them wore any clothes, and the one Drafli was looking at was the tallest of them all, and very blatantly well-built, with beautifully striking black-painted eyes.

Alma's breath caught in her throat, her eyes fixed to the carving, to how those strangely familiar eyes were seeing her, *knowing* her—and she felt her head bowing, her own fist coming to her heart. "Skai-kesh," she whispered. "My lord. It is an honour."

And was she talking to Drafli, or to his god, or both, and when she belatedly glanced back at Drafli, his face had gone entirely unreadable, his fist still over his heart, too. While on Alma's other side, Baldr had huffed a soft snort, his head shaking.

"I ken Draf has taught you of Skai-kesh, then," he said. "Skai oft seek comfort here under his eye, and show him their truth. They would also never speak false here before him, ach?"

Never speak false. And wait, was that why Drafli had wanted them to come here? Because he'd wanted Alma to know that he was telling her the truth?

"And if a Skai ever wishes Skai-kesh to grant his blessing

upon another," Baldr continued, even quieter, "he comes here to ask for this, ach?"

There was something too meaningful in his voice, in his eyes on Drafli's—and to Alma's rising confusion, Drafli nodded, the movement quick and sharp, his gaze shifting between Baldr and her. Saying something, betraying something, and...

You will present yourself here, Bright-Heart, Drafli ordered her. *To me.*

37

---

lma would present herself. To *Drafli*?!

Her heart had surely stopped beating, her eyes gaping at Drafli's face—but oh gods, oh Skai-kesh, he was signing it again. Gesturing at the nearest fur-covered bench this time, making his meaning far too clear.

Present yourself. To me.

Alma's breath shuddered from her lungs, her hands quivering against her skirt—and Drafli was still looking. Waiting. And he'd apologized to her, he'd told her the truth, he wanted Skai-kesh to bless her...

And in the mess currently swarming Alma's thoughts, there was somehow, somehow the courage to... obey. To lurch toward the bench Drafli had indicated, and to awkwardly climb onto it, on her hands and knees. And then, keeping her face toward Skai-kesh, she shakily yanked at her skirt and her cape, and let them fall to the bench beneath her.

It meant she was kneeling here, fully bared, in what surely a public room, where anyone could walk in and see—but there was no shame, and Drafli had taught her this, Drafli wanted this. So she swallowed hard, and took a deep breath, and... presented herself. Her knees spread wide, her back arched, all her hidden places wide open and exposed for the taking.

The room had gone utterly silent, but for Alma's gulping breaths, and the faint, betraying sounds of her own hungry clenching heat. And were Baldr and Drafli looking at her, were they judging her, what were they going to do next...

And finally, finally, there was the touch of a hand, against her bare hip. And when Alma's head reflexively twisted to look, it—it wasn't Baldr this time. No, it was Drafli, standing tall and powerful behind her, his eyes fixed on Skai-kesh before them, his trousers hanging low on his hips. And his scarred, swollen heft was already bobbing in his hand, he was stroking it up and down, coating it with slick, gleaming white. As if... as if...

Alma's breath audibly choked, her eyes frozen on Drafli's face—but he was still looking at Skai-kesh. And then, so briefly, toward Baldr, who had somehow moved to stand before Alma, his body close and restless, his big hand trembling against her hair.

"Peace, Bright-Heart," Baldr murmured. "He shall be careful with you, ach? He was gentle my first time, also."

Oh, *hell*. And Alma was blinking, searching Baldr's eyes, because surely that didn't mean what it sounded like, but—

But oh, oh, it *did*, and Alma yelped aloud at the sudden, staggering feel of it. Of Drafli, of that part of Drafli, *touching* her. Not where she was already so wet and open, where he might risk sparking his son upon her—but further up. To the forbidden place where he'd asked her to keep using her tools, where Baldr had used his finger—but oh, this already felt so much weightier, so much more *alive*. And he was shuddering as he nudged against her, he was leaking out that slick sweetness, putting it *inside* her...

Alma's yelp was more of a moan this time, and in return that slick, delving hardness flexed and swelled, sputtering out more liquid heat against her. Enough that she could feel it dripping, pooling downwards, while her hungry empty heat seemed to clutch at it, tasting it, wanting it inside...

"Ach, this is it, Bright-Heart," Baldr breathed, his fingers carding deeper into her hair. "Deep breaths. Feel him thus, and learn him. Think of being open and soft for him, ach?"

Alma gulped and nodded, holding his beautiful, reassuring eyes as she dragged in one breath, another. Thinking of being soft, open, welcoming that prodding pulsing heat, welcoming... *him.*

But Drafli still wasn't pushing, or demanding more. No, he was just waiting there, feeling her there, seeping more of his hot sweetness against her, into her. Wanting her to open even more, to bloom beneath his touch...

And when Alma heaved in another full breath, and let it out again, she could feel Drafli pressing a little closer, a little deeper. The tip of him easing just slightly inside, opening her around him—and oh, the *feeling* of that, oh gods, oh *gods.*

"Good woman," Baldr murmured, one hand now stroking down her hot cheek, the other still deep in her hair. "This feels good, ach? Think upon this, and welcome this. Think of how it shall feel even better, once he is seated deep within you."

Alma couldn't help another low moan at the words, her body clamping hard against where yes, Drafli was actually *inside* her now. That hard, slick head throbbing within her, holding her open around it, and Drafli was doing this, Drafli was really, really doing this...

"More, Bright-Heart," Baldr breathed, and oh, Alma was nodding, again and again, as she felt herself slowly relaxing again, as that solid, uncompromising heft kept slipping deeper, deeper. Feeling so, so full now, and so strange, like Drafli was truly part of her, piercing her whole upon his strength.

And she could feel the grip of his strong hands on her hips now, could feel the hard exhale of his breath on her bare back. Could feel him shuddering inside her, taking her as his own while his god watched. *Need to keep you happy, safe...*

And suddenly Alma was twitching, blinking up at Baldr, while something dipped and pitched in her belly. "But you—you're sure," she gasped. "Both of you. You—want this. *Truly*."

Baldr's hand stilled on her face, his eyes flicking back to Drafli—but then, oh thank the gods, he nodded. Quick, fervent, *sure*.

"Ach, we do," he whispered. "You are *ours*, Bright-Heart. And you have never looked or smelled lovelier than you do at this moment, on your knees for my mate, taking his prick inside your sweet little rump, ach?"

Alma's moan was harsh and heated this time, and Baldr actually chuckled, tilting her chin up, brushing his thumb against her parted lips. "There is only one way you could be any more stunning," he purred, "and that is if you would also welcome me into your sweet little mouth, ach?"

Alma's nod jerked on its own—yes, *gods*, yes—and Baldr's smile slipped even higher as he drew down his trousers, and that familiar, gold-tipped length bobbed out.

Alma didn't even wait for him to guide it to her, just lunged for it, hungrily sucking it inside—and Baldr's low laugh rippled all through him, enough that she rippled against Drafli, too. And she could feel his answering exhale on her back, his instinctive thrust deeper, and oh that felt so strong, so impossible, so *glorious*—

"Good, Bright-Heart," Baldr was breathing, his voice husky and thick, his gold-tipped heft slipping deeper into her mouth. "Good. Now, you shall welcome the rest of him inside you, ach? You shall feel what a gift it is, to be ploughed by the Right Hand of the Skai, both before his god, and his mate?"

Oh hell, Alma's shudder was wracking through her again, ripping her apart—but she needed more, more, and surely Drafli knew it, his fingers gripping harder against her hips, his heft easing deeper. Plunging slow but sure, opening her wider and wider around him, trapping her on his power, his intensity, his command. Owning her, invading her, her entire body flaring and trembling upon him, until—

He slid home with one last, certain thrust, his hips pressed hard to her backside, his heavy bollocks swelling against her open, dripping heat. And the rest of him—that scarred, vicious, deep grey brunt of him—was *inside* her, filling her, opening her wide and wanton upon him, while his mate did the same with her mouth.

"Ach, Bright-Heart," Baldr was breathing, his voice breaking, his eyes half-lidded on Drafli behind her. "This is so good. You are so soft and tight upon my mate, I ken. I can taste how this feels for him, how your sweet little rump seeks to milk him dry. You wish to drink all his seed inside you, you wish to prove to his god how much of him you shall take. How you shall welcome him with such eager yearning, and now you shall always, *always* scent of him, ach—"

And it was then that Baldr bent double, his fullness already spraying out into Alma's mouth—while behind her, Drafli's entire body stiffened, his claws digging sharp into her hips. And then he was flooding out too, that strength inside her flaring again and again, filling her with his hot, roaring ecstasy—and when his hand dropped around in front of her, rubbing at where Alma most desperately craved it, she actually screamed around Baldr's still-spurting heft, the pleasure surging and soaring and shrieking, the sparks streaking bright white behind her eyes.

It took some time for awareness to return again, to trickle in past the wheeling, tilting contentment. But when it did, Alma distantly realized that both her orcs were still inside her, both slightly softer than before—and that she was spilling their hot, thick, slippery seed in both places, pooling down her chin, her crease, her thighs. Because they'd both taken her, Drafli had taken her, *there*, while his god had watched—and that surely meant something, it had to, it *had* to.

And yes, yes, her hazy glance up at Baldr found him gazing

at Drafli, his eyes glimmering with meaning—and when Alma wrenched to look behind her, Drafli was... signing. Signing, the movements slightly shaky, his own eyes fixed to Skai-kesh before them.

Bless her, he was saying, over and over again, his hand touching her back. *Bless her. Guard her. Claim her as yours. Keep her safe. Grant her to me, and to Pure-Heart. Bless her. Guard her.*

There was a strange, compelling fervour to the words—the prayer—and Alma could feel the hushed stillness that seemed to surround it, curling close and quiet in her chest. Drafli was asking—he was begging—his god to bless her. And it wasn't making sense, why would he do this, why would he lie, why would he risk his relationship with his god like this. He hated her, he was only doing this for Baldr, for his absolution...

Or... or was he? And as Alma watched Drafli signing those words, repeating his prayer again and again, something seemed to shift, odd and stilted, in her stuttering thoughts. He was inside her. He'd taken her. He'd been gentle with her. He'd apologized to her. He was asking his god to bless her.

And... he'd brought her help. He'd brought her a cat. He'd allowed her to use the threat of him as she wished. He'd complimented her, he'd taught her his language, he'd taught her to swim, he'd given her unthinkable pleasures, he'd made her a *vow*. And he was trying to learn, to be a better mate, and a better father, because—because she'd *asked*.

And somehow, somehow, Alma was shifting backwards—giving Baldr's softened strength one last, reverent kiss as she slipped away—and then bowing her head, and signing her own prayer, too. *Bless them. Honour them. Keep them safe. Claim them as yours. Please, my lord, please.*

She kept signing as Drafli slowly pulled away too, as more proof of what he'd done spilled thick and hot from inside her. But his hand still lingered against her back, and as she kept signing, the certainty—the peace—kept growing, edging away the whispers of darkness. She was theirs. Safe, for always. A *family*.

When she finally lifted her wet-feeling eyes again, she found herself kneeling on the fur, with Baldr and Drafli now kneeling on either side of her. And Drafli's hand was still touching her back, his gaze still fixed to Skai-kesh, while Baldr was watching her, watching Drafli, with something strange in his eyes. Relief, surely, and happiness, but also... guilt?

Alma tried to smile at him, wiping at her still-wet cheeks, and Baldr twitched a smile back, slow and bittersweet. His eyes again flicking toward Drafli, to where he was now just staring up at Skai-kesh, his jaw set, his eyes blank. Almost as if he hadn't at all found the peace Alma just had in this, in seeking the favour of his own god.

And that was something, something important, that surely needed to be said. And Alma again glanced between them, squaring her shoulders, taking a breath—

"My lord," she whispered, "why did Narfi believe that Skai-kesh has punished you for your sins? And that you will surely soon be punished again?"

And Drafli... froze. Not blinking, not even breathing, as he stared straight ahead, toward Skai-kesh's suddenly unnerving eyes. As if he was somehow stunned by Alma's question. As if he was almost afraid to answer.

On her other side, Baldr had shifted, and when Alma glanced toward him, he was watching Drafli too, his head tilted, his brows deeply furrowed. Waiting, surely, for Drafli's answer—but it didn't come. Only that same stillness, as Drafli kept staring, unmoving.

"You have served Skai-kesh faithfully since the day we first met, Draf," Baldr said slowly, his eyes searching Drafli's hard profile. "You have kept your clan's ways, again and again, against your own wishes, at great cost to yourself. At great cost to—"

To me, he was surely about to say—and beside Alma, Drafli twitched. *Flinched*. Betraying, surely, his agreement. His guilt.

And blinking at his set, stiff body beside her, it occurred to Alma that surely, Narfi hadn't been lying, when he'd claimed that Skai orcs weren't supposed to make vows of fidelity to other orcs. That according to their clan's ways, Skai were expected to freely share their affections with one another, even if that hurt someone they loved.

And Drafli had done that, he'd kept his clan's ways, even though he'd deeply wounded Baldr by doing so—and then he'd waited for his clan's approval before taking Baldr as his mate. Right? So why was Drafli still frozen like this? Why did he look so guilty? So *afraid*?

"Draf," Baldr said, quieter, but now with a sharp thread of command in it. "How did you break the Skai ways? And when? Tell us. The *truth*."

And once again, Drafli flinched. The movement somehow seeming to flare the rest of him into motion, his hands signing with jerky urgency, his eyes still staring empty toward Skai-kesh.

"You broke the Skai ways when you... took your first *mate*," Baldr said aloud, slowly, the confusion clear in his eyes, his voice. "But you... hunted her, as your Skai ways command. You alone sought her out, you watched her, you followed her to her home, and claimed her there. Ach? Simon has said this, and the captain, and..."

Baldr's voice faded into silence, his head tilting further, while grim comprehension flared across his face. "You... did *not* hunt your first mate?" he said, incredulous. "Then what—what did you do?!"

Drafli kept staring forward, but his hands again signed a curt, forceful answer. Something about... being introduced, at an orc camp, when he'd been out scouting, alone.

"So to keep your clan's ways, you should have then led a rut upon her instead, and thus shared her with them," Baldr said, his voice heavy with more grim comprehension. "Or walked away. So ach, of course you lied to your clan about this, but why"—his voice dropped—"why did you lie to *me*? *Again*?"

Drafli's eyes had finally snapped sideways, glinting hard and bright on Baldr's face. *I no lie to you*, he signed. *You no ask, and I no speak of this.*

But Baldr's face was visibly crumpling, his head whipping away—and suddenly Drafli had leapt off the bench, lurching to stand tall and jittery before Baldr's still-kneeling form.

No, Pure-Heart, he was signing, the movements almost frantic. *No. No. Listen.*

Baldr still wasn't looking at him, his eyes squeezed shut, and Alma could see Drafli dragging in breath, his shoulders squaring. "I *never*," he said aloud, his voice a hoarse croak, "wished you to think you were no good enough. That I should break Skai ways for *her*, but no for *you*."

Baldr still wasn't looking at him, and Alma could see the rising desperation in Drafli's eyes, how his throat was swallowing, flitting pain across his face. "I was *wrong*, for breaking Skai ways, for *her*," he rasped. "For speaking false to my clan thus. I fell to my weakness, and my *longing*. And for this, Skai-kesh smote me. He took all from me. *All*. My mate. My son. My honour. My *hope*. And all that was left"—he drew in a shuddering breath—"was *shame*."

Oh. Ohhh. And as those heavy, horrible words sank between them, Alma could almost taste that shame, could feel it, dark and heavy in her gut. Enough that her hand had somehow reached to clutch at Drafli's, grasping it tight, while words tumbled choked and erratic from her throat.

"So you couldn't risk breaking the Skai ways ever again," she gulped at him, nodding so hard it hurt. "You couldn't bear the thought of losing Baldr the same way you lost your first mate. Or"—her eyes kept searching Drafli's, studying that shimmering, sickening *fear*—"or the thought of Baldr *ever* going through what *you* went through, after your mate sold you to those horrible men. You couldn't bear the thought of Baldr suffering the way you did. Right?"

She could see Drafli swallowing again, his eyes shifting, his hand gone slack in hers—but then he jerked a small, twitchy nod.

Yes. Yes.

"So you kept your clan's ways this time," Alma continued, faster now. "You did everything that was expected of you, as perfectly as you could, until you finally gained your clan's permission to make Baldr your mate. But some Skai, like Narfi, still think you're breaking the Skai ways. And"—more understanding flashed across Alma's thoughts—"*you* still think that too, don't you? You still fear that someday, Skai-kesh will come for you. For... *Baldr*."

Drafli didn't nod this time, but his thick swallow surely again meant, *Yes.* And gods, it was all making so much sense, finally, all the little bits and pieces pulling together to make a bitter, horrifying whole. The way Drafli had pushed Alma to make that secret vow. The way he'd done everything he possibly could to make her stay. The way he'd dragged her into his bed, and his relationship, and his *life*.

And gods, even the way he'd kept the news of Mr. Pembroke from her. Because the last time she'd heard such things, she'd run away, hadn't she? She'd put Baldr in danger. Her actions had threatened the fulfillment of all Drafli's greatest fears, and in return he'd done everything—*anything*—to keep his mate safe.

I shall give all, he'd told her. And maybe even this—bringing Alma to this shrine, claiming her before his god—was even more of the same. Begging his god for mercy. For *absolution*.

Bless her. Guard her. Claim her as yours. Keep her safe. Grant her to me, and to Pure-Heart.

"But—*Drafli*," Alma choked, pleading at his face, clutching his limp hand tighter in hers. "Skai-kesh wouldn't do that to you. Surely he wouldn't. He *sees* you. He knows how faithful you've been. You are a good Skai. A good mate."

Something twisted on Drafli's mouth, and Alma kept gripping him tighter, feeling the truth of it, the strength of it. "And there is no shame, remember?" she breathed at him, hard and fervent. "None. *Ever*. Not with Skai-kesh, and not with his mother Akva, either. And if she doesn't hold with such things, why would she ever tolerate her son doing so?"

Drafli's mouth spasmed again, but Alma was not done, she wasn't. "And Baldr was absolutely right, because your first mate's choices were her own. Not yours, and *not* Skai-kesh's. And"—she gulped down another breath—"there is no need whatsoever for your penance, or for absolution, because it is not too late for you. It is *not*, Drafli. We are here, and we love you, and no god worth serving would punish you for that. *Ever*."

And wait, wait, what the hell was she saying, because Drafli was staring blankly at her now, and surely Baldr was too—but she was finishing this, she would be honest, she would do better, she *would*.

"So now, my lord," she gulped at him, "you will apologize to your loyal mate, won't you? You'll tell him how much you regret keeping this secret from him, all this time. How much you regret putting your own fears above your honesty toward him. Your *respect* toward him, and your *trust*. You will promise to keep learning, to keep doing better. Please, my lord. *Please*."

A thick, ringing silence seemed to follow her words, echoing against the stone walls, the watching gods before them. While Drafli's body had once again gone stock-still, his hand briefly convulsing against Alma's, his eyes still blank and entirely unreadable on her face.

And then—then he glanced at Baldr. And Baldr looked just as stunned as Drafli did, his tooth biting at his lip—and suddenly Drafli yanked his hand away from Alma's and began signing, the movements so fast she could only catch bits and pieces of the words.

I love you, Pure-Heart. I am sorry. Loyal, true. Fear, Skai-kesh, wrong. Learn. Better. Son.

Baldr was watching it all, and blinking hard, his throat bobbing. Watching, watching, not speaking, until Drafli gingerly stroked a hand to his cheek—and then Baldr slowly leaned into that touch, his expression full of pain and longing and... relief.

And when Drafli bent forward, and pushed Baldr down on his back on the bench beside Alma, Baldr didn't resist. Only stared up at Drafli with bright, glistening eyes as Drafli pulled back to yank his trousers off, irritably hurling them away, before settling between his bare, parted thighs. And then sinking inside, slow and steady and sure, while Baldr gasped and flailed up beneath him, his hands clutching tight at Drafli's back.

It was surely the sweetest Alma had ever seen them together, their bodies rocking together with smooth, fluid familiarity, their eyes fixed to each other's face. So beautiful that she couldn't seem to resist a touch, light and furtive, against Baldr's hand—and he instantly clasped her fingers in his, and again gripped at Drafli's back.

It meant that Alma could feel Drafli's smooth skin beneath her fingers, the shift of sleek muscle as he filled his mate again, again, again. Showing his regret, his affection, his *hope*, in the most powerful way he knew. Because—because of her.

And gods, Alma was somehow actually weeping, the wetness streaking down her cheeks—but she didn't even care. And instead, her other hand had begun to sign toward Skai-kesh, repeating Drafli's prayer as best she could.

Honour them. Bless them. Guard them. Keep them safe. Love them.

Drafli had glanced toward her as she did it, his eyes

blazing—so she drew her other hand away from Baldr, and said it again, properly this time. *Love them. Love you.*

And. Without once breaking his fluid, stunning rhythm, his sweet claiming of his beautiful mate, Drafli leaned over, and *kissed* her. His mouth so soft, so clever, so utterly perfect on hers. It was a reward, it was his blessing, and Alma moaned as she met it with desperate eagerness, drinking him up, shivering all over in the raw, reeling strength of it.

And when he pulled away, it was right that his parted lips should just slightly quirk like that—*So easy, Bright-Heart*, they seemed to say—before his mouth next dropped to Baldr's. Kissing him with just as much firm, gentle intensity as he'd kissed her, while Baldr moaned and arched with pure, unabashed pleasure—and then his release suddenly sprayed wide, splattering both him and Alma with thick spurts of messy, fragrant white.

Drafli had pulled up just in time, watching it with glittering, half-lidded eyes—and then he was the one grinding deep, his head tilted back, his lashes fluttering low. While Baldr again writhed and moaned beneath him, his face flushed, his claws spasming against Drafli's skin.

And then, finally, it was done. And Alma found herself kneeling naked on a rather sticky fur, and spattered all over with slick wetness. While beside her, her two orcs were still locked together, and Baldr—who had still been wearing a tunic—looked even messier than she did, his seed streaked all over the fabric, and on his reddened face, and even in his hair. And when Drafli slowly pulled away from him, that was even more mess, filling the air with its sweet, succulent scent.

There was an instant's silence in its wake, Baldr's breath inhaling deep—and then, out of nowhere, he *laughed*. The sound bright, and warm, and tinged with unmistakable, shuddering relief.

"So you truly betrayed me with all those Skai, all that time," he breathed at Drafli, "because you thought if you did not, your Skai god would *torture* me? Or *kill* me?!"

Drafli twitched and grimaced, and then cast a rather alarmed glance over his shoulder toward Skai-kesh—but Baldr was laughing again, and shaking his head, and rubbing at his sticky face. "You stubborn, single-minded Skai *prick*," he breathed, with a sigh. "You just *wait* until I tell Maria about this."

Drafli's eyes had gone even more alarmed than before, his lips pulling back to bare his sharp teeth, but Baldr just laughed again, and that was surely affection in his eyes, in his sticky hand reaching to spread wide against Drafli's chest.

"I was still better than the rest of them, though, ach?" he whispered, soft. "You wanted me the most?"

And that flare in Drafli's eyes was surely regret, and pain, and affection. *Ach, Pure-Heart,* he signed. *You were always my mate. My heart. Always.*

Baldr's smile back was so slow, so warm, it hurt Alma's chest—and she abruptly found herself smiling too, and sniffing, and wiping at her eyes. And now Baldr and Drafli were looking at her, Baldr with that same tilting affection, Drafli with a careful, studied watchfulness. Perhaps regretting all he'd betrayed just now, or how Alma had pushed him into all this— but she still felt herself beaming tearfully up at him, and clasping her hand against her heart.

"Thank you for bringing us here, my lord," she murmured at him. "I know Skai-kesh has blessed us, in this. I *know*."

She'd waved a shaky hand down at her own messy, sticky body, and then at Baldr's, too. And then at Drafli's glossy, half-hard heft, still jutting out over his trousers—and she felt herself flushing at the very sight of it, at the undeniable truth that he'd taken *both* of them with it just now. And oh, he knew she was thinking that, because he was smirking at her, and signing something she only half-understood.

"He says that Skai-kesh's blessing," Baldr murmured, the

laughter close in his voice, "is not gained only by taking a Skai prick up your arse, Bright-Heart."

Alma shuddered all over, because oh, the truth of Drafli saying that, acknowledging that, was almost too powerful to be borne—and above her, his smirk had slightly softened, his hands signing even faster than before.

"But he says that this was a good start," Baldr continued, quiet. "And you have shown yourself eager, and sweet, and true. And Skai-kesh bringing you to us"—Baldr cleared his throat—"mayhap this *was* a blessing, ach?"

Oh. And surely Drafli was just saying that, surely—or was he? Because he wouldn't speak false before Skai-kesh, Baldr had said, he wouldn't. And even that look in Drafli's eyes as he watched her, that look was almost indulgent, or maybe even *grateful*.

You are ours. You are safe. Your new home.

And Alma was smiling again, her eyes blinking, her head nodding. "I'm honoured, my lord," she whispered. "And if you really think this is a good start—maybe this could be a—a *new* start, for us? For all three of us? And we could all be honest with each other, with no more secrets? No more—"

No more vows, she'd been about to say, but she broke off just in time, her eyes still fixed to Drafli's face—and then darting to Baldr's, too. Because gods, she suddenly wished more than anything that she could go back in time, and undo all those secret promises she'd made. That she'd just dragged them into a room together, and blurted out everything, and made them face all their fears together, like the bonded, devoted mates they were.

But they could still start fresh now. They could. And oh, Baldr and Drafli were even glancing at each other, as if they were considering this... and *nodding*?

"Ach, Bright-Heart," Baldr finally said, his eyes shifting, shining, as the slow, stunning smile again spread across his mouth. "We shall make a new start. Together."

38

For the rest of the day, Baldr and Drafli kept to their word, and showed Alma a glorious, perfect new start.

It began with Drafli swiftly snatching up all their discarded clothes, and then again parading Baldr and Alma through the corridor—both of them fully bared this time, and liberally dripping his slick, sticky seed down their thighs. And as brazen as it was, Alma could only seem to find peace in it, and perhaps even a quiet, shimmering *pride*.

Her gorgeous, virile lord had finally, fully taken her, together with his equally gorgeous mate. And now he was blatantly flaunting the proof of his favour, and his ownership. His casual command over not only one worshipful Grisk, but two.

Drafli didn't even glance at the various orcs they passed this time, or acknowledge their envious, admiring glances—and only stopped once he'd reached the door to the baths. Waving both Baldr and Alma in before him, and even lightly slapping Alma's sticky bare arse on the way by.

The pool's heated water—now freshly replaced after the cleaning spree the day before—was yet another delight, and so was the way Drafli again tackled Baldr into it, wrestling and splashing together with bright, unfettered ease. And Baldr's laugh seemed to come easier than Alma had ever heard it, the sound echoing in beautiful rippling waves throughout the room.

Once they had both resurfaced near Alma, their faces flushed and dripping, even Drafli was smiling, his eyes glinting on hers. And then he and Baldr promptly launched into another round of swimming lessons, punctuated by frequent groping, and pouncing, and finally by Drafli and Alma lavishing Baldr together with their hands beneath the water. Until he came apart between them, howling at the ceiling, while Alma grinned at Drafli behind him, drinking up the sheer satisfaction in his eyes.

So beautiful, she signed at him, over Baldr's shoulder. *So perfect*.

And that was recognition in Drafli's eyes, *appreciation*, as he signed back. *So perfect*, he repeated, dipping his head to nip at Baldr's scarred neck. *So sweet*.

And perhaps they might have started it all over again, if not for the sudden arrival of several new orcs, striding into the room. Several Skai orcs, it turned out, come to speak with Drafli and Baldr, and Alma hung back uncertainly as they talked and signed together at the edge of the pool, speaking with low, intent-sounding voices.

But then, to Alma's genuine surprise, Drafli glanced over his shoulder, and waved her toward them—and once she complied, he actually *introduced* her. The pair of tall, lean, stern-faced orcs were two of his scouts—Killik and Halthorr—and the third, alarmingly huge with a massive bare chest and shoulders, turned out to be Maria's mate Simon, who had just returned from a scouting trip that morning.

"Ach, I have already heard much of you, woman," Simon said to Alma, with a toothy, gleeful smile. "I never should have *dreamt* a woman could trounce my coldest brother thus, ach?"

Drafli's eyes had dangerously narrowed on Simon, his

graceful, dripping-wet body leaping up out of the pool, as he signed something back at this Simon that looked rather like, *I'll trounce you, you great prick*. While beside Alma in the pool, Baldr barked a merry laugh, and then met her questioning glance with a broad, contagious grin.

"This means we are headed to the Skai arena, ach?" he explained, leaping out of the water too, and then reaching to pull her up after him. "They shall show us a fierce match, I ken."

This prediction turned out to be alarmingly accurate, Alma soon discovered, as she sat between Baldr and Maria in the Skai arena, her hands clapped over her mouth. While before them, Simon and Drafli punched and kicked and tackled each other with capable, calculated viciousness, until they were both covered with welts and cuts and bruises, and dripping *blood* on the freshly washed floor.

It was strangely engrossing, watching Drafli's lean body jump and kick and whirl with such effortless skill—but it was also highly terrifying, Alma's heart wildly leaping in her chest with every blow he took. Until finally Drafli signed for a break, and then stalked over toward her and Baldr, grasping for a waterskin that had been lying nearby.

You are distracting me, he signed sharply at Alma, before dumping out the waterskin over his face. *Deal with her, Pure-Heart.*

With that, he spun and stalked back toward Simon again, while beside Alma, Baldr was giving her a rather devious, calculating look. And without warning, he reached over to grab her by the waist, and unceremoniously plopped her into his lap.

"We cannot have you affecting Drafli's match, Bright-Heart," he informed her, as his warm hands slid purposefully up her thighs. "Mayhap this shall help cover the taste of your fear, ach?"

And oh, oh, he was spreading her thighs apart, his hand

slipping up beneath her skirt—and that was his finger, stroking up and down her hot, slippery crease. Making Alma shudder and gasp upon him, her wide eyes darting around to meet his, but he only grinned back, and gave a low laugh in her ear as one of those fingers slid slow and smooth inside.

"Ach, now that is better," he said, with satisfaction, as he inhaled against her ear. "Now look at our Skai, ach? He is so good, mayhap the best unarmed fighter in our mountain. That was *such* a clean kick—Simon had no hope of dodging it. Or that! *Destroy* him, Draf!"

Beside them, Maria was yelling equally impassioned curses toward Drafli, and gods, Alma could scarcely keep up at this point, between the feel of Baldr's hard, twitching body beneath her, that finger still absently toying inside her. While he himself still seemed fully engrossed in the match, shouting praises and surprisingly filthy profanities, as Drafli just kept showing off his deadly, devastating prowess before them.

A killer, Alma's deepest thoughts abruptly whispered, *he'd lied*—but she gripped tightly at Baldr's thigh beneath her, and firmly thrust that thought away. No. No. They were fixing this. A family. A fresh start. And truly, Drafli was breathtaking like this, it was almost a fluid, calculated dance, the way he was whirling around Simon with pointed intention, his arm snapping hard around Simon's throat—

"He got him!" Baldr shouted, and surely he would have leapt to his feet, had Alma not been still pinned on his lap. "He won, Bright-Heart! Is he not magnificent?!"

He truly was, and Alma felt herself smiling up at Baldr's flushed face with genuine, lurching fondness. And when Drafli swaggered over toward them, covered in sweat and blood and bruises, she smiled up at him, too, her shaky hands furtively signing. *You are stunning, Golden-Tongue.*

He answered this with a haughty-looking toss of his head—*I know*, it could have said—and then a blatant clutch of his hand at his swollen trousers. Saying, perhaps, *What are you going to do about it?*

Alma's breath caught, her eyes darting uncertainly around the busy room—and then settling on Simon, who had come over to grumble good-naturedly at Maria about cheating, show-off Skai brothers. And who was now glancing toward Drafli—toward Alma—with keen-eyed interest, his heavy brows rising.

But Drafli's cool, imperious eyes were still only on Alma, and she swallowed, and felt her face flushing as she signed up toward him. *May I suck you, Golden-Tongue?*

And though she knew it was just for fun now, Drafli's dismissive, casual shrug still shot straight to her groin, clamping her tight around Baldr's finger. And Baldr huffed a low, approving laugh as she reached for Drafli's trousers, and drew them downwards. Finding him already rock-hard and dripping-wet, that delicious white actually dangling from him in a long, succulent stream.

It led to her and Baldr again taking turns sucking him, lavishing him with lips and tongues, while Baldr's fingers kept playing inside her, and Drafli coolly stood over them and watched. And while Simon kept watching, too, looking almost as if he was *judging*, his bloody trousers visibly tented, his huge hand rubbing possessively against Maria's hair.

And gods, even Maria was watching too, her eyes still markedly suspicious, and she even muttered something at Simon about cheating Skai, indeed. To which Simon huffed a low laugh, his big hand clapping over her mouth, his head nodding with approval as Drafli abruptly poured out into Alma's gulping throat, flooding her with his thick, delectable sweetness.

"Ach, you ken you have my blessing," Simon told Drafli. "But if you wish to fully claim this woman as your mate, you must yet lead a rut upon her, before all our kin, as our clan's ways command. Ach?"

Drafli didn't immediately reply to that, his eyes intent on where Alma was still suckling at his softened, sputtering head. *Ach*, he finally signed at Simon, as he drew out of her. *I ken.*

And oh, did Drafli mean he might do that, he might really take her as his *mate*?!—and Alma's heart was desperately, furiously thudding, her eyes fixed to his dispassionate face. *Please*, she wanted to sign at him, *please, my lord, please...*

But then Drafli purposefully glanced away, to where yet more orcs were approaching. And then he'd pulled out and away, tucking himself into his trousers as he went to meet them, his hands swiftly signing while the orcs spoke in hushed, urgent voices.

"I ken Draf shall need to address this," Baldr said to her, his eyes narrowing as he watched. As Drafli actually reached a hand back toward them, clearly signing something at Baldr, while his other hand kept speaking to the orcs before him.

"Ach, we shall meet with him again soon," Baldr said now, his voice rather thin, as he frowned at where Drafli was now striding out of the room, the new orcs following close behind him. "Until then, Bright-Heart, mayhap you and I can spend the rest of the afternoon together? I could show you all my favourite places in the mountain, should you wish?"

Alma immediately agreed, of course, though she couldn't help giving Baldr a worried, sidelong glance as they stepped out into the corridor again. "Is... everything all right?" she asked. "This doesn't have anything to do with... Mr. Pembroke, does it?"

Baldr winced, his eyes briefly meeting hers—and it was like something ice-cold had been dumped down Alma's spine, her feet stumbling over the floor's smooth stone. "It does?" she gulped at him. "What—what's happened now? What does he want?!"

Baldr winced again, his steadying arm sliding around her back as he drew her to a stop beside the corridor's stone wall. "This foul man only wants what he cannot have," he said flatly. "And thus, he seeks more allies to flail and whine against this."

More allies. More *allies*?! "Like who?" Alma demanded, her voice shrill. "Tell me, Baldr. Please."

Baldr's other hand was rubbing intently at his nose, his eyes flicking to something beyond Alma's head. "Pembroke has gained promises from the province's ruling lord, Otto," he said, "to help him move against us, if you are not soon returned to him. In five days."

What?! Mr. Pembroke had gained the support of the province's actual *lord*, in this?! And Alma's fear was shouting and jangling, her eyes frantic on Baldr's face—on where Baldr was rapidly shaking his head, his hand now clamped over his nose.

"No, Bright-Heart," he breathed. "No. You must not fear this. Otto is a cousin to the captain's mate, and this is in turn only a ploy against her, ach? I told you, we have faced this man countless times before, and gained the upper hand each time. We shall face this again, with ease. So there is nothing to fear. You are ours, and you shall *never* return there. I shall *die* first."

Oh. The intensity in his voice and his eyes seemed to shudder away the coldness, drawing out Alma's exhale—and even stronger when both his hands came to her face, tilting it toward him. "You are *ours*," he said again, heated and low. "Drafli has even claimed you before his god. And if he next does this before his clan"—his throat bobbed—"they shall all defend this. All our mountain shall defend this, for you shall be our mate. *Forever*. Ach?"

Their mate. Alma's breath had caught, her body stilled under his touch, and the fear slipped a little further, lower. "Do you really," she gulped, "think Drafli will? You told me he would—never."

But Baldr's nod was just as fervent as his eyes, his hands spasming on Alma's face. "You have honoured him," he said. "Gained his trust. Shown him your true heart. And in this"—he breathed out, shaky—"you have shown me great kindness also. Thank you, my Bright-Heart."

Oh. Alma swallowed hard, blinking up at his glittering eyes—but the fear had settled even lower, and Baldr was nodding again, his mouth pulling into a wavering smile. "So you shall not fear this," he said thickly. "You shall trust us to face this. And now, you shall come with me, and first I shall show you the view from the mountaintop, ach?"

Alma felt her shoulders dropping, her own smile twitching back toward him. Flashing more beautiful warmth across his face, and a certain, stunning relief. And it was enough to shove back the last of the fear, the uncertainty, as Baldr drew her to a walk again, leading her in the direction of the Ash-Kai wing.

"Now, Bright-Heart," he said lightly, "you are not afraid of high places. Are you?"

Alma hadn't thought she was—but once Baldr had taken her up a narrow corridor, and led her out onto a grassy, sunny, windswept bluff, she felt her breath choking in her throat, her eyes staring in shock at the sweeping vista before them. At the mountain's sheer, rocky descent, the sprawl of surrounding forest below, the distant fields and settlements. All painted in rich deep yellow by the golden sun, just beginning to lower in the western sky.

"Good *gods*, Baldr," she breathed. "Your home is *spectacular*."

He'd come around behind her, his arms circling her waist, drawing her close against the strength of his chest. "Ach, it is," he said, quiet. "And now, it is your home, too."

Her home. *Home*. A truth that kept resonating as Baldr led her back inside again, his hand clasped tightly in hers—and then proceeded to take her on a delightfully intriguing tour of Orc Mountain. Focusing not on the multiple areas she already knew, but instead showcasing a variety of less-obvious nooks and tucked-away secrets.

And there were so *many*. Things like a room full of glowing mushrooms, presided over by a proudly grinning Joarr. A massive underground cistern of fresh water, just as large as the heated baths above. A stunning, ice-cold waterfall deep in the Skai wing, leading to an entirely hidden secret tunnel, connecting the Skai, Ash-Kai, and Ka-esh wings. And the Ka-esh wing turned out to be an entire marvel of its own, with an actual laboratory, and a beautiful, tucked-away sunroom.

"Do you mind stopping by the sickroom next?" Baldr asked Alma, his voice a little too casual, once they were heading toward the Grisk wing again. "There is just something I wish to check with Efterar."

Alma couldn't help a curious look toward him, but didn't argue, of course. And once Baldr and Efterar had disappeared into the adjoining back room together, Alma took a few moments to catch up with Kesst, who had apparently taken it upon himself to polish all the brass-framed beds to a brilliant, sparkling shine.

"They really look wonderful, Kesst," Alma said, as she found a spare rag, and joined in. "This whole room already looks so much better. I must say it was an excellent choice on my part, hiring you."

She shot him a teasing grin as she spoke, and in return Kesst gave an irritated roll of his eyes, even as he kept scrubbing harder at his bedpost. "It's something to do, I suppose," he said flatly. "I'm better off cleaning beds all day than I am curling up and wallowing in my ongoing existential dramas, you know?"

Alma's head tilted, her hand briefly stilling, her thoughts flitting backwards. To earlier that day—had it just been that morning?—when Tryggr had shared all those revelations about Kesst's past. About how Drafli had killed that horrible Ofnir orc who'd hurt him.

"Are you all right?" Alma asked Kesst, her voice lowering. "I'm sure that must have been a lot to digest, this morning."

"Just a bit," Kesst replied, clipped. "I mean, it's bad enough that I need to re-evaluate all my preconceptions about that infuriating Skai of yours. But add in the fact that they all knew about it? That loudmouth fuckboy *Tryggr* knew about it? I'm losing my edge, sweetheart, clearly."

Alma's rising sympathy was briefly thwarted by a surge of indignation, her hands come to her hips. "Tryggr is a *treasure*, Kesst," she retorted. "And of course you're not losing your edge, or any other such rubbish. I'm sure it was just far more comforting to—"

She bit her lip just in time, wincing—but Kesst's grimace was far too knowing, his eyes darkly glinting. "To keep using the Skai as a dumping ground for my pent-up bitterness?" he finished coolly. "Yes. Probably. Instead of putting it toward Ofnir himself—who's no help, being dead and all—or toward my own clan. Because they *didn't* protect me. They didn't do fuck all against that bastard. My own *brother* ran away without a word, and left me here for the *wolves*."

Kesst's voice had gone hard and thin, his hand frantically scrubbing at the bedpost, and Alma felt her stomach twisting as she watched. "But have you ever wondered," she said slowly, "whether maybe your brother might have been struggling, too? Maybe he had his own challenges you weren't aware of?"

Kesst's answer was half-snort, half-laugh, his head shaking. "Rathgarr was completely incapable of keeping his fat mouth shut," he said. "And that belligerent prick used to be one of the best fighters in this mountain. He would've given Grim a damned good run for Captain, if he'd stayed. No one was taking advantage of *him*."

The words were flat and angry, but Kesst's brief, bitter glance toward Alma showed his eyes glittering, his mouth tight. And now there was only sympathy, clamping in Alma's chest, choking at her throat.

"You miss him," she said, quieter. "Don't you?"

Kesst half-laughed again, but didn't meet her eyes this time. "Painfully on-point again, sweetheart," he said thinly.

"But Rath's probably dead. So there's no point in raging at him either, is there? Or in worrying that maybe—maybe you're right, and maybe I've been wrong about *him* all this time, too?!"

Kesst's voice had risen dangerously, his eyes blinking—and Alma was almost staggeringly grateful when Efterar and Baldr abruptly reappeared out of the back room. Efterar taking one sharp-eyed glance toward Kesst, and then striding over to embrace him from behind, pulling him close.

"Ach, you," he murmured in Kesst's ear. "You'll get through this. You *will*, my fierce-tongued flower."

Kesst's face had flushed a becoming shade of pink, and Alma could see his expression softening, his body sagging back into Efterar's arms. "Did you just," he said to Efterar, "call me a fierce-tongued *flower*?! I think you're still drunk on all that sleep, Eft."

Efterar, who was indeed looking more awake and alert than Alma had ever seen him, darted an embarrassed glance toward her, and then toward Baldr, who was now standing beside her. But Baldr was looking surprisingly cheerful, and flashing them all a rather cheeky grin.

"That is a very sweet pet name," he told Kesst. "My father oft spoke of how the orcs of old liked to use such names for their hearth-mates. He called my mother Sweet-Strike, for her scent felt like a felling blow whenever he came near."

It was the most Alma had ever heard Baldr voluntarily say about his parents, and her warm, curious glance toward him found him betraying a faint wince. "And your scent is much the same, Bright-Heart," he said quickly. "Now, do you wish to keep exploring?"

Alma did, of course, but she couldn't help hesitating, her eyes glancing back toward Kesst. Thinking, oddly, about what Tryggr had said, about Ash-Kai pretending they were fine, when they really weren't. About them not asking for the help they needed.

"Baldr," she said slowly, "did you ever meet Rathgarr? Kesst's brother?"

Kesst had abruptly stiffened in Efterar's arms, frowning darkly at Alma, but Baldr was already shaking his head. "No, Rathgarr had gone away before I came here," he said. "Why?"

"Well, everyone says you have the most skill with scents of any orc in the mountain," Alma said, a little shyly now. "Do you think—do you think you might be able to help find this Rathgarr? Or figure out if he's still alive, somehow?"

Kesst still wasn't moving, now staring at Baldr with unblinking eyes, while Baldr tilted his head, biting his lip. "Mayhap?" he said thoughtfully. "If we had something with Rathgarr's scent—clothing would be best—I could at least begin to cast about for it."

Alma beamed up at him, and then over at Kesst, who was still looking thoroughly dumbfounded. "That sounds wonderful, Baldr," she said. "Kesst, I don't suppose you have anything of Rathgarr's on hand?"

Kesst didn't immediately reply, and behind him, Efterar gave him a gentle little shake. "You put Rath's things down in the crypt, right?" he asked quietly, and when Kesst didn't reply, Efterar shook him again. "Right, Fierce-Flower?"

That seemed to twitch Kesst to life again, his eyes glancing with reluctant amusement toward Efterar. "Yes," he murmured back. "You ridiculous prick."

"That's Sweet-Prick to you, Fierce-Flower," Efterar countered. "Or maybe Great-Prick. Golden-Prick?"

Kesst gave a halfhearted smile, shaking his head, but behind him, Efterar was looking unmistakably relieved. "You really wouldn't mind doing that, Baldr?" he asked. "It would really mean a lot. To both of us."

But Baldr was already nodding, and waving it away. "Of course, I am happy to help," he said. "And mayhap Alma would indeed like to see the crypt next, ach?"

Usually, the thought of visiting a crypt wouldn't even be

slightly appealing, but Alma was surprised to find herself nodding, and meaning it. "Yes, I'd love to see everything you can show me," she told him. "And I'm sure it would be helpful to know for the Keeping, too."

Baldr replied with a broad, approving smile, and soon the four of them were walking down toward Orc Mountain's crypt together. It turned out to be a good distance beneath even the Ka-esh wing, and it was blocked by several large, cleverly engineered stone doors, upon which Baldr seemed to press specific combinations with his palms.

"The crypt is sacred to orcs, so the doors' patterns are marked by scent, to keep it safe from men," he told Alma, as he heaved one of the doors open, and lifted his lamp. "This will now lead us to the antechamber, where the newly dead are kept."

That sounded rather ominous, and Alma braced herself for unnerving sights, or scents, or both—but as Baldr led them into a large, rounded, high-ceilinged chamber, she was surprised to find that it was... lovely. Not dissimilar to the Skai shrine, really, with five arched doors cut into the rounded walls, and more stone, life-sized carvings in the middle of the room. And while the air smelled old and musty, it wasn't nearly as foul as Alma might have expected, either.

"Our newly dead are kept in sealed chests, until the scent has passed," Baldr explained, as they stepped deeper into the room. "And then they are moved to their clan's cells within the crypt. Each clan has its own ways in death, as we do in life."

Alma nodded, and then hesitated as she studied the chamber's stone carvings. There were only two—a tall, powerful, fully bared orc, with a huge pickaxe over his shoulder. And beside him, tucked under his arm, was an equally bared, voluptuous woman. A woman who looked a lot like... Akva?

"This is our father, Edom, the first of the orcs," said Baldr's quiet voice. "And his mate Akva, the mother of our five clans.

They watch over our newly dead, and see them into the afterlife."

Oh. Because these long, narrow boxes, radiating out from around them in a ring—these were *caskets*, with dead orcs inside, and studded between them were a smattering of large urns, as well. And blinking at the nearest urn, Alma was suddenly, viscerally reminded of the jar of ashes back at Mr. Pembroke's, tucked under her bed. Or perhaps now lost, gone, forever.

"I stuck Rath's stuff in the Ash-Kai cells," Kesst voice cut in, and he was already striding away, toward one of the doors carved into the rounded wall. "This way."

Alma exhaled, and followed along with Baldr and Efterar. Feeling foolishly, desperately grateful for the strength of Baldr's hand, slipping into hers and holding tight, as they stepped into another narrow passageway. But along the sides of this one, there were what looked like multiple stone bunks carved into the walls—and within each bunk, there was an orc-shaped form, tightly bound with thick strips of fabric and furs. Some bunks had more than one body inside—families or mates, surely—and some had small ones, too.

But Kesst didn't stop to look, and he kept his eyes straight ahead as he stalked deeper and deeper. Turning around one corner, and then another, until he halted beside a bunk that had two silent, still forms inside.

"Father," Kesst said flatly, to the larger of the two wrapped figures—and then he put his hand to the smaller one, resting against what was surely its head. "And—mother. And—"

He'd snatched up an urn that had also been sitting there, close at his mother's side. And then he just stared down at it, blinking, until Efterar silently reached over, and lifted the lid. Revealing what seemed to be a surprisingly mundane collection of possessions tucked inside—clothing, a leather purse, a gleaming steel dagger.

"Would this do?" Efterar quietly asked, pulling out what

looked like a tunic, and handing it over toward Baldr. "Can you smell Rathgarr's scent on that?"

Baldr was already bringing the tunic to his nose, inhaling slow and deep, his eyes gone distant—but then he nodded, and handed the tunic back. And this time it was Kesst who snatched it, stuffing it back down inside the urn, and shoving it into the bunk again.

"Thank you, Baldr," Efterar said. "And Alma. And now"—he slipped his arm around Kesst's hunched shoulders—"back to work, Fierce-Flower? Do you want to take bets on how many bloody Bautul will be waiting for us up there?"

Kesst reflexively sniffed, wiping at his eyes with a shaky-looking hand, but nodded. "A dozen," he said thickly. "No, a hundred. And Fierce-Flower sounds so ridiculous, Eft, you know I don't smell good at *all*."

"You do," Efterar said firmly, as he steered Kesst back down the way they'd come. "Like the sweetest, fairest bloom I have ever known. How about Fair-Bloom, then?"

"No, you Smart-Arse," Kesst's distant voice replied, but at least there was a faint hint of laughter in it. And then they were gone, and Alma and Baldr were left looking at each other, amidst an audience of silent, long-gone Ash-Kai.

And for a choked, stalled instant, Alma couldn't seem to shake the odd, twitching darkness of this place. The heaviness in it, maybe, or the grief. A grief that had perhaps been deepening in Baldr's eyes too, dragging against his shoulders.

"I don't suppose," Alma heard herself whisper, without at all meaning to, "you have family down here, too?"

Baldr's mouth twisted, his head nodding—and then he guided Alma back out, into the larger, rounded antechamber. And then into another one of the doors, this one with a similar narrow corridor, and more bunks carved into the stone walls.

But here, the bunks were all larger, because most of them had multiple sets of remains. Surely orcs, and women, and children, and relatives, all lying close together in death, as families.

At least, until Baldr halted beside a bunk—and within this one, there was just a single wrapped form, lying silent and still.

"Here," Baldr said, his voice thin. "My father. Barden, of Clan Grisk."

Oh. Alma looked at the bunk for a long, stilted moment, and then she put her hand to her heart, and gave a little bow. "It is an honour, Barden of Clan Grisk," she said, low. "Thank you for giving us your son."

It ought to have helped, maybe—but Baldr's eyes were still strangely dark, his mouth grim. And there was still something to his reluctance around this, something important, and Alma studied him for a long moment, felt her heart skipping beats in her chest.

"How did your father die?" she whispered. "You said you and your mother were attacked at your home in the east, right? Was he killed then, too?"

Baldr's hand jerked up roughly between them, signing side-ways, saying, *no*. "My father was killed in a human attack on a Grisk camp," he said, "when I was mayhap thirteen summers old. But I did not learn this"—he swallowed—"until many years later, when the captain finally found us, and told me."

What? Alma stared at Baldr, her head tilting, her hand clenching against his. "You mean," she breathed, "you didn't *know*? That your own father was dead? For *years*?"

Something briefly flared in Baldr's eyes, and was gone again. "No," he said, his voice cracking. "He came every winter, ach? But that winter, we waited, and waited—but he never came. Not then, or the next winter, or the next, or..."

His voice trailed off, and Alma's disbelief was surging, the vision of a lonely, waiting, grieving Baldr twisting horribly through her thoughts. "So you didn't know," she gulped, "if your father was dead... or if he'd just... *left*?"

And oh, oh, she'd surely hit the truth of it, Baldr's wince contorting his mouth. "No," he replied, his voice hard. "And I know he loved my mother, but it was not always—easy, between them, either. And he promised, if anything ever befell him, that his clan—his perfect, precious Grisk clan—should surely come for us, and help us. But no Grisk never came. *Ever*. And mayhap they truly could not find us, mayhap they thought they would be followed, mayhap all his closest brothers were dead too, but"—he gulped for air—"I have never been able to learn why. *Never*."

Cold, miserable chills were streaking up Alma's back—what a horrifying, appalling uncertainty to live with—and she frantically searched Baldr's eyes. "But you said—your captain came," she breathed. "Grimarr came. Right?"

Baldr's mouth contorted again, and he jerked a nod. "He came as oft as he could," he continued, without inflection. "But he was always too busy to stay, ach? He wished to bring us back here, to safety—but my mother refused, again and again. And I—I ken it was because of the Grisk, ach? She could not bear to face this clan—the clan my father so trusted, the clan he spent his *life* serving—after they *failed* us. She did not wish to hear their excuses. Their apologies. Their *cowardice*."

Oh. Oh, gods, oh how *devastating*, and that surely explained everything, *everything*. Why Baldr avoided his clan the way he did. Why he wanted to be Skai, rather than Grisk. And maybe—maybe even why he hadn't trusted Varinn to help him, back when Alma had first come here, because the Grisk had always failed him before. Even his own *father* had failed him.

"And then we were found by men," Baldr said woodenly, his eyes closing. "And my mother was—killed. And I was defeated, and left for dead in the river. I tried to help her, I fought so hard, but I—I failed. I was useless. Worthless. A pathetic, shameful *coward*, just like the rest of my clan."

The words struck against Alma like blows, each one a dizzying, sickeningly familiar pain. Because gods, she'd said those things herself, she'd thought them about herself, and she couldn't bear for Baldr to think them, she couldn't—

"No, Baldr," she gulped, and she was suddenly, frantically

shaking her head, whipping her hair in her face. "No. That is not true. It isn't. There is no shame. That was *not* your fault. And no one is worthless, or useless. *No one.*"

But it wasn't even slightly working, Baldr was shaking his head too, his eyes far too bright. So Alma gulped for more air, grasped for both his hands, gripped them as tightly as she could.

"I—I lost m-my mother too," she said, speaking too quickly, stumbling over the words. "And I also did everything—*everything*—I could. I did all the work, I took on all the debt, I cared for her night and day. And I—I failed too. She still died, and I'll never, *ever* get her back."

Baldr's throat convulsed, his eyes still so painfully bright on hers, and Alma dragged in breath, courage. Thought of Kesst, of Drafli, of penance, guilt, absolution...

"But you wouldn't tell me it's my fault," she gulped at him. "Would you? Just like it isn't Drafli's fault, because he failed with his mate. It's not our fault that the world is a cruel and unjust place sometimes. It *isn't.*"

Her voice was so fervent it shook, her hands shaking on his, too. "And it might even be easier to blame ourselves, isn't it?" she managed. "So much easier, than blaming the people we loved, after they're gone. But maybe—maybe you *are* still angry sometimes too, right? Because maybe you'll never get those answers—not from the horrible people who took your mother from you, and most of all not from her. You'll never understand why she stayed. Why she didn't do more to protect you. Why she never just *told* you, and—"

And oh gods, now Alma was sniffing, and rubbing painfully at her leaking eyes. "And she's still gone forever," she whispered. "And you won't even get her ashes back, from the person who hurt her the most, who's really at fault. And how do you ever move past that? How, Baldr? What do you *do*?"

And was she asking him, she was, but surely he didn't have an answer, either, blinking back at her with such glimmering, miserable eyes. His own chest erratically heaving, his shaky hand swiping hard at his wet cheeks, as his gaze darted up, toward—

Toward *Drafli*? And oh, oh gods, it was Drafli, stalking tall and silent up the narrow passage toward them. His dark, disapproving eyes flicking back and forth between them as he approached, as if he were about to scold them, or judge them, or—

And then he strode straight between them, and dragged them both into his arms. Circling them tight in his powerful, almost-painful grip, pressing their heads close against him. Making them feel his certainty, his command, his safety.

It was almost as though it released something, broke something, deep in Alma's chest—and beside her, Baldr was surely weeping too, his head buried in Drafli's shoulder. But Drafli didn't move, didn't sign, didn't complain—only stood there and held them, his strong hand now curving firmly around the back of Alma's neck.

And it... helped. Gods, it helped so damned much, just feeling him here, settling the chaos, the grief, back into its place again. Because their lord was here, he would do anything to protect them, and keep them happy, and *safe*.

A new start. *A family*.

And in it, somehow, Alma found the courage to lift her wet eyes, to meet Drafli's impassive, unreadable gaze. And maybe even to attempt a small smile, full of relief, of gratefulness.

"Did *you* know your mother, my lord?" Alma heard herself ask, her voice still wavering. "Or your father?"

Above her, Drafli audibly snorted, his hand moving from her neck to sign an answer—and Baldr had tilted his head to watch, his mouth slightly twitching.

"Draf says he did not know his mother," Baldr replied, hoarse. "But he says he well knew his father, and he is glad that prick is dead. And that if he ever dares to come back"—Baldr's mouth twitched higher—"Draf will be glad to kill him again, upon first sight."

Alma blinked at Baldr, once—and then oh, gods, she burst into sudden, helpless laughter. The sound giddy and shrill, carrying bizarrely through the crypt, her body wildly shaking against Drafli's solid strength. While Drafli's hand again just came back to her neck, his fingers spreading wide, as though nothing out of the ordinary was occurring.

But once the laughter had faded, in its place was again that odd, stilted peace, settling Alma's breath, stilling against her heart. And it felt so instinctive, so natural, to again glance up at Drafli, to give him another slow, affectionate smile.

He didn't quite smile back, but it was close, softening his mouth, warming his eyes. And when he silently led her and Baldr back through the crypt, it didn't feel nearly as dark or oppressive as it had before. Instead, Alma found herself eyeing Drafli's straight bare back, the prowling certainty in his steps. Drinking up the rising, whispering awareness that surely, their devil wasn't done with them yet—and beside her, Baldr was even biting his lip, his still-wet eyes half-lidded on Drafli's shoulders.

Drafli didn't look back as he led them up through the narrow corridors again, into the Ka-esh wing, and then the Grisk, and the Skai. And finally, back toward their familiar room—and before Alma had taken a single step inside, Drafli's tall body lunged for Baldr, and hurled him onto the bed.

Baldr's moan tore through the air, harsh with shock and hunger and surely relief. And he didn't even try to resist as Drafli tore off his clothes, tossing them to the floor, and then beckoned Alma closer, with a sharp wave of his hand.

Undress, he signed at her, as he shoved his hips between Baldr's bared, sprawled thighs. *And come here.*

Oh, gods. Alma frantically nodded, first shucking her own clothes with fumbling fingers, and then lurching toward the bed. And before she could ask Drafli what he wanted, he'd grasped her by the waist, swung her up over Baldr, and settled her down upon him. So that she was facing toward Drafli rather than Baldr, with her thighs straddled wide over Baldr's hard abdomen, his swollen, gold-tipped length already flaring up against her parted, clutching crease.

Baldr had gasped and shuddered beneath her, his big warm hands gripping at her hips, while Drafli's hungry eyes dropped to look—and oh, *oh*, now his hand had dropped too, catching with proprietary ease against Baldr's still-bobbing shaft, and guiding it upwards. Notching its dripping gold head into Alma's swollen throbbing heat, and then spreading his hands over Baldr's on her hips, and driving her down deep upon him.

Alma and Baldr cried out in unison, Baldr's strength vibrating and spurting hard inside her, while she desperately clamped around him. And while Drafli just kept watching with cool, glinting satisfaction, one hand now dropping to circle around Baldr's bollocks, while the other signed an order toward Alma.

Ride him, it meant. *Hard.*

The heated relief kicked and flared, and Alma instantly obeyed. Plunging herself down again and again upon Baldr's thick, powerful invasion, while Drafli kept standing so close before her, watching. One hand still fondling between his mate's legs, while the other one slipped up to circle casually around Alma's neck, his clawed thumb stroking at her swallowing throat. And she felt herself leaning into the touch, into that sharp, shocking scrape of his deadly claw. He could so easily silence her, kill her—but he wouldn't, he never, ever would, and she was so sure of it now, she almost felt dizzy with its truth. She was his. Theirs. For *always*.

And it felt so instinctive, so natural, for her own hands to slide downwards, too. First feeling the hard strokes and tugs of Drafli's long fingers against his mate's bulging bollocks, and then slipping even lower. Deep between Baldr's legs, now, to where she'd never touched him before, not yet—and she could hear his gasps fraying as she softly, carefully caressed him, finding that secret, shuddering heat. Feeling it clutch and caress against her in return, almost as if it truly wanted her *inside* him—

And when she nudged her finger a little further, she could feel him actually flexing *around* her, drawing her deeper. Into where it was hot, tight, and astonishingly smooth, pure sweet silk gripping against her touch. And Alma gasped aloud as she felt herself gripping against his body inside her in return, her eyes fixed wide and shocked on Drafli's intently watching face.

"Oh," she gasped, her throat convulsing against Drafli's still-pressing claw, as her delving finger slipped a little deeper inside his mate. "He's so tight. So hot. So *hungry*."

Drafli's nod was curt, knowing, satisfied—and Alma felt his hand slipping downwards too, prying his mate wider open. So that Alma could sink her finger even deeper into that hot silken grip, all the way to the knuckle, while Baldr choked and flared beneath her, around her, *inside* her.

Drafli was watching again, his mouth smirking, and Alma could feel his hand shifting again, settling closer. So that his fingers—two of them, both with their claws pulled back— could nudge close against hers, prodding at Baldr's tight heat. And then they sank inside too, hard and purposeful, making Baldr again flail and shout, his body clamping reflexively against them.

Keep riding, Drafli mouthed at Alma, because oh, she'd somehow forgotten that, caught in the sheer power in this— but moving again, like this, with Baldr inside her, and her and Drafli together inside *him*, felt even more surreal, more impossible. The sensation fierce and wheeling, flaring out from every plunge of Baldr's strength within her, with how he clutched back against their fingers with the exact same rhythm. How his hands now clenched almost painfully on Alma's hips, his voice moaning in a steady stream behind her.

And when Drafli swiftly pulled out first his fingers, and

then Alma's, it was as though she could read his intent, without him signing at all. Her eager hands opening his mate for him, pulling him wide, showing off that open, tempting heat for his glinting, approving eyes.

Drafli gracefully shucked his trousers, releasing his own bobbing, dripping heft, and slicking it all over with a few easy swipes of his hand—and then he grasped Baldr's thighs, tilting his arse further upwards, as he leaned closer. Catching his scarred, glossy head on that open sweetness between Alma's fingers, on where he belonged—and then stroking in, smooth and sure and deep.

Baldr's desperate shout seemed to reverberate inside Alma, all around her—and then again, as Drafli eased into a swift, forceful rhythm. Pushing Baldr's hips up further with each thrust, until Alma bodily sank backwards upon him, her back pressed flush to Baldr's sweaty, heaving chest. While Drafli only shifted closer, now kneeling on the bed between their splayed legs, his eyes flashing with hunger, his lean body driving with fluid, furious ease.

It was nearly impossible for Alma to move like this, stuck and pinned upon her lord's mate, while he took his pleasure above them. And every sharp slam of Drafli's hips seemed to drive Baldr harder and fuller into her, almost as if he were the one doing this to her. As if *Drafli* were the one inside her, opening her up, pouring her full of his certainty, his safety.

And as Alma jolted and juddered beneath him, searching his glittering eyes, it belatedly, hazily occurred to her that this, too, was still about... *that*. About him calming them, comforting them, reminding them who they belonged to. And even doing it like this meant that he could see them both, he could touch them both—and yes of course his hand should drop behind Alma, to grip at Baldr's neck, to pin him firmly to the bed. And yes, Alma could feel Baldr shuddering harder beneath her, his hips jerking up, his breath ragged and hot in her ear, against her throat—

And wait, that was Drafli's other hand, guiding Alma's head further back too, closer into the heat of Baldr's mouth. Into the tentative, careful touch of Baldr's *teeth*, oh hell, and Drafli surely didn't mean that, or did he, he was signing another order, pounding in deeper. *Drink her, Pure-Heart, drink our woman up.*

And even as Baldr's teeth bit deep, flashing yet more furious chaos across Alma's already-screaming thoughts, there was no unease, no fear. Only the dazzling, utterly surreal wonder of this moment, impaled between two huge, powerful orcs, her body arched and wide open, giving all it would give, all they could take. And those teeth in her skin, that hot mouth clamped upon her, that steady series of hungry swallows in her ear, suddenly seemed a crucially important rite, or perhaps even a vow...

And Drafli was still here, leaning over her, watching. His long black hair now hanging loose around his flushed face, his lips parted, his breath slowly inhaling. His eyes shifting and flaring on the sight, on his mate's teeth in Alma's neck—and it was only right, only natural, for her to slide her shaky hand up, into the silk of his hair. And then to draw his mouth down too, guiding it to the other side, to where she most craved it, needed it...

And Drafli didn't resist. Didn't shudder or flinch away. Only came forward as Alma wished, smooth and easy and eager. Until his mouth, and his own sharp teeth, had also settled close and deadly against her skin. Against the same place, perhaps, where he'd first almost done this, back when he'd threatened her, what felt like years before...

But everything was different now, everything, and Alma gasped as she felt his teeth stroking, scraping, searching. Taking their time, finding their place, perhaps even making her feel it. Making her wait, even as his mate kept desperately gulping on the other side, because he was still the one in charge, he was her devil, her lord—

His bite clamped down strong and deep, far more painful than Baldr's had been—but oh, the pain was already skittering away, scattering into a raging, whirling pleasure. Into the staggering truth of being locked between two orcs, trapped beneath their heat and their teeth. Being made part of this, part of them, her very life's essence filling their gulping throats, while their bodies drove up harder and tighter. Coiling them together, binding them deeper, stretching so taut they might shatter—

And then the strength inside Alma jolted—and exploded. Surging out deep inside her with hot, frantic spurts of slick molten heat, as Baldr's low, shuddering moan vibrated into Alma's actual skin—and then oh, oh, Drafli was moaning into her too, his own body flooding his mate with enough power that Alma could feel it all through her, inside her, warming her blood, her womb, her heart.

When it finally finished, the world seemed to be spinning, twirling slow but steady above Alma's blank, blinking eyes. And she could feel Drafli shifting, his mouth carefully detaching, easing away from her—and then the feel of his soft, slippery tongue. Licking, so gentle and careful, against the wounds he'd made.

And once he'd seemed satisfied, he nudged at Baldr, even giving a harsh little snarl, until those teeth reluctantly pulled away, too—and again there was again the touch of Drafli's tongue, stroking, caressing, approving.

Alma felt herself sinking into his care, his safety, the world again slipping away—until she felt Drafli leaning back, and easing sideways. Settling himself onto the bed beside them, before his strong hands reached for her waist, and eased her off toward him, too.

It released the hold between her legs, spewing bubbling heat in its wake—but wait, that was the feel of a cloth, stroking gentle against her, mopping up the worst of the mess. And then something was nudging against her mouth—a waterskin—and

The Maid and the Orcs

Alma eagerly, frantically drank, gulping the cool liquid until it was gone.

And then, somehow, all was still. At peace. With Alma still tucked between her two orcs, facing toward her lord's bare chest, while her beloved's warm, sticky body curled close behind her, his arm settling heavy over her waist.

It was contentment unlike anything she had ever known, and she drifted into it, quiet, away—until there was a shift of her lord's body against her, a twitch of purposeful movement. And wait, that meant—surely it meant—he was going to take her away again, he always took her away, but—

But when her bleary eyes blinked up at him, she found he wasn't looking at her at all. Instead, his head above hers was nudged against his mate's, because they were... kissing. Their dripping-red lips and tongues softly caressing, licking, tasting each other—and in an odd, shivery shock of awareness, Alma realized they were tasting *her*. They were licking her off each other, oh gods above, and it was quite possibly the most beautiful thing she had ever witnessed in her life.

But even better was the way her lord's hand dropped to her head, tucking it back down against his chest. *Sleep, Bright-Heart*, his hand signed, before her eyes, even as his mouth kept licking the taste of her off his mate's lips. *Stay.*

Stay. And surely he didn't mean it. Surely. But his strong hand had once again come to her head, guiding it closer against him, against the warm skin of his chest, the steady thud of his own lifeblood within it. Stay. Stay.

Stay.

And with a full heart, a rippling impossible hope, Alma nodded, and obeyed.

39

A lma slept long and deep that night, curled close into the safety of her orcs. Knowing, once and for all, that they'd fixed this. They'd faced this. A family.

And when she finally blinked awake again, she found herself still there. Still curled up against Drafli's lean, warm body, while Baldr faintly snored behind her, his heavy arm still slung over her waist.

Alma stayed there for a few long, silent breaths, while her happiness seemed to bubble up, nearly enough to burst—when beside her, Drafli's solid body shifted. Leaning down and sideways, perhaps, and he couldn't be leaving her now, he couldn't—

But no, there was only a sharp flick, and then a flare of light. He'd lit a candle, illuminating the room with a soft glow, and now he was sinking onto his back on the bed beside her again, his long body stretching as he yawned.

It felt oddly, powerfully intimate, suddenly, waking up here in bed with him, knowing Drafli had lit the candle for her. And she felt herself give him a slow, grateful smile, her hand moving up to sign toward him.

Thank you, she told him. *For all of this.*

He shrugged against the bed, and his hand lifted up, signing too. *No, I thank you*, it said. *This is... good.*

This meant *them*, his hand doing a fluid little circle that encompassed Alma, and Baldr, and him—and the warmth seemed to bubble even higher in Alma's chest as she kept beaming at him, smiling so wide it hurt. It was *good*, he'd said. A family.

Pure-Heart tell you of the Grisk, last eve? Drafli asked now, signing slowly enough that Alma could follow. *His mother? His father?*

Alma nodded, and grimaced. *Yes*, she signed back. *It was awful. Poor Pure-Heart.*

Drafli nodded too, his eyes sliding up toward the ceiling. *It is good for him to speak of this*, he signed. *Mayhap this will help.*

Oh. And looking at Drafli's sharp profile, now with a faint tightness around his mouth, Alma wondered, for perhaps the first time, if speaking about his own past—or at least, acknowledging it with them—had maybe helped him, too. And if maybe Baldr had been right, and Drafli doing all this with her—finding a way to trust a human again—really had served as his vicarious vengeance, after all. If it really *had* given him a way to move beyond his anger, and his grief.

Something seemed to be knocking against Alma's ribs, her eyes blinking on Drafli's impassive face. And before she could start weeping here before him, she flashed him another hopeful little smile, her hand again raising up between them, catching his gaze.

I think so too, she told him. *And maybe some day, Pure-Heart will even dress like a Grisk, too. Make you happy.*

Drafli instantly angled her a dark, disapproving look—though Alma didn't miss the movement of his hand, casually adjusting something in his trousers. And wait, he was adjusting his rapidly swelling *bulge*, the transparent devious bastard—and Alma choked down a laugh as she grinned at him, shaking her head.

I see you, Golden-Tongue, she signed at him. *You would love that.*

Drafli made a face at her, but his mouth was very slightly quirking, too. *His clothes are so vexing*, he signed back. *Always mess. Always in my way.*

Alma was still grinning at him, and also nodding, because Baldr's clothes *were* quite annoying, she had to admit. *Pure-Heart would be so pretty in Grisk clothes, right?* she signed at him. *Maybe you will give him more jewels, too.*

Drafli arched a cool eyebrow at her, surely meant to be dismissive—but its effect was thoroughly blunted by how his hand was again adjusting his trousers. To which Alma choked back another laugh, again shaking her head, even as she felt her eyes searching his.

But you will, won't you? she signed at him. *Maybe here, like you promised him?*

She'd dropped a finger to brush against her own nipple, and Drafli followed the movement, his brows rising even higher. *Mayhap you like this too, Bright-Heart*, he signed. *You wish for my gold in your teats?*

Alma's desperate, reflexive shudder surely answered for her, and Drafli's mouth again quirked up, into something very like a smile. And gods, Alma was suddenly hot and flushed all over, her gaze again darting down to that bulge in his trousers. To where his hand was blatantly stroking it now, his mouth still smirking at her, and she'd already raised her hand to start signing at him, *May I—*

When behind her, there was a yawn, and then the feel of Baldr shifting and stretching, his arm circling tight around her waist. "Ach, now *this* is a way to awaken," he murmured, close against her hair. "Were you about to suck out Draf's morning seed for us, Bright-Heart? He is an ogre all day if this is not dealt with, you ken."

Alma laughed, the sound bright and merry, and wriggled a little closer into Baldr's delicious, heated touch. "Do you really mean our devil could be *worse*?" she murmured, grinning at how Drafli was glaring at them, with a not-quite-genuine frown. "Of course, I would do anything to avoid such a dire fate. And then maybe"—she twisted to smile at Baldr—"*you* could have a turn?"

Baldr was already smiling back down at her, his eyes almost painfully warm on hers, shimmering with bare, fervent affection. "Ach," he replied, soft, as his finger gently stroked down her cheek. "This should be—"

But then he broke off there, his eyes gone abruptly, strangely still—and his body against her had stiffened, too. Gone hard, tight, *wrong*.

Alma blinked uncertainly up toward him, her mouth opening to speak—when Baldr suddenly snapped his face down into her neck, and inhaled. Filling his chest with sharp, inexplicable purpose, and when Alma darted a glance toward Drafli, she found him looking just as wary as she felt. His eyes rapidly narrowing on Baldr as he shoved himself upright on the bed, without any of his usual gracefulness.

"What is it, Baldr?" Alma asked, breathless, wavering. "Is— is something wrong?"

Baldr's taut body twitched against her, and he recoiled back too, away—and oh, something was wrong, it *was*. His jaw was set, his mouth contorting, his eyes shifting between something that might have been joy, or maybe also shock, or grief, or... guilt.

What is it, Drafli was signing, the movements tense and forceful before Baldr's eyes. *Tell us. Now*.

And yes, surely that was guilt now, shining brightest in Baldr's eyes, as he shot a glance toward Drafli, and then squeezed his eyes shut. His throat swallowing, his hand coming up, rubbing hard against his twisting mouth.

"You are... with child, Bright-Heart," he finally breathed, thick, through his fingers. "I can smell him upon you. Your... your *son*."

Oh. Oh. Her *son*. That single, plummeting word so powerful, so impossible, spoken with such hushed, palpable reverence. Alma was with child. Pregnant. With their *son*?!

"Truly?" she gulped at Baldr, at Drafli, her heart suddenly
kicking, and then roaring to life in her chest. "You mean it? You
can really *smell* him?!"

And in no world, at no time, had Alma ever fully imagined
how this moment, this revelation, might feel. How she'd shot
up to sitting too, her hands wildly wringing in midair before
clasping against her belly. Her heart still thundering in her
ears, her blood on fire, while the joy—the pure, ringing
elation—swarmed out her throat, escaping in a bright, astonished laugh.

"Truly?" she said again, her eyes now frantically darting
between Baldr and Drafli's oddly stiff faces. "We—we really
made a *son* together? Oh good gods, oh Akva, oh"—her shaky
hands wiped at her leaking eyes—"oh, we're going to be a
family. Together."

And she was beaming at them, and somehow sobbing too,
and clutching her hands tighter against her belly. They'd done
it, she was going to give them this, they'd fixed everything,
together, *forever*. And she couldn't seem to stop laughing, or
perhaps still weeping, as she smiled tearfully at her beautiful
orcs, her lovers, her son's own *fathers*.

But... wait. Because Baldr was smiling back at her, with sure
affection, indulgence, flitting through his eyes—but stronger
still, so much stronger, was that guilt. The... *regret*. And Alma
could see his throat bobbing, hard and meaningful, as his eyes
again flicked toward Drafli.

And. Drafli—Drafli wasn't smiling at all. And instead, his
eyes were glittering narrow slits, snapping between Alma and
Baldr—and without warning, he lurched downwards on the
bed, and put his face to Alma's belly. And now inhaling hard
and deep, while the warmth flooding Alma's chest seemed to
catch, curdling dark and uncertain. Drafli... wasn't happy? He...

hadn't wanted this, after all? Had he—had he changed his mind?

"What," Alma choked at Baldr. "What is it. Did I—did I do something wrong? Or is there something wrong with—with my smell? With—our *son*?"

And oh gods, the fear of that thought suddenly seemed to crash over all else, crushing the last of her happiness beneath its strength—and before her, Baldr clapped his hand to his nose, his head whipping back and forth. "Nothing is amiss, Bright-Heart," he said, his voice badly wavering. "Nothing at all. Your scent is perfect. *Perfect*. It is only—"

But he broke off there, his head still shaking, his eyes again squeezing shut—while before Alma, Drafli was rising again. The movement slow and menacing, his teeth bared, his eyes vicious and flashing with rage. And he was looking at her, he was furious with *her*, and why, why, *why*—

"What, Baldr," she gulped, her eyes wide and terrified on Drafli. "Please, Baldr, tell me!"

And finally, finally, Baldr looked at her, and squared his shoulders. As if he were facing their demise, their *doom*.

"Your son," he whispered, "is not mine. It is—Drafli's."

lma's son was... Drafli's.

Drafli's?! Her son was *Drafli's*?!

The sheer, sweeping shock seemed to strike Alma to stillness, her eyes seized on Baldr's wan, grim face. Her son was—Drafli's? But—*how*?! When Drafli had never, *ever* taken her that way, not once, while Baldr had done so again, and again, and again?!

"That's—" she began, faltered—when suddenly, Drafli flew into motion. His lean, deadly body flashing up over her, like a raging avenging god—and then she was crashing back onto the bed, hard enough that her breath slammed from her lungs. While something heavy and powerful circled tight around her neck, pinning her to the fur.

Alma fought for air, for words, but there was nothing, nothing. Nothing but Drafli, oh gods, leaning down over her, with murderous, terrifying rage screaming through his eyes.

"How you do this," he croaked at her, as he brandished his other hand before her face, his claws curving and lethal, a stark, horrifying threat. "How. Tell me!"

Alma was staring, flailing, panicking, there was still no air, no possible way to escape, to speak—when oh, thank the gods,

Baldr's big body rammed into Drafli's, shoving him sideways on the bed. Not enough to fully release Drafli's grip on Alma's neck, but enough that she could try to breathe again, her throat coughing and convulsing as she dragged in long, rattling gulps of air.

"I—I didn't," she gasped, between coughs. "I didn't. I swear to you. I *swear*."

And there were tears running down her face, her coughing throat now also choking on its sobs, and she could even feel something hot and sticky—her blood?—trickling down her neck. But it didn't matter, none of it mattered, but the sickening, harrowing sight of Drafli's betrayal, and his rage. And he might have even lunged for her again, if not for Baldr again shoving between them, his elbow slamming into Drafli's belly, his claws actually swiping hard against Drafli's cheek.

"Stop!" he bellowed, straight into Drafli's face. "Stop this, *now*. I did it, Draf. *I* did it!"

He did it. Those bizarre, unthinkable words shuddering the room to a dangling, menacing silence, broken only by the ragged sounds of Alma's coughing, rattling breaths. And Drafli's body had frozen in place, his eyes now fixed to Baldr's, his face a haggard, hollow-looking mask.

"I did it," Baldr repeated, in a rush. "I mean—not making *your* son, Draf, but I stopped—mine. After we—after we first made the deal. I—I went to Efterar."

The silence kept twisting, churning, tangling between them—and Baldr gulped for another breath, rubbed his hand hard against his nose. "You ken how I—I fought Varinn, how this near halted his seed," he continued. "And then Efterar himself did this, to help Varinn heal. So after this, I asked Efterar to do this. For *me*."

What? Baldr had—he had purposefully gone to Efterar, and asked him to prevent him having any sons? Because Baldr... hadn't wanted a son? With... with *her*?

Alma's hand had clapped over her still-coughing mouth,

while something plunged deep in her belly. Baldr truly hadn't wanted this? He hadn't wanted... *her*? To the point where he'd secretly made sure he would never, ever have a child with her? So he could—what? What? Leave her? Or—or send her—away?

The raw, ragged sob seemed to escape Alma's throat on its own, her face crumpling into her hands. Oh, gods, oh please, she had pushed Baldr into this, he hadn't even wanted it, hadn't wanted her, oh gods what had she *done*—

"Wait," cut in Baldr's voice, close and frantic, and she could feel his hands trembling as they found her face, and tilted it toward him. "Wait, Bright-Heart. No. Do not weep thus, *please*. It was not that I did not wish for this, or for you. I did wish for this. I *did*."

Alma was blinking at him, staring at him, desperately clinging to that fervour in his voice—and his head was furiously nodding, his face deathly pale, his eyes alarmingly bright. "I longed for you, and for our son," he breathed. "Our family. But I only"—he swallowed, the sound audible in his throat—"I only wished to be sure of this first, ach? Of us."

Of us. His eyes darting sideways at Drafli as he spoke, brief but unmistakable—and oh. Oh. The comprehension finally swarming, spinning the room before Alma's eyes. Baldr hadn't been sure that *Drafli* had meant it. Or, perhaps, that Drafli would be able to follow through with it. Baldr had done it to protect his mate, to give him more time, a way out if he needed it.

And maybe—maybe he'd even done it to protect Alma, too. To make sure that Drafli truly wanted her. That they could truly be a family.

And as much as it hurt that Baldr hadn't told her—that he'd kept this a secret—Alma could at least understand why he'd done it. Why he hadn't wanted to rush. And perhaps even why he hadn't told them. Because Drafli had been so damned adamant about all this, he might very well have ignored Baldr's concerns, and pushed him into it anyway.

Just like, perhaps, he... *had*.

And glancing at Drafli's drawn face, Alma could see that he'd followed that, just as clearly as she had. Baldr hadn't trusted Drafli to listen to him, to respect his decisions—so he'd lied to him, to both of them. And worst of all, he'd been justified in it. Hadn't he? Not only because of Drafli, but because of...

"I never meant it to be permanent," Baldr was saying, still speaking far too quickly. "In truth, I asked Efterar to remove it yesterday, ach? And I *never* thought you would take her yourself, Draf, at least without me there to witness this, so I thought—"

But now Drafli was finally lurching into motion, signing at Baldr, again and again. *I didn't*, his hand snapped. *I didn't. I didn't.*

"Ach, I ken," Baldr replied back, his own hand snapping sideways, his voice wavering. "I can still *smell*, Draf. It was surely just—from the shrine yesterday, ach? When you took her as you did. You were not careful with your seed, and I did not think to speak of this, and now—"

And now his hand was giving a shaky, dismissive wave toward Alma, toward their son. And Alma felt her own trembling hands curving closer against her belly, almost as if to protect their son from these dark, painful truths. He hadn't been conceived on purpose. He hadn't, perhaps, even been *wanted*.

And maybe Baldr had seen that, because he was grimacing again, rubbing his hand to his mouth. "But I still wished for this," he continued, hoarse. "I did. I only wished for a little more time. I even spoke to you of this, ach, Bright-Heart?"

He had? *When*? And Alma could see her own confusion suddenly reflected in Baldr's eyes, in how they were frantically searching hers, almost as if pleading with her to agree—while beside them, Drafli had again flashed into motion, his body whirling powerfully toward Alma.

You knew?! he signed at her, the motions hard and furious. *You knew of this? And you no tell me?*

Alma flinched and scrabbled backwards, her hands instinctively come to her neck, her head shaking. "I—I didn't," she gulped, glancing between him and Baldr. "I—I didn't know. I swear to you."

But Baldr was looking bewildered now, shaking his head, too. "You did," he insisted. "I told you. That day I overheard you—speaking—in the corridor, with Kesst. I told you I wished to wait a little longer—for a month—before any lasting choices were made."

What? And that didn't make sense, that hadn't at all been what Baldr had meant... had it? And Alma couldn't stop staring at him, searching him, fighting to find some sense amidst the havoc still screeching through her thoughts.

"But that month," she gulped, "that was my—my deadline. You gave me a month to—to make friends of Drafli. To gain his trust. One month. Right?"

And surely that was right, because gods, how many times had she thought of that one-month deadline—but wait, wait, this was more confusion in Baldr's eyes, and in Drafli's, that was...

"No," Baldr said, slow, uncertain. "That was—that was not what I said. That was not meant for—for *you*."

He looked even more bewildered than before, and Alma surely wasn't following either, staring at him with dazed, blank bafflement. While Drafli had abruptly snapped between them again, his hand fiercely signing toward her.

What did he say, it demanded. *Tell me everything. Now*.

Alma winced and cringed backwards, but fervently nodded, her sweaty hands wiping against her belly. "He said—he wanted to give it one month, before any lasting decisions were made," she gulped, toward Drafli's dark, unreadable eyes. "And in that time, I was to do everything I could to gain your trust. To honour you. *Obey* you."

For a hanging, horrible instant, Drafli just stared at her—and then he closed his eyes. And it was almost worse than the rage somehow, worse than when he'd pinned her to the bed, because it was shutting her out, putting her away, it was him thinking Alma had only done this—all of this—because—

"But it was—it was more than this, ach, Bright-Heart?" Baldr said, the words tumbling too fast from his mouth. "You did not only do all this with Drafli for *me*. You did not truly think I would give you only one month here? Before I—what, I cast you *out*?!"

The last bit came out as a laugh, sharp and incredulous—but then it rapidly, abruptly faded, his eyes gone wide and disbelieving on Alma's. His face almost draining of colour, leaving him looking pale, hollowed, horrified.

"You did not truly believe this?" he said now, high-pitched. "This was not—this was not why you sought so strongly to please Drafli, ach? Because you thought I should throw you *away*, if you failed?"

And gods, it was like he'd struck Alma straight across the chest, and she felt her breath unnaturally heaving, hitching out her still-sore throat. While before her, Baldr had begun to look truly ill, and Drafli—Drafli might well have been carved from stone, his black eyes staring beyond Alma, his body utterly still.

And what was Alma doing, what the fuck was she implying in this, and she somehow grasped more air, words, anything. "It wasn't only that," she managed. "It really wasn't. I still—wanted Drafli. I—*liked* him. Respected him. He is—"

But Drafli had again flashed into motion, both his hands forcefully signing between them. *Stop. Stop. Stop.*

"No, you fool woman," he spat at her, his voice a brittle croak. "No. You shall stop speaking so false to us. Between this, and our vow, and my *gold*, we all know why you sought so hard to please me!"

What?! Alma felt herself recoiling, her eyes shocked wide on Drafli's cruel, contorted face. Because surely he didn't think—he couldn't think—that she was a fool? That she cared about... his *gold*?!

"What gold," cut in Baldr's voice, far sharper than before. "*And what vow,* Drafli."

No, no, no, they weren't doing this, they weren't getting into this, they weren't—but that was already pure suspicion in Baldr's eyes, and accusation, and anger. "You made a *vow*?!" he demanded, staring back and forth between them. "To each other? Without me? With *payment*?!"

Gods curse them, gods curse the vile mess they'd made of this, and Alma wildly shook her head, and groped for an answer. "It didn't mean anything," she gasped. "It *didn't*. Most of all the payment. And I *did* tell you Drafli promised to help me, if I left, right? But I want to stay, Baldr, you know I've always wanted to stay, more than anything, *please*."

And why couldn't she stop babbling, why couldn't she make sense, why couldn't she wash away that stunned, shaken betrayal from Baldr's blinking eyes. And oh, she'd already failed, his hand already snapping up, signing, *No. Stop. Stop.*

"I want to hear it from Drafli," he said, his voice hard and grim. "Every last fucking bit of it. *Now*."

But beside Alma, Drafli had again gone starkly, unnervingly still. His eyes staring blankly at Baldr's face, his jaw set, his hands clutched into fists against his knees.

"Tell me, Drafli," Baldr hissed, low. "The truth. Or I will never, ever believe anything you tell me, ever again. *Ever*."

And that, surely, was the fear, flashing bright and dangerous across Drafli's deadened eyes. And suddenly he flared into motion again, his hands signing with such urgent rapidity that Alma could only catch pieces of it. But he was surely doing it, telling Baldr about his fear, about the contract, the vow, the gold. And then, about how—how he'd threatened Alma, and sworn to kill her if she ever told Baldr the truth.

And as he signed, it was almost as though Alma could see Baldr shrinking, his shoulders hunching, his body curling in on itself. His eyes dropping, until he surely couldn't even see Drafli's signs anymore—and that was a sudden, single streak of wetness, slipping down his cheek.

Drafli had finally dropped his hands, his face gone truly haggard now, his bones standing out in stark, sharp relief beneath his skin. And Alma couldn't bear it anymore, any of it, and she clutched for Baldr's hand, squeezing it tight within hers.

"But Drafli didn't mean it, Baldr," she gasped at him. "Any of it. He didn't. His threat was rubbish, I *knew* it was rubbish, he was only afraid for you, and terrified of what the bond between us could do to you. He was just trying to keep you *safe*."

But it wasn't working, it still wasn't changing anything, *no*—and Baldr snatched his hand out of her grip, his head wrenching back and forth. "Ach, keep me *safe*," he sneered at her, at them. "Whilst he *lied* to me, again and again! Just like how he lied to me about his mate. How he lied to me about why he fucked half his clan before my eyes. How he did not think to tell me that he lived in *fear* that his fool Skai god would *kill* me!"

Alma flinched, and beside her, Drafli had perhaps flinched too—but Baldr leapt off the bed, now pacing back and forth, his hands scrubbing against his face. "Why," he gasped. "Why do I keep believing you, Drafli. Why do I keep coming back to you, when you have betrayed me again, and again, and *again*!"

Drafli had jumped to his feet before Baldr, fervently signing an answer—something that ended with, *I love you, I love you*—but Baldr wasn't even looking, and now he'd spun back toward the bed, toward—toward *Alma*.

"And *you*," he growled at her. "You lied to me, too. Kept this from me, all this time! You swore a vow to *my* mate, you swore to take his *gold*? In exchange for my *son*?! No wonder you were so damned eager all the time, always splaying yourself for me, *begging* for me. Just like a shameful little—"

And oh, oh, he couldn't finish it, he couldn't, and Alma frantically flailed her arms toward him, and somehow found that she'd burst into desperate, coughing sobs. "Please don't," she pleaded, as hot shame streaked down her face. "Please. I'm so sorry, Baldr. I'm so, so sorry. I loved you. I *love* you. I swear to you. *Please*."

But it still wasn't working, it was ruining everything, and Baldr was reeling back, away, his palms pressing to his eyes. "Stop," he gasped. "Stop. I need to go. I should have gone back then. I knew it was wrong, it was too good to be real. I *knew*."

And he was weeping too, oh gods, and Drafli was lunging for him again, grasping both his wrists with strong hands. "No," he rasped. "No. You no go. You stay. Teach me to fix this. We have *son* now."

But Baldr was whirling away, shoving Drafli backwards, his head still whipping back and forth. "No," he choked. "No. You do not touch me, Drafli. You do not speak to me. I have given you so much, I have sought to be all you wanted, to be a worthy mate, to earn your truth. And you return all that with *this*?! I was still not good enough for you? I was not your partner, I was *never* your partner, I was your pretty, foolish, pliant Grisk *pet*! Just like—"

He broke off there, but his hand had furiously waved toward—toward *Alma*. Striking her with one last, horrible blow, before he spun away, toward the door. And Drafli was shaking his head, tripping as he shot around Baldr again, whirling up between him and the door, his hands still desperately signing. Saying, *I am sorry, Pure-Heart. I love you. I love you.*

Baldr wasn't looking, wasn't listening, and he grasped for Drafli's hands, and shoved them downwards. "No," he hissed. "We are done, Drafli. I am finished. And if you try to follow me, I will never, ever speak to you *again*."

And that, finally, seemed to snap Drafli back to stillness

again. His tall body just standing there, not moving, while Baldr strode past him, toward the door. And Alma wanted to yell at him, to beg him, to apologize, to weep—but she couldn't seem to move either, just huddled alone on the bed, her eyes frozen on Baldr, the rest of her wet face half-hidden behind her knees. Shameful. A pretty, foolish, pliant Grisk *pet*.

"Goodbye, Alma," Baldr said from the door, his voice stiff. "I am—sorry. I—"

But he didn't finish, his eyes squeezing shut—and then he spun and rushed away, without looking back.

41

Alma didn't know how long she sat there alone on the bed, weeping into her knees. While all of those horrible words of Baldr's kept ringing through her skull, echoing with such awful, sickening finality.

Shameful. Always begging. A pretty, foolish, pliant Grisk *pet*.

A servant. A... *harlot*.

Gods, it hurt, to think that Baldr had truly thought of her that way—and it hurt even more to think that perhaps she'd deserved his contempt, and his fury. She should never have lied to him like she had. She should never have kept that vow from him. She should have been honest from the start, damn Drafli, damn all those promises.

But she couldn't even seem to rage at Drafli, either, not after how he'd staggered back against the wall, and then sunk down against it, his face in his hands. Not looking at her, not signing, not speaking. Not saying, *There is no shame, I shall care for you, this is good. You are ours.*

Because maybe—maybe Alma *wasn't* theirs anymore. Most of all if Baldr had truly gone, because where did that leave her, with Drafli? With their vow? With—with their *son*?!

The fear and the dread seemed to again strike through her chest, her arms shuddering tighter around her knees—when suddenly, there was a sound at the door. A tap. And when Alma's head jerked up—please let it be Baldr, *please*—she found herself blinking at Tryggr, who was glancing between her and Drafli, and letting out a low, hissing whistle.

"Trouble, then, Boss?" he said, quiet. "Anything I can do to help?"

Drafli seemed to twitch on the floor, and though he didn't raise his head, his hand flicked up, signing with pointed, careful precision. Something about... Alma, and about her throat, and... their son.

"Right, then," Tryggr said, with a rather false-sounding cheerfulness, as he strode across the room toward Alma, swiping for her clothes on the floor as he passed. "Come along to the sickroom, then, woman, won't you? Get a good look-over, make sure your orcling's knitting together as he should?"

Oh. Alma stared blankly up toward Tryggr, and he gave a too-understanding smile back, holding out her clothes. "C'mon, then," he said. "Boss just needs a bit of time, to think things through. He'll sort it out, he always does."

Alma swallowed, her eyes again darting toward Drafli, who hadn't acknowledged any of this, or even raised his head—but she finally somehow nodded, and numbly reached for her clothes. Pulling them on with shaky fingers, while her thoughts kept whispering, dragging dark and despairing through her skull.

Shameful. A pretty, foolish, pliant Grisk *pet*.

"That's it," Tryggr said, once she'd finished dressing, and somehow staggered to her feet. "All good. Here, just don't trip over Cat."

With that, he'd reached down, and indeed produced Cat— and while Alma should have been surprised to find Cat skulking around in their bedroom, she couldn't even seem to nod. And thankfully, Tryggr didn't seem offended, and instead plopped Cat up on his shoulder, and ushered Alma toward the door.

But that meant she had to pass by Drafli, just sitting there immobile on the floor—and oh, he wasn't even going to look up, he wasn't going to even pretend that he'd ever cared. He was just going to send her away, like he always had—

Until his hand snapped up, catching against Alma's skirt. Pulling her to a halt beside him, and Alma shakily complied, staring blankly down toward his dark, messy bowed head. And though he didn't look up, his hand was signing toward her, far slower than he had with Tryggr.

You rest, and heal, it said. *I am sorry I frightened you, and hurt you.*

And with that, his hand dropped again, his body gone small and silent. And Alma stood there staring for far too long, until Tryggr loudly cleared his throat, and gingerly tugged against her cape.

Alma ducked her head and nodded, following Tryggr out into the corridor, but it almost hurt to leave Drafli behind like that, so quiet and alone. And where had Baldr gone, had he really *left* them, and what would happen next, what would become of her, of their son, their *family*?

But there was no answer, not from the dim familiar corridor, not from Tryggr beside her. Only silence, and darkness, and grief.

"It'll be all right, woman," Tryggr finally said, his voice cutting into the thick silence. "Boss will clear it up. No need to weep, ach?"

But Alma was frantically shaking her head, and fixing Tryggr with her wet, molten eyes. "He can't," she gulped at him. "Baldr will never forgive us. And he thinks I'm a—a *harlot*. A foolish, shameful Grisk *pet*."

Tryggr loudly snorted, and made a gesture with his hand that Alma couldn't follow. "Ach, then you can be sure Boss shall thrash him," he said, "for thinking thus of his sweet, lovely woman. You shall see."

Alma's head was shaking again, her hands wiping at her wet eyes. "But it—it's *true*," she choked at him, around another muffled sob. "I *was* Drafli's... pet. His *servant*. And you know it's true, you even said so, you said *you* wanted one, too!"

Tryggr gave a sharp exhale, running a clawed hand against his hair. "Ach," he replied, "that's truth. But that don't mean a pet's *only* a pet, you ken? It's more just—how you play and fuck together. It's... *fun*, to throw out orders, and have 'em obeyed by a sweet, pretty thing who knows exactly how to please you. But that don't mean we don't care about *you*."

He'd jabbed his claw toward Alma's chest, surely implying that Drafli had cared about her—but her head was still shaking, because it had gone well beyond that with Drafli, hadn't it? *Honour me*, his contract had demanded. *Obey me.*

"An' look," Tryggr continued, with another heavy sigh. "Likely Boss did take it a bit further with you, and his other Grisk, too. But it's not about him seeing you as less, ach? It's seeing you as *more*, and wanting to honour you, and take good care of you, and keep you happy and safe. It's what he's always done, it's what Skai are *s'posed* to do, ach?"

And it likely should have helped, maybe, maybe—but now Alma was thinking of Baldr, leaving them, running off unprotected and alone. Making another failure of Drafli, again. And maybe Drafli had deserved it—*she* deserved it—but surely it wasn't safe, was it? What if Baldr ended up trapped, or attacked? And hadn't they said Mr. Pembroke was sending men, the province's *lord* was sending men, and—

"Here we are, then," Tryggr's voice said, sounding distinctly relieved, and when Alma blinked up, she found herself inside the sickroom. And across the room, both Efterar and Kesst had snapped to look at her at once, Efterar with surprise in his eyes, and Kesst with a swiftly darkening frown.

"What the hell happened to you, sweetheart?" he demanded, as he stalked over, and joined Tryggr in marching her toward her old, familiar bed. "And why the hell are you *bleeding*?!"

Alma winced as she sat on the bed, her distracted hand fluttering toward her neck, and finding it sticky and stinging. Not from a new wound, maybe, but—she winced again—from where Drafli had *bitten* her, the night before.

"Ach, that'll heal," said Efterar gruffly, and he'd come over too, reaching his hand to hover against her neck. "Looks like the wound just pulled open. Although"—he grimaced—"it'll probably scar. The other side too, most likely."

Alma couldn't seem to muster a response to that, but even the memory of last night—of that perfect, beautiful happiness—seemed to wrench the misery even harder, colder. It was over. She'd failed. Again.

"And you know, I'm guessing," Efterar said now, his voice careful, "about your son?"

Alma jerked a nod, her eyes again prickling with yet more shameful heat. "Yes," she gulped. "Drafli's. Because Baldr, he—he came to—to *you*—"

Her voice cracked and broke, but the accusation in it kept ringing, scraping toward him—and above her, Efterar gave a slow sigh. "Right," he said. "Baldr didn't tell you that, then. I thought—I thought surely he would. I'm sorry."

Alma shook her head, the wetness now spilling from her eyes, streaking down her cheeks. "It's n-not your fault," she choked. "It was his truth to tell, I know—but he didn't, to either of us. And now I'm pregnant, and he—he *hates* us, and he's g-*gone*."

Above her, Kesst and Efterar were exchanging meaningful glances, and Efterar gave a grim, bracing smile. "I'm sure Baldr doesn't hate you," he said firmly. "And I'm sure he hasn't gone far, either."

But he didn't understand, he didn't, and Alma frantically shook her head again, while more wetness spilled from her eyes. "Baldr is finished with us," she gasped. "With... *me*. I—I lied to him. I swore a vow without telling him. It was so perfect, we were so happy, we were going to be a *family*—and I ruined everything. I ruined *everything*!"

Her voice sounded painfully shrill, grating through the room, and Kesst actually flinched, his eyes gone sober and dark. "You didn't ruin anything, sweetheart," he said, quiet. "You've been a gift from the gods to those two. To all of us. And if they're too blockheaded to see it, that's on them. *Not* you."

But the sobs wouldn't stop coming now, wracking through Alma's chest, escaping out her mouth. "I lied," she gulped. "I *failed*. I was their *harlot*. Their stupid, shameful Grisk *pet*."

By the end of it, she was weeping too much to speak the words, her hands clutching around her waist, her body shuddering with bleak, broken misery. With all the horrible, harrowing loss, of everything she'd ever, ever longed for. Gone. *Failed*.

"*Eft*," Kesst breathed above her, and Alma only distantly noticed him tugging on Efterar's arm, his hand clapped to his mouth. "Do something. Help her. Gods. *Please*."

And oh, Alma's eyes had snapped up again, desperately searching Efterar's pale face. "Please," she begged him. "Just— make it stop. Make me sleep. Please."

Efterar's shoulders rose and fell, his brow heavily creased with concern—but Alma kept staring at him, silently pleading, while the tears kept pouring down her cheeks. Until he finally nodded, raising his hand to her face, hovering it over her eyes.

And finally, Alma sagged to the bed, her sobs silenced, as the world slipped away into emptiness.

When wakefulness next came, it was with a pounding headache, a bone-deep chill, and a cold, barren misery.

Alma had failed. She'd ruined *everything*.

"Is she awake?" whispered a hushed, familiar voice. "She smells like she's awake. Is she?"

"Yes, Sweet-Fang," replied another voice, Efterar's voice. "But give her a moment, all right?"

Alma's swollen-feeling eyes slowly blinked open, and she found herself lying in her familiar sickroom bed, with Kesst's familiar face peering worriedly toward her from the bed opposite. While Efterar stood behind Kesst, his hand gripping his shoulder, and sitting beside them was Jule, giving an encouraging smile, with a squirming Bitty-Grim in her lap.

Alma stared blankly between them, and for an instant, it was as though time had dragged her into its depths, and spat her out again. Back into a world before Baldr and Drafli, before the Keeping, before—she shoved up to sitting, her hands clenching at her waist—before her *son*.

"How are you feeling this morning, Alma?" Efterar asked, his eyes wary on her face. "Any fatigue, or nausea?"

Alma twitched and shook her head, her hand giving a numb-feeling wave, her eyes darting between the assembled grim, watching faces. "What's happened?" she croaked. "Where's Baldr? And Drafli?"

They all seemed to grimace in unison, exchanging significant looks—until Jule cleared her throat, and held out a folded piece of paper. "We don't know where Baldr went," she said, her voice low. "And now Drafli's taken off, too. But he asked me to give you this."

Wait, Drafli was *gone*?! And Alma's shaky hand could barely seem to clutch for the paper, her fingers fumbling as they unfolded it, while time again seemed to bend back on itself. Back to another similar-looking, world-altering piece of paper, with Drafli's clear, careful script inside.

But this one—Alma stared down at it, motionless—was far shorter. Consisting only of a few brief lines, written in sharp black ink.

I must go after Pure-Heart, it read. *I know not when I will come back.*

While I am away I wish you to stay here, and stay safe.

If you wish to end our son, I shall not hold this against you.

I am sorry.

Alma read it again, and then again, as something in her belly began to wrench and heave. Drafli was gone? He didn't know when he'd be back? He didn't care if she *ended their son*?!

She only vaguely noticed Kesst's low hiss, or the way Efterar had abruptly stepped closer, his hand reaching to hover over her waist. "Deep breaths," he said. "You'll be all right."

But Alma was precariously close to sobbing again, her hands twitching up to her face—but that meant she'd dropped Drafli's letter, and she frantically clutched for it again, cradling it close. Drafli was gone. After Baldr. Into...

"But," she gulped toward Jule, her thoughts spinning, swerving, scattering. "Isn't it dangerous to be out there alone right now? Aren't there soldiers everywhere? Have you dealt with Mr. Pembroke yet? With the province's *lord* yet? How many days do we have left?"

Her voice had risen higher with every word, and she didn't miss Jule's faint but unmistakable flinch. "We have three days, until Pembroke's bands start attacking orcs on sight," Jule replied, voice strained and thin. "Not that they aren't already, but without Baldr—"

She stopped there, her lips pressing together, and Alma stared at her, while the distant roar of her heartbeat rose higher in her ears. "Without Baldr what?" she demanded. "*What*?!"

Jule hesitated again, clearly reluctant to elaborate, until Kesst gave a careful little shrug beside her. "It just gets a bit more complicated, right, Jules?" he said, in a voice that was perhaps supposed to sound light. "Baldr's spectacular nose makes it a hell of a lot easier for the rest of us to still travel, hunt, forage, get supplies—you know, live our *lives*—without getting attacked. Without sending more of *this* back here for Eft to deal with."

He'd jerked his head toward the rest of the sickroom, toward where—Alma's breath choked in her throat—there were multiple wounded, immobile orcs occupying the sickroom's beds. Five orcs, no, seven, no... ten?!

And rather than the usual sparring-related injuries Alma had become accustomed to seeing—the cuts and bruises and broken bones—these wounds seemed more... sinister, somehow. The nearest sleeping orc's bare, shuddering chest seemed to have multiple deep holes in it, as if he'd been pelted with arrows—and that orc's entire face had been bandaged, his eyes fully covered. And that orc—Alma gasped as she twisted to look—was *Thrain*. His usually smiling face gone pale and gaunt in sleep, his lean body mottled with vicious, painful-looking welts and gashes.

It felt as though something had kicked Alma in the stomach, her eyes frozen on the horrifying sight—that was Thrain, Thrain had been *attacked*?!—and she felt herself flinch again as another orc strode over. It was Varinn, his steps sharp and jerky, his clawed hand gripping a full waterskin. And though he thankfully appeared uninjured, his face was just as drawn and haggard as Thrain's, and he didn't even seem to notice the rest of them as he bent down over Thrain, and pressed his mouth to his forehead.

"*Ach, krútt,*" he said, his voice barely audible. "*Ansans kjánaskapur.*"

Alma couldn't understand the words, but Varinn's anguish—his *helplessness*—felt almost palpable as he stood up again, and carefully placed the waterskin by Thrain's head. And then just stood there blinking down at him, not moving, but for the hard swallow in his throat.

"Ach, he'll be all right, Grisk," cut in Efterar's gruff voice, and he abruptly strode over toward them, his hand reaching out to hover above Thrain's head. "Should be able to wake him by this time tomorrow."

Varinn nodded, but otherwise still didn't move, his eyes fixed on Thrain's face. And Alma's heart was now roaring in her ears, her hand clasped to her mouth, her head twitching back and forth.

"So—*Baldr* has been preventing this kind of thing, all this time?" she breathed at Jule, her voice cracking. "With his—*smelling*? *That's* how he's been spending his days, ever since I came here?"

Jule winced, and exchanged another meaningful glance with Kesst. "Well, our scouts obviously help prevent these situations, too," she said bracingly. "And Baldr's work extends far beyond that, as well. He's always involved in multiple projects, both in and out of the mountain."

If that was supposed to be comforting, it utterly failed, and Alma's stomach was heaving again, her face burying itself in her shaking hands. Baldr's impossible skills had been crucial to his people, he'd been keeping them safe, from her own horrible employer. And now he was out there somewhere, in the midst of all this, *alone*?!

"And you can't—you can't find him?" Alma's strained voice demanded, her head jerking up again, her eyes darting toward—toward *Varinn*. "You can't find a way to follow his scent, and bring him back?"

But Varinn hadn't even seemed to hear her, his eyes still blinking down toward Thrain's face, and finally it was Jule who spoke again. "No one's been able to find even a hint of Baldr's trail," she said heavily. "Grimarr says if he doesn't want to be found, he won't be. Drafli's our best hope, since he knows his scent better than anyone else—but even that's not promising."

Good gods. And now Alma's brain was twisting back again, back to when she'd first come here. When Baldr had wanted to run east, far away...

Because of her. Gods curse it, because of her. And Pembroke was because of her too, and now Baldr and Drafli were both gone, alone, facing horrifying danger—and now they were leaving everyone behind in horrible danger, too. Because of her.

"But look, I'm sure Baldr won't stay away long," Jule added, her voice back to bracing again. "He and Drafli have gone through rough patches before, and he likely just needs some time to cool off. This will all sort itself out sooner or later."

But Alma's head was suddenly, fervently shaking, her fingers crumpling the paper still clutched between them. Because what had Baldr said to Drafli, before he'd left? *If you try to follow me, I will never speak to you again.*

And Drafli knew that, he *knew*—and he'd still gone. He'd still run straight toward that fate, toward the certain rejection of the person he loved most. *I must go after Pure-Heart*, he'd written. *I must.*

It meant... this was dangerous. This was deadly. This was about Baldr's *life*. And just look what had happened to these orcs, to Thrain...

Because of her. Because of Pembroke. And Pembroke had destroyed Alma's mother, he'd tried to destroy her, and now he wanted to destroy Baldr and Drafli? He wanted to destroy all the orcs? He wanted to destroy Alma's new home, her family, the family of her son... and for what? His selfishness? His pride? His retaliation toward her for defying him, and escaping him? His revenge?

Three days. Three days, until this became worse. *Worse.*

And Alma's eyes were fixed to Thrain, lying so still and lifeless in that bed, with Varinn standing just as still above him. Worse. Her home. Her clan. Her *family.*

And there was only one way left. One way for Alma to fix this, to bring Baldr back. To finish what she should have finished so, so long ago.

"Then it's settled," she told them, quiet but sure. "I'm going back to Ashford."

43

Alma's announcement was met with a predictable assortment of gasps, frowns, and protests. Jule and Kesst and Efterar all speaking at once, all spouting the various excellent reasons that Alma had already heard last time.

"I'm sorry," she heard herself reply, once they'd quieted again. "But I need to go back. It's the only way that makes sense."

There were more rising protests, about risk and danger and her health and the treaty, but Alma again waited until they stopped, and gulped down a thick, shaky breath. "First of all, me returning deals with Pembroke," she continued, as if they hadn't spoken. "It meets his three-day deadline, and destroys his most obvious reason to keep attacking you. It would also cast into doubt the claims he's made to Lord Otto, and possibly even cause Otto to withdraw his involvement altogether. Right?"

Jule's eyes had narrowed, but she thankfully didn't argue this time, and Alma dragged in another breath. "And it might—it might help with Baldr, too," she said, a little shaky now. "I've been told"—she shot a furtive glance toward Varinn—"that

Baldr would be able to smell me returning to Pembroke's, no matter where he is. And maybe that might encourage him to—to come back."

She couldn't help a wince as she spoke—gods only knew if Baldr would be willing to come back at this point, or whether everything between them had been ruined beyond repairing. But if there was anything Alma could do to try, to silently speak to him across the distance, surely, it was this.

"Not only that," she added, a little faster now, "but when I first came here, Drafli was—concerned, about Baldr being separated from someone he'd bonded to. He was worried about how that might affect Baldr's—mind. And I know others"—she again glanced toward Varinn—"shared that concern. And Baldr was upset and angry when he left, so he may not have thought properly about whether that might continue to affect him. And even if it doesn't, even if he's fully over that now"—she looked back at Jule with pleading eyes—"it's still a risk, isn't it? Far too great a risk, for someone who's so important to our mountain. To all of us."

She'd still been speaking too quickly, the words tripping over one another, but she couldn't seem to stop, her clammy hands twitching on Drafli's letter. "And finally," she choked out, "going back helps—*me*. It gives me a way to—to break out of this mess. I *want* to disobey Drafli. I *want* to break my stupid secret vow to him. I *need* to. In the clearest, most blatant way possible, so Baldr knows, too. So he doesn't go on forever believing that I did this for Drafli's coin, or that I meant to steal his mate from him. I can't add another Grisk betrayal to his life, or another failure from a woman he trusted. I *can't*."

She finally stopped there, her breaths heaving from her constricted throat, her wet eyes still blinking at Jule's face. To where Jule stared back, her head slowly tilting, her shoulders sagging.

"But going back there is dangerous, Alma," she finally replied. "It's so dangerous. Pembroke is unpredictable and enraged, and he's sure to take any disruption to his plans very badly. He's sure to take it out on *you*."

But Alma already knew that, of course she knew that, and she gave a tight little nod. "So perhaps you'll try to help me," she said. "You'll safely escort me there, and monitor my whereabouts. You'll watch for any signs of Baldr returning. And if the situation becomes truly dire, you'll step in. Show up at the door claiming to be my long-lost cousin, or something."

Jule was clearly considering this, biting worriedly at her lip, but beside her, Kesst gave a sharp shake of his head. "And how long do you get stuck in that house with that raging crackpot?" he demanded. "What if Baldr's on a ship across the sea right now, and never comes back? And what about the fact that you're still pregnant? With an *orc*?! You really think Pembroke's going to tolerate *that* in his house?!"

Right. Alma's stomach pitched in her belly, sharp and nauseating. "Well, I should still have a while before my pregnancy becomes obvious, right?" she managed. "So I'll stay as long as I can, give Baldr as much time as possible. And if he doesn't come back, I"—her voice faltered, but she made herself keep going—"I would hope that maybe—maybe if Drafli comes back, maybe he would still take pity on me. Even without our vow. And that he might—"

The words had again died in her throat, her eyes dropping to the paper in her hand. She hoped that Drafli might... what? Tolerate her? Take care of her? Find a way to support her? Acknowledge the unwanted son that he'd just given her permission to *end*?

Kesst was cursing again under his breath, but no one else spoke. And as Alma blinked down at Drafli's paper—at Drafli's rejection, perhaps, just as blatant as Baldr's—she felt herself swallow hard, against the odd, stilted certainty in her throat. A certainty that felt familiar, suddenly, like a new cloak she'd forgotten she was wearing.

She couldn't control Baldr and Drafli. She couldn't change their motivations, or their choices, or their actions.

But she could still change her own. She was a Grisk, she was loyal and hardworking and true, and soon, perhaps, she would even be a—a mother. And even if Baldr and Drafli wanted no part of that, she could still do it... for herself. She could make her own family. Her own way.

And there was no shame in that. No shame in making her own choices. In being... herself.

"I'm so grateful for all your kindness these past weeks," she whispered. "I'm so glad I've met you all. I've had such a wonderful time here. But..."

Her eyes flicked back up to Jule, to Kesst, to Efterar, even over to Varinn. Who was now watching her, too, his head tilted, his eyes shifting, maybe even approving.

"But I'm making my own decision on this," Alma continued, without hesitation this time. "I'm going back, with or without your help. *Today*."

44

A short while later, Alma found herself dressed in warm clothes, and once again walking through a damp, dark tunnel, with Varinn by her side.

Getting to that point had taken a good deal more stubbornness, and even a few regrettable threats—but in the end, Jule had gone and collected the captain himself, who had listened to Alma's proposal with surprising willingness. And instead of refusing to cooperate, as Jule had clearly anticipated, Grimarr had finally given a slow, thoughtful nod.

"You are more like your two mates than I knew, woman," he'd told her, his voice firm and decisive. "They would gladly face such dangers, to keep safe one they loved. And were this not his own tangle, Drafli would be the first to demand we send you to Ashford, to better draw out this man, and finish this."

He'd said this with a rather regretful glance toward Jule, who'd frowned back at him with surprising vehemence. "You just want Baldr and Drafli back at your beck and call as soon as possible, don't you," she'd snapped at him. "Gods forbid you try to survive a week or two without them?"

Grimarr had shrugged, and given Jule an affectionate half-grimace, half-smile. "I ken not what you speak, woman," he'd said lightly. "Now, when shall we begin this? Today?"

Thus had begun a whirlwind morning of preparations—planning, packing, discussing possibilities and contingencies. Grimarr had quickly brought in his full team of advisors—including Maria and Simon, Ella and Nattfarr, and Rosa and John—and while Maria had glowered darkly at the news of Drafli's departure, she thankfully hadn't protested, and had willingly joined in the discussion. Much of it entirely incomprehensible to Alma, focusing on scouts and bands and various plans for surveillance—but by the end of it they'd all seemed satisfied, even Jule.

"We'll do our absolute best to keep you safe, Alma," she'd said. "And now, who's going to serve as your escort to Ashford?"

At that, Alma had again glanced at Varinn, who had already been giving a decisive nod. And after another rapid round through the Grisk storage-room, Alma had once again been dressed in rather uncomfortable, constricting human clothes, and ready to return to Ashford.

Throughout it all, the entire endeavour had begun to feel distant and surreal, as though it had been happening to someone else—but now that Alma was doing this again, walking through this exact same dark, dripping tunnel, the truth of it seemed to weigh down against her shoulders, dragging her feet against the hard stone beneath them.

She was going back to Ashford. Going back without Baldr and Drafli. Risking everything, for a distant foolish hope. For two orcs who might not even notice, or care...

But then she squared her shoulders, let out a harsh breath. There was no shame. She was doing this, for herself.

"Thank you for escorting me, Varinn," she made her thick voice say, toward his silent striding form beside her. "I know you can't find Baldr's scent, but have you noticed any hint of Drafli coming this way?"

Varinn gave a wan half-smile back, and shook his head. "I

ken Drafli went above ground," he said. "This would also make it easier for Baldr to scent him. And it sends a message, just as you are doing, ach? It says that he is searching for his mate, and wishes for his safe return."

Right. Baldr's words were again surging through Alma's thoughts—*if you try to follow me, I will never, ever speak to you again*—and she shook her head, wincing. "But—Baldr was so angry, Varinn," she whispered. "At Drafli, and at—at me. We—lied to him. And the son he wanted—the son we planned for—Baldr isn't—he isn't—"

He isn't our son's father, she was supposed to say, but the words broke again, as quickly as they'd come. Because she couldn't even bear to speak them aloud, to give life to the thought that Baldr might forever reject not only her and Drafli, but the son they'd all made together.

"Ach, I ken," Varinn said, voice low. "But I cannot see how Baldr would meet this with anything but gladness. Drafli is his mate, and thus, they are both your son's fathers, ach? The truth of a healthy, hale son, made by the orc you care for so deeply, and thus scenting always of him"—he jerked a shrug—"this would be an unthinkable gift. A joy to carry through all the rest of your days."

Alma felt herself giving Varinn a sidelong look, considering that—but then there was another thought, weighing even heavier than before. "You don't think," she whispered, "Baldr planned for it on... *purpose*? Because you knew, didn't you? What Baldr did with Efterar? How he didn't *want* me to have his son?"

She was thinking about Varinn's odd comment in the corridor, that day they'd cleaned the floors—*mayhap soon you shall choose to make a son after all*, he'd said—and she wasn't at all surprised to see him nodding, slow.

"Ach, I could smell this upon him," he replied. "I thought surely you and Drafli were part of this. But"—he dragged a hand through his hair—"you yet cannot think that Baldr would have meant to trick you, ach? He would have only sought to care for his mate, and protect you and your son. He would wish to be sure his son was wanted, and loved, and *safe*. As any Grisk would, in his place."

Alma's steps had slightly faltered, her eyes blinking blankly at Varinn's hard profile. Because of course Baldr would have been thinking of their son, too. Of course he would have wanted their son to be safe. As any Grisk would...

"But the Grisk *haven't* always cared for their sons," Alma countered, her voice more accusing than she meant. "Baldr's own father failed him. All the Grisk failed him. And Baldr has never been able to find an answer for that, *ever*."

Varinn's shoulders rose and fell, his eyes now fixed straight ahead. "Ach, we have all lost much, and failed much," he said. "I know not what befell Barden's plans for his son, or why these failed—but I met Barden many times as an orcling, and I well remember how deeply he cared for his mate and son, and how hard he fought to keep them hidden, and safe. And ach, mayhap he failed—and mayhap the Grisk failed him, too—but he tried. He sought to do his best. There is no cowardice in this. No fault. No shame."

Oh. Oh. And the truth of that, the pure resonant power of that, suddenly seemed to burrow deep into Alma's belly. There was no cowardice. No shame. *He sought to do his best, keep his son safe, as any Grisk would...*

And now here were Alma's own words, words she'd said to Drafli, to Baldr. *There's no need for your penance. It's not our fault that the world is a cruel and unjust place sometimes. We are here, and we love you. There is no shame.*

It all seemed to keep twining deeper as they walked, weaving itself into Alma's thoughts, into her very soul. There was no shame. She was doing this. Doing her best. As any Grisk would. As Baldr had. As Drafli had. As maybe—maybe even her own mother had, too.

And somehow, it was enough. Enough to keep her feet

walking, her head held high, her thoughts steadily focused forward. Even as they stopped to camp for the night, sleeping in a chilly mud-walled room, before waking up the next morning, and setting out again. Finally moving above ground, over rough terrain that slowly became smoother and easier. Until they reached a familiar wide river, and crossed it over a thin wooden bridge, the sight and sound of the rushing water making Alma's heart thunder against her ribs.

But she kept moving, kept doing this, now following Varinn along a narrow path through the trees. Closer and closer and closer, one step after another, until she was blinking up at the familiar sight of Pembroke's house, looming large and menacing before them.

Her steps had faltered, her clammy hands rubbing at her skirts, her eyes. Willing her thoughts to settle again, thinking of all she'd accomplished, all the friends she'd made. All the wonders she'd discovered, all the pleasures, the joys of having had two orcs to love, for even a short time. Having a family.

And now—now she was doing this. Doing her best. No shame.

So she drew in a breath, and profusely thanked Varinn for all his support and kindness. And then she hoisted up her pack, walked up the lane, and rapped on the front door.

45

Alma had fully expected her return to Pembroke's would be met with shock, or disbelief, or fear. But what she hadn't expected was... excitement?

"Alma?" said the footman—Karl—who'd opened the door, his mouth widening into a broad smile. "Alma! You're alive?!"

A passing housemaid—Caroline—had skidded to a halt in the hall behind him, her hand clapped to her mouth. And before Alma could speak, Caroline had rushed over, and thrown her arms around Alma's neck.

"You're finally back!" she gasped. "And you're alive, and well! Please say you've come to work again? You would not *believe* the state we're in, we've lost six staff this past month, and last week Fred ran off all the horses, and then set the stables on fire! Just like Cook with the kitchen!"

Alma blinked bemusedly at this, and abruptly found herself confronted by another former colleague—Yvette, a scullery maid. "Oh, thank the *gods*," she said, with palpable relief. "You know how to make that pie Pembroke prefers, right? Could you please write down the recipe, we can't remember it at all, and he's been raging about it all week!"

"And did you know that Pembroke found Cook, and made

her come back?" demanded Jane, another housemaid. "But then he went and caned her, so we've been needing to cover for her while she heals, and I've barely slept in a fortnight!"

Alma winced, but squared her shoulders, and attempted a smile toward the lot of them. "I'd be happy to help you however I can," she replied. "But speaking of Pembroke, I should probably meet with him first. Is he at home?"

The two housemaids exchanged meaningful looks, but nodded in unison. "He's in his office," Jane said flatly. "Perhaps we'd best come with you this time, though? In case you need witnesses, or protection?"

She'd frowned darkly toward Karl, who had surely been one of Alma's pursuers, that day Pembroke had fired her. And to Alma's vague surprise, Karl actually gave a shamefaced wince, and nodded. "Let me call Franz, too," he said. "Just in case."

With that, he ducked into the side hallway, and soon reappeared with Franz at his heels. And close behind Franz were two kitchen maids, and even Cook, running her shaky hands against her silver-streaked hair.

"Thought for sure you were dead, sweet girl," Cook croaked, as she pulled Alma into a surprisingly tight hug. "I'm so, so sorry about the fire. Shoulda known you'd end up taking the blame for it."

A thick lump was rising in Alma's throat, and she squeezed Cook back, as tightly as she could. "I'm glad you're all right, too," she whispered. "Though I'd hoped you'd be able to get away and start a new life, for good."

Cook shook her head as she pulled back, her eyes bright. "This bastard doesn't let go that easily," she said, jerking her head in the direction of Pembroke's office. "As I'm sure you well know. He's been losing his damned mind without you. Throwing out soldiers and threats and ultimatums all over the place."

Alma made a face, but felt herself nodding. "I've heard," she said. "It's about time we had a talk, I think."

With that, she took a breath, and set off in the direction of Pembroke's office, her chin held high. She was doing this. Her best. No shame.

The rest of her former colleagues trailed along behind her, whispering and jostling one another—though they seemed to quiet all at once as Alma stepped into Pembroke's open doorway. As she blinked down at the cruel man who had threatened her. The man who had almost killed her. The man who surely bore the brunt of the blame for her mother's death, as well.

Pembroke's grey head had snapped up toward Alma in the doorway, his furious eyes narrowing, his face already flooding with red. A sight that would surely have set Alma trembling and apologizing, once upon a time—but now, staring down at his paunchy body and his beady grey eyes, Alma felt her arms folding over her chest, her teeth gritting together. This man. This horrible, hideous, greedy little man, who had done so much to hurt the people she loved.

"I've returned, Pembroke," she said, her voice clipped. "As you've repeatedly demanded."

Pembroke kept frowning up at her, his wet little mouth opening and closing, and Alma felt herself huffing a short, contemptuous laugh. "So you will now send word to Lord Otto at once," she said, "and inform him that your missing employee has returned safe and sound. And that you have *no reason whatsoever* to continue warring against the orcs."

Pembroke's blank-faced mouthing at empty air had finally ceased, his meaty hands clutching at the side of the desk. "I have every reason," he hissed back. "My longtime employee was kidnapped by orcs, and held hostage in that vile mountain for weeks! Then, those foul orcs refused to return you, thereby breaking multiple terms of their so-called *peace-treaty*!"

Alma heard herself huff another laugh, her head shaking. "You fired me, and nearly chased me to my death," she replied coldly. "Fortunately, I was rescued by an orc, and stayed with his people until I had healed from the injuries that *your* orders inflicted. And now I've returned, just as you've demanded. So you *will* call your men off, Pembroke. Today!"

Her voice rang through the room, cutting through the collective whispers and gasps behind her. And Alma could see Pembroke glancing nervously at their audience, taking in the footmen, the housemaids, the kitchen maids, the scullery maid, and Cook.

"You—ought to have sent word," Pembroke finally said, his bottom lip jutting out. "I was only looking out for you, girl. And you can't honestly expect me to believe that those orcs didn't compromise you? *Impregnate* you with their vile spawn?!"

He'd cast a baleful, accusing glare down at Alma's still-flat belly, and she felt her hackles rising, her anger snapping out sharp and cold. "The orcs helped me, and healed me," she growled back. "All of which they communicated to you, multiple times. And for their trouble, you have broken your treaty, and attacked them without cause, and called for another unjust war against them! Your actions have been ill-reasoned, ill-founded, and utterly irresponsible, and unless you want me to inform Lord Otto of your grave mistakes at once, you *will* call off your men! Now!"

Pembroke was staring blankly at Alma again, his face gone an unnatural shade of grey. His eyes repeatedly glancing between Alma and their audience, while visible sweat beaded on his forehead.

"There, there, girl," he said thinly. "I can see there must be some—misunderstanding. I'll send for Otto, and you can rest assured we'll straighten this out. And look, I'll even"—he hesitated, one of his hands fumbling for his desk drawer—"I'll even hire you back on as my housekeeper, with a full three-month advance. See?"

He'd produced a small bag, tossing it across the desk—and when Alma didn't move to take it, Jane darted around her, plucked it up, and thrust it into her fingers. It felt like coins—it *was* coins—but Alma felt her head tilting, her eyes narrowing on Pembroke's sweaty face. It couldn't be that easy. Surely it couldn't.

"You'll see, girl," he said, wetting his lips with his little pink tongue. "I'll call for Otto. We'll leave off your orcs, and you'll get to be a housekeeper again. You'll see."

The words felt like sickly, weeks-old rubbish, pouring off that foul little tongue, and Alma couldn't seem to stop glaring down at him, her lip curling. At least, until Jane tugged at her arm, her eyes pleading.

"We'd love to have you back, Alma," she said. "You can show me how to open that linen closet on the third floor, and how to properly black the stove. And perhaps you can make that pie for supper?"

Alma had finally torn her eyes off Pembroke, her shoulders sagging. Because yes, he was surely a foul lying swine, but she didn't want to risk being kicked out again, either. Not now. Not yet. Not until there was some word from Baldr, some sign.

He had to come back. He *had* to.

So Alma gave a slow exhale, and clutched tighter at her bag of coins. She was doing this. Her best.

"All right, then," she said. "Let's get to work."

———

46

Much later that evening, Alma finally stepped into her cramped old bedroom, set down her candle, and shut the door behind her.

It had been a long, exhausting, and thoroughly bizarre day. A day that had again felt like time folding in on itself, and dropping Alma out the wrong end. Twisting her back into this house, this job, this life.

And while Alma had truly enjoyed seeing her old colleagues again, and helping them work through the various problems that had arisen in her absence, she'd also found herself seeing their lives in an entirely new light. They worked from dawn until dusk. They wasted inordinate amounts of time serving Pembroke's every whim, no matter how absurd. They had no allotted time for leisure or family or pleasure, so instead they cut corners, told convoluted falsehoods, and sneaked around in spare bedrooms, surely spending far more time and energy in such pursuits than if they'd just been granted the evenings off.

And worst of all, they all lived in terror of Pembroke. Of being caned, as Cook had been upon her return, or of being cut off and run out, as Alma herself had been. And they were afraid to leave their remaining colleagues with even more work and grief, more aches and malaise and frustrations. More overall ill health, perhaps hinting at more serious ailments, like the one that had killed Alma's mother.

It was... appalling. And as Alma had worked throughout the day, she'd again and again found herself comparing her old existence here with her new life and work in Orc Mountain. With how she'd been respected, and appreciated, and free to manage her own time, and direct her own days. How no one had noticed or complained if she'd gone off swimming, or exploring, or visiting her friends, or spending time with her orcs.

And that, perhaps, grated even harder than the rest, burying it all beneath a wash of brittle, bone-deep loneliness. Because gods, she missed them. She missed Kesst and Efterar, Tryggr and Dufnall, Varinn and Thrain, Nattfarr and Ella and Rakfi, Rosa and Maria and Gwyn and Stella, all the friends she'd made. The freedom she'd had among them, to just be herself, without shame.

And most painful of all, she missed Baldr. She missed Drafli. She missed their easy shared understanding, their support and their comfort, their pleasure and their joy. And it truly felt like an age had passed since she'd lain tucked between them in bed, companionably signing with Drafli, feeling Baldr's laughter in her hair.

Ach, now this is a way to awaken, Baldr had said, and Alma could still feel the contentment in that, the rightness. The quiet, fundamental peace that had curled between them, drawing them close. Safe. A family.

But now—she sagged against the room's little door, her head thudding back against the solid wood—Baldr was still gone. Drafli was still gone. They were still alone, and unhappy, and in very real danger. In a war. While Alma had worked all day in their enemy's house, blacking his stoves and unlocking his closets and cooking him a fucking *pie*.

She exhaled hard, her eyes squeezing shut, her head twitching back and forth. No. She was doing this. Doing her best, as any Grisk would. No penance. No shame.

It was enough to ease the tightness in her shoulders, her chest—until she dropped her hands. And found herself staring at the bed in the candlelight, blinking at where she'd kept her mother's ashes beneath it.

But the jar—that large, white, constantly distressing beacon of her misery and grief—was gone. Gone. *Gone*?!

Alma choked a cry, and rushed toward the bed. Dropping to kneel beside it, to plunge her hand beneath—but there was nothing. Nothing. Gone.

And finally, finally, after all the confusing miserable hell this day had been, Alma sank down onto her bed, and buried her face in her hands. And felt the sobs wracking through her, shuddering her shoulders, shaking the little bed beneath her. Her mother was gone. Her orcs were gone, and in very real danger. She was back in this hellish house, trapped serving this horrible man, who was waging war against the people she loved. And what if her best wasn't enough, what if she failed, what if it was too late, what if she ruined everything...

When suddenly, there was a sound. A low, purposeful exhale, from the corner of her room. And it sounded familiar, it *felt* familiar, Alma's heart abruptly galloping, her body leaping to her feet, her eyes searching in the darkness.

It was—him. Him. Tall and silent and waiting, his arms crossed over his chest, his eyes gleaming on hers.

Drafli.

47

I t was *Drafli*.

Drafli was—here? In Alma's room? At Pembroke's?!

Alma stared for a long, hitching moment, her body frozen, her heart thundering in her ears. Drafli. Was here.

And suddenly he was striding toward her, closing the small space between them—and Alma was being dragged into his arms. His lean body hard and rigid against hers, his claws pricking her back, his face ducking into her neck. His familiar scent swarming her breath, flooding her with sweetness, safety, *relief*.

And Alma was clinging to it, to him, with all her strength. And gods, she was weeping again, streaking wetness against his bare chest, but if he'd noticed he didn't let on, his strong hand now stroking her hair, pressing her even closer against him.

Ach, you are safe, it meant. *I am here.*

Alma fervently nodded, and clutched at him, and kept weeping, until the sobs seemed to sputter themselves out. Leaving her still here, in her cramped old bedroom, held tight in an orc's arms, tucked against his solid, sweet-scented safety.

"You are well?" he finally whispered, his voice close and hoarse. "No pain?"

Alma shook her head, even as she twitched a little away from him, meeting his bleak black eyes. "And you?" she gulped. "And Pure-Heart?"

Drafli visibly flinched, his eyes closing—and then he jerked a swift shake of his head, saying no. *No.*

He hadn't found Baldr. Baldr was still out there somewhere, in danger, alone.

Alma gulped another helpless sob, again pitching into Drafli's chest—but again, he only held her close, one hand sharp and firm against her back, the other stroking against her hair. Saying, again, *I am here. You are safe.*

And he was, she was, it was truth, it was *everything*—until Alma felt herself flinch away again, her wet eyes desperately searching his set face. "And—my mother," she gulped. "Her ashes. She's gone, too, and—"

But Drafli's strong hands only drew Alma close again, folding her back against the strength of his chest, his heart. "I sent for her, after I heard you speak of this, in the crypt," his voice whispered. "She is safe at our home, waiting beneath the earth with the other Grisk, until you come back to her."

Oh. Oh, *gods*. And the emotion welling up in Alma's throat seemed to burst again, breaking out into more harsh, wracking gasps, more wetness leaking onto Drafli's skin. But he was still here, still caressing her, still caring for her, safe.

"Th-thank you," she finally choked, squeezing him as hard as she dared. "*Thank* you, my lord."

But at that, he seemed to stiffen, even as his hands kept stroking her. And when Alma again drew back, she could see the darkness clouding his eyes. The... regret.

You no need to speak thus now, he signed at her, his hand moving before her eyes. *You have... disobeyed me. Broken my terms. Ach?*

Alma swallowed, her gaze dropping, because gods, she'd been trying not to think about that part of it, about what Drafli would think, what he would say. About how this was without question yet another betrayal, from yet another woman who'd gained his trust, and then broken it.

But maybe Drafli didn't care—he'd left, he'd wanted Alma to end their *son*—and she still couldn't meet his eyes as she nodded, jerky and quick. *Yes*, she signed at him. *I want to break our vow. I'm sorry.*

There was a sudden empty silence, swinging far too powerful between them, and Alma finally dragged her eyes up again, met his stark, unreadable face. "You know I would never have been able to follow through with it," she whispered. "Taking your payment, or leaving our son. I"—she squared her shoulders, made herself say it—"I should never have agreed to that vow in the first place, Drafli. We should never have lied to Pure-Heart like that. It was cruel, and unfair, and disrespectful, and *wrong*. He didn't deserve that from us. Not after all the kindness he's given us. The *joy*."

She'd braced herself as she'd spoken, because surely now Drafli would retaliate, rage at her, leave—but he didn't. He only kept standing there, looking down at her with those dark, so-still eyes.

Ach, I ken, he finally signed at her, the movements careful and smooth. *I thought only of my fear, and not of Pure-Heart, or his wishes. He was right to spurn me, and to run.*

Alma couldn't seem to find an answer for that, and Drafli's chest filled and emptied, his eyes still unmoving on hers. *If we find Pure-Heart*, his hand slowly continued, *I ken he will forgive you, in time. I wish you will return to him. I wish you to—*

His hand stuttered there, briefly rising to rub at his mouth, and then dropping again. *I wish you to—forget*, he signed, the movement a swift swipe of his claws across Alma's forehead. *Forget me. Forget my—*

With that, his hand dropped down to Alma's belly, making the exact same sign. *Forget him. Forget my son. End him.*

Alma's stomach plummeted, her breath frozen in her throat—Drafli truly still wanted her to end their *son*?!—but then she realized that his other hand was still there, too. And it was clutching tightly against her waist, long fingers spreading wide, and... trembling.

Forget him, that hand kept saying, while the other kept... staying. As if to protect their son, to guard him there, even as the rest of him kept trying to say, *forget*. *Forget*. His eyes glittering on hers, pleading with hers, brighter than she'd ever seen them—and now his head was shaking too, twitching back and forth. Saying, *No. No. No.*

No.

And Alma was suddenly twitching too, her breath shuddering out hard, her hands fumbling toward her waist. Toward Drafli's hands, not only the one against her—but also the one still saying, *forget, forget*. And she clutched them both close, holding them both here against her. Against their son.

"No," she gulped. "I can't forget him. Can't forget *you*. We're a *family*, Drafli."

Drafli's bright eyes stared at her for another long, unblinking moment—and then they fluttered closed, his head tilting back, his brow creased deep. As if he were exasperated, or in pain, or... confused.

So Alma kept his hands clasped in hers, and she raised her arms, and crossed them against her chest. Holding there until his eyes slowly opened, found hers again—and then she lifted their joined hands to cross against his chest, too. Waiting, saying it, shouting it.

I love you. I love you.

Drafli's throat bobbed as he looked, his eyes blinking—but then his head began shaking again, his chest heaving beneath her crossed hands.

"No," he croaked at her, his voice harsh. "I no deserve this. I frightened you. Threatened you. Harmed you. I *failed* you."

And Alma was nodding, jerky and fervent, even as she blinked back the wetness again pooling behind her eyes. "But—I know you were trying your best," she croaked back.

"Trying to do better. You—listened to me. Took care of me. Defended me. Comforted me. You—*saw* me, Drafli."

Drafli was still shaking his head, his mouth contorting, but Alma kept nodding, defying him, disobeying him. Breaking her vow to him, and still honouring him, as best as she possibly could.

"And if you want to keep doing better," she whispered, "you'll keep listening. You'll honour me, and respect my own choice in this. And you won't make me or our son part of your penance, or your absolution, or whatever the hell you're thinking. You'll accept"—she inhaled, let it out—"that even if you failed, that doesn't mean you need to go off and drown alone in suffering and shame. It *doesn't*. There is no shame, remember?"

Drafli's body shuddered against her, and he'd stopped shaking his head, his eyes again bright and still. "But," he whispered, almost inaudible. "Still did much wrong. Still ought to make amends. To you, and to Pure-Heart. I *must*."

And blinking up at his glittering, grieving eyes, Alma again felt herself nodding, while one more surprising truth seemed to settle into place. She didn't want Drafli's guilt, his shame, his penance—but she would willingly accept his amends. His continued efforts to do better, to be a better mate. A better father.

"Then maybe," she replied, her voice hitching, "you'll—stay. Even if Pure-Heart doesn't come back. You'll still be the father our son needs. And maybe you won't treat me as just his mother, or your pet, but maybe—if you felt the same—someday you might even take me as your—your—"

She couldn't seem to finish it, her hands clutching tighter to his, lightly bumping against his chest. "Your hearth-mate," she finally managed, her voice cracking. "Yours."

There was a sudden, strangled stillness, Drafli's body again shuddering against hers. His bright eyes flaring with something she couldn't follow, his throat convulsing, his tongue briefly flicking against his lips...

And without warning, he *tackled* her. His strong hands grasping her waist, shoving her down onto her back on the bed behind her, while his tall powerful body crushed down against her. Covering her with his lean strength, his hot sweet scent, his protection, his approval.

Alma had already arched up into it, meeting it, craving it with a sudden ravenous ferocity—and oh, he was just the same, his face already buried deep in her neck, his strong hand purposefully yanking up her skirts. And he was between her legs, shoving her knees apart with his, and that was—that was—

That was him. There. That hard, pulsing, dripping-wet heft, so familiar, and yet so foreign. Because Alma had never felt it like this before, felt it seeking its way between her parted folds, finding her throbbing swollen heat. Finding the place where he'd never, never taken her, never done this, he wasn't going to do this, was he truly doing this—

But oh, he'd yanked back to look, to sweep his blazing eyes over Alma's flushed face, her gasping mouth, her own frantically fluttering eyes. To briefly bend down, biting at her lips with a vicious kiss—and then to pull back again. To hold her gaze with dark, glittering purpose, *look at me, look at me...*

He sank inside with one smooth, devastating stroke, plunging himself to the hilt within her. While Alma kicked and arched and very nearly screamed, impaled fully upon his furious strength. On how it felt so different, and oh so glorious, so hard and deep and demanding. Flexing and pulsing within her, pumping out steady spurts of hot sweetness, driving tight against her womb, against her very soul...

He kept watching her as he held there, still making her meet his eyes—but that was surely pleasure in his eyes, too. Pleasure, and perhaps even a twitch of surprise, as his hips ground a little against her, as she flared and clamped back against him. And oh, he was biting his lip as he did it again, his breath heaving out harsh, because he liked it, he liked it, he liked *her*.

The truth of that had Alma clutching back at him, clinging to him, clamping even tighter against his beautiful invasion, yes, oh gods, *yes*. And in return Drafli actually moaned aloud, the sound broken but true, his head tilting back, his eyes squeezing shut.

Alma kept drinking it up, drinking him up, her hands now scrabbling greedy and desperate over his back, his shoulders, his neck. He was here, he was so stunning, he was strength and safety, he would comfort her and protect her and keep filling her like this, keep making her feel him inside her, and—

And then he drew away, swift enough that Alma choked and keened, her frantic eyes caught on his—and oh, he sank back in, in another smooth carving stroke. Again holding himself there, his eyes burning on hers, as she thrummed and thrashed upon him—and then he dragged out again, slow, soaring ripples of agonizing ecstasy in his wake...

Until he drove inside again, and then again, and again. Easing into a fluid, vehement rhythm, piercing Alma over and over with his power, his pleasure, his approval. His glinting, hooded gaze now flicking between her face and her still-wounded neck, his tongue slipping against his lips...

But when Alma's shaking hands found his head, guiding it downwards, she felt him hesitate over her, inside her. His strength giving a heavy, purposeful spasm against her womb, while his eyes again flashed with doubt, with guilt. With shame.

But Alma shook her head, watched her hand flutter to the hard line of his cheekbone, his jaw. To the surprisingly soft warmth of his mouth, the heat of his breath.

"No shame," she breathed, holding his eyes. "Mine."

And she could see those eyes shifting, flashing, falling into the deep—and then he was there. Here. His face shoving hard into her neck, his teeth already searching, scraping, while his power between her legs again drew out, and slammed inside. Driving even harder and faster than before, her body jolting with every movement, as those teeth kept teasing, tasting, firing her full of heat, anticipation, fear, craving. He was here, he was hers, he was honouring her, he had to, he had to—

And when those sharp teeth sank deep, it was as though the last of Alma's uncertainty skidded, smashed, shattered— and then exploded. Rushing out in stream after stream of storming, slamming euphoria, seizing her against Drafli's stricken shuddering heat—until it shattered apart, too. Surging out into her again and again, answering her body's convulsive milking strokes with spurt after spurt of hot molten sweetness. While his mouth still latched to her neck moaned and drank, gulping again and again, swallowing her inside him, just the way she was swallowing him.

Alma couldn't tell how long it kept swirling, shimmering, the room slowly spinning behind her eyes—but she couldn't stop stroking him, running her hands over the silk of his hair, the sweaty strength of his back. He was here. Honouring her. *Hers.*

She shivered all over at the feel of his teeth carefully pulling out again, his warm tongue gently lapping against the wounds he'd made. Easing the faint twinges of lingering pain into something more like pleasure, like peace.

And that peace only sank deeper as that warm mouth softly kissed up the side of her neck. Moving slowly, sweetly over her jaw, her cheek—and then finding her mouth. Meeting it with a slick, heady blend of salt and sweetness, danger and safety, hunger and relief. And Alma met it, welcomed it, let herself bask in the truth of it. Here. *Hers.*

When Drafli finally pulled away again, his mouth was streaked with red, his eyes still oddly bright as they searched hers. As she blinked back up at him, her hands again caressing him, her head slightly nodding.

"Thank you, Drafli," she whispered. "My lord."

His throat audibly swallowed, his eyes closing—and then he lowered his head, until his forehead rested against hers. His breath still shuddering from his mouth, unfurling sweet across her face.

"No need to call me this now," he whispered, hoarse. "I no deserve this, Bright-Heart."

Gods, not this again, and Alma felt her chin jutting up, her nose bumping against his. "I want to," she whispered back. "I like it."

He'd opened his eyes again, the sight so close it was blurry, but Alma didn't blink, or flinch away. Because there was no shame, and she was making her own choices, and Drafli was honouring that, he was—and even the way he was still searching her perhaps confirmed it. Not judging, not frowning, just... searching.

"You being my lord, it just... takes it back, you know?" she continued, with a rueful little twitch of her shoulder. "Takes that power away from Pembroke, and gives it back to me. Maybe like with you and women, and your first—"

She belatedly winced, breaking off there—gods, of all the times to bring up Drafli's horrible first mate—but his mouth abruptly made a sound that might have almost been a huff. A... laugh.

"Ach," he finally rasped, with a sigh. "Take women from blood and shame and death, and cover with *this*."

This. He'd again bumped Alma with his nose, and she couldn't help a twinge of uncertainty as she blinked up toward him—and he gave another wry huff, shaking his head. "So sweet," he whispered. "So bright and eager and true. Always speaking this... wisdom, even when I no wish to hear it."

Oh. An odd, trembly heat was swirling up Alma's spine, and Drafli drew in a slow breath. "So quick to learn," he continued, even softer. "To give. To please. To... *meet* me. As if Skai-kesh make a second Pure-Heart, and drop her into my bed."

Alma felt her lips curve up, even as the pooling warmth

slightly stuttered—and she could feel Drafli catching that, his face pulling back, enough that his eyes came into focus again. "I ken you are no him," he whispered. "You are you. And he is..."

His voice caught, his mouth grimacing—and he abruptly ducked his face into his elbow, and coughed. The sound thankfully—hopefully—muffled enough that it couldn't be heard, though Alma flinched at the feeling of his body wracking over her, inside her, speaking his still-present pain.

And when he looked back down at her, that brightness was finally spilling from his desolate eyes, streaking down his harsh cheeks. And Alma only clutched him tighter, loved him harder, with all her strength.

"Baldr's still your mate," she whispered at him, nodding as fervently as she could. "Your home. Your *heart*."

Drafli was nodding too, fierce and forceful, as more of that wetness streaked from his eyes. As he ducked his head back into Alma's neck, his breaths juddering through his chest against her. His grief strong enough that Alma could taste it, could feel it pooling behind her own eyes, prickling and hot.

"We'll find him," she gulped, stroking his hair again and again. "We'll get him back. He loves you too, Drafli. He *does*."

But Drafli didn't answer, perhaps couldn't, between the sobs straining him, breaking him apart. And Alma kept holding him, kept stroking him, until the room finally faded, and slipped away into darkness.

48

Morning came with the sudden ring of a bell, jangling far too loud in Alma's ears.

She jolted up in her bed, rubbing painfully at her eyes—she was at Pembroke's, that was Pembroke's bell, what could he possibly want so early—and then she realized that there was still something slung over her hips, pinning her to the bed. Something warm, and heavy, and wait—

Wait. It was Drafli. It was *Drafli*, still sprawled here in Alma's little bed, his legs dangling off the end, his long body arching as he yawned. Good gods, Drafli was *here*, in Pembroke's house, he'd been here all night, and now Pembroke was ringing for her—and suddenly that was terror, streaking through Alma's thoughts.

What if Pembroke came up here, now?! What if he found Drafli here, and attacked him, and destroyed the peace-treaty? Destroyed everything?!

But Drafli's hand had slid over to grip against Alma's wrist, his eyes frowning toward her. *You no fear this foul man,* he signed, complete with a disgusted-looking flourish up at the still-ringing bell on the wall. *He is no more your lord.*

Alma twitched a grateful half-smile toward him, but her

heart was still hammering, her body still angling off the bed—until Drafli's hand snapped up higher, his long fingers curling around her *neck*.

Alma stilled beneath his touch, her eyes frozen on his face—and he actually gave a dark little smirk as his hand flexed against her throat, and then pressed downward. Pushing her upper body back down onto the bed, oh hell, while he himself flipped up over her, and knelt between her thighs.

He is no your lord, Bright-Heart, he signed, while his other hand kept coolly caressing her neck. *I am.*

Alma's breath escaped in a choked, hungry gasp, even as her cursed eyes reflexively angled back up toward the bell—until she felt something give a pointed, purposeful prod between her legs, and then a hard, heavy slap down from above.

And wait, that was—*that*, it was him, and he was again slapping his swollen heft down against her, his tapered tip smearing wetness into her coarse hair. *I am your lord*, he signed at her, and then his hand dropped again, gripping casually at his base, and then slowly sliding the tip back down her crease. Making her feel it, blatantly smearing her with more sticky white—and then nocking himself there, oh gods, *there*. To where she was still open and dripping wet, from when he'd taken her the night before.

I am your lord now, his hand repeated, as his other hand finally dropped from Alma's neck, in favour of gripping powerfully at her thigh, and yanking her lower half higher up into his lap. *Thus, you serve me first.*

With that, his hips canted forward, driving himself deep inside her. While Alma arched and trembled all over, her hand clapping against her gasping mouth, her eyes wide and shocked on Drafli's face.

But Drafli's head was tilting back, his long lashes fluttering, both his hands now gripping tighter to Alma's hips, better positioning her upon him. And then he launched into a swift, punishing rhythm, his strength snapping deep again and again, plunging into where it felt so much looser, wetter than before. The thick warm liquid from last time already spurting, pooling down her crease, while the sounds rose sloppy and obscene between them. But Drafli clearly didn't care, and only pumped in harder, faster, his eyes now half-lidded on the sight, as Alma helplessly moaned and writhed beneath him.

The bell on the wall was still ringing, but it had become a vague distant whine—especially once Drafli's hand had curtly grasped for Alma's wrist, and pulled it downwards. *Bring yourself relief,* he signed at her, sharp and commanding, his eyes flashing on hers. *Milk the seed from me.*

And oh, hell, Alma had already been close, caught in the danger, the disbelief, the craving—and it was far too easy to oblige. To grind her hungry fingers against where it felt best, to let them nudge against that slick scarred strength pounding her, ramming in again and again. Taking her there with such fluid, familiar ease, as though he'd done this a hundred times before, as though Alma were his to use as he wished.

And she was, she *was.* He was here, he was hers, *I am your lord now*—and the truth of that was enough to pitch her over the edge, the pleasure wheeling and screaming, while her body wildly convulsed against Drafli inside her. Milking him, just as he'd commanded—and oh, now he was the one convulsing, wringing himself out deep within her, his head bowing low, his chest heaving, his loosened hair hanging around his face.

The sound of the bell had abruptly stopped, the silence ringing uncomfortably in its wake, and Alma could feel Drafli giving a heavy sigh as his hand dropped to his trousers. To where he'd apparently had a rag, and he slipped it down between Alma's legs as he drew out of her, even tucking it a little inside.

Ought to hide proof of me for now, he signed, glancing up at her, his eyes far milder than before. *Are you well? Any pain?*

His hand had slid up to spread against her belly, against

their son, with something much like concern, or even reverence—and Alma's heart lurched a little as she shook her head.
No, she signed back. *Thank you, Golden-Tongue.*

But at that—that use of Baldr's sign for him—she could see
Drafli's eyes briefly stilling, slipping again into darkness, his
throat visibly swallowing. And then he gave a curt nod as he
leapt off the bed, striding over toward the door, and... *smelling*
it?

Get up, he signed at Alma, over his shoulder. *This man is
coming here.*

Oh. Oh, gods. Alma's heart was hammering in her chest,
and she awkwardly scrambled out of bed. She thankfully
hadn't undressed to sleep, she was still wearing the human
clothes they'd taken from the mountain, and while there was a
distinct wet patch on the skirt, perhaps Pembroke wouldn't
notice, perhaps—

But then that thought flailed away, her eyes frantically
searching Drafli's set face, because they hadn't even talked, had
they? They hadn't sorted out any kind of plan whatsoever, did
he even know everything they'd discussed at the mountain,
what was she supposed to do next—

But suddenly Drafli was here, his strong hands brushing
out Alma's clothes, and tucking her loose hair behind her ears.
I shall watch, and keep you safe, he signed at her. *You keep with
plan, and pretend to obey until Pure-Heart returns. Ach?*

Wait. *You know the plan?* Alma signed back at him, frowning—and in return he rolled his eyes, and tugged up the neck-
line of her dress, covering the fresh bite-marks on her neck.

Ach, I know plan, he replied, his eyes narrowing toward hers.
I am Right Hand of the Skai.

Oh. Alma couldn't help a reluctant little smile toward him,
and Drafli twitched a small smile back, before giving her cheek
a light flick with his claw. *Be brave, Bright-Heart*, he signed at
her. *I will be with you.*

And after everything they'd been through, all the misery

and betrayal and secrets, Alma still found herself... nodding. Saying, *Yes. I trust you.*

Drafli nodded too, his eyes shifting—and then he leaned down, and gently pressed his mouth to hers. His warmth and his tongue and his sweetness all swarming her in a heady dizzy rush, even as he eased her around, and reached for the door...

And without warning, he'd released her, and nudged her out the open door. His hand giving one last little swat at her arse on the way, one last little rush of warmth, until...

Until Alma was standing out in the chilly narrow corridor, and blinking into the darkness. At the emerging sight of a hunched, menacing figure, stalking straight toward her.

It was Pembroke.

49

"Where have you been, girl," Pembroke growled as he strode toward her. "I've been ringing for you!"

Alma's heart was still thudding in her chest, but the truth of Drafli, hidden just behind that door, made it easier to lift her chin, and hold Pembroke's beady eyes. "I'm here now," she said. "What do you need?"

In response, Pembroke only grasped for her arm with his meaty hand, and began roughly dragging her down the corridor. Not toward the main part of the house, as Alma might have expected, but toward the servants' back stairs. And she felt her heartbeat thundering even louder as she followed him all the way down the narrow stairwell, and toward the servants' side entrance.

"Where are you taking me?" she heard herself ask, her voice not quite steady. "Are you—firing me again?"

"Quiet, girl," barked Pembroke in reply, as he yanked the door open, and thrust Alma out into the cool open air. "We're going to a... meeting."

A meeting. Alma's eyes darted uncertainly around her, taking in the quiet grounds, the dim morning light. It was still very early, the sky only barely beginning to brighten, and the rest of the servants were surely either occupied with their morning tasks, or still asleep.

"What kind of meeting?" Alma asked, still glancing uneasily at the surrounding darkness. "And where?"

Pembroke loudly huffed, and began dragging Alma across the empty grounds, in the direction of the forest. "With Lord Otto, girl," he snapped at her. "Just like you wanted, remember? He's set up camp with a band in the forest, and he said if I bring you by early this morning, he'd be willing to hear your side. About the... *orcs*."

His mouth twisted as he said it, and the thunder of Alma's heartbeat briefly stuttered, scattered into disbelief. The province's ruling lord was truly here? Truly willing to hear her side? To possibly stop the fighting, and return the peace again?

And gods, that was precisely what Alma had hoped for, one of the crucial reasons she'd come here—so she jerked a shaky nod and quickened her steps, while the too-vivid vision of Thrain's silent, immobile body filled her thoughts. She would do this. She would do anything she could, for her home. Her clan. Her family.

Her hands had fluttered to her belly as she walked, her thoughts clinging to the truth of Drafli's nearness—his promise to keep her safe—as she followed Pembroke into the thick line of trees. Onto a narrow, twisting path, taking them into the midst of a tangled mass of alders and birches.

But the sight suddenly felt darkly, horribly familiar, whirling up memories of running through these very woods, the thin branches scraping and whipping at her face. Her feet tripping, her breath burning, the distinctive sound of the rushing river, rising just ahead...

Alma shivered all over, clutching her arms tighter around her waist, and cleared her choked-feeling throat. "How far in is Lord Otto camped?" she asked, toward where Pembroke was purposefully stomping along in front of her. "And how many men does he have with him?"

Because it was strangely quiet, unnervingly so, beyond the steady, ever-rising sound of the river. And surely if there was a camp nearby, there would be the sounds of voices, of horses, of men preparing for the day to come...

But there was still nothing, no telltale sights or sounds. Only the river, its bank now visible just ahead, the sharp drop off the edge far too familiar, far too clear.

And Drafli was with her, Alma's distant brain chanted, he'd promised—but her heartbeat was still surging, roaring in her ears, as she felt her steps halting, her eyes gone wide and fearful on Pembroke's back.

"Why did you bring me here?" her thin voice asked. "There's no sign of a camp here. No sign of *anything*."

Pembroke had hesitated too, and Alma could see him glancing around, his eyes lingering on the cliff of the riverbank just ahead. As if he were looking too, searching for something, something hidden under the brush at his feet...

And without warning, he grasped up a coil of rope, and *lunged*. Lunged straight for Alma, oh gods, knocking her off-balance, and flinging his rope over her—over her *head*?!

Alma screamed and scrabbled against him, her fingers desperately clutching at the rope—but Pembroke was already thrusting it down over her shoulders, and reeling backwards. Yanking the rope hard and painful around her chest, clamping her arms tight against her sides. Trapping her, oh gods, he was *tying her up*—and now he was wrenching her forward, sending her feet stumbling over the uneven ground toward him.

"This is why you're here, fool girl," he hissed at her, his mouth widening into a cruel, horrifying smile. "To finish what you started, when you *dared* to run away from me!"

Alma's entire body was shuddering, her tingling hands still frantically fighting to grasp at the rope. But the way he'd trapped her arms made it impossible, *impossible*—and

Pembroke was still smiling as he watched her struggle, both his hands still clutched tight to the rope's other end.

"You tried to defy me," he snarled at her. "You tried to humiliate me, and ruin all my plans. So now"—his horrible smile broadened even wider, his beady eyes glinting with vicious satisfaction—"you're going to run away again. For good, this time. *Forever.*"

What? *What?* Alma's head was desperately shaking, her hands still wildly fumbling at the rope, the panic screaming in her skull—and wait, what was Pembroke doing. He was kicking aside more mounded brush, and bending down, and grasping for something. Something large and heavy and—

No. *No.* It was a rock, a massive grey stone, and it was—it was tied. It was tied to the *rope.* The rope around *her.*

And Pembroke kept giving that awful, triumphant smile, as he began dragging the rock toward... the river. Toward the cliff, only a few short steps away from him, and no, no, no, he couldn't, Alma's son, her life, her family, the war, Baldr, Drafli, please—

She kicked off, running toward him, her shoulder heaving into his chest, her legs kicking as powerfully as she could, aiming for the bastard's groin. And for an instant there was the hope, bright and screeching, that maybe she could do this, she could fight him off, if she just—

But then the rope around her yanked, wrenching her downwards, dragging her to the earth. Flashing pain through her knees, sparking wheeling white stars behind her eyes. Enough that she almost couldn't see Pembroke, lunging for his rock... and heaving it over the cliff.

"No!" she croaked, her hands flailing, her body staggering toward the edge. "Drafli! *Baldr!*"

But it was too late, it was over now, it was done. And Alma screamed as she dropped back through empty air, and crashed into the deep.

50

Drowning was still a horrifying way to die.

The slam of the river's ice-cold water on Alma's back felt even more shocking than last time, flashing her full of excruciating, devastating agony. And though she instinctively knew how to react this time—keep her nose and mouth closed, kick up with her throbbing legs, aim for the surface—it wasn't working. Not with her arms trapped like this, not against the relentless weight of the rope, the rock, plummeting her steadily deeper, dragging her toward her death.

It was over. Finished. She'd failed.

But as Alma's furiously flailing body sank further into the icy darkness, there was at least one distant certainty, thudding in time with the echoing drive of her heart. There was no shame. She'd tried. She'd done her best, as any Grisk would.

And in it, she'd found love. She'd found purpose, and strength, and happiness. She'd made peace with Drafli, with her mother, with *herself*. And maybe she'd even helped a few others find peace along the way, too.

She'd done her best. She *had*.

When suddenly, something—was here. Something large and shadowy, bobbing in the water before her—and then lurching for her. Or rather—Alma's hazy, burning eyes blinked against the darkness—for her rope. Sawing against it with fierce, frantic urgency. With—his claw?

Drafli, Alma's distant thoughts shouted, Drafli had come— but as the weight dragging against her abruptly lessened, bobbing her upward, the arm circling powerfully around her didn't feel like Drafli's. It felt like... like...

Alma joined him in kicking upwards, surging toward the light—and as they broke through the surface of the water, she reflexively clutched for her rescuer, clinging to him with all her might. Dragging in the familiar, head-spinning scent of him with every coughing, gasping breath.

"It's you?" she gulped, her eyes painfully blinking at the hazy, greenish outline of the orc holding her, grasping her tightly in his strong arms, as his legs easily kicked below, keeping them safe above the rushing water. "*Baldr*?"

Yes, yes, oh thank the *gods*, it was Baldr. And as he slowly came into focus before her, Alma could see his head fervently nodding, the water streaming down his face. His black hair plastered to his cheeks and neck, his eyes wide and blinking and horrified on hers.

"Ach," he whispered, his voice wavering. "It is me. And you. *Ach*."

With that, he yanked Alma close again, his big hand pressing tight against her back, his solid body shuddering with his breaths. "Ach," he breathed again. "I am here. Will keep you safe. I am so, so sorry you had to face this. So sorry, my Bright-Heart."

Alma clutched even tighter against him, dragging in the impossible, tenuous promise of those words. Here. Sorry. *Safe*.

When behind them, suddenly, there was a shout. A sharp, purposeful splash. And Alma's blinking, clouded eyes darted back, just in time to see someone kicking and thrashing in the water. It was... Mr. Pembroke?!

Alma's fear flashed white and sickening—was Pembroke

still chasing her, was he still trying to *kill* her?!—when someone else surged up out of the water behind Pembroke. Someone who was grinning maniacally as he snapped a rope down over Pembroke's head, and yanked it tight.

Drafli.

Pembroke shouted and flailed, clawing desperately at the rope around his neck—but behind him, Drafli just kept grinning as he wrenched the rope tighter. And then gave it a hard, vicious yank, almost as if *testing* it, while Pembroke sputtered and screamed before him.

"Mayhap best not to look, Bright-Heart," cut in Baldr's low voice, as he drew Alma around in the water, and kicked toward the bank. "Drafli has this in hand. Come. This way."

Alma certainly wasn't about to argue, and felt her shaky body swimming along beside Baldr toward the shore. Until she could find her footing on the rocky riverbed, and Baldr's strong arm kept her steady and close as he guided her up over the bank, onto a flat, grassy little knoll.

But from behind them, Alma could still hear Pembroke shouting, cursing, railing against foul orcs, against *her*. His panicked voice rising and thinning, becoming increasingly frayed and shrill—until it was broken by a sudden, decisive-sounding splash.

And then... quiet. Only the odd, relatively silent sounds of the river, rushing smooth and steady behind them, as though nothing out of the ordinary had occurred.

But Alma's breaths were still erratically gulping, her shocked eyes staring up at Baldr beside her. At where he was looking unmistakably... *relieved*, his shoulders sagging, his breath exhaling. And then he drew her even closer, and heavily sank down onto the earth, dragging her into his lap.

"Did that foul man harm you?" he breathed now, his gaze sweeping up and down her torso, as his claws yanked through the fabric against her neck. Slicing it away, so that he could carefully tilt her chin, inspect the skin of her throat. "Do you feel any wounds, or pain?"

Alma swallowed, and desperately fought to consider that through the still-driving beat of her heart. "I... think... I'm all right?" she whispered back, between gulps of air. "I didn't—hit anything, other than the water. Or—swallow it, this time."

Baldr was rapidly nodding, his lips pressed tightly together, his eyes still fixed on her throat. On... oh. Where Drafli had *bitten* her, the night before.

"Good," he whispered, hoarse, as his eyes purposefully dropped, his claws again slicing at her sodden clothes. Yanking them off her breasts, her torso, her hips, until she was sitting entirely bared in his lap, and his big hand was carefully running all over her, clearly checking for any sign of injury.

But then he'd hesitated again, his hand held over her groin this time, his eyes blinking toward it. And in a sudden flurry of motion, he'd shifted her down onto the earth, so that he could bend over her and inhale, his lashes fluttering, his chest filling against her.

And wait, he was smelling—their *son*, and Alma's heart suddenly kicked up again, her hands snapping down to clasp against her belly. "Is our son—still there?" she choked. "Still alive?"

Baldr jerked a nod, his gaze flicking uncertainly up to her face. "Ach, he is well," he whispered back. "Stronger. Smells more like—"

But then he winced, and twitched to look up over his shoulder. Toward—Drafli, oh gods, *Drafli*, who was striding purposefully over the bank toward them, his lean body streaming water, his eyes flashing hard and intent.

Alma could feel Baldr stiffening, almost as if bracing for a fight—but as Drafli halted to stand beside them, his hand only reached down to grip at Baldr's shoulder, giving it a firm, companionable little shake.

Good to see you, Pure-Heart, his other hand signed, the movements very pointed and deliberate. *Any wounds? Or pain?*

His too-intent eyes were flicking between Baldr and Alma, clearly including them both in this—and gods, had Alma even thought to ask Baldr if he was hurt?—but Baldr was already shaking his head, his shoulders rising and falling, his eyes angling back toward Alma.

"She says she is well," he croaked. "And I can smell nothing amiss. Not with her, or"—he winced, as his shoulders rose and fell again—"or with your son."

Alma could see Drafli's already-coiled body hardening tighter, his clawed hand very carefully moving to flick at Baldr's cheek. But Baldr quickly twitched away, his eyes closing, his swallow visibly convulsing in his throat.

"So you mean to keep your son after all, then?" he asked, his voice very thin. "And I can now taste your scent all over Alma also, so I ken you—you mean to keep *her*, too?"

To keep her. Oh. As if Baldr thought—as if he thought Alma was still only Drafli's—pet. *Your pretty, foolish, pliant Grisk pet*, he'd called himself, when he'd left. When he'd gestured at Alma like that, clearly calling her a foolish pet, too. A... *servant.*

The hurt flashed through Alma's chest, pooling cold and bitter in her belly—and above her, the barely contained tension in Drafli's tall body seemed to shudder, and burst. Flashing into a sharp streak of motion, into his hand grabbing for Baldr's loose hair, and dragging him around to look at him. His other hand rapidly signing, so fluid Alma couldn't fully follow, but it kept coming clearer as he kept repeating it, over and over again.

You want to know? it surely meant, his hand yanking even harder at Baldr's hair. *You want to know what I want, you stubborn, provoking Grisk brat? You want to know?*

His tension seemed to be seeping into Baldr's body against him, into the way his eyes were flashing too, his hands clutching to fists. "Ach, speak all you wish," Baldr sneered back, "but you ken I shall not believe a word of it, from a lying, cheating Skai!"

The rage sparked higher in Drafli's eyes, his rigid form almost seeming to ripple in place—and then he again flashed into movement. Hurling himself straight down toward Baldr, his body twisting and wrenching with astonishing speed as he threw Baldr onto his back on the earth.

There was a moment's flat stillness, their breaths gasping—until Baldr suddenly flared up beneath Drafli, his elbows and knees driving at Drafli's chest, his neck, his groin. Striking with raw, genuine aggression, with fury that seemed just as brutal as Drafli's. Wringing Drafli's rage even higher, his teeth bared as he swiftly dodged and countered Baldr's blows, as he shoved himself down harder onto him. As one clawed hand thrust between them, slicing and shoving with frenzied intent. Yanking at... Baldr's trousers.

And oh, Baldr knew it, he was flailing up with even more purpose than before, his elbows slamming painful-looking blows against Drafli's neck, his face. The last one hard enough that Drafli growled and reared back, his wet hair flying out behind him—and then he seemed to redouble his efforts, tearing out the seams of Baldr's trousers with sharp, forceful yanks. While Baldr's now-bared legs kicked and kneed at him, and Drafli growled again as he thrust Baldr's thighs apart, and shoved himself between them.

"Still want to know?" Drafli snarled, as he ducked another blow, and cuffed Baldr straight across his cheekbone with his fist. "Ach?!"

Baldr's head had snapped sideways, his mouth hissing, but he wasn't refusing, he wasn't. "Still won't believe you," he grunted, as his leg again kicked at Drafli's side, betraying a glimpse of his own thick, heavy hardness, lying swollen on his belly between them. "You sneaking—lying—"

But his voice cracked there, because Drafli's thighs had shoved up harder against his, splitting them wider—and oh,

Drafli had somehow yanked down his own trousers, and thrust himself there. Prodding up hard and purposeful against Baldr, against where Baldr had abruptly stopped fighting, his chest heaving, his eyes glittering on Drafli's face.

"Ach?" Drafli hissed at him, as his hands grasped for Baldr's wet tunic, hauling it off over his head, revealing the damp, gleaming skin beneath it. And Alma could see Baldr's throat convulsing, the heft on his belly shuddering, his expression warring between fury, and hunger, and misery.

But then he twitched a short, furtive little nod. And in return, Alma could almost taste Drafli's relief, blazing across his eyes—and then he drove forward. Slamming inside Baldr without warning, without tenderness, with only vicious, furious force.

Baldr flared up beneath it, another guttural growl burning from his throat—and suddenly he was swinging up again, striking for Drafli's neck and face. Almost as if to take advantage of the fact that Drafli was now locked inside him, good gods—and Drafli knew it, hissing as he swung back, as he yanked out, and slammed inside with another fierce punch of his hips.

Baldr again arched up, his shout tearing through the trees, his heft now flexing between them, his claws dragging down Drafli's front. Leaving long red lines behind, but Drafli didn't even seem to notice, and only knocked Baldr's arm aside as he pulled out, and plunged in again. Driving another desperate shout from Baldr's throat, his swollen heft spraying a sharp little splatter of white onto his bared belly.

It almost felt like Alma had been watching from somewhere else, from a world very far away—but at that, she could feel her own breath exhaling, her eyes caught on the sight. On Baldr's shuddering, gleaming skin, ridged taut over hard muscle, and spattered with that pearly, glistening white. Bared, seething, vulnerable, hungry.

Wanting this. *Needing* this.

And wait, now Baldr's movements had stilled again, his eyes catching on Alma's—and Drafli was looking too. His eyes boring into hers, burning, *wanting*.

And then Drafli's head jerked toward her, the movement curt but purposeful. Saying, *Come. Over here. Now.*

So Alma did, crawling closer toward them on the grass, keeping her gaze on Drafli. On how he was blatantly looking her up and down, leering with shameless, glinting hunger. With... appreciation.

Good, he coolly signed at her. *Now, you will feed my stubborn mate. With my seed.*

She would... what? Alma's head tilted, her brows rising, but beside her Baldr still hadn't moved, but for his heaving breaths. His eyes flicking uncertainly between her and Drafli, while Drafli's smirk only seemed to sharpen, his hand waving purposefully between Alma, and... Baldr's *face*.

A low, ragged moan escaped Baldr's throat, and Drafli kept giving that wicked smile as he reached for Alma's hand, and drew her forward, up, closer. So that she was now kneeling too, facing toward him, her knees on either side of Baldr's head, and—

Oh. *Oh.* And Drafli's hand had come to her shoulder, guiding her downwards, because—because he wanted her to lower herself onto Baldr. That part of her. Onto his... mouth.

And yes, Baldr had tasted her there before, but never like this—and Alma felt her breath choking as she glanced down at his flushed-red, wide-eyed face between her legs, and then back up at Drafli again. To where Drafli was raising his eyebrow, and jabbing his claw downwards. Saying, *Sit, Bright-Heart. Now.*

So Alma... did. Again keeping her eyes on Drafli as she slowly lowered herself closer, closer. Until she could feel the heat of Baldr's breath, tickling so close against her swollen, spread-open warmth—and then, oh hell, a quick, furtive little lick of his tongue.

"Oh," Alma gasped, shuddering all over, and Drafli gave another dark, approving smile as he ground his hips deeper inside Baldr, and then reached for the leather on his wrist. For Alma's leather, that he'd still been wearing—and once he'd tugged it out long and thin, he coolly grasped for Baldr's still-swollen length, and threaded the leather through his *ring*. Pulling it until both ends were even again, and then giving it a casual, experimental little tug. Watching with hooded eyes as Baldr growled and flared, his now-trapped heft bobbing straight up on its string, and spraying out another splatter of thick white.

"*Fuck*, Draf," Baldr croaked, the words hot and desperate against Alma's trembling, hovering heat—and Drafli's grin went even more devious, more devilish, as he coolly thrust the leather's loose ends into Alma's hand.

Here, he signed at her. *Now sit. Ride him. For me.*

Oh, gods above. Alma couldn't seem to breathe, let alone speak, but she nodded, and lowered herself a little downward. Down toward the shuddering exhale of Baldr's breath, closer, closer—until oh, she was touching him, meeting him, kissing him. And he was carefully kissing her back, tasting her with his lips, his tongue, and oh it felt impossible like this, unbelievable, *obscene*—

And it was that word, that thought, that suddenly had her eyes darting at the forest around them—the still-rushing river—while a distant vague shouting began reeling through her skull. They were out in the open, she was fully naked and straddled over Baldr's *face*, while Drafli was still grinding bollocks-deep inside him. After he had just—he'd just—

But then Drafli's hand snapped forward, and circled around Alma's neck. His thumb tilting her head up, making her meet his eyes, his claw gently prodding up beneath her chin.

No shame, his other hand signed at her, his eyes hard and meaningful. *Need to show him. Show him we see him. We hunger for him. We love him.*

And that made no sense, or did it, because Alma could feel Baldr giving another shuddering exhale against her, followed by another furtive, careful kiss. As if, perhaps, he wasn't sure, either. Wasn't sure if this was truly his. If *they* were truly his.

And that was their fault, they'd been the ones who'd done this to him, lied to him, made that stupid secret vow without him. But Baldr was here now, he was doing this, he wanted this—and now it was up to them to show it. To prove it. To do better. To make amends.

So Alma shuddered, nodded, understood. And then, holding Drafli's crackling eyes, she leaned back again, into that still-tentative touch of Baldr's tongue. And instead of carefully kissing him back, she sank herself hard against him, crushing her folds against his mouth, burying his face deep.

His harsh, muffled groan quivered all through her, his tongue driving up with far more purpose than before—and Alma cried out at the unreal sensation of it, the impossible, brazen intimacy of it. At how his strong hands had come up, gripping at her thighs, and how her body willingly sank closer, meeting his urgent, desperate licks with slick, lurid caresses of her own. The wetness already shockingly intense, throbbing out of her in pulse after pulse, and wait, that was because of Drafli, Drafli had poured her full of him just a short time before, and now she was pouring it out into Baldr's mouth, oh gods, oh fuck.

Her wide eyes had found Drafli again, drinking up the sharp smug satisfaction in his glittering, watching gaze—and now he was plunging forward again, too. Driving into Baldr with hard, powerful strokes, making his body beneath them judder and arch, his moans vibrating deep into Alma's core.

Oh, it felt good, so good, and Drafli raised his brows toward Alma as he kept pumping, his gaze dropping to the leather in her hand. His silent command all too clear, and she shivered all over as she gave the leather a gentle little tug, as Baldr shouted and flailed and desperately licked *inside* her. Into where she was flailing too, and flooding his mate's seed into his mouth.

Fuck, it was *magnificent*, so Alma tugged again, watching, feeling, greedy and lurid and desperate, as Baldr again flared up, his throat frantically swallowing. His heft on a string—on *her* string—spurting out another spray of glossy white, and this time Alma's fingers fumbled down to catch it, to slip its rich sweetness between her parted, gasping lips.

And that was a nod from Drafli, *approval* from Drafli, as he dropped his clawed hand to grip around Baldr's plump length, to pump up with a firm stroke, in perfect time with his next plunge inside. And Baldr's shout was even louder this time, pure choked pleasure into Alma's clutching dripping heat, and she gasped too, and yanked on her string as she ground a little harder against him. Then again, and again, while Drafli plunged and pumped, and Baldr kept shouting into her, his rigid body writhing up beneath her, this tongue stuttering deep inside.

The feeling was like nothing Alma had ever known, wheeling and swooping with reckless abandon, and she held her eyes to Drafli's brash, burning gaze as they worked Baldr together. He was here, he was theirs, they were doing their best for him, they were...

Speak to him, Drafli mouthed at her, as he slammed in again, again. *Speak for us.*

And yes, Alma would, of course she would, and already the words were rising, ripening with every desperate writhe and kick from Baldr beneath them. "You're so beautiful, Pure-Heart," she gasped. "So gorgeous, when you're stuck and screaming for us, aren't you?"

She punctuated the words with an extra-hard tug of her string, and she could feel him arching up even further, his shout long and sustained against her, as another spray of white flared out against his ring.

"So pretty, with our devil inside you," she whispered,

dropping her other hand to stroke at his flexing, gleaming chest as she kept riding him, in time with Drafli's movements before her. "And with you drinking his seed from me, like you should. So good. So sweet."

And oh, the way Baldr shuddered, the way Drafli's eyes were burning on hers, with appreciation, with affection. "So *perfect*," she continued, breathless, her thumb sliding against one of Baldr's hardened greenish nipples. "We love feeling you like this. Love your tongue. Love being inside you. Love making you beg and scream for us."

And yes, Baldr was screaming, his body thrashing up, and Alma was lost, found, utterly enthralled, one hand tugging at that leather, the other pinching his nipple, feeling his throat gulping as he swallowed her, feeling his tongue thrusting inside her. Feeling how Drafli was ramming into him with such pure reckless devotion, with the silent promise that he would do anything, destroy anyone, for this. For them.

"And Drafli loves you so much," Alma gasped, drinking up the truth of that in Drafli's wild, frenzied eyes. "You're his mate. His heart. The pure heart he didn't get to have. But now he has you, we have you, and we would give anything for you, love, *anything*."

She'd been yanking at the ring as she spoke, driving home every word, every shining, perfect truth—and Baldr roared up into her as he sprayed out, spurting thick and messy all over her hands, her leather, her breasts, her belly. While between his legs, Drafli stiffened, his head thrown back, his claws sunk deep into Baldr's skin, dragging him up harder, tighter, into pain and pressure and deliverance—and Alma could see him pouring out inside, could feel it in Baldr's desperate cry inside her, in his own claws digging into her hips. In the sudden surging crush of her own ecstasy, milking itself out around his tongue, flooding more of his mate's seed down into his gulping, groaning throat.

The impossible pleasure seemed to keep circling, careening

back and forth between them—until finally, finally, it filtered down again. Settling into something almost bearable, something Alma could almost touch at... when Drafli surged forward, and kissed her.

It was hard, possessive, approving. Full of firm lips and seeking tongue and sharp dragging teeth, and Alma met it, moaned into it, her tingling fingers slipping around the back of his neck, and up into his hair. Into his warmth, his strength, his fierce, unflinching affection. While between her legs, another mouth kept kissing her too, with just as much fervour as this one.

Alma let herself sink into it, soar into it, kissing both their mouths, whirling into the truth of their hungry tongues and lips and teeth. And when Drafli finally drew away, his eyes soft, his claw flicking her cheek, she signed at him, quick and instinctive and raw.

I love you, my lord, she said. *I love you.*

Drafli's eyes on hers shifted, changed, glimmering with bright, tolerant approval. *Good*, he signed back at her, his mouth a little saucy. *You should. This pleases me.*

Alma actually felt herself laugh, shaking her head—and in return Drafli again flicked her cheek, and then twitched his head sideways. Saying, *Get up, then*, and then adding a few swift signs, too. *More later, ach?*

Alma nodded, and carefully eased herself up, and off to Baldr's side. Wincing a little at the sight of his face, bright red and slicked all over—but oh, that was his tongue, licking at it, sweeping over his mouth. Still wanting to taste her, oh hell, or wanting to taste his mate, or both.

He was looking just as dazed as Alma felt, his chest still heaving with his breaths, his eyes gazing blankly up at the sky. Or rather, up at Drafli, because Drafli had now eased down to lie on top of him, holding himself up on his elbows, so he could look down into Baldr's eyes.

And Baldr was looking, blinking, his throat visibly

convulsing—and then Drafli bent down and kissed him, too. Just as hard and purposeful as when he'd kissed Alma, full of tongue and force and teeth, and deep, vehement thoroughness.

Mine, it seemed to say, as his hand slid into Baldr's hair, drawing him closer. *Mine. My heart.*

Alma could feel her eyes prickling as she watched, as she felt her heart skipping at the relief of it, the rightness of it. They were finally together again, safe again. A family.

And as if to prove that, Baldr's arm reached for her, and pulled her into his side. So that she was lying tucked against him, her head on his shoulder, while above him, Drafli shifted too, his arm settling against her back, his claws sinking into her hair. Wanting her close, wanting her here with them, together.

And the peace of that, the rightness of that, only swelled higher as Drafli gently drew away from Baldr, and flicked a claw at his cheek, too. And then tilted Baldr's chin toward Alma, while he himself slid the wet hair away from Baldr's neck, and eased his face down against it.

Baldr shuddered all over, his breath hissing as Drafli bit down—but his hand had skittered up, stroking gently at Alma's face, and nudging her closer toward him. Careful and tentative, almost as though he wasn't sure she would want it—but she was already there, here, pressing her lips to his. Feeling him shiver, and open—and then he was kissing her too, frantic and desperate. Silently shouting of his regret, and his relief.

"Ach," he whispered, as he finally pulled away, his warm hand still trembling against Alma's cheek. "I am so sorry, Bright-Heart. I ought never have run and left you thus. I never wished to place you into danger. Never wished to hurt you, or frighten you."

Alma nodded, and stroked his dear, beautiful face. "I know," she whispered back. "And I'm so sorry, too. We should never have hidden that vow from you the way we did. We should have told you the full truth from the start."

She could feel Baldr's swallow, his shoulder jerking against her. "But I hid the truth from you, also," he replied thickly. "I did not tell you what I had done with Efterar, when you had every right to know this—you and Draf both. And I foolishly made you think you only had this one month to please us, and this"—he swallowed again—"this must have felt so cruel to you. It must have caused you so much *fear*, Bright-Heart."

Alma couldn't find a way to counter that, and Baldr's bright eyes squeezed shut, and opened again. "And worst of all," he whispered, even quieter, "I failed to show you how much you meant to me. How deeply I have prized and cherished you, and all the great gifts you have granted us. You have shown yourself such a faithful partner and friend, and in return, I"—he winced—"I made you think you were only a servant. A *pet*."

Alma winced too, and felt herself searching his glimmering eyes, so close. Remembering all those painful words he'd shouted at Drafli, the day he'd left. *I have sought to be a worthy mate, to earn your truth. I was not your partner, I was your pretty, foolish, pliant Grisk pet.*

"But you saw *yourself* that way, too," she croaked at him. "And you're not, Baldr. You're *not*. You've never been Drafli's servant, or his pet. You're his mate. His *heart*."

Drafli's head hadn't lifted from Baldr's neck, but Alma could see him nodding, silent and quick. And his hand had slipped down from Alma's head, back over to Baldr, his fingers spreading wide against Baldr's heart.

Baldr's chest rose and fell beneath Drafli's touch, his eyes fluttering closed. "Your heart is a *fool*, Draf," he croaked, and in reply Drafli's mouth shifted against him, his jaw visibly flexing, while a brief flash of pain—and then pleasure—shot across Baldr's face. "Ach, ach," he murmured. "I ken."

Drafli's hand again came up, patting lightly at Baldr's cheek, approving, before sliding back up into Alma's hair. As his body eased down closer onto Baldr, like he was settling in for a long proper meal of him, good gods—but Baldr didn't look in the least unsettled by this, and even gave Alma a rueful, relieved half-smile. While his hand slid up into her hair, too, his fingers catching there with Drafli's, and curling together against her, their joined claws brushing her scalp.

It was quite possibly the most glorious thing Alma had ever felt in her entire life, so content, so safe—and she snuggled even closer, breathing in their warm, succulent scents. And perhaps even slipping off toward sleep, full as she was of such warmth, and light, and ease.

At least, until a familiar, horrible smell stole into her breath. The smell of... smoke. And Alma felt her head jerking up, her eyes snapping open, searching the brightening morning light. Where a growing grey cloud was rising above them...

Something was burning. On fire. And it was close.

51

Alma scrabbled up to her feet, her heart furiously pounding, her eyes wildly sweeping across the sky. While memories of the last fire she'd faced poured through her thoughts, clamping at her suddenly tight throat.

They were in danger. They had to run. *Now*.

She'd whirled back around to Baldr and Drafli, who had both risen to their feet, too. Both of them studying her, Baldr's head tilting, Drafli wiping at his reddened mouth.

"Fire," she gulped at them, her voice cracking. "Fire! We have to run! We have to—"

But before she could finish, she suddenly found herself caught between them. Her face tucked firmly against Drafli's strong chest, his hand stroking at her hair, while Baldr's strong arms circled her from behind, holding her close and safe.

"Do not fear, Bright-Heart," Baldr murmured, into her hair. "There is nothing to fret over. You are safe with us. Ach?"

Alma was still shivering between them, but she could feel the panic fading beneath their closeness, their certainty. "But," she gulped, "why? What is it? Why aren't you—"

But Drafli only kept stroking her, while behind her, Baldr huffed a hoarse laugh. "Because Draf started that fire, ach,

Draf?" he replied. "Or ordered your scouts to do so. Same thing, in the end."

Wait. Alma twitched backwards, frowning up at Drafli's face—and he was indeed looking very smug, with that familiar devilish glint in his eyes. *Ach, I did*, he coolly signed at her. *I wished to see this foul man's house burn.*

Alma's breath choked, her eyes darting back to the smoke—because yes, oh gods, it was from precisely the direction of Pembroke's house. Drafli was burning down Pembroke's *house*?!

"But—the staff!" Alma's voice rasped. "My colleagues. They're just as trapped as I was, they—"

Ach, we ken, Drafli swiftly signed at her, as his other hand came up to her face, his fingers pressing gently against her lips. *We make sure humans are safe. But for that one.*

His mouth was curling into that alarming smile again, his eyes alight as they glanced toward the river. *They now think he die in fire*, he continued. *But he lie rotting at bottom of river instead.*

Alma gaped at Drafli's smug face, while an incomprehensible surge of guilt, and relief, and maybe even *amusement* swarmed through her thoughts. "But—*Drafli*," she gasped at him. "You can't just go around *killing* people! Even ones as vile as Mr. Pembroke!"

But Drafli's eyes had slightly darkened, danger glinting in their depths. *I can*, he signed back at her. *This man sought to kill you. He sought to destroy what is mine. For this, he had to die.*

Oh. Alma couldn't seem to find an answer to that, blinking up at Drafli's set, triumphant face—and behind her, she could even feel Baldr giving a low growl, his arms circling a little tighter. "This man also caused grave harm to your mother," he said. "And likely to many others. We could not allow him to run free again."

Alma swallowed, her eyes glancing uncertainly up at the smoke rising behind them. "And this won't—come back to haunt you, though?" she asked, her voice still wavering. "With your captain, or the peace-treaty?"

Drafli's eyes were again betraying that devilish glint, and she could feel Baldr shaking his head. "The captain shall sort it out," he said. "But it shall not take much effort, I ken. It is due to this man's own cruelty that his own servants have twice sought to burn his home, ach? If the third attempt should be successful, taking his life with it—and mayhap yours, Bright-Heart, as well—how is this the fault of orcs?"

Ohhhh. Oh, that was clever. And Alma felt her body relaxing, sagging back into Baldr's strength behind her—and she could hear Baldr exhaling, too. "This was a good plan, Draf," he said, quiet. "I—thank you, for thinking of this, and carrying it through."

And wait, was Baldr implying that this—this had been the orcs' plan all along? And Alma hadn't known of it? Because the plans they'd discussed back at the mountain had included scouts, and surveillance, and various contingencies until Baldr returned... but certainly no burning, or *killing*. Had it?

But Drafli's hand was already giving a dismissive wave, his eyes angling between Alma's and Baldr's. *I only decide it today*, he signed. *Only after I see what this man mean to do. And after—* his other hand reached up to Baldr's face behind Alma, perhaps flicking at his cheek—*I scent you, Pure-Heart.*

Alma could feel Baldr stilling, and when she twisted up to look, he was frowning at Drafli, his head tilted. "You scented me," he said slowly. "When? Where?"

Drafli signed something that might have been a place name, and Baldr's frown deepened. "You were not supposed to," he said, under his breath. "Did your scouts scent me, too?"

Drafli shook his head, his eyes gone decidedly smug again. *You are my mate*, he signed back. *I learn your tricks, Pure-Heart.*

Baldr's mouth was hanging open, his expression caught somewhere between disbelief and admiration. And looking up at his face, thinking back to all the various hints around this, Alma realized that this was something she wanted to know too, once and for all.

"So how does that... work, exactly, Baldr?" she asked him, as she pulled away a little, out of their embrace, to better see their faces. "You're not only able to follow others across large distances, but you can hide your scent, too? At will? Even from those you're close to?"

Baldr grimaced at Drafli, who was fully grinning now, and again flicking his claw at Baldr's cheek. *Ach*, Drafli signed back at her. *His scent, and that of others, also. He is most gifted orc in all our mountain. Most powerful. Most... perfect.*

Drafli's eyes had sobered at the last, his thumb brushing against Baldr's lips. And then his throat convulsed, his shoulders squaring, as he briefly glanced down toward Alma. Almost as if needing to see her. Needing her... help.

And Alma was already nodding back up at him, her hand spreading against his back, pressing him her affection, her encouragement, her trust. Knowing he could do this. He could do better. He would.

I am sorry, Pure-Heart, Drafli signed toward Baldr, the movements very slow, very careful. *I ought never have sworn this vow without you. Ought never have pushed you into this. Ought never have broken your trust.*

Baldr's mouth spasmed, but he didn't speak, and Drafli kept signing, faster now. *I wish to learn*, he said. *I wish to be a better mate. Wish to gain your trust again. Your heart.*

Baldr still didn't reply, and Drafli again glanced down at Alma, and back at Baldr again. *You are no just my pet, Pure-Heart*, he continued. *You were never just this. You are sweet and fair, ach—but you are also strong and fierce and true. You are a great gift to me. I love you.*

There was a long, shuddering silence, thick and choked between them—and then Baldr's hand rubbed at his face, his gaze dropping. "But—you are wrong, Draf," he replied, his voice thin. "I am not strong, or fierce, or true. Instead, I proved myself a true Grisk in this, ach?"

Drafli was frowning at him, Alma shaking her head, but

Baldr still wasn't looking at them, and exhaled a heavy sigh. "I left you, Bright-Heart," he continued, even quieter. "I was weak. I ran away like a coward, and left you in danger, and failed to keep my word, and my vow. Just like my own—"

But both Alma and Drafli had lunged for him at once, Alma clutching at his chest, Drafli's arm whipping around his waist, and yanking him close. "No," Alma hissed at him. "You are *not* weak, and you are *not* a coward. We hurt you, and lied to you, and your response to that was perfectly valid and understandable. Not only that, but"—she darted a confirming glance up at Drafli's glittering eyes—"you still kept your word. You still came back when we needed you. You still saved my life. *Again.*"

Drafli was fiercely nodding beside her, his rapidly signing hand echoing her words, and Alma jabbed her finger into Baldr's chest, and held his blinking eyes. "You are a fierce and faithful Grisk," she continued, "and we *adore* you, just as you are."

Drafli punctuated this with a sharp slap at Baldr's arse, enough to make him jump—to which Baldr huffed a helpless-sounding gasp, and then a short, breathless laugh. "Gods above, you two," he said, running his hand through his hair. "Shall I now always be thus accosted, whenever you disagree with me?"

"Probably," Alma said cheerfully, while beside her, Drafli gave a broad, terrifying smile. And then he bent down to give a sharp little nip at Baldr's neck, his hand still blatantly groping at his arse.

Baldr huffed another laugh, his body visibly leaning into Drafli's touch, but Alma could still see a twinge of darkness in his eyes. In the way those eyes slid uncertainly back toward her, or rather... to her waist.

"But," Baldr said, his voice gone very quiet. "Now you two will have—a son. Both of you. *Together.* Without me."

And thank the gods, the indignation again flashing across Drafli's eyes was just as strong as what Alma felt, hard and furious and perhaps even insulted. Not only on her and Drafli's behalf, but on their son's.

No, Drafli was signing at Baldr, the slice of his hand fierce and uncompromising. *No. We have son. We. All of us.*

His hand was angrily circling between them, his eyes still thunderous on Baldr's. *We are family*, he continued. *We are scent-bound. We make bonds together. Ach?*

Baldr was watching this very intently, his tooth biting his lip, and Drafli kept signing, his hand wheeling even stronger than before. *We even make son together*, he signed, *beneath Skaikesh's watching eye, upon his own altar. And next we will name our son together, and raise him together, and keep him safe together. We teach him the ways of the Grisk, and the Skai. Ach?*

Baldr twitched again, and that was surely longing, *craving*, in his too-bright eyes. "But," he breathed, "*you* want that, Draf. *You*."

His eyes had again flicked to Alma, again speaking of uncertainty, of guilt—and to Alma's vague surprise, Drafli seemed to be considering that question, with all seriousness. His gaze dropping to Alma too, his finger gently tilting up her chin.

"Ach," he whispered, aloud this time. "You chose well with her, Pure-Heart. She... pleases me."

Oh. Alma's heartbeat was oddly skipping, her eyes frozen on Drafli's, and his mouth quirked, his finger angling her chin a little higher. "She is much like you, ach?" he continued, hoarse. "Brave, and kind, and true. She is quick to learn, and eager to please. She shall stay faithful to us, and care well for our son. She"—his head cocked, again as if he were truly considering this—"*sees* us, and herself, as a Skai's woman should."

The warmth was racing up Alma's spine, pooling on her cheeks, and Drafli gave her chin a gentle shake, his mouth still quirking. "And," he added, almost inaudible now, "I like how she squeals. How she begs. How fiercely her little womb seeks to suck me inside, and milk me dry. You did not"—his eyes flicked coolly to Baldr, his brows raised—"speak truth to me of how sweet this felt, Pure-Heart."

Alma's face was smarting with heat now, her eyes darting toward Baldr—and to her genuine astonishment, he was actually giving Drafli a slow, relieved smile. "Did not wish to make you too jealous," he said softly. "It is good, ach? You liked?"

Drafli's nod was firm and decisive, his eyes gone rather speculative on Alma's face. "I shall not be denied this again, woman," he continued, the command still ringing through his near-silent voice. "Henceforth, you shall welcome my strong Skai ploughing each day, just as Pure-Heart does. You shall both bend over for me, and I shall use all your tight pretty holes, as oft as I should wish."

Alma nearly choked on her own breath, and beside her Baldr sounded like he was choking too, even as his chest convulsed with laughter. "*Draf*," he murmured, warm, affectionate. "We cannot have you scaring her off now, ach? Not after we have finally gained her for our own."

Drafli's eyes had dangerously flashed at Baldr, and then down at Alma. *She is no afraid of me now*, he signed. *Though I ken I shall take great joy in testing this.*

With that, he purposefully dropped his claws, scraping them against her throat—and in return, Alma betrayed a loud, desperate gasp. Flaring more smug satisfaction across Drafli's eyes, and another one of those terrifying, breathtaking grins across his mouth.

This shall please you too, ach, Bright-Heart? he signed at her. *You wish to squeal and beg and open wide for your lord, ach?*

Alma's head was nodding, her eyes surely shining on his, and his smile slipped into something more genuine, even more stunning than before.

Good, he replied. *This honours me. You honour me.*

She honoured him. And beaming back up at his shifting eyes, Alma could feel the impossibly powerful truth of that, settling between them. Even though she'd broken her vow to him, in the end, she'd still honoured him. She'd still gained his trust. His heart.

And behind her, Drafli's heart was clasping her even closer, rocking back and forth, his face buried in her neck. "I am so glad," he whispered, his voice catching. "So glad you came to us, Bright-Heart, and shared all your gifts with us. Now, will you come home with us? And stay, this time?"

And somehow Alma was nodding, and clutching at him, and smiling, and maybe even weeping, all at once.

"Yes," she said. "Yes. I will."

52

Alma's journey back to Orc Mountain was delightful.

It began with a brief visit from two of Drafli's scouts—Killik and Halthorr—who had appeared out of nowhere, signing updates toward Drafli, and thrusting a large pack into Baldr's hands. Which had turned out to contain food and furs and waterskins, and even a fresh set of Alma's beloved, cozy Grisk clothes.

"None of *my* clothes?" Baldr had asked Drafli afterwards, with an exasperated glance down at the sodden, torn trousers he was yanking back on. To which Drafli only smirked at him, and then rummaged through the pack again, and held out a vaguely familiar-looking little bag toward Alma.

This is yours, he signed at her, clinking the bag, making the coins inside it jangle. *From that man.*

He'd given a vicious smile back toward the river, and Alma wryly shook her head as she took the bag into her fingers. Feeling the weight of it—three months' salary—and belatedly realizing that of course Pembroke had never intended for her to keep it. He'd meant to kill her, and promptly take it back again.

The horror of that was suddenly crawling up her spine, and Alma thrust the bag back toward Drafli again, shaking her head. "You keep it," she told him. "I've been wanting to pay you back for all those lovely clothes and gifts anyway. I never wanted you to think I would take your coin, and..."

Her voice trailed off there, because Drafli's expression had gone alarmingly ferocious, his eyes flashing with disbelief, his teeth bared toward her. *No*, he signed back. *I care for you in this. I dress you, and please you, and honour you. This makes me good Skai. Good lord. You no take this away from me!*

Oh. Alma blinked at him, and then down at the bag of coins, and then up at Baldr. Who was watching Drafli with his head tilted, his hands fidgeting on the waist of his torn, filthy trousers.

"Right," Alma belatedly said, with a small, genuine smile toward Drafli's murderous face. "In that case, thank you for taking such good care of me, my lord. And"—she eyed the bag for an instant, chewing her lip—"what would you think of me putting this toward my mother's medical debts, then? Even if I am supposed to be dead to the world now, I would feel better having those dealt with. Taking that back from Pembroke too, you know?"

Her questioning glance up at Drafli's rapidly softening eyes confirmed that he did know, and he jerked an approving little nod, and snatched the bag out of her hand again. And then snapped a sign up at the nearest tree, from where—Alma gasped, and then laughed—Killik was leaping down, swiping the bag from Drafli's hand, and coolly striding away, as though this were a perfectly ordinary thing to do.

Alma exchanged an amused grin with Baldr, and then all three of them set off into the trees together. Drafli leading in front, as usual, while Alma followed behind with Baldr, her eyes lifting to the beautiful sight of Orc Mountain in the distance, streaming its smoke to the sky. They were going home. *Home.*

She could feel Baldr's hand squeezing tighter on hers, and another glance toward him found him still smiling, too—

though his eyes had gone rather pensive, or perhaps even longing, as they slid down Alma's form. Lingering on her fur cape,
and then her kilt, as he again yanked up his own sodden
trousers, and cleared his throat.

"You know, I was thinking," he said, a little awkwardly.
"Once we are home again, mayhap"—he angled a look up at
where Drafli had hesitated, glancing over his shoulder—"mayhap you will choose some Grisk clothes for me also,
Draf. Should you still wish for this."

For an instant, Drafli's eyes had widened, looking truly
astonished—but when he spun around and prowled back
toward them, there was only pure, devious satisfaction on his
face. *Ach, yes,* he signed. *Finally.*

Alma was delightedly grinning between them, her eyes
sweeping up and down Baldr's half-bared body. "Finally,
indeed," she said, her voice husky. "And we'll go shopping for
them together in the Grisk storage-room, right? And maybe
Ella and Nattfarr could help, too? And Rosa, and Maria?"

Baldr and Drafli groaned in unison, and Drafli abruptly
spun to face her, his glinting eyes somewhere between exasperation and amusement. And before Alma could speak, he'd
shoved her down to her knees on a soft patch of moss, yanked
down Baldr's sodden trousers, and fed Baldr's swollen, dripping, gold-tipped head deep into her mouth.

Better, he signed smugly at her, grinning—and then he
eased around behind Baldr's back, and yanked at the trousers
there, too. And then drove inside, again, while Baldr shouted
and staggered against him, his heft wildly bobbing in Alma's
mouth.

But it was magnificent, utterly glorious, their beautiful
Grisk again being lavished, cherished, overcome. Being
worshipped, like the adored partner he was, reassured of his
place between them. And Drafli was even whispering in Baldr's
ear as he ground inside, telling him how pretty he was, how
good he was, how perfect.

And after they'd finished, with Baldr pouring out into Alma's throat, and Drafli pouring out into Baldr, there was only more warm, wonderful satisfaction. In the way Baldr was slightly weaving on his feet as he blinked at them, his heft still glossy with Alma's saliva, while Drafli's wetness streaked down his thighs. And Drafli looked just as pleased as Alma felt, grinning and swatting Baldr's arse before yanking off the last of his trousers altogether, and once again striding off ahead, the torn trousers' remnants clutched in his claws.

"This shall yet... take some getting used to, I ken," Baldr murmured as he and Alma followed, their hands again tightly clasped together. "I have never before known him to be so free with his words, ach? Or with"—he shot a teasing glance toward Drafli's back—"this... *smiling*. This is most unnatural, ach?"

As he spoke, he'd swiftly ducked down, because Drafli had thrown a pinecone at him, with alarming accuracy—and without warning, Baldr kicked off and lunged ahead, tackling Drafli from behind. Which Drafli met with a clever little roll sideways onto the path, twisting Baldr on top, grinning up at him with breathtaking fondness—and Baldr's joyous laugh rang through the trees as they wrestled and rolled together, playing like two exuberant, carefree orclings.

When they finally came up for air again, Drafli's hair was a mess, and Baldr's already-sticky body was covered in twigs and leaves. And thankfully, it turned out that there was another stream nearby, and they all washed up and then ate beside the stream, talking and signing and laughing together. Baldr and Drafli willingly telling Alma highly entertaining stories of their early relationship, like the time they'd ended up trapped in a tiny cave together, or when their captain had gotten so annoyed with their ongoing animosity that he'd ordered Drafli to plough Baldr over the table in the middle of an important meeting.

Ach, you liked that, Drafli signed at Baldr, again flashing his breathtaking grin. *All that sweet envy choking your breath.*

"I did *not*," Baldr retorted, though his face was vividly flushing. "*You* were the one who dragged it on for the entire meeting!"

Ach, I did, Drafli said, his smile gone decidedly smug again. *As you shall do also, next time Bright-Heart comes to a meeting, ach?*

His eyes were dangerously lingering on Alma now, his tongue brazenly licking at his lips, and Alma laughed, and shook her head, and attempted to glower back toward him. "Oh, no," she said. "You are not making me come to *any*—"

But her voice twisted into a squeal, because without warning, Drafli had leapt up, and *pounced* on her. Tackling her down into the grass with fluid, impossible ease, kicking her legs apart, finding that place between them, and—

Alma shrieked and shuddered as he drove deep, his breath chuckling low and hot into her ear. "You shall come," he whispered, "whenever your lord tells you, ach?"

Alma was writhing and moaning far too much to argue, and beside them Baldr had swiftly settled closer to watch, his tooth biting his lip, his own bared heft already bobbing in his hand. "Ach, you two," he breathed through his teeth, sounding almost reverent. "Ach, so pretty. Smells so good. Have so oft *dreamt* of seeing—"

But his voice had also sharpened into a shout, because Drafli's hand had dropped to knock Baldr's away, gripping that plump length in his own firm fingers. Sliding up in perfect time with every plunge of his hips inside Alma, making both Baldr and Alma gasp and flail in unison—until the pleasure once again splashed out between them, the warmth charging and careening as they came apart together.

This of course necessitated another intensive round of washing up, but once they'd finally set back on their way again, the rest of the trip seemed to pass with unaccountable speed. With so much more easy laughter and banter between them, and even the occasional bout of flat-out running, with Alma alternately clinging to her racing orcs' backs, while their mountain kept rising closer and closer above them. And as they finally approached its bulky, rocky base, Alma found her happiness swelling even fuller as her eyes drank up the sight, lingering on the towering, powerful stone, streaming its smoke to the late afternoon sky. They were together, and they were home. Home.

And it felt like something almost sacred, somehow, with Drafli and Baldr's hands both clasping to hers, and drawing her together into the mountain's lamplit warmth. Into where it already felt so cozy and familiar and safe, as if it had perhaps even missed her, too.

"Ach, there they are!" boomed a deep voice—and when they all whirled to look, it was Grimarr, their captain, barrelling out from a nearby corridor, and flinging his big arms around Baldr and Drafli's shoulders. "And with their woman, also! It gladdens my heart to see you, brothers. It has been too long!"

From behind Grimarr, Jule had suddenly appeared too, wryly smiling as she darted over to hug Alma with one arm, while holding a wide-eyed Bitty-Grim above the fray with the other. "Yes, it's *so* good to see you safe and sound, Alma," she said. "I hope it all went well? The scouts' reports today have been *quite* astonishing, I must say."

She accompanied this with a dark look toward Drafli, who had already ducked out from beneath Grimarr's arm, and was now smoothing out his hair. *Too bad*, he signed at Jule, without looking even slightly repentant. *I wished to kill that foul swine, and taste the sweet scent of his fear, while his fancy house burned. You ought to be happy I did not take my time and make him—*

"Draf says he did the best he could," Baldr croaked, from beneath Grimarr's still-punishing embrace. "But under the circumstances, this was the best we could come up with. I hope it does not cause too much added trouble, Captain."

Thankfully, Grimarr was still giving a relieved-looking grin, enthusiastically rubbing his big hand against Baldr's already-messy hair. "Ach, we shall sort this out, brothers," he said firmly. "I am only glad you are here again, and safe."

"That goes for all of us," Jule added, with another rueful grin toward Alma. "It turns out that Grimarr's dependence on these two is far more dire than I knew. One would have thought they'd both run off and *died*."

Grimarr shot Jule a distinctly mulish frown, his arm again yanking around Baldr's neck, while Baldr gave him a sheepish, ruffled-looking smile. "We missed you too, Captain," he said. "We are happy to be home."

"Good," Grimarr said gruffly. "And now that you shall have both a woman and son to look after, neither of you shall leave here again, lest I command you. Now, woman"—his eyes settled on Alma—"shall you grant your orcs to me, for only a short time, whilst we seek to clean up this mess they have made?"

"Grimarr!" Jule hissed beside him, clearly disapproving of this plan—but Alma had caught sight of a few familiar faces poking out around the corner up ahead, and she laughed as she gave a quick little wave toward them.

"It's fine," she said firmly, to Jule and Grimarr. "I promise. It seems as though I ought to stop by the kitchen for a while anyway. So I'll see you soon?"

Her eyes had darted to Baldr and Drafli, while perhaps the faintest twinge of uncertainty coiled in her belly—but Baldr was fervently nodding toward her, his eyes still shining, while Drafli swiftly stepped forward, and pressed a hard, no-nonsense kiss to her mouth.

Soon, Bright-Heart, he signed at her, with a sharp slap to her arse. *I shall be ploughing your sweet little womb again before night-fall. Ach?*

Alma shyly nodded in return, and felt her lips curving into a slow, genuine smile. *Good*, she signed back. *I can't wait, Golden-Tongue.*

He gave her another approving swat as she walked away,

and she had to make her hazy eyes focus on the smiling faces up ahead. On Tryggr, and Dufnall, and Gegnir, and Timo—and that was even Cat, loudly purring from where she was curled up in Dufnall's arms.

"Welcome back, sister!" Timo said, grinning up at her as he bobbed from foot to foot. "We hope you had a good trip, ach? We have been waiting for you! Come, and see the scullery!"

Beside him, Tryggr's eyes were far more knowing, and he gave Alma a purposeful little wink. "Boss sorted you out, did he?" he said lightly. "Told you he would. C'mon, you'll wanna see. Right, Duff?"

Dufnall gravely nodded, his clawed hand carefully petting Cat in his arms. "Cat ate seven rats, whilst you were gone," he told Alma, with the air of one sharing a great secret. "Good Bautul come by again, too. Feed him *many* tasty treats."

Tryggr elbowed Dufnall in the side, but then exchanged a conspiratorial grin with Gegnir. "We mighta offered 'em your desk, while you were away," he said to Alma. "You don't mind, do you?"

Alma gave a choked laugh, and tried not to wince. "As long as they didn't touch my ledgers," she said, eyeing Tryggr's suddenly blank face. "They didn't touch my ledgers. Did they?"

Tryggr's face was still far too innocent for Alma's liking, and he jerked his thumb up the corridor. "You know, I'm just gonna go ahead," he said casually. "Just—check on a couple things."

With that, he sped off up the corridor, while Alma laughed again, and fought to shove the horrible image of seed-soaked ledgers from her mind. "So how have things been in the kitchen?" she asked Gegnir. "Other than the rat situation?"

"Ach, well, Narfi has gone," Gegnir replied, with a disgruntled frown. "Sent off digging tunnels, I am told. And thus, I have had to handle all the deliveries and payments, and all the meals, all alone! I have missed you, woman."

Alma gave him a wincing smile, but she was tapping her chin, her head tilting. "You know," she said slowly, "I have a few former colleagues who may be looking for work, Gegnir. If you wouldn't be opposed to working with a human or two?"

Gegnir scoffed good-naturedly as he waved the question away, though his eyes had gone rather piercing. "What kind of humans?" he demanded. "Any who are more in their prime? Not that I cannot bear to work with young'uns such as you, but more seasoning makes for a better meal, you ken."

He was now eyeing Alma expectantly, his tongue licking hungrily at his lips, and she chuckled as she followed Timo into the familiar warmth of the kitchen, and toward the scullery. "I'll see what I can do," she promised. "But—"

Her voice broke off there, her eyes frozen on the scullery— because somehow, impossibly, it had been *transformed*. The floors and counters pristine and perfectly smooth, as though the stone itself had been polished, and buffed to a beautiful shine. There also appeared to be brand-new, expanded drying racks installed on the walls where the rickety old racks had been, and the old wooden washbasins had been replaced with shiny new steel ones. And sitting on one of the washbasins was a strange, complicated-looking steel contraption, topped by what seemed to be a large wooden handle.

"You like it?" asked Timo, who was eagerly grinning up at Alma, and waving her further into the room. "We fixed it all up for you while you were gone! And finished all the laundry, too!"

Alma's breath was choking in her throat, her hand trembling against her heart as she blinked at where the mountain of laundry had been—and where there now only stood a small stack of folded, clean clothes.

"This is unbelievable," she gasped at them. "How did you— why did you—"

Tryggr had abruptly reappeared too, flashing Alma a wry grin as he leaned back against the nearest counter. "Boss, actually," he said. "Before he took off after his mate the other day. Said he wanted us to do something nice for you. Not that we wouldn'a anyway, of course"—he gave an apologetic smile—"but he's got the clout and the credits to get things rolling, you know? Get those pretty Ka-esh off their pretty arses."

Alma's hands were fluttering over her mouth now, her breaths seizing in her chest. *Drafli* had done this? *Before* he'd gone off after Baldr, and left her that note? He'd wanted to give her a gift?

And gaping around at it, Alma belatedly realized just how damned meaningful this gift was. It had been Drafli telling her, surely, that he'd wanted her to stay, no matter what she'd decided about him, or his son. And not only that—but in it, he'd clearly shown his respect toward her, and her chosen work, too. Treating it not as something shameful to be ignored and forgotten, shoved away behind the kitchen—but instead as something worthy of attention, of support. Of care.

Alma felt herself laughing, suddenly, even as her throat dangerously spasmed, very near to a sob. "Thank you," she choked at them. "Thank you. All of you."

They collectively waved it away, all grinning at her at once, even Dufnall. And Timo cheerfully skipped over to the counter, and plucked up the last few piles of clothes, thrusting one into Alma's hands. "These are Kesst's, if you should like to deliver them to him," he said. "And these"—he brandished the others—"are all Grisk. I shall take them now, so we shall be done, even for a short while, ach?"

Alma profusely thanked him, and fondly watched as Timo took off out the door again. "Ach, he's a good one," Tryggr said softly, speaking Alma's own thoughts aloud. "And he—ach, Ka-esh!"

He'd abruptly twitched and lurched toward the door, his eyes wide and alarmed—and when Alma whirled around, it was Eben. Carrying another one of the strange washbasin contraptions, and nearly staggering sideways under his weight—but thankfully Tryggr was already plucking it out of his arms, and carefully setting it down on top of one of the new washbasins.

"Watch yourself, Ka-esh," he said sharply. "Or call for help when you need it, ach?"

Eben's face had flushed a deep pink, his head ducking. "Sorry, sir," he said, in his quiet voice, before raising his big dark eyes to Alma's, and giving her a careful smile. "And welcome back, Keeper. We are glad you are home again."

Alma smiled back toward him, as a bright thrill flared up her back at that beautiful word *Keeper*—while beside them, Tryggr loudly cleared his throat, and kicked at the washbasin. "Well, don't keep her in suspense, Ka-esh," he said. "Show her how it works, will you?"

Eben's face flushed even redder, but he quickly nodded, and bent over the new contraption he'd brought. "This is a washing machine," he explained, as his trembling hand found the handle, and showed Alma how it turned. "We had heard of them being used in the north, and it is a simple concept, so we made our own, ach? You turn the handle, and the paddle beneath shall wash your clothes for you."

He waved for Alma to take a turn, so she did, feeling the ease of the handle, the way the large paddle swung powerfully below. "It's brilliant," she told him, her voice fervent. "And so well crafted, too. This will save us so much time, Eben. Thank you."

He gave a bashful wave, surely dismissing what had been a massive amount of work, especially on top of his usual tasks in the sickroom. "Ach, I was happy to help," he said softly. "We all wish you to feel welcome, and stay."

There was a beat of silence, in which Alma felt her own face slightly heating—and beside them, Tryggr huffed, and shifted against the counter. "Maybe you haven't noticed, Ka-esh," he said flatly, "but this woman's spoken for. *Permanently*."

Alma's face flushed deeper, and so did Eben's, too. "Ach, I— I ken," he stammered, his voice even softer. "She has gained the most fearsome Skai in our mountain as her lord. Through not her beauty or her strength, but through... her hard work. Her kindness."

Oh. It distantly occurred to Alma that perhaps she should have been insulted by that—but she was far too busy staring at Eben, while comprehension twined through her thoughts. Eben hadn't been interested in her, all this time? He'd been interested in... being *like* her?!

Tryggr was looking just as astonished as Alma felt, his jaw dropping open—and then snapping shut again, while a slow, devious little smile curled at his lips. "Is that so, pretty Ka-esh?" he said, his voice pitched far lower than before. "You like the idea of catching a hungry Skai's eye, do you?"

Eben's face had gone even redder, his eyes wide and dark on Tryggr's face. While behind them, Gegnir huffed a wry laugh, and muttered something about smelling a rat in the kitchen—to which Dufnall immediately perked up and launched out the door, with Gegnir close behind him.

That left Alma and Eben alone with Tryggr, who had begun to look distinctly wolfish, prowling closer toward them. "Then why don't you bend over, little Ka-esh, and show us this again," Tryggr said, kicking his boot at the washbasin. "Give us a better look this time, ach?"

Beside Alma, Eben had visibly shuddered all over—but then, to her amazement, he... obeyed. Carefully bending forward, his long lashes fluttering, his shaking hands clutching at the steel basin beneath him.

"Ach, just like that," Tryggr purred, as his clawed hands settled against Eben's hips, and then smoothly began guiding his trousers downwards. "You *are* eager to please, aren't you?"

Alma's mouth had fallen open—wait, Tryggr was truly doing this, here, *now*?—but Eben had already twitched a furtive nod, his breath exhaling harsh, because oh, Tryggr had indeed dropped his trousers, and was now sliding his hand down the curve of his bare arse. "Ach, just as I thought," Tryggr continued, his voice even lower. "So pretty, Ka-esh. Bet you're nice and tight too, ach?"

Eben replied with another harsh, shuddering exhale, as Tryggr's hand smoothly explored upwards again, and perhaps even delved deeper. "You ever take a Skai in here before, Ka-esh?" he murmured. "Ever have a strong Skai ploughing, and get pumped full of good Skai seed?"

Eben's gasp was surely a moan this time, his body pushing back into Tryggr's touch, and Tryggr gave an amused chuckle, a gentle slap at Eben's arse. "Ach, ach, you'll get it," he drawled, as he shoved down his own trousers, revealing a brief glimpse of his long, greyish heft, which was—like Drafli's—heavily scarred with teeth-marks. "You're gonna suck me all the way inside you, aren't you, pretty Ka-esh? Show me what a good little pet you could be?"

Eben was again frantically nodding, his entire body trembling over the basin, while Tryggr leaned forward, slicking himself, settling closer. His own eyes fluttering closed, his head tilting back in a manner very similar to Drafli's, as he gripped at Eben's hips, and slowly sank inside.

Eben shook and moaned, his hands skittering on the basin, his teeth biting sharp against his lip. His eyes dark and liquid and pleading, as they furtively blinked up toward—toward *Alma*.

And good gods, what the hell was Alma doing? She was just standing here like a lump, and *watching* this? In her clean new scullery? And wait—who had gone and shut the door behind her?

"Tryggr!" she hissed, as she belatedly clapped her hands over her eyes, blocking them from view. "You can't just go ahead and—"

But she couldn't even finish, and she could hear Tryggr chuckling again, and perhaps again slapping Eben's arse. "Ach, sure I can," he said back, with surprising coolness. "Boss had you in here while we watched, didn't he? And it seems to me this Ka-esh likes it just as much as you did—and he even likes you watching, too. Don't you, my pretty pet?"

This was accompanied by another telltale swatting sound, and then Eben perhaps drawing in air, his breath ragged. "Ach," he croaked. "Sir."

Tryggr's laugh was warm and approving, and maybe a little breathless, too. "Then see, woman, you ought not deny him this," he said smugly. "Most of all after he has shown you such kindness."

There truly were no words, though Alma was becoming more and more reminded of Drafli with every passing moment—and she huffed an amused sigh as she finally let her hands fall from her face again. Once more confronting her eyes with the shocking sight of this, with Tryggr blatantly waggling his eyebrows toward her as he caressed Eben's shuddering flanks, and drove deeper and deeper inside.

"Ach, that's it," Tryggr breathed, his eyes back on Eben, his own chest heaving now, too. "That's nice, little Ka-esh, real nice. Good and tight and sweet, ach?"

Eben whimpered as Tryggr finally sank all the way in, grinding hard against him, his half-lidded eyes still intent on the sight. "Just like that," Tryggr rasped. "Even better than I thought. *Ach.*"

Eben's whimper had steadily risen into a sustained moan, his head arching back—and Tryggr's hand swiftly snapped up, catching the end of Eben's long braid. Pulling his head up a little higher as he leisurely drew out again, and then drove back inside.

Eben bucked and squirmed this time, his mouth barking a helpless-sounding shout, while a dark, delighted smile curled across Tryggr's mouth. "You like that too, little Ka-esh?" he purred. "You like your Skai being a bit rough with you? Making sure you feel it?"

And oh, Eben was eagerly nodding again, while Tryggr chuckled and settled himself closer, wrapping Eben's braid

firmly around his palm, and giving it an experimental little tug.
"Even better, little Ka-esh," he breathed, as he slowly drew out
again, and then drove back inside, with far more power than
before, while Eben shouted and flailed beneath him. "Ach,
you're so pretty, aren't you? So sweet, when you're being railed
by a good Skai prick?"

Eben desperately nodded and cried out, his voice rising
with every purposeful plunge of Tryggr's hips, and Tryggr's
eyes were blazing now, one hand still yanking at Eben's hair,
the other stroking at his flank. "So sweet," he gasped again, his
voice catching. "And you're gonna smell even sweeter when
you're chock-full of Skai seed, aren't you? When you're walking
around here reeking of *me*?"

His voice had badly frayed by the end, his hips grinding
hard against Eben's arse—and then he was groaning, guttural
and deep, his head tilted back, one hand still caught in Eben's
hair, the other digging its claws into Eben's hip. While beneath
him, Eben jerked and shouted, his body wrenching tight—and
suddenly he was spraying out too, painting the shiny new
washer beneath him with thick spurts of sticky white.

For a long, dangling moment, no one moved, including
Alma—and then Tryggr cleared his throat, and palmed at
Eben's arse. "Look at you, pretty pet," he murmured. "Messing
all over your brand-new gift. You're gonna lick that clean for me
now, aren't you?"

To Alma's ongoing astonishment, Eben jerked an ashamed
little nod, his face now flushed fully scarlet—and then he
indeed ducked his head, and began licking. While behind him,
Tryggr gave a low, breathless moan, his hands spreading wider
on Eben's shivering skin, caressing him with surprising
gentleness.

"That's good, pretty pet," he breathed. "Real good. Now tell
me, sweet thing"—he leaned forward, gently pressed his
mouth to the back of Eben's neck—"what's your name?"

Alma felt herself give a short, disbelieving chuckle, her

head shaking—but this suddenly seemed a moment of unmistakable intimacy, one that ought to be shared between just the two of them. So she slipped out into the kitchen again, fanning her hot face with her hand, while across the room Gegnir gave her a wry, knowing grin.

"Knew it was only a matter of time before that Skai went at it in there," he said. "They will only work for so long, you ken. Cake?"

Alma couldn't help another choked laugh, but she shakily stepped forward, and gratefully took the proffered cake. Which turned out to be delicious, and just the sustenance one needed, after unexpectedly witnessing a Skai claiming his brand-new pet.

"Thank you, Gegnir," Alma told him, with all sincerity, once she'd polished off her cake, and he'd thrust another entire wrapped cake into her hands. "You've been so kind. Truly."

Gegnir waved it away, rubbing at the back of his neck. "We are only glad to have you back again," he said firmly. "You have been a great gift to us all. Now"—he gestured at the cake, and the fabric still clutched in Alma's other hand—"off to the sickroom with you, ach? The boy shall be pleased to see you, too, I ken."

The sickroom? The boy? Alma blinked at Gegnir, and then down at her hand—where somehow, she was still holding Kesst's clean clothes. And she gave another wry laugh, shaking her head, as she thanked Gegnir one more time, and headed off for the sickroom.

"Sweetheart!" Kesst exclaimed, the instant she stepped through the door—and then he dropped the armful of furs he'd been carrying, and rushed over toward her. Not to embrace her, as Alma might perhaps have expected—but instead to whip his clean trousers out of her hand.

"You brought my *trousers*!" he crowed, clutching them to his chest, and then to his nose, inhaling deep. "And they're *clean*! Eft, she brought back my *trousers*!"

Efterar had already been striding over too, his eyes crinkling into a warm smile as he clapped his hand against Kesst's shoulder. "Ach, I can see, Sweet-Fang," he said. "And she's brought herself back, too. I hope you're well, Alma? And Baldr and Drafli, and your son?"

Alma's eyes were inexplicably prickling, and she earnestly nodded, and grinned between them both. "Very well, thank you," she said. "We all met up at Pembroke's, and then Pembroke tried to kill me, so Drafli killed *him*, and set his house on fire, and—"

"Ooooh, oooh, oooh," Kesst interrupted, wildly waving his trousers. "You need to sit down and tell this one properly. And come on, I'm sure these two will want to hear it, too."

These two turned out to be Thrain and Varinn, both sitting up on Thrain's bed. Thrain was still looking distinctly pale and weary, his head resting on Varinn's shoulder—but he was awake, and he was blearily grinning at Alma, and then at the wrapped packet in her hand.

"Gods bless sweet Grisk sisters," he said to Varinn, his voice still a little slurred. "Tha's cake, isn't it? For us?"

"Of course," Alma replied, beaming as she thrust the cake down toward them. "I hope you're feeling better, Thrain? And that your journey back here was uneventful, Varinn? And that there haven't been any more attacks?"

It turned out that there hadn't been, thankfully, and that Varinn's trip back had indeed gone well, though he'd been wondering about the distant scent of smoke in the air. Which led to a thorough retelling of Alma's adventures in Ashford, from Pembroke's failed murder attempt, to Drafli's successful murder attempt, to all of them making up again.

"And now the most important question, sweetheart," Kesst said, leaning forward, stuffing his mouth with a large slab of cake. "What did Drafli do to punish Baldr, once he finally came back to you again? You can't expect us to believe he just patted him on the arse, and let him off easy, after a stunt like that?!

Running out on quite possibly the sweetest woman who ever existed? While she's *pregnant*?!"

Alma's throat spasmed around the cake she'd been eating, and she swallowed with effort, and smiled as she shook her head. "Um," she managed, "I don't really think—"

"Ach, Draf let me have it," cut in a beautiful, familiar voice, and Alma sat up straight, her smile broadening into a delighted grin, as Baldr himself strode across the room, and settled down on the bed beside her, his strong arm circling around her waist. "Pounded me within a breath of my life, whilst she sought to drown me with his seed, ach, Bright-Heart?"

He actually chuckled as he spoke, his eyes wry on hers, while across from them Kesst gave an affronted gasp. "That damned Skai is getting soft," he announced flatly. "That is not even a *punishment*. You've probably been dreaming about them doing that for *weeks*."

To Alma's surprise, Baldr laughed again, the sound light and merry, and then gave a companionable little shrug of his shoulder against hers. "Ach, mayhap," he said. "He was showing me what I would be missing, I ken."

At that, his eyes had slightly sobered, his arm drawing Alma closer against him. "I missed you both so much," he whispered, as he bent to kiss her hair. "You ken I would never have been able to stay away from you, ach?"

Alma fervently nodded against him, and she could feel his chest filling and emptying, his body sitting a little straighter on the bed. "And—Varinn," Baldr said, more careful, now. "I wish to thank you, for your great kindness toward me, even when I was not worthy of this. You have shown yourself a true and faithful Grisk brother, and I am forever in your debt. I"—his chest rose and fell again—"I should be honoured if you should grant me a chance to be a better Grisk brother to you, in return."

Something warm was pooling in Alma's belly, sparkling

even brighter as Varinn swiftly waved Baldr's apology away. "Ach, there is no debt," he said firmly. "Only—"

"Only him teaching us some of those rubbish Skai fighting tricks," Thrain's groggy voice interrupted, his hand snapping up to clutch at Varinn's. "That rubbish is deeply unfair. An' *rubbish*. Almost castrated Varinn! Who needs sons. So rub—"

"And that's enough for you for now, I think," interjected Efterar, raising his hand over Thrain's face—and without warning, Thrain dropped sideways into Varinn's lap, his eyes closing, his mouth already lightly snoring. While above him, Varinn gave his sleeping face a rather unsteady-looking smile, his hand carefully brushing the black hair out of his eyes.

"Gods, you Grisk," Kesst muttered under his breath. "All of you, so sweet and scent-bound to each other, falling all over yourselves with cuddles and apologies. My poor *teeth*."

He did look legitimately pained, his lips pulled back, his tongue rubbing gingerly against one of his sharp white fangs. While Efterar, who had been standing behind him, gave a low chuckle, his hand sliding down Kesst's front, his fingers splaying wide against his bare chest. And against—Alma blinked, and looked closer—something she hadn't noticed Kesst wearing before. A long, beautifully braided chain, with a smooth, iridescent black gem hanging from the end of it.

"Ach, you are just as sweet," Efterar murmured. "But with an exquisite tinge of sharpness, too. You're such a great gift to me, Sweet-Fang—even more now that you're properly working together with me. Using all your cleverness to help me. Bringing even more of your light into my days."

To Alma's vague surprise, Kesst didn't even flinch at Efterar's use of the pet name, and his hand had snapped up to curl around that lovely new black gem, clutching it closer against his chest. But there was still sadness in his eyes, in the twitch of his small smile. "Thanks, Eft," he whispered. "You're so good to me, too. To all of us. You deserve all the best things."

"Ach, I have them," said Efterar firmly, his hand nudging

harder against Kesst's chest. While Kesst rapidly blinked, his head furtively nodding, his other hand coming up too, and clinging tight to Efterar's wrist. To which Efterar bent down, and took a long, deep inhale before pressing a kiss to the top of Kesst's black head.

And watching them, in the strangely stilted silence, Alma felt a painful tightness in her throat. While her own hand grasped at Baldr's beside her, and something seemed to snap through her thoughts, flailing out sudden and sideways. An awareness. An idea. One more way they might be able to help.

"Wait," she breathed. "Baldr. Not only can you find scents... but you can also *suppress them*. On yourself, and others. Right?"

She was sitting up straighter on the bed, silently pleading at him with her eyes, and he tilted his head as he warily nodded. And Alma was nodding too, clutching even harder against his hand. "And on Drafli," she continued, her voice rising. "He doesn't smell like—you know—when he should. Right? And that—that must be because of you. Right?"

Baldr was still nodding, his brow furrowing. "Ach," he said. "He no longer wished to smell—you know. So I altered this, upon him."

"Right," Alma said, nodding even harder, beaming toward him. "So you could do it on someone else. Right?"

Baldr gave another wary nod, though his brows had furrowed even closer together. "Ach," he replied slowly, "but I could not remove a live bond, like the one we have between us. And I should still very clearly know my own scent, wherever I had done this, so this is why I did not—"

Too late Alma realized what she'd been implying, and she flapped her other hand toward him, shaking her head. "Not *me*," she said. "*Him*."

She'd glanced meaningfully toward Kesst, who was now staring back toward them with clear disbelief in his eyes. "Grisk, right?" he muttered up toward Efterar. "Do *you* understand any of this, Eft?"

But Efterar's eyes had gone very sharp on Baldr's, his body strangely stilled behind Kesst. And Kesst gave a rather high-pitched laugh, his eyes again intent on Baldr. "*Can* you?" he demanded, his voice shrill. "Suppress scents? On *other people*?!"

And oh, thank the gods, Baldr nodded again, the comprehension now flaring across his eyes. "I would need to touch, though," he said, his gaze flicking thoughtfully between Alma and Efterar. "But over your hands may work?"

Kesst was still looking thoroughly stunned, but behind him Efterar was rapidly nodding. "Then—try it," he said, his voice hoarse. "If you—if you wish, Sweet-Fang."

Kesst gave a twitchy nod too, his eyes still uncertain on Efterar's face—and Alma could hear Efterar's thick exhale as his suddenly shaky hands skittered up, gently cupping around Kesst's neck. While Baldr stepped forward, his hand reaching to rest against Efterar's, his eyes distant and unfocused as his hand moved forward, around, over to the other side.

But when Baldr finally pulled away, he was looking unmistakably pleased—and Efterar had ducked his head down, inhaling against Kesst's neck. His breath deepening into a dark, hungry growl, his teeth suddenly scraping against Kesst's skin, while beneath him Kesst startled, and then drew in a quick, astonished gasp.

"You—Grisk—*genius*," he gulped, his eyes shining, as he frantically waved Baldr closer again. "Do the rest. More. Oh gods. *Please*."

Baldr willingly nodded, while Kesst dropped back onto the bed, and furiously kicked off his trousers. And then he and Efterar worked their way down Kesst's bare body, bit by bit, in a manner that might have raised Alma's jealousy, in another life—but as she watched, there was only hopefulness, and a hitching, twitching anticipation. This had to work. It *had* to.

And once Baldr finally stepped away again, meeting Efterar's eyes with a knowing kind of warmth, Kesst abruptly curled up on himself, dragging in a long, endless-feeling breath, his chest filling, his shoulders rising, as if he were about to burst—

And without warning, he broke into gales of shrill, giddy laughter. His body shuddering on the bed, his hands wildly groping for Efterar, and yanking him down tight and close.

"I smell—good," he choked, his arms and legs wrapping around Efterar, his claws digging into Efterar's back. "I smell so *good*, Eft. Just me. Just—*you*."

Efterar was nodding too, his face already buried in Kesst's neck, and Alma could see the mingled joy and pain and ecstasy on Kesst's face as Efterar bit down, their bodies arching up together, Kesst's claws dragging deep.

"Oh, fuck," Kesst gasped. "Oh, Eft. Yes. You devious—*ack!*"

He shivered all over, while Efterar laughed darkly against him, and pinned him harder to the bed. And Alma's own relief—her own happiness—seemed to be flaring, flying, and she flailed toward Baldr, and squeezed him tight.

"You are a god," she whispered into his chest. "A *god*, Baldr of Clan Grisk."

He was slightly trembling against her, perhaps with relief, or laughter, or both. Too much for Alma to follow, to face, her own wetness streaking down her cheeks, her throat gulping for air, for anything—

When thank the gods, someone new stalked in. Someone tall and powerful and gorgeous, whose disbelieving eyes swiftly swept across the room—and then he strode over to Alma and Baldr, and yanked them into his arms.

It was Drafli.

53

Even a few days ago, Alma would never have imagined herself so happy to see Drafli, or to find herself tucked tight against his chest, her breath dragging in heavy gulps of his sweet scent. Drafli. Her lord. Here. Safe.

"What have you two done now?" he hissed between them, his hoarse voice thoroughly exasperated, but not quite—and Alma felt herself laugh a sob as she clutched him closer, felt his claws pricking into her back in return. Promising her that he was here, he would do all within his power to comfort her, calm her, help her.

"Pure-Heart is just being a god, again," she whispered into Drafli's chest. "Making everyone's lives better. Like he always does."

Drafli loudly huffed, but Alma could feel him looking over at Kesst and Efterar, and then bending closer into Baldr, perhaps nibbling at his neck. "And *you* had naught to do with this?" his hoarse voice demanded at Alma, once he'd come up again—but again, there was no real heat in it, and instead, it might have even sounded amused. "I ken better, Bright-Heart. Now come. I have surprise."

Alma willingly followed him toward the door, darting only

a brief glance back toward where Efterar was now pounding Kesst into the bed with hard heavy thrusts, while Kesst writhed and whimpered beneath him. And Alma caught Baldr looking too, his eyes just as bright on hers, brimming with warmth, with satisfaction.

Do you know what Golden-Tongue means? he signed at Alma, behind Drafli's back. *What surprise?*

No idea, Alma signed back at him. *He didn't tell you?*

Ahead of them, Drafli had glanced backwards, his eyes flaring with disapproval—but beneath that, again with unmistakable amusement, too. And his hands snapped back to swat both their arses at once, gently shoving them out the door before him, and guiding them down the corridor. Until he thrust them into a large, lovely, familiar room, filled to bursting with shelves and goods.

It was the Grisk storage-room, of course, and gathered here inside it—Alma's mouth twitched into a delighted smile—were multiple waiting women and orcs, many of them excitedly grinning back toward them. Ella and Nattfarr, Rosa and John, even Simon and Maria.

"There you are, brother," Simon said in his deep voice, his huge hand clapping against Baldr's shoulder. "I hear we are to dress you, like pretty Grisk doll. In maker-upper."

"Make-*over*, Simon," Rosa corrected him, without looking up from the little book she'd already buried her nose into. "Oooh, look, John-Ka, there's a section on Grisk orc outfits here, too! This piece is quite intriguing—do you think it's merely decorative?"

John, who had been looking vaguely disgruntled by all the commotion, visibly perked up as he considered the book, his claw tapping his chin. "Ach, that is a garrotte, I ken," he said, with genuine-seeming interest. "Now this is curious, for I would not expect *Grisk* to choose this, but..."

His eyes had slid toward Nattfarr, who was indeed wearing the exact same item—an intricate cuff of flexible-looking braided ropes, stretched over his bicep. And Nattfarr accordingly shook off the cuff, and then snapped it out with a quick flick of his fingers, into a long, shimmering string of braided gold.

"Natt!" Ella exclaimed beside him, looking legitimately shocked. "That's a *weapon*?!"

Nattfarr flashed her an apologetic smile, and showed her how the chain hooked back on itself, making it look much like a noose. "Ach, I did not even think to speak of this," he said ruefully. "It is for if you are captured, I ken, or find yourself one-handed in bed with an enemy. Naught that I need to fear now, lass."

He gave Ella a cheerful little wink, and in return she sputtered at him, and plucked the garrotte from his hand. "Well, maybe I ought to have one, too," she said, as she tested the chain's mechanism, and then waggled it teasingly toward him. "Just in case."

"And maybe Baldr should have one, also," Maria pointed out, with a not-so-nice smile toward Drafli—to which Drafli instantly bared his teeth at her, and Simon and Baldr both groaned in unison.

"We no start this here, my Maria," Simon told her, circling his big arm around her waist. "Our brother has brought us here to help *honour* his mate, no to grant him weapons to kill him in bed, ach?"

Drafli and Maria were still glaring at each other, and Simon gave a rather Drafli-like swat to Maria's arse as he guided her away. "Stubborn woman," he said affectionately, before twitching sideways to intently study a nearby shelf. "Ach, mark this blade! I no have one thus, yet."

Now it was Maria's turn to groan, while everyone else— even Drafli—laughed behind them. And Ella was excitedly waving Baldr further into the room, while Rosa began eagerly recounting a list of essential items, and Baldr gave Alma and

Drafli a flushed, sheepish-looking smile as he squared his shoulders, and followed them deeper.

But already Alma and Drafli were by his side, Alma giving his arm a reassuring squeeze, Drafli making a fluid sign that meant something like, *Tell us. Out with it.*

Baldr shook his head, smiling, but then furtively signed an answer. *I have only—never before come in here. Too many scents, ach?*

Drafli had shot Baldr a searching look, his hand again signing, even faster than before. *Your father?* he asked. *You wish to leave, Pure-Heart?*

No, Baldr signed back, slow but sure. *I wish... to face this. To accept this.*

Alma squeezed his arm even tighter, and then signed at him, too. *But if you want to stop, just say this*, she told him. *Please, Pure-Heart.*

Ach, ach, you two, he replied, wryly shaking his head—and then pulling up short, because the others had halted here, and were now all staring at them. Looking surprised, and curious, and—in Rosa's case—delighted.

"Oooh, I didn't realize they'd taught *you* sign language too, Alma!" she exclaimed. "How *exciting*. I don't suppose you might be willing to share some pointers? I've always wondered about the syntax, and we really ought to create a dictionary of common terms, don't you think? Come to think of it"—she bounced excitedly in place—"we really should pull together a *class*! Drafli, might you be willing to teach one for us?!"

To Alma's surprise, Drafli had been listening to all this with his head tilted, looking almost *interested*—at least, until that last question, which flashed an incredulous, too-familiar hostility across his eyes. And thankfully, John had abruptly steered Rosa away, loudly pointing out some new discovery in their book, while Simon gave Drafli a commiserating half-grin, and Ella purposefully began yanking items off the shelves, and thrusting them into Baldr's arms.

"You'll need to start by smelling, of course," she said firmly. "And then we'll go from there."

Baldr meekly obliged, and soon they were caught in a dazzling flurry of fabrics and furs, in a bewildering array of styles and colours and sizes. The strength of Baldr's scent preferences were quite remarkable—some items he thrust away with immediate revulsion, while others he considered longer, sometimes handing them over to Drafli for approval as well. And to Alma's ongoing amusement, Drafli actually inspected them with surprising care, sniffing them, and even holding them up against Baldr— and she couldn't help noticing, when Baldr perhaps hadn't, that Drafli immediately threw away all the trousers, and several other items with plenty of coverage, too.

And when Baldr's suddenly shaky hands passed Drafli a grey fur cape, with what looked like a gold torc attached, Drafli smelled it for a long time—and then stepped forward, and carefully slung it around Baldr's shoulders. Turning him around so he could fasten it in front, while Baldr's throat convulsed, his shoulders heaving up and down.

You really think it is good? he signed at Drafli, without quite looking at him. *It suits me?*

Ach, Drafli signed back, with a light flick of his claw to Baldr's cheek. *Perfect, Pure-Heart. As always.*

Alma was fervently nodding beside them, stroking her hand against the soft fur. "Gorgeous," she said, soft. "And maybe together with this?"

This was a black leather kilt that had met the approval of not only Drafli, but Ella and Nattfarr and Rosa too, and Baldr willingly shucked his trousers, and pulled it on. Stepping back so Drafli could see—and Drafli was indeed eyeing it with blatant eagerness, his eyes hungrily flicking up and down, his tongue sweeping against his lips.

"Ach, let him finish, brother," Simon cut in, grinning as he clapped his hand to Drafli's shoulders. "He yet needs weapons, ach?"

"And multiple outfit options," Ella added cheerfully, "in case his clothes are stuck in the laundry. We wouldn't want to add any extra pressure onto our Keeper, you know."

Drafli gave a wry glance toward Alma, and jerked a curt nod. Though the hunger in his eyes only kept rising as he watched, as Baldr's pile of new clothes—kilts, capes, belts, baldrics, cloaks, and indeed several new weapons—grew higher and higher beside them.

By the time they'd finished, Baldr was looking flushed and surprisingly happy in his beautiful new Grisk clothes, while Drafli had become alarmingly twitchy and restless, his trousers tented, his hands fidgeting in his pockets. Looking hungry, yes, and approving, but also almost... nervous?

Are you well, Golden-Tongue? Alma surreptitiously signed at him, but the movement had caught Baldr's eyes, too. And now he was studying Drafli with her, his head tilting, as Drafli drew in breath, and let it out.

Now... gifts, for my Grisk, he signed at Baldr, his eyes gone unreadable. *Should you wish.*

Baldr slowly nodded, his head still tilted, and Drafli abruptly clasped Alma's arm, and thrust her over to stand beside Baldr. Placing them side by side, his two watching waiting Grisk, both dressed in matching leather and furs.

Drafli's throat visibly convulsed as his eyes swept over them, his hands again twitching in his pockets—and then thrusting out toward them. And something in each hand was glittering, sparkling blue and green. Flashing almost like water, beneath a sunny sky.

Alma's breath choked, her hand fluttering to her chest—because she'd seen these before. They were the same jewels Drafli had offered to pay her with, so many days ago. The jewels he'd wanted to use to buy Baldr's son.

But this time—this time they were different. Rearranged.

Remade. And it took far too long for Alma to realize that the one he was holding toward her was a ring, its slim gold band beautifully twisted, its large sapphire clustered close with smaller stones of twinkling green.

Beside Alma, Baldr had gone just as still as she had, his breath just as frozen in his chest, his eyes staring down at Drafli's hand before him. At where Drafli was holding out a second, almost identical ring, but much larger, its band thick and gleaming.

"*Draf,*" Baldr choked—but then his shaky hand fumbled closer to Drafli's, his fingers spreading out wide. And as Alma stared, Drafli slid the ring onto Baldr's finger, his lashes lowered, his eyes fixed to the sight.

They were both still for a long moment, both staring down at it, at how Baldr's hand shivered, his fingers flexing, as if to test if the ring was real. And oh, it surely belonged there, blending beautifully against his green knuckle, speaking of light and strength. Of even water, perhaps, and how it had helped to bring them together, and given them life again.

They were hers, ach? Baldr's other hand signed, quick and furtive. *Your mating-gift to her?*

And even without the name, Alma knew very well who he meant. Drafli's first mate. And Drafli was grimacing, but nodding, and squaring his shoulders.

Ach, Drafli signed back. *But I wished to—remake this. Face this. Keep making new start. New family. Together.*

Oh. Alma's heart was knocking against her ribs, her eyes prickling hot. Drafli *had* faced his past through all this, after all. Just like Baldr had. Just like she had. And they'd done it together, they'd learned together, and challenged and encouraged each other, and helped each other. Together. A family.

And oh, they were both turning toward her now, Baldr's now-glittering hand lifting to wipe at her wet cheek, while Drafli raised his brows toward her. And Alma was desperately nodding, and smiling, and still weeping, as Drafli next slid her own ring onto her finger, and then flashed her a stunning, sharp-toothed smile.

Knew this would please you, he signed at her, while an unmistakable smugness crept across his eyes. *You wished for these since you first saw them, ach?*

Alma sputtered at him, flailing her hands at his infuriating chest—but then stopped short at the astonishing sight of that beautiful, brilliant sparkle, glittering on her finger. It was *hers*. Drafli had freely given it to her, to *keep*.

She only distantly registered Baldr laughing, the feel of his hand sliding against her bare back. "Ach, I ken she likes it, Draf," he said, the warmth almost shimmering in his voice. "It looks so pretty upon her, ach?"

Drafli was actually nodding, his eyes again glinting with smug satisfaction. *Mine*, he signed coolly toward her, and Alma tearfully smiled back, nodding as hard as she could.

Yours, she signed back. *And Pure-Heart's. Together*.

Drafli was still nodding too, his eyes catching back on Baldr's—and suddenly they were all locked together, clutched into each other's arms, rocking back and forth. And if Alma was weeping again into Drafli's chest, he certainly didn't seem to care, and only kept petting her, holding her, tucking her and Baldr tighter against him. Safe. A family.

By the time they finally pulled apart again, Alma had almost forgotten they had an audience—but they were all smiling too, Simon reaching over to clap Drafli on the back, as Maria gave him a grudging nod. And wait, Rosa and John appeared to be taking *notes*, while Nattfarr had drawn Ella close into his side, both of them watching with indulgent, satisfied eyes.

"So are we finished, then?" Ella asked, her eyes giving an assessing glance up and down Baldr's newly Grisk-ified form. "Is he missing anything?"

Ach, he is, Drafli signed, drawing all the room's eyes toward him—and his smug smile had sharpened, his eyes flicking between Baldr and Alma gone dark and dangerous.

You ken I am done with you yet? he signed at them, as he again reached his hand into his pocket—and this time he pulled out four small, shining gold rings. All seeming perfectly smooth, except for their slightly flattened sides, which—Drafli's fingers snapped one of them open—each hid a gleaming, deadly-looking point, tucked deep inside.

Now come, my pretty angels, he signed at them, all beautiful, breathtaking wickedness. *And take your devil's gold inside you.*

54

It turned out that being pierced by one's lord was both surprisingly painful, and thoroughly, deeply gratifying.

Before he'd done the actual piercing, Drafli had marched Alma and Baldr back down to the sickroom, and—with surprising politeness—asked Efterar to supervise. Efterar had been lying tangled in a bed with a soundly sleeping, sated-looking Kesst, but he'd clearly been awake, and had thankfully agreed with all apparent willingness. So after a few moments' preparation, including dousing the piercings in some sort of Ka-esh antiseptic, Drafli had drawn Baldr close, slid open his new cape, and grinned dangerously toward him as he'd lanced his greenish nipple with his gold.

There had been far more than just pain in Baldr's cry, his eyes gone hooded on Drafli's, his tooth biting his lip—and Drafli had taken his time with the other side, letting his fingers linger, letting Baldr feel it. And once he'd finally finished it, driving another hoarse cry from Baldr's mouth, Drafli had bent his mouth to each one, stroking with his tongue while Baldr had watched, his chest heaving, his eyes on fire.

And when Drafli had pulled away again, the sight he'd left behind had been... stunning. Their beautiful Grisk orc standing huge and hungry before them, his shoulders looking impossibly broad beneath his new fur cape, while his brand-new gold rings glinted underneath, matching the torc that bound the cape across his chest. And his handsome face was suffused with pink, his muscled arms and legs bare and power-ful, his rugged leather kilt visibly tented, his clawed hands—one of them with that gorgeous ring—hanging sharp and deadly at his sides. Looking more like an orc, and perhaps also more like *himself*, than Alma had ever seen him.

Drafli had stepped back to stare too, momentarily looking just as stunned as Alma felt—and his hand very rapidly signed something that looked rather like, *Thank you, Skai-kesh*. His eyes repeatedly flicking up and down, as a distinct flush of red gradually crept up the back of his neck, and his hand casually adjusted the visibly pulsing bulge in his trousers.

Beside them, Efterar had cleared his throat, his hand reaching to hover over Baldr's new piercings—to which both Baldr and Drafli seemed to startle awake again. Baldr giving a warm, sheepish smile, while Drafli spun to look at Alma, his eyes almost predatory on hers.

Your turn, Bright-Heart, he coolly signed at her, as he beck-oned her closer, and thrust back her own fur cape. *Are you ready?*

Alma swallowed hard, but fervently nodded, as she held Drafli's eyes. And this time, he and Baldr did the piercing together, Baldr's hands carefully cupping her breast for Drafli, while also murmuring a steady stream of encouragement into her ear.

The flash of pain was truly shocking, enough to bring tears to Alma's eyes—but Baldr kept whispering soft praises, and frantically waved Efterar over. And thankfully, the pain imme-diately faded, even as Baldr and Drafli swiftly moved to the other side, and yet more pain bloomed in their wake.

But that faded just as quickly too, thank the gods—and Drafli had again bent down, taking Alma's new piercing into his mouth, gently stroking it with his tongue. Sparking a new, astonishing sensation deep into her skin, and she startled at the feel of it, at the heat flaring hard in her belly. And then even harder at the feel of Baldr bending down too, taking the other side into his mouth, and blinking up at her with hungry, worshipful eyes.

Oh. Oh, gods. It should not have felt this good, this powerful, both of her breasts sucked deep into warm, reverent orc mouths, both of them tasting and caressing at once. And oh, now Drafli was looking at her too, his eyes gone suddenly, strangely vulnerable—and Alma swallowed as her shaky hand caressed the silk of his black hair. Revelling in how his lashes fluttered, his tongue lingering soft, his breath exhaling hard through his nose against her skin.

And for a brief, dangling instant, Alma was utterly caught in it, her hand stroking Drafli's hair, her eyes drinking him up. The most fearsome orc in Orc Mountain, the orc who'd been a terrifying enemy, had saved her life, fathered her son, and given her his gold, and his affections, and his safety. And now this, this impossibly intimate, unguarded moment, this *offering*.

And surely he knew it too, his eyes shifting, his tongue giving one more gentle stroke—and then he softly drew away again. Leaving behind Alma's peaked, flushed nipple, now with a ring of gleaming gold embedded within it. His ring.

On the other side, Baldr had drawn away too, his eyes sliding between her and Drafli, glowing with so much bare, burning affection that Alma could almost taste it. And then he abruptly fumbled at his new kilt, at where there seemed to be a clever little pocket tucked into the side of it—and he yanked something out, something that was also bright and gold and shining.

"And now a gift for you, Draf," he said, his voice husky. "If you should accept this, from us."

From—us? But wait, yes, that was a knowing twinkle in Baldr's glance toward Alma, a brush of his other hand on her back. And as he held out his gift toward Drafli, Alma realized it was another one of the cleverly fashioned, braided Grisk cuffs, with the garrotte hidden inside.

"Ach, I smelled you, when you saw Nattfarr's," he murmured at Drafli. "And I know you have liked having this one, to bind us with."

With that, his hand had skated over the leather still coiled around Drafli's forearm—Alma's leather—and Drafli's eyes had dropped to watch, the rest of his body unmoving, as Baldr slid the new gold cuff over Drafli's hand, up past the leather on his arm. Settling it into place upon his bare bicep, where it glinted beautifully against his scarred grey skin.

Drafli still hadn't moved, his eyes holding to the sight for a long, juddering moment—and when he finally glanced back to Baldr again, he again looked almost vulnerable, somehow. Surprised. Pleased.

You are... sure, his hand rapidly signed at Baldr. *You have enough credits for this? You ken I have no need, I no find enemy in bed now, I—*

But Baldr's hand had grasped for Drafli's, guiding it downwards, as he smiled at him with slow, stunning fondness. "I want you to have it," he murmured. "Want you to wear it. To... use it on us."

That flashed a new, glimmering danger across Drafli's eyes, as his hand shoved up under Baldr's kilt. Making Baldr shudder and gasp, and Alma felt herself reaching to pull the kilt aside—so much easier than trousers—and revealing the glorious sight of Drafli's claw, imperiously caught in Baldr's gold ring. As if...

There was a sudden cough nearby, loud enough to make Alma jump—and when they all twitched to look, it was Efterar, his expression somewhere between irritation and amusement. "Before this goes any further," he said, "did you want those fully healed, or not?"

His eyes had dropped to Alma's new piercings, and Baldr

and Drafli both gave jerky nods, their hands snapping up to cup at Alma's breasts. So that Efterar could hold his hands over theirs, his brow furrowing, while Alma felt an odd tingling, deep within.

"That should do it," Efterar said firmly, as he drew away again. "You'll still want to always be careful with them—no hard yanking—but light traction should be fine. Come back if there's any pain or problems with them, all right?"

Alma gratefully nodded, and gave him a warm, sincere smile. "I will," she replied. "Thank you so much, Efterar. For this, and for so thoroughly healing my throat and lungs too, and just—everything. You're *wonderful*."

She tried not to notice how Baldr and Drafli had exchanged a dark, disapproving glance at that last bit, but thankfully Efterar hadn't seemed to notice, either. "I'm glad I could help," he said, with a dismissive wave of his hand. "And in truth, I ought to be thanking you. Not only for your kindness toward me, with organizing those arena closures, and giving me a chance to rest, but also"—his eyes glanced over his shoulder, to where Kesst was still sound asleep in the bed—"for your great kindness to my mate. You have changed his life. All three of you."

Efterar's gaze had swept over Baldr and Drafli as he'd spoken, his eyes gone sober and heavy with meaning. "The two of you destroyed his greatest enemy, all those years ago, without seeking any redress from him, or even any acknowledgement," he said, quiet. "And then"—his eyes flicked to Alma—"*you* came along, and listened to him, and *saw* him. You thought to offer him credit on his *own* terms, and recognition for all he was already doing, when even I didn't think to see this. And now, all this with his scent—he has always smelled exquisite to me, but I know how much this meant to him. And in helping him with this, you have also helped grant him the peace he has always, *always* deserved."

Efterar's flinty eyes had darted back to Baldr as he'd

spoken, again including him in this, as his palm pressed to his chest, making Drafli's sign for *thank you*. "And even this hope of Rathgarr," Efterar continued, his voice thick. "Even if he's never found. Before this, Kesst refused to even hear his name for many, many moons—but to now visit the crypt, and to freely speak of him, it is—"

Efterar's voice halted there, his shoulders rising and falling, his lips pressing together—and Baldr cleared his throat, his eyes glancing between Alma and Drafli. "Speaking of Rathgarr," he said. "While I was away, I think—I think—I may have caught scent of him, far to the north. I do not wish to raise Kesst's hopes without cause, but—"

His eyes angled to Drafli, shifting, almost as if silently speaking—and Drafli was already nodding, and signing something in return. Something about coordinates, and scouts, and reports.

"But Draf will send out scouts to confirm," Baldr continued, his attention back on Efterar again. "And we shall hope for good news, ach?"

Before them, Efterar was dazedly staring, his big body actually swaying on his feet—and then he abruptly dropped backwards, sitting down hard onto Kesst's bed. "This is—" he began, rubbing at his mouth, his eyes blinking bright between them. "This is so good of you. Thank you. Again."

But now Baldr and Drafli were both waving it away, and Drafli was signing again, swift and sharp. *There is no debt*, he said, *only brotherhood. You saved our mate, we saved yours—and we shall all do this again, whenever it is needed. Ach?*

Baldr had quietly spoken that for Efterar, his eyes catching brief but meaningful on Drafli's, while something raw and fierce seemed to blaze up in Alma's chest. Had Drafli just called her... their *mate*? *Theirs*?

Her heart was erratically thumping, her eyes whipping back and forth between them, her body stilling at the sight of Drafli signing at Baldr, each word a swinging flying hope.

Are you sure, Pure-Heart, he said. *Forever sure.*

But Baldr was already nodding, signing back, speaking it with his hands and his voice. "I am sure," he said. "If you are, Draf."

And Drafli had nodded too, his eyes sweeping back to Alma, and gleaming with warmth, with indulgence, with unmistakable flaring heat.

And you, Bright-Heart, he said, as he raised his hand, gently flicked her cheek with his claw. *You wish for this. For us.*

"Yes," she whispered. "Yes, Drafli. My lord. Always."

He inclined his head as his hand dropped, catching on her brand-new ring. Tugging her a little closer, while a hoarse, hungry gasp choked from her throat.

Ach, then, he signed, with a dangerous, diabolical grin. *Follow me, and obey.*

55

All too soon, Alma once again found herself being paraded after Drafli down the corridor, with Baldr prowling close and powerful by her side.

But this time—Alma's eyes fluttered as her new piercings tugged again—it was their most blatant, most brazen display yet. Because Drafli, walking tall and proud before them, was pulling them along after him. Not by their clothes, but by two slim, taut strings, held casually in his hand.

One was Alma's leather, and it extended down beneath Baldr's new kilt, looping through his ring—and the other was Drafli's new gold cuff. Which he'd uncoiled into its long, shimmering cord, before stringing it through Alma's shiny new piercings, and gently pulling it taut.

Now, my pretty Grisk, he'd signed at them, all devious satisfied arrogance. *Come and show yourselves to the Skai.*

With that, he'd turned and led them out into the corridor, his hand lightly tugging on his strings. On his two Grisk worshippers, held fast by his own gold, sunk deep into their most intimate places, at his bidding and pleasure.

And in this moment, with Drafli leading Alma through a corridor by her nipples—and leading his mate by his *prick*—it almost did feel, perhaps, as though Drafli was their lord, and they were his pets. His obedient, adoring followers, bound to his whims and his will, meant only to suckle and to serve.

But there was no shame, Alma told herself, lifting her head higher. And she and Baldr had both defied Drafli, dishonoured him, disobeyed him—but despite all that, he was still here, still with them, still wanting them. Still honouring them.

It's not about him seeing you as less, Tryggr had said. *It's seeing you as more, and wanting to honour you, and take good care of you, and keep you safe.*

And as they passed more and more Skai orcs in the corridor—many of them stopping to stare—Alma could see that. Could appreciate that. Could feel herself shivering all over in the raw, raging power of that, her hand squeezing against Baldr's, earning a gentle squeeze against hers in return.

Are you ready? he signed at her, his eyes hooded and hungry. *You ken what is coming, ach?*

Another furious thrill chased up Alma's back, because Drafli was taking them to the Skai, he'd said. And though he'd called Alma their mate, that couldn't be true, not yet—not until Drafli claimed her before his clan. Until he led a *rut* upon her—showing her off to his clan—while they all bore witness.

And of course Baldr needed to be part of that too, and beside her, he'd begun to look even bigger and hungrier than before, his mouth curving into a sharp, surprisingly dark smile. While his hand had dropped to stroke all the way up his massive heft, up to his ring, to the leather string caught within it, pulling him out straight toward Drafli before them.

Ach, Bright-Heart, he signed back, slow and sultry. *You shall be flooded so full of us, you shall forget all else, but begging for more.*

Alma's gasp was surely more of a cry, drawing a too-aware glance from Drafli over his shoulder—and oh, he was giving a dark, deadly smile too, as he smoothly drew them sideways, into a dim, fur-strewn room. The Skai common-room, Alma knew, and it was already occupied with multiple orcs. Most of them also in a state of blatant undress, and shamelessly taking their pleasure together.

There was Simon, sitting on a bench with a pregnant, loin-cloth-clad Maria squirming on his lap, and beside them were Joarr and Gwyn, Gwyn grinding up against him, while Joarr complacently smiled toward her. And wait, on Simon's other side, that was *Tryggr*, his long legs sprawled wide—and crouched between his knees on the floor, that was surely Eben, sweetly sucking on the tip of Tryggr's scarred grey length, while Tryggr fondly rustled his hand in his messy black hair.

"This way, Bright-Heart," Baldr murmured, as his hand—together with Drafli's chain—gently tugged her forward, toward the middle of the room. Toward where there stood a large, flat table, covered all over with soft-looking furs.

Alma willingly went, though she could hear the room rapidly quieting around them, could feel the strength of multiple eyes on her prickling skin. But Baldr and Drafli only drew her closer, Drafli now slowly easing out his gold chain from her new piercings, as Baldr's warm hands began deliber-ately undressing her. First sliding her fur cape off over her shoulders, and then loosening her skirt, dropping it to the floor at her feet. Leaving Alma fully bared before the entire room of orcs, wearing only her lord's gold.

"Speak for our Right Hand, Baldr," came a deep, carrying voice from across the room, and when Alma glanced over to look, it was Simon, surveying all this with glinting, attentive eyes. "For what does Drafli wish."

Baldr was already glancing back at Drafli, even as his hands firmly guided Alma closer to the fur-covered table, oh gods. While beside them Drafli slid his new cuff back into its place on his arm, and signed toward Baldr. Saying, *You know*.

"Our Right Hand wishes," Baldr replied, his voice low and melodious, "to take this woman, Alma of Ashford, as his second bonded mate, in the ways of the Skai. And thus, he wishes to lead a rut upon her, while his clan bears witness."

There were a few murmurs and nods around the room, but no obvious dissent—and Simon was nodding too, his dark eyes warming with approval. "And do you wish for this from our Right Hand, Alma of Ashford?" he asked back, waving his big hand toward her. "Shall you accept Drafli's rut—from both him and his first mate—and thus become his second mate, in the ways of the Skai?"

Alma's already-pattering heartbeat was now thundering in her chest, so loud she could scarce hear anything else—but she felt herself nodding, frantic and fervent. "Yes," she breathed. "Yes, I want it. Please."

Her eyes had again found Drafli's, found them flashing, approving. And his hand had signed a fluid, nonchalant order, so quick that she almost didn't notice the slight trembling of his fingers.

Then present yourself, it meant. *To me.*

Alma gave another shaky, shuddery nod, her body still oddly caught in the impossible truth of this moment—and thankfully, Baldr's warm hands were still here, helping her up onto the table. Waiting until she was steady on her hands and knees, and then he gently, inexorably guided her legs wider. Opening her, showing all her most secret parts, for all these watching eyes—and oh, those were his fingers, tracing all the way up her bared crease. Spreading her apart for his mate, for his taking. His... rut.

There was a breath of total silence, of palpable anticipation—and suddenly Alma was slammed full of hard, unforgiving orc. Of *Drafli*. His long throbbing heft buried to the hilt inside her, impaling her upon him, driving a harsh, helpless shout from her mouth.

There were a few low, approving chuckles from the watching orcs, but far stronger was Drafli's pulsing strength within her, jutting so hard and deep, in bizarre contrast to Baldr's careful hands still pulling her apart. Holding her there, exposed and wide open, while Drafli slowly eased out again, until it was only his tip, bobbing against her—and then he drove inside again, as Alma's shout again rang through the room.

She was already arched and shivering all over, clutching at Drafli's invasion inside her, willing him to stay, if only for a moment—but no, he was already sliding out again, and then punching back inside. Wanting her to flail and shriek upon him, wanting to show his power over her, his ownership of her, his honour of her.

And Baldr's warm hands were still there too, still supporting this, guiding this. Opening her for his mate's claiming, his conquest, his *care*. And that was gratefulness—or perhaps even relief—as Drafli slammed in again, as another shout tore from Alma's gasping mouth.

"More, my lord," she somehow managed, as he drew back again—but it twisted into yet another shout as he again snapped inside. And then again, and again, and again, swifter and stronger with every thrust forward, with every drive of this impossible truth. He'd filled her with his son, he'd taken her before his god, and now he was claiming her before his clan, before his mate—

His position had suddenly shifted as he pounded her, his body leaning sideways—and oh, that was because he was kissing Baldr, biting hard at Baldr's trembling lip, without once losing his fierce furious rhythm upon her. Reminding Baldr that he was still his first mate, that he was still part of this, still his heart—and the awareness of that seemed to scrape Alma's shouts even higher between them. Yes, her lord was making her his—she *was* his—but he would never ignore or abandon his first mate, either. They were together. A family.

Something had sharply stuttered within Alma—Drafli, that truth, the utter perfection of this moment—and suddenly she could feel him breaking, spraying, pouring himself out inside her. Filling her with surge after surge of hot, rich Skai sweetness, his strength jabbed as deep as it could go, surely jutting tight against her already-full womb. As if making doubly certain it was his, she was his, opened and pierced and filled upon him, for all his clan to witness...

But then, without warning, he yanked fully out of her, the movement swift and shocking—but before Alma could feel the full loss of it, there was something else. Someone else. Someone blunter and smoother, with cool metal that whispered and sang against her hot skin as it found its place, and sank slow and steady inside.

And oh, the comparison was so beautiful, so strange. This one opening her even wider, but feeling far less powerful, less dangerous. Meeting her, rather than conquering her. Giving her time to adjust to him, to clutch at him, to welcome him there, to revel in him...

At least, until it suddenly slammed forward, too. Plunging another shocked shout from Alma's gasping mouth, even louder than before, while a surge of indulgent laughter rose around the room. And too late, Alma realized that Drafli had circled around the table, now standing tall and commanding before her eyes, and signing imperious orders toward Baldr behind her.

Ach, better, he was signing. *You make her scream, whilst I make her choke.*

And gods, Alma was already shouting again, because Baldr was indeed driving in again, just as hard as Drafli had—but wait, now Drafli's slick, swollen, dripping-wet heft was here, nudging between her lips. And then slamming in too, in perfect time with Baldr behind her, and fuck, Alma was choking, and screaming, and writhing between them, while Drafli's hand coolly tilted her head up, made her meet his eyes.

And oh, he was *smiling*. Smiling with such graceful, devilish danger as he blatantly used her mouth, as Baldr kept driving in between her legs. And Drafli was even signing at her, commanding her, while she sputtered and gagged on his plunging heft.

Suck me, woman, he said. *Drink up my good Skai seed. Feel my perfect mate ploughing you, owning you, on my command. You like that? Wish for more?*

Alma was nodding, feverish and desperate, her face burning, her body shuddering all over—and oh, the way her lord smiled, full of satisfaction, of triumph. The way he yanked out of her mouth, his scarred, gleaming heft bobbing into his waiting hand—and then he sprayed out not down her throat, but straight into her hot, gasping face. Shamelessly painting her with him, oh gods, spewing it back and forth, while his entire clan watched.

And in this, maybe, Alma ought to have felt shame—but that thought vanished as quickly as it had come, lost in the pure glory of this moment, in the way Baldr's breath had caught and choked, his body bearing down even deeper inside her. And suddenly Alma could feel him firing too, flooding her with yet more hot seed, while Drafli's claw casually drew open her lips wider, so that the last of his own spurting seed might catch upon her tongue.

He kept pumping himself until it was a slow drizzle, until his slick head had somehow met Alma's parted lips again. Allowing her to lick and suckle him clean, while his eyes watched with raw, glinting hunger, and he calmly signed a fluid order toward Baldr behind her.

Get out of her, Pure-Heart, it meant. *I want in there again.*

At that, Baldr actually chuckled, husky and affectionate, and accordingly drew backward. Leaving Alma empty and gaping in his wake, and—she gasped aloud—spurting out an astonishing quantity of hot, thick liquid, pouring slick and fragrant down her thighs.

And was it more shame, perhaps—but no, wait, here was Baldr, shifting around to hover with blazing eyes before Alma's face, his slightly softening heft already swelling again as he tilted up her chin. As he drank up the sight of her, so thoroughly drenched in his mate's fresh seed.

"So pretty," he purred at her, his thumb smearing the mess wider, as he gently fed his own heft between her wet parted lips. "So sweet. *Ach*, Bright-Heart."

He groaned as Alma willingly sucked him deep, his rich liquid already spluttering out onto her seeking, hungry tongue. While behind her, Drafli's hard, prodding strength was slipping up and down against the still-pouring mess, almost as if relishing it, coating itself in it—and then plunging in again. The sound slick and truly obscene, while more hot seed spluttered out around him, and poured down Alma's shaking thighs.

"So sweet," Baldr was gasping again, as he slid in and out of her mouth. "And you smell so good, when you are so full of us both, ach? When my mate ploughs you thus, taking you amidst my fresh leaking seed, ach—"

His voice had cracked, his body bending double over her— and then he was already pouring out again too, flooding himself down her throat. While Alma desperately sought to open for him, to swallow down every last drop of his hot surging release.

And oh, she'd almost succeeded, only a little escaping her mouth as he pulled away. And his approving hands were stroking her face, spreading the mess even wider, as his eyes watched with hushed, fluttering awe.

"So pretty, Draf," he croaked, his gaze flicking up behind her, to where Drafli was still plunging in and out, spurting out more hot fluid around him. "You like, ach?"

Drafli had surely agreed, and that was the feel of his *hand*, giving Alma's bare arse a gentle but purposeful slap. While Baldr huffed an unsteady laugh, his thumb brushing at Alma's swollen, parted lips.

"And you like too, ach?" he crooned at her. "You wish for our devil to fill you again? To bless you with his good Skai seed?"

Alma was wildly nodding, her mouth somehow speaking, babbling, begging. And Baldr's shoulders were shaking, *laughing*, as she felt Drafli plunging in, holding, grinding—and then again spraying out deep inside, his body curling low over her back. And oh, that was because he was kissing Baldr again, their tongues and teeth clashing against each other, while Alma's own pleasure raced and reeled, another scream tearing from her throat.

Drafli waited until it faded, his heft still slightly pulsing inside her—and then he yanked away again, while yet more hot seed flooded in his wake. Surging out like a fountain now, the sound of it even louder and more lurid than before, and Alma's face again swarmed with heat, with distant whispers of shame. She was being shared, used, packed full by her orcs, and now—now—

And now, oh hell, Drafli had slid deep inside her mess again, his strong arms clamping around her—and somehow, he'd lifted her up against him, and then dropped down onto his back on the fur. So that Alma was still pinned upon him, her back to his front, her pierced, juddering breasts now pointed toward the ceiling, while Drafli's heft circled and ground within her from beneath.

Come here, he'd signed at Baldr, with an inscrutable wave at Alma's breasts, and in return Baldr nodded and groaned, while his big body eased up onto the table, straddling over them both. So that he could—Alma trembled all over, her eyes seized on the sight—lower himself down over her, clutch her breasts with both hands, and slide his slicked, swollen heft deep between them.

"Ach," he hissed, his head arching back, his hips already driving forward, plunging his flushed, pierced, dripping pink head straight toward Alma's gasping face. "Ach, Draf. So *good*."

Beneath her, Alma could feel Drafli nodding, his chest heaving, his own hands coming up to grip over Baldr's against her breasts. Pressing them harder, closer together, his claws grazing at her new gold rings, while Baldr's moans sharpened, his thrusts and breaths quickening—and then he spewed out again, the streams of fragrant white spattering up over Alma's neck, her collarbones, her face.

And oh, Drafli was twisting up around her, so that he could lick at where Baldr had sprayed her, his tongue swirling slick against her skin. While Baldr watched with ravenous eyes above them, his body steadily lowering, his face coming closer, his breath inhaling. His tongue flicking out too, meeting Drafli's as it tasted Alma's cheek, tangling hot and hungry together.

It led to another fierce, vicious kiss between them, their teeth biting and scraping each other, so close beside Alma's face—and Baldr was again moaning, his body now lying long atop her, his slippery heft grinding against her groin. Rubbing up hard against where Drafli was still plunging inside her, still spurting and sloshing out more thick fluid with every driving thrust.

Gods, it was so much, so intense, whirling and battering against Alma's awareness, her senses. The world beginning to coil, to tighten, drawing in on Drafli inside her, on Baldr grinding in time with him just above. As if he wanted to be inside her too, buried in her slick leaking heat with his mate. Where it felt so stretched and used and open, so drenched in the same seed that coated Alma's face, her neck, her breasts. Theirs. *Hers.*

And was it shame, or something else, if Alma slipped her shaky fingers downwards, finding Baldr's slippery hardness. And then carefully, purposefully, nudging it up against Drafli's, against the open streaming mess they'd made.

She could feel them both briefly stilling, their eyes blinking toward her—and then a hard, full-body shudder from Baldr, while Drafli's hand came up to sign before her face, the movement not quite steady.

You are sure, it said. *You wish us both inside you.*

Alma nodded, even as she felt herself slightly grimacing between them. "As long as you don't," she whispered, hopefully soft enough that only they could hear it, "think it's shameful? Wrong?"

But above her, Baldr was whipping his head back and forth, so hard that his hair fell loose in her face, while Drafli gave a sharp, disapproving pinch to her pierced nipple. *No shame*, he signed at her. *We honour you, when we plough you, and fill you with our good seed. And you honour us when you accept this. When you welcome this. When you welcome... us.*

Oh. And that was one more revelation, spinning wide through Alma's already swirling skull, as she felt herself nodding, her relief sagging her back into Drafli's strength beneath her. Accepting them. Honouring them, in the way they were honouring her. Her mates.

And there wasn't even a whisper of shame, now, as Alma's tingling fingers found Baldr again, curving around his slick straining heft. And then guiding him further downward, nudging him just above where Drafli had eased almost all the way out, lining himself up with Baldr, making more room.

It meant that Alma could now circle her shaking hand around them both, feeling their combined swelling strength pulsing and dripping in her fingers—and then she carefully guided them toward her again. Nudging both their oozing heads against her own clutching, pouring-wet heat.

She could feel Baldr flaring hard at the touch, while Drafli spluttered out onto her fingers—but then they were moving in gentle unison, bearing up against her, seeking their way inside her. Into where it already felt impossibly, dangerously tight, oh fuck—but Drafli was easing in and out a little, surely opening her a little more, while above him Baldr barked a choked-sounding howl, and buried his face in her neck.

"So good," he gulped, and in the midst of the sheer wheeling sensation, Alma somehow found that it did feel good. Gods, so, so good, both her orcs sliding their way into her at once, impaling her, filling her to her utter limit...

"More," she gasped, clutching her hands at Baldr's bare

arse—and in return he moaned into her throat, driving a little deeper, while Drafli's teeth skittered against her neck. Speaking, again, of his approval. His honour.

The pressure was unthinkable, unreal, splitting Alma wider and wider as they bore down, deeper, breath by breath. As she was filled, speared, cleaved apart, her body frantically seizing against the powerful, pulsing orcs inside her. Feeling them shudder and spurt in return, winding each other higher, closer, fuller. Pumping her with even more molten heat, but there was no possible way for it to escape now, not with two orcs blocking her, stoppering her, driving her so full and so tight there was only this, nothing but this...

"Fuck," Baldr was gasping, his entire body hard and taut over her, perhaps with the effort to keep himself still—while beneath Alma, Drafli was dragging in long, desperate breaths, his teeth scraping even harder against her neck. And Alma scarcely noticed his claws scraping too, drawing up her flank, while his other hand twitched up toward Baldr's head, and yanked it downwards.

It meant their faces were both in Alma's neck now, their movements inside her a little more jerky, less controlled, tilting into chaos—and oh, it was Drafli who snapped first. His teeth clamping down hard against Alma's skin, while his hips slammed upwards, sinking him the rest of the way inside her. Gorging her impossibly full of him, oh—and then he grasped for Baldr's arse, and plunged him deep, too.

Alma's scream felt like someone else's, her body flung from itself, swept inside out, rammed full of huge, rutting orcs. So full she couldn't even move, her open heat stretched almost to breaking. Locking her upon her mates, them locking into her, into her womb her neck her heart. And the last thing missing was this, Baldr's teeth scraping her shoulder as he desperately moaned above her, until Drafli's hand again found his head, shoved it hard, as his teeth sank deep.

And it was that, finally, that took the wheeling sensation,

the fullness, the rising shouting storm—and shot it off into roaring, ravaging oblivion. Into Alma's choking, chock-full body screeching its raging release, wrecked and ruined and recklessly milking the orcs crushed into her. Demanding their honour, their favour, now—

And oh, even Drafli gave a hoarse, strangled shout as they both shuddered all over, and surged out into her. Their invading bodies firing off together, flexing and flaring, flooding her already distended core with torrents of hot swelling seed. Glutting her, bloating and bulging inside her, so much, too much, she was going to explode—

Until Baldr gasped and yanked away, his body still wracking with pleasure above her—and in his wake, surging out around Drafli's still-invading strength, was a thick, bubbling deluge of slick fragrant heat. Gushing out in a cascading rush, swarming between them, coating them all in the furious proof of their brash, beautiful ecstasy.

And then, somehow, it was over. Over, with Drafli's teeth carefully detaching from Alma's neck, his trembling hands slipping down her sides, and up again. While above her, Baldr kept heaving for breath, his eyes still on fire, his tongue sweeping against his red-stained lips—and then he rushed down, and met Alma's mouth. Kissing her with desperate surging craving, with gratitude and affection and admiration, pouring off his tongue into hers.

And then he'd pulled away, his shaky hand tilting Alma's head sideways—and that was so Drafli could kiss her too, his hungry tongue tasting of iron and salt, his teeth scraping hard and possessive against her lips. While above them, Baldr stroked her face with gentle fingers, his breath now inhaling deep against her throat.

"So good, Bright-Heart," he whispered, while Drafli's glorious golden tongue kept caressing her, tasting her, perhaps speaking too, agreeing. "So pretty. And your scent thus, so drenched in both of us, it is all I could ever long for. All I have ever *dreamt* of. Perfect, Bright-Heart, so *perfect*. And now you shall be ours, *forever*."

Forever. And lying here between them, lost in the stunning, utterly wondrous truth of these words and this kiss and this moment, there was a tilting, twirling, impossible peace. She was here. Home. Safe. Theirs.

And they kept pressing that truth into her, kept whispering it, kissing it, caressing it into her very skin, her soul. Theirs. With a solid, heavy certainty that hadn't ever been there before. Theirs, hers, forever. A family.

Alma couldn't have said how long they stayed there, kissing and stroking each other, swirling together in the peace, the relief—but at some point, Baldr's stroking hand had found a cloth, wiping up some of the sopping mess, while Drafli finally stretched his long limbs beneath her. His body arching up with a smug, blatant satisfaction that almost reminded Alma's stuttering brain of Cat, after she'd gone and caught a particularly juicy rat.

That smug satisfaction only seemed to sharpen as Drafli craned up to look over Alma's shoulder, his eyes swiftly surveying her sprawled, sated body upon him. Lingering on her surely reddened, white-smeared face, her swollen mouth, her streaked, sopping-wet body. And then particularly hesitating on her swollen-looking belly, his mouth quirking higher—and then his hand slid down, and gently pressed against it.

The resulting surge of heat from between Alma's legs spattered all over Baldr's still-wiping hand, and Baldr huffed a low chuckle as he shook his head. "*Draf*," he murmured, reproachful—while Drafli's mouth flashed into a dark, wicked grin. And then he pressed down again, spraying even more mess across Baldr's hands and torso—and Alma somehow found herself laughing together with Baldr, her eyes warm and knowing on his. United in their affection for their contrary, beautiful devil, and all his devious, outrageous demands.

But Alma had perhaps never felt trust like this, safety like this—even when Drafli's finger lightly flicked her hot cheek, and he nudged her sideways. So that he could fully ease out from beneath her, and then rise to his feet beside the table, his clawed hand still firmly gripped to her sprawled thigh.

But he wasn't looking at her now, or even at Baldr, whose body had gone still beside her—and instead, his glittering gaze was sweeping over the room. Over all the gathered watching Skai, his clan, his witnesses, with something much like a challenge in his stance and his eyes. As if to say, *She is mine. Ours. Shall you fight me upon this?*

But thankfully, none of the Skai seemed to take that challenge, and instead returned it with nods, and even with signs of affirmation and approval. Tryggr was actually grinning toward them, signing, *Nice, Boss,* while beside him, Simon had put his fist to his heart, and given a decisive nod.

"We see your gain, Skai," he called out, his voice firm. "You have our blessing."

Alma could see Drafli's shoulders slightly sagging, his head bowing, his own fist pressing over his heart. And then his fingers slowly spreading out wide, shifting into, *Thank you. Thank you.*

But then his hand dropped, his lean body again whipping back toward Alma and Baldr—and oh gods, his smile was lighting up his face, crinkling his eyes, flashing all his sharp teeth. Flooding Alma with his warmth, his light, his approval. Home. Hers.

And it kept swinging, surging, as Drafli swept closer again, his hands reaching for both her and Baldr, catching with possessive familiarity on their chins. Drawing them both toward him, so he could keep grinning back and forth between them—and then he actually *laughed*. The sight almost astonishing in its beauty, in their lord with such delighted ease in his eyes, with his triumph written all over his fluid body. In the way both his thumbs were swiping at their mouths, his eyes fluttering as their tongues slipped out, met him, adored him.

It was almost as though the world had stuttered again, as though Drafli might again tackle them down onto the table, and take turns with them—until he glanced down at the messy fur beneath them, and visibly grimaced. And then reached and drew Alma upwards, his arm solid and steadying around her waist.

Come, pretty Bright-Heart, he signed at her, as he slowly guided her bared, shaky, still-sticky body across the room, and toward the bench. Toward where Simon, Joarr, and Tryggr were all still sitting, with Maria still curled onto Simon's large lap, Gwyn clasped in a smugly grinning Joarr's arms, and Eben still crouching hazy-eyed between Tryggr's knees, and carefully licking at his half-hard heft.

"Ach, we are most pleased for you," Simon told Drafli, his eyes warm and approving, as Drafli smoothly sank onto the bench between him and Tryggr, and then drew Alma down on top of him. "It is not every Skai who gains not only one, but *two* pretty mates for his own."

Maria, who was only wearing her Skai loincloth and dagger, had visibly bristled as Simon spoke, elbowing him hard in the belly—and Simon chuckled as he blatantly slipped his fingers beneath her loincloth. "Ach, my Maria, you ken you are all I have ever longed for," he murmured. "But Drafli knew that his beloved mate longed for a woman and son, ach? It is thus only good Skai care, to offer him this."

At that, Alma exchanged an uneasy glance with Baldr, who—in the absence of more room on the bench—had slipped down to the floor with Eben, leaning against Drafli's sprawled thigh. "You did not *need* to offer me this, Draf," Baldr said, his brow creasing, his eyes searching Drafli's. "I did not expect this of you. Ever."

But behind Alma, Drafli's eyes were surprisingly mild, his shoulder giving a dismissive shrug. *Ach, I ken*, he signed back. *But mayhap I wished for her, too.*

On Alma's other side, Tryggr had paused his lazy petting

of Eben's head long enough to nudge Drafli's knee with his own, flashing him a teasing grin. "Ach, don't 'mayhap' us, Boss. You've been fussing over your pretty new pet ever since she came here, ach? Giving her all those costly trinkets, dressing her up so fine, and teaching her how to speak to you, and how to please you and your mate. Not to mention giving us constant grief for not helping her more! As if I could sort out that flaming laundry disaster in a coupla *days*?"

He waggled his eyebrows at Drafli as he spoke, and Alma was thoroughly unsurprised by Drafli's hard knock back at Tryggr's shoulder, the not-quite-disapproving frown in his eyes. *Then mayhap you need another broken knee*, he signed back, *until you finish that laundry for her, ach?*

Tryggr twitched with visible chagrin, his hand reflexively dropping to rub at his knee. "The laundry's done, Boss, I swear!" he squeaked. "Knew you'd want it sorted by the time you got back, so we hustled night and day on it! And as fun as it's been, woman"—he shot Alma a rapidly warming grin—"I refuse to be on laundry duty forever, ach? But I'll come visit— gotta check on Duff, of course—and maybe you'll stop by the arena more often, too? Get Boss to teach you a few lessons?"

Alma shot a brief glance backwards, to where Drafli was actually shrugging—saying, maybe?!—and she found herself nodding, and giving Tryggr a fond, genuine smile. "I'd love to," she said. "And I'm just so grateful for all your help, Tryggr. You were *wonderful*."

Tryggr cheerfully waved it away, though Alma didn't miss how both Baldr and Drafli were now frowning at him, their foreheads almost identically creased. *Our mate needs a drink*, Drafli signed at him, the movements far sharper than before. *And a snack, also. And a fresh towel.*

Tryggr gave a good-natured roll of his eyes, a reluctant glance down at Eben—and then his mouth quirked as he caught Eben's chin, and lifted it up toward him. "Do me a favour, sweet thing?" he purred. "Go fetch me some food and water, will you? And a clean towel, too?"

Eben had nodded, his eyes rapt on Tryggr's face—and he instantly stood up and padded out, belatedly yanking up his fallen trousers around his slim hips. While Tryggr watched him go with visible appreciation, his eyes lingering on his arse.

"Thanks for the suggestion on the pet, by the way, Boss," he said lightly, with another meaningful elbow at Drafli's side. "I only snagged him today, but I'm already thinking he'll work out real well. After a bit of proper training, of course."

Drafli was looking reluctantly amused again, and perhaps rather mollified, too. *He is pretty*, he replied to Tryggr, with the air of one making a great concession. *But not as pretty as mine. Or as sweetly scented, either.*

His hand had dropped to tilt up Baldr's chin, as his own head bent into Alma's neck, breathing deep—while beside him Tryggr loudly scoffed. "For the love of Skai-kesh, give me time, Boss," he replied. "Also, for all they reek of you, it still seems to me like you missed an important spot on your woman just now, didn't you? Simon's *way* ahead of you there."

He was giving a sly wink across Alma and Drafli, toward where—Alma's breath caught—Simon was in the process of intently lowering Maria down onto his alarmingly massive heft. And not in the place Alma would have imagined, either— because he was still blatantly playing there in front with his fingers, while that gigantic beast slowly slid up into—well.

"Ach, we do this to honour Drafli, you ken?" Simon said smugly, while upon him, Maria's face had flooded a deep red, her breath catching as she sank a little deeper, her eyes darting a frown at Simon behind her. Who only kept grinning back toward her, now with a rather dangerous, Drafli-like gleam in his eyes. "I well ken how it pleases him to see my pretty mate honour me."

Ach, for she cannot grouse at me with that inside her, Drafli signed back, with a glance of deep dislike toward Maria—who, to Alma's surprise, was suddenly looking sharply offended, her hand reaching to clutch against her dagger.

"You slimy, domineering—" she began, but then her voice broke into a ragged gasp, as Simon's enormous bulk sank deeper into her. "I have no idea how you—*you!*—got *them!*—some kind of—*trick*—"

But Simon had thrust up a little harder, wringing Maria's voice into a desperate shout, while his fingers clearly increased their efforts beneath her loincloth. "Ach, this is better, woman," he said smugly. "We shall honour our Right Hand's gain, on this happy day."

Maria had furiously sputtered again, but no actual words came out, and Drafli was indeed looking darkly pleased as he watched her writhe and moan, while Simon chuckled affectionately into Maria's neck, and Joarr openly cackled on his other side. And Alma only belatedly realized that Drafli's own hands were also casually shifting her atop him, raising her upwards, so that he could—

She yelped as he prodded her, just there, just like Simon was doing to Maria—and the orcs all merrily laughed, Baldr's hands even moving up to *help* Drafli, oh hell. Lowering Alma slow but careful down onto him, plunging her full of more hard hungry heat. And surely, this would have been far more difficult, if not for the fact that she was still dazed and sated and thoroughly relaxed all over, and still generously and copiously drenched in thick, slippery white.

"Ach, this is it, Bright-Heart," Baldr was murmuring, his eyes on a level with the surely shocking sight of this, with how the pressure was squeezing even more thick seed from Alma's still-stretched crease before him. "Ach, so pretty. Smells so good. *More.*"

He'd leaned closer into her, deeply inhaling—and as Drafli finally sank all the way inside, settling Alma's full weight back onto his lap, his indulgent hands slipped down to Baldr's face, caressing him, opening his mouth. And then guiding him forward, pressing his face deep into Alma's open, dripping heat.

"Oh gods," Alma gasped, as Baldr obligingly, eagerly began kissing, licking, swarming his hot clever tongue against her, while Drafli ground into her from behind. "Oh, gods, my lord!"

But her helpless glance up at Drafli showed him looking even more pleased than before, one hand gently stroking her still-bulging belly, the other tangling in Baldr's hair. While beside them, Simon was giving Drafli a knowing smile, even as he did something that made Maria loudly screech upon him— and on their other side, Eben had finally returned, indeed carrying all the items Drafli had requested. And after shunting them off toward Drafli, Tryggr wasted no time in yanking down Eben's trousers, and coolly telling him to have a seat upon his Skai, too.

Eben obliged with unabashed eagerness, shivering all over as he lowered himself down onto Tryggr's waiting length, while Tryggr murmured a steady stream of praises into his ear. Until Eben's head had fallen back onto his shoulder, his eyes squeezing shut, as Tryggr's teeth purposefully scraped at his exposed neck.

It was all utterly, thoroughly surreal, and even more so once Drafli began feeding Alma bits of the meat and fruit Eben had brought, in between long drinks from the waterskin, while also gently wiping her clean with the towel. As if he wasn't even slightly affected by the fact that he was still *inside* her, and that Baldr was still voraciously feasting between her legs, his face now coated with their wetness, the sounds slick and obscene.

But Alma's pleasure kept wheeling, swirling with peace, contentment, ease. With *care*. With the sure, certain awareness that Drafli was honouring her in this, pinning her here safe upon him, feeding her and cleaning her, while his mate knelt before her, lavishing her with his tongue. Wringing her up higher and tighter, her body writhing against Drafli within her, but he had her, he was inside her, she was his, *safe*—

The rush of pleasure felt more like a wave this time, rising and rising, surging Alma upon its steadily soaring tide—and then crashing into a million swarming, shuddering flares of ecstasy. Into her entire body convulsing with raw, reverent bliss, lost in such closeness, such care, such safety. She was theirs. Their own.

And when Drafli gently eased her up and off, and then swept her into his strong arms, that certainty only swelled higher, sinking her ever safer against him. He'd claimed her before his mate, his god, and now his clan. His.

And Baldr's too, her contented thoughts whispered, feeling his warm hand stroking her hair as Drafli carried her out the door, and into the corridor. And for a strange, juddering instant, Alma's thoughts had whirled back to the first day they'd met, to the way Baldr had carried her to his home, just like this. When he'd promised her she wouldn't interfere. When he'd promised to keep her safe.

And even if there had been all those challenges along the way—Alma blinked her bleary eyes open, and found Baldr's beloved face, his eyes shining on hers—they'd still found a way forward, together. As friends, as lovers, as co-worshippers of their beautiful devil. As... mates.

But that last one still felt far too new, and perhaps not quite real—at least, until Drafli had settled Alma down onto their familiar bed. And blinking up at him, at the room, she only vaguely registered that her things—her trunk, her pillow, even some of her furniture—were here. In their room. Theirs.

But even more important, more meaningful, was that look in Drafli's eyes. The way they were shifting and changing on hers as he knelt beside her on the bed, his throat bobbing, his hand rubbing at his mouth.

You say it, he signed at Baldr, the movements oddly furtive. *For both of us.*

On Alma's other side, Baldr had nodded, his eyes now

shimmering just as strangely as Drafli's. His breath inhaling, exhaling, inhaling again.

"We see you, our sweet Alma," he whispered, so soft. "And with this, we pledge you our troth. We grant you our swords, and our favour, and our fealty. We shall keep you safe, so long as we are able, and so long as you shall wish."

And as he'd spoken, Drafli had signed the words beside him, matching them, confirming them. The signs not all familiar, but enough that Alma could follow, could feel her heart surging as she blinked between them, as wetness streaked from her wide, astonished eyes.

This was... their vow. Their promise. Making her their mate. For good.

And oh, she couldn't even speak, her throat thoroughly blocked in the unthinkable, impossible strength of their promise—and suddenly she was frantically signing back, the movements wild and shaky, pouring out her soul.

Yes, she was saying, her eyes desperately searching between them. *Yes, please. I see you, I love you, I pledge you my loyalty, my honour. I am yours.*

Baldr was drawing in more breath, nodding, his palm rubbing at his blinking eyes, while on her other side, Drafli was watching her with silent, serious intensity. Almost as if he were digesting her answer, absorbing it, committing it to memory. Contrasting it, maybe, with all the anger from when they'd first met, the mistrust, the hatred.

I no like you, he'd told her, with such loathing in his eyes. *I hate you.*

But there wasn't even a trace of that now, only that watchful waiting stillness, that... reverence. Watching Alma signing to him, speaking to him in his own way, with the words he'd taught her.

I am yours, she told him, again and again, her arms crossing over her chest, and extending toward Baldr, and then toward him. *I love you. I love you.*

And finally Drafli nodded too, his own eyes also gone unnaturally bright, as his arms slowly crossed over his chest, and reached toward Baldr, while Baldr did the same—and then Drafli leaned down, and pressed his sign against her. Holding it there, his breath heaving, as Baldr slid his sign down too, his hands gripping Drafli's wrists, binding them together.

We love you. We love you.

And suddenly Alma's tingling arms were clutching against theirs, saying it too, holding them close. Saying, *yes. Yes. I love you too. Always.*

An unexpected sob had choked from her throat, shuddering her chest against them—and beside her, wetness was streaking down Baldr's cheeks, too. While Drafli had gone still, blinking back and forth between them, his eyes incredulous—and with a heavy sigh, a fluid flash of movement, he'd dropped down onto the bed, and yanked both Alma and Baldr into his arms. Burying their faces into his chest, caressing their heads with his strong steady hands.

"Ach, my sweet mates," he whispered, hoarse. "Always so soft. So *needy*."

But he didn't sound upset—quite the opposite, really—and when Alma stole a peek up at his face, he was actually half-smiling up at the stone ceiling, his eyes unusually warm, as his hands firmly stroked at their hair. And Baldr was looking up at him too, his own eyes shining, and his glance over at Alma was so knowing, so beautiful.

Our devil likes it, he signed at her, as Drafli darted a sharp, disapproving glance downwards. *He wants us like this, forever bound to him, needing him, caught in his thrall.*

And Alma was laughing, and still weeping a little, and clinging to Drafli, and his strength, and his safety. "Of course he does," she whispered. "Bringing us both firmly to heel, and laughing all the while."

With that, Drafli had abruptly stiffened beneath them, something wicked flashing behind his eyes—and then he'd swiftly thrust them both down to the bed, while he himself hovered over them, all sheer, smiling, breathtaking danger.

You wish to see me laugh, my pretty angels? he signed at them, the movements swift, sure, spectacular. *Present yourselves to me. Now.*

And there was only warmth, only joy, as Alma beamed up at her lord's dark, dangerous eyes. And then, together with her fellow favourite worshipper, she turned around, raised her arse, and obeyed.

EPILOGUE

Drafli was dreaming again.

Alma could feel the brittle tension of his body in the bed against her, the way he kept flinching, as if from a series of invisible, painful blows. And worst of all, as always, was the unnatural way he was dragging in air, the way it whistled high and panicked in his throat.

"*Nei*," he croaked. "*Hættu. Ég bið þig.*"

But thank the gods, on Drafli's other side, Baldr was already shifting awake, too. His hand squeezing brief and reassuring to Alma's arm in the darkness, before stroking back against Drafli's heaving chest.

"Ach, Draf," he murmured, soft. "*Við erum hérna. Þú ert heima.*"

It was the orcs' spoken language—Aelakesh, it was properly called. And thanks to some helpful classes from Rosa, Alma now knew enough to at least follow Baldr's words—especially given his flatter, common-tongue accent.

We are here, he'd told Drafli. *You are home.*

But Drafli was already flailing up again, and Alma could feel his rigid arms clutching for Baldr, yanking him nearer in the blackness. "*Kona*," he rasped. "*Sonur. Dáinn.*"

Woman, it meant. *Son. Dead.*

Baldr replied with a low shushing sound, his big body guiding Drafli back down to the bed. "No, Draf," he said, as his hand again found Alma's arm, and drew her a little closer. "They are here, too. Alma, and our son. You can smell them, ach?"

"*Nei*," Drafli gulped, and Alma could feel his head shaking back and forth, hard enough that his hair whipped across her face. "*Nei, ég verð—*"

His voice abruptly broke into a harsh, hollow cough, painfully loud in the previously quiet darkness, and Baldr made the shushing sound again, his hand on Alma's arm now nudging her a little downward. But this wasn't new to her anymore, and she'd already been shifting lower, easing her way down Drafli's taut body in the bed, while Baldr held him still beneath her.

"You wish to feel her, Draf?" Baldr murmured, low, reassuring, as Alma kept sliding downward. "Wish to feel our woman sucking you?"

Drafli had surely nodded, his hands clutching and skittering, grasping for Alma's head. Saying yes, like he always did— and though Alma and Baldr always asked, they knew they always had his permission, too. *Ach, you ought to always be sucking me*, he'd smugly told Alma, months before. *Awake or asleep.*

So Alma carefully settled in between Drafli's still-twitching thighs, and slowly, gently found his rigid heft in the darkness. Giving it a few soft, sweet kisses, before slipping its smooth head into her mouth.

Drafli had abruptly stopped moving, though his body remained solidly unyielding beneath her, and Alma took him a little deeper, while Baldr's hand gave an approving rustle against her hair. "You feel her now, Draf?" he murmured. "You feel our mate's sweet mouth suckling you? Her clever little human tongue kissing you?"

Alma's tongue was indeed delving a little inside Drafli, feeling him clench and flare against it—and oh, thank the gods, it was working. The rest of his body slightly sagging back against the bed, his breath exhaling hard, his hips snapping up, grinding him deeper into Alma's mouth.

"Ach, this is it," Baldr continued, and Alma could hear his hand stroking Drafli, rubbing up and down his flank, softening his tension further. "Feel how she is here in your bed, seeking to please you. She loves having you in her mouth, ach, Bright-Heart?"

Alma murmured her agreement around Drafli's steadily pulsing heft, feeling his body sag a little more, his hips canting up harder. While Baldr kept murmuring and stroking too, until his own voice broke, his muscles flexing rigid—and then Alma could hear Drafli swallowing, the sound hard and rhythmic, his teeth surely now buried deep in Baldr's neck.

Baldr's moan was low and needy, his hips bucking against Alma, but he still kept stroking Drafli, reassuring him, whispering comfort and praises, while Alma kept sucking him, lavishing him, seeking her tongue inside him. Until Drafli finally arched up and surged out into her mouth, flooding her with pulse after pulse of his hot, succulent sweetness.

And like always, it seemed to sweep away the last of the tension, the fear—and Alma could hear Drafli's gulps slowing, fading, as he sank back toward sleep. His body beside them again gone limp and relaxed, his chest inhaling and exhaling in a deep, steady rhythm.

Alma could feel Baldr relaxing too, his own breath exhaling—and then his hands reached down toward her, and bodily pulled her up again. Nestling her close between him and Drafli, his front to her back, his strong arm around her waist.

"Thank you," he breathed, soft, in Alma's ear, as his hand spread wide against her rounded belly. "He is getting better, ach?"

Alma gratefully nodded, twining her fingers together with

his, and settling closer into the comfort of his embrace. She'd become deeply familiar with Drafli's dark dreams these past months, and with how the truth of their growing son had perhaps made them even more frequent, more intense, than before. But Baldr, who had already been well used to them, had continued to meet them with unflinching steadiness and acceptance, and Alma had quickly learned to do the same.

And it was odd to think, now, of how these dreams had so clearly been a crucial part of why Drafli had kept sending Alma away at nights, when she'd first come here—and why Baldr hadn't ever argued that at the time, either. Because to Drafli, Alma now knew, the dreams were still signs of his shame, his weakness, his defeat. Too-vivid reminders of a past he longed to forget.

But Baldr was right, and lately it had been getting better again, too. Easier to calm and soothe Drafli, most of all with Baldr offering his hands and voice and neck, while Alma offered her mouth. Working together to honour their lord, to help him, to ease him away from pain, and back into pleasure again.

But there was one major drawback, Alma had quickly discovered—the fact that their concerted efforts often left them both feeling twitchy, and hungry, and thoroughly unsatisfied. A situation that currently wasn't being helped by the feel of Baldr's thick, pulsing length, bobbing with thwarted eagerness against Alma's bare thighs.

"Oh," Alma gasped, arching back toward it, without quite meaning to—and in return Baldr gave a low, husky moan, his hips reflexively grinding back up against her. Making her arch and gasp even more, her own hips now angling backwards, brazenly seeking his prodding heft where she craved it most.

"*Alma*," Baldr groaned, with palpable exasperation, as his smooth head found her too, nudging hungrily against her slick heat, and then slipping just slightly inside. "*Ach*. Draf shall *not* be pleased with this, you ken."

But Alma gasped again, and shook her head as she pushed back a little harder. "No," she breathed. "He'll be *very* angry."

Baldr moaned again as he sank deeper, his teeth nipping at her ear, his claw gently thumbing at her pierced nipple. "He shall surely," he whispered, "punish us."

Alma fervently nodded as she shoved back the rest of the way upon him, burying him to the root in her clenching, craving heat. "You most of all," she whispered back, "for this is *your* doing, Pure-Heart."

Baldr's low laugh was warm and appreciative, his fingers giving her nipple-ring a delicious little tug as he ground deeper inside her. "You think he shall spare you?" he purred. "He knows what a greedy little Grisk you are. Always seeking your next strong ploughing."

"And *you're* any different?" Alma scoffed back, even though she was vibrating with laughter against him, and she turned her head to find his mouth, to taste his beautiful twining tongue. Gasping against it as his hips bucked harder against hers, his stunning strength gouging deep inside, plunging again and again and again—until it poured out into her, filling her with glorious heat, while his hand firmly ground against her in front, flaring out her own release, too.

And oh, it was so much better, sinking back into the safety of his arms, of his softening bulk still buried within her. Feeling so sweetly sated that sleep seemed to swirl all at once, curling her into its embrace, into the safe quiet darkness...

Until light suddenly blazed to life in Alma's eyes. And something sharp was jutting under her chin, tilting up her head. A hand. *Drafli's* hand.

What is this? he demanded at her, his other hand waving down toward his groin. Toward where—Alma gulped—her bare thighs were still painted in sticky white, and Baldr's softened, gold-tipped head was guiltily peeking out between them.

"Um," she began, "well, it's not *quite* what it looks like, and—"

But Drafli's hand had clapped over her mouth, his eyes glinting with danger—and perhaps with amusement, too. *Get up*, he ordered her. *Present yourself. You too, my disobedient Pure-Heart.*

This was said with a sharp slap of his palm toward where Baldr had been lazily yawning behind her—and Alma could feel the thrill running down his big body, his claws slightly clenching against her skin.

"It was not my fault, this time," Baldr protested, his voice still thick with sleep, but surely with hunger, too. "*She* was the one who began this, and tempted me, and sucked me in so sweetly, and—"

But this resulted in a sharp yank of Drafli's claw against Baldr's still-poked-out ring, hard enough to make him gasp. *I told you*, Drafli signed, *to present yourself, Pure-Heart.*

"Ach, ach," Baldr choked, as he scrabbled to extract himself from Alma, shoving up onto his hands and knees—and earning in return another stinging slap from Drafli's hand against his arched, exposed arse.

And you? Drafli demanded at Alma, who was belatedly shoving up into the same position as Baldr, tilting her arse up into the air. Showing Drafli everything he wanted to see, including the blatant truth of Baldr's fresh mess, streaming liberally down her thighs.

And oh, Drafli was watching it, his lashes fluttering, his breath hissing out through his teeth. *You ken I would not smell this, or see this?* he signed at her, at them, as he palmed his hand in the mess, and spread it wide over Alma's arse. *My woman, dripping my orc's fresh seed? Flaunting my commands, yet again?*

With that, he gave Alma's arse a gentle but purposeful swat, firm enough to make her twitch. *What do you say to me*, he demanded at her. *How shall you make amends to your lord.*

Alma shivered all over, her body flushed and prickling, her breath choking in her throat. "Forgive me, my lord," she gulped. "Please. I'll do whatever I can to make it up to you. *Please.*"

The words sounded vaguely familiar, like something she might have said once, in another life—but there was only eagerness, and hunger, and a reckless gleeful craving, as Drafli's hand again slapped her arse, his claws lingering this time, caressing, teasing.

Ach, he signed at her, as one of those fingers found her dripping-wet heat, and thrust inside. *You shall.*

Alma arched and shouted at the touch, already begging for more—but Drafli was smirking again, yanking his hand away, *depriving* her, as he eased over behind Baldr instead. And then he slammed deep, without warning or kindness, while Baldr frantically flailed and keened beneath him, his body spasming all over at the next sharp swat of Drafli's hand.

Alma watched them with breathless, writhing longing, biting her lip as Drafli coolly shook her leather off his arm, and snapped it out long. And then—Alma moaned aloud—Drafli strung it across Baldr's *mouth*, pulling it back like a bridle, while Baldr reared up hard, choking out a hoarse, muffled cry around it.

Look what you have done, Drafli signed at Alma, giving Baldr another firm swat as he kept riding him, pounding away inside him. *Look how he suffers for you. You still wish for forgiveness now? Still wish to pay your penance, naughty pet?*

Alma frantically nodded, her tongue helplessly licking her lips, her body shuddering with sheer, unfulfilled craving—and suddenly Drafli dragged her over closer, shoving her beneath Baldr's kneeling form, prodding Baldr's swollen, bobbing heft against her slick open heat, oh hell.

Ach, and you wish for my *orc*, Drafli smugly signed at her, his hand moving before her fluttering eyes. *So you shall have him, but only whilst he keeps bearing the brunt of my wrath, on your behalf.*

With that, he again slammed himself forward into Baldr—

this time driving Baldr deep into her, sinking them both to the hilt. While both Alma and Baldr desperately howled, and she could hear another satisfied swat at Baldr's arse, and a sound much like a laugh behind them.

And then it was only sheer flying sensation, shouts and slaps and squelches and moans as they rocked and soared together, as Drafli's strength rode them, pummelled them, as his claws scraped red penance against their sweaty skin. As Baldr finally shouted and broke, his teeth sinking hard into Alma's shoulder, around the leather still in his mouth—and then Alma and Drafli both pitched over the edge too, Alma screeching into the fur, while Drafli gouged deep into Baldr, and finally poured out his forgiveness.

It took some time to wash up, after that—Drafli had thankfully made a habit of freshening the water in the pitcher each evening, for just such events—and once they were all clean and dry again, Drafli helped Baldr and Alma dress, too. It was something else that had just become habit these past months, Drafli casually picking out their clothes for the day, fastening their furs on over their shoulders, before buckling on their kilts, and helping them comb and braid their hair. And then, finally, he would choose simple jewels for the workday, too— today a glittering green earring for Baldr, and a delicate gold bracelet for Alma.

"Thank you, my lord," Alma murmured, standing on tiptoes to kiss his cheek. And once he'd given her an approving little once-over in return, his hand gently swatting her arse, Alma went over to collect the bed's extremely messy fur, grimacing as she folded it up for the laundry.

But without warning, Drafli was once again looming here before her, plucking the fur from her arms. *Wait, Bright-Heart,* his other hand swiftly signed at her. *Are you hurt? Tired? In pain?*

Alma blinked up at him, and then felt her face soften into a smile, her head shaking. "Oh, no, I'm fine," she said. "Just thinking about the laundry. But thankfully"—her smile twitched higher, with genuine relief—"it's Duff's day on wash-basin duty, since I'll be busy preparing for the party."

The party was one Alma had been eagerly anticipating for days now—it was the orcs' traditional half-year celebration for young orclings, and was being held in honour of Ella's son Rakfi—but Drafli didn't look even slightly appeased by this, and he irritably tossed the fur aside, in favour of furiously beckoning Baldr over. *Smell her, Pure-Heart*, he swiftly signed. *Is aught amiss?*

Baldr obediently ducked his face into Alma's neck, his breath inhaling, while Drafli's hands dropped to slide against Alma's swollen belly, his long fingers spreading wide. His eyes narrow and intent on Baldr, who was looking unmistakably relieved as he pulled back, his head shaking.

"Ach, she smells fine," he said to Drafli. "I made doubly sure not to ride her too hard, ach?"

Drafli's dark expression still hadn't changed, his claws clenching on Alma's belly before drawing away. *You take her to Efterar, after your prayers*, he signed at Baldr. *If aught is amiss, you send for me. And you*—he jabbed his claw at Alma—*you are not to work too hard on this foolish party, ach? You ought to rest. Mayhap I ought to tell Efterar to command you*—

But Alma couldn't help a warm, affectionate grin, a shake of her head as her hand signed, *No.* "I'm fine, Drafli," she told him. "I promise."

She truly did mean it—so far, her pregnancy had been blessedly uncomplicated—but Drafli kept fiercely glowering at her, enough that Alma began to suspect that he was contemplating tying her to the bed. When thankfully, at that very moment, something black and furry streaked through the air toward Drafli's head, and landed with surprising agility on his shoulder.

Alma startled, but then laughed aloud, because it was Cat, of course. Looking supremely satisfied as she stretched out to lie across Drafli's shoulders, her fluffy black tail curling to swat against his nose. Once again entirely ignoring the fact that Drafli had continued to treat her with the utmost disdain these past months—a state of affairs which had inexplicably spurred Cat into overcoming her enmity toward him, and choosing him as her second-favourite person, after Dufnall, of course.

Damned provoking pets, Drafli signed irritably, perhaps more toward himself than anyone else—but the glower in his eyes had slightly faded, and Alma took advantage of the opportunity to give his cheek another quick kiss, while Baldr leaned in to do the same on the other side.

"See you at the captain's, after prayers," Baldr murmured, into his neck. "And you ken I shall come for you at the first scent of trouble."

Drafli's shoulders had sagged a little beneath Cat, and he nodded, palming his hand at Baldr's arse under his kilt. And then, before Drafli could change his mind, Baldr swiftly ushered Alma out of the room, giving her a wry, knowing grin as they walked down the corridor together. Not talking about Drafli, of course, because hard-won experience had taught them that he was subsequently liable to materialize out of the nearest shadow—but still smiling about him, all the same.

"So how is our mountain this morning?" Alma asked instead, leaning a little into Baldr's solid warmth beside her. "Any new developments?"

"Ach, not much of note yet today," Baldr replied, though he'd tilted his head toward a passageway as they passed, his breath inhaling. "One of the new Ka-esh tunnels has flooded again—John-Ka will not be pleased—and the Bautul have caught a large buck for the party tonight. And a band of Grisk have come from the west for the party, also—I ken they are staying in the Speaker's rooms, should you wish to send some bedding there."

Alma gratefully nodded, and next asked how many people she needed to prepare for, and whether Baldr knew their names—and soon they were caught up in their usual easy morning conversation. Discussing their beloved mountain—and all its inhabitants and friends—like the genuine partners they were, combining Baldr's daily knowledge of the mountain with Alma's daily caretaking of it. And together, working to make their mountain a better, brighter, cleaner place for all its people. Keeping them safe. Making a home.

"Ach, and Thrain has gotten into the berry-juice *again*?" Baldr added, wryly shaking his head, as he guided Alma into the cozy, familiar Grisk shrine. "The sun is scarce over the horizon, brother!"

He'd grinned at Thrain as he'd spoken, and Thrain gamely raised a goblet toward him, from where he was leaning against the shrine's back wall. "Och, 's a special occasion," he said, barely concealing a hiccup. "Li'l brother becomin' one of us for good!"

Said little brother—Rakfi—was currently squirming frantically in Nattfarr's arms, clearly attempting an escape toward Ella, who in turn was obviously trying, and failing, to have a quiet moment for her prayers. "The party isn't until tonight, Thrain," she said, with an exasperated glance over her shoulder. "At this rate, you'll be too foxed to make it through the day."

"Are you questioning my stamina, sister?" Thrain shot back, with a broad, rather alarming grin. "Absurd. You ought to see my—"

"Ach, no, not again," interrupted another exasperated voice—Thrak, Thrain's brother—as he lurched forward, and swiped the goblet from Thrain's hand. "We have all seen your stamina, brother, and none of us wish to do so again. Well, except"—his dancing eyes angled downwards—"mayhap Varinn here, ach?"

Varinn had clearly also been trying to pray, but was now looking rather hunted, his knees edging slightly away as his eyes darted up toward Thrain behind him. Toward where

Thrain was brazenly looking back at him, and slowly licking the berry-juice off his lips—to which Varinn twitched, Thrak groaned, and Baldr had actually winced and covered his nose, drawing the rest of their attention toward him.

"Ach, you're going to knock our brother out if you keep that up," Thrak said, giving Baldr a bracing clap on the back, as he thrust Thrain's goblet down toward Varinn. "Drink, Varinn?"

Varinn promptly grasped the goblet, pouring its remaining contents down his throat, while the rest of them merrily laughed. And then—perhaps taking pity on Varinn—they finally settled down to say their prayers together, with Alma kneeling between Baldr and Ella, and fervently thanking Akva and Skai-kesh for her family, and her home.

After they'd finished, Baldr indeed took Alma to the sick-room, as he'd promised. These days, the sickroom was looking brighter and cleaner than it ever had before, thanks to Kesst's ongoing Infirmarian efforts—which had so far included the installation of dividers between the beds, lamps that could be controlled by the patient, an assortment of soft, comfortable furniture, and even a little bookshelf, which had been helpfully stocked by Rosa with duplicates from the library.

"Morning, sweetheart," Kesst said to Alma as he strode over, both his pointed ears glittering with dangling black jewels—recent gifts from Efterar, Alma knew. "I hope you're here to tell me the latest gossip? Or wait"—his eyes flicked to Baldr, his lip curling—"has your mangy Skai gotten it into his thick head again that he's irrevocably harmed you somehow?"

Alma couldn't help a laugh, even as Baldr slightly stiffened beside her. "Maybe a little of both?" she replied, giving a teasing elbow into Baldr's side. "What's new? Are you coming to the party tonight?"

"Of course we are," Kesst said over his shoulder, as he stalked away toward Efterar—who had been working over yet another bloody Bautul—and bodily steered him back toward

Alma. "Now please look her over, Eft, and tell her she's fine, will you? *Again*?"

Efterar easily complied, reaching his hand to hover over Alma's belly, and then further down. "You're fine," he said firmly. "And your son's growing beautifully, too. Double the nourishment is certainly paying off. Anything else?"

Alma smiled and shook her head, noticing—once again—that Efterar was looking remarkably awake, no doubt thanks to her latest arena closure the day before. She'd kept on with the weekly cleaning schedule, and while Efterar no longer slept the entire day through anymore, the regular rest still seemed to have done him a world of good—in a recent development, he'd even begun remembering multiple people's names, without any prompting whatsoever.

"How about with you, Baldr?" Efterar asked now, his brows rising. "Any news?"

Baldr returned this with an easy grin, a knowing shrug of his shoulder. "As far as we know, Rathgarr is still headed this way," he replied. "The latest word from Killik is that he still brings the woman with him, also."

Efterar had smiled and nodded, angling a warm glance toward Kesst—who in turn was looking genuinely gleeful, rubbing his clawed hands together. "We are *so* going to be uncles, Eft," he said, with relish. "No matter how infuriating Rath is, he cannot take our nephew away from us! You know"— he whirled toward Efterar, pinning him with a surprisingly powerful glare—"we really ought to come up with a contingency plan to steal away our adorable nephew, in case Rath really is as rubbish at fathering as I expect he'll be. Don't you think?"

Efterar's mouth had opened and closed, his mouth quivering up, his eyes warring between disbelief and affection. And before Baldr and Alma could become party to yet another Ash-Kai kidnapping scheme, Baldr quickly ushered her back out the door again—only to discover that Drafli was waiting for them, lurking in the shadows outside the sickroom, his arms crossed over his chest.

You're late, he signed at Baldr, the movements sharp. *What news?*

"She is fine, Draf," Baldr said, with a rueful pat at Alma's rounded belly. "And our son is fine too. Growing beautifully, Efterar said, thanks to all the extra nutrition we keep giving her."

His chest had puffed out a little as he'd spoken, and Drafli was suddenly looking decidedly smug, too. *Good*, he signed, maybe at Baldr, or Alma, or both. *And now that we know you are well, Bright-Heart*—he snapped his fingers at a nearby empty room—*come.*

Alma meekly obliged, and soon found herself bent over against the room's stone wall, her short skirt rucked up around her waist, while Drafli and Baldr took several thorough, purposeful turns with her. Drafli driving in hard and smooth and powerful, Baldr slower and softer, murmuring how perfect she was, how beautiful, how sweet. How she was the gorgeous, generous, scent-bound hearth-mate they'd always dreamt of, and how he was so glad she'd come to them, and brought such joy into their lives.

Drafli, of course, didn't bother with such niceties—but once he and Baldr had both finished, flooding Alma with yet more hot orc sweetness, he flicked her cheek, and thrust a fresh rag into her hand. And then firmly slapped her arse before striding out the door, yanking along a sheepish-looking Baldr after him.

Alma was still smiling to herself when she reached the kitchen, some time later—and her smile only broadened as she waved toward Cook, who was busily working beside Gegnir at the counter. Cook—or rather, Olga, her actual name was—had arrived at the mountain soon after Pembroke's demise, and had settled in with surprising ease, darkly informing Alma that compared to Pembroke, these orcs were merely hungry, lusty, oversized kittens. And ever since her arrival, the mountain's daily meal offerings had considerably expanded, and now always included cooked food, too. Not only for the mountain's humans, but also for the sickroom, and any orcs like Drafli who needed it.

"There you are, girl!" Cook—Olga—was calling out now, waving Alma over with her mixing spoon. "Come, try this."

Alma eagerly complied, trying a careful taste of what looked like berry pudding—and oh, it was delicious, and she couldn't help a delighted grin toward Olga's flushed, beaming face. "It's lovely," she said. "What a treat! Is it for the party tonight?"

Olga proudly nodded, and elbowed at Gegnir beside her. "*He* thinks it's too sweet," she said archly, "but I keep telling him, he needs to leave the human meals to me. Can't take orders at *all*, this one."

She shot a decidedly saucy look at Gegnir, who was indeed looking rather devious, as he blatantly poked his claw into Olga's pudding, and then flicked it at her apron. To which Olga plucked up her rolling pin, and attempted to swat him over the head with it, while Gegnir barked a gleeful-sounding chuckle, and brandished a wooden spoon back toward her.

Alma laughed as she watched, and then shot a sideways smile toward where Kalfr had appeared, carrying a gigantic basket of fresh vegetables. "If you shall be so kind as to write this up," he told her, "I shall go wash it, and—"

But then his nose wrinkled, his eyes twinkling in the direction of the scullery. "Do I smell Gaukr and Dufnall in there again?" he said. "Ach, and a dead rat, too. Mayhap the washing can wait."

Alma wholeheartedly agreed on that front, making a mental note to avoid the scullery for the foreseeable future, and instead settling back into her snug little office to do her morning reconciliations. Followed by a jaunt over to the main Grisk common-room, discussing party plans with Ella and Nattfarr and several other Grisk helpers, before launching into menu planning, and entertainment organizing, and the optimal distribution of lamps and table-games and snacks and fresh furs throughout the room.

Baldr and Drafli each stopped by to check in, too—Baldr to let Alma know of a few more recently arrived guests, Drafli ostensibly to bring her some fresh fruit from the garden. Half of which he then ended up eating himself, as he made thorough use of Alma's throat in the next room—a highly enjoyable diversion that quickly drew the attention of Baldr's vigilant nose, and soon he'd popped by for a turn, too.

The rest of the afternoon passed far too swiftly, consumed by ever-rising activity and excitement. And finally, Alma was again convening with Baldr and Drafli in their bedroom, and preparing for the party together. Drafli first dressing Alma and Baldr in clean furs and kilts, and then again pulling over their little box of glittering, colourful jewels. Choosing gold chains for around their necks and wrists, and then multiple dangling earrings for both their ears, and then even smaller, sparkling blue and green gems that hung on their nipple-rings, sending out fiery twinges of pleasure every time they moved.

And for Baldr, Drafli finally pulled out their favourite heavy gold ring, perhaps as big around as his palm—and while Alma hungrily watched, Drafli swept aside Baldr's kilt, and slid the ring down his rapidly swelling length. Tugging his full bollocks through too, before settling the ring tight and close against Baldr's groin, thereby putting his own precious jewels on delicious display, as well.

Alma almost whined as Drafli dropped Baldr's kilt again, hiding the stunning sight away—but Drafli had only grinned smugly toward her, and had then gone and made the situation even worse by dressing himself. Pulling on the tight black leather trousers Alma had had made for him, and then his garrotte-cuff, before loosening his long hair, and letting it fall down his back in a silken, shining black sheet.

It made it very difficult to stop staring at him as they set off to the Grisk wing together, Baldr's tongue regularly slipping against his lips, Alma's breaths gone short and shallow in her throat. And she was genuinely, absurdly grateful for the sudden, all-consuming distraction of the party, swarming to life in the Grisk common-room before them, swelling it full of noise and warmth and laughter.

There were surely a hundred—or more—orcs gathered inside the room, talking and laughing, eating and drinking, playing and dancing. Alma was briefly gratified to note that there was still plenty of food—for now—and that the room's occupants were well spread out on the furs and furniture she'd so carefully arranged, and that they were all clearly revelling in the party's varied entertainments. Table-games in one corner, an open area for drumming and dancing, another cordoned-off ring for sparring and wrestling. And even a little circle for storytelling, which was currently being presided over by a beautifully dressed Kesst, speaking animatedly to a rapt, wide-eyed audience.

Where do we start? Baldr excitedly signed at them, but Drafli's narrow gaze was already fixed to the sparring-ring, where Simon was heartily laughing as his huge body sprawled back onto the floor, while a small, delighted-looking orc— Simon and Maria's adopted son Bjorn—brandished a wooden sword over him. And Alma and Baldr exchanged an amused, affectionate glance as they followed Drafli over, to where an extremely pregnant Maria was cheerfully watching, too. And once Bjorn had scampered off, Drafli and Simon promptly launched into a thrilling sparring-match, while Alma, Baldr, and Maria shouted curses and praises toward them.

Simon ultimately emerged as the victor, much to Maria's satisfaction, and Baldr and Alma's displeasure—and next Drafli took out his frustration by launching into another match with Baldr, who put up an excellent fight, but was soon roundly defeated. A typical outcome, to be sure, but one that neither Baldr nor Drafli ever seemed to mind, and Drafli was currently grinning at Baldr's happy, sweaty face, and signing, *Better and better, Pure-Heart, as always.*

And then, his eyes gone rather speculative again, Drafli glanced toward Alma, and waved her in for an impromptu sparring lesson. This had been an ongoing project of his, one that had met with varying degrees of success—Alma was certainly not a born fighter—but Drafli had turned out to be a surprisingly patient teacher, and a deviously clever one, too. And one of his frequent tactics—Alma half-laughed, half-groaned as he smirked darkly toward the sidelines—was Maria.

Get in here, you harpy, he was now signing toward her, his lip curling with contempt. *And see if you can defeat my sweet angel.*

Maria viciously glowered back toward him, while beside her, Simon barked a deep, approving chuckle, and firmly nudged Maria forward. And by now, Maria didn't even bother pretending to resist, though she still cursed Drafli under her breath as she handed Simon her dagger, and then stalked into the ring toward them.

"I am *not* doing this for you, you arrogant swine," she snapped at Drafli as she passed. "You're just damned lucky you managed to hoodwink such a lovely woman into mating you."

With that, she flashed Alma a warm, rather rueful smile, and settled into position. And Alma scarcely had time to react before Maria lunged toward her, her hand jabbing out, and landing a near-fatal strike on Alma's shoulder. The "strike", of course, being more of a tap, since neither Drafli nor Simon would countenance even the idea of their pregnant mates actually harming one another—but Simon was already hooting his approval, while Drafli swiftly signed at Alma, saying, *Watch your stance, be light on your feet, destroy that harridan where she stands.* Earning himself another sidelong snarl from Maria as she flew at Alma again, but thankfully Alma had ducked just in time, even managing a brief tap on Maria's back in return.

That one had Baldr yelling too, joining the chorus of equally enthusiastic exhortations from Simon, and soon Alma was entirely caught in the match. In leaping and striking and dodging and laughing, while Drafli watched with glinting eyes from the sidelines, both he and Simon now sporting unmistakable bulges in their trousers.

In the end, Maria was still undeniably the winner, despite her very pregnant state, and she grinned as she clapped Alma on the shoulder. "You're really improving, sister," she said, between heavy breaths. "Another match soon?"

Alma was gulping for breath too, but grinned back as she eagerly nodded. And then glanced up at Drafli, who was giving an approving little nod, too—*Good work, Bright-Heart*, he signed—before his eyes narrowed sharply on her sweaty face. *Are you still short of breath?* he demanded. *Do you feel dizzy? Shaky?*

Alma laughed and shook her head, but it was to no avail, and she soon found herself being unceremoniously marched over toward Efterar. Who was sitting in the story circle together with a variety of familiar friends—including Dufnall, Timo, Jule, and Bitty-Grim—and intently watching Kesst as he weaved a tale before them, his rings sparkling as his hands gestured through the air.

"And thus, the proud warrior rested deep beneath the earth, together with his devoted hearth-mate," Kesst said, his voice smooth and expressive, with a lilting, oddly compelling cadence. "And the warrior found no cause to leave his hearth again. For in her great wisdom and kindness, his hearth-mate had tended and strengthened his home, thus granting him all the respite and relief he had lost. She filled his belly with sweet meat and gladness each day, and flooded his soul with not only her pure scent and dazzling beauty, but with her many secret gifts, granted to him alone. And he named her Star-Seed, for she had taken a piece of his heart, and grown it into a mountain."

The tale had surely ended there, but the silence somehow seemed to shiver out beyond it, quieting the raucous noise of the surrounding party. Holding Kesst's rapt audience in a strange, stunning stillness, and Alma couldn't have said how long she stood there, feeling the shimmering hopeful warmth of the tale, pooling deep into her belly.

But then Drafli sharply twitched beside her, and when Alma blinked at him, he was frowning mightily toward Kesst— whose glittering hands were still gently sweeping in midair— and then toward Efterar. Who was currently gazing at Kesst with starry, reverent eyes, and a dazed, awestruck smile on his half-open mouth. Looking so blatantly, hopelessly worshipful that even Kesst was darting him a swift, unreadable look, his face visibly flushing as his hands dropped again.

That almost seemed to break the spell, somehow, the rest of his audience stirring, and smiling, and rubbing at their eyes. Several of them fervently thanking Kesst, but he dismissively waved them away, his attention back on Efterar again. On where Efterar had been slowly sidling toward him on the fur, still with that stunned look in his eyes.

"Sweet meat and gladness," he mumbled at Kesst, unsteadily lurching closer, and burying his face in his neck. "Pure scent, an' dazzling beauty. Great wisdom and kindness."

Kesst was looking even more flustered than before, his slightly trembly hand patting Efterar's hair as the rest of their audience slowly dispersed. "There, there, Eft," he said, his voice soft. "It's only a story."

But Efterar just kept nuzzling at Kesst's neck, his chest filling as he inhaled. "Sweetest hearth-mate," he murmured. "Many secret gifts, just for me. Grant me one, Sweet-Fang? Suck me?"

Kesst's face had flushed even redder, his breath huffing out, his tongue brushing his lips. "Soon, love," he murmured back. "I think you've gotten into the berry-juice. Or the ale?"

But beside Alma, Baldr had given a low laugh, shaking his

head. "I cannot smell a single drink upon him, Kesst, and surely, neither can you," he said lightly. "And, er, do you think you might spare him a moment?"

Baldr was glancing sheepishly toward Alma, and then toward Drafli, whose eyes were still glaring at Kesst with mingled impatience and rage. And Alma could see Kesst blinking up at Drafli, and then stiffening and glowering straight back, while gathering Efterar's pliable body closer into his arms.

"No, you paranoid Skai," he snapped, his voice far sharper than before. "He's busy with his hearth-mate, so you can fuck the hell off, and go get busy with yours. And if you *dare* interrupt us again, I *will* tell him to castrate you, and I promise you, in this state, he'll do it!"

Drafli was looking truly thunderous now, his hands clenched to fists at his sides—but then he spun on his heel and stalked off, furiously signing for Alma and Baldr to follow. Which they did, exchanging knowing half-smiles as they trailed him across the room, over toward where Tryggr was sitting sprawled on a bench, with a curled-up Eben in his lap.

Eben's face was buried in Tryggr's shoulder, and Tryggr had been murmuring in his ear, his fingers gently tracing against the thin gold band encircling Eben's neck. It was the same kind of Ka-esh jewelry Rosa wore, Alma knew, except that Eben's currently had a long, shimmering gold chain attached, its other end linked to the matching gold bracelet on Tryggr's wrist. And as Tryggr glanced up at Drafli approaching, he gave the chain a gentle little tug, instantly turning Eben's face toward him.

"Boss needs help, pet," Tryggr said lightly, nodding up at where Drafli was still looking mutinous. "Likely needs his own pet looked over, I ken. Ach, Boss?"

Drafli jerked a sharp nod, and luckily Eben—who was well used to this by now—swiftly snapped to attention, and reached beneath the bench to pull out his little medical kit. Which he'd taken to carrying around with him, no doubt for precisely these occurrences, and he flicked it open, first pulling out Alma's chart, and then a variety of shiny steel tools.

His examination didn't take long—he took Alma's temperature, and checked her heart rate, then listened to their son's. And then asked Baldr to describe very slight variations in her scent and taste, which he immediately did, the words nonsensical to Alma's ears—but Eben had nodded as he jotted some notes in her chart, and then handed over a small stoppered vial.

"Your salt levels are mayhap just a little too low, sister," he told her, with a soft smile. "You must always make sure you pair your exercise with good sustenance, ach? I ken your mates should usually offer their seed, but"—he cast a knowing glance around at the variety of assembled ages present—"until then, this ought to help. You may wish to speak to your midwife upon this, also."

He'd angled a brief glance toward Gwyn, who was currently leaning against a nearby wall with a rather ferally grinning Joarr, and helplessly giggling as she popped a mushroom into his mouth. A sight that had Drafli loudly huffing beside Alma, dismissing both Gwyn and Joarr with a curt wave of his hand, and irritably signing something toward Tryggr that looked much like, *Foolish lovesick brothers.*

To Tryggr's great credit, he didn't even blink at this, but instead gravely nodded, even as his hand gently kept rubbing up and down Eben's back. Waiting as Alma drank her prescribed medicine—some kind of salty-sweet milk—before helping Eben pack up his kit again. "Just come back if you need anything else, Boss," Tryggr told Drafli, with a wink. "Always happy to help, ach?"

Drafli was thankfully looking mostly mollified again, and even signed his thanks toward Tryggr and Eben before leading Alma and Baldr back into the party again. First over to the food, which all of them happily tucked into—Alma *had* been feeling rather hungry—and then just wandering and talking and laughing together, catching up with their many friends and acquaintances. And also saying hello to a few unfamiliar guests, one of whom turned out to be none other than Roland, the mountain's former Keeper.

Roland was far more fierce-looking than Alma had imagined, with hulking shoulders, pure white hair, and heavy, bushy grey brows. And in contrast, the woman tucked beneath his huge arm—a small, plump, silver-haired woman named Margret—smiled warmly toward Alma, and firmly shook her hand.

"We're so delighted that the Keeping is in good hands, aren't we, Roland?" she said, glancing up toward him. "I know he's been worrying about it, leaving you all in the lurch the way he did."

Roland's severe expression looked rather the opposite of worried, but he jerked a nod as he tightened his grip around Margret's shoulders. "Had more important work to do," he said gruffly. "Glad you picked it up, woman. This grand old place needs the care of someone living in it, tuned to it. But I got my head turned elsewhere, ach?"

This was said with a rather fearsome smile down toward Margret, and Alma found herself smiling too, and suddenly feeling in utter, shining accord with him. "I know everyone here is so grateful for all your past efforts, Roland," she told him. "And I promise you, we've been doing our best to catch up, and give the mountain our best possible care. Although, I would love to know"—her head tilted—"how *did* you ever get Gaukr to work, anyway?"

Roland's face had flushed, his eyes guiltily glancing down to an amused-looking Margret beside him. And thankfully Baldr jumped in there, quickly asking about some water pipe that had been inexplicably blocked for years, and soon they were caught up in cheerful, companionable conversation together.

Finally, the sound of a loud whistle tore through the air,

drawing the partygoers' collective awareness toward the reason for the party in the first place—Ella and Nattfarr's tiny, squirming son Rakfi. Who was suddenly looking delighted at all the attention, stopping his furious wriggling in Ella's arms, in favour of blinking bright-eyed at his rapt audience.

"Welcome, friends!" called out Thrain beside them, his hands upraised, his voice carrying through the room. "*Okkur hefur verið gefinn sonur og í dag fögnum við.* A son is given to us, and today we rejoice!"

This was met with a raucous whirl of claps and stomps and cheers, which was soon followed by a round of lovely gift-giving, with representatives from each of the clans. All welcoming little Rakfi into their lives and their home, and wishing him good health and good luck. While Nattfarr and Ella both beamed, though Ella had begun looking rather teary-eyed, leaning gratefully into Nattfarr's embrace as she clutched Rakfi close.

After the gifts were done, Grimarr stepped forward, and called down the gods' blessing upon their beloved Grisk brother. And once the cheers and stomps had again subsided, and the younger ones had been sent off to bed, the party seemed to swell even louder and more boisterous than before. The ale and berry-juice flowing freely, the dancing becoming far more flamboyant, while many of the party guests began turning hungry eyes toward one another.

Finally, Drafli had signed, as he'd hauled Alma and Baldr over to a wide, fur-covered bench against the room's back wall, and sprawled down onto it. *Undress each other for me. Now.*

Alma's own relief seemed to stutter wide and warm, her eyes eagerly meeting Baldr's equally heated gaze. And already her hands were sliding up his broad chest, unfastening his fur, easing it off his shoulders, as he did the same to hers. Dropping her fur to the floor, and revealing Alma's full breasts and pierced nipples, their dangling jewels sparkling with every thick, shuddering breath.

But there was no shame, none at all, and Alma moaned as Baldr gently tweaked one of her dangling jewels, before moving his hands to her skirt. Shoving that down, too, and leaving her fully bared before him, but for her piercings, and the gold sparkling all over her.

Leave those, Drafli coolly signed, in response to Baldr's questioning glance toward him—and oh, Drafli had already taken himself out of his leather trousers, and his hand was now smoothly stroking up, slicking himself, while his other hand kept signing toward them. *Keep going,* it meant. *Show me my orc, Bright-Heart.*

Alma nodded, biting her lip as she glanced back at Baldr again. As her hands shakily unbuckled his kilt, too, letting it fall to his feet, and showing off everything beneath.

And gods, he was beautiful. That plump green length not only pierced with Drafli's gold, but also firmly encircled with it, flaunted by that thick ring at its base. Making him look even larger, more intimidating than before, jutting out with greedy shamelessness over those bulging bollocks, bobbing up into Alma's waiting fingers.

"So pretty," she murmured at him, as she stroked all the way down that silken pulsing length, and back up again. "So good, Pure-Heart. Want to feel it, inside me."

He groaned as he bobbed up harder into her hand, streaking her palm with hot hungry wetness. And Alma's pleading glance down at Drafli thankfully found him waving her forward, toward where another beautiful hungry cock was waiting, visibly throbbing in his fingers, angling hard and powerful toward her.

"Oh, *thank* you, my lord," Alma breathed, as she swiftly straddled him on the bench, lining him up with her craving clenching heat—and then sank down onto him, crying out as that glorious strength rammed deep. Filling her all the way with hard, hot orc, pulsing and flaring inside her, while she clamped back at him, revelled in him, adored him.

He'd been watching her do it, of course, his eyes glinting approvingly beneath his lashes—and then his hands found her bare hips, spreading wide, letting her feel the bite of his claws. And then grinding her down, while he drove up, making her shout and shiver upon him—and then again, again, again.

He kept watching her as he did it, his eyes drinking up her hot cheeks, her gasping mouth, the jangling jewels in her nipples. And then her bare swollen belly, rubbing against his muscled torso with every thrust, speaking of what he'd put inside her, of how he owned her...

And that ownership only wheeled higher, harder, as one of his hands came to her back, pressing her further forward against him. And then both hands were on her arse, tilting her up, pulling her apart, oh hell—because he was opening her, wide and shameless, for their mate. Showing her, offering her, please, *please*, and Alma whimpered at the feel of Baldr settling close behind her, straddling Drafli's knees on the bench, while something hard and familiar nudged there against her.

Alma cried out, pushing back toward it, needing it, oh—but she could hear Baldr chuckling as his strong hand held her still, as that beautiful hardness slipped up, down, around. Coating her, she knew, easing his way, but oh it was so hard to wait, the sheer shaking anticipation squirming her against him—at least, until there was a gentle slap at her hot face, a meaningful tug at her pierced nipple. Drafli. Her lord.

You wait, my greedy angel, he signed at her, holding her eyes to his. *You let our mate ready you for him. Ach?*

Alma had obediently shot to stillness, other than her frantically nodding head, her tooth biting at her lip—and oh, Drafli's smile, Drafli's hand stroking her cheek, Drafli's seed pulsing steady within her. *Good*, he signed at her, and oh, Alma could have preened in it, holding herself here for him, while their mate finally, finally prodded a little inside her. Making her twitch and shake all over, but Drafli kept holding her, safe in his eyes and his strength, as that thick, seeking head delved deeper, gently opening her upon it.

And while Alma was used to this now—it had become one of her favourite ways to do this—she still clamped and keened as Baldr slowly, surely sank his way inside. The feeling so impossibly, mind-meltingly full, with both her orcs easing within her, using both her holes for their pleasure.

And oh, Drafli's eyes kept watching, glittering with such hard, vicious satisfaction, as his first mate skewered his second, as she screeched and flailed upon him. Even as she desperately fought to hold herself still, as he'd wished—and he knew her struggle, he liked her struggle, he was smiling with such dark wickedness as his hands slid around to his mate's arse, and shoved him the rest of the way inside.

Alma's scream was shrill and scraping this time, rivalling the thudding drumbeat, earning a few indulgent laughs behind them—but oh, her orcs were here, they were both locked deep inside her, where they belonged. And Drafli was still smiling at her, with such devious fondness, as he snapped his hips up, and again watched her scream.

And then it was pure chaos, raw and primal and wildly surging, with her orcs first taking turns plunging into her, and then driving in together. Holding her up between them while they slid deep again and again, as first Baldr's teeth found Alma's throat, and then Drafli's. Honouring her, drinking her, making her theirs, splitting her apart upon their massive driving strength—

And this time it was Drafli who broke first, his head tilting back against the wall, his sharp red-rimmed teeth biting his lip, his hands holding Alma down as he spasmed and sprayed inside her. While behind her, Baldr was moaning, surely watching this, his hips bucking up hard and furious—and then he was spraying, too. Filling her second hole with just as much hot surging heat as the first, pouring her full of their bright, blazing bliss.

And then, oh, it was over. But with Alma now so full, so sated, so dazed and soft and content. Sagging forward into Drafli's waiting strength, knowing he would catch her, just like this, settling her closer into his arms. And then pulling Baldr forward, too, his sweaty chest heaving against Alma's back, one of his strong arms around her waist, the other slipping over Drafli's shoulders, his face burying itself into Drafli's neck.

Their breaths rose and sank as one, their bodies sagging even closer, settling seamlessly together, belonging together. At peace. At home. A family.

"See, this wouldn' be so bad, right?" cut in a familiar, slightly slurred voice—and when Alma peeked a hazy eye open to look, it was Thrain. Lying sprawled on the other end of the bench, with his messy head in Varinn's lap, and a goblet still clutched in his clawed hand.

Behind Thrain, Varinn had winced, angling Alma an apologetic grimace before plucking the goblet from Thrain's hand, draining it, and tossing it away. "Quieter, *krútt*," he murmured, his claws scraping purposefully at Thrain's head. "They are trying to rest, ach?"

Thrain showed no sign of having heard this, and instead vaguely waved his hand down the bench toward them. "I'm just saying," he continued. "Why the hell not, Varinn? They're happy. They like it. *She* likes it. They're havin' a *son*."

He tilted his head back at the last bit, so as to better pout up at Varinn's face—but Varinn was looking at Alma again, his mouth thinning, his expression genuinely pained. "You know why, you vexing prick," he said, the words darker, more forceful, surely meant to create more distance between them—even as his claws kept scraping at Thrain's hair, caressing, *longing*. "It is impossible enough to find a woman who wishes for one orc, ach? We would never find one who wanted both of us. *Ever*."

Alma could see Thrain's throat bobbing, his hand again waving down the bench. "But *they* did it," he said stubbornly. "Why can't we?"

Varinn sighed, his eyes still pained on Alma's, his hand briefly stilling on Thrain's hair. "That is *Baldr*, remember?" he said, quiet. "Mayhap the kindest orc in our mountain, and bearing mayhap its greatest gift, with his scenting. And he is very pleasing to the eye, with such a fat, pretty prick, too. Women *love* him, ach?"

He sounded almost despairing, and Thrain loudly huffed, his bleary eyes now glaring toward Baldr. "He's not *that* pleasing," he protested. "An' you're just as good-hearted as he is, Varinn, and your prick is just as pretty, too. I *know*."

This was said with a dark, mulish frown up at Varinn's face, and Varinn sighed again, and shot a longing glance toward the empty goblet he'd thrown away. "*Thrain*," he said, his voice strained, pleading. "You ken I want a woman, and a son. I have always longed for this. I *need* this. And I could not bear"—he drew in a shaky breath—"to draw even closer to you, to taste you thus... and then, to someday need to break this. To seek to forget this. Forget you. Ach?"

Thrain's bottom lip was jutting out even more, his long-lashed eyes far too bright as they blinked up at Varinn's drawn face. "You wouldn't actually *forget* me, though," he said thickly. "Would you, Varinn?"

And suddenly Varinn looked like was about to weep too, his head shaking, his hand trembling in Thrain's hair. "No, *krútt*," he whispered. "Would never forget you."

Thrain jerked a nod beneath his still-stroking hand, his eyes squeezing shut. "'Course not," he said, his voice harder than before. "'Cause if you do, I'll haunt your dreams. Steal all your cake and berry-juice. Leave stink-beetles in your bed. Beat you in sparring, *again*, like I always—"

"You do *not* always," Varinn snapped back, though that was surely relief in his eyes, too. "And if you dare bring a stink-beetle anywhere near me, I shall make you *eat* it. Also, you ought to listen to me for once, and scotch the berry-juice for good, you ken? After today, I shall now smell it souring on you for *days*, making you reek of foul old vinegar—"

"I do *not reek*, you fun-sucking *liar!*" Thrain retorted, flailing up beneath Varinn, swinging his fist toward his head—and suddenly they were squirming and wrestling together, so ferociously that they fell off the bench, and rolled away on the floor, while the sounds of grunting and squealing trailed behind them.

"Ach, I ken it may not be easy to find a woman for those two," Baldr murmured sleepily behind Alma. "But we shall yet keep our scents open, ach?"

Alma felt herself giving a shaky laugh as she nodded and settled closer against Drafli's warm chest, her eyes fluttering closed—and suddenly there was just stark, staggering gratefulness, flooding full and deep. She was so, so blessed. So spectacularly fortunate, to have found her orcs. To have found meaningful work, scores of new friends, and such a beautiful new home. Such love, where once there'd been so much emptiness.

"Thank you," she whispered, to her orcs, her gods, her mother, her son, her mountain... and perhaps, even to herself. "I love you."

And her orcs both whispered it back, echoing it like a vow, a prayer. One voice soft and melodious, the other harsh and broken, but both here. Both hers. Home.

And Alma smiled as she settled in closer, warmer, *forever*, and then sank into the deep.

BONUS EPILOGUE

Alma blinked awake to the familiar feeling of a tall, lean body, sliding into bed behind her, and drawing her close.

Drafli.

She turned to burrow into his chest, inhaling his sweet, succulent scent as her hand slipped up and down his bare back. "Hi," she whispered. "How was your trip?"

She felt him shrug against her, but when she shot a questioning look toward where she knew his face to be, she could feel him twisting around, reaching toward the lamp. Flaring a warm, flickering glow across their room, and Alma gratefully smiled up at where she could now see Drafli's harsh, gorgeous face. He'd only been gone for four days, on urgent Skai business, but gods, it felt so much longer, and Alma drank up the sight of him, her lord back in their bed again, where he belonged.

Ach, it was fine, he signed at her, as he bent his head down, and inhaled against her hair. *Mess cleaned up now. Missed you all.*

Alma nodded and snuggled closer against him, squeezing him as hard as she could. "We missed you too," she whispered.

"Barden even demanded we make you a pie. Thinking you would smell it, and come back faster."

Drafli twitched a little against her, his expression gone both pained and pleased, and she could see his throat convulsing, his eyes flicking over toward the orcling in question. Toward Barden, their son.

And even before Alma turned to look too, she knew exactly where she would find him. In the same place he always slept, sprawled wide on Baldr's chest, his little grey body rising and falling in time with the sound of Baldr's faint snores.

Alma settled in to watch them, blinking her prickling eyes, as Drafli's arm pulled her closer against his front. Both of them drinking up the beautiful, surreal sight of it, Barden's wispy black hair fanned out on his father's greenish skin, his little pointed ear poking up, his little hand—with its tiny claws—spread wide against Baldr's shoulder. His mouth hanging open as he breathed, showing his sharp little teeth—and then his teeth snapped shut, as if he were dreaming about some particularly tasty treat.

Alma could feel Drafli's huff of laughter behind her, followed by a hard swallow from his throat. Surely feeling just the same as she did, still not fully believing—even after almost three years—that this was real, this was theirs.

It was a feeling that Alma had never quite overcome, since the first moment she'd set eyes on her beautiful, grey-skinned little son. Her pregnancy had truly gone as well as they could have possibly hoped, but labour had still been its own particular hell, lasting for the better part of an entire day. A day that had left Baldr increasingly pale and silent, while Drafli had paced and snarled and raged, to the point where Simon had ended up dragging him bodily away, and forcing him to punch out his fury in the next room, until they'd both been breathless and bloody all over.

But then—then, finally, there'd been their son. Their tiny, slimy grey son, clinging to Alma's chest, and staring at her with huge, reverent black eyes. And Baldr's breath had lurched as he'd buried his face in the orcling's hair, dragging in hard, shaky breaths, while on their other side, Drafli had just stared, stunned and frozen, gone utterly still for the first time in a full day.

It had finally been Baldr who'd taken Drafli's hand, and put it to their son—and as Drafli's hand had curved around the orcling's little grey back, his face had seemed to crumple, his head shaking, his eyes pouring wetness down his stark cheeks.

By then Baldr and Alma had been weeping too, all of them clinging to each other—and their son—while Gwyn, Stella, Eben, and Efterar had helped clean things up again. Efterar and Gwyn both reassuring them—before Drafli could recollect himself and begin making demands—that Alma was still in excellent health, and their son was whole and hale and safe.

It had taken a few days to decide on a name, but in the end, they'd all settled on Barden, Baldr's father's name. A very Grisk name, to be sure—but that fact had felt right, somehow, especially when weighed against Alma's realization that despite his mixed parentage, their son was still instantly considered Skai, by every single orc who met him.

"Ach, it is mostly just his scent," Baldr had explained to Alma that first night, watching fondly as their son eagerly nuzzled and nursed at her breast. "He smells so sweet, just like Draf, ach? All Skai have this, and"—he'd bent his head to that soft black hair, inhaling deep—"it is perfect upon him, ach? So perfect. So—*you*, Draf."

His voice had hitched there, his eyes angling up to where Drafli had been watching this, his eyes glimmering with bright, dangerous affection. *Ours*, Drafli had signed at him, his hand still visibly trembling. *Ours, even if he is Skai.*

Baldr had nodded, and smiled tearfully between the three of them. "Ours," he'd whispered. "And we shall teach him Grisk ways too, ach, Bright-Heart?"

Alma had fervently agreed, weeping again too, and clutching their son closer into her arms. Theirs. A family.

And ever since then, they had indeed done their best to make sure Barden was exposed to both clans, and that Baldr and Drafli were equally recognized as his fathers. A fact that had impacted Barden in curious ways over the past three years—because while he very much looked, smelled, and behaved like Drafli, he'd also seemed to adopt multiple characteristics and interests from Baldr, too. Including a whole-hearted love for the water, a deep awareness of the mountain, and an uncanny ability to isolate and track scents that seemed very advanced for his age.

And that particular ability was becoming more and more evident in this very moment, as Alma and Drafli both watched Barden and Baldr beginning to stir together. Baldr's breath inhaling very deep, lifting up Barden's little grey body upon him, while Barden's tiny nose twitched and wrinkled, his long-lashed eyes blinking open, and frowning first toward Alma, and then Drafli behind her.

"Da-pa?" he said, his small voice thick with sleep—and then Alma could see the delight flashing across his little face, brightening his dark eyes. "Da-pa home!"

With that, he hurled his little body across the bed, scrabbling over Alma, and into Drafli's arms. To where Drafli was already catching him, and drawing him close, pressing his little black head into his shoulder.

On Alma's other side, Baldr was grinning too, and stretching as he shifted closer, his arm encircling all three of them. "Finally, Draf," he said, his voice thick with sleep, too. "So good to scent you so close again, ach?"

Drafli flashed Baldr a quick smile back, signing behind Barden's head—*You shall soon more than scent me, Pure-Heart*—but Barden, who missed very little, had twisted around to frown suspiciously at Drafli's hand. And Drafli's smile twitched higher as he again began signing, before Barden this time, so he could see.

I missed you so much, Golden-Heart, he signed at him. *I hear you make pie for me?*

Barden brightened and proudly nodded, signing back with his little clawed hands. *We make you good pie, Da-pa. You smell and come back, ach?*

Ach, Drafli signed, his eyes gone unmistakably bright. *It smell so good, Golden-Heart. But you ken I come back first for you, and Mama, and Bapa. You all smell best.*

Barden beamed back at Drafli, and then toward Baldr and Alma, too. "Ach," he said. "We are best."

Alma's eyes were prickling again, and she couldn't seem to hide her reflexive little sniff—earning a narrow, watchful glance from Drafli, and then a longsuffering roll of his eyes. And in a sudden flare of movement, he'd passed Barden over to Baldr, and then plucked Alma into his arms, before yanking Barden and Baldr close again, too.

It meant that they were all piled on Drafli, now, Baldr and Alma tucked against both his shoulders, with Barden now contentedly sprawled between them on his chest. And Alma's happiness seemed to shudder and swell, escaping in the wetness streaking from her eyes, while Drafli firmly caressed her, held her close and safe.

They ended up dozing there for a while, just revelling in the closeness, in being together again—until Barden began squirming, clearly ready to begin the day. *Hungry*, he signed imperiously at them, his bottom lip jutting out—but then he whipped around, and blinked curiously toward the door. Toward where Simon and Maria's son Arnthorr—who was also three years old, and already nearly twice Barden's size—was poking his head in, excitedly waving toward Barden.

"Come to arena, brother!" he said. "Papa and Bjorn taking us!"

Arnthorr had grinned up behind him as he'd spoken,

toward where Simon was now looming in the doorway, his big arm slung around a gangly-looking Bjorn, who'd now grown almost to his shoulder. "Ach, come along, little brother," Simon told Barden, with a wink toward Drafli. "Your Dapa needs a spell with his mates, I ken."

Drafli was looking markedly grateful, signing, *Skai-kesh bless you, brother*, behind Barden's back—but again Barden whipped around to look, his little brow furrowing with displeasure. "You come too, Papas," he demanded. "And you, Mama."

Alma couldn't help a fond smile toward him, but was also thoroughly thankful when Drafli firmly shook his head, and signed, *Not yet, Golden-Heart. I must care for my mates. Then we come meet you, ach? Eat second breakfast together?*

Barden's little mouth pursed, but then he cast a longing glance over his shoulder toward Arnthorr, and jerked a nod. And after a quick round of hugs from all three of them, he scampered off toward the door, leaving them smiling together in the bed behind him.

Now, my pretty angels, Drafli signed coolly toward them, his eyes flaring with that familiar wicked gleam. *Who gets breakfast first?*

Baldr had given a low hiss, his hand already sliding toward Drafli's tented trousers—but Alma was much faster, lurching down Drafli's front, and yanking him out with hungry, desperate fingers. Taking only an instant to revel in the wondrous, familiar sight and scent of that hard, scarred grey cock, before sucking it greedy and deep into her mouth.

"*Alma*," Baldr whined, his voice thick with thwarted exasperation, his own hips bucking helplessly against Drafli's side. To which Drafli complacently smiled, and kept watching as Alma gouged his heft into her throat, sucking his succulent sweetness as hard and powerful as she could.

Too slow, Pure-Heart, Drafli languidly signed at him. *But ach, look at our pretty mate, so full of Skai prick. You practice for me, Bright-Heart?*

He was eyeing Alma with his brows raised, his hips giving an experimental little thrust upwards. Burying him even deeper in her throat, as she frantically sought to keep it open, to welcome him there, to breathe. Her lips nearly sunk to the base of him, but not quite, and Drafli gave another little roll upwards, sinking him even further, blocking her throat with him, oh *hell*.

"Ach, we have been practicing for you," Baldr murmured now, his voice far milder than before—no doubt because of how Drafli had pulled him out of his kilt, and was now casually stroking him with firm fingers. "She took me easier than she has yet, ach, Bright-Heart? But you are yet longer than I am, Draf, so—"

But he'd broken into a hoarse, amused laugh, because Drafli had bucked his hips up just a little more, while also pressing Alma's head down closer against him. Meaning that she was indeed sucking him all the way, too, her lips stretched around the very base of him, her nose buried in the sweet scent of his coarse hair.

"Ach, so pretty," Baldr crooned now, his ire clearly entirely forgotten as his hand came down, and caressed against Alma's hair. "Ach, look at you, Bright-Heart, with your throat stuffed so full of our Skai. You look so good thus, ach? So pretty. She deserves your sweet Skai breakfast for this, ach, Draf?"

He'd cast a pleading, reproachful glance up at Drafli, who was still coolly watching, his fingers absently tugging at Baldr's swollen heft, toying with his ring. *Ach, mayhap*, Drafli signed, with almost-convincing nonchalance. *Drink up, Bright-Heart.*

With that, he bucked up once more, his body stiffening, his eyes rolling back—and then he poured himself out deep into Alma's throat, his invading flesh pulsing again and again as it held her open, flooding its bounty straight into her belly.

Alma desperately kept him there, fighting to drag in air as her throat convulsed, her watering eyes held to Drafli's face. As the cool command in his eyes slowly softened, in time with the softening heft in her mouth, its strength gently contracting from her throat.

This pleased me, Bright-Heart, he signed at her, his breath shuddering from his chest. *Honoured me.*

He accompanied that with a flick of his fingers upwards—*come*, it meant—so Alma obeyed, her body still a little shaky. And thankfully, Drafli grasped her with his strong hands, drew her close, and brought her mouth to his.

His kiss was hard, purposeful, thick with affection and approval. Flashing wild streams of heat and hunger to Alma's groin, and oh, Drafli's hand had dropped first to yank off her sleeping-kilt, and then to stroke deep beneath. His fingers slipping first with proprietary ease through her wet heat, feeling her clench and caress against his touch, before rising up to toy with the delicate gold ring at the top of her crease. A ring that was far smaller than Baldr's, but otherwise identical, down to the vow engraved inside it in beautiful, tiny script.

I see you, my sworn mate. I pledge you my troth, and my favour, and my fealty.

Alma was already moaning again, even hungrier than before, rubbing herself against her lord's fingers—but then Drafli huffed a laugh, and slid his hand away. Toward—Alma's breath caught—toward Baldr, his dripping-wet fingers slipping into Baldr's mouth, lingering against his swirling, hungry tongue.

You be patient, Bright-Heart, Drafli signed at her with his other hand, his eyes watching half-lidded as his fingers delved deeper into Baldr's mouth. *Our mate needs a turn.*

With that, he tugged a little at Baldr's mouth, pulling him sideways, on top. So that Baldr was straddling Drafli's hips, his heavy bollocks rubbing against where Drafli's glossy grey length was already swelling again, pulsing larger with every breath.

Ride me, Pure-Heart, Drafli signed at him, his tongue licking at his lips. *Whilst you touch him, Bright-Heart. Show me my orc.*

Alma moaned and furiously nodded, shoving up to her knees beside Baldr, pulling off his kilt with eager hands. Revealing his rippled abdomen, his powerful thighs, and—most beautiful of all—that thick, bobbing green length, already leaking a steady string of white from its plump, pierced pink tip.

Baldr gasped as Alma's fingers circled around it, stroking up slow and firm, pumping out more thick white, while her other hand caressed up his thigh, his hip, the hard muscle of his torso. Flicking at his gold nipple-rings, revelling in how he moaned and shuddered, in how that fat green cock in her other hand swelled and strained, drizzling out even more thick white onto Drafli beneath him.

Drafli was watching, of course, his hooded eyes hungry and approving, his grey heft blatantly flexing up between Baldr's thighs. Making its order very clear, and Alma willingly took that pulsing grey cock in hand, guiding it upwards. While Baldr lifted up to shift over it, angling a little backwards, so she could settle that slick scarred head deep between his muscled arse-cheeks.

Alma had promptly returned both hands to stroking him again, showing off his hard, virile body for his watching mate—and oh, Baldr was so gorgeous like this, his muscles taut, his green skin gleaming, his cheeks and ears flushed with pink. His eyes fluttering, his tooth biting his lip as he slowly, slowly sank down, easing Drafli inside him. That scarred grey length slipping deeper and deeper, swallowed breath by breath into what it owned, where it belonged.

And even after years together—after seeing it hundreds of times now—Alma had never, ever tired of this sight. Of her two beautiful, powerful mates locking together, connecting to each other in perhaps the most primal of ways, sharing their devotion and their joy. And the way Baldr always looked like this, his face gone rapt with ecstasy, with *relief*, as he settled all the way down, seating Drafli fully inside him.

And Alma now understood, when she perhaps hadn't before, that this still bore a trace of their old challenges, of Drafli's bitter betrayals. That Drafli still bore the scents of all those Skai, even if Baldr could have used his spectacular skills to diminish them, hide them away. But he hadn't, they hadn't, because this way, they were conquering those scents through their own continued pleasure together, their own choices together, with every day that passed.

They fade a little more each time, Baldr had long ago confided to Alma, his face grimacing with something that had looked almost ashamed. *And I cannot smell them at all anymore, when he is inside me. When I am... drowning them. This is... pleasing to me.*

But there was no shame, of course, and Alma had firmly reassured Baldr of the rightness in this, the justice. And perhaps she'd even leaned into it afterwards, tentatively at first, but now with a brazen, breathless ease that only ever seemed to ramp their collective hunger higher.

"So pretty," she murmured, licking her lips as she watched Baldr grind deeper against his mate, his lashes fluttering, his breath inhaling with deep, desperate gulps. "So perfect. Our mate is the most beautiful orc you've ever seen, right, my lord? The most beautiful one you've ever felt?"

She kept caressing Baldr as she spoke, smoothing one hand over his silken skin, pumping the other up his thick, leaking length. Showing off all his raw, stunning beauty, flaunting him for his mate, his lord, while Drafli watched with visceral appreciation, with rabid hunger, with glittering, greedy pride.

Ach, he signed back. *Our mate is the most beautiful. The most perfect.*

Gods, yes, he was, and Alma's face was in Baldr's gleaming shoulder, inhaling the scent of him, glorying in the perfection of this moment. "You've never wanted another orc the way you want him," she continued. "You've never needed to be inside one the way you need to be inside him. Right?"

Baldr's moans were scraping darker, desperate, as he kept

grinding, as he watched Drafli nod. *Never*, Drafli signed back. *Never hungered for any orc how I hunger for you, Pure-Heart. They never feel so hot, so sweet upon me, so—*

But then he'd snapped to a stop, his eyes narrowing on where Baldr's body was arching, stuttering, surely about to blow—and his hand swiftly dropped to Baldr's glinting, dripping-wet ring, and gave it a firm little yank with his claw.

No yet, my pretty angel, he signed at him. *Be patient, and I shall reward you.*

Baldr's face had contorted with both pain and pleasure, his breath heaving hard, his head frantically nodding, his eyes squeezing shut. And Drafli's eyes again flared with pride, with wicked satisfaction, as he abruptly grasped for Alma, pulling her over to straddle above him, too. And before she'd quite realized what was happening, he'd tilted her arse up, yanked her open, and impaled her deep upon Baldr's swelling, throbbing cock.

"Fuck!" Alma gulped, as Baldr bucked and howled behind her. His invading strength wildly bulging and bobbing inside her, almost as if it were both astonished and delighted to find itself encased in her clutching desperate heat. In how Drafli was already plunging her up and down upon it, his eyes glinting dangerously between her and Baldr's shouting faces as his strong hands gripping her hips bodily pumped her again and again. Blatantly using her to whip up his mate's shudders and shouts, to stroke at him with furious powerful thrusts, caressing him, consuming him, rewarding him...

Baldr sprayed out with a sudden, strangled-sounding roar, his massive cock kicking and convulsing inside Alma, flooding her full of hot, molten pleasure. Emptying out in burst after burst, while Alma's own pleasure soared closer and closer, oh, oh please, oh—

But then, without warning, Drafli yanked her off Baldr's still-sputtering heft, the sound thick and messy between them—and for a jolting, twisting instant, Alma nearly whimpered at the loss, the emptiness. At least, until Drafli heaved her hips powerfully upwards, making her scrabble to keep up, clutching at the bed for balance—and then he crushed her open, pouring-wet heat against his hungry, sucking mouth.

Alma's ecstasy escaped in a shrill, high-pitched scream, her entire body flailing against Drafli's face, shuddering out in stream after stream of flashing, flying euphoria. Lost in the impossible, unthinkable sensation of her lord drinking her from the inside out, swallowing his mate's fresh seed in gulp after hungry gulp, while his own seed shot out of his straining, tightly encased cock, and back up into his grinding, shouting mate upon him.

And oh, it was so good. It was all of them back together, bound together, pouring each other full of life and pleasure again. Of their very essence, their ownership, the constant confirmation of those vows they'd made, spoken with hands and seed and mouths. *We see you. We love you. We grant you our favour, and our fealty.*

And as lovely as it was—it always was—between just Alma and Baldr, it always felt fuller, somehow, with Drafli here like this. Stronger. With his commands, his devious satisfaction, his unspeakable comfort. With how even now, he was giving a gentle, purposeful nip of his teeth at Alma's ring—something Baldr would never have done—and smiling with lazy, sated amusement as she yelped and twitched away from him.

I ken our mate has one more load, Bright-Heart, he signed coolly at her. *Suck it out for me, ach? Show me how deep you can take him, also?*

Behind Alma, Baldr was moaning again, but surely not arguing with this, and Alma gave a jerky, flush-faced nod as she shakily obliged. Shifting backwards and around on the bed, and bending herself over where Baldr was still pinned on Drafli's strength, his slick green cock already swelling full again, and nudging itself hungrily toward her mouth.

But this time it felt slower, sweeter—and it was also

another kindness on Drafli's part, Alma knew. Always making sure things were fair between her and Baldr, taking care to notice both their needs, and providing for them. Giving Baldr a tight, sucking mouth to help soothe and soften his still-straining cock, even as—Alma moaned around Baldr's thick flesh gouging in her throat—the two of them began signing back and forth, clearly discussing Drafli's trip and its outcomes, while Baldr kept sputtering and swelling into her mouth.

But this was something Baldr needed too, Alma now knew. The reassurance that he was a valued, respected partner in his and Drafli's work together, and how sometimes that took precedence over pleasure. And how sometimes it needed to be shared just between the two of them, just the same way she and Baldr shared their work on the mountain, or the way she and Drafli shared their worship of Skai-kesh together.

So Alma eagerly stroked and sucked their beautiful mate, lavishing him without jealousy or shame. Until he again shattered and sprayed within her, his shaky hand caressing against her hair, even as his other hand kept signing at Drafli, clearly answering whatever he'd just asked.

But then she could feel him softening, relaxing, and that was the certain sense of Drafli relaxing more beneath them, too. His claws giving an approving little scratch at Alma's back as he tugged her up toward him again, tucking her sated, trembling body close into his chest. And then pulling Baldr down onto him, too, so they were again both curled against him, sweet and safe in his arms.

It meant that Alma was looking across Drafli's chest at Baldr's eyes, seeing her own contentment reflected back toward her. Smiling slowly at him, and watching as he smiled back, so warm and genuine, his eyes bright and shimmering, and—

And then stilling. Blinking. And then a flash of sudden, flaring movement, as Baldr shoved up onto Drafli, and thrust his face down into Alma's neck. Inhaling sharp and deep, filling his chest with fierce, inexplicable purpose, while his entire body shuddered against them.

Alma had gone utterly still, her gaze darting up toward Drafli, who looked just as nonplussed as she felt. His eyes rapidly flicking between her and Baldr, and then he abruptly shoved them all up to sitting, giving Baldr's shoulder a purposeful little shake. But Baldr didn't even look, because he was too busy inhaling again, his face pressing even harder into Alma's neck, his tongue now dragging desperate and hungry over her skin.

"What," Alma managed, breathless. "What—is it?"

Baldr's taut body gave another hard, sustained shudder, but he finally drew back again, nodding. His body slightly swaying, his eyes shining, his hand rubbing at his mouth.

"You are... with child, Bright-Heart," he breathed, against his fingers. "With our—our son."

Oh. Oh. Their—son. And Alma had again frozen in place, the shock washing over her, flooding from her head to her feet. She was pregnant. With their *son*.

"Truly?" she gasped at him, at Drafli, her heart suddenly flaring up, roaring to life in her chest. "You mean it? You can smell him?"

And oh gods, Baldr was nodding, and beaming at her, as wetness streaked from his eyes. And Alma's hands were wildly flailing in midair, her heart now thundering in her ears, while the joy—the raw, rising elation—swarmed out her throat, escaping in a bright, bubbling laugh.

And before her, Baldr was laughing too, and wiping at his face, while Drafli—who had gone alarmingly, impossibly still—stared back and forth between them with wide, disbelieving eyes. His own head very slowly tilting toward Alma's neck, his breath inhaling slow and careful against her skin, his tongue gingerly brushing against it, against the many scars he'd made, his chest filling so full she thought it might crack—

And then, suddenly, perhaps it did. His body snapping into

a sudden, surging swell of laughter as he whirled away again, and surged toward Baldr. Throwing his arms around Baldr's shoulders, and yanking him tight as they rocked back and forth.

"Smells like you," Drafli's hoarse voice croaked, his face now buried in Baldr's neck. "Both of you. Like perfect Grisk son."

He sounded truly awed, somehow, wondering—and Baldr was still laughing, and weeping, and he'd suddenly flailed for Alma, yanking her close, too. "I ken not why," he gulped, "you smell *surprised* at this, Draf."

That was surely in reference to the fact that Drafli had planned for this, and had indeed pushed for it far harder than either Baldr or Alma had. Not the son himself—they'd all been united in their eagerness to make and meet another one—but in the fact that Drafli had wanted a Grisk son this time. *A son to carry on our mate's great gifts*, he'd told Alma, with grave seriousness. *To help lead our kind in the years to come.*

Baldr had tried arguing, telling Drafli that it didn't matter, that he loved Barden with all his heart, that he would weep for joy at another son scented of his mate—and while Alma had fully agreed, she'd also supported Drafli in it, too. Because in truth, despite his constant commands in the bedroom, Drafli actually asked for very little, from either of them. He was so often the one to offer them his strength and help and care—sometimes, Alma suspected, to his own detriment. And if they could care for him in this, offer him something he craved so strongly in return, then, she'd rather felt, they should.

So they'd all agreed, in the end, and they'd gone and spoken to Efterar and Gwyn together, discussing the optimal timing to ensure the health of both Alma and the orcling, and a plan for bringing it about. And now it was here, it had happened, and Alma was still desperately clinging to her mates, and tearfully smiling at where Drafli was elbowing

Baldr in the side, even as his other arm surreptitiously wiped at his eyes.

"No knew," Drafli croaked, his face again thrusting into Alma's neck, "he should scent so *good*, upon our mate."

Baldr sniffed and grinned, fervently nodding, and when his and Drafli's eyes met again, there was a new shared understanding there, shimmering between them. And then they were all clutching at one another again, rocking back and forth together, until they'd collapsed back on the bed again, sprawled in each other's arms. Lost in the pure, tilting joy of this truth, of each other, of their family.

Alma didn't know how long they stayed there, swirling in the unreal contentment of it all—but it must have been longer than she'd thought, because Baldr eventually pulled up the fur over them, and purposefully lifted his head up, looking toward the door. Toward where Barden was suddenly barrelling into the room, his little face straddling something between eagerness and exasperation.

You late, he signed at them, once he'd swiftly clambered up onto the bed. *I already eat breakfast,* and *beat Arnthorr in match!*

"Ach, this is good, Golden-Heart," Baldr said, smiling and rubbing a fond hand against Barden's black head. "We did not wish to make you wait, but we have had news, ach? Can you scent aught new, upon Mama?"

Barden's eyes had flared with interest—he loved Baldr's ongoing scenting challenges, Alma well knew—and he accordingly squirmed on top of Alma, and pressed his face into her neck. His little chest filling as he inhaled, his snub nose gently sniffing against her skin.

"Smell... new," he said decisively, pulling away, and tilting his head toward Baldr. "Smell like... *you*, Ba-pa. Like Grisk. Like"—he stuck his face into Alma's neck again, frowning as he pulled away this time—"like *me*."

And oh, Alma was surely about to start weeping again, and Baldr perhaps felt that way too, his smile slightly wavering.

"Ach, like all of those," he said, husky. "For he is your new brother, ach?"

They'd talked to Barden about his forthcoming brother before, of course, but Alma was still relieved to see his eyes light up, his mouth flashing an approving, pointy-toothed grin between them. "New brother," he said, with satisfaction. "Name him Bitty-Bardy."

Alma and Baldr both laughed—Kesst's nickname for Bitty-Grim had unfortunately held on to a surprising degree—while Drafli firmly shook his head, his hand signing, *No*.

"No Bitty-Bardy," he hissed flatly. "I am father, I say no. He shall be"—his mouth pursed—"Drathkarr, mayhap. Or Dreng-fall. Good Skai name, ach?"

Alma's chest was still swelling with warmth, with pride, with impossible happiness—and she felt herself easily nodding, and meeting Baldr's warm, shining eyes. "A good Skai name," she repeated. "I'd like that."

"Ach," Baldr said, with a decisive nod, and a searching glance at Drafli's still-frowning face. "I like Drathkarr, Draf. Shall speak of you, ach? We could call him Drath?"

Drafli's expression had abruptly softened, his eyes looking both surprised and pleased. *You are sure?* he signed at them, very quickly. *You ken you can choose aught else, I no mean it must be this, but—*

But Baldr was already catching his hand in his, and Alma had leaned up closer to nuzzle at his sweet-smelling neck. "We're sure," she whispered. "Drathkarr it is, then. Of Clan Grisk."

Drafli's throat audibly swallowed, his eyes sweeping back and forth between them—and then he'd again yanked her and Baldr close, dragging them tight into his shoulders. "Ach, my angels," he murmured, hoarse, but perhaps almost reverent. "So kind. So sweet."

Alma was blinking back tears again, clutching at both him and Baldr, and at Barden, too. Who had squirmed up onto

Drafli's chest, sprawling out with a happy little sigh, nestled close and safe between them.

"Brother," he mumbled contentedly, as his little hand patted the fur covering Alma's waist. "Bitty-Bardy."

And the laughter and the warmth was everything, everything, all Alma had ever wanted, here in her arms, in her overflowing heart.

She'd made her family, and she was home—and she couldn't wait for whatever came next.

THANKS FOR READING
AND GET A FREE BONUS STORY!

Thank you so much for reading this book! It's such an honour to share my orc adventures with you. :)

And if you're not quite ready to leave Orc Mountain yet, please come join my mailing list at www.finleyfenn.com for some fun extra content, including artwork from this book, and a free Orc Sworn story. I'd love to stay in touch with you!

FREE STORY:
OFFERED BY THE ORC

The monster needs a sacrifice. And she's on the altar...

When Stella wanders the forest alone one fateful night, she only seeks peace, relief, escape. A few stolen moments on a secret, ancient altar, at one with the moon above.

Until she's accosted by a hulking, hideous, bloodthirsty *orc*. An orc who demands a sacrifice—not by his sword, but by Stella's complete surrender. To his claws, his sharp teeth, his huge muscled body. His every humiliating, thrilling command...

But Stella would never offer herself up to be used and sacrificed by a monster—would she? Even if her surrender just might grant her the moon's favour—and open her heart to a whole new fate?

FREE download now!
www.finleyfenn.com

ACKNOWLEDGMENTS

Once again, I am just so, so thankful for my incredible community of readers and friends. This book ended up being much more epic (and time-consuming!) than I'd originally expected, and I've been so touched and encouraged by your patience, kindness, and enthusiasm. Not to mention all the highly entertaining memes, fics, jokes, and sexy artwork! It's been such a delight!

I especially want to thank the awesome group of advance readers and proofreaders who've supported this book: Erin, Jennifer N., Jen R., Judi S., Lauren Maunchley, Lexi K. Jordan, Line Vienneau, Serena, Sue Philips from Australia, and my dearest heart Amy F. And huge thanks to Stacy for being my sign language expert, and to Þórey H. for the ongoing support with my Aelakesh (aka Icelandic).

I also need to extend my wholehearted gratitude to writing goddesses Ruby Dixon and Eris Adderly, both of whom have given me shocking amounts of their time, expertise, and utter brilliance throughout the process of writing this book. You are both geniuses, and I remain in complete awe of your generosity and greatness! (And to anyone who hasn't read their spectacular books yet, you must!)

I also want to specifically mention just a few of the many fabulous folks who've supported me this past year. A huge thank-you to the multi-talented MK, for being the extra brain I desperately need; Elizabeth for all the gorgeous art and general awesomeness; Katie for the unflinching and hilarious enthusiasm; Jane M. for hosting the Orc Sworn Awards; and Amy,

Angie, Coco, and Morning Dove (among MANY others) for sharing so much orc love with the rest of us on Discord and Facebook (join us at Finley Fenn Readers' Den)! And as always, I am just so grateful to my fellow indie authors who have given me so much guidance, commiseration, and inspiration throughout this strange and wonderful journey.

And finally, of course, I need to thank my own gorgeous, generous Skai mate, who takes such constant good care of his needy Grisk wife, and thereby makes all my writing possible. Thank you, my lord.

ALSO BY FINLEY FENN

THE LADY AND THE ORC

He's the most feared monster in the realm. And she's what he needs to win his war...

In a world of warring orcs and men, Lady Norr is condemned to a childless marriage, a cruel lord husband, and a life of genteel poverty—until the day her home is ransacked by a horde. And leading the charge is their hulking, deadly orc captain: the infamous Grimarr.

And Grimarr has a wicked plan for Lady Norr, and for ending this war once and for all. She's going to become his captive—and the perfect snare for Lord Norr.

There's no possible escape, and soon Lady Norr is dragged off toward Orc Mountain in the powerful arms of her greatest enemy. A ruthless, commanding warlord, with a velvet voice and mouthwatering scent, who awakens every forbidden hunger she never knew she had...

But Grimarr refuses to accept half measures—in war, or in pleasure. And before he'll conquer Lady Norr's deepest, darkest desires, she needs to surrender *everything*.

Her allegiance.

Her wedding-ring.

Her future...

And with her husband's forces giving chase, Lady Norr can't afford to play such a dangerous game—or can she? **Even if this deadly orc's plans might be the only way to save them all?**

ALSO BY FINLEY FENN

THE HEIRESS AND THE ORC

Once, he was her dearest friend... but now he's a brutal, terrifying monster.

In a world of recently warring orcs and men, Ella Riddell is determined to ignore it all. She's the wealthiest heiress in the realm—and soon, she's to wed a lord, and become a real lady.

Until the night her engagement-party ends in utter *disaster*, and Ella runs for the forest—and straight into the powerful arms of a hulking, deadly orc.

And it's not just any orc. It's *Natt*. The orc Ella made a secret, foolish pledge to, many years past...

He's huge and shameless and vicious, not at all the gangly, laughing daredevil Ella remembers. And he's here with one shocking, scandalous aim: to wreak vengeance on Ella's betrothed. With *her*.

With her hunger.

Her surrender.

Her undoing.

Ella knows she should run, even if this deadly enemy was once a friend. Even if his scent drags up a dark, forbidden longing. Even if his kisses are the sweetest, filthiest thing she's ever tasted in her life...

But will Ella truly risk her perfect future, for an orc? Will she face the bitter truths of the past, and brave the terrifying Orc Mountain, before more war rises to destroy them all?

He's a massive, mocking, murderous monster. And there's only one thing he wants from her...

In a world of recently warring orcs and men, Maria is desperate for escape. She's trapped in an opulent prison, tainted by rumours of madness, and wed to a cold, vindictive duke who hungers only for war.

But with no family, no funds, and no hope, there's nowhere left to run—except for the one place even a duke can't reach. The place where women almost always meet their doom...

Orc Mountain.

It's a grim, deadly fortress, filled with fierce, bloodthirsty beasts—**and the first orc Maria meets is the most terrifying of them all.** A huge, hostile, hideous brute, hardened by hatred and war, who instantly accuses her of foul trickery, and threatens her with death—

But this orc also wants something. Something that kindles deep in his gleaming black eyes, in his rough, rugged scent, in the velvet heat of his voice. Something that just might grant Maria his safety... but only if she grants him *everything* in return.

Her defeat.

Her dignity.

Her devotion...

And surely, a duchess wouldn't dare make such a shameful deal with the devil—or would she? Especially when surrender might spark yet more war... or bring the mighty Orc Mountain to its knees?

ALSO BY FINLEY FENN

THE MIDWIFE AND THE ORC

Orc Mountain needs a midwife. And this devious, deadly orc is determined to find one...

In a world of recently warring orcs and men, Gwyn Garrett is a lord's daughter on a mission—to escape her lord father, dump her cheating betrothed, and pursue her true calling as a plant-obsessed midwife.

Until the night her brand-new house is invaded by an *orc*. A tall, taunting, treacherous monster, with sharp teeth, vicious claws, and gleaming black eyes. And worst of all, a blatant, brutal mission of his own...

He's come to court her.

Claim her.

Compromise her.

But Gwyn is far too clever to fall for this sneaky orc's schemes—right? Even if he moves like a graceful god, if his voice is sweet syrup in her ears. If his low, mocking laugh sparks something hot and reckless, deep in her soul...

It's hunger, it's *home*, it's everything Gwyn never knew she needed—but in its wake, there's only devastation. Defeat. And the realization that she's forever linked with this horrible orc, and his horrible plans...

And with the war. The fates of hundreds of women like her. And the truth that **Orc Mountain desperately needs her, and maybe this proud, lonely orc does too...**

ABOUT THE AUTHOR

Finley Fenn has been writing about people falling in love for as long as she can remember. She creates steamy fantasy romance tales with cranky-but-sexy men and monsters, loads of angst and drama, a dash of mystery and action, and wholehearted happily ever afters.

When she's not obsessing over her stories, she reads everything she can get her hands on, and drools over delicious orc artwork (find her latest faves on Facebook at Finley Fenn Readers' Den). She lives in Canada with her beloved family, including her own cranky-but-sexy husband, and her cranky-and-hungry dog.

To get free bonus content, character illustrations, and news about upcoming books, sign up at www.finleyfenn.com.